SHADOWS IN THE WATER OMNIBUS VOLUME ONE

BOOKS 1 - 3

KORY M. SHRUM

Cover Design by Christian Bentulan
http://coversbychristian.com/

TIMBERLANE
PRESS

SHADOWS IN THE WATER OMNIBUS VOLUME ONE

GET THREE FREE BOOKS NOW

Connecting with my readers is the best part of my job as an author. One way that I connect with my readers is by sending newsletters with give-aways, exclusive free material, and bookish finds for bookish fiends like you.

In exchange for trusting me with your email, I send you three FREE ebooks right away. I also promise never to abuse or sell that email address. And if you don't enjoy my newsletter (sent 3-4 times a month) for any reason, you're free to unsubscribe at any time. No questions asked.

So if you're interested in receiving free books, learn more at www.korymshrum.com.

SHADOWS IN THE WATER

SHADOWS IN THE WATER BOOK 1

Thus did I by the water's brink
Another world beneath me think;
And while the lofty spacious skies
Reversed there, abused mine eyes,
I fancied other feet
Came mine to touch or meet;
As by some puddle I did play
Another world within it lay.

—Thomas Traherne, "Shadows in the Water"

PROLOGUE

N o, no, no." Her daughter's hand shot out and seized Courtney's slacks. "Don't leave me."

"Jesus Christ." She tugged her pants from Louie's dripping grip and shoved her back into the tub by her shoulders. "What is it with you and water? It isn't going to kill you. You won't drown! And I have to finish dinner before your father gets home."

Louie's chest collapsed with sobs. "Please. *Please* don't go."

"Stop crying. You're too old to be crying like this."

Louie recoiled like a kicked dog, her body hunching into a C-curve.

God almighty, Courtney thought as shame flooded her. *What am I supposed to do with her?*

The illogical nature of your daughter's fear doesn't negate the fact her fear is very real, the therapist had said. Dr. Loveless must have repeated this a hundred times, but it didn't make these episodes any easier. The fat-knuckled know-it-all had never been present for bath time.

Most ten-year-old girls could bathe on their own. No handholding. No hysterics. No goddamn therapy sessions once a week. And somehow this was supposed to be *her* fault? Why exactly? Because she'd gotten pregnant at eighteen?

No. She did everything right. She married Jack, despite her reservations. He was too young, uneducated, and a dreamer. Triple threat, her Republican father called it.

She read all the pregnancy books. She quit her managerial position at the insurance company and stayed home with Louie, practically giving the girl her undivided attention for the first five years of her life. If she was guilty of anything, it was over-attentiveness.

But Courtney didn't believe for a second this was her fault.

It was *Jack's.*

Jack was the one who insisted on renovating the upstairs bath and then insisted his friend do the renovations. Three years. *Three years* it sat unfinished and oh no they couldn't go to another builder because Jack *promised* Gary the job. Jack and his misplaced loyalties. What did it get them? Bum friends who always borrowed money and *three years* with only the clawfoot bathtub to share between them.

Things worth having are worth waiting for, Jack had said.

This philosophy worked for a DEA agent like Jack, someone who had to track criminals for months or years, but Courtney had never been good at waiting. She preferred what her alcoholic father had called *immediate gratification.*

Within a week of switching from the shower to the clawfoot tub, Louie's episodes began. After three *long* years, Courtney felt she'd had more than enough. God, it would be wonderful to shove a valium down the girl's throat and be done with this. She wanted to. *God almighty,* she wanted to. But Jack had been firm about pills. Courtney loved Jack, but goddamn his self-righteous "drugs are drugs" bullshit. Any half-wit knew the difference between valium and heroin.

You will have to be patient with her, Mrs. Thorne, if you want her to get through this without any lasting psychological damage.

Apparently, the therapist didn't know a damn thing. The damage had *already* begun to show. Louie not only feared water now but dirt also. The child who used to come in at night covered head to toe in grass stains and palms powdered with pastel sidewalk chalk, now crept around as if playing a constant game of The Floor is Hot Lava. This morning, Louie had burst into tears when Courtney asked her to pull weeds from the hosta bed. Even after putting her in coveralls and peony pink garden gloves, the girl had whimpered through the task, ridiculous tears streaming down her cheeks.

Now, hands on hips, Courtney stared down at her hunched, shaking daughter. She could count the vertebrae protruding through her skin. She'd grown so thin lately.

It could be worse, she told herself. She could have a child with quadriplegic cerebral palsy like her book club buddy Beth Rankin. Would she rather have a kid who screamed in the bathtub three or four times a week, or a man-child who had to be pushed in a stroller everywhere and his shitty diapers changed and drooling chin wiped?

Courtney forced a slow exhale through flared nostrils and pried apart her clenched teeth.

"Okay," she said in a soft, practiced tone. "Okay, I'm here. I'm right here."

She knelt beside the tub and grabbed a slick blue bottle of shampoo off a shelf above the toilet. As she squeezed the gel into her palm, Louie still cowered like a beaten dog, head and eyes down.

"I'm sorry," Courtney said, her cheeks flushing hotly. "But it's hard for me to understand this fear of yours."

The girl's teeth chattered, but she said nothing. Only one of her eyes was visible from the slate of black hair slicked against her head.

Courtney massaged the soap into her hair. Thick white bubbles foamed between her knotty fingers, her skin turning red from the pressure and steam. Her gentle massaging did nothing to relax the girl.

"Isn't this nice?" Courtney asked. "I'd love it if someone washed *my* hair."

Louie said nothing, her arms wrapped tightly around her knees.

"You have to lean back now." She trailed her fingers through the gray water. "So we can rinse."

Louie seized her mother's arms.

"I know." Courtney tried to add a sweet lilt to her voice, but only managed indifference. Better than angry at least. "I'm right here. Come on, lie back, baby."

She thought *baby* was a nice touch. Wasn't it?

But Louie's chest started to heave again as her head tipped back toward the soapy gray water.

"Breathe, *baby*. The sooner we do this, the sooner you can get out of the tub." Courtney hoped the girl wouldn't hyperventilate. That would be the fucking icing on the cake. Dragging her wet body out of the tub would be hell on her back, and she'd already had her valium for the night. She'd risk taking another, but she knew Jack counted them.

As the back of Louie's hair dipped into the water, her golden eyes widened. Her fingers raked down Courtney's arms as she clung tighter. All right. It only stung a little, and it would be something to show Jack later when she complained about his lateness.

It was your turn for bath night and look what happened. She might even get away with a second glass of wine at dinner sans lecturing if the marks were red enough.

This made her smile.

With one arm completely submerged under Louie's back, buoying the girl, she could use her free hand to rinse Louie's hair. Thick clumps of soap melted into the water with each swipe of her fingers.

"There."

Louie's muscles went soft, her nails retracting.

"Not so bad, is it?" Courtney cooed with genuine affection now. "I love baths. I find them very relaxing."

Louie even managed a small smile.

Then the oven dinged.

"My ham!" Courtney clambered to her feet.

"No, no, no!" Louie frantically wiped water from her eyes and tried to pull herself into an upright position. "Don't! Please!"

And just like that, the hysterics were in full swing again. *Fucking Jack. I'm going to kill you.* "Breathe, baby."

Shaking suds off her arms, Courtney jogged toward her glazed ham and caramelized Brussels sprouts three rooms away. The sweet, roasted smell met her halfway. "The door is open, *baby*. Keep talking so I can hear you."

"Mom!" Louie screamed. "Mommy! It's happening!"

"I'm right here." She slipped a quilted oven mitt over each hand. "Talk to me. I'm listening."

The girl's escalating hysteria cut off mid-scream. For a moment, there was only a buzzing silence.

Courtney's heart skipped a beat. Her body froze instinctually. Her reptilian brain registering *danger* entered a mimicked catatonia. For several heartbeats, she could only stand there before her electric range, in her gloved hands, the oven mitts spaced equidistantly as if still holding the casserole dish between them.

Her eyes were fixed on a spaghetti sauce splatter to the right of the stove, above a ceramic canister holding rice. She stared without seeing.

Then a chill shuddered up the woman's spine, reactivating her systems. As her muscles cramped, she thought, *fear trumps valium*. She yanked off the oven mitts, throwing them down beside the casserole dish steaming on the stovetop. She jogged back to the bathroom, the silence growing palpable.

"Louie?"

The tub was empty. No shadows beneath the soapy gray water.

In a ridiculous impulse, she looked behind the bathroom door and then inside the small cabinet beneath the sink, knowing full well Louie couldn't fit into either space.

The bathroom was empty. "Louie?"

She ran to the girl's bedroom.

It was empty too. And the wood floor tracing the entire length of the house was bone dry. Louie's soft Mickey Mouse towel, the one they bought on their trip to Disney World two years ago, still hung from the hook by the tub.

She searched every inch of their house, and when she couldn't find her, she called Jack. When he didn't answer, she called again and left a frantic message.

He arrived twenty minutes later.

They searched again. They called everyone. They spoke to every neighbor and the police. If Courtney thought Dr. Loveless was a ruthless interrogator with his second chin and swollen knuckles, she found the authorities much worse.

"I didn't kill her!" she said for the thousandth time. "Jack, do something! These are *your* friends!"

For three nights, they had no peace. Courtney doubled the wine and valium, but it wasn't enough currency to buy sleep.

In the early morning hours, she would find herself wandering their house, wearing down a path between the clawfoot tub and Louie's empty bed. Sitting on the firm twin mattress, she would pull back the Ninja Turtle comforter hoping to find her underneath.

In her mind, she apologized for every frustration, every cruel thought. *I'll do anything—anything. Bring her home.*

The call came on the fourth day.

Sixty miles east of the Thorne's home in St. Louis, Jacob Foxton was interviewed many times by the police, but his story never changed.

His nieces were coming down from Minnesota for the Memorial Day weekend, and he and his wife were very excited to see them. They'd changed the sheets on the spare bed and stocked the fridge with root beer and Klondike bars. The pool was uncovered and cleaned, and the heater turned on. All that was left to do before their arrival was mow the yard.

I was cutting my grass, and she...appeared.

As the police tried to pin the abduction on the man, the lack of evidence made it impossible. Foxton had no priors, and a neighbor confirmed Foxton's rendition.

Billie Hodges had been washing her Chevy Tahoe with a clear view of the Foxton family pool. Like Foxton, Hodges swore the girl simply appeared.

As if from thin air.

After thirty-six fruitless hours, the Perry County Sheriff's Department was forced to believe Jacob Foxton had merely cut a left around his rudbeckia bushes with his squat red push mower and found Louie Thorne standing there, on the top step of his pool.

Naked. Soaking wet. Her dark hair stuck to her pale back like an oil slick. Foxton released the lawnmower's safety bar, killing the engine.

"Hey! Hey you!" He rushed toward her, clumps of fresh cut grass clinging to his bare ankles.

The girl turned toward the sound of his voice, and his scolding lecture died on his lips. It wasn't only her fear that stopped him.

It was the blood.

So much that a cloud of pink swirled toward the drain in his pool.

The girl's body was covered in lacerations, the kind he got on his arms and legs as a kid, hiking through the woods. A great many of them stretched across her stomach and legs and a particularly nasty one across her cheek.

She must have run through the forests of hell, he thought.

But it wasn't the scratches that frightened him.

A ring of punctures encircled the girl's right shoulder. A ragged halo from neck to bicep. Like some hungry beast larger than the girl had grabbed ahold of her with its teeth. Long rivulets of blood streamed down her pale limbs, beading on her skin.

"Honey." Jacob pulled off his T-shirt and yanked it down over the child's head. If she cared about the sweaty condition of the shirt, the grass stains, or Jacob's hairy belly, she didn't show it. "Are you all right?"

"Is it still on me?" she whispered. She turned her face toward Jacob, but her eyes didn't focus. His mother called that *a thousand-yard stare*.

"Who did this to you, honey?" Jacob asked. He took her hands in his. The hairs on his arms rose at the sight of blood pooled beneath her nails.

"Jacob?" Called Billie from across the stretch of lawn between their two yards. "Is everything all right?"

"Call an ambulance," Jacob yelled. He saw the girl's mouth move. "What was that, honey?"

"Is it still on me?" she whispered again. "Is it?"

And that was the last thing she said before collapsing into his arms.

1

Fourteen years later

Lou unfolded the tourist map and eyed a man over the rim of the creased paper. A boxy man with a crooked nose and a single bushy brow stood on the harbor dock, smoking a cigarette. He draped an arm around a woman's shoulder while he joked with another guy twice his size, a hairy bear as wide as he was tall. The woman was a little more than a caricature to Lou. Big hair and a big mouth, made bigger by the annoying smack of bubblegum between her magenta lips. Her clothes were too tight in some places and nonexistent in others. *A Jersey girl*, Aunt Lucy would've called her.

Lou scowled at the tourist map, pretending to read about the seaport's attractions, and wondered if the girl under Angelo Martinelli's arm would feel half as cozy if she knew what a monster he was.

If Bubblegum Barbie was observant, she might have noticed Martinelli's penchant for leather, Dunhill cigarettes, and pointy shoes. Maybe Barbie even suspected the Martinelli family was responsible for fueling the heroin problem in Baltimore. Hell, she probably tolerated this aftershave-soaked prick *for* the heroin.

Whatever Barbie thought she knew of the Italian draped over her, Lou knew a hell of a lot more.

She should. She'd been hunting Angelo since she was fourteen.

Lou looked away as if to read the street sign, her heart fluttering with anticipation. A steady pulse throbbed in the side of her neck and in her hands. She was thankful her dark shades and windblown hair hid her excitement. And grateful that Martinelli was too nearsighted to see the map tremble in her sweaty grip.

Her mind kept turning toward the future, when he'd receive a shipment at Pier C and insist on counting everything himself. Better yet, because he'd want to be discreet as to how much dope he imported, his security detail would be thinner. He'd invite enough muscle to get the job done. No more.

Lou wouldn't get him entirely alone. A man like Angelo was *never* alone. He didn't even fuck without an audience. She knew this because she'd considered the possibility of going O-Ren Ishii on his ass. Before fully exploring this option, Lou realized she'd forsake her vow of revenge and blow her own brains out long before trying to seduce a Martinelli.

Tonight there would be guns, of course. And the ones chosen for this evening's mission would be fighters. Perhaps a few even better than Lou herself.

And there was the water to consider. The harbor sparkled in the late afternoon sun. Looking at it made Lou's skin itch.

Angelo ran a thick hand through his oiled hair and tossed his Dunhill butt on the ground. He smashed it out with a twist of his boot and hooked an arm around Barbie's waist.

Tonight, she thought, as a swarm of tourists swelled on the pier. *I'm going to kill you and love every minute of it.*

Her sunglasses hitched higher on her face as she grinned.

Before Angelo could turn toward her and spot a familiar ghost in the crowd, Lou did what she did best.

She disappeared, not returning until well after dark.

By 2:00 A.M., all the tourists were in bed with dreams of the next day.

Lou, on the other hand, wasn't sure she had another day in her. That was okay. She didn't need to see another sunrise as long as Angelo Martinelli didn't either.

Lying on top of one of the shipping containers, Lou had a great view of the docks below. Her forearms and body were covered in leather and

Kevlar, but her palms were bare. The metal container serving as her lookout was warm under her palms, sun-soaked from the day. She was small enough to fit into the grooves in the top of the container, making her invisible to those below. Unless of course, Angelo arrived by helicopter.

Her body squirmed. Despite the pleasant breeze rolling off the deep harbor, sweat was starting to pool at the back of her neck beneath her hairline. Her feet twitched with excitement.

Death by waiting, she thought.

She was desperate to swing at something. She imagined certain animals felt this way during the full moon. Hungry, unsettled, itching all over.

Do it already, her mind begged. *Slip*. A heartbeat later she'd be standing behind Angelo. So close she could run her hands through his greased hair.

Boo, motherfucker.

Not motherfucker, she thought. Mother *killer*.

True, Courtney Thorne was hard to love. Her compulsive and domineering behavior, her impatience. Her tendency to chide and scorn rather than praise. Her face a perpetual pout rather than a smile.

But Louie also remembered how hard her mother had hugged her the day after she was found in Ohio. Louie had sat in the sheriff's office for hours, wrapped in a scratchy wool blanket consuming all the soda and peanut butter cups she could stomach until her parents arrived.

Louie! Her mother had cried the moment she stepped through the station's glass doors. Louie had only managed to put down her soda can and slide out of the chair before her mother fell on her, seizing and squeezing her half to death. She smelled like makeup powder and rose water. Like the old woman she would never become.

Courtney wasn't her favorite parent, but she didn't deserve to die either.

Louie's fists clenched at her side.

Angelo's men stirred on the pier. To anyone else, it seemed as if an innocuous few stood around, smoking, and talking. Apart from the hour, nothing suspicious there. But Lou glimpsed blades catching moonlight and saw the bulging outlines of guns under jackets.

Jackets in this heat were clue enough.

Cops stopped patrolling the harbor at midnight. Lou wondered if that could be blamed on budget cuts, ignorance, or money from Angelo's own pockets. *A little of each*, she thought.

She'd almost succumbed to drumming her fingers on the shipping container when a car pulled into view.

The black sedan was like so many others Angelo had rented in cities where he'd done business before: Chicago. San Francisco, New York, Atlanta and now Baltimore.

As soon as she saw the car, she started to slip. Bleeding through this side of the world. *No. Not yet*, she scolded herself. *Don't fuck this up.*

She'd only have one good shot. One chance to catch him off guard.

Tonight she would finish what her father started so many years ago.

Someone opened the back door, and Angelo stepped out. He adjusted the lapels of his leather jacket. She took a deep breath and let it out slowly. Again. Because the sight of him was enough to make her heart hammer.

Angelo called out to someone in Italian, then pointed at the boat. "Ho due cagne in calore che mi aspettano ed un grammo di neve con il mio nome scritto sopra."

Louie only understood a little Italian and caught the words *two whores* and *waiting*. Enough to get the gist of his harsh tone and thrusting hips, and comprehend why the men leered. One whistled through his teeth.

Angelo cupped his hands around a fresh Dunhill. A flame sparked, illuminating his face. With a wave, Angelo led his entourage to the pier where the boat sat tied to the dock. The boat rocked in the waves, straining against its rope, like a tied horse ready to run.

As soon as Angelo placed one foot on the boat, then dipping his head to enter the cabin, Lou let go.

She bled through. One moment she lay on top of the shipping container, the next, she stood in the shadows beneath the cabin's stairs. Her eyes leveled with Angelo's heels. It was hot in the unventilated room.

Angelo Martinelli descended the stairs with a man in front and one behind him. Lou smelled the leather of his boots and the smoke from his cigarette. *I can grab him now*, she thought. *Reach between the steps and seize his ankle like in a horror movie.*

Someone turned on the overhead light, and the interior of the boat burned yellow in the glow of the 40-watt bulb. Lou jumped back into the corner without thinking. An honest reaction to the sudden influx of light.

But her shoulder blades connected with a solid wall.

Heads snapped up at the sound of Lou searching for an exit that had been there only a moment before but was now gone.

She had only a second to decide.

She drew her gun, one fluid and practiced movement, and shot the overhead light. The 40-watt bulb burst, exploding in a shower of sparks. It was enough to throw them back into darkness and provide Lou with her exit. She slipped behind the stairs, then emerged from a narrow pathway between two shipping containers. Gunfire erupted inside the boat behind her. The ship strained against its rope again, and the wooden docks creaked.

More men came running, guns drawn.

She cursed and slammed her fist into the shipping container. So much for the surprise.

The chance to grab Martinelli and slip away undetected was gone. As her target emerged from the boat, gun at the ready, the weight of her mistake intensified.

He was spooked. Now he looked like the horse ready to run.

He inhaled sharp breaths of salty air as he hurried toward his car in short, quick strides. Fifty steps. Thirty-five. Twenty and he'll be gone.

It was now or never.

Fifteen steps.

Ten.

The thick tint of Angelo's car might work to her advantage, but her timing had to be perfect. Her blood whistled in her ears as she counted his last steps.

3....2...1...

She stepped from the edge of the shipping container into the back-seat of Angelo's car. The leather seat rushed up to greet her, bending her legs into place.

But it was her hands that mattered. And she had plenty of time to position them.

Angelo turned away from her, pulling the car door shut. She pressed her gun to his temple the second the door clicked into place.

The driver began to turn, pulling his weapon up from his lap but he was too slow. Louie lifted a second pistol from her hip and shoved it to the back of his neck, to the smooth nape. His neck tensed under the barrel, shifting the gun metal against her fingers.

"Don't," she said. Her eyes were fixed on Angelo. "I have a better idea."

"You were not in the car when I opened the door," Angelo said. His tobacco breath stung her nose. "I'm certain of this."

"Imagine how quick I am with a gun." It was a bold bluff given her predicament. His men were abandoning the boat. Some were moving the heroin. Others were lumbering toward other vehicles. If even *one* of them got into this car, she was screwed.

She could produce a third gun, sure. But not a third hand to hold it.

"You were also on the boat." Angelo's eyes shined in the dark, reflecting light like the black sea in front of them. "Or one like you."

"That would put me in two places at once," she said. She arched an eyebrow. "Impossible."

The driver remained very still, his hands at the ten and two positions on the wheel. Lou didn't recognize him, but she doubted that she'd ever forget the thick stench of Old Spice turned sour with sweat. It made her head swim.

If he was new, he was probably uninterested in doing anything that would cost him his life. She'd have to test this theory.

"What do you want?" Angelo asked. He shifted uncomfortably. Lou had found her silence made men nervous. Or maybe it was her gun. Difficult to tell. "Money? The drugs?"

"Driver?" she said.

The driver didn't turn toward her or even make a small sound of acknowledgment.

"Do you see the pier?" she went on, eyes still on Angelo. One of his greased curls fell across his forehead, and one corner of his lip curled in a partial sneer. His cheek muscles twitched. "Beside the pier is a space between the guardrails. Do you see it?"

The driver remained mute. His shoulders remained hunched, eyes forward. It was as if he'd had guns pressed to his head before and had since learned how to keep even a single muscle from twitching.

Lou saw all this in her perfect peripheral vision, not daring to look away from the man she wanted most.

Angelo Martinelli. This close he was smaller than she'd imagined.

She smiled at him, the taste of victory on her lips. "Drive into the bay."

When the driver didn't move, she smacked the gun against his occipital bone. "If you don't do it, then you're useless to me, and I think you understand what happens to useless people."

If he refused to drive, she'd shoot them both. It would be messier. Riskier. But if she couldn't get Martinelli into the water, she wasn't going to let this opportunity escape.

Yes. If Lou had to, she'd shoot them both and drive the car into the bay herself.

"Make your choice, Martinelli," she said. His eyes were pools of ink shining in the lamplight.

The confused pinch of his brow smoothed out. The curling sneer pulled into a tight grin.

"Drive," he said.

Without hesitation, the driver put the car into motion, and the sedan rolled forward.

"Faster," Lou said, grinning wider.

"Faster," Angelo agreed. A small chuckle rumbled in his throat. He slapped the back of the driver's seat like this was a game. "*Faster.*"

The driver punched the accelerator, and the car lurched forward. As it blasted past the men on the docks, shouts pinged off the windows. Angelo's laugh grew more robust, pleasing belly laugh.

He's high as hell, she realized. *High as hell without any idea of what's happening to him.*

They hit a bump when flying past the guardrails and onto the pier. The wooden slats clunked under the car's tires.

In the wake of Angelo's mania, Lou couldn't help but smile herself. She didn't lower the gun. "You're crazy."

This proclamation only made him laugh harder, clutching at his belly. His laugh warped into a wheezing whine.

The thrum of the wooden slats disappeared as the car launched itself off the pier. The sharp stench of fish wafted up to greet them as they floated suspended above the ocean. Her stomach dropped as the nose of the car tipped forward and the windshield filled with black Atlantic water.

There was a moment of weightlessness, of being lifted out of her seat and then the car hit the water's surface. Her aim faltered on impact, but she'd righted herself before either man could.

Cold water rushed in through the windows, trickling first through the corners, filling the car slowly as they slid deeper into the darkness. It seeped through the laces of her boots.

"Now what?" Angelo asked. He seemed genuinely thrilled. As if this was the most exciting experience of his life.

"We wait," she said.

"She's going to shoot us and leave our bodies in the water." The driver's voice surprised her, higher and more childish than she imagined. No wonder he'd kept his mouth shut.

The driver could open the door and swim away for all she cared. "I don't—"

The driver couldn't wait for any reassurance. He whirled, lifting his gun.

Without a thought, she fired two shots into his skull, a quick double tap. His head rocked back as if punched. The brains splattered across the windows like Pollock's paint thrown onto a canvas.

She was glad she'd decided on the suppressor. Her ears would be bleeding from the noise if she hadn't. The smell of blood bloomed in the car. Bright and metallic. It was followed by the smell of piss.

Angelo's humor left him. "Is it my turn now, ragazzina?"

Water gurgled around the windows as the car sank deeper into the dark bay.

"No," she said, her eyes reflecting the dark water around them. "I have something else for you."

2
_____

Will you do it?

The question looped in King's mind. *Will you do it, Robbie?*

At the corner of St. Peter and Bourbon, Robert King paused beneath a neon bar sign. Thudding bass blared through the open door, hitting him in the chest. The doorman motioned him forward. King waved him off. He was done drinking for the night. Not only because the hurricane was getting acquainted with the pickle chips he'd eaten earlier, but because the case file under his arms wasn't going to examine itself.

Despite the riot in his stomach, he hoped the booze would help him sleep. He was overdue a good night. A night without crushing darkness and concrete blocks pinning him down on all sides. A night where he didn't wake up at least twice with the taste of plaster dust on his lips. Leaving the bedside light on helped, but sometimes even that wasn't enough to keep the nightmares away.

Drunk revelers stumbled out of the bar laughing, and a woman down the street busked with her violin case open at her feet. The violin's whine floated toward him but was swallowed by the bass from the bar.

King paused to inspect his reflection in the front window. He smoothed his shaggy hair with a slick palm. He could barely see the scar. A bullet had cut a ten-degree angle across his cheekbone before blasting a wedge off his ear. The ear folded in on itself when it grew back together, giving him an elfish look.

A whole building collapsed on him, and it hadn't left a single mark. One bullet and...well, he supposed that was how the world worked.

Calamity didn't kill you. What finished you was the shot you never saw coming.

He straightened and smiled at the man in the glass.

Good.

Now that he didn't *look* like a drunk, it was time to make sure he didn't *smell* like one. He pinned the file against his body with a clenched elbow and dug into his pocket for mints. He popped two mints out of the red tin and into his mouth, rolling them back and forth with his tongue as if to erase all the evidence. Satisfied, he continued his slow progress toward home.

The central streets of the French Quarter were never dark, even after the shops closed and all that remained were the human fleas feeding in the red light of Bourbon Street. The city didn't want a bunch of drunks searching for their hotels in the dark, nor did they care to provide cover for the petty pickpockets who preyed on them. There were plenty of both in this ecosystem.

At the corner of Royal and St. Peter, King paused beneath a metal sign swinging in the breeze rolling in off Lake Pontchartrain and wiped his boots on the curb. Gum. Vomit. Dog shit. A pedestrian could pick up all sorts of discarded waste on these streets. He balanced his unsteady body by placing one hand on a metal post, cane height and topped with a horse's head. The pointed ears pressed into his palm as he struggled to balance himself.

A fire engine red building stood waiting for him to clean his feet. Black iron railings crowned the place, with ferns lining the balcony. Hunter green shutters framed oversized windows overlooking both Royal and St. Peter.

The market across the street was still open. King considered ducking in and buying a bento box, but one acidic pickle belch changed his mind. He rubbed his nose, suppressing a sneeze.

Best to go to bed early and think about all that Brasso had told him. Sleep on it. Perhaps literally with the photographs and testimony of one Paula Venetti under his pillow for safe keeping.

And with his gun too, should someone come in during the night and press a blade to his throat in search of information. It wouldn't be the first time.

Will you do it?

King supposed if he thought this case was hot enough to warrant a knifing in the night, he should've said *no*. He should remind his old partner he's retired. Brasso should find some young buck full of piss and vinegar. Not a man pushing sixty who can't have two cocktails without getting acid reflux severe enough to be mistaken for a heart attack.

The case file sat heavy in his hand. Heavier than it had been when he'd first accepted it. He clutched the folder tighter and crossed the threshold into Mel's shop, the lights flickered, and a ghostly moan vibrated the shelves.

A gaggle of girls looked up from their cell phones wide-eyed. Then they burst into laughter. One with braces snorted, and the laughter began anew.

Mel's sales tactics may not be old hat to them, but King found the 10,000ᵗʰ fake moan less thrilling than the first. Funny how it had been the same with his ex-wife.

It's all about theatrics with these folk, Mel had said when she forced him to help install the unconventional door chime. *They come to N'awlins for the witchy voodoo stuff, and if you want to keep renting my room upstairs, Mr. King, you best clip these two wires here together. My old fingers don't bend the way they used to.*

And he did want to keep renting the large one-bedroom apartment upstairs, so he offered no further resistance to her schemes.

The store was smoky with incense. Ylang ylang. Despite the open door and late breeze, a visible cloud hung in the air, haloing the bookshelves and trinket displays full of sugar skulls, candles, statues of saints, and porcelain figurines. The fact that he recognized the scent spoke of Mel's influence on him these past months. If someone had bet him he would know the difference between ylang ylang and geranium two years ago, he would have lost the shirt off his back.

Apart from the four girls clustered by a wall of talismans, only one other patron was in the store. A rail-thin man with a rainbow tank top and cut-off jean shorts showing the bottom of his ass cheeks plucked a *Revenge is Love* candle from a wooden shelf. He read the label with one hand on his hip. When he scratched his ash blond hair, glitter rained onto the floor.

King's heart sank. Despite Mel's endless tactics, business was still slow. At ten o'clock on a Friday, this place should be packed wall-to-wall with tourists, ravers, or even drunks. Five customers did not an income make.

Behind the counter, a twenty-two-year-old girl with a white pixie cut took one look at the falling glitter and her nostrils flared.

Piper wore a sleeveless tank top with deep arm holes revealing her black sports bra beneath. A diamond cat earring sat curled in the upper curve of her ear and sparkled in the light of the cathedral chandelier overhead. A hemp necklace with three glass beads hung around her neck. Every finger had a silver ring, and a crow in flight was tattooed on her inner wrist. She managed to mask her irritation before Booty Shorts reached the counter with his purchase.

"$6.99." Piper slipped the candle into a paper bag with the *Madame Melandra's Fortunes and Fixes* logo stamped on the front.

Booty Shorts thanked her and sashayed out into the night. A glow stick around his neck burned magenta in the dark.

"I don't see what a candle can do that a hitman can't." Piper blew her long bangs out of her face.

"Why would you have someone else fight your battles for you?"

"I don't hit girls." Piper scoffed in mock indignation. "Anyway, my point is it's a waste of time sitting up all night with a candle praying to some goddess who doesn't give two shits about my sex life. Don't cry about your sour milk! Go get another fish! A cute, kissable fish who'll let you unsnap her bra after a couple tequila shots."

"Be grateful for the candle-burning crybabies," King adjusted the folder under his arms. "Unless you want to be a shop girl somewhere else."

Her nostrils flared. "*Apprentice*. I'm learning how to read fortunes. Sometimes I set up a table in Jackson Square and make shit up. People *pay* me! It's unbelievable."

"The Quarter is a dicey place for a young woman to be alone."

"*Awww*. I've always wanted a concerned father figure." She pressed her hands to her heart. Then she rolled her eyes. "Who said I was alone?"

"Were you with Tiffany?"

"Tanya," she corrected. "And *no*. We broke up weeks ago."

King rubbed the back of his head, leaning heavily against the glass case. "That's right. You left her for Amy."

"Amanda," she said. "Keep up, man."

He'd never been great with names. Now faces—he never forgot a face. "I'm sorry. How's Amanda?"

"She's—"

A teenage girl burst from behind the curtain, clutching her palm as if it'd been burned. Fat tears slid down her cheeks, glistening in the light until her friends enfolded her in their arms.

The velvety curtain with its spiraling gold tassels was pulled back again and hung on a hook to one side of the door frame. From the shadows, a voluptuous black woman with considerable hips emerged. Mel's kohl-rimmed eyes burned and an off-the-shoulders patchwork dress hugged her curvy frame. Gold bangles jangled against her wrist as she adjusted the purple shawl around her.

"Bad news?" Piper arched a brow, and King realized she'd begun to mimic Mel's dramatic eye makeup.

Mel crossed the small shop, and King straightened again. He hoped his eyes weren't glassy, and the mints had done the trick.

Mel stopped short of the counter and put one hand on her hip.

"Crushing hearts?" Piper asked, and she sounded excited about it.

Mel rolled her eyes. "I only suggested a book."

Piper frowned. "What book?"

Mel puckered her lips. "*He's Just Not That Into You.*"

Piper's grin deepened. "You're so cruel. Do you want me to talk to her? I'm *really* good with damsels."

"They're release tears. They're good for the soul. She'll wake up tomorrow and feel like the sun is shining, the baby bluebirds are singing, and—"

"—she'll be $80 lighter for it," Piper muttered.

"She'll be fine." Mel tapped her long purple nails on the checkout counter and turned her dark eyes on King. "You, on the other hand, you're in trouble. *Big* trouble."

King felt the sweat beading under his collar. He resisted the urge to reach up and pull at it. It was the chandelier overhead, beating down on him. Or he could blame the muggy night. New Orleans was hot as hell in June. Sweating didn't mean a damn thing.

"You're awfully quiet tonight, Mr. King."

He shrugged.

Mel stopped tapping her fingers on the glass countertops. King noticed reflective gems had been glued to the end of her index finger-nails. "I see a woman in your future. She's someone from your past. Pretty little white thing. Blonde. Big blue eyes. And she needs your help."

His ex-wife Fiona had brown eyes, and no one would have called her *a pretty little white thing.*" She'd been nearly six feet tall with the body of a rugby player.

Lucy.

"Is this a real fortune, Mel?" he asked his tongue heavy in his mouth.

Mel wrinkled her nose. "As real as the booze on your breath, Mr. King."

He adjusted the file under his arm. "It's mouthwash."

"I've done told you when you signed your lease, I wouldn't let no drunk man in my house again."

King found it amusing when Mel's southern accent thickened with her anger. Amusing, but he didn't dare smile. Mel hadn't wanted to rent her spare apartment to anyone, let alone a man. It had taken two weeks of wooing and reference checking to convince the fortune teller an ex-DEA agent was an asset rather than a liability.

"At least he's not an angry drunk." Piper tried to pull the file free from King's underarm. She bit her lip as she tried to peel the flaps apart and glimpse the contents within.

He slapped her hand lightly. "I'm not even buzzed."

Mel's eyes flicked to the case file then met his again. She arched an eyebrow.

King didn't believe in palm reading or fortune telling. Ghosts only existed in the mind, and he would be the first to admit he had a menagerie of malevolent spirits haunting him.

But despite what his mother called a healthy dose of skepticism, he believed in intuition. Intuition was knowledge the frontal lobe had yet to process. He trusted his instinct and he respected the instinct of others. No one person could see every angle. Shooters on the roof.

Boots on the ground. You had to rely on someone else's eyes, and this was no different.

Did Mel sense something about the case Brasso brought him? About a witness on the run and the man hunting her? And this mysterious woman from his past...

Mel spoke to the gaggle of girls. "Who's next?"

Three hands shot up. Someone cried, "Me!"

Clearly, they were eager to have their hearts broken.

"Wait." King touched her shoulder, and she turned. "Were you serious about the woman?"

"I don't need to be a fortune teller to know there's a woman, Mr. King." Mel tucked one of the girls behind the curtain and met his eyes again. She looked at him through long, painted lashes. Candle flames danced on the walls behind her. "She's in your apartment."

"You let a woman into my apartment?" His heart took off. "There's a woman in my apartment? *Now?*"

Mel grinned and dropped the burgundy curtain.

"Good luck with your ex-girlfriend." Piper swiped at the floor with a corn husk broom, doing no more than smearing the glitter. "Hope you have better luck than I do with mine."

"I'll be okay." King stood at the base of the stairs, looking up at his dark door. "Probably."

3

The moment the water overtook the car, Lou made her largest slip yet. She took Angelo, the car, and the dead driver. She didn't know if this was her doing, or if some things slip through on the current of their own desire. After all, there were enough rumors. Ships found floating without people. The Bermuda triangle. Planes disappeared and were never seen again. No debris ever found. She wasn't so egotistic to assume she was the only one who could slip through thin places.

Once the dark water turned red, became a different lake in a different place and time, Lou kicked out the window and swam.

She surfaced beside the body of the driver. He floated face down in the water. His shirt was puffed up in places where the air had entered beneath his collar. The water of Blood Lake, always the same crimson hue, added a surreal dimension to the floating body. As if the driver floated in an ocean of his own blood.

A large splash caught her attention, and she paddled in a half-circle. Her heavy boots tugged at her ankles, making it harder to stay afloat.

It wasn't Angelo. He was moving slowly toward the shore, making poor progress under the weight of his leather jacket. He slapped at the surface of the lake, each clumsy stroke of his arm like an eagle trying to swim. She spun further to the right in time to see a large dorsal fin dip beneath the surface about ten yards away.

She didn't need to be told getting out of the water was a good idea. Blood in the water was sure to attract any predator, earthly or otherwise. The splattered brains on the sinking car's window was an added draw.

And she didn't have much time. The ripples of the creature's descent were already lapping at her breast bone.

She swam for shore in slow, controlled movements. Not panicked. Not like prey. Yet she expected at any moment to find herself jerked under. Each easy stroke toward Angelo was an act of self-control.

Yet she emerged from the lake unharmed. Her heart hammered, but her body was whole. Angelo inspected a cut on his hand. He hadn't been careful enough with the broken window he'd pushed himself through.

Lou watched him, waited for him to adjust to his surroundings.

Finally, he looked up. He made a small sound of surprise, and Lou followed his gaze toward the water. The body of the driver bobbed once. Then a harder jerk submerged all but the puffed shirt. A flick of a large grotesque tail covered in purple spines slapped against the surface. One more tug and the body was gone. Only ripples on the surface suggested an exchange had happened.

Angelo stared gape-mouthed at the sky, transfixed by the two moons sagging there. "We are dead."

Lou tried to imagine what this place looked like to him. What it had looked like to her on her first visit.

The red lake. The white mountains. The strange yellow sky. A black forest with short trees and heart shaped leaves. Incongruous colors that were so different than those of her world.

"You are a demon." He crossed himself and kissed a saint pendant hanging from a gold chain around his neck.

It was the smell of sulfur that made him think of Hell, no doubt. It hung in the air and would cling to her hair and skin until she bathed. She shook water off her hands. "This is not some Roman Catholic parable." *Though you will learn a lesson here*, she thought.

"Who are you?"

"Jack Thorne's daughter."

Angelo's eyes widen. "No. She hit the bottom of the pool and didn't come up."

I didn't *come up*, she thought. *I went down. Sometimes the only way out is through.* And Lou thought there wasn't another person on Earth who that could be more true for.

She remembered every detail of that night, of her father's final hours. As if those moments had been burned like images onto film, forever preserved in her mind.

On the last night of his life, Jack Thorne entered their Tudor house in the St. Louis suburbs. He stood there in the doorway, wearing his bulletproof vest and badge. He was an intimidating sight, over six feet tall and filling the doorway like an ogre from a storybook. His gaze was direct and cumbersome most of the time. Only when he smiled, and the lines beside his eyes creased, did the gaze feel friendly.

"I want to talk to you," he said.

Louie, twelve, had slowly lowered her book, mentally marking her place on the page, before looking up from the window seat where she sat.

Her father had laughed, his grin transforming his face. "You're not in trouble. Scout's honor."

He'd never been a scout, but that hadn't stopped him from hailing the three-finger salute.

He ruffled her hair before heading to his bedroom where he changed. She'd listened to him, to the sound of his holster buttons snapping open. The clunk of the gun being placed on the dresser. One boot falling with a thud to the floor. Then the other. The Velcro of the bulletproof vest ripping free. These were the sounds of him coming home, and they had comforted her.

At dinner, she pushed a piece of soft, over-boiled broccoli around her plate, and waited. She listened to her mother complain about her day, about her part-time job at the chiropractor's office.

"They don't even vaccinate their children," her mother sneered between sips of red wine. "Six children and no vaccinations. Haven't they ever heard of herd immunity?"

"Mmmhmm," her father said companionably and scraped up the last of his turkey and broccoli with a fork. The turkey was dry as sandpaper, and the broccoli was practically mush. But Jack Thorne ate it with the same relish he would have a 24 oz. Porterhouse because of his respect for the woman who made it. *Tasteless food never hurt anyone*, he'd told Louie once. *But cruel words do.*

"Dr. Perdy said, 'my children have never been sick.' I wanted to ask, 'do you know why, Dr. Perdy?' Herd immunity, *that's* why. And do you know how we gained herd immunity?"

"Hmmm?" her father prompted, as he was expected to. He sat back in his chair, unbuttoned his jeans and began reviewing his teeth with a toothpick.

"He's supposed to be a medical professional." Courtney finished her glass of wine. "A medical professional surely understands what could happen if we sabotage our herd immunity."

Her father took a swig of beer. "Do you want to do anything special this summer, Louie?"

Louie looked up from her broccoli and shrugged.

Her mother made a *tsk* with her tongue, a sound which she reserved to express her annoyance. In this instance, it was about her husband's unbuttoned pants at the table and his attempt to shift the conversation to their daughter.

Louie's showers usually ended with such a *tsk* of her mother's tongue and a complaint about her aching back. Other times, her mother would thrust the towel past the curtain and hold it there until Louie wiped the water out of her eyes and took it. She hadn't been allowed to bathe alone since she'd returned from Ohio.

"She should do summer school this summer," Courtney said with arched brows. "Her social studies grade was dismal! We need to get serious about this, Lou. You only have four years before you start applying to college."

Louie opened her mouth but caught her father's slight shake of the head. She shut her mouth and resumed her assault on the vegetables.

Courtney topped off her glass of wine and retired to the bedroom, with the cordless phone as she did every night. She'd call her sister, and they'd talk while watching the DVR recordings of her favorite soap operas.

As soon as the bedroom door closed, her father nodded toward the back door. "Last one out is a snot-covered Wheat Thin."

Louie wrinkled her nose. "Gross!" Any lingering hunger from her unsatisfying meal was squashed by this disgusting image. She pushed back from the oaken table.

Despite his playful attempt to put her at ease, her heart knocked wildly against her ribs and her legs dragged beneath her like two bags of wet sand. She wasn't sure if it was the prospect of going near the pool or the pretense of their conversation.

Her father turned to find her trailing reluctantly behind.

She closed the door and stepped out into their fenced backyard. She skirted the kidney bean-shaped pool. Her eyes transfixed on the dark water. "What's wrong?"

"Come over here and sit with me," he said. He slipped into one of the poolside chairs and patted the seat beside him.

Her arms and legs felt ten pounds heavier, but Louie obeyed, inching toward him. Once they were knee to knee, he spoke up.

"I want to talk about the pool."

The pulse in her ears blocked out all sound.

"Stay with me, Louie," he said as she instinctively stepped away from the water. "I know this scares you, but it's important."

When she didn't answer, he put his hand on her shoulder, cupping the large scar encircling her upper arm and clavicle. Twenty-three stitches and months of physical therapy to combat the scar tissue which formed after.

"Louie, Louiiii. Oh baby," he sang. If he wanted her to smile, he sang mumbled nonsense from some '60s cover song. "Do you trust me?"

She did. But she only managed a small nod despite her father's pleasing baritone.

"Do you remember me telling you about Aunt Lucy?"

Her brows pinched together. "The one you named me after?"

"That's the one. I want you to go stay with her."

"You're sending me away?" She swayed on her feet. The shadows dancing at the edge of the motion lights pressed in on her, swiped at her neck and face with cold fingers. And the water—the godawful water—seemed to roll toward her like a hungry, anxious tongue, lapping at the sides of the pool.

"No, no," her father said, squeezing her shoulders. "Aunt Lucy can help you."

"Summer school," she blurted. "Mom said I—"

"You don't need to learn about wars, Lou-blue. You need help."

"I'm sorry about—" Louie stammered. "I know it's not normal. I—"

"No, no, hey," he said. He pulled her into his arms. She collapsed completely even before he kissed the top of her head. A whiff of beer burned her nose. She liked the smell. She wrapped her arms around him.

"This isn't a punishment. You haven't done anything wrong. Do you hear me?"

"I don't want to leave." Tears stung the corners of her eyes. Her fists balled behind his back. "Don't make me leave."

I only feel safe with you. She wasn't sure if it was merely his size or the steady calm of his presence. He wasn't reactive like her mother. He wasn't volatile in his responses—one minute pleased, the next panicked —he was even. Predictable. A cool, unmovable stone to rest her hot face against.

He grounded her in a world where she felt on the verge of falling through at any moment.

"Maybe Lucy can come here," he said, kissing the top of her head. "But you need to see her. I think she can help you. When we were children, she would disappear like you did."

She pulled herself out of his lap. Like her. Someone in the world like *her.* "Why didn't you tell me?"*An aunt. An aunt like me.* "Why didn't you tell me about Aunt Lucy?"

"I had to find her first." He considered the beer bottle as if the answer was hidden in the bottom. He looked up and saw the questions in Lou's eyes. "Aunt Lucy and I didn't always get along. I didn't believe her. I thought she disappeared for attention. I figured she liked scaring our grandmother half to death."

Louie cupped her elbows with her palms and chewed her lip. *An aunt. An aunt like me.*

"But I believe you," he said and pushed her hair out of her eyes. "And I don't want you to be afraid. When you're out of school this summer, we'll have three whole months to work on this. We'll figure this out."

"This isn't a trick?" Louie whispered, squeezing her elbow tighter. "I'm not being sent away to an insane asylum or something?"

"No," he said, firm. "Lucy wants to help. She thinks she can show you how to control it—"

Louie's voice bursts from her throat. "I'm not going in the water!"

"You can control it," her father said again. He pressed her hands to his beard, trapping them beneath his own. She loved this beard and thought it made him look very handsome. But it wasn't enough to soothe her blind panic. Not now. When the pool seemed to swell in her vision.

"No." She tried to pull her hands away from his. "You don't understand. There are things over there."

He wouldn't let go of her. "You can conquer this. And I'll be right here."

Nightmares reared in her mind. A great yellow eye. Rows of stained teeth. Hooked talons reaching.

"Master this, Lou-blue. Don't be its victim." He cupped her cheeks this time and kissed the tip of her nose. "Promise me."

Gunfire erupted in the house. Their heads snapped toward the sound of it in time to see strobe lights flash in the bedroom window. The noise of glass shattering wafted through the open bedroom window. No screams. Then the gunfire ceased, and the bedroom fell dark again except for the soft blue light of the television.

Seconds later, only long enough for her father to stand from the pool chair, men burst through the side gate into their backyard. A hand shoved aside a lilac bush. Petals the colors of bruises rained down on the lawn.

Louie saw a specter, a phantom illuminated by the motion lights. And that was all she saw before her father lifted her off the ground and threw her into the pool.

Her body hit the surface, and on impact, the air was knocked out of her, swallowing her scream. The cold water engulfed her, enclosed her limbs like tendrils of seaweed. Through the aqua distortion, she saw her father turn and run, his white shirt an ethereal target drawing the gunfire away from her.

But even as she tried to frantically swim toward the surface, screaming and reaching out for him, she felt herself falling through.

But she never forgot the face of the monster.

Angelo Martinelli. And here he was at long last.

"The kid's dead. We made sure."

"Sorry to disappoint you." She kept one eye on Angelo, but her attention was on the trees. She had only one reason for bringing Angelo here. *Where are you?*

"What are you looking at?" Angelo turned toward the trees and peered into the black forest.

Her shoulder burned. The warped flesh and old scar tissue was a reminder of the beast's stealth. Of its ability to appear suddenly no matter how quiet or careful she was.

It's close.

The dark seemed to ripple, and Lou had only a second to prepare herself.

A beast with skin the color of tar leapt from the trees. Angelo screamed the way she must have the first time she saw the animal. If it could be called an animal. Six legs with scaly feet. Pus-colored talons and eyes. A face and round belly could be mistaken for cute, as long as it didn't open its mouth and hurl its death screech into the sky. Or bared its double row of jagged shark teeth.

Lou put one foot in the water, making Angelo the closer target. His decision to scream and run only sealed his fate. She knew she should jump into the water. Slip through before the animal could catch her.

When she used La Loon to dump dead bodies, she never stayed longer than a minute. But Angelo was alive. She wasn't leaving until she saw him dead.

The beast's serpentine back contracted, black muscle stretching long as it lurched forward onto its anterior feet. Screaming louder, Angelo dashed for her as if to throw himself at her feet and beg for mercy.

"You can't run from it," she said. Her voice was weakened by her throbbing shoulder. Her old scars were alive again. "It'll catch up to you every time."

One snap of its jaws brought Angelo down. A second tore open his belly, spilling his guts onto the wet earth. The flesh stretched away from his rib cage, the scraps of leather jacket serving as inadequate protection.

He stayed alive much longer than Lou expected, long after his intestines erupted, spilling out of his abdomen as if spring loaded. Then his screams weren't much more than gurgling sounds. The water's edge grew darker, thicker with Angelo's gore.

Lou took a step toward the creature. Its yellow eyes contracted at the sight of her. The eyes, forward facing like the predators of her own world. Its lips pulled back in a recognizable growl.

Master this, Lou-blue. Don't be its victim. Promise me. The sound of her father's voice in her mind winded her. Her sweet father who was dead because of the man at her feet.

The beast's nostrils flared.

"Am I still prey?" Lou asked, and slid one heel behind the other. She assumed a fighter's stance and curled her fingers around the handle of her knife. "If you think so, then I still have business here."

Lou waited for the pounce. A lunge. The way it would rise on its hind legs like a fox.

But the beast didn't pounce. It regarded her with its acid-yellow eyes and then much the way a hyena protects its kill, the monster seized one of Angelo's legs in its mouth and dragged his body into the woods to eat in privacy. It kept one great yellow eye on her as it went.

4

King found Lucy Thorne stretched on his red leather sofa, an icy glass of sweet tea balanced on her pale knee. Her body was ethereal in the moonlight coming through the open terrace door. It was if she'd never left him. In twelve years, the only discernible change was her hair. She wore it longer now. It fell over her shoulders and hung halfway down her back like a curtain. It had been pixie short, a cleaner version of Piper's style when he met her.

"Nice place you have here, Robert." Lucy put the glass of ice tea on a coaster, one of the many mismatched rounds of cardboard King had stolen from local bars. He had quite the collection. He worried she might notice how many bars. Or he *would* have worried if the top of her red sundress hadn't stretched across her chest, showcasing hard nipples. It was difficult to worry when faced with hard nipples.

She caught him staring and grinned. "The pension must be good."

"I'm a kept man," he joked, heat filling his face. "I hooked up with the rich widow downstairs, and as long as I pleasure her when she calls, all my expenses are paid."

Lucy barked a short, sharp laugh. "I'm glad to hear you're putting your talents to good use."

Your talents. The words were like a cold hand on the back of his neck.

If anyone knew anything about his skills, it would be Lucy. He'd never worked so hard to please a woman in his life.

It hadn't been enough to keep her.

Lucy ran a thumb down the side of her thigh, wiping up a glistening trail of moisture left by her tea glass.

He realized he was standing in his apartment staring down at her like an idiot and not because she was beautiful but because he wasn't sure what to do with the file. If he set it down, there was the chance she'd scoop it up. And while he didn't think Lucy had any connection to the Venetti case, and wasn't sent to steal the file from him, he also didn't know why she was here.

"Were you in the neighborhood?" *Or feeling horny? Please god, say horny.* He didn't mind being used for a night. He would brush his teeth first. If he could squeeze one last dollop out of his crushed tube.

Lucy's coquettish face tightened around the mouth and eyes. "Right to the chase. I like that about you. Who has time for banter?"

"We can banter," he said, trying to recover the ground he'd apparently lost. Her tone had changed the way a woman's tone always changed when he said the wrong thing. Was it because he kept standing over her? Did he seem hurried?

He went to the leather armchair in the corner and sat down. He tucked the folder between the rolled arm and the cushion wedging it there.

"No," she said, not bothering to hide her curiosity. She tilted her head as if in question at the folder. Was he giving the game away like a first-year rookie?

She looked away. "You're in the middle of something. So I won't keep you."

Keep me, he thought. *I don't mind.*

His aging and pitifully nostalgic mind accosted him with bright images of Lucy the last time he'd seen her. The way her long body had looked in the morning sunlight. She was naked, tangled in his sheets. When she smiled, he knew she'd caught him staring. She'd rolled over, exposing her breasts. On the small side but perfectly sized with dainty nipples the color of cotton candy. And Lord, what a carnival ride their lovemaking had been.

"You're less reputable than I remember," she said, her elbows balanced on her knees.

King blinked away his thoughts. "What?"

She took a drink of tea, crunching a piece of ice between her teeth. "I—"

"Nothing damning," she said. "But you had such a hard stance on drugs sixteen years ago."

Her eyes slid to the Bob Dylan vinyl lying beside a record player. That's where he kept his weed and a half-used pack of rolling papers. How had she known about that?

"You searched my place?"

"A little snooping," she admitted with a coy smile. "I wanted to make sure you were still an okay guy."

"Okay is a low standard." She'd hurt his feelings. When was the last time someone had been able to hurt his feelings? "I haven't turned into a drug dealer or pimp. I don't torture animals."

His buzz was gone.

She frowned. "I'm not criticizing you. I'm only saying you seem less self-righteous than I remember. It's a good thing, Robert. I always thought you needed to relax more."

Says the tofu-eating yoga teacher, he thought. He said, "Only young men can afford to be self-righteous. At my age, you realize we're all equally fucked."

Lucy's smile tightened, and her gaze slid away toward the balcony. They're in the dark and yet he couldn't bring himself to turn on a light. He believed she would disappear if he did. He wasn't ready.

"You didn't come here to listen to an old man rant." His chest clenched. "Tell me what you need. You know I'll do it."

She looked up at him through her lashes. "What makes you think I want something from you?"

"The fact that you're here," he said. "And you're not the begging type. It's important."

"Or maybe I do plenty of begging these days."

He said nothing.

Lucy looked toward the balcony, her gaze growing distant. "Jack worshiped you, you know."

It was like she'd slapped him across the face.

Jack Thorne.

When King broke three ribs during a drug bust, he'd been asked to do a term teaching at Quantico while he healed up. Jack Thorne, with sandy hair and big brown eyes that made him look like a goddamn doe in an evening field, was one of his first students. But Jack was brilliant. Smart as a whip. A damn hard worker. And sharp instincts. When Jack graduated from his DEA training, King himself put in the request to have Thorne transferred to his department in St. Louis.

The years he spent mentoring Thorne were the best in his life. King had his balls back post-divorce and he'd thrown himself into his work without apology for the first time. He'd always loved his job, but now the work had been great because he had this bright, smart-ass kid at his side. Pushing him. Challenging him. King had never felt so alive, and they had the success stories to prove it.

They were the golden years. Until Thorne and his attractive, if uppity, young wife got killed by the Martinelli family. Their deaths were on King. He was the one who'd given Thorne the bust. Asked him to do the press. Put his fucking face all over the goddamn media.

He wanted Thorne to take the credit, him and his pudgy partner Gus Johnson. Hoped the recognition would give him the promotion he deserved.

It got Thorne a medal and nine bullets to the chest.

The worst of it: Jack Thorne's name was trashed, dragged through the mud by anyone who could get their hands on it. Overnight, he went from hero and family man to master manipulator. The media found a more sensational, better-selling tale. The murder of Jack Thorne and his wife wasn't a revenge killing for Thorne's arrest of Angelo Martinelli's brother. It was gang shit gone wrong. Thorne had been aiding the Martinelli clan all along. He was a mole. A snitch. He betrayed his comrades and closest friends. And it hadn't been enough to play both sides. When he'd gotten too greedy, the infamous crime family lit him up like flashing Christmas lights.

It was all bullshit. The press and the department slandered a good man to save their own asses.

Lucy was talking again. "He said you got through to him in a way no one ever could. And you may have changed, but you're still a good teacher. Your students say so."

So she even knew about the occasional adjuncting for LSU's criminal justice department. She'd been digging. For what? "If you're looking for my references, there's a job. What's the job?"

Lucy worried her lip.

"Spit it out while I'm still riding the tail of my buzz. You know I'm very open to suggestion when inebriated." It was a joke meant to put her at ease, even if he couldn't ease his own dark thoughts.

In his mind, he bent down beside a black body bag. His shaking hand pulled the zipper tab to reveal Thorne's face. So young. So goddamn young.

A fly landed on the dead man's face, twitching its wings.

"Lou is just like him. Tough. Smart. *Too smart.*" She barked another laugh. "Stubborn. Determined. Focused. A complete disregard for authority."

King grinned. "Quite a combination."

"She's a challenge, but she is an achiever."

A letter of recommendation, maybe. King did the math in his head. Thorne's kid would be 25? 26? Too old for college so it would be for the force then. Perhaps she wanted him to pull some strings and get her a job in one of the safer departments. But if she were even half as good as Thorne, she'd be wasted on a desk job. "You want me to put in a good word with someone? That's no problem. I'm happy to help."

And he was. It didn't matter that the minute Lucy learned her brother was dead, she'd dropped King like panties on prom night and assumed the mantle of guardian to the girl. It hurt. He'd missed her like hell for a long time too. Looking at her on his red leather sofa in the moonlight coming from the terrace he wondered if he'd ever stopped missing her.

He didn't blame the kid.

He'd lost Lucy, and it was his own fault. He hadn't gone after her because his guilt wouldn't let him. It was his responsibility for getting Jack killed and for not working harder to salvage the man's reputation when the whole fucking ship started to sink. Everyone took hits when Jack's loyalty had been pulled up and examined. He saved his own ass, and he knew it.

Louie would face her own problems in the force. Overcoming her father's reputation was only the beginning.

A cloud passed over the moon, and Lucy's face was hidden in shadow. Only her mouth shown, her teeth glowing in the light as she let go of her bottom lip.

He realized what she *wasn't* saying. No, *thank you*. No *that would be great*.

Not a recommendation then. "Is she in trouble?"

King's mind ran wild with the possibilities. Drugs. Prostitution. Kidnapping. She'd been kidnapped by a new drug lord, and he would have 32 hours to bring her back alive. He sure as hell hoped not. He was no Liam Neeson.

Lucy shook her head. "She's not a victim."

"I'm a piss poor guesser." *And it's been a long night for cloak and dagger meetings*. He ran a hand over his head. He moved from the chair to the coffee table so he could be closer to her. Right across from her. The wood groaned but didn't break. He was close enough to smell her lotion now. She still smelled like sandalwood and peonies. He prayed she couldn't smell his pickle-booze breath. "This is going to take all night if you make me guess, Lucy. If you want to stay the night, I can think of better things we could be doing."

She flashed him a weak smile. "I want you to promise that you won't go to the police with this. Hear me out and if you don't like what I tell you then forget I said anything."

"Kids make mistakes." He immediately drew up a list of twenty or thirty of his own fuckups. Some of them committed in the last few months.

"Do you remember Gus Johnson?"

"He disappeared."

Lucy gave him a look. "And the crime family who killed Jack and Courtney."

"Wiped out one by one," King said. "But they never found a body. Or a weapon."

Lucy's hard look lingered.

A pinpoint of surprise dilated in his mind, expanding into full-blown awe. "You're saying Louie's working with a team? She fell in with some mercenary group or gang—"

"No." Lucy shook her head. "Lou works alone. She's not...a people person."

"Lou." He laughed. "A girl named *Lou* single-handedly destroyed an entire crime family? You're fucking with me."

Lucy's face was disturbingly calm.

"When you took her in, did you send her to ninja school?" He couldn't believe this. There's no way she pulled off those jobs alone. When King himself had heard about the Martinelli's destruction, he assumed it was a rival crime family. There were enough of them out there, vying for supremacy. And he knew some thought Martinelli's iron-clad rule had gone on for too long.

If Lou killed even *one* of the Martinellis, she had combat skills. Intel gathering skills. Espionage. A fuck ton of guns. Not to mention balls, or in this case ovaries, the size of Texas.

How did she come by that training? Certainly not from her Buddhist aunt who wouldn't even eat a bacon cheeseburger for fear of the animals' suffering. Lucy wouldn't have even let the girl kill the flies in her house, he was sure of it. Unless she was carting the girl off to some shaolin temple on the weekends...which begged a lot of questions.

So how was she trained? How did she pull it off?

No *one* person had it all. It's the reason mercenaries often worked in teams. "Logistically, what you're saying is impossible."

Lucy's face hardened. "She's Jack Thorne in miniature, with Courtney's cold heart. And she got a little something from me too."

His humor dried up like a creek bed in July.

She placed the empty glass on the table and leveled her gaze on him. "Do you remember?"

"No," he said. Doors in his mind began to slam shut. Memories tried to surface, and he shoved them down with a rough hand.

"The night those men came for you...?" she probed gently. As if she knew he was lying to himself as well as her. "She's hurt. She's angry. I think Lou hunts these men as a way to pay homage to Jack."

"I don't know what you think I can do." He grabbed her glass off the coffee table and dumped the rest of the ice into his mouth.

"Give her a case, anything that'll help her see there's another way to use her abilities." Lucy slid off the couch and knelt in front of him. She took his free hand in hers and squeezed it. "Please, Robert. *Please.* I've tried everything. I've lectured. I've chanted. I tried to get her into yoga."

"Yes, that's how we tame all the would-be assassins." The empty tea glass grew warm in his hand. "Down dog."

It was Lucy's turn to pull at her face in exasperation. "If she keeps going on like this, she's going to end up dead, and she's all I have left."

You could have me.

"I promised Jack."

We all made promises to Jack we couldn't keep.

"It's too much to expect her to stop..." Lucy searched for a word. "...*hunting*. I can accept her nature but she needs guidance. Please."

So will you do it?

He knew his answer. He would do it. For Jack. For Lucy. And tomorrow he knew he'd tell Brasso the same thing. *I'll do it.*

And just like that King found himself with not one but two jobs in less than twenty-four hours. Two faces from his past surfacing. What was it his mother loved to say? Some old proverb?

Trouble travels in threes.

What could he expect next?

King took Lucy's hand and squeezed it. It was as cold as a corpse's hand, sending a chill through his body. "When do I meet her?"

5

Konstantine stood in the alley with blood drying in the hairs on his arms. His chest heaved as he struggled to catch his breath. A wind rolling through the narrow alley hit the back of his neck and the sweat beading there. It itched, and when he reached back and raked his nails along his occipital bone, his fingers came away wet.

Now that the excitement was over, the .357 in his hand doubled its weight.

He pulled a purple rag from his back pocket and wiped his face and neck. Then he tucked the gun into the waistband beneath his black shirt and the cloth back into his pocket.

Konstantine turned away from the body and searched the alley. A gray cat with white paws washed its ears on a stone stoop. Otherwise, no witnesses. No allies either.

The bells of the Duomo began to ring, loud clangs vibrating through the city center.

Where the fuck are they? Konstantine looked up between the buildings but saw only the clear blue sky. Then a sound caught his attention. *Speak of the devil, and he appears.*

A red Fiat 500 rolled past the alley and then the brakes squealed.

The car whined as it reversed, backing into the tight space between the two stone buildings where Konstantine stood over a dead man.

It backed over the cobblestones, tires bumping as Konstantine used his hands to direct the driver. *Left, a little to the right*, and then a fist. *Stop.* The brake lights flared red.

The doors on both sides popped open, and two men climbed out, one with obvious difficulty. The passenger had to grip the roof and haul his massive body out of the small seat. Once he'd cleared the door, his enormous belly flattened against the wall, causing him to sharply inhale until he could squeeze through. Calzone was what they called him, at least amongst the Ravengers. His mother, whom he still lived with, called him Marcello.

Vincenzo, the driver, was rail thin and his limbs twitchy like a rat's. He jerked himself from the car, stopped toe-to-toe with the body bleeding out on the stone walk.

"O Signore, what a mess," he whined and turned his head away, puffing his cheeks. He grabbed a cigarette from behind his ear and a white plastic lighter from his front pocket. He didn't look at the body as he lit the cigarette, indulged in a slow drag, and blew the smoke skyward in a long dramatic exhalation. Then Vincenzo's eyes slid to the corpse again. "A fucking mess."

"You bitch like a woman," Calzone said. His fingers disappeared into one of his many chins, and the fat jiggled as he scratched himself. "Hurry up, I'm hungry."

"You're always hungry," Konstantine said, but he tempered the words with a good-natured smile. Now that they were here, filling the alleyway with meaningless prattle, the knot in his chest loosened.

Another squeaking sound caused all three men to freeze and turn toward the opposite end of the alley. An old man with a shopping cart full of plants shuffled past. He wore an enormous hat and round spectacles with thick lenses magnifying his surprise. The old man froze under their gaze and his mouth opened in question.

Then he saw the purple rags hanging from back pockets. The old man howled like a theatrical ghost and threw his cart into traffic.

Calzone started after him, but Konstantine reached out and barred his path with a straight arm. Let the old man get away. What could he do?

Konstantine nodded toward the corpse. "You'll never get lunch if you waste any more time."

"You've got to be heading out too," Vincenzo said. He pushed a button on the Fiat's fob, and the trunk popped open. The interior was lined with thick plastic, not unlike the kind one might place along the floor before painting. "Padre's asking for you."

Vincenzo's black hair fell into his eyes as he squatted down to grab the dead man's arms. Still stooped, he looked up at Calzone. "You gonna help me or stand there looking pretty?"

Calzone grunted and bent to grab the dead man's legs. The jeans slid up revealing cotton socks. One shoe, an American sneaker, wobbled, threatening to fall off. Then it did.

They dumped the body onto the plastic without ceremony, and the Fiat bounced under the weight before the rubber tires settled. Vincenzo was forced to pretzel the dead man's limbs into the trunk. Calzone had one enormous hand on the trunk lid, waiting.

"Hold up," Vincenzo said and scooped up the sneaker. "What do you think this is, an 8 or 9? I bet I could wear these."

Konstantine turned in the direction of the fleeing man. He didn't want to watch Vincenzo strip the dead man of his shoes. And he wanted to wash his hands and face before seeing Padre.

"Well *arrivederci* to you too," Vincenzo called after him.

Konstantine didn't stop. He marched to the Piazza six blocks away. There had not been much blood spray from the gunshot, and what little there had been was hidden by his dark clothes and shoes. A thin mist of blood had dried on his forearms, but no one in the streets looked too closely at him. It could be the purple rag in his pocket. Or it could be the way he walked the streets as a man who was not to be deterred in any way. Shoulders high. Chin tucked and eyes hidden behind dark shades.

Three guys lingered on the cathedral steps, smoking. Only one, Michele, greeted him before he ducked into the church. At the nave, he went right and stepped into a modern bathroom with a faucet. He'd seen no one in the church at this hour. No one on their knees asking for forgiveness.

He washed up without looking in the mirror. If he could help it, he went weeks without looking at himself in the polished glass, afraid of what he might see.

He would find Padre Leo in the basement.

In the chapel, the urge to kneel before the Blessed Mother overwhelmed him like a rising choir. He kneeled, crossed himself, and kept his eyes lowered. He had no problems worshipping Mother Mary. The idea of a mother goddess rang true. Mothers were love. Peace. Fierce protection. It was the heavenly Father he could not believe in. There was no such man in his world worthy of such reverence. Except perhaps Padre Leo. But Padre Leo was only a man as flawed as the rest of them.

Konstantine ducked into a stone stairway leading to the basement. Unlit torches hung on the wall, long ago rendered obsolete with the installation of electricity. His boots scuffed along the steps until the narrow passageway opened to the lowest level.

Men stood in groups of three or four. Some were laughing, oblivious to Konstantine's presence. Others had placed their hands on their guns, eyes sharp.

He waved a hand, and they relaxed. Shoulders slumped. Breath exhaled.

"He's in there," said Francesco. His new buzzed haircut made his ears look twice as large.

Konstantine fell on heavy doors made of redwood and stained-glass windows. The brass handles turned, and the hinges creaked open under the weight of his body. Slowly, an inner sanctum was revealed. Straight ahead, a desk sat with high bookcases behind it. The wood of the bureau, doors, and furniture was all the same rich wood. Cherry perhaps. Or oak with a sangria finish. The room was messy, looking more like the enclave of a professor than the head of one of the most notorious gangs in the world.

But Konstantine's lord and master was not at his desk.

A deep, whooping cough echoed from the bathroom. The door stood ajar. From Konstantine's place on the dusty rug, an outline of a man hunched over the sink was clear enough.

"Padre?"

Leo opened the bathroom door, and his lips pulled back in a grimace. "Close the door."

Konstantine leaned on the heavy doors again, sealing them up in the enclave.

Padre Leo shuffled across the dim room toward the desk and collapsed in the high-back chair, a hacking cough shaking his thin frame. He held a purple, silk handkerchief over his pockmarked face.

It was a long time before Padre caught his breath. Konstantine kept looking to the bathroom, wondering if he should fetch a drink or wet rag.

"Should I—?" Konstantine began.

"No need," Leo said, his face red with exertion. "This will not take long."

Konstantine felt as if he had been slapped across the face. The man owed him nothing. If he had decided Konstantine should stand on one foot from dawn until midnight, it was expected he would do so without question or protest.

The muscles in Konstantine's back twitched. "I am not in a hurry, Padre."

The man wiped at his mouth with his purple silk, and it came away wet with blood.

"Are you okay?" Konstantine's heart hammered at the sight of blood. It always did.

The man smoothed bony fingers over his gray hair and gave a snide snort. "I am not. Or so the doctors tell me."

"Is it serious?" Konstantine asked. Then seemed to catch himself and the absurdity of the question. "It's none of my business."

Leo waved him off. "Drop the ass-kissing. Frankly, we don't have time for it. I need to make my wishes clear while I still have the breath to do so."

As if to emphasize this, he began coughing again. The sound was wretched, shaking the man like a toy in the jaws of a great dog. The cords in his neck stood out. Sweat gleamed on his forehead even in the chilled basement of the old church. The purple rag was darker still with his bloody spittle by the time he caught his breath.

As Padre drew in a few shaky breaths, he motioned for Konstantine to sit in the leather armchair beside the desk. Konstantine understood and obeyed. He pulled the .357 from behind his back when he sat and laid it on the desk, pointing away from his boss.

"As you can see," Leo said at last. "It is challenging for me to talk. In truth, it's difficult to do anything. I've stopped eating. I've stopped sleeping. It is too painful to lay down. Even my mattress hurts my chest. The doctors say I have a month at most."

"What could act so quickly?" Konstantine asked. A red-hot flood of shame washed over him, but per Padre's wishes, he didn't apologize again.

"It wasn't fast. It's only I can't hide my illness any longer." He snorted, threatened a laugh but then pressed one hand hard on his diaphragm to stop himself, as if the cost of laughing was too high a price to pay now.

Padre fell back against the chair. He slumped like a child at the dinner table. Konstantine sat up straighter as if to compensate.

"This organization is my lifeblood, Konstantine. I believe you understand."

"Yes, sir." Konstantine expected some important task. Some last command or dying wish. He would honor it as he had every other request from Padre Leo since he joined the Ravengers fifteen years before.

Leo's breath remained shallow. "I have bled and dreamed and built this empire from the ground up."

"I know."

"When I am no longer in this world, I want to know my legacy is preserved, my ambitions honored. Change of power is a turbulent time for any group, but the right man can make the transition easy. A steady hand can take the ship's wheel and steer her fine."

Konstantine's heart sped up. "I will support whomever you choose. If others object—" because Konstantine knew that no matter who was selected, someone would object. The most ambitious would see themselves supreme. Others would consider their loyalty to the Ravengers finished, their contracts terminated upon the death of the man who had recruited them. "If others object I will persuade them."

Padre wiped at his brow with his bloody rag, seemingly unaware of the blood he smeared across his forehead. Konstantine leaped up, wet his own cloth with fresh water from the sink and offered it to the man. Leo's fingers trembled when he took it.

"I will name you as my successor, Konstantine."

"Me? Why in god's name? I am no one."

"You want my reasons?"

He knew he had no right to ask them. And already the older man's face was burning red, his breath shortening again. Padre spoke anyway.

"You understand this new age in a way most Ravengers do not. You are strategic. You are futuristic. You are adaptable. Who better to leave my empire to? You do things with computers most of my men cannot even fathom."

Leo pulled up his dress shirt and revealed his left forearm. He placed the arm, belly up on the desk so Konstantine could see the tattoo clearly. Not that he needed to see it. Konstantine bore the same mark on his own skin. A crow and crossbones. The crow, wings spread as if in flight and the two bones crossed beneath.

"The raven is a symbol of longevity. Of intelligence and stealth. It is why I chose it as my emblem."

Only Konstantine did not see a raven. He saw a crow with blunt and splayed wings rather than a raven's pointed tips. He saw the small flat bill without its tuft. They called themselves Ravengers—a poetic condensation of *raven* and *ravager*. But Konstantine alone seemed to see the difference between the cousin birds. He knew that while a raven could live for thirty years or more, a crow was lucky to see eight.

"You have the global perspective and technological comprehension to take us into the new age. Furthermore, I trust no one else."

"Padre—"

"Would you reject me?"

"No." He did not hesitate. "Never."

"Because I have already contacted those people whom I believe will be most beneficial to you during the transition. I will give you their names, and I want you to reach out to them immediately and make your intentions clear. Despite your reservations, sound sure of yourself and your plans for the Ravengers. It is easier to support a man who is sure of himself."

Your plans for the Ravengers. Konstantine had none. His heart pounded. He wet his lips with his tongue but still found no way to express his thoughts.

"And here is where I ask something *truly* difficult of you," the man said, and he extended his open palm to Konstantine. Konstantine had not held the man's hand since he was ten and Padre Leo had invited him into the fold in exchange for his mother's immunity and protection.

Konstantine could only look at the open palm.

Padre Leo smiled. "Indulge a silly old man."

Konstantine took his hand.

"Be a Martinelli," Leo said, and when Konstantine tried to jerk his hand away as if burned, Leo clamped down on it. Surprising power pulsed through the old man's grip as if Death itself lent him his indomitable strength. "You have rejected your father's name, but I ask you to embrace it now."

"You ask too much," Konstantine said, yanking the way an animal might jerk if caught in a trap, ready to rip off its own paw to be free.

Leo did not let go. "The only flaw the Ravengers bear is their youth. They wait for us to be foolish in the ways young ones always are. We are democrats, not aristocrats. New money, not old. But you can bridge that gap, Konstantine, with the Martinelli name alone."

Be a Martinelli. But he could never. How could he bear the name of a man he despised?

"I know you hold no love in your heart for your father, but others do. And I have heard the loyalists are desperate for any link to the family they've lost. With Angelo's death, you are the last. *Use* it. For all they know, he groomed you himself. A bastard son is still a son. Be a Ravenger, my boy, but also be a Martinelli. There is no one to oppose you! And taking up the mantel of an old, distinguished line will offer opportunities for expansion and unification. I am sure of it."

Angelo's death. He had not heard. So it was done then. She had her revenge. Good.

"No one will oppose you," Padre Leo said as if trying to read his silence. Konstantine knew he was wrong, but he let the man hold his arm and make his demands.

"Power comes with benefits," Padre said, eyeing Konstantine in his stillness, measuring his silence. "With my money and your father's name, you could have whatever you desire. Is there nothing you can think of having for yourself?"

Yes.

He wanted *her*. The girl who'd appeared one night, curled in his bed like a kitten by a fire.

With Padre Leo's resources, he could find her. As a Martinelli, she might find *him*.

6

Lou bolted upright in her bed, head throbbing with adrenaline. She had the gun pointed without consciously choosing a target.

"You've never been a morning person," Aunt Lucy said, closing the closet door behind her and stepping into the studio apartment. "But this is a tad extreme."

Her aunt stood by the closet with two take-out cups in hand. A long skirt rubbed against her calves and the tops of her sandals. *Jesus sandals* Lou called them. Like Lucy should be trudging across the desert preaching love and forgiveness to anyone who would listen.

Lou lowered the gun to the soft coverlet draped across her legs.

"Where have you been?" Lucy shifted her weight to one hip. "It's been hard to track you down."

In the three weeks since killing Angelo, she'd been restless. She'd hardly slept. Hardly ate. A pervasive feeling of loss surrounded her, like she'd forgotten something and couldn't stop searching for it.

But everywhere she searched, she only found violence.

Last night she'd ended up in a dive bar in West Texas, beating the shit out of six bikers in a parking lot. She'd only wanted one of them— Kenny Soren. But when his friend grabbed her ass, she'd broken his wrist instantly. Then introductions were made by all.

She looked down at the dark purple and rose colored bruises across her knuckles. A marble-sized pocket of fluid rest above her second knuckle. She'd obviously busted a vein.

Lucy's breath hitched, and her eyes slid away. "You need ibuprofen."

"I don't have any."

"Here," Lucy said and gave Lou one of the Styrofoam cups. When Lou reached to accept it, the aches and pains from last night made themselves known. She'd done something to her shoulder. It screamed when the arm extended. It was probably the baseball bat that'd come down on her shoulder blade. She raised her arm overhead, rotated it until the tension eased. Then her neck cramped.

"You need to do bhujangasana," her aunt said. She put her own coffee cup on the counter and went into the kitchen, which was really still the living room, and the bedroom given the studio design. Drawers opened and closed loudly. Ice rustled in the freezer. Then Lucy reappeared with an ice pack wrapped in a dishcloth.

Lou accepted the ice pack. Her aunt's cheeks were flushed, and her jaw worked furiously. And if Lou wasn't mistaken, a hint of wetness glistened near her temples, as if she'd quickly scrubbed at her eyes.

They wouldn't talk about Lou's injuries. Lucy wouldn't ask how she got them, no matter how much she might want to. Lucy had set this policy herself and the fact that she'd taken her tears to the other room was proof this rule had not changed.

Lou's stomach turned. "Bhujangasana. Is that what the kids are calling it?"

She swung her legs out of the covers and put her bare feet on the cool wood floor. She let her hand rest between her thigh and the ice pack as she drank the coffee using her free hand.

"It's yoga," Lucy said, her voice strong again. "Cobra pose."

Lucy laid on the floor in demonstration, belly down, and pushed away from the floor with her forearms. "It opens up your chest and shoulders and feels *so* good."

Yoga. Of course.

Lou had no idea why she thought her aunt would even suggest drugs for her aching body. As a child, when Lou got migraines, her aunt would boil her tea rather than fill her prescription for Sumatriptan. Lou would be an inch from a brain bleed, and Lucy would hand her a steaming cup much like the one she held now and say some shit like *all the love and none of the side effects.*

"Or!" Lucy said, her eyes widening and lips breaking into an *ah ha* grin. "You could do Thunderbolt, Vajrasana." She rose into a lunge, arms out in front of her.

Lou tuned out the woman doing yoga in her periphery and lifted the cup to her nose. She inhaled. The scent of roasted coffee shifted the whole world into focus. The harsh sunlight softened to a warm glow. Her aches seemed to relax with the rest of her body. She was wondering if this was how cocaine addicts felt after their first line of the day.

"Le Bobillot?"

"It's still there," Aunt Lucy said, her face smashed into the wood floor as she held her next pose. "As charming as ever, though I see no one is adhering to the smoking ban. *Gah.*"

Sunlight streamed through the large windows and warmed the back of Lou's neck. She sipped her coffee and pictured the Paris café in her mind. A corner building across from a boulangerie. Round tables were evenly spaced in a row on each side of the door, so if a patron so wished, they could drink their coffee while watching the 13th arrondissement buzz around them. Across the way, an ancient church, beastly the way only churches in the Old World could be, rang gigantic bells on the hour.

A month after her parents had died, Aunt Lucy had brought her to this café. Bought her a baguette from the boulangerie across the street. She drank espresso from the tiniest cup she'd ever seen and nibbled her warm loaf. It was the first happy memory she'd had since her father died.

Lou stood, leaving the warmed ice pack on the bed and stretched her arms overhead. She was careful not to dump coffee on herself and then padded over to the window.

Aunt Lucy continued to prattle off yoga poses behind her, building her own flow. It was hard for the woman to stop once she began. Besides, yoga always calmed her aunt. The tension that had erupted between them at the sight of Lou's injuries had diminished, like a mist slowly dissipating from the room.

Lou kept her eyes on the window, on the pool glistening two stories below. The sparkling water surrounded a lush garden with white and pink roses twining the fence. Petunias in patio planters and a creeping morning glory reached for the No Lifeguard On Duty sign.

Stretching out beyond the pool and its walled garden was the St. Louis skyline. The arch cut the sky with a delicate whoosh. The river coursed behind it, shimmering like melted silver. A boat with a large red wheel churning at one end cut through the waters. People as small as ants roamed the boardwalk.

This was the way with Lou and her aunt. Together, perhaps even occupying the same space, yet with an undeniable distance. Sure, each tried to cross the barriers to the other's side, out of love or respect, yet never quite breaking the borders of their own worlds.

"What are you doing tonight?" Aunt Lucy asked. She was on her knees, looking up at her. The yoga flow had ended, and Lou's coffee was nearly gone.

Lou thought of Jimmy Castle.

She'd been in Texas looking for names. Names of anyone associated with the Martinelli crew. Pimps. Drug pushers. Traffickers. She'd weed out all the rats who'd served him, starting with the worst. Before she put a bullet in Kenny Soren, he'd blabbed about Jimmy Castle, a dealer in Dallas, an old-time peddler who still carried the Martinelli torch.

Lou intended to pay Mr. Castle a visit tonight.

"I'm busy." Lou kept her eyes on the St. Louis skyline, on the cars speeding from one end of the bridge to the other. A hand clamped down on her shoulder and turned her around.

"With what?" Lucy demanded. Her blue eyes shimmered with the threat of tears. "They're all dead."

Lou's skin iced and she put the empty Styrofoam cup on a cinder block serving as a bedside table. "How would you know? Is there some Martinelli bulletin board I don't know about?" She forced a smile. She was aiming for joviality, but came up short.

Lucy's lip trembled. "Your father gave you to me—"

Like a goddamn coffeemaker, Lou thought bitterly. She stared at the callus on the side of her thumb.

"—because he wanted me to keep you safe. He wanted you to live, and you're trying your damnedest to get yourself killed!"

They'd begun with the usual cold silence and now the argument.

Lou's shoulders relaxed as the conversation turned familiar. She was on solid ground again.

Her aunt drew a breath, seemed to draw on some inner reserve and stilled herself. "I know you can't stop cold turkey."

Lou snorted. "As if I'm an addict."

Lou thought it was her one good quality. She'd never fallen prey to drugs or alcohol, no matter how deep she went into the underbelly of the world. Lou was her father's daughter in that respect. She could walk beside the derelict without succumbing to the temptations herself.

"Aren't you?" Lucy spat. "Normal people have jobs and friends. Relationships. You're too self-serving for that."

Lou flinched as if slapped.

Lucy grimaced. "I'm sorry."

"Self-serving," Lou repeated. *Self-serving* was her least favorite word in the world. That's what the papers and media had called Jack Thorne. Self-serving. They claimed he'd forgotten his purpose. Forgotten his duty as a public servant. He'd turned *self-serving* in a quest for more money. More power. And this greed had gotten him killed. "Like my father."

"Those were lies," Lucy said. Tears broke the surface and spilled over her aunt's cheeks. "Your dad was a good man."

Lou turned toward the window so she wouldn't have to see those tears. She didn't overlook the fact Lucy was professing Jack's innocence, not hers.

And her aunt was wasting her breath. Lou didn't believe the slander printed on every front page in June of 2004, yet it still stung to hear even the suggestion Jack Thorne had been *self-serving*. Her mother? Without question. Lou loved her mother, but Courtney had been a cold and selfish woman. Every inconvenience was taken personally. Every mistake a personal insult.

But not her father.

"I'm at my wit's end. Every night you go out, you hunt down some criminal and—"

Lou's headache worsened the harder she worked her jaw. She turned when Lucy appeared beside her at the window.

Lucy reached up and brushed the hair out of Lou's face. "I want you to have a life."

"Because your life is *full* of people," Lou said, knowing it would cut her.

Lucy's hand fell away. For a moment, she looked unsure what to do with it. Then she settled for putting it on her hip. "I want more for you. I want you to be happy."

"That's the thing about happiness. It's different for everyone. What makes the executioner happy? You need to understand that's what I am. You preach acceptance. So accept it."

Her aunt reached up and pinched the bridge of her nose. Lou couldn't count on all ten fingers and toes how many times she'd seen her aunt do this. *Here it comes*, she thought. *All the patience is gone, and we'll jump right to the demands now.*

Lucy took a breath. "Your father had a friend, Robert King. He's a private detective in New Orleans. He's offered you a job. He thinks your skills would be useful for his current investigation."

Lou blinked. The conversation had gone in a direction she hadn't expected. She searched for purchase, hoping to pull herself upright again. But her aunt charged on.

"He's an old friend. And he likes to bend the rules like you do. I think you'll like him."

"I don't like anyone."

"He can be trusted."

"No one can be trusted."

Lucy pinched her nose again harder. "He's known about me and what I can do for sixteen years. He hasn't told anyone. *I* trust him."

And now he knows about me.

"Everyone needs allies, Lou. Even you," Lucy said, and it was her own father's words from long ago.

Lou understood what allies were. A big fat liability.

"He wants to meet at the Café du Monde, tonight at eight o'clock. Please be there."

Lucy marched toward the closet and stepped inside. Lou thought she was alone until her aunt reappeared and hurled a bottle of ibuprofen at her.

It hit Lou square in the chest before she caught it.

"And don't shoot him," Lucy commanded, before disappearing again.

Sunset was at 8 o'clock in New Orleans. She wouldn't show up to the café before 8:15. Maybe he wouldn't wait, and this whole situation would dissolve like ice in water.

Fine. She would indulge her aunt if only to buy her a month or more of peace before the nagging resumed. And by then, she'd have followed the Castle trail to new monsters in the dark.

A Martinelli was best. They slaked her hunger better than any other kill. And she had to accept the possibility she would never know peace, no matter how many men she bled dry.

But she had to start somewhere, and there *were* other demons in the world worth hunting.

7

King tore open three sugar packets and dumped them into a large cup labeled Café du Monde in curvy black letters. Beneath the words was a cartoon image of the café where he currently sat, a sienna-colored building with green awning and chairs.

Coffee and beignets, it promised.

And it delivered, as King had a generous portion of both spread before him on the table.

He showed up thirty minutes early. Not because it was his favorite café in New Orleans, but because he wanted time to look at his file again, and to think about what he might say to Lou.

Lucy hinted that while Lou agreed to come, she wasn't sold on the idea. It would be up to King to sell it to her. He had to admit, if only to himself, he *wanted* the girl's help. If he intended to follow through with the Venetti case, her ability would be an asset. He could also use the gun power and someone to watch his back. Getting around without drawing attention would be easier, provided the girl was as discreet as Lucy.

Lucy claimed Lou had Jack's sensibilities, his mind. What would King say to Jack to win him over? He tried to imagine a bloodthirsty Jack Thorne and what words could be spoken like an incantation to bring him back from the dark side.

Yet in practice, a conversation never went the way King envisioned.

It didn't matter who the person was or the circumstances. People were the final variable, and he found success most often when he was willing to follow their lead.

He'd chosen the right place, at least. It was crowded enough, with light flooding the eating area beneath the green tent. A woman could feel safe here, speaking to a man she'd never met before. It had the added bonus of coffee and deep fried donuts covered in powdered sugar. And an attentive teenager walking up and down the aisles, sweeping scrunched straw wrappers and crumpled napkins into an upright dust pan.

Of course, King had the feeling Thorne's kid might not be into crowds, lighted places, or deep fried confections. If she mopped up the Martinelli family the way Lucy thought she had, she probably didn't need some overhead bulbs to make her feel safe.

By the time King polished off the third of four beignets, he knew she wasn't coming. The Jackson Square crowd was thinning. A human statue painted to look like stone stepped down from her crate at sunset and packed up for the night. The artists who'd laid their canvases against the iron fence, on display for the day's passing tourists, they were packing up too. They stuffed paintings into large black sacks and picked up the blankets or jackets they'd been sitting on. King watched one man rub his half-finished cigarette out on the bottom of his shoe before tucking it behind his ear for later.

People shuffled deeper into the quarter with thoughts of after-dinner drinks on their minds. King kept waiting even as the last of the orange faded to black, and the only lights were the artificial orbs overhead and the streetlights growing brighter as the world dimmed.

King thought of Brasso, the way he looked the night before, sitting across from him at the high-top table. A toothpick bobbed in his mouth as he twirled a coaster on the smooth wood. His bright face had glowed in the tiki lights, and his smiles had been too quick to come and go.

A witness has skipped out on a high-profile case. Find her, bring her back, and there's a big fat retainer in it for you. We need her. These women keep disappearing and she's the only one who's survived. We need her if we hope to can this bastard.

Not the most compelling case, if Lou was as half fire-forged as Lucy made her out to be. *We're going to look for someone* couldn't compare to *let's kill off the mafia.*

And there was Brasso's story itself.

You came all the way down here to ask for my help? King had asked, doing the St. Louis to New Orleans math in his head.

You're retired. You can take a lengthy road trip, and no one is going to ask you to account for your time. And you're the most trustworthy guy I know.

It was bullshit flattery and only made sense if Brasso believed there was a rat in the department, tracking his movement.

There was another reason why he would have said yes to about any request from Chaz Brasso.

Brasso's face had been the first he'd seen after three days in the dark. The hand that had grabbed onto his and pulled him from the rubble.

What the media would later call the Channing Incident, had been the worst days of King's life.

Eleven enforcement individuals had gone into a building for drugs and a mob boss, and only one had come out alive. King was beneath a set of stairs when the bomb went off, bringing down the Westside brownstone they were searching. Four days he laid in the dark, trying to breathe, trying to stay alive.

At 8:30, King stood from his wobbly little chair and went to the pick-up window for another order of beignets.

When he came back to his table, she was there, at *his* table, as if she'd been waiting for him all along. He slid into the chair across from her. "Lou Thorne?"

She nodded, and he sat the plate of beignets, coffee cup, and three sugar packets on the table. Then he extended his hand, noticing a smudge of powdered sugar on his fingers.

To his surprise, she accepted it, sugar and all. She shook it firm, but not too hard. She wiped the transferred sugar off her hand with a couple of sharp slaps against her thigh.

"And you're *Detective* King," she said.

King snorted. "Is that what your aunt told you?"

She stilled. "You're not a detective?"

"Not legally, no. I never was. I have the skill set. I was a DEA agent. I taught your old man at Quantico. Got him straight off the bus. He was brilliant. And a hard worker."

The girl's ears perked up at the mention of Jack. King filed this observation away as well. Then he kept on, riding this train for as long as the rails were there.

"DEA agents do a bit of everything. Investigation. Undercover work."

He gave her a long look, waiting for questions.

Her brown eyes held his unblinking. Her face was unreadable. She might be Jack's kid, but those cold, flat eyes were Courtney's and damn unsettling.

"You'd make a hell of a poker player."

She considered this comment without smiling. Then she leaned back in her seat, a slight arch to her back. *She's packing*, he realized. "Lucy said you want my help with a case."

Ah, there was Jack. Right to the point. No time for bullshit. Now to see if she had Jack's patience. He didn't know how long the kid had been at this game. She could've survived this long purely by coincidence.

"This is an interview, Lou. You can't expect me to hand over secrets about a high-profile case to a stranger. No matter what kind of past I've got with your aunt."

That got a raised eyebrow. So Lucy hadn't told her about the two of them. King wasn't sure if his feelings were hurt or if he was relieved. Surely she hadn't kept their brief but intense relationship secret because she was ashamed. Lucy once tried to get him to go to a naked hot yoga class with everyone's *bits* flapping in the wind. Lucy Thorne didn't do shame.

He saw Lou's curiosity now. She was looking him over with a different expression on her face.

"Ask your questions."

He took a long drink of coffee then began. "What kind of training do you have?"

"My dad taught me to shoot when I was a kid. He didn't want me to be afraid of guns or blow my own brains out."

King remembered this himself. A memory, warped with age, bloomed behind his eyes. "Maybe I saw you at one of the family picnics."

"There were a lot of people and a lot of picnics," she said, looking out over Jackson Square. She shifted in her seat.

She'd been a shy, forlorn kid, he remembered. All the other children had been little bullets of motion and chaos, running, screaming, laughing. And Louie had been at the picnic table with a book. When Lou disappeared, scaring the hell out of Jack, they'd stopped coming to functions.

However else she might have changed, the perfect stillness hadn't left her.

"Apart from guns, I know some hand to hand. I studied aikido and Uechi-Ryu."

"When you were a kid?" He sipped his coffee. He was trying to gage how much experience she had. Ten years? Fifteen? Of course, if she was hunting and murdering regularly, he supposed that would keep her sharper than most cops who sat behind desks eating fast food for lunch.

"I wanted my father's service weapon, but Lucy has a stance on guns in the house. So we compromised. She agreed to send me to the dojo when yoga didn't work out."

He couldn't suppress a grin. "Do you have your own gear? Vests? Concealed weapons?"

"Yes."

King imagined what kind of apartment this young woman had. Did she push a dramatic red button and walls moved away, exposed studs and an arsenal worthy of a Colombian drug lord?

"Ever been tortured?" he asked.

She glared at him. "I've never been caught."

"Do you have a boyfriend?"

Her teeth clenched. "Is that relevant to my job duties?"

"In this game, if they can't catch you, they lean on someone you love. I've seen it enough it's cliché."

He thought she would shrug him off again, fall back on the false bravado today's youth relied on. But her face remained pensive. She was serious. God, she was too young to know this was serious.

Goddamn, Jack. I'm sorry.

Sorry for giving him the case and the credit. For painting the target on his back. But most of all he was sorry for this hardened kid left behind.

"Lucy is the only one they can lean on," she said at last. "And she can take care of herself."

He took another sip of coffee. "Yes, she can. And from what I've heard, so can you."

"Do you want my help or not?"

"I do," he said. He grinned and shoved one of the beignets in his mouth. Sucking powder sugar off his fingers. "So you want to know about the case before you say yes? It's dangerous."

She gave him a flat, humorless smile. "I appreciate a challenge."

"My old partner still works for the DEA. He's got a partial case built but not enough to charge or convict. A senator invites women out onto his boat, only they don't always come back. One woman took a boat ride into the Texas bay and barely escaped with her life. She agreed to testify against the senator, but then she disappeared. She's either dead or on the run. We need to find her and convince her we can keep her safe until the trial. Bonus round: We find even more damning evidence on this guy."

"Why doesn't your partner want to look for her?" Lou asked.

She asked the right question, without accepting something at face value. Questioning people and their motives was what kept you breathing. Maybe he could keep her alive after all.

King smiled. "Good question. It's because of who he wants to convict."

She waited for him to go on, her flat shark eyes never leaving his. It was enough to make his skin crawl.

"Most drug trafficking is a front. A way to generate funds for more ambitious projects. It's not unlike municipal bonds actually. And when you work within the law, you've got to follow the law. And powerful men like Ryanson always have the law on their side."

Lou arched an eyebrow. "Senator Greg Ryanson?"

King nodded, knowingly. "I know. Pristine public image. Philanthropist wife. His two daughters serve charities that make you feel all fuzzy inside."

"I saw the picture of Ryanson holding the baby panda."

"His eldest Emma runs the wildlife charity, and she isn't afraid to use dear old dad's face for publicity."

King slid the file across the table and watched her open it.

"But this is him, in the photos, and it's..." Her voice trailed off.

"Looks damning, doesn't it?" he agreed. "So we're going to dig deeper, starting with Paula Venetti. She was his girlfriend for a long time. If she's still alive, I want to interview her in person. We'll ask better questions and build on what she gives us."

"Leads," she murmured, her face still focused on the photos.

Like a fish to water.

"According to your aunt, we should be able to figure out if she is still alive fast enough."

Lou didn't smile. She flicked her eyes up to meet his.

"This case is a chance to expose a horrible man for what he is. Maybe save some lives," he said. But he didn't think she cared about the heroic shit one bit. "At the least, we might defund some horrible projects."

She pushed the folder back over to him but didn't answer. Her eyes were roaming along the square, taking in the crowds shuffling beneath the streetlights. It was late, but jazz music still played, and the tarot readings over shaky card tables were in full swing. Several cigarettes burned in the dark as peddlers and pickpockets watched the crowd with hungry eyes.

"I've only got one last question," he said, vying for her attention. "I'll ask it while you're walking me back."

She looked at him warily as he slid the folder under his arm and stood. They exited Café du Monde's congested patio, stepping out into the hot summer night. She moved through the crowd effortlessly, cutting the waters without bumping into the drunks or the beggars with their hands out.

She'd be a hell of a stalker.

They'd made it to St. Peter Street when he stopped her. "Your aunt seemed to think you were in some kind of trouble. Maybe it's too late to get out. That's why she asked me to hire you."

Lou leaned against a brick wall at the mouth of the alley. Most of her was in shadow, with only a square of light from an adjacent shop, a closed antique store, cutting across her face.

"She said you've been killing off the men responsible for your old man's murder." He waited for her to speak. When she didn't, he backtracked. "What?"

"I'm listening for the question," she said.

Smart-ass. King wasn't sure if she'd gotten that from Courtney or Jack. "Are you in trouble?"

"If you want a partner," she said, turning away from the lit mannequin in the window to face him. "Don't talk to me like I'm a victim. I don't need your protection."

"There's nothing wrong with accepting help," he said. He felt stupid as soon as the words left his mouth. He didn't know her. And the idea she needed help from this old man with a gut was patronizing at best. "I'm not going to sell you out. I'm just wondering if you're in too deep to surface on your own."

"You have your own problems, King."

He had no time to react before she pulled herself up onto her tiptoes and clasped her hands on the back of his neck. She brought her face close to his, and for a horrifying moment, he thought she was going to kiss him.

She was beautiful. No question. Her body was young and tight in all the ways his had gone soft. She had Courtney's full jaw and Jack's big eyes. Her slender neck gave way to sharp collar bones.

He tried to pull away, but the hand on the back of his neck tightened, locking him in place. Any illusion he had about how easy it would be to disentangle himself evaporated. His pulse leapt. She could snap his neck if she wanted.

She brushed her lips against his ear. "You have a man following you, and he looks like a professional asshole. What do you want to do about it?"

He plastered on his own fake grin, seeing his reflection in the shop window do the same. He hated the look of it. An old man preying on a girl half his age. *Less* than half his age.

Lou stepped away from him, placing herself entirely in the alley's shadows. She was impossible to see. In darkness, the eye relied on movement, but Lou was perfectly still. Invisible.

"$300 an hour," he shouted. "That's outrageous!"

He heard her dry laugh.

King made a big show of patting himself down. Then he whipped his head up. "You stole my wallet! Hey, come back here!"

He pretended to chase her down the alley, stepping off the side street into the dark. He fumbled through the darkness until she took pity on him and seized his arm.

"Get us a better view," he rasped. He was embarrassed how winded he was from shouting.

The world was yanked out from under him.

His stomach dropped as if he'd reached the top of a roller coaster and was now sailing down the other side. He was falling.

Then they were on a balcony. They stepped away from the corner of a privacy wall, dividing the balcony for two separate units' use. Lou grabbed his arm and yanked him down, so they were hunched behind the iron rails. She pulled apart a nest of fern tendrils and peered at the street below. King did the same. His knees popped when he crouched, and already his lower back burned. He had little confidence he would be able to get up from this crouch quickly.

"Look," she said, still watching the street. The stalker entered the alley, then came back out. He threw up his hands, apparently angry he'd lost his target. Then he headed up the block, presumably to catch King further up.

"The question is, was he tailing you or me?" he asked.

She looked ready to dismiss him outright, but then she hesitated.

"No one tails me." She met his gaze, her eyes shimmery in this streetlight. "Maybe they know your game for Ryanson."

If they did, that was damn fast.

He stood slowly, slipping back into the shadow of the overhang. He leaned against a dark window. As soon as he did, a light kicked on in the bedroom, and a woman shot straight up in bed, screaming. Lou grabbed his shirt and shoved him into the corner.

Another roller-coaster drop and they were by the river beside a streetcar stop. It was abandoned this late at night, the tram running only during reasonable hours. They were alone except for the homeless man sleeping beneath the bench, a brown bottleneck protruding from a paper sack inches from his face. He was snoring too damn loud to give a shit about what they were saying.

"God, how can you stand that?" he asked, one hand on his stomach.

"What?"

He described the feeling to her. "It's jarring."

"I don't feel anything," she said.

King wanted to ask more, part horrified, part fascinated by her strange gift, but she looked ready to run. He would've bet a twenty spot she had somewhere to be.

"Are you sure you want to work this case?" he asked. He ran a hand through his hair. Sweat had beaded along his scalp, and his palm came away damp. "If those men were looking for me, then this is hot. And it's only going to get hotter."

"Are you sure you want to work with *me*?" she countered. "You'll have twice as many enemies."

He smiled at that. He saw Jack standing at ease in the Quantico gym as King paced in front of the men and women with their hands clasped behind their backs, chins up.

Are you sure you want this job? It's not all party dresses and tea time. DEA agents die every day. Some hard ass motherfuckers roam the streets of America. He'd stopped in front of Jack Thorne, speaking to him for the first time. *Are you ready for them?*

Are they ready for me? Jack had asked.

"You're more vulnerable than I am," she said. Her lip pouted out when she was thinking. It was cute. "If anyone sees us working together, they might kill you thinking you were part of..." Her voice trailed off. "... of what I've done."

He considered this. It wasn't bravado. Lou wasn't blowing smoke up his ass or puffing her chest. She was stating a fact.

"You *are* in deep," he said.

Lou smirked, a cold, hard twitch of her lips. "I've no illusions as to how this ends. I know what happens to people like me. People like my dad."

People like me, he thought.

"Live by the sword, die by the sword," she said.

The skin on the back of his neck stood up.

She turned, giving the impression she was about to leave him there by the streetcar stop.

"You're right," he blurted out, hoping to stop her. He gestured around them. "I am vulnerable. But you'd save me a lot of time. It takes hours and hours to research and hunt. More if I have to fly or drive. I can't say you're not a preferable alternative."

Not to mention her skills. She'd spotted the men in the crowd when he hadn't. She was young. Sharp. And he preferred working with a partner to working alone. He always had. Some people need to be alone to think. He needed a sounding board.

She gave him another once over. "When do you want to talk to Paula?"

"Tomorrow?" he asked.

She agreed to his suggested time and meeting place before she disappeared, leaving him alone at the deserted trolley stop.

He thought, *Lucy is going to kill me.*

8

As soon as she could, Lou ditched King and went looking for Castle. She made only a quick stop at her apartment for a wardrobe change, having left the heavy stuff at home lest the retired cop turn out to be a snitch for Aunt Lucy.

Sitting on the edge of her bed, Lou slipped her feet into black sneakers. Then she pulled her dark hair into a low ponytail and brushed her teeth. It was a waste of time to wash her face. She'd be filthy again by the end of the night.

Ready, she stepped into an empty closet and waited in total darkness.

When she rented this studio apartment, the very first thing she did was remove the four flat wooden boards serving as shelves within the linen closet. She swept the square of wooden floor at the bottom and wiped the corners of cobwebs and dust. A few short steps from her bed, from the bathroom and from the kitchen, she could reach this exit at a moment's notice.

Even with the three walls bare, it wasn't a large space. Only one other person could fit inside the closet with her, if necessary, and even then, it would be a negotiation of elbows and angles. Her shoulder blades shifted against the bare wall as she tried to focus on her target. She pictured him in her mind.

The cowboy coat he favored. His shaved head. The three vertical cuts in his eyebrow made by a razor. A prison tattoo of a devil fucking a woman from behind on his bicep.

She fed her intuition these markers, letting her compass zone in on the man she wanted.

Then she saw him, in her mind first, as the compass swirled inside her, orienting herself appropriately.

Castle marched down a nighttime street with his arm around a girl's waist. He had a Marlboro between his lips. And a white ten-gallon hat with a brown and gray pheasant feather protruding from one side of the cap. A gold ring on each of his pinkies, one bearing the crest of the Martinelli family. An ornate capital *M* and two dragons chasing one another head-to-tail around the letter. Ahead of the man was a bright flashing sign for a bar Lou recognized.

Downtown Austin then. Same time zone, so no problem there. Much hotter than St. Louis, but she didn't want to step out of the closet and change. She wasn't going to stay in the city any longer than she had to. She held the image of him in her mind as the pull intensified, the wire on her imaginary compass vibrating stronger.

She'd learned how to do this, strengthen the bond between herself and her prey before slipping. By twenty-four, her control had improved. She traveled with intention now. She could step into the full darkness and remain right where she was for as long as she needed. That had not been the case when she was a child. As a child, she was prey to the darkness. Whenever it wanted her, it could open its fanged mouth and swallow her whole. Sleeping at night was always a risk when the world was darkest and her mind most off guard. She couldn't count the number of times she'd laid down in her bed, safe in her aunt's Chicago apartment, only to wake up halfway across the world.

It was the same for water. She would never be like her mother, who'd enjoyed sliding into a hot bath with a book and a glass of wine.

She found this new development in her gift, the most useful advancement. Slipping blind had huge risks. No one knew what waited in the dark better than she did.

The girl at Jimmy Castle's side was a brunette in a tight, short skirt and five-inch heels. The night air in Austin was humid as hell and sweat had already begun to form at the back of Castle's neck. Even though she stood in a pitch-black box 800 miles away, Lou could smell his thick cologne and the cigarette smoke haloing his jaunty hat.

When her skin and limbs felt like they were on fire, she let go and slipped.

The hum of her apartment's refrigerator and whirling A/C were exchanged for the blast of car horns and a wall of heat. It felt like someone had thrown a blanket over her head and she was trying to breathe through its tightly meshed fibers. She stepped out from behind a dumpster, wrinkling her nose at the smell of garbage rotting in the heat. A cat hissed at her sudden intrusion, back arching. She hissed back, and it ran.

It was cooler in the alley than in the main drag, all lit up with its cars and stoplights and people on their phones. Little screens like sentient eyes burning in the dark. People were laughing too loud. Talking too loud. Trying to hear one another over the din of the throbbing traffic. Lou's eyes slid over the bodies, over the collective slithering movement until she found her target.

And there he was.

Lou leaned against the wall of a building and pretended to scroll through her own phone. It was turned off, but no one was looking closely. She stole glances at her target when he wasn't looking.

Castle stood on a corner with his arm around the brunette Lou'd seen in her mind first. Now she took in the details her mind's eye had missed. Penciled eyebrows. A mole on the cheek. The way she grinned at Jimmy over her cupped hands as she lit herself a cigarette. Lou had learned not to overlook or dismiss the girls she saw with her targets.

If she had to track someone in the daytime or slipped only to find herself in broad daylight, she'd have to rely on other skills to track her prey. And following their girls always proved easier. In her experience, Lou found that no one kept track of men better than their women.

Jimmy fist-bumped another man on the sidewalk before turning toward the entrance of the building she leaned against. A green awning reminding her of the Café du Monde illuminated the sidewalk and a doorman checking IDs. He grinned at Jimmy and slapped him a high five. More machismo bullshit. Then he waved Castle's group inside, bypassing the long line waiting to get into the club. A girl near the back groaned.

Lou turned and walked back down the alley, past the reeking garbage. She pressed herself into the deepest corner between the two buildings, shrouding herself in darkness. A heartbeat later, she was standing in a closet, listening to the hard *dhump dhump dhump dhump* of the club's bass.

The door flew open, and Lou barely had a moment to register the stockroom surrounding her.

"What the hell are you doing in here?" a bartender in a white shirt and black vest hissed.

Lou faked a slur. "Where's the fucking bathroom?"

The bartender grabbed her by the arm and steered her out of the closet. She resisted the urge to break all his fingers. Hurting him would draw attention to herself, and she worked best when no one noticed her. No one to remember her. No one with questions that could lead back to her.

Still holding her elbow, the bartender spun her toward the mouth of the hallway. The music was louder, and up ahead laser lights in purple, pink, and neon green shot through the air. "Go back to the dance floor then hook a right. Take the *other* hallway, and you'll find the bathrooms."

He slapped her on the ass and pushed Lou toward the dance floor.

She might murder him after all.

She slid through the dark searching for Jimmy. Her internal compass told her he was somewhere near the dance floor, on its outer fringes. She found him in a velvet booth with four girls and three men. They were doing shots and laughing like the world was ending.

Not the best place to grab him, but Lou was patient. She ordered a drink. She paid cash.

She sipped her virgin daiquiri and kept an eye on the man in the booth with his friends. His girls. Lou didn't mind being in the clubs. They were dark. And darkness was her element. But there was also a vibrancy to this atmosphere that she could appreciate. It wasn't unlike the vibrancy she felt in her little closet back home in St. Louis, or when she slipped through the thick shadows clinging to doors and buildings, or even a thick knot of trees.

No one needed to tell her the darkness was alive.

Anyone who'd spent a moment standing in a dark room knew. They could feel the energy along the back of their neck. Their pulse rose.

Some primal part of them sensed creatures lurking just on the other side. Most people didn't slip through the thin membrane as she did, but they *knew* what was there.

Castle was on the move. The girls were scooting out in their tight skirts so he could stand. He had another cigarette between his lips even though smoking was forbidden in this club and all other watering holes from Boston to Seattle.

She watched him over the sparkling rim of her daiquiri as he exited the booth and moved toward the bathrooms, lit cigarette bobbing in the low light. The music thrummed in her chest as she watched him go. The crushed ice against her lips cooled her.

As soon as he ducked into the hallway, she set her daiquiri down and glanced around the room for any eyes trained on her. The club was full of convulsing bodies, too drunk or high to be capable of coordination. No one watched her.

She was only another face in the crowd, and not even a very memorable one considering the painted peacocks with iridescent blue eye shadow and shimmery shirts on the dance floor. She cut through the crowd easily. Behind a booth much like the one Castle had vacated, she found a thin spot in thick shadow and slipped through. Then her hands were on the back of a stall door.

It was a single-room employee bathroom. Why would Castle bother to wait in the piss lines like everyone else?

The light flicked on as Castle entered the bathroom and locked the door behind him.

Castle's slurring voice hummed out of tune. He swayed before the porcelain, and after one precarious lean, his arm shot out and grabbed at the concrete wall to steady himself.

"Oops." He looked down at his pee-splattered boot.

Lou watched him through the gap between the stall walls. Castle's back was to her as he shook his dick over the basin. She made her move.

She grabbed him and twisted his arm behind his back, immobilizing him.

He wailed and fought her hold, throwing a blind elbow strike which she ducked easily, given the difference in their heights and his sluggish movements. Fortunately, she only needed to hold onto him for a heartbeat. She hit the light switch on the wall with one quick swipe of her hand and pulled him through the dark.

Once the fresh air hit her, she stopped clinging to Castle and let him tumble to the grassy knoll at the edge of the lake.

His drunk ass hit the dirt, and he cried out.

The crickets fell silent at having their concert interrupted. The other night sounds swelled, oblivious to their intrusion. So far into the wilderness, scuffles happened all night long. Beasts tearing apart one another wasn't newsworthy. So the night went on.

An owl hooted. A fish jumped up before belly flopping the surface of the water. Something on the opposite shore slid into the water, a silver trail cutting the surface behind it. Ducks maybe. She wasn't sure. Surprisingly, despite all her gifts, Lou's night vision was unremarkable.

She loved this place. A small placid lake in the Alaskan wilderness. The evergreens thick with snow. A caribou on the opposite edge darted away at their intrusion, but otherwise, perfect silence. Perfect stillness as snow fell from the sky. Standing in this snowy world of eternal night calmed her in a way no other place on Earth could.

And not only because it was the entrance to her dumping ground.

When she killed, she brought them here, got them into the freezing waters and slipped to La Loon. They were miles from anything. Perfectly secluded, in a world that was night for months on end.

It calmed her every time.

Castle pulled himself to his feet, clawing at the small of his back.

"Looking for this?" Lou asked, pointing his gun at him. A night bird cawed.

Castle stopped slapping his lower back, and his jaw fell open. "Oh fuck. It's you."

She stopped.

He finally pulled up his pants. "You're Konstantine's bitch."

She grimaced. "I'm no one's bitch."

"No, you're her. I've seen the fucking pictures. I thought he was jumping at shadows and shit but look at you." He waved a hand up and down her body. "Oh fuck, are you going to kill me?"

She should've said yes. That was her intention. But she was hung up on the words *fucking pictures*.

"God, I'm too high for this right now." He ran his hands over his face. Then he dropped down by the lake and started splashing water onto it. His white cowboy hat with the fancy plume fell off his head and into the water. He fished it out and shook it before laying it aside. A strange expression seized his face. He was going to puke.

She lowered the gun. This was new. Usually, when she came across a hired hand from the Martinelli drug ring, it had a predictable pattern. It began with threats.

There was the name calling.

The threat to kill off her family.

Too late, she'd said. *You've already killed them. I'm here to return the favor.*

Or some variation. It was all pretty much the same. These men weren't great conversationalists, with their limited vocabularies.

When they found her unmoved, they tried to strike first. Then she killed them and shoved their bodies and all the evidence into the water.

The end.

No one had ever recognized her before. Mentioned pictures before. Collapsed to their knees and started vomiting before the first threat was even made.

"Jesus fucking Christ. What did I ever do to you?" He sounded as though he would cry.

Lou lowered the gun even more. She kept the pistol cupped in her hands, ready to raise and shoot at any moment. She thought the best way to proceed in an uncertain situation was to check her facts.

"You're one of Martinelli's mules."

"What does that got to do with you?"

"The Martinellis are dead, but you're still selling. *Why?*"

He turned and heaved into the lake again. When he stopped vomiting, he added, "Like you said, I'm a mule. It's what I do. I gotta pay bills, don't I?"

"I don't like drugs."

"Fuck, then don't do them!" he said with a wild shrug. "I never held you down and forced you, did I?"

"Good point. I'll cut you a deal." Lou flashed a smile. Only this seemed to frighten Castle more than the gun.

The man begged. Literally begged on his hands and knees. Hands clasped.

"You stop muling, and I won't kill you."

His Adam's apple bobbed in the moonlight.

"You don't like my deal, Jimmy?"

Jimmy ran his hands down the front of his pants. "Come on, man. Be reasonable."

She pistol-whipped him.

Castle touched two fingers to his bloody cheek. It swelled a dark purple in the moonlight. "If I quit I'm as good as dead. Konstantine will cut off my balls and stuff them up my ass."

"Ah, so that's the real reason. You have a new boss." Lou grinned. Why did pain compliance work so well? Hurt them a little, and they spilled their guts. "So who is he? Konstantine?"

Her pulse leapt at the idea of a bigger fish. A worthier opponent.

His bald head gleamed in the moonlight. His hat lay against one knee, and he studied it intensely. He said nothing.

Okay. Crime lords were all the same to Lou anyway. "He's another roach that'll run under the fridge when the light comes on. I'll get to him."

Castle's head snapped up. "He ain't no roach. He's Martinelli."

She raised her gun and shoved it between his eyes. "There are no more Martinellis."

"Missed one. And the things I've heard about him, you wouldn't believe it. Truly fucked up shit."

"And he has pictures of me?"

Castle tugged the damp hat back onto his head. "He sent them around. I thought it was a story to keep all the good little mules in line. But here you are, and you look like your fucking pictures."

Keep the good little mules in line.

Because they hadn't been in line. Lou saw the infighting herself. But she thought the chaos was the result of her murdering everyone in charge. She'd cut off the thumb holding them down, and now every dealer with an ounce of ambition was vying to be on top.

Of course, this Konstantine would have to be a bloody bastard. He'd never re-establish the pecking order or the fist of power the Martinelli family had built with soft tactics. The clans and other crime families would eat him alive.

Alive. There was at least one more Martinelli alive. She couldn't help but smile. Grin like it was Christmas morning and she'd found a present under the tree, wrapped and ready for her. Before she could stop herself, she laughed.

"Get up," she said.

"Oh come on." Castle pulled himself to his feet. The sight of her jubilation intensified his horror. "Please don't fucking kill me. You want money? I've got—" His voice broke, and his face screwed up like he was going to burst into tears.

"Don't cry. It pisses me off," she said.

"Please."

"I'm not going to kill you."

Castle's face lit up. "You're not?"

"You sound disappointed."

"No, no!" he begged. "I'm not ready to die."

"Everyone dies, Castle." She stepped into the shadow of the tree and slipped, leaving Castle with wide, glassy eyes.

She didn't go far. Across the way, she peered from beneath a Sitka pine. He turned a circle, searching. He went to the tree where she'd been and looked beneath it as if expecting to find her there.

When he seemed satisfied that she had left, he lifted his hat and ran a hand over his gleaming, bald head again, before walking south, away from the moon-filled water.

She wasn't going to let him get far.

If he kept wandering his current direction, he wouldn't last two days. There was nothing but Alaskan wilderness that way.

And this place was sacred to her.

It had taken her a long time to find one so perfect. Its silence. Its eternal night. The magic way the lake did not freeze with more than a thin layer of ice, no matter how cold it got. It told her the dark waters underneath were deep.

She wouldn't let him ruin this place for her.

She slipped through the trees, staying on his heels as he navigated the forest. Coyotes yipped nearby, catching her scent and no doubt Castle's. It didn't matter. As soon as he passed beneath the next shady limb, she was going to grab him.

The arm of a mighty fir tree stretched overhead. As soon as the shadow cast itself over Castle's body, she caught him. He yelped, as expected. And he was still howling when she dropped him on the side-walk beside the downtown alley.

She ducked out of sight before he could turn and look for her.

Let him think she's a ghost. A boogeyman.

Power was only powerful when no one knew how much you had. It was better if they believed her invincible. She was in trouble if they realized how many limitations she had.

From beneath an awning across the street, she watched Castle clamber to his feet and turn in all directions. He peered into the dark alley, searching for her. Some of his friends called from the club's entrance, and he turned, wide-eyed and bewildered. He lifted his hat and ran a hand over his bare head.

Lou smiled. She could go straight to this Konstantine. Murder him outright. But she'd had nights and nights with no Martinelli in the world. And it had been cold and dull playing without a target.

Oh, he would die. Of course. But she would take her time with this.

Draw it out.

Enjoy every minute.

Run rat run, she thought, watching Castle disappear into the throng of sweaty parasites feeding on the night. *Take me to your leader.*

9

Lucy stood in Lou's dark apartment. One of the windows was open, and a light breeze blew through, rattling the blinds and mangling the slats. The moonlit sheets stirred, and a paperback opened face down, spine creased, ruffled in the breeze. Outside, a train whistled and huge iron wheels scraped against their rails. Horns blared even at this hour. God, how could she sleep with all this noise? Maybe she couldn't. Lou's bed was empty after all.

The moonlight falling across the bed between the blinds brightened the white sheets to an ethereal glow. It was rumpled the way Lou's bed was always rumpled, even as a child. Unlike Lucy and her brother Jack, God rest his soul, who made their beds first thing in the morning as their Nana had taught them, Lou could tumble in and out of a messy bed with little concern. If the sheets and blanket weren't in perfect alignment, who cared?

Lucy crossed the room and sat on the edge of the mattress, a hard, unforgiving foam pad resting on a box spring. She exhaled and ran a hand over the coverlet and sheets, smoothing it. No girl. No gun either.

She was out hunting then. Did she do it every night? Every night that Lucy had dropped in unannounced, she'd found the bed empty, no matter the hour.

She stuck her hands under the pillow, still expecting to find a gun, but it was bare underneath.

Something like cardstock scraped the back of her hand. She frowned, her brows knitting together, and lifted the pillow. Nothing lay beneath. So she turned the pillow over in her lap and traced the fabric. Her fingers probed the pillow case and found it smooth until her nail snagged on a rectangle with soft edges.

Lucy slipped her hand into the pillowcase and grasped the edge of the card. She pulled it out.

Not a card. A photograph with a glossy image on one side and a cool white backing on the other, the kind developed in those one-hour photo labs found at most corner pharmacies.

Lucy's heart hitched. In the picture, Jack smiled up at her. His teeth were perfect, the product of braces he'd absolutely hated wearing for four years, but oh how they'd provided so much ammo for his tween sister. *Metal mouth. Brace face.* Or when she was feeling less imaginative, plain ol' *gummy dummy* worked. In her mind, Lucy could still see the little rubber bands, so many small bands, and the way he would shoot them at her, once catching the corner of her eye and throwing their grandmother into hysterics.

In the photo, Jack's hair was wet and falling into his eyes, and he had one massive arm around Louie. She was *Louie* then, no more than seven or eight years old and grinning at the camera, tucked into the crook of her father's big arm, one ear pressed to his chest. One of her front teeth was missing. But whether or not Jack would have submitted his own daughter to braces would never be known. He was dead four years later.

Their last visit burned in Lucy's mind.

You have to help me. I don't know what to do, Jack had said.

He was in head-to-toe black. Muscle shirt to combat boots, standing in the Walmart parking lot off Exit 133.

Help you? Lucy had said, spitting the words at him. *The way you helped me?*

On a warm July night, she'd seethed like the boiling blacktop under their feet. Decades of anger crouched inside her, waiting to tear her treacherous brother apart.

I'd never ask you to do this for me, Jack had pleaded. *But Louie is scared out of her mind. She needs someone. And we both know I'm not that person.*

No, you're not. The only thing you're good at is abandoning the people who need you.

Lucy wished she could take those words back. *What if—as he lay dying he thought—*she squeezed her eyes shut and sucked in a tight breath. When she opened them, Jack was still smiling at her.

Louie's hair wasn't wet even though they were at the beach. Lucy understood why—*she never goes into the water.* Hadn't Jack told her that? *I try to put her in the bath, and she screams bloody murder. The therapist and Courtney are brushing it off as a phobia. There was even a word for it. Aquaphobia. But we both know it's more than that.*

But when she'd first heard of her niece's fear she didn't make the connection. After all, Lucy herself had never been able to slip through water the way she did through shadow. She couldn't imagine it was possible. Yet Lou did both, and the water didn't even have to be dark water. But from what Lou told her, this mutation of their shared family trait did have its limitation.

Lou could slip in water, but she only went to one place. Every slip took her to *La Loon.* Their name for a strange world with a purple sky, red lake, and two moons. Lou could travel by water but always washed up on the shore of Blood Lake. And when she used the lake to return it was also into water. Never water to darkness. They didn't mix. If Lucy got into the car and drove north on I-80, she could only reach Chicago, not Paris. And it seemed the same was true for Lou's watery roads. She couldn't climb into her bathtub and pop up in the Atlantic Ocean. Perhaps her bathtub to La Loon, and then to the Atlantic Ocean, but never without that first stop.

Lucy worried about it. What was Lou's connection to that strange place full of monsters? Worse still, Lucy suspected that Lou had come to use it as a sort of dumping ground for the men she killed—and that notion frightened her more.

I'm sorry I didn't believe you, Lucy. I'm sorry I didn't protect you.

I didn't need you to protect me, she'd argued. And it had been a bold-faced lie. *I needed you there.*

There. When the darkness grew thin and swallowed her up. *There.* When one by one she lost her friends and jobs because of her "delusion." When their own grandmother had called her a liar. A demon.

Think whatever you want about me, but please help her. I don't want her to feel alone.

Like me, Lucy had said bitterly.

Lucy frowned down at the photograph of her dead brother and rubbed her forehead. *I'm sorry, Jack. I'm trying. I really am.*

All the old blame rose, flared its cobra head and hissed. A cold voice enumerated her sins.

You blame Jack for abandoning you, for not being there when you needed him, and yet you weren't there for him either, were you? You could have saved your brother from those men if you'd been paying attention instead of fucking his boss.

She'd gone to Jack as soon as she knew something was wrong. She dumped King off at his sister's, and a heartbeat later crawled out from under a sedan in the driveway across the street. But she was already too late. Cop cars and unmarked SUVs lined the curb outside Jack's home. His two-story suburban house modeled after some quaint Tudor manor stood wide awake with all the lights in the house on. Dozens of officers passed behind the windows as they moved from room to room. Others clustered together behind the yellow tape.

Then she was across the street, lifting the yellow tape up over her head.

"Ma'am." A woman in a uniform held up a hand. "You can't come in here."

"Where's Jack? Is he okay? Where is he? Where's Louie?"

"I can't answer those questions," the officer said.

"What do you mean you can't answer my questions? Are they dead? Is my family fucking dead or not? It's a simple question!"

Her voice boomed across the damp lawn in the early hours. Across the street, lookie-loos were pulling back curtains, blue-red-white flashes dancing across their own homes. Several officers who'd been busy chatting with one another until that moment turned toward her. Lucy was about to storm away, slink around the side of the house, perhaps beneath the shade of a bush and slip into a closet. She had to get into the house. She had to see what was going on for herself.

Before she could, a wall of a man was coming across the lawn, his big boots stepping right through Courtney's begonias. He was calling her name.

"Lucy?"

Lucy didn't recognize his face until he stepped into the light.

"Detective Chaz," Lucy said and then realized it wasn't right. Chaz was his first name. But at that moment, she didn't give two chickens or a pile of shit about remembering his last name. "Is Jack okay?"

Brasso ran a pudgy hand across his brow. "I'm so sorry to be the one to tell you this. Jack is dead. His wife is too. It looks like a break-in. They were both shot."

Lucy's guts cramped as if a massive fist had been slammed into it. "Louie—"

"We can't find her. We're looking. High and low, we're looking."

Tears streamed down her cheek for Jack, and surprisingly, for Courtney too, though the woman had never shown an ounce of kindness to her—Jack's *insane* sister. Sorrow swelled, then the wave of it crashed down on her and under the sorrow, a chord of terror. *Oh god, where is Louie? Did she get out? She could have slipped through the dark when the gunshots started. Or god forbid, they took her. They took her and—*

Lucy whirled away from King's partner. "I have to go."

Brasso started after her. "Are you sure you should drive? Hey, how did you know? Did someone call you?"

"Yes," she lied, saying anything to get him off her. "I came as soon as I could."

"That explains the lack of shoes." Brasso pointed down at her feet. He wet his lips and shuffled on his feet. "Who called you?"

"I'm sorry, but I have to go." Lucy was already jogging across the dark street toward the parked car.

"I don't have your number!" he yelled after her. "Why don't you give me your information so—" but whatever he intended to do with her information, she didn't hear. She was going down on her belly and rolling under the sedan.

He'll get it from King, she thought. *If he needs it.*

On her belly under the car, she heard a door open, heard someone say, "Where the hell did she go?"

She didn't wait to assure the owner she was no car thief. She slipped through the dark, desperate to find her niece.

Despite her night-long efforts, she didn't find Louie. She got a call from King the next day. Louie had come back to the house on her own, dripping wet. It would be months before Lucy learned why she couldn't find Lou despite all her searching.

Lou had been in La Loon, the one place where Lucy couldn't go. That strange world wasn't on Lucy's map. It could be Europa or in the Andromeda galaxy for all she knew.

And King. What a fuck up that had been. The first time she loved someone, and she threw him off the bridge like a discarded cigarette butt the moment life got hard. And what had been her excuse? *Louie needs me.* Bullshit. The truth, as she'd come to accept it after $5,000 in therapy and countless hours of self-reflection, was that she'd refused King out of guilt. She'd failed Jack. Failed his daughter. And she didn't *deserve* to be happy. And no matter how many self-help workbooks she read, or positive affirmations she recited while looking at herself in the bathroom mirror, she couldn't seem to make herself *un*believe this self-evident truth.

Lucy kissed the photograph and slipped it back into the pillowcase.

Think of all those years wasted, giving Jack the cold shoulder, and why? Because he hurt your feelings? Because he'd refused to blindly believe the wild stories you told him about your abilities? When Lou tried to tell you about La Loon, how did you react? How did it feel? To know you were as close-minded as you accused Jack of being? He died with your words in his ear, Lucy. He died thinking he'd abandoned Lou as you told him he would.

Lucy tried to shake off this dark voice. The one which would have her drown in her own regrets and sorrows. Buddhism had taught her to embrace her sins. To forgive herself as a work in progress. To know she was perfect as she was, but there was also room for improvement.

On most days, as long as she didn't neglect her yoga, or chanting, or meditation, this personal mantra worked.

She had only one way to honor the memory of her older brother and his legacy now. Only one way to prove to the universe and herself that she loved him and forgave him, in death if not in life. She would do more than *show* Lou she wasn't alone. That she wasn't abandoned.

She had to keep her alive.

She stood, and her lightheadedness spun the room. A wave of nausea bubbled up into her throat. She put one hand on her stomach and one hand on her head until it passed.

It was to be expected, she supposed, given her condition.

This reminder of her body's frailty was a warning, a nudge. She would have to move fast if she wanted to make good on her promise to her brother.

She had to. She was running out of time.

Konstantine walked from the Duomo toward his apartment as the lively summer day danced around him.

He loved Florence. With its cobblestoned town center and statues as old as civilization itself. Loved the stone walls, bridges, and ancient churches. Loved the river cutting through it as pigeons the color of sheet rock perched on buildings.

It was an old city built on the blood and corpses of men. Countless bones lay in the earth beneath his feet. Kingdoms rose, flourished, and fell. And it would be the same with his own empire.

Walking around the city made him think of his mother. While his mother had sold postcards from a squeaky cart she pushed around the city center, he would ask tourists if they wanted a tour for 5000 lire. He could get four or five takers a day during the low season and as many as twenty in high season, his sandaled feet wearing the cobblestones smooth before and after school.

His mother made enough with her postcards, keychains, and umbrellas. She had a sweet smile and bright voice. People liked her. And she let Konstantine use his money to buy treats from the countless vendors lining the streets.

When Konstantine did have money in his pockets, he spent it on koulouri and pide, Greek sweets that came from a shop by the Ponte

Vecchio. He loved the koulouri and pide, but he also liked the immigrant shop owners' little girl. A dark beauty with big black eyes like polished river stones and hair like raven feathers. He'd discovered the shop with his mother, who favored it, insisting a Greek shop was incredibly rare in Florence, and therefore, should be appreciated.

Konstantine had loved the treats, but the girl was even better. He brought her little gifts. A two-scoop gelato, a frog made of blown glass. He'd buy his warm bread and then go down to the water with his treasures in his pockets, watching the gulls bob on the river Arno. Sometimes the Greeks, who were mostly amused by Konstantine's affections, would let their girl, Dica, go with him.

But when the lire were replaced with expensive euros, the Greeks closed shop and moved without warning. Konstantine did not even get to say goodbye. And not long after, his mother stopped pushing the postcard cart around the city center, and she accepted his tour money, more heartily than ever before. It would be much later before Konstantine understood what had actually chased his mother indoors.

Konstantine checked the time and realized he would be late if he did not hurry. On the steps outside the Uffizi, Asians posed with rabbit ears in front of the grand wooden doors. Teenagers with their tight jackets and scooters swerved around pedestrians, and the beggars lay prostrated, face down with their open palms cupped. A lovely girl in a sundress, no more than sixteen, stood outside his favorite gelateria, gobbling limoncello sorbetto with a girlish smile. She wiped at her dripping chin with a paper napkin as the breeze tousled her skirt.

Konstantine stepped through a portico into an atrium and courtyard. He passed beneath the rounded archway and ascended the old stone steps to his attic apartment overlooking the lush courtyard and fountain. Water poured through a cherub's mouth, his delicate stone fingers ready to play the lyre held up in his hands.

This courtyard always made him think of his mother. Of the roses she tried to grow on the balcony of their apartment. When he was a good boy, his mother would let him watch the old black and white American movies in her bedroom.

He'd been watching *The Godfather* the night he decided to join Padre Leo's gang. It wasn't the glorified life of a criminal portrayed in the movie that had sparked Konstantine's interest. In fact, having watched the film about a hundred times, Konstantine was sure all gangsters died horribly, looking like bloody pincushions or with their brains sprayed all over everything.

But that night itself had changed everything.

Go into my room and watch your movie, amore di mamma. Let me talk to Francesca.

She disapproved of *The Godfather*, Konstantine being only eight years old. She wanted him to watch a cartoon or something like it. But he also knew she hated to raise her voice in front of others. If he kept the volume low, she might not even notice the gunfire and swearing. If she caught him anyway, the punishment would be light given Francesca's presence. So he'd turned on the movie and pushed the volume all the way down until only one bar showed at the bottom of the screen. Oh, how thrilling childhood deviance had once seemed. Now Konstantine only felt such delicious panic when dumping a body into the Arno River.

Fifteen minutes into the movie, Konstantine had wanted a drink. He went to the kitchen for water and caught a scrap of conversation between the two women. His mother sat at their bistro table with her head in her hands. Francesca was rubbing his mother's shoulders.

It doesn't have to be so garish as all that. No street corners in broad daylight, Francesca said. *Well, go on! He's waiting. Try to relax.*

His mother nodded and left the apartment, closing the door softly behind her.

Where's she going? Konstantine had asked.

Francesca paused in lighting her cigarette and turned to the boy. Her lips were pursed and her eyes wide. Then she forced a tight smile. *She went to my apartment to get something for me. She'll be right back. Go watch your movie.*

She was lying in that way adults lie, pulling a curtain to hide their adult world.

Konstantine returned to his movie having entirely forgotten about his thirst. And somehow, despite the rampant bloodshed and gun fighting on the screen, he'd dozed off. When he woke, the movie was off, the night was dark and quiet. Someone, his mother no doubt, had tucked him in tight. It took him several moments to realize it had been the sound of his mother crying that had woken him. Lying beside him, he could see the slender plane of her back beneath her thin nightdress. Her shoulders trembled.

Konstantine knew Francesca by reputation. Boys his age gossiped like anyone else. He understood then, with a child's clarity, what had happened. He visited Padre Leo in the basement of his old church the very next day.

It was easy enough to find him. All the boys in the city knew of Padre Leo and his small army. If a boy agreed to take a package across town without any questions, he could have a pocketful of candy and lire by the end of the day.

And by the afternoon, Padre Leo was sitting in his mother's apartment, drinking coffee and assuring her everything would be all right.

And it was, because Konstantine never saw Francesca again. And he never woke to the sound of his mother crying again. His mother was happy and safe. Until his father's enemies caught up to them.

Konstantine stepped into his apartment and an arctic blast of air hit him, like entering a meat locker. It was a pleasant change from his warm walk in the afternoon.

He opened his laptop with his thumb recognition software. The screen whirled to life, loading his programs. He checked his watch again. His video conference call was in two minutes.

He arranged himself at the desk, adopting a relaxed posture purposefully. He turned on the camera to inspect himself. He made sure the lighting was right. A giant oil painting of a man with a sword raised high hung behind him. Otherwise, the stucco was bare and the room nondescript.

He could be anywhere.

Perfect.

He looked at the man framed in the video screen. His wavy black hair was neatly trimmed in the current style, short on the sides and a little long on the top. He left his mirrored shades on. He tightened his jaw to hide the fullness of his lips. He looked too much like a pouty little boy with his lips parted. He'd shaved that morning, but black stubble was already poking through. That was okay too.

Best not to look too polished, too refined. That sent a very different kind of message about the sort of man Konstantine was and how he would conduct his business.

The computer trilled with the sound of an incoming call.

Konstantine sat back in his chair and composed himself. He placed his arms on the chair, clenched his jaw again and let it ring. *Best to never let people think you're too eager.* Wasn't it his beloved Padre who had said this?

"Hello?" he said at last. He liked the sound of his English. Accented, but not unpleasantly. In the movies, he would be the love interest of a beautiful woman who would love him for this voice, going wet between her legs at the sound of it.

The chat program opened by voice recognition and Julio Vasquez appeared on the screen. A cigarette dangled from between his lips, he sat back away from the screen as if to give Konstantine some room. As if the ocean and half a country weren't enough space between Texas and Florence.

Julio's hair was greased back, slicked against his head. He wore a black tank top, and hair protruded from everywhere. From under his arms, and from his chest, great black tufts of it. Julio was one of the men who Padre trusted. His open acceptance of Konstantine had been jarring at first, in the weeks following Padre's death. The way he performed duties without question. But now Konstantine was starting to appreciate the man's swift execution and efficiency.

Konstantine waited for him to speak. Men in power never spoke first. It was beneath them. It was Julio's place to explain, Julio's place to ask for instruction. Not his.

"We've got Castle here." Julio plucked his cigarette from between his lips and exhaled blue smoke toward the ceiling. "He's got news about that bitch you're looking for."

Konstantine focused on the light behind Julio's head and the five-gallon paint bucket, orange with white splatters, overturned in the middle of the scene.

Konstantine considered correcting him. *She's not that bitch.* But it was too soon in his reign to start showing weakness. Infatuation counted as weakness in the eyes of most men. It was natural to want something and desire it. Having something you love within arm's length was stupid.

"Put him on," Konstantine said. He kept his tone even, checking his image in the box at the lower right of the screen. He looked a tad eager. He leaned back in his chair and straightened his spine.

Julio slipped out of sight, and another man appeared. He had a deeply pit-marked face and a tall, white ten-gallon hat on his head with a ridiculous feather jutting from one side. His eyes were glassy in the camera, either with fear or narcotics. The two men escorting him pushed him down onto the overturned paint bucket converted into a seat. The plastic scraped along the concrete floor.

"Hello, Mr. Castle." Konstantine laced his fingers. "How are you this evening?"

The man licked his lips and hesitated. His shoulder jostled when someone nudged him. Konstantine heard Julio say, "He's talking to you, dude. Don't be fucking rude."

"I'm good," Castle stammered and ran a hand under his nose. "How-how are you?"

"Fine," Konstantine answered with a smile. It wasn't a friendly smile. It was the smile he'd learned how to make from the gangsters in his American movies. His mother called it an I'm-so-hungry-I-could-eat-you-up smile. "I have heard something fascinating about you, Mr. Castle."

"Yeah, what's that?" Castle asked. He fidgeted, trying to get comfortable on the overturned bucket.

"Julio says you were kidnapped. By a woman."

"Hell yeah!" the man said, indignant. Relief was palpable on his face. Whatever he'd initially thought this conversation was going to be about, it wasn't about his woman. "She snatched me right out of the goddamn bathroom. Then we were in a fucking forest in the middle of fucking nowhere. It was cold. I don't even think we was in America. Well, maybe Montana, some shit like that."

"Slow down," Konstantine said. His own voice had sped up with excitement, and he was speaking as much to himself as to the dealer. He took a breath and reasserted his self-control. "Mr. Castle, what you're saying seems rather remarkable. You expect us to believe you were kidnapped by a woman, and then magically transported thousands of miles away?"

He heard Julio and the others laughing.

Castle's mouth dropped open in outrage. "But it's fucking true! I swear it."

Julio cackled like a hyena. "Perhaps you need to sell more snow than you're using, man."

"Where were you when this happened?" Konstantine asked, measuring each word.

"Tito's place."

Julio bent down so that his face was visible in the camera. "It's a cowboy bar off 6th street. Up in Austin."

Konstantine flashed another one of his controlled smiles. "Mr. Castle, is it also true you only escaped because you, how did you put it, 'gave her the best fuck of her life'?"

Julio and the others roared. Julio slapped his thigh and reached up to wipe tears from the corners of his eyes while Castle continued to defend his ridiculous story.

She would slit you, navel to nose, and leave you for dead before you even touched her.

Konstantine felt his anger rising. He let a controlled breath escape his nostrils, trying not to let them flare and give away his irritation. He would kill Castle for touching her.

She's mine, his brain whispered. *She's mine until the day she dies.*

"Settle down boys," Konstantine said once he felt he could trust himself to speak. "Castle may be a beast for all we know."

It was a cruel jibe and Castle's face crumpled, wounded. "I saw her. I swear I did."

"*That* I believe." Konstantine sat back in his chair. "So my next question is, why did she let you live? Every one of the mules she's taken has never been seen again. Yet here you are. Why do you think that is?"

Castle stiffened in his chair.

His reaction was a clue to guide Konstantine's questioning. He steepled his fingers. "Did you tell her anything?"

Castle didn't answer. His mouth hung open, and his stained, yellow teeth gleamed in the computer's shitty resolution.

Julio smacked Castle upside his head. "Do you have enchiladas in your ears? The man asked you a question."

Castle set his jaw. "No. I didn't say anything. She grabbed me from the bathroom and dropped me off in the woods. She pointed the gun at me, I talked her down. Then she brought me back."

"You talked her down?" Konstantine grinned. How would one coax down such a creature? Whatever means necessary would be beyond a man such as this.

"Yeah, you know. I was fucking *nice*. I made her see she had the wrong guy."

Castle's cheek twitched.

"And who was the *right* guy?" Konstantine leaned forward and peered into the camera, seeing his face large in the small window within the chat box. "Me?"

"No, man, no." Castle was quick to rebuke. "I didn't say anything about you."

"Julio?" Konstantine said, part question, part call for attention.

Julio didn't even have to ask. The two men who'd escorted Castle in seized his shoulders, forcing him to sit still on the overturned paint bucket. Julio held a gun to his head while the others held his arms.

"Have you ever played the game twenty questions?" Konstantine asked. Sweat had begun to form on his brow, but his voice remained perfectly even.

When Castle didn't immediately answer, Julio slid the safety off the gun and chambered a round.

"Yes, yes!" he moaned. "Yes, every fucking body has played twenty questions. What about it?"

"I love twenty questions." Konstantine smiled. "I would play this game with my mother for hours, and she always indulged me. She was a very patient woman. Wasn't she?"

Before Martinelli threw her to the wolves.

"A fucking saint," Castle said, squirming beneath the pistol pressed against his temple.

"I want to play twenty questions with you now. But the version I play with you is going to be a little different than the version I played with my mother. With you, when I ask you a question, if you lie to me, Julio is going to blow off one of your fingers. If we run out of fingers, then we have your toes."

Without having to be told, Julio moved his gun to Castle's left hand. He pressed the barrel to the man's pinkie, holding it out to the side so the bullet could blast right through without hitting either Castle or the two men holding him.

Castle squirmed. "But I haven't lied to you!"

"Be still, or I might blow off your fucking finger accidentally, you dumb fuck," Julio warned. Sweat gleamed on the back of the Mexican's neck in the overhead light.

"And if we run out of fingers and toes, then we must find something else to shoot off. Can you think of anything else on your body which resembles a finger or toe?" Konstantine asked. The men, who weren't being threatened with a bullet, laughed.

Castle began to let out a high-pitched whine. "Come on, man. I haven't done anything."

Konstantine wet his lips. "Question one: Did you tell the woman anything about me?"

Castle hesitated. Julio pulled the trigger. The report crackled through the sound feed, and the black room momentarily lit up with light revealing exposed beams and rafters. They were in one of the unfinished condos then. Konstantine noted Julio's smart choice. It was as important to keep track of the honorable mules as it was of the naughty ones. Sometimes more important. The video lagged for a heart-beat then skipped, catching up.

Castle screamed. Blood gushed from the partial stump of his pinkie, pumping over his hand. He kept screaming as Julio moved on to the ring finger, grabbing the man's slick finger as if the blood didn't disgust him.

Konstantine's stomach turned.

"Question two," Konstantine said, without looking directly at the blood. "Did you tell the woman who kidnapped you about *me*?"

"Yes!" Castle screamed. "Fuck yes. I might've said your name. But I swear to god I didn't say nothing bad about you. Not a goddamn thing."

"Question three. What did you say about me *exactly*?"

When Castle didn't answer after a few tense moments, Konstantine nodded to Julio. The gun went off again, severing the ring finger from Castle's left hand. The finger dangled in Julio's grip before it was dropped to the floor. Konstantine was thankful for his dark shades and the privacy they afforded him. He could close his eyes, and they would be none the wiser.

Castle's screams intensified. "Fuck man, I was thinking! I was fucking thinking!" Tears streamed down the man's face. It had become so red, Konstantine had to remind him to take a breath or he was going to pass out.

"At the rate we are going, I don't think you'll live to see the end of the game, my friend. You're bleeding too much," Konstantine said. He managed to add a patronizing lilt to the end of his words.

"Don't shoot so fast," Castle begged. He wiped his snotty nose on his sleeve. "I got to think."

Ah, the begging. It came whenever they tried to slow down the pain.

"I can't think so fast with my hand hurting, man. It hurts like a bitch."

"Is that my fault?" Konstantine asked.

"No, man, no."

"I want you to try very hard to answer my questions as quickly as possible," Konstantine said. "I have appointments this evening. You wouldn't expect me to be late, would you?"

"No sir," the man said, spit clinging to his lips as he spoke. He looked like a bawling child, but he didn't yank his hand away from Julio as the middle finger was grasped and bent straight. Maybe Castle was not as stupid as he looked.

"So I'll ask again. What did you say about me exactly?"

"She told me if I didn't stop muling she was going to shoot me, and I said I couldn't stop muling because you'd kill me."

"And then?" Konstantine encouraged with a little wave. He noted the spray of blood across the man's white hat.

"She said you were another roach or rat or something."

Julio raised his gun and pressed it against the middle finger on the left hand.

Castle's voice took off like a shot, rising fast. "God, I don't remember. An animal, some kind of animal that scurries. I swear to god that's what she said."

"And then?"

"I told her no, you were the new Martinelli. And she said there's no fucking Martinellis because she killed them all. And I said, no there was you. That's it. I swear on my fucking mother that's it. That's all she said."

His anger surfaced. His pulse throbbed in his ears. *The new Martinelli*. "And then she took you back to Austin."

"Yes."

Konstantine sat back in his chair. The new Martinelli. So that was why she'd cut Castle loose. No doubt she'd been furious at the idea of a Martinelli living. Breathing.

After a moment he said, "Did she realize you recognized her?"

"Yeah," he said. He was looking like he might vomit. A sheen of sweat coated his face.

"Did she ask how you recognized her?"

"The pictures," he said without hesitation. He was going to pass out from blood loss, Konstantine realized.

"And then she brought you back," he said again, but he was grinning now.

"Yeah, man. I told you. She dropped me off outside Tito's place."

Konstantine's anger softened. *Tricky, tricky girl.*

"Julio?"

"Yeah, boss?"

"Please help Mr. Castle attend to his wounds. He has been very helpful. It would be unfortunate if anything were to happen to him."

The two men who'd been holding him down moments before now helped him up, slapped him on the back and escorted him from the room as if he were nothing more than a buddy who'd had too much to drink. Meanwhile, Julio barked orders to have the concrete floor hosed down and the fingers collected off the ground.

"Stay for a moment, Julio," Konstantine commanded before he could terminate the call.

Julio pulled the overturned bucket up to the computer screen, the perfect height to frame himself in the camera. Two men discussing business. The blood-soaked bucket and fingers on the floor already forgotten.

"Make sure Castle doesn't die. I want him sewn up and back on the street tomorrow at the latest."

"You got it."

"She's going to track him. So we are going to track him too. Send a few men up from San Antonio, men Castle won't recognize, and have him followed. *Everywhere.* But don't be obvious. She will know we are onto her if she sees too many men standing around, obsessing over Castle."

"No problem," Julio said, slipping a new cigarette between his lips and lighting it behind a cupped palm.

"Should we give him his fingers?" Julio asked. "If we get them on ice, he can sew that shit back on."

"No," Konstantine said, his voice cold. "We are going to kill him, if she doesn't do it first. No need to go out of our way."

"She's only a girl," Julio said, scratching his hairy chest.

Konstantine grinned. "You have no idea what she's capable of."

She would come back for him. She would come for Konstantine and he couldn't be more excited. Even if it meant his death, he would see her again. And truly, she deserved her revenge. What his brothers did to her family, it was unforgivable. Why shouldn't she seek his blood in return?

"I started looking into her family the way you wanted," Julio said. He placed his thumb in his mouth and began to chew it. "It was Angelo's kill, like you said. But I'm hearing other shit too, man."

Konstantine leaned forward, unable to hide his interest. "Tell me."

11

At five past eleven, Lou stepped into her apartment. She'd only come back for a wardrobe change. She removed the machete from her back and switched to thin, efficient blades, easily concealed in her inner arms and boots. Their handles were sleek metal meant to keep the weight of the blade even if she needed to throw it rather than plunge it into her target's neck. Black metal would neither reflect the light nor draw attention to itself.

Killing, not intimidation, was the order of the evening.

She pulled four S&W blades from their hook on the wall and slipped them into place. Then she loaded six clips. Six was a tad much for a simple stakeout, but she'd only been expecting to meet her aunt's friend for coffee, and look how that turned out.

Someone was watching her. Tracking *her*.

It was a new sensation and unpleasant.

The part she loved most about her ability was the way she moved through the world. Like a ghost.

She blended into a setting, observed, took what she wanted, and was never seen again. And the men she seized, they never lived to tell the tale. Her anonymity was her greatest power, and she fully understood this. Even if she hadn't been raised in an age where starlets were displayed on magazine covers, and their sex tapes rampantly devoured, she would have understood this. His face and name had gotten her father killed after all. Even before the internet, five minutes on the television was all the Martinellis had needed to track him down.

Castle was the first man Lou'd let go since she killed Gus Johnson at the tender age of seventeen.

And the fact that this new Martinelli, *Konstantine*, had photos of her, shopping her face around, meant the number of men who could recognize her on sight was rising. And what the hell was his game anyway? He must want revenge for his murdered family. That was the only connection between them. And yet, she was certain she'd been careful. Left no witnesses. Konstantine shouldn't even have the smallest idea of who the hell he wanted revenge *from*. So where had she fucked up?

Fuckups happened, but they had to be cleaned up. The only problem was, Lou was in a boat on the open sea. It was filling up with water, and she had no idea where the leak was.

That simply will not do, as Aunt Lucy liked to say in a fake and poorly rendered British accent, and probably misquoted from some old movie launched before Lou's time.

The moment Lou realized the not-detective King was Aunt Lucy's ex, she wasn't surprised. Aunt Lucy was too romantic. Of course, she would run to her ex, some man she probably still coddled a burning love for, and ask him to swoop in and save her wayward niece from self-destruction. The idea that a woman needed a man to help her do anything was ridiculous and five minutes with King was enough to tell her he was no saint on a white horse. His apartment reeked of marijuana. He had no food in the fridge. He was at least forty pounds overweight, and yet he'd gobbled those beignets like he hadn't eaten in three days, sucking the powdered sugar off his fingers with relish.

She loaded a magazine and then inserted it into the butt of her gun. She chambered a round. She didn't need some bored ex-cop to give her direction. She'd call her own shots, *thank you very much*.

She slipped the extra magazines into the pockets of her cargo pants and the inside pockets of her vest. Again, it was a lot of ammo for stalking. But Lou felt the heat of the situation rising, and she'd rather be ridiculously over-prepared than ridiculously stupid. Besides, this was one of her father's vests. She ran a hand down the front of her chest over the Kevlar, and the muscles in her body went soft.

She'd had to sneak into their home to get it.

After her parents were killed, Lou returned to her house. Lucy had forbidden it, but Aunt Lucy couldn't watch her 24/7. The moment her aunt's snores turned soft and steady in the next room, Lou had slipped through and found herself in her house. Her *old* house.

The grief had welled fresh then, as her mind tried to sort through its options for reclassification: *my old house, my childhood home, my parents' house, where I used to live—*

She'd appeared in her room. The twin bed was there, and her covers rumpled. Most of her stuff was still there since they'd forbidden her from taking anything away from The Crime Scene. That's how they said it, as if in all caps, THE CRIME SCENE.

Lucy had slipped her back in of course, after a few hours, but only to get clothes. *Nothing they'll notice*, she'd said. But it wasn't enough. Lou knew the cops didn't give two shits about her books, clothes, or music. Her rollerblades with the one cracked wheel or the drawings she'd done herself and stuck to the wall with Scotch tape. She could've stuffed all her things into her camo backpack or her Hello Kitty suitcase, and they'd never question where the shit went. But she'd wait until Saturday for those, the day she was allowed to take what little was left of her former life.

Aunt Lucy was left with the task of going through her parents' stuff and determining what should be sold and what should be boxed up for Lou.

Sell it all, Lou had told her.

Because it wasn't all her mother's worthless shit that she'd wanted. All the throw pillows and doilies and ceramic vases and china figurines.

She'd wanted her father's things.

And she knew that's what the cops wanted too, so she had to be first. She went into her parents' bedroom and froze. Blood stained the mattress, one side of the sheets had been stripped back to reveal the mattress and the stain spread in an oval on her mother's side of the bed. The cordless phone was still on the floor where her mother had dropped it. And a glass of wine, with a thin layer of dried wine coating the rim, lay on the carpet beside the phone. Her mind kept trying to put the two together, the overturned wine glass and the blackish stain on the mattress. *She spilled her wine*, her mind said. A lot of *wine*.

The shattered lamp which had caught a bullet.

She'd torn her eyes away from it and went into her father's closet. Not her mother's, which had been the walk-in on the left, but the one on the right. She pulled the brushed aluminum handle, and the door came open with a *pop,* the frame sticking in the heat of summer.

She stepped inside and closed the door. The world wavered, threatening to pitch her through, but she turned on the light, and it became steady again. Her father's dress shirts were organized by color, Courtney's doing. At first, Lou could only run her fingers along the sleeves and feel the different fabrics. Mostly cotton. Some of them the flannel he loved.

She reached her arms out and squeezed the shirts into a giant ball and cried. They smelled like him and her mother's detergent, and she would never smell it again.

She had no idea how long she stood in the closet, sobbing into her father's shirts. But she took the flannel, still had it, though it fell to her thigh when she wore it. And she had to roll the sleeves up above the elbow. In addition to the shirts, she took two other things. Cut-resistant Kevlar sleeves which had to be resized later, but she'd found someone to do it. And his adjustable vest. Her father had worn it at the biggest size, the straps stretched fully extended. She wore it at the smallest, with the Velcro overlapping. Before she grew up and found a use for her father's vest, she would wear it on the nights she couldn't sleep. She'd put it on, tighten the straps, and crush it against her. It didn't fit, but it was something of his. A poor substitute for his arms around her.

Lou blinked back tears and the St. Louis skyline came into focus, locking on the searchlight from Busch Stadium. A distant roar of loudspeakers and cheers swelled. There was a game tonight. Some man in a red and white uniform was dreaming he'd hit it out of the park.

Lou stepped into the closet hoping for the same.

When she stepped out of the closet, she was on a rooftop in Austin. She crouched in the shadow of a bigger building, standing tall beside the one she squatted on. The buildings were right against one another. She leaned one arm against the sun-warmed brick and watched the downtown strip below. From here she could see the evening in full swing. Women in fish scale or leopard print skirts prowled the four-lane boulevard. Men in jeans or leather stalking them or possessively holding onto their hips in a display of dominance. Cigarette cherries burned in the darkness beneath the pulsing lights, and music blared through bar doors, mingling with the sound of honking horns and squealing brakes on the street.

She could see everything from up here. And she could thank King for the idea. When he asked her for a better view of their stalkers, she knew what he meant immediately. She preferred to slip laterally. She could put real distance between herself and her attackers. It was easier to track from underneath, following the sounds of footfall through floorboards overhead. She had gone high for a vantage point, an idea she credited to King.

But it seemed perfect for her current predicament.

If Konstantine was looking for her and Castle was alive and spouting tales of his escape, he would put men on the ground. She had no idea if Castle had had time to talk yet. He could be dead for all she knew.

But he wasn't.

She pulled the scope from the front pocket of her vest—her father's vest—and lifted it to her right eye.

The boulevard was blown up to movie screen proportions.

It took her a moment of sweeping the walkway to find Castle. He still wore the tall white hat with feathers, making him an easier target. Tonight he wore jeans, black cowboy boots with steel toe tips and a black vest. A leather choker with a large turquoise medallion lay against his throat and bobbed up and down as he laughed.

He stood on the corner outside a bar smoking a joint and chatting with three men and two women. He showed them something in his hand, weaving some long, bullshit tale about his exploits no doubt. Some female conquest or a close battle won. She'd shadowed enough bars to know how men spoke when they were together in large, hungry groups.

Castle's audience bent down to look at something close, and then suddenly, they jumped back. One of the women shrieked. Her friend beside her clutched her arm, laughing, but the laugh was hollow. Pure fear.

When one of the men looked aside, creating a gap in the circle, Lou saw his hands.

They were empty. It wasn't what he held that was the spectacle. It was the hand itself. Two fingers had been severed from Castle's left hand.

She adjusted the scope.

Thick black stitches knotted the skin together. The flesh was torn, puckering between the black twine. A home job. And the fingers hadn't been severed cleanly with a knife.

Had Konstantine ordered they be torn off? Brutal.

But the wound was fresh, no doubt, as Castle had had all ten fingers when she dumped him on the avenue the previous night.

So Konstantine moved fast.

She lowered the scope and tried to think. Why would they sever the fingers? To send a message? Because he was angry? Because he hadn't captured her himself?

Perhaps.

Yet if he'd wanted his dealers to capture her, he would kill Castle and send a stronger message. Give them a strong motivation to come out of this alive, should one of them find themselves at the wrong end of her gun.

No, he must've wanted something else.

Lou lifted the scope again and started searching the walk for tails.

It was hard to tell who might be following Castle as he stood on the sidewalk showing his war wounds to his friends. The tails would only move when he moved. And if they were following him to find her, she had to be careful of her own movements.

If she moved when Castle moved, it would draw attention. Like prehistoric reptilian beasts, her movements would attract their eyes and bring her into sharp focus.

She would have to confine her actions to slips, sticking close to the shadows.

Castle's phone rang, and he fished it out of his back pocket with his good hand. He used his thumb to mash the button to take the call. After receiving some instruction, he returned his phone back to his pocket and nodded down the street. Castle wrapped the pinkish white gauze over his hand as he walked. He moved in her direction, his face hidden behind the large brim of his hat as he focused on his hand. His group kept him encircled in a cozy knot as they walked.

In the scope, she could see the blood splattered across the brim of his hat. A grim reminder a lot could happen in twenty-four hours. Castle had lost two fingers. A shiver ran up her spine. What would happen to her by the time the sun rose on the next day?

She kept her arm pressed to the side of the warm brick building. Unmoving, only her eyes tracked Castle down the sidewalk.

A group of drunks bumped into Castle's front line and another man shoved them off. The belligerent drunk's eyes going wide when a knife was pulled and pressed to his throat. The victim looked like a bleating goat from where Lou stood. His eyes wide and lips blubbering. But the man with the knife let him go, laughing.

Lou wanted to put her knife to his throat and see how he liked it. In her mind, she moved this mule to the top of her list beneath Castle. She killed Martinelli mules in order of importance. Who moved the most dope? Yank the biggest fish out of the sea, and the ecosystem collapses. She had to keep these objectives in mind. What would she do when Konstantine was dead? The listlessness would not overtake her a second time. And King's pathetic interest in witnesses would never be enough to stimulate her or put her skills to good use. No. Rank the mules. And perhaps she would have something worth doing once this was all over.

Movement caught her eye.

The moment Castle and his group walked beneath an awning, a shadow emerged from the alley one block up. She marched up the street in platform heels the color of bubblegum and a black skirt barely covering her ass. Her breasts were falling out of the front of her denim shirt, which looked like an ordinary garment, though molested. The sleeves had been rolled up above the elbows. The bottom had been knotted above the navel rather than buttoned correctly.

She wobbled down the street on thin legs, a cigarette burning between her fingers.

When Castle stopped to smash out the butt of his cigarette, she stopped. She shot a look across the street and met eyes with a man leaning against a light post, pretending to look at his phone. His face was aglow in the light of the screen. He made a nod toward Castle, and the girl started teetering after them again.

At least two tails then. But Lou figured where there were two tails, there were more. A horrible thought bloomed in the back of her mind.

She tore her eyes from the ground and looked up. She searched the windows and balconies of the buildings for eyes.

Her heart sped up as she counted. Two. Three. Five. *Seven* pair.

Two men sat on a balcony with beers balanced on their legs, the picture of casualness if not for the perfect synchronicity of their heads turning toward Castle. Three were watching from the windows of two different buildings as he passed. One leaned down and spoke into a phone.

Her heart pounded in her ears.

She'd walked right into a fox den and hadn't even realized it.

There were too many men on Castle. She'd greatly underestimated Konstantine's interest in her. She needed to get the fuck out of here.

She looked into the window directly across from hers at the man speaking into his phone. The room behind him was dark and his face as translucent as a ghost, reflecting the light from the boulevard below. He scanned the rooftops. His eyes two buildings to her left and moving in her direction, his head did a slow, dramatic turn that made her heart hammer even faster.

She shrank against the building and slipped through this side of darkness.

The world solidified again with her in her closet, heart pounding. She sucked in deep breaths and tried to steady herself. Had the scout seen her? Had someone else watched *her* while she was all doe-eyed over Castle?

"Fucking stupid!" she punched the inside of the closet. Anger rose inside her.

The fear never lasted in her experience. This old familiar hate would always draw itself up, its head opening like a cobra hood, flaring to life around her. Hate she understood.

Konstantine thought he was smarter than she was? Thought he could overwhelm her with his muscle and use her own tricks against her? Because Castle had been her trick. She'd cut the rat loose and sent him running, hoping it would lead her back to the den.

Instead, the wolves came out, looking for her.

If he dared to use her trick against her, she would repay him in kind. She could slip to him right now if she wanted. Fall right through the closet and pop up wherever the bastard was hiding and cut his fucking head off. *Hunt this!* she'd say as his slit throat gurgled blood all over her hands and forearms. *Here I am, you fucking cunt.*

Easy girl, her better judgment began. The leash on her anger tightened. Her father's voice echoed through her mind. *Stay with me, Lou-blue.*

The anger broke on the shore like a wave. Each wave that followed less angry than the one before. She saw his beautiful face. Felt his scruffy beard under her small hands, remembered the way it would tickle her nose when he kissed her. How he would lift her whole body off the ground when he hugged her.

She hadn't had one of those great encompassing hugs in sixteen years.

Stay with me.

"I can't," she whispered in her dark closet. Her chest ached. "They sent you somewhere I can't go."

re you sure this is the right finger bone?" King asked. He looked at the disconnected phalanges in his cupped palms and frowned. The plastic rolled in his palm as incomprehensible as the entrails of some gutted animal. "They aren't matching up."

Mel placed one hand on her hip and glared at him. Her voice rose. She'd reached the limit of her patience and no more questions were to be asked. "You have these bones in your own fingers, don't you? Can't you figure it out?"

Her lipstick was a dark purple today, the color of bruises or rotting meat. And every time he looked at her, his stomach turned. He kept his eyes on the mess in his hands.

"I've never seen the bones in my fingers," King countered. "Fortunately."

Why did assemble-yourself projects have to be so goddamn compli-cated? The only easy part had been the one-piece jaw, which snapped into place and hung from the base of the skull. Every other step in this endeavor was like pushing a boulder up an oil-slicked hill.

"This skull face is so awesome." Piper leaned forward and adjusted the hood on the skeleton. Every time she leaned toward the skeleton, the ladder beneath her wobbled and King's heart hitched.

His emotions warred. He was both furious she might touch the skeleton in a way that'd decimate his hard-earned progress, and simultaneously fearful she would fall off the rickety ladder and break her neck.

"Can't you be careful?" King snapped, uncomfortable with the tight whine of his voice.

Piper ignored him. "It's going to scare the bejeezus out of the customers."

"Are you sure that's what you want?" King asked, looking from the finger bones to Mel hopefully. "You don't want people to run screaming from the shop, do you?"

"I'm tellin' y'all. Spooky foo sells! Since I installed the door chime—"

"Mel, that isn't what spooky foo means," Piper interjected.

"—since *we* installed," King said, seizing the ladder as it started to tip.

"Sales have gone up by 200%. This guy here is going make it even better."

"200%?" Piper snorted, righting herself. "So what? $50 this month?"

Mel cast her a sharp sideways glance. "Perhaps you haven't seen the full vision yet." The fortune teller reached behind the skeleton and flicked a switch on his back. "Piper, go on outside and then come back in."

Piper descended the ladder and King was grateful for a chance to let go. His arm ached from clutching its rails. A warm breeze followed Piper into the shop as she strolled in, and King became aware of the time. Morning was nearly over and he hadn't made any of the phone calls he'd intended to make on the Venetti case. But he'd promised Mel he would help her with this skeleton and he couldn't duck out before he'd finished, no matter how strongly the case file called to him from his coffee table upstairs.

A shriek blared through the shop and King fell back, dropping the ladder. It was as if someone had grabbed a cat and swung it overhead, helicopter style. No. *Five* cats howling in fear and fury as the skeleton's jaw dropped down low enough to accommodate an infant. The eyes burned bright red. Twin bulbs shone in their sockets.

King's body flushed with adrenaline. An immediate tremor seized his hands.

Then the sound ceased, the jaw closed, and the red lights dulled to a flat black.

For a moment, no one spoke.

"That's—" Piper searched for a word, eyes wide, one hand on her chest.

"Perfect!" Mel clapped her pale palms together.

"Shocking," Piper said, licking her lips. "Uh, what's the return policy on this thing again?"

"We're not returning it. We're going to move it closer to the door," Mel said, her face lit up with her excitement. She practically danced from foot to foot.

"Okay but you better add some good health insurance to my work benefits package. Every time this thing goes off, I'm sure I lose a decade of life. By the end of the week, I'll have gray hair."

King pointed at the gold Mardi Gras beads hanging from her neck. "Did you have those a moment ago?"

Piper grinned and wagged her eyebrows. "Nope. I just got them." She jabbed a thumb over her shoulder at the street beyond the windows as if this explained everything.

Mel's excitement dimmed. "Must I remind you that while you work for this establishment, you must maintain a respectable reputation? This isn't Bourbon Street."

Piper pursed her lips. "I know. I don't get paid enough to forget it. And haven't you ever heard of gender equality? Or I think your generation called it 'women's lib'? Bottom line: I'll show *what* I want, *when* I want."

King shoved one finger bone onto the peg of another, trying to arrange them from smallest to largest. This must have upset the skeleton because it emitted another toe-curling shriek.

Once Mel's shoulders dropped away from her ears she said. "It has a 60-day return policy. But we won't need to return it, because we're going to see sales skyrocket."

"Oh, so we're going to make $100 a day," Piper huffed. She rolled her eye. "Sounds magical."

King felt Mel go still beside him.

"Pippy, go to the back and see if we have anything that'll go with this."

"What goes with a plastic skeleton?" Piper snorted, twirling her newly earned beads between her fingers.

"Look around," Mel said. But King heard the hard edge to her voice despite the simple instruction. And he thought it was no coincidence Mel wouldn't look at the girl as she spoke.

Piper disappeared down the aisles toward a door marked Employees Only to the left of the curtained nook where Mel dispensed fortunes.

"You all right?" King asked. He hoped he sounded nonchalant, but he didn't. As he shoved the stump of a hand onto its wrist, the force and irritation with his task bled through.

"God help me, I love that girl, but sometimes..." her voice trailed away. King thought she was finished, but Mel's voice came hot and fast on a fresh wave of anger. "I mean, does she think I'm *trying* to tank my business? Does she think I've got nothing better to do than let this place eat me out of house and home?"

"She's a kid," he said. "She doesn't realize what she's saying."

And this is my home too. Even though he'd only been in the city for a few months, it *was* home. He had a breakfast place which served buttermilk flapjacks and the best eggs hollandaise, with a thick yellow sauce he could mop up with a salty biscuit. He had his coffee place. They knew not only his name but to put four sugars and a creamer on the counter with every order. What would horrify Mel, he knew, was his first-name-basis with a few of the bartenders at local watering holes, and he knew what drinks they did best. Kevin made a smooth dirty martini. Hank was a master of whiskey sours. Gemma made an unbeatable gin and tonic.

And there were the places themselves. The quiet streetcar stops. The steps outside the aquarium and Spanish plaza, a place perfect for an afternoon stroll-and-sit. And he could have a beer there too.

All of this on top of the place where he put his head every night and the balcony from which he said goodnight to the world.

"You could raise my rent," he said and gave her a nudge with his shoulder.

Mel stilled beside him. She considered the face of the skeleton with the same intense stare she gave young girls with their smooth palms in hers. What did she see in those black sockets? The dark glass of the unlit bulbs shining in the dim light around them.

"We're gonna be all right," she whispered to the boney man. "Life is all about cycles. Up and down. The tide in and out. We're down and out now, that's all. When I saw this broken shop, I knew I could make her fly. I believe it, Mr. King. After these ten years, for better or worse, I still believe it."

Her eyes were glistening and wet when she met his gaze again.

Hurricane Katrina swallowed up the city and spit her out the other side, and many of the shops and businesses in the French Quarter were damaged. Fresh from a divorce with money in her pocket after a hefty settlement, Mel bought the place on the cheap from a couple of northerners who had neither the interest nor the patience to deal with FEMA or the insurance company in order to rebuild. One breaking dam was enough for those New Englanders.

And King couldn't help but wonder if she'd seen something of herself in the boarded-up shop. Hollowed out, half-drowned in an ugly divorce and nowhere to go but up. She had to remake more than these four walls. She had to rebuild a life after thirty years with a man who drank too much Johnny Walker and couldn't tell a punching bag apart from a jaw bone.

"I'm going to have to let Piper go. At least for a while. I can cover her this week and next, but after—" Mel's voice hitched in her throat. She sucked in a deep breath through flaring nostrils. "It's gonna break her heart."

The muscles in King's chest tightened. "Don't do that. What do you pay her? $10 an hour? Twenty hours a week?"

"There about."

"I'll cover her. I can get her to do some of the little jobs for my case." King's offer was out of his mouth before he could consider what he was saying. But he was right. He *could* cover her. Brasso had hired him as a freelancer to find the Venetti woman, and he'd added the open-ended *plus expenses* clause. Piper could be his *plus expenses*.

He wasn't sure how long he could draw out the case, but if he could ease Mel's financial burden for a while, he'd do it.

Mel's black hawk eyes narrowed and her lip curled. "Out of the cast iron and into the blaze!"

"Not dangerous work," he said, pretending to be wounded. "Photocopying. Googling. Maybe a few innocuous phone calls."

King hated making phone calls. He'd pay anyone to do that unpleasant task for him.

Mel worked her lower lip, chewing off a great deal of the purple lipstick. "She'll love it. Any excuse to be nosey as hell."

"I'll talk to her if you want," King asked with raised eyebrows. "Or she doesn't even have to know I'm paying."

"No, I'll talk to her," Mel said scratching at an elbow absent-mindedly. "You know she's here morning and night. Yesterday I gave her a shift from 10-2. So, I had enough time to run to the bank and pick up a shipment from the French market. Then at midnight when I was taking out the garbage, I caught her sitting on the curb across the street, smoking a cigarette and playing on her phone."

King didn't add anything to this. He wondered what Piper's home life was like. The girl lived with her mother, he knew, but this wasn't unheard of for a twenty-year-old. Young women came by the shop asking for her. Never boys, or men. Mel didn't mind, because sometimes they bought candles or incense. But the fact remained these girls weren't meeting Piper at *home*, or at least, he didn't think so. And King's nose told him there must be a reason.

The door banged open behind them, and their conversation ceased. Mel and King turned in unison, reluctantly pulling their gaze away from one another, and saw Piper's butt first. White jean shorts cut off mid-thigh and halfway through an almond-colored birthmark. Then the rest of her came up, and she straightened, smiling.

She wore oversized sunglasses, a feather boa the color of wine, and a red and yellow foam finger with Loyola Wolf Pack printed on it. She shook her hips in time with her pumping arm while humming the basketball team's entrance tune.

"How's this for our slender man?"

Mel's eyes met King's. "She's all yours."

13

T he line was quiet.

"Well?" Konstantine urged. He tried not to let his desperation for answers seem too obvious. He feared it was too late for such caution.

"Nah, it's nothing," the lookout said at last. "The roof is empty."

Konstantine's disappointment fell like a weight against his shoulders. His phone beeped. The number was blocked, but he knew whose voice he would hear when he answered.

"Report to me in an hour," Konstantine said and terminated the call. Then he switched lines. "Hello?"

"Konstantine? Mr. Konstantine?" An American voice with an exaggerated drawl responded immediately. His name was like rocks in the man's mouth. Kon-stan-teee-nnna. Horrible. Who taught him how to speak?

"Yes? Who is this? How did you get this number?" Konstantine hoped his irritation was authentic. He was disappointed his crew had not spotted the girl, but he wasn't surprised. He knew what she was and how difficult it would be to snare her. He hoped the trap he was laying for this caller proved more fruitful.

"I've heard your name around, in certain company. I hear you are a man of many talents, Mr. Konstantine. I'm looking to employ those talents."

Good. The bait Julio had placed worked.

"I am a busy man," Konstantine said, soaking his words with indifference. He dragged his fingers across his forehead and thought of the stakeout happening on the Austin rooftops as he spoke. It was difficult to switch the mind from one task to another. "Please skip the flattery and tell me who you are and what you want."

The man laughed. "Direct! I can appreciate that."

He told Konstantine who he was and what he wanted.

Konstantine's heart was pounding by the time the man finished.

"Are you still there?" the man drawled. "Did I lose you?"

"I'm here," Konstantine managed to say. He'd broken into a sweat and his shirt stuck to the high back leather chair in which he sat.

"After Colorado legalized marijuana, we have five other states trying to push the same bill," the man said. He spoke as if Konstantine should find this news horrific. "We've got to curb this as fast as we can. And it will be beneficial for your own enterprise, won't it?"

"We do not deal in marijuana," he said, digging deep for calm. He'd wanted the man to take the bait and he'd taken it. *Don't fuck this up now.*

"They'll legalize marijuana now and cocaine tomorrow and heroin the day after. It will be a *disaster*. Did you know they have clean needle exchanges on the streets?"

Konstantine knew of the same policy in the EU. Mitigating the spread of blood borne pathogens was more important to health departments than keeping drugs off the street.

"Come here, on my dime of course, and get the information we need. Information is as good as gold to these men. If we have the right information, we can swing the votes. We can keep the system running the way we like it. I'll make it worth your time. I promise."

This man was willing to pay a gross sum to protect his larger investments and wealth.

Konstantine thought Americans fretted over their money the way one worries over their children. They had no idea how much they truly had—or didn't—or where the bottom of the barrel sat.

So much of the world suffered from this illness. These men believed their money made them powerful. Omnipotent.

They sit on mounds of money and wish for more. But money makes a man lazy. Unimaginative and limited. Those who do without are forced to be clever, forced to keep their claws and minds sharp.

He had money from Padre Leo and a name from his father. True. But he would not let it weaken him. He eyed a more valuable prize than an unending bank account—true freedom. True and limitless power.

And once he had Thorne's daughter, it would be his.

"I do not have to come to America in order to do what you ask," Konstantine said, wearily. "I can produce information on these men here."

Silence on the line.

"I prefer to work with men I know. Whom I've actually seen," the man said. His tone set the hairs on the back of Konstantine's neck to rising. "And you should come to Texas so you'll have a chance to see how your stateside affairs are working. I understand you have contacts right here in Texas."

Julio had done his job well.

"I do," Konstantine said cautiously.

"Perhaps they would benefit from direct attention."

And if I came to America, did this hacking job for you, then I would have a chance to look for her myself. I could come to her.

"If this price is right, I will come," Konstantine said. He imagined the moment of meeting her. In a dark club, seeing her at the bar watching him, measuring him the way she had measured Castle. Would she take him there? Kill him in this winter paradise Castle spoke of? Would he learn firsthand what happened to Angelo and the others?

He knew encountering a leopard in the wild was a death sentence. But he still sought her out, convinced that if she only heard him out, she would know the truth of his vision. Of his plans.

"Can you come tomorrow?" the man asked.

"No," Konstantine refused. Outright. On principle. He agreed to board a plane, a private jet sent by the man himself, in three days and then terminated the call.

Konstantine turned his cell phone off and sat back against the headboard.

Again, he saw her. Tight black clothing hugging her firm body. The way she looked up at him through her lashes. The glint of metal pressed to his cheek.

He reached up and touched the small scar under his chin. It was rough, catching on his fingernail. It was an old wound. The skin puckered into a line where no hair grew.

He would never forget what she'd looked like that night, the moment she stepped out of his closet and pressed a knife to his throat. The way she'd made his heart race.

She wasn't more than nineteen or twenty and it had been at least a year since he'd seen her last. This was the first night she'd appeared to him awake, and not as a sleeping doll in his bed.

The sight of her body so close to his, the smell of her sweat and skin. It gave him an erection. Then and now. Already his hand was on the button of his pants, undoing them, slipping a slick palm beneath the waistband.

Blood thrummed between his legs as he saw her lying beside him. Her hair fanned over his pillow. Her cheeks flushed with color as her brows knit together against dark dreams.

"I want you," he whispered to the woman made of darkness, the woman unfurling in his mind. As if admitting it aloud, he could summon her across the distance. But she did not come when called.

He would see her again. He'd find a way.

Unlike the lazy and greedy American, he knew true power when he saw it. And what was worth having was worth waiting for.

14

Lou paced her apartment. She felt the weight of her father's vest in one hand. She opened and closed it, mashing the Velcro together only to rip it apart again. The angry tearing sound soothed her. It soothed her the way the smell of beer on a man's breath soothed her. Remnants of her father's life still alive in the world.

Once when she was a child, her father had taken her to the zoo. She hated it. The large-eyed lemurs, the great wildebeests, and even the capybaras looked depressed to her. All the animals, which had once been free in the world, now confined to cages.

One animal had cut her deep.

Inside an exhibit, a black panther paced back and forth in front of the glass. It looked utterly exposed and vulnerable in the bright sunlight. Its big eyes followed her from beyond the glass as it walked up and down in front of people.

As she watched her pace back and forth in her cage, Lou had begun to cry.

She was grateful for the full sunlight of the day. Her sympathy for the animal was so great she would have slipped into the enclosure.

That night as she lay in bed, the only thing keeping her from visiting the beast was the fear she'd be eaten alive. And she was too small to move the animal back to the South American jungle and keep all her limbs attached to her body as well.

But her heart hurt no less.

Now, as she walked back and forth in her apartment, opening and closing the vest, she knew exactly how the panther had felt.

Prudence her mind whispered. She knew she was being hunted, and the way the hunted survived was by hunkering down until the hunter walked past, unaware. Then when his back was to her—*pounce*. That was the moment to sink one's teeth and crush the skull.

Threat eliminated.

Hide her inner wisdom counseled, the part of her that had saved her skin so many times in the past few months. Hide and emerge only to cover her tracks. Because that was another consideration. If this Konstantine were half as smart as his predecessor—because of course the other Martinellis had tried to find her—he would try to learn of her identity. She had no driver's license or government ID. She did not vote. She had no medical or dental records to speak of, if only because hospitals scared her. Too much bright light and not nearly enough shadows to hide in.

She had no phone number and no friends. The apartment was in her aunt's name with her aunt's billing information. All her bills were paid for automatically from the trust established by her father before his death. The fact that her father had life insurance and a trust established the moment Louie was born, told her he had doubted he would see his daughter grow to adulthood.

This thought alone broke her heart—or it would have if she'd had much heart left.

With only minimal public documents, would he make the connection between the murder of Jack Thorne and his wife and their surviving daughter?

And that was the problem, wasn't it? She couldn't predict how much this Konstantine knew and how accessible she was to him. He had pictures but perhaps not a name.

She knew he would be heavily guarded, like his brothers. So the idea of jumping right into his dark bedroom some night and killing him was suicidal.

Maybe she could *see* him.

She looked up at the lit skyline and smiled. She laid her father's vest down gently on her bed. Then she ducked into her closet and closed the door.

Her body softened in the darkness. The thin veil between this side of the world and Konstantine's thinned even more. It began to give, sliding out from under her. Her hand shot out and touched the grainy wood of the closet's opposite wall. She held this space, keeping her body rooted in place.

She heard sounds. A car honked. A bicycle horn blared in response. A dog was barking, and the bells of a church began to chime. She counted the toll—seven. She quickly did the math. Not America then. He was somewhere in Europe, in an industrialized city with a church old enough that the hour was kept by bell tolls—which hardly narrowed it.

He could be in Sweden, Poland or Algeria. Italy seemed the most obvious guess, given what she knew about his family, but it was dangerous to make assumptions when working with such a man. Only one thing was for sure.

Wherever he was, the sun had already risen over the horizon, and the shadows would be thinning. Tracking him openly in the daylight would be more dangerous than overtaking him beneath the cover of night.

Of course, if he was a world away, it meant Lou had more room to breathe than she thought. There was an ocean between them. And while Castle might have been heavily guarded and maybe most of the dealers holding the Texan line were off limits, for now, the world was a big place. The list of dealers she wanted deported to La Loon was fifty. *At least.*

He had mules in Chicago, Orlando, New York. And it was only one o'clock in the morning.

She grinned and placed her other hand against the closet wall, relieved to find a reasonable way to burn off steam.

She could accomplish a lot before dawn.

At 1:07, she grabbed Yorkie Hankerton off Michigan Ave where he'd been trying to finalize the deal between two sex workers and a tourist from Albuquerque.

Yorkie, with his chest swelled up and a hairy navel protruding from beneath a tight shirt, postulated like a gorilla at the zoo. His back grazed the giant reflective bean in the Millennium Park and his mirror image mimicked his movements, mocking him behind his back. A shadow from the enlarged bean stretched out behind him, darkening the walk. The girls stood ten yards away on the corner, smiling, giggling provocatively until the tourist pulled out his calfskin wallet and began counting out bills in the chilly Chicago night. He looked up, money ready, and found the pimp gone.

The tourist circled the bean twice, $300 still clutched in his hand, but Yorkie was gone. The girls were clever, though. Before the man had the good sense to put his money away and slink off into the night for easier prey, the girls descended on him. One took the money. The other looped her arm in his, and the trio shuffled toward the river. Only one of the girls looked over her shoulder with a frown on her face.

AT 1:47, ANTHONY BORTELLO STOOD ON A PIER IN BALTIMORE. HE was shaking with cold. With a cigarette balanced between his lips, he waved an arm in the air in a grand sweeping gesture, much the way a bullfighter waved his red flag in the face of El Bullo. A man driving a forklift carefully slipped the forklift's prongs into the two-way pallet. With a clank, it lifted over three hundred kilos of cocaine off the loading dock. With a great *beep beep beep*, the machine reversed and the pallet was carried toward the warehouse, toward the light emitted from the raised door.

Anthony heard the whiz of the next forklift accelerating toward him. He took this moment to lean against an empty transport container and relight his cigarette. He barely felt the hand on his shoulder before the dock and machinery disappeared.

AT 2:23, HANK KENNEDY WAS BUSY BEATING HIS WIFE. HE'D COME home to a dirty house and no dinner. Instead of finding her working hard on putting things right, he'd found her in bed, pretending to sleep. He'd yanked her from the bed by her hair, still wet from a shower, and proceeded to slap her across the face until she awoke screaming. She hit him back, slapping wildly until she saw who it was.

He'd cracked two of her ribs with a swift kick to her side as she tried to crawl away. She braced herself for a second kick, but it didn't come.

When Janie Kennedy looked up, only a woman stood there, bending down with Janie's cell phone in her hand. She pressed it to Janie's ear, and held it until the woman took the phone.

Then the bedroom was empty again, the silence pressing in on her.

"911," the voice in her ear said. "What is your emergency?"

AT 4:11, TYLER PINKERTON WAS IN THE SHOWER, SCRUBBING AT HIS eyes and hair with the dry soap provided by the hotel. It was dark out, and it would still be by the time he reached the opium farm in Gostan. But the workers started at dawn, and he wanted to be there when they did and get a proper count and gross product projection. Rinsing the soap out of his hair and eyes, he optimistically figured he could have the numbers run by lunch and spend the rest of the night in a little bar he'd come to favor. The waitress had big tits and made a habit of pressing those breasts to his arm as she leaned across the table to collect his empty bottles.

It was a bonus they didn't water down his drinks like some of the other bars in the most touristy districts.

He was smiling when he stepped naked out of the shower, thinking about the hard nub of a nipple trailing across his forearm.

He stopped smiling when a young woman clad in black, blood smeared across her cheeks and caked under her nails, stepped into the bathroom with him. And turned off the lights.

LOU STEPPED OUT OF THE CLOSET INTO THE PINK DAWN LIGHT saturating her apartment. She was naked and dripping wet. *I should hang a towel in here*, she thought as she crossed the hall to her bathroom. She flipped the switch, flooding the small room with artificial light.

She preferred the dark, without question. But she was exhausted and didn't want to struggle to keep her body on this plane, in this room with no windows.

She turned on the shower and climbed into the cold stream even before the water heater had a chance to kick on. Her limbs were begin-

ning to stiffen and she would have to rely on the heat to loosen the overworked cords of her flesh again.

She wasn't worried about evidence.

Her cleanup process was more thorough than any on Earth.

She took them whole and unharmed to La Loon. The beast disposed
of the body. And then Lou stripped and returned naked. The Alaskan
Lake, her entry point, was always freezing, but never more than a stone's
throw from a shadow leading home.

No clothes to wash.

No bullets to test.

No blood splatters to examine.

No body or weapon to find.

It was perfect.

If a witness saw a brief glimpse of a woman, how would they find
her? And even if they did, they'd find evidence she was also a thousand
miles away on the same night. How would they reconcile this
discrepancy?

Reason would seal tight the small gaps in her dealings. After all, she
had been in New Orleans earlier. There were witnesses to this. How
could she also have visited Chicago? New York? Afghanistan? *And*
Baltimore?

Impossible.

With her hair wrapped in a towel, so as to not dampen her pillow,
Lou fell into her bed beneath the window. The sunlight was orange
now, the color of the sherbet coated ice-cream she'd loved as a child.
Summers all heat, sunlight, and the taste of Creamsicles in her
memory.

A memory surfaced from its depths.

Her mother was bitching about dinner, something Lou hated. Cranberry dressing? And she'd heard the front door open. She heard the
rattling box even before her father called out to her.

She ran to him and found him grinning ear to ear, a box of Creamsicles pressed between his two large palms.

"It's cranberry surprise for dinner," Lou had said, or something like
it. She remembered how her stomach turned on itself greedily at the
sight of her favorite treat.

Her father had wrinkled his nose in sympathy and handed her the box. He gave her his customary welcome hug and whispered in her ear, *clean your plate, and I'll let you eat two.*

He put her on her feet and pretended to lock up his lips with a key.

A whistle blasted for the 606 Eastbound train, dragging Lou back to the present. A steam engine honked on the river. And Lou's heart wobbled with heartache in her loft above the pool.

She knew peace only with another man's blood on her hands.

15

Paula Venetti rented a room in the basement of a record store in San Diego. During the day, she worked at a drive-thru. Burgers, milkshakes, and fries with banana ketchup, fast food for the eco-conscious consumer who dabbled in animal rights activism.

Lou and King gained two hours slipping from New Orleans to San Diego, and found themselves beneath an enormous tree on the edge of a parking lot. The streetlights overhead flickered on, marking the end of twilight. The drive-thru was spotlighted by these street lamps and it gave the impression a show was about to start and they'd arrived just in time to see it.

"Vegan fast food," Lou mused aloud, nodding at the sign. "Lucy would love this."

King remembered the first time he'd taken Lucy on a date to a steakhouse and had been affronted when she'd only eaten a few iceberg leaves with olive oil. Before that, he'd never even heard the word *vegan*.

"There she is," Lou said, giving a slight nod toward a woman framed in the drive-thru window.

Venetti was handing over a basket of fries to a kid with dreads. One of his feet balanced on a skateboard as he asked for ketchup.

"So she *is* alive," King said, his stomach settling.

Venetti was younger than King expected, or at least she looked younger than the age listed on her testimony. Of course, these men liked to run with younger women, didn't they? So why should it matter that Venetti was thirty years younger than the senator who'd courted her?

They approached Venetti with casual strides. Her strawberry blond hair was tied up in a Rosie the Riveter handkerchief. A black Marilyn Monroe mole had been penciled onto her face near her upturned nose. Her eyes were coated in thick green eyeshadow which made King think of mermaid scales shimmering beneath the surface of an ocean tide.

"What'll it be?" the woman asked, a pen gripped in her fist. Her Texan accent was strong.

"The facon-bacon cheezeburger and almond-vanilla shake, please," Lou said.

King looked at her, surprised. "You eat this shit?"

Venetti looked up from the order pad and arched an eyebrow. She said nothing, as if waiting for King to dig his own grave.

"You don't grow up with a Buddhist yogi and not develop a taste for vegetarian food," Lou said. "And I'm hungry."

"It comes with fries," Venetti said. "You can upgrade to sweet potato fries for $1.00."

"Regular fries. Add avocado to the burger, too," Lou added. "Thanks."

"And for you?" Venetti arched her perfect eyebrow at King. The flannel shirt rolled up to her elbows was a faded yellow with brown stripes. "Any of this *shit* for you?"

Lou snorted.

"Fries," King said. His eyes were roving over her exposed skin, looking for bruises. He saw none. "I'd love an order of fries, thank you. And a Coke."

"Organic cola okay?"

Lou's grin widened. "Lucy would *love* this place."

King's voice caught in his throat. "The cola is fine."

Venetti scribbled something on the notepad, tore off the sheet, and then clipped it to a string overhead. The paper whirled out of sight, pulled down the line by some imaginary force.

"That'll be $16.92," she said, and King fished a twenty out of his worn leather billfold.

"I can bring it out to you," Venetti offered and pointed at a picnic table on the grass beside the parking lot.

King sat first and Lou took her place opposite him. She was scoping the area. King could tell. She was doing a good job of looking like she was doing nothing at all. But when she leaned down to scratch an ankle, her eyes swept the perimeter. When she stretched her arms and then rolled her neck, she managed a full 360. Her eyes gathered intel in quick, nearly imperceptible glances. If King hadn't been less than a foot from her, he'd have never noticed her do it.

"So are you going to eat your fries and *organic cola* or are you going to ask her some questions?" Lou taunted. The streetlamp overhead grew brighter as the world darkened.

"The place closes in twenty minutes," King said. He couldn't stop staring at her. She stared right back with flat, black shark eyes. "When she brings the food, we'll tell her our intentions and then hope she sticks around after her shift."

"Is that the official protocol for interviewing witnesses?" Lou asked.

King found it difficult to gauge her emotions. Her face was expressionless. No happiness. No sadness. A perfectly serene face. And her tone lacked proper inflection. No hints of interest or boredom. Fatigue or curiosity. What was he supposed to do with that?

All the charm and normal effusiveness she'd shown toward Venetti was gone. He didn't like how she could turn it on and off again. Apparently, she viewed emotion only as a tool, to wield when necessary.

He tried to remember if Courtney had been like that. Cold. Unreadable. If her voice came out in a perfect uninflected tone...yes. He thought she had.

"You're staring," Lou told him, in the same steady voice.

"Sorry," King said. "I'm trying to read your face."

"And?"

"And it isn't working."

He hoped his honesty would throw her off guard.

She didn't even blink.

"I did a lot of interrogations for the DEA, I'm pretty good with body language but I'm getting nothing from you. Even the involuntary stuff, what a famed psychologist called micro-expressions. I thought I caught some excitement earlier but it's gone."

"I'm excited about my bacon cheeseburger," she said. With about as much excitement as someone who says, "I'm getting a kidney out next week."

"That's a lie." King glanced over his shoulder at the drive-thru, making sure Venetti wasn't walking up on him this very second. "All of it. The bacon. The burger. The enjoyment. *Lies.*"

"I'm beginning to see why Lucy dumped you," Lou said.

"I'll have you know I ate all the tofu she cooked without a single complaint," he said.

Lou arched an eyebrow.

"Maybe *one* complaint," he said.

Venetti appeared with a milkshake in a to-go cup.

"Can I get a straw?" Lou asked. The normal cadence had returned, even the apologetic smile women often used to soften their requests.

"Sorry, no straws. We have to think about the sea turtles."

King forgot all about Lou's body language. "Sea turtles?"

"Yeah, the sea turtles. All the straws we use end up in the ocean." Venetti reached inside the black apron tied around her waist and pulled out a picture. She flashed it at Lou first and then King. A sea turtle was swimming around the ocean with a drinking straw stuck out of its nose. When she turned the photo over, it was the turtle having the straw removed, blood streaming from its nostril. "So sad, right?"

"Tragic," Lou offered, and King thought he saw real anger flash there, but it was gone before he could be sure. "Hey, do you think we can ask you some questions?"

Lou smiled up at her. Venetti shrugged. "Sure."

Lou turned to King and waved a go-on gesture.

"Ms. Venetti, my name is Robbie, and this is my—"

"Partner," Lou offered.

"We want to talk to you about Greg Ryanson."

Venetti froze. All the muscles in her body appeared to stiffen to statue-like rigidity. Her eyes went from casual interest to round half-dollars, dilating with fear.

Lou reached up and placed one hand on the girl's forearm. "Easy there. We aren't the bad guys."

"You can't," Venetti said. She was looking around and was none too subtle about it. "You *can't.*"

"Can't what?" Lou asked. King saw the grip on Venetti's arm tighten. Not enough to cause real pain, but it was a good grip. Venetti wasn't going to cut and run, even if she wanted to.

"Did he find me?" Venetti asked.

"No," Lou said, her voice low and steady. "And he won't because we found you first."

"Have you gone to the police?" King asked, sitting up taller.

"I tried. I wanted to be a witness. For Ashley and Daminga...they deserved better." She fell silent, probably as the memories of Ryanson began to surface. Then she said, "but the police are on *his* side."

"Why do you say that?" King prompted gently. He'd pulled a thin pad from his pocket and had a pen in his hand. He was ready to collect any golden nuggets falling out of this woman's mouth.

"I was halfway through the interview when I realized I was fucked. I was talking to a spy. I don't know why I should be surprised. He owns everything."

A spy.

"But how did you know?" King asked, his hand still hovering above the notepad. Thoughts swirled and collided in his mind, but nothing cohesive yet. He'd need a minute to put the words on the page properly.

"Look at you!" Venetti said. She jabbed a finger at King and his little pad. King began to pull back reflexively. If she didn't like the pen and paper, he would hide it. He'd simply memorize what she said and make notes later. He'd done it before. No amount of nodding or soft smiles reassured the naturally paranoid. "You're writing down what I'm saying."

"I haven't—" King began.

But Venetti shook her head. "The man who interviewed me didn't write down anything. And he kept telling me to lower my voice. And when he said he needed to call his superior to get the okay to proceed, I watched him dial the number. It was *Ryanson's* number. I should know because I had it memorized. His and my mother's in case I ever got into trouble but didn't have my cell phone on me. Fucking pathetic, I know, but it's true."

"You ran," Lou said.

"Why do you think I'm here?" she asked. She waved at the fast food joint behind her. "I asked myself, where is the last place Greg would look for me? Last place in the *world*? A vegan fast food place in San Diego sounded about right."

"Good choice," Lou agreed. Her eyes were checking the dark around them again. Venetti didn't seem to notice.

"Right?" Paula said with a casual wave. "I didn't even know what the word vegan meant. I had to look it up."

"What did he look like? The cop you spoke to?" King asked. *Who was the rat?*

"Medium height. Average weight. Dark hair and eyes."

Damn, King thought. *That was half the force, at least.*

"When I came to the station, a man asked me my business and I told them I wanted to report a murder. They were helpful until I said Ryanson's name. Then I was sent straight to some detective. He wouldn't even give me his name. What kind of detective or cop or whatever he was, won't give a name? Everyone else gave me their name."

"You sensed their involvement," Lou said, chiming in again at the right moment and it was good one of them was focused on the momentum of the conversation because King was drowning.

Ryanson owned the DEA? And the local police department?

"It was smart to run," Lou said. She didn't look away from Venetti as if she knew doing so would break the trance and send the girl running.

Venetti nodded. "I wasn't going to be another dead bitch at the bottom of the bay."

King could see Lou's interest was apparently piqued. "Does he kill a lot of girls in Houston and dump their bodies in the ocean?"

Venetti laughed, a hard cough-like sound. "Who knows how many have been swept out into the Gulf of Mexico by now."

King saw a gleam in Lou's eyes. If he didn't find a way to reinsert himself into this conversation and take control of it, Lou might slip off and kill the senator before he'd had any chance to gather a single piece of evidence that'd be admissible in court.

He could hear himself saying *sorry, Chaz. But I took care of it. Or rather my new pet mercenary took care of it.*

"Yeah, he's a real piece of work." Venetti wrapped her arms around herself. "The fucked-up part was I really liked him, you know? Most of the girls were only interested in his money or the drugs. And we all thought he was handsome. But I thought he was sweet. How messed up is that?"

Lou gave him a sharp glare which King could read perfectly. *Any time you want to jump in, Mr. Detective.*

But he couldn't get over the idea a senator owned an entire police department and at least one DEA contact. There were always snitches, of course. But this was different. The infection was spread far and wide or Venetti was unlucky enough to have found the one corrupt cop.

He didn't think so.

The girl was talking again. "He was rich. He was gorgeous. He had this classy vibe going on that none of my exes had. And he liked to give gifts. Even when he was mad, he never hit me or anything. He was always ready to party. He made me feel like the only thing that mattered to him was that I had a good time."

"Until he tried to blow out your brains and dump your body in the bay."

"Pammy, order up!" A boy called from the window. It broke the spell. Venetti blinked several times and then went to the window for the two baskets. One with a bacon cheeseburger and fries and the other fries only. She went back a second time for a bottle of organic ketchup.

"How did you find me?" Venetti asked. She seemed to remember who she was and why she had run.

"We're not with Ryanson," King answered, finding himself on familiar ground again. He'd spoken to witnesses on the run before, and this fear was always the same. That if they could be found once, they could be found again. Therefore, it was time to go. "We're trying to build a case against him. We want to prosecute."

"Prosecute," she repeated the word. "That's the word they used in the station when I told them what happened. "The spy had asked, *do you want to prosecute?*"

"Do you?" Lou asked, taking a huge bite of her burger.

"What happened to Ashley was—bad. I'd want someone to do the right thing if it was me. But I don't see how dying is going to make it any better. Men like that always walk. The men with money and power—I'll never see the inside of a courtroom. They'll kill me first. My only choice is to keep running if I want to live."

"No." Lou's voice was a mountain. Insurmountable.

"If you know where I am then..."

"He doesn't know," Lou said. "Even if he found out, he can't get to you faster than I can."

Venetti turned to Lou then. She stared down at her, mouth hanging open. *Catching flies,* his mother had called it.

King was looking at Lou too.

"No offense, lady," Venetti said. "But you're crazy. You can't be faster. Nothing travels faster than money."

"Do you want to get out of here before ten or what?" the boy called from the drive-thru window after a couple in their Subaru drove off with their evening meal.

"I've got to help close up," Venetti said. "Stick around and I'll tell you what I know. But I can't testify."

They watched Venetti disappear back inside the squat, tangerine building.

"Twenty bucks says she runs," King said, chasing a handful of fries with his soda. It was flat, and the sweetness was off. But the fries were good. Of course, it would be hard to fuck up fries.

They ate in silence. King thought of his Plan B. He would take Venetti's statement. He'd get all the details he could on Ryanson and his wrong doing, and then he'd look for another girl. One who would testify against the senator. It might take them longer, but they could build the case.

But that isn't what Chaz is paying you for, a little voice said. *Chaz wants you to bring Venetti back. You're hooked, Robbie Boy. Better detach now or you're going to choke on this lure.*

When the boy stepped out at 9:45 and locked the door, Venetti crossed the parking lot toward them. Before she even reached the table, Lou was up on her feet, gesturing toward her, beckoning Venetti to follow her around the side of the building.

King started to rise, but Lou held up a hand in a halting gesture.

"We'll be right back," Lou said, her eyes were dark water in the light of the streetlamp, her skin a soft tangerine color. "Finish your drink."

They stepped behind the building, which was a soft gray in the colorless light now. The two women were out of his range of vision, and he didn't like it. But he'd learned long ago the best way to gain trust was to give it. Lucy had begged him to let Lou learn how to work a legitimate case, and he knew unless he wanted to buy a plane ticket back to New Orleans, he had only one way home tonight.

He'd reached across the table and begun to finish off Lou's fries when the two girls reappeared. Lou's face was hard, unreadable. Courtney's cold glare firmly in place.

Venetti, however, was grinning, eyes wide and her hair blown back like a kid who's just exited the most exciting rollercoaster. Venetti rushed over to King and placed both hands on the picnic table, slapping them down like a player tagging home base.

"I'll do it! I'll testify." Her ecstasy was palpable and her words rushed out of her in one breathy exclamation. "What do you want to know?"

16

In the back room of the corner market where King liked to buy his late-night sushi rolls and vinegar chips, Lou and King stepped out from behind a crate of 7-UP bottles. Without a word, the pair opened the back door quietly and slid into the vacant alley, closing the door to the market behind them. On this side of the door, the exit was a smooth metal slab without a handle, looking more like the sort of steel plate one would hammer into their head rather than seal an entrance.

King placed one hand over his rioting belly and placed a forearm against the brick alleyway. He'd never get over the 90-foot-drop feeling. When he was sure he could speak he said, "You gave her your phone number. I don't even have your phone number."

"It's not a phone number." Lou turned over her wrist and pointed the black face of a wristwatch at King. She clicked a button and the hour changed. A world clock, he realized. Displaying her time via GPS, in military time. After another click, a bright green ZERO appeared on the screen. "No messages. If I have one, it will buzz. Then I go. Depending on the time of day or my situation, response time varies. But it isn't registered or traceable like a phone."

"How the hell did you get it?" he asked. He thought this question was better than: *who the hell would page you?*

"Aunt Lucy. I refused a phone and she wanted a way to call on me, in the event she couldn't..." she searched for the word. "Reach me any other way. I think she got it from Germany. It has a global SIM card."

"I want the number," King said, remembering the business card she'd given Venetti. "In case, I need to page you too."

Lou forked one over. He let go of the brick wall for support and accepted it with two fingers.

It was a slip of cardstock. Cream with black numbers. No name, only the 11-digit call number, including country code.

King frowned at the plain scrap of paper. "You're displaying a shocking amount of organization for the rough brute your aunt told me about. Rogue gunslinger. A vigilante with *business* cards. And you handled Venetti as if you'd interviewed a hundred girls before."

Lou's gaze slid away. She wasn't uncomfortable. She was searching the area again. King knew there was nothing he could say that would make this woman squirm.

"You weren't talking," she said when her eyes met his again. "We were there to ask her questions, and you kept shoveling fries in your mouth."

He barked a surprised laugh. "I was assessing the situation. And preparing my attack."

"She'd be packed and halfway to Sacramento by the time you stuffed the cannons, Captain."

"You milked her like a cow." He couldn't let it go. She was proving impossible to read and he didn't like it. "How did you learn to do that?"

He could read anybody. *Anybody.* All he needed was one meeting and a serious conversation. But trying to get a handle on Lou was like trying to hold water. The tighter he squeezed, the quicker she slid through his fingers.

"I did not milk her." Lou wrinkled her nose. "I don't waste time. Mine or anyone else's."

"Is that a personal code?" he asked, wondering if she'd written herself a manifesto somewhere, perhaps tacked up in her apartment.

"One I wish everyone subscribed to," she said. She was looking bored again and at least that part King had gotten right, because she stepped away from him and started walking. He had to jog a little to catch up.

They came around the corner and a wall of warm summer heat hit them the same moment as the bright French Quarter lights fell on their face and shoulders. They faced Madame Melandra's Fortune and Fixes. Lou didn't go inside.

She feels safer in the dark, he realized. Even the soft glow of Mel's chandelier and the flicker of candle flames in the window were too much. Thick shadowed alleys and obscured doorways were as comfortable as worn chairs with their coffee stains and ass cheek imprints to her. His eyes slid over the sidewalks of the crowded quarter. At this hour, it was in full swing. A lot of noise. A lot of bodies. But Lou didn't seem to mind.

"You took an unnecessary risk," he said. He lingered on the curb with her so she would not be forced to go in. "The fewer people who know about your talents, the better."

"She'll keep my secret," Lou said, letting her eyes wander down the street.

"How can you be sure?"

"Because she wants to live. And if she was the kind of girl who liked to talk, she'd be dead now."

King couldn't argue there. Talkers ended up dead sooner rather than later. Of course, he could think of one exception to this. Brasso's mouth ran like a steam engine, and yet he was as free as a wildebeest.

Lou flicked her gaze up to meet his. "Do you care what happens to her once you're done with her?"

He flinched as if slapped. Her black water eyes held the twin flames of the streetlight overhead. Her dark hair was haloed with a ring of gold. "I don't *want* her to die."

"Hmmm."

"Don't you believe some people should be protected?"

"Yes," she said. "Truly defenseless people. People who are preyed upon by the weak bastards looking to extort or abuse them. Capable people can save themselves. There are enough of the first in the world, why waste my time on the second?"

Certainly no hero complex, he thought.

"Is that what you want to do now that the Martinellis are gone?" he asked. "Will you use your abilities to save the *truly defenseless*?" He used air quotes.

Her eyes bore into his. The gaze so heavy it made the hair on the back of his neck rise. For a moment, a crazy moment where his front mind clicked off and his reptilian brain slithered into the driver's seat, he nearly pulled his gun. He *wanted* to pull his gun. Maybe the air quotes were a bad idea.

She hadn't moved.

Her expression hadn't changed, and yet the overpowering sense of danger welled inside him.

Her voice was shockingly soft when she spoke. "I have to go. Your landlady is giving me the finger."

King turned to look into the shop and found Mel standing there in full gypsy garb, her braids pleated over each shoulder. She wasn't flashing the middle finger salute. She was making the sign of the cross, touching each bare shoulder then her forehead.

King turned back, ready to offer reassurances, serve as Mel's character witness, but he was alone on the sidewalk.

Lou was gone.

Mel's arm brushed his. "Who are you looking for Mr. King?"

"A girl," he said. "But I think you scared her off."

"That was no girl," Mel said and reached into the folds of her skirts. She pulled out a pack of Camels and lit one with her Bic. She dragged hard on the filter and then blew the smoke out of her nose, reminding King of those cartoon bulls he watched on Saturday mornings as a kid. "She was the angel of death."

The angel of death.

He didn't even argue.

His adrenaline had spiked under Lou's cold stare and now it crashed. His stomach hollowed out. His head buzzed between his ears.

He was starting to think he'd like to smoke a joint before he called Brasso and told him about Venetti. But maybe the call should wait until tomorrow altogether. Or even, the day after.

If he was too quick in his turnaround, Brasso might wonder how he managed to track a girl to the West Coast so damn fast. Finding Venetti and getting to San Diego should take some time for an old man with no leads.

And there was Paula's testimony itself. King wanted to chew on it for a moment.

"What are you playing at, Mr. King?" Mel arched an eyebrow and inhaled a second time.

An excellent question.

What *was* he doing? He wasn't an agent anymore. He wasn't even a private investigator. In Louisiana, he needed a license. His DEA experience would qualify him, and what knowledge he might lack in regulations he could easily acquire in a certification course offered by the Louisiana State Board of Private Investigator Examiners.

But he wasn't certified and he hadn't considered it before Brasso showed up with this case. Could he even call it a case? He was looking for a missing person. Was he a liaison then? That too required documents and clearance through special channels.

What are you playing at?

"I've taken up a hobby," he said at last. "I hear it is very important to keep yourself active once you retire, lest you die of boredom."

At least that was the truth, in part. Something about Brasso's request had sparked him. He was awake, engaged with the world in a way he hadn't been for the months since he'd left the bureau and headed south like a snowbird.

King often envisioned his mind as a police station. Rows of desks and men—all looking like King himself—working furiously. Each one processing a part of his task or problem.

Right now, one considered how to talk to Brasso.

Another formed a list of all the reasons he couldn't simply turn Venetti over to his old partner.

He wasn't a search dog that could be put away once it'd found the cocaine hidden in a suitcase. He had Venetti, but he didn't have answers. He didn't have *closure*.

Third, he had to consider Mel and Piper. What he was doing was dangerous. He'd known it the second two men tried to tail him. What if they came to the shop looking for trouble?

But what about paying the Piper? If you cut this case short, how will you compensate her? How will you pick up the slack for Mel? The longer King worked on the case, the more expenses he'd accrue. The more expenses the larger the burden he could carry on his landlady's behalf.

And it wasn't safe to turn over Venetti now. *He owns them,* she'd said.

If he had Lou pack the girl up and send her to Brasso, she could very well find herself in the bottom of the bay after all.

All of this was his mind avoiding the biggest question of all.

Lou.

The angel of death.

He swam to the surface of his thoughts and caught Mel watching him through the haze of her cigarette smoke. Her lips pursed around the filter.

"Come on. Don't look at me like that, Mel. This is another source of income. We can hang a sign from the balcony, Robert King's Detective Agency. You can charge me commercial property rent, if you like. Steady income. Isn't that what you were hoping for?"

Mel dropped the spent cigarette and stamped it out with a fierce twist of her boot. "Hope is a demon, Mr. King. And don't you forget it."

17

Konstantine opened his suitcase on his bed and unpacked a stack of dress shirts. Then he removed the row of dress pants all the same shade of midnight. And in the third row, his underwear, socks, gray silk pajama bottoms and two pairs of sweatpants. He considered the contents for a moment, wondering if he should put them in the dresser provided by the hotel, or if it was better to leave his suitcase packed, in the event he had to leave immediately.

His computer pinged. He went to the desk and opened the chat program.

"Konstantine," he said, hoping there was no hint of the eagerness straining his muscles in his voice.

"Hey boss, it's me, Julio."

"Go on."

"We checked the surveillance for the club and think we found your girl. I'm sending you the pic."

Konstantine's heart sped up. "Sure." *Sure* was casual enough. Neither eager nor indifferent, but ice slid down his spine. It was sheer force of will that kept him from shuddering.

Julio was one of Padre Leo's most trusted servants, and was recommended by the benevolent father himself.

The chat box pinged again, registering a receipt of the image Julio had sent. Konstantine waited for the rainbow wheel to stop turning and the fully downloaded image to appear.

A black and white photo popped up on the screen.

"Down in the left corner there's a woman by the bar," Julio went on though his face was hidden behind the expanded photo. "You can't tell, but she's looking in Castle's direction. And when he goes to the bathroom so does she."

He hadn't needed Julio to point her out to him. He'd spotted her immediately. The remarkable exactness between his imagination and reality made the hairs rise on the back of his neck. Her hair was shorter now, only shoulder length. A short ponytail pulled all the hair from her face. He imagined sliding a finger beneath the black elastic, and plucking the band out of her hair. The hair would fall across her thin, feline throat. It was so small he was sure he could wrap his entire hand around it.

He was sixteen when he first saw her.

He had killed his first man a week before and had barely slept. Instead, he'd toss for hours and when that failed to settle him, he would quietly leave the apartment and walk the city streets until exhaustion won at last. When he left, he left a note. He had not wanted his mother to get up in the night, see him gone, and worry.

It had been his mother's only stipulation. *At night he will be home in his bed, Padre Leo. You cannot imagine the terror a mother feels when the night grows long, and she doesn't know where her child is.* So Padre sent him home at sunset each day.

He ate dinner with his mother. He kissed her goodnight. And when her gentle snoring rumbled from the adjacent bedroom, he would be gone again, knowing Padre would have a job for him if he wanted it.

The night he saw Castle's huntress for the first time, he was also sleepless. He'd been lying on his back, reading a spy novel in bed, one hand under his head. His mother's snores caught up to him at the end of the next chapter. Then he was up, shoving his feet into his Adidas sneakers with their white diagonal stripes—nice, beautiful shoes. A gift from Padre Leo. What better recruitment tool than a well-dressed boy? What kid didn't want the *cool* American clothes and expensive Swiss watches? All his boys were dressed to the nines.

It was better advertising than a billboard in the piazza.

He'd adjusted the waistband on his track pants and had turned to look for a T-shirt to pull down over his head.

And there she was.

A girl. In his bed. Thick dark hair fell over her cheeks and face in delicate strands. It cascaded nearly to her waist. Her arms and legs glowed in the moonlight coming from his high windows. Her lips were parted, split like a cherry. She was the most beautiful creature he'd ever seen.

His thighs pressed to the side of the bed, and he peered down at her. He was half certain she was a trick of the light. Somehow the moon had met his rumpled bed sheets and created this magic.

But her brow knit, and her hand kept opening and closing on her chest. The small movements of a living creature. Not a moonlight illusion.

He watched her, barely breathing until it struck him this was the way his mother slept. Fitfully, until she woke with a scream.

He reached out to touch her pale cheek. As soon as his fingertips brushed her warm flesh, the girl shot up in bed. A sharp intake of breath passed her lips. Her wide eyes searched his room.

He stepped back. He held up his hands in apologetic reassurance.

She squeezed his sheets to her chest as if she was undressed beneath it and Konstantine had been the one to intrude upon her.

It's okay, he said first in Italian, the language he used with his mother. When her brow creased deeper, he said it again in English.

He took a step toward her, and the moment he did, she rolled right off his bed onto the floor. The sheet went with her, pulled right off the bed—except it kept going. Something about it reminded Konstantine of a magician's trick with silk scarves and a hat.

He ran around the bed to the other side, expecting to help the surprised girl off the floor.

Only there was no girl on the floor. The girl and his bed sheet had both disappeared.

All that was left was a thick patch of shadow between his mattress and the closet.

Konstantine understood this about her. Especially now with his father and brothers dead, he understood she traveled by the dark. Somehow, she rode the darkness like a passenger train. And though she had appeared in his bed only four or five more times when he was young, he never woke her again. He learned his mistake there. If she woke, she ran. But if he was still and quiet, then he could watch her sleep. He could lie beside her, breath held until she winked out again. Enjoying her scent. Her warmth and how it radiated off her like the fire in Padre Leo's office. Sometimes she spoke in her sleep. Once she cried for her father, bright wet tears sliding from the corners of her closed eyes and onto his pillows.

"Is it your girl?" Julio asked.

"Yes," he said and realized he hadn't blinked since seeing the image. "Any other sign of her?"

Julio paused. "Not on camera."

Konstantine reluctantly closed the image so he could see the man's face. "What do you mean?"

Julio worked his lower jaw as he mustered the courage to give his boss the bad news. Konstantine waited, more out of fear for what might be said than patience.

"She was busy last night," Julio said finally. He slapped the back of his neck, crushing a mosquito. A smear of blood dragged across the man's neck when he pulled his hand away. "I've had reports coming in all day. We're missing a lot of mules."

Konstantine wet his lips and steadied his voice before speaking. "How many?"

"Nine," Julio said. "So far."

Nine.

She was angry. Obviously. The question was why. What had he done to piss her off?

"What do you want me to do, boss?" Julio asked. He'd begun chewing on the meat of his thumb.

Konstantine's appreciation for Julio swelled. He'd executed the task of finding the girl flawlessly. And now he wanted another job. The man's work ethic was admirable.

"Kill Castle," Konstantine said. "We don't need him."

Julio nodded as if he expected this. "And the girl?"

"Track her movements, if you can. But make no move against her. I will deal with her myself."

"When do you arrive?" Julio asked, his spatulate fingernails scratching at the blood drying on his neck.

"I'm already here."

18

Melandra turned over the first tarot card, the reversed Queen of Pentacles. A woman in dire financial straits. She rolled her eyes heavenward and cursed the spread forming on the glass jewelry case.

"Tell me something I don't know," she murmured to the worn deck in her hand.

She looked up and surveyed her empty shop. It was late afternoon, and the sunlight slanted along the topmost shelves as it prepared to dip behind the buildings. It was warm, collecting the heat from the June day between its walls.

The virtuoso was back, busking on the adjacent corner, and her song drifted through the open door along with the warm air. At least she'd gotten better, Mel thought. When the girl had begun to play on the corner six months ago, each note screeched like a cat with its tail caught in the door.

She hadn't had a single customer all day.

It was true magic shops had more appeal in the nighttime hours, when people found it easier to believe in ghosts and voodoo and all that lay in-between. But she could usually count on *at least* a *few* tourists to stream in during the day. Coming or going from the gumbo shop down the street. Or sugared up on beignets from the square. Foot traffic was good in the quarter, and she had an exorbitant mortgage to prove it.

She kept doing the math in her head. She counted the purchasing customers needed to keep her shop afloat. How many palm readings? How many past life regressions? How many tarot readings? Or maybe someone would want a picture of their aura. She hadn't done one of those in a while.

*If five people come in and buy one thing...*but this was where her mind split. Would they buy the mix and match incense sticks? Ten for one dollar. It wasn't enough to pay the electric bill. *But let's say they bought a candle, anywhere from $5.99 to $9.99...in that case I'd have to sell...*

Why do I do this to myself?

Calculations for sales that aren't happening is one way to drive yourself mad, she thought.

She was half mad already, she knew.

Here she was.

Alone on a gorgeous afternoon, reading her own fortune because there was no one else to peddle truth to.

Oh that's not all, and you know it, she chastised herself. This was no mere reading out of boredom. She'd been itching to turn over the cards ever since that woman came to see King.

The ex-girlfriend, Lucy, was sick. That much Mel knew. As soon as she'd shaken the woman's damp hand, she'd known it. And whatever she had wouldn't be fixed by juju beads or a gris gris bag. Maybe Grand-mamie could have taken the sick demon out of her, but Mel couldn't.

She didn't have that kind of power.

She thought of Grandmamie. They'd called her a faith healer in their little town outside Baton Rouge. A Priestess. The Mother or sometimes Mamie Blue Jeans because no matter how hot it got down in the bayou, Grandmamie wore blue jeans.

Mel could see her in her mind, her saggy breasts lying on a great round belly and balloon arms on either side as she raised a sweating glass of sweet tea to her lips.

"Mmm hmm," she said to the thickening twilight.

"Uhhh huhhh *what?*" Mel had asked, a stick creature with dirt splotches from head to toe.

"Can't you feel it, girl?"

Mel had looked out from their porch into the growing dark. The trees were crowded against one another, and the smallest of spaces between them were black as a cottonmouth's back. But she didn't *feel* anything. She heard the chickens cooing in the grass and the squirrels yammering in the trees. And a jay screeching off somewhere. She smelled the beans on the stove. She could taste the licorice in her mouth.

But no *feelings* of any kind.

"Change is in the air," Grandmamie said and turned to her. She smiled at her through the round spectacles sitting halfway down the bridge of her nose. "You got to learn how to feel change a'coming, girl. It don't do you no good to be numb to it."

Change came as a decree from the governor buying their land so they could run a highway through it.

Change is a'comin', girl.

"I know it," Mel said in her quiet shop because she'd done as Grandmamie had asked. She'd learned all right. And now she felt all kinds of things she wondered if she had any right to be feeling at all.

She flipped the second card and lay it perpendicular across the first. *This is what crosses me.* The five of wands glared up at her. A war party in full swing. Staffs slammed against one another and faces contorted in hate. Conflict. War.

"Because that's what I need," she sighed.

She flipped the third card, the crowning position, meant to tell her the atmosphere of what was unfolding.

Death. A hooded skeleton with a scythe grinned its bone white grin at her. Not very different from the one now standing by her shop door.

This was Grandmamie's deck, or it had been a long time ago. And she had a faith in these old worn cards that she didn't have for any others. She sold cards in the shop. Glossy, unbent pieces of commercial trash, most of it. Sometimes a deck arrived and Mel would get a feeling when she turned the pack over in her hand. Sometimes she'd put one of those decks aside for herself. But not even those decks compared to the one she'd inherited on her nineteenth birthday, two weeks before Grandmamie died.

So she believed in the power of her grandmother's cards, but that didn't mean she had to like what they said.

She put the cards down and rubbed her forehead. "If you ain't got nothing nice to say, I best stop right there."

Before she could push away from the glass case holding protective amulets, the breeze rustled the deck. The black cards with gold trim fluttered, and an unmistakable pull centered in her chest. She looked down at the cards, expectantly.

She waited.

Mamie Blue Jeans had taught her more than how to feel change.

She'd taught her to listen.

She'd taught her how to treat snake bites and read clouds as well as bones. She'd learned a spider taking down its web meant rain was on its way.

So when the breeze flipped over the Tower card, she didn't dismiss it as coincidence.

Unlike Mr. King, Melandra was a believer.

She placed the Tower as the center piece and then flipped the next several cards, rounding out the spread. Longing. Danger. A secret. Lies revealed. Disease. And a man, face down with seven swords protruding from his bleeding back. Betrayal.

The swords gave her pause. It was the suit she associated with Mr. King. The King of Swords being he himself, the other cards from ace to ten, his journey.

She pressed the fingers of her right hand to the Death card and the two fingers of her left hand to her forehead. She closed her eyes.

First only darkness. Bland and flat. Then the darkness swirled like water, gained dimension, and a woman, pale as moonlight, surfaced. Her name—Louise. No. That wasn't quite right, but close.

Mel pushed deeper, following Louise into the water. Men dropped like offerings at her feet. A mound of bodies, broken and bleeding. Blood on her hands, up to the elbows. Smeared across her mouth and cheeks. She was eating...Mel pushed harder and saw...a heart. Louise held a heart in her hand and was eating it. And when she was done, she danced on their bodies, danced like the death goddess Kali on what little remained of them.

Mel let go of the card and crossed herself. "Holy mother of god."

"Holy mother what?" Piper said. She stopped short of the glass jewelry case and plopped her backpack beside the register. Her brow scrunched up. "Whoa, Mel, are you okay? You look like you saw the devil."

Piper leaned over the glass jewelry case and peered at the cards.

"Oh," she said, frowning at the cards. "Not the devil. The tower. And someone is feeling stabby."

"Seven of Swords," Mel managed to say around her tight throat. She swore she could taste blood.

"And that means... Wait. I've got this." Piper tapped the side of her head, a pensive gesture. "The swords are about thoughts. Brain stuff. Seven is delivery. Or an arrival. So the arrival...of brain stuff."

She didn't wait for Mel to correct her. She powered on to the next card.

"And the tower..." her voice trailed off as her face screwed up in concentration.

Mel gazed down at the tower silhouetted against a stormy sky. Noted the body twisted and falling through the darkness. "The end of life as we know it."

19

King sat on the balcony overlooking Royal Street. The ferns waved in a gentle breeze. The sweat on the back of his neck chilled and offered some relief from the heat of the day.

Sometimes when the heat was too much, his apartment felt too small. He had to open all the windows and let in the breeze. And if that wasn't enough to loosen the crushing hold the walls had on his heart, he went out onto the balcony. The sunlight, the people, the elevation, and open space—that usually did it. With a melting glass of Mel's sweet tea balanced on his knee, he felt more than fine.

King reviewed his notes.

He reviewed everything Paula Venetti had given them, which amounted to five and a half pages in his tight script on his yellow legal pad. It was quite a haul.

As Venetti told it, on a warm night in late September, she witnessed the murder of Daminga Brown. She also assumed a third girl on the boat that night, Ashley DeWitt, was also dead.

Or worse.

He was getting ahead of himself.

King took a deep breath and put down the glass of tea.

He settled back in his chair and laced his fingers over his belly. He closed his eyes and reconstructed the scene Venetti had given them.

He replayed it step by step, slowly. He wanted to see what questions arose. What needed clarification. He wanted to turn this puzzle over in his mind and see its shape clearly.

And doing so began with this reimagining.

He saw Venetti stepping out of the shower and into her closet, selecting a tight red dress. He imagined how the thin material must have cupped the curve of her ass. Watched her remove a blue dolphin ecstasy pill from a cigarette case and dissolve it on her tongue. He spared no details. The water droplets dripping from the end of her hair as she combed it out. The floral design of the cigarette case.

It was pure imagination, based only on the details the girl had provided, but it was incredibly effective in helping his mind see what the witness may have missed.

She was feeling better than good by the time Ryanson's private car turned up at her apartment. A silver luxury car, the lights reflected in the polished exterior.

Two other girls were already in the back seat, drinking and rubbing their bodies against Ryanson's. Venetti didn't mind. It was hard to mind anything when you were on X. She joined right in and started nibbling the red lipstick off the closest pair of lips, bucked against the hand slipping under her dress.

The group traveled twenty minutes from the Baybrook Mall area down I-45 to Tiki Island where Ryanson had his Rizzardi CR 50 docked and ready for their arrival.

They all got on the boat—Ryanson, two guards and three girls—joining a captain already on board. Seven in total. The captain took them out on the water until the lights of the city were like pinpricks on the horizon. Far enough away the music and loud voices wouldn't disturb other seafarers. Ryanson kept the cocaine and alcohol flowing. The captain, a gold-toothed man with a crow and crossbones tattoo, slapped Venetti's ass when she leaned over the rail with a bout of nausea. She wanted to slap him. Instead, she smiled.

There was only one rule on this boat: no matter what, everyone had a good time.

Venetti sucked in the fresh salty air, trying to steady herself. When she opened her eyes, she saw a light burning in the darkness. Not in the direction of shore, but in the direction of the unbroken horizon. She stared harder, trying to comprehend the floating orb bobbing in the night.

"What is that?" Venetti pointed at the light, and the captain left his hand on her ass as he peered around her to see for himself.

His hand fell away. "Sir? There's another boat."

Venetti could see it now that it was close enough to fall into the light of their own vessel. The boat was smaller but still beautiful. Venetti didn't have a better description. *I don't know boats.*

King didn't know boats either, but for this exercise, he imagined a sleek speed boat with wooden side board. It didn't matter if this was accurate. King was more interested in the men who'd boarded.

They had matching tattoos. It was some kind of animal and a flag.

Five men got off the other boat and came onto Ryanson's. King did the math in his mind.

Now we have twelve people who know what happened that night.

As soon as they stepped on to the boat, I knew we were in trouble. Ryanson's mood had changed when the fifth man boarded. He was wearing a pinstriped suit and hat.

Before anyone spoke the captain pulled a gun. One of the men put a bullet between the captain's eyes. The girls started screaming, a natural reaction to seeing brains spill across the deck of a boat, and the men turned those guns on the girls.

If you don't want to die, you better sit down and shut your fucking mouths.

All three women sat down on the padded cushions of the bench and shut their mouths.

Ryanson was pistol whipped straight away, as if to set the tone for the interrogation that was to follow. *Where is it? Tell me where it is. If you don't tell me where it is, I'm going to put a bullet in her head.*

Venetti looked away. The violence only made her nausea worse. When she could bear to open her eyes, she saw a scuba tank hanging on a hook beside her. She knew the tank would be heavy because she'd dived with Ryanson before. And she wasn't sure she could grab it and a buoyancy compensator before someone put a bullet in her head. But a little farther away hung a scuba tank with an *attached* BC.

I'm ashamed to admit it but I knew Ashley or Daminga would be shot, if I jumped overboard. But I didn't care. I wanted off the fucking boat.

Where the fuck is it, Ryanson?

Ryanson didn't answer, and Daminga's brains were splashed along the Rizzardi's deck.

The warm spray of blood and bone matter on Venetti's own feet made a scream boil in the back of her throat. But somehow she'd managed to swallow it down, until Ashley bolted. She was up and trying to throw herself into the water.

Two laughing men pulled her back into the boat. All eyes on her like predators attracted to movement. Venetti saw this as her only chance to escape. She leapt up, grabbed the tank with its attached BC, and rolled over the rail of the yacht.

A bullet grazed her shoulder, and the cut ignited in the salt water. White hot pain bit into the flesh of her upper arm.

With the tank, she dropped like a stone. She tried to equalize the pressure on her way down, but her limbs were sluggish from pain and fear. Then, at last, she managed to find the BC's release button in the dark water.

She stopped sinking and began to swim.

She held her breath for as long as she could, already swimming underwater toward the direction of the shore. When her lungs were about to burst, she took sparing sips of air from the regulator. She had no idea how much oxygen she had, because she couldn't read the air gauge so deep in the dark, nor see how far she was from shore. So she sipped and swam until she thought she was going to die.

She never thought she would make it, swooping her arms out in front of her in the pitch black water. She couldn't be entirely sure she was moving at all. She was certain sharks would get to her long before she reached shore. Her bleeding arm would attract them, and everyone knew they fed at night. And if not some underwater monster, then a bullet to the back of the head would finish her. But nothing took a bite out of her. No bullets came.

She surfaced and saw the lights of a distant pier. She finally made it to the pier and pulled herself out of the water, collapsing on the planks with shaking arms. Her whole body shook. She didn't dare check Ryanson's stall on the marina's far dock to see if he returned. She went straight to the marina's entrance and hailed a taxi. She cut in front of a line of patrons leaving a restaurant and commandeered the first cab.

People shouted. She didn't care. The driver took one look at her and didn't seem to care either. He pulled away without even asking her where she wanted to go until they were on the interstate.

Venetti didn't go home. Her body hurt. She was cold and wet. But she wasn't stupid.

She went to Merry Maids, a housecleaning business on the north side of the city. She convinced one of the housekeepers to enter her apartment and pack up her essentials—some clothes, jewelry, toiletries and a stash of cash all packed inside a pink backpack. The maid hid them in her cleaning cart.

Venetti hoped this act would avoid suspicion, since Merry Maids entered her apartment once a week anyway. They would only be entering the apartment two days early and they could be doing it for any number of reasons.

Before noon, she was on a bus from Houston to San Diego without looking back. She'd chosen San Diego at random from a travel guide. She'd been inside a bookstore café, eating a sandwich and an orange juice. She bought the bus ticket next door. Next thing she knew, she was in San Diego with a rented room and a job.

Venetti had done more than recount the traumatic event which sent her running for the West Coast. She gave them details about Ryanson's habits and connections, everything she could think of.

For all her faults, King thought as he surveyed the massive amount of information scribbled on his pad, *she's a good witness*. This was more than he would have been able to wring out of most witnesses.

Of course, he would have to do some fact-checking on dates and times to see if the girl's memory was as reliable as it was detailed. He also had his doubts that all the details were precise, given Venetti's own admission to drug and alcohol use.

But if Venetti's memory was half right, they had a lot to go on. And they had other leads. Ashley DeWitt for one. If she was alive, Lou would find her and they would have a second witness to interview. If it didn't pan out, they had the boat at Tiki Island. It could be swept for evidence. King knew the bodies were long gone, but it was hard to remove all evidence of a murder unless the murder was performed in a certain environment.

He wondered how Lou had managed to be so thorough in her own cleanups.

On second thought, he wasn't sure he wanted to know.

King hoped DeWitt *was* alive. It was the men King was interested in and she would have spent the most time with them. He could set Piper on the task of researching the animal and flag tattoo. Who were they, and what was their interest in Ryanson?

Who was Ryanson working with and to what end? Either Ryanson was involved in a turf war or made a shady deal with a gang.

It was clear Ryanson hadn't been killed. His pretty-boy face was all over the news, as he was the face for Don't Legalize Marijuana in his party. So despite the hardballing from the pimp in the pinstripe suit, as King had come to call him in his mind, he'd survived the night Daminga Brown had not—how? With promises? Was a deal struck? How many pies did Ryanson have his thumbs in?

The fire escape rattled as someone from the street started to ascend.

King leaned over the railing fingers twitching above his gun. Piper was climbing up the ladder. He relaxed with a muttered curse under his breath. Less than two days on the job and he was jumping and starting like a rookie.

"Shouldn't you be opening the shop?" he grumbled.

"Mel sent me up. She said she's pimping me out to you." She paused on the ladder and looked up at him. "Is that right?"

"Yeah, come on up," King shuffled his papers in a way so that nothing important could be read at a glance. Then in a wave of paranoia, he turned the notebook over so only the cardboard backing of the legal pad showed and placed his cell phone on top, to pin it in place.

Piper appeared, clutching her side, chest heaving. "Whew! I think I deserve a Snickers bar. I'm so athletic!"

King arched an eyebrow. "You're too young to be out of shape."

"Not all of us have exciting jobs chasing bad guys. I pay my bills by stuffing candles into bags and sweeping glitter off the floor."

King remembered the glittered raver and grinned. "I knew he'd pissed you off."

She scratched the back of her head and then shrugged. "It's fine. I get it. Sometimes you've got to sparkle. So what bitch work do you have for me?"

"Do you have a problem helping an old man?"

"You're not old."

King compressed his lips. Of course, he seemed old to someone who was barely old enough to buy alcohol.

"Is Mel going to fire me? Is this like a *He's Just Not That into You* hint? She's been talking about that book a lot lately."

King tapped his pen on the folder. "She doesn't want to fire you."

"Yeah, but she might have to. It's been dead around here. And not the kind of dead that sells."

King gave a weak half smile. "Business is slow. It'll pick up."

Piper snorted. She pulled up a chair and plopped into it. "Man, you suck at lying. And I thought you already had help. I saw you walking around the Quarter with a girl the other night. Dark hair. All black clothes. She kind of has this strut."

King stopped tapping his pen. "Lou?"

"*Lou!*" Piper shook in her seat. "That's her name? Oh god, it's *cute*."

"What about her?"

"Is she your girlfriend?"

King snorted. "I'm not a cradle robber."

"She's an adult. It's not cradle robbing."

"You know, some men actually see women as partners, not sex dolls."

Piper widened her eyes in mock surprise. "I had *no* idea. So, if she's not *your* girlfriend, does that mean she's someone else's girlfriend?"

King burst into a grin and tilted his head. "Are you milking me for info?"

The grin was accompanied by red cheeks. "*Maybe.*"

King crossed his ankle over his knee, not speaking.

"Don't set us up or anything!" Piper said, her face burning brighter. "I'm perfectly capable of orchestrating my own *accidental* introduction. I'm trying to get a sense of her availability."

"What if she doesn't like girls?" King asked. He bit back, *sorry kid, but I don't think she likes anyone.*

"Who cares! All the girls I slept with in high school were 'straight.'" She used air quotes. "And I get this very ambivalent vibe from her." Piper made a so-so gesture with her hand. "I don't think she cares about a person's gender." Her face lit up. "Maybe she's pansexual! I've never met one of those. It's kind of fascinating."

"Do you think you can help me with my investigation, or will you be distracted by the brunette with a gun?"

Piper sat up straighter. "She has a gun? On my god, that's *so* hot."

King wrangled Piper's attention long enough to give her two tasks, both research-based, and a $50 bill for any expenses. "I don't want you to use your computer."

Piper waved the fifty between her fingers. "Paranoid much?"

"Paranoid is my default setting."

"Don't get killed and stuffed into a trash bag. Got it." Piper leaned forward. "Okay, but about *Lou*. Has she said anything useful?"

"Useful? Of course. She's very capable."

"Favorite food? Television show? Favorite color? It's probably black, which isn't technically a color. It's a shade, but let's overlook that for now."

King could feel a headache building behind his eyes. "We don't talk about colors."

Piper frowned. "What do you talk about?"

"Dead people, mostly."

Piper rubbed her chin. "Maybe a ghost tour then. It's half-off if you go during the day."

"She doesn't come out in the day. Pretend you're trying to woo a vampire."

Piper nodded thoughtfully, completely missing the joke in King's voice. "Well, the tours run until midnight."

"Piper," King said, rubbing his forehead. "When do you think you'll have this information for me?"

Piper's embarrassed grin returned. "Not sure. I've never researched street gangs before. While I'm gone, feel free to put in a good word if you have the chance. Play up my best qualities."

"Maybe Lou isn't interested in someone with *qualities*. She's interested in someone with a special skill set."

Piper paused at the top of the fire escape. She grinned. "Even better."

King listened to her descend the steps, the rattle of the latch and the slow squeaking groan as the ladder lifted and returned to its resting position.

The skeleton shrieked and ghosts howled as Piper reentered Madame Melandra's Fortunes and Fixes below.

Now to buy more time.

King picked up his cell phone and dialed a number jotted at the top of the yellow legal pad.

His old partner Chaz Brasso answered on the third ring. "Brasso."

"We found Venetti and verified her testimony," King said.

"You found her? Honest to god?" Brasso said. "Where the hell was she holed up?"

"San Diego. In a vegan fast food restaurant of all places."

"There can't be many of those," Chaz said. "That was a quick trip! Did you fly out there?"

King's stomach turned, but the lie came easily. "Yeah. I'm still here actually. I won't get back until tomorrow morning."

There was silence on the line.

Then Chaz said. "So what did she say?"

20

Lou stepped into King's apartment and found herself staring at two wet ass cheeks. Not the smooth sculpted muscle one could find in the Louvre, which she wandered sometimes. But dimpled and hairy flesh.

As soon as she saw the naked man toweling his hair and whistling a tune to himself, Lou stepped right back into dark corner from where she'd entered the apartment, and disappeared again. This time, she emerged on the balcony outside the window and rapt a fist against the glass.

"King?" she called through the cracks.

"Just a minute!" She heard his muttered curse and the sound of bone knocking on something. He clipped his elbow on the sink maybe. Or his toe on the side of the toilet. He was too large for that bathroom. His knees must sit against his chest when he shits.

Loud footsteps rumbled through the apartment, the glass windows trembling as he darted past the windows into the bedroom.

"Hold on!" he called again as if she'd given him any indication to hurry. She leaned against the balcony and scanned the streets below. The man who'd been following King, and she was certain he *was* following King, was on the street corner. He sucked on a cigarette, the cherry burning orange with his inhalation. A large hat hid his face.

She'd already pointed these men out to King. She wouldn't do it again. Hell, maybe King would get himself killed and she could stop this charade. Her aunt would be sad, sure, but Lou would have fodder for any future attempts at rehabilitation. *Because it went so well last time*, she would say, and that'd be the end of it.

The balcony door creaked open and King appeared, hair still dripping. "All right, come on in."

Lou squeezed past him into the apartment. He was in jeans but barechested. A gold chain hung in the nest of his chest hair, and his feet were bare. It was always strange to see men barefooted. And he had old man feet. Toenails gnarled and yellow. He pulled a white polo shirt down over his head.

"Thanks for knocking," he said with a tight smile. "You would've gotten more than you paid for if you hadn't."

"No problem." She let her gaze glide along the apartment's interior and the brick façade of one wall. The steam had rolled out of the shower and now hung in the air reminding her of European bars where smoking was still allowed.

Her hair began to curl at the nape of her neck and temples from the humidity. The smell of his musky shampoo or soap permeated the whole apartment. A male scent like cologne. The way it had smelled when her father had bathed.

There was also something fried and meaty, perhaps chicken, that'd been microwaved within the last hour.

King continued to ruffle his hair with the white towel. "Let me run a comb through this and we'll check on Ashley DeWitt."

"If she's alive."

"Yeah about that," King said throwing the towel over one shoulder. "Explain how it works."

Lou arched an eyebrow. "Well, if the air is going in and out and she has a pulse—"

"No, your, what did you call it? Compass? Has it ever led you to the wrong person?"

"That's why we'll begin with, '*Hello. Are you Ashley DeWitt?*'"

"You don't want to talk about your compass I take it?"

The muscles in Lou's back stiffened. "No."

She didn't want to talk about waiting in darkness. How she could clear her mind and hear what was on the other side. Or car horns. Or church bells. She didn't want to talk about the way she felt pulled, like her legs were in a great river, and all she had to do was let go and be swept away with its current to some unfathomable shore.

Because the conversation would do two things. First, it would give King the very inaccurate belief that he had any right to her business. Aunt Lucy's approval or not, she didn't know this man. Lou had assessed that King was benign, mostly. But he was a man with mental issues and a gun. That wasn't the kind of friend she needed. Secondly, such a conversation would inevitably lead to where she'd gone and hadn't wanted to. La Loon, without question. But there'd been other times and places as well. And Lou didn't like to think about her compass as having an intelligence of its own. Doing so forced her to consider an uncomfortable truth: she wasn't as in control of her ability as she wanted to be.

As a child, this was apparent. Every slip was accidental and seemingly unprovoked.

As an adult, she'd convinced herself she'd grown into it. *She* chose her locations and moved where she wanted.

But she knew a lie when she heard it.

"Do you close your eyes, click your heels and *badda boom?*" King asked. Obviously, he'd missed her subtle clues to drop it. "Do you need a picture or object or—"

Her jaw tightened. "It's not hocus-pocus."

He frowned. "I wasn't trying to insult you. I'm curious. How do you navigate?"

Her unease grew. There was something about having a question she'd asked herself said aloud to her.

"If it's some big secret," King said, looking slightly hurt. "Then forget I asked."

You don't owe him anything the cruel voice inside said. *Tell him to mind his own damn business.*

"I don't know what to tell you." Her voice sounded cold even to herself. Never a good sign.

King arched his brow. "You don't know?"

"Can you ride a bicycle without knowing how you can do it?"

"Hogwash. Everyone can ride a bike. Not everyone can do what you do."

"Tell that to an amputee without arms and legs."

King shut his mouth.

"You might understand there's balance involved and the pedals have to be moving. Otherwise, it's more practice and instinct than anything else. This is no different." She felt stupid suddenly and that sent her itching to pull her gun. Fuck people and their questions. What did she look like? Their schoolmarm? If he didn't understand why the sun was orange instead of some other color, why should she have to explain why she could do the impossible?

She turned away from him.

"But is it like—"

"Ask Lucy how she slips," she said. *She'll have more patience.*

"You call it slipping."

"Yeah," she said, breath softer now.

"Why?"

"Jesus Christ, you're like a five-year-old tonight. Why? Why? *Why?*"

Lou considered slipping King to the top of the empire state building and then letting him drop. That would shut him up. She already felt hemmed in by Konstantine's hunt. She didn't need to feel hounded by someone's curiosity on top of it.

"Did you ever end up somewhere you didn't want to go?" he asked, tugging at his shirt.

Oh, look. He'd reached the question on his own anyway. "You know the answer."

"Your dad didn't talk about your disappearance much, but I read the report." King stopped in front of her, buttoning the top of his shirt. "That's how I met Lucy."

Lou stopped imagining his demise. "You met her when I disappeared?"

"About two days after you came back, Thorne—your father—asked me to hunt her down. I did."

Lou heard her father's voice in her mind. She heard his sharp intake of breath as he lifted her and threw her into the pool before drawing the gunfire away from her. Asking her if she wanted to spend time with Lucy was only a courtesy. He'd already decided for her.

King pointed at the glistening scar tissue encircling her upper arm, visibly protruding from the edge of her sleeveless black shirt. The scars were faded now. Time did that to every wound, no matter how bloody.

She hoped.

"What took a bite out of you?" he asked as he slipped on his boots.

"I call him Jabbers. Or her. I haven't tried to lift its skirt to verify gender."

King snorted. "You named the thing that took a bite out of you. What was it? A wolf? Did you end up in the Michigan wilderness or something?"

"No," she said. She refrained from defending the wolves. Healthy wolves didn't attack humans. That was a misconception. Her heart hitched, and she stepped toward the window.

"I didn't mean to pry."

"Yes, you did." She didn't turn around.

He didn't argue. Instead, he said, "The night isn't getting any younger, and neither am I. Let's go."

Lou searched the room for a deep pocket of shadow. In the corner stood a television armoire weighing no less than two hundred pounds. It was ancient and was probably in the apartment long before King ever showed up. Otherwise, she had no idea how anyone got it up here.

A diagonal shadow stretched from the side of the dresser across the wall, thickest in the corner.

"Turn off the lamp," she said. And when King did, her hand was already on his arm, pulling him toward the armoire.

She paused a moment beside the armoire and listened. Pressing her ear to the ground and listening, feeling the vibrations through her body like a snake.

Silence. Absolute silence.

"What's wrong?" King asked.

Instead of answering, she pulled him through the thin membrane with her.

The first thing to catch Lou's attention was the swelling cacophony of sound. Crickets rubbing their legs together and frogs belting songs from their bloated throats.

The moon was full and bright, eerie light stretched across an overgrown field.

Lou took a step forward, still holding King's elbow, and her boots disturbed soft earth. A dirt floor. No. Dirt. They stepped from the doorway of a...what? Barn? A building of some kind. She closed her eyes counted to five and then opened them again, allowing her pupils to dilate and adjust to the light.

Then she caught the smell. Soft hay. Earth. Animal piss.

Horse stables.

A paddock stood empty a few yards away. They'd entered from the corner of the dark barn, standing in an empty field. The dilapidated barn barely stood. Boards jutted in all directions like crooked teeth. The stalls were empty, their doors slung wide. Hungry black mouths hanging open, waiting to be filled. And an unlatched door swinging slightly in the breeze was like a tongue lolling in the mouth. Begging for its thirst to be quenched.

"Where the hell is this?" King asked softly. He stepped away from her into the moonlight washing the land. A field stretched in all directions, interrupted only by trees as a border. "Have you ever been wrong?"

"No," Lou said, anger rising in her chest. "She's here."

She closed her eyes and listened. A pull formed down her right arm, and she turned in that direction. Leaving her eyes closed, she followed the pull. She let it lead her. A sharper right and then a throbbing from her belly.

Then the smell hit her.

She opened her eyes. She stood in one of the stalls. Half of the stall was clotted with broken boards from the exterior wall having fallen in. The rest of the soft earth was covered in a mound of sweet hay. More white moonlight filtered through the broken boards, painting the hay silver.

"Shit," King said behind her.

She swept her boot over the hay, pushing clumps to the left and right, inching closer and closer to the floor with each pass. Then her boot hit something hard. This time, it wasn't only hay turned over by the swish of her foot. A white bone revealed itself, its glow preternatural in the moonlight.

"So she didn't end up in the bay. But why would they bring her here?" Lou asked, bile burned in her throat. But these bones had been picked clean. Given the teeth marked on the bone itself, Lou guessed animals did the job for the killers.

"Where's here?" King asked.

"I don't know." Lou toed the bone with her foot. *It's the radius or the ulna*, she thought. She had no desire to uncover the rest of Ashley DeWitt to confirm this, or even to lean in for a closer look.

King left the barn, stepping back into the open night, raising his cell phone toward the sky. The bright blue screen blazed in the darkness.

"You probably won't get a signal out here," she said.

"Oklahoma," he said. He lowered the phone and pressed a series of buttons. It clicked, the recognizable sound of a screenshot being snapped. He waved it at her. "So maybe they killed her on the boat, and instead of dumping her in the bay, they drove her north and dumped her here."

"Or they didn't kill her on the boat," Lou offered. "Maybe she ran to Oklahoma, and they caught up." A darker thought surfaced. "Or they killed her on the boat but couldn't dump her right away."

King shrugged. "If she ran, there must be someone here. In Oklahoma, I mean. Parents. Grandparents. A sibling. Someone worth running to. And maybe said person heard an interesting story in the hours before she was killed. We should find out and talk to them."

"Or they're dead too," Lou said, stepping out of the stable. "I wouldn't have left the family alive if I thought she had talked."

King stared at her. "Any chance you can find Daminga's body? We might find usable evidence."

Lou closed her eyes and strained. But the needle spun and spun. Nothing.

"I think she's in the bay." And Lou couldn't slip into the middle of ocean.

A cold wind blew through the sagging building, and a chill ran up Lou's spine. She didn't like this place. She wasn't sure what it was. Not the corpse. But something. And she knew better than to question it. Her instincts about places were never wrong.

Lou reached out and grabbed King. One sidestep into an adjacent stable, one with its rear wall still intact, and then they were in his apartment again, standing in his bathroom. The toilet pressed against the back of Lou's leg.

"That was abrupt," he said. He frowned at her. "We could have gotten pictures. Taken notes. I could have swept the barn for evidence. Tire tracks. Fibers. Anything."

"It wasn't safe to stay there," Lou said. "I need to go."

What she hadn't said was, *or run the risk of stranding you there.*

Standing in the darkness, she'd felt her compass whirling. Had the barn been unsafe, or was it the pull of something greater that had triggered her?

Threaded tendrils of nervousness tugged on her arms and legs, whispering into her dark heart there was another place she needed to be. Another place she had to go.

She knew this feeling and recognized its meaning. And with understanding, the heartbeat in her chest began to thump unevenly, as if straining under the pressure of wanting to be in two places at once.

"Yeah, okay. I can do the rest alone," King said. He shifted his weight. "Hey, are you okay?"

She didn't answer him. She gave herself over to the current and was gone.

W hen Lou woke, something was wrong. The light streaming from the high windows was purple. The sun was dipping low behind the trees, its last eye open on the horizon. Under her pillow, her fingers curled around her gun and found the metal warm from the feathers incubating it throughout the day.

She heard a noise again. A small sound jerked her upright, gun pointed.

"Two for two." Lucy placed a sandwich wrapped in glossy newsprint on the counter and stuck her hand into the brown paper bag again. She gave Lou a half-smile from the kitchen island as she peeled back the wrapper. "One of these days you're going to blow my head off and save me the trouble of worrying about you."

"Stop creeping up on me." Lou lowered the gun. The smell of red onions flooded the studio. Her stomach rumbled its response. When was the last time she'd eaten? She wasn't sure. Sometimes when she was working, she'd forget to eat. The task distracted her. It was only when she worried her weak limbs or unclear head would cost her that she bothered to make time for the inconvenient task.

The burger, she remembered. She'd eaten a burger at the vegan fast food place about twenty hours ago.

"What are you doing here?" Lou asked.

"Can't a loving aunt bring her niece a veggie loaf sandwich when she wants to? I got your favorite. Extra avocado, extra oil, and extra oregano. Come eat with me."

Lou thumbed the safety back on and disentangled her limbs from the bedding.

"Don't you get hot sleeping by the window?" Aunt Lucy asked. She nodded at a barstool by the island where she'd spread the sandwich on its wrapper.

Lou slid onto it, placing her gun on the counter beside the wrapper. It clanked heavy against the granite surface. "It's the best light in the apartment. I don't have to worry about waking up in Bangkok."

Aunt Lucy popped open a bag of chips and dumped them onto the paper spread beneath Lou's sandwich. BBQ. Her favorite. But Aunt Lucy was frowning. "Do you still slip in your sleep?"

"No," Lou said, stuffing three chips into her mouth at the same time. The oils began melting the moment they hit her tongue. The muscles in her back loosened. "Because I sleep by the window, in full daylight."

Her aunt plucked a chip off her spread and made a pensive sound. "I thought that was something you'd outgrow. I did."

"We've already established I'm different."

Lucy squeezed her elbow. "Different in the most charming ways, my love."

Lou arched an eyebrow.

"What did you really come for?" Lou knew the food was her aunt's way of disarming her. After all, if someone shows up with a pint of ice cream or a pan of tiramisu, it's hard not to welcome them with open arms.

Lucy put a chip into her mouth and said, "How is it going with Robert?"

"*Robert?*" Lou laughed, charmed by her aunt's growing blush. "I've been calling him King. Aren't cops last-name-only?"

Lucy gave a curt nod, conceding the point. "You're right. Your father went by Thorne."

Her heart fluttered at the mention of her father. Somewhere in her stomach a snake coiled tighter. She could feel his scruffy cheeks against hers. The sound of his boots hitting the floor when he came home.

Lucy's voice yanked her back to the present. "What does he have you doing?"

Lou spoke around a mouthful of sandwich and wondered if they were moving toward the reason for this visit, or away from it. "Witness protection. We are making sure this woman's ex-boyfriend doesn't find her until she can testify."

Lou had to convince King that partial truth was better than an elaborate story. Lucy's bullshit meter was razor sharp. Always had been. Lying to her was fruitless and only got her into deeper shit. King seemed rather horrified by this truth.

The crinkles in Aunt Lucy's forehead relaxed. "Do you enjoy it? Or is this too boring for you?"

Lou sensed the trap in the question. If she claimed to *love* working with King, Lucy would be suspicious why. If she said she hated it, Lucy would also expect an explanation. And it wasn't just the lengthy discussion Lou was avoiding. It was the concern. Her aunt's worry turned her stomach and made her feel guilty. She could put down ten men in one night and not feel the guilt she felt when confronted with Lucy's stricken face.

Lou settled on, "I'm giving him a chance."

Lucy's shoulders relaxed. "Good. That's all I can ask."

Lou's gaze slid to the gun on the table, saw her aunt looking at it too, and moved it into her lap out of sight. "King said he met you right after I went to La Loon for the first time."

Lucy froze, a chip halfway to her mouth fell to the paper. "You're gossiping about me?"

Lou laughed. "Wouldn't you like to know?"

Her aunt couldn't hide her smirk as she licked her lips and then crumpled up the glossy newsprint, stuffing it back into the brown sack. Then she folded down the top, once, twice, three times, far too much consideration for a brown bag smeared with avocado.

"Is it true?" Lou pressed. "How you met?"

"Your father and I had a falling out in high school. I...took off. We hadn't spoken for about ten years when he figured out you were...like me."

What was your last fight about? Lou wanted to ask. But she didn't ask personal questions, not just as a courtesy, but because she didn't want to open that door. If you asked questions, you had to answer them too. Lou was uncomfortable with simple questions like: *What are you doing tonight?* The notion she might have to respond with something as personal as *It must've hurt when he rejected you* was unfathomable.

And truly, she didn't need to ask. Lou could piece together much of the story herself. Somehow Dad had discovered Lucy's ability, and his reaction wasn't good.

If Lucy loved her brother half as much as Lou did, of course it had hurt. The smallest admonishment from her father—*Lou-blue, I'm disappointed*—had wrecked her.

She sucked in a breath. "Dad was motivated to find you because I disappeared."

A statement, not a question. Less emotional entanglement.

"Yes. But he couldn't find me. So, he sent King. The rest is history," Lucy gathered up the trash of their lunch and began separating it for the recycling bin. Paper in one pile. Plastic in another. "How does he seem to you?"

Lucy bent under the sink to retrieve the blue recycle bin and frowned.

Fuck.

Her aunt pulled out a cardboard toilet paper roll. "This is recyclable."

"I must have missed," Lou said. No other response would do.

"Well?"

"I'll work on my aim. It's dark under the sink. Sometimes the trash can and the recycle bin look alike." Not much of an apology.

She tossed the cardboard tube into the bin with a shake of her head. "No, King. How does he seem to you? Be honest."

She thought of his wet ass cheeks, caterpillar brows, and yellowed toenails. "Old."

Lucy's frown deepened. "He isn't old. I think he's very handsome."

Lou did not find King attractive, but she couldn't tell her aunt that. It would be like leaning into a stroller and informing the mother it was the ugliest infant you'd ever seen.

"He reminds me of Dad," she said instead. And she hadn't realized it was true until it was out of her mouth.

Lucy straightened slowly. "How do you mean?"

Lou felt the ice cracking beneath her and tried to ease some of her weight off the frozen lake of her mind. The wrong step and she'd be submerged. "They're a particular breed."

"Thrill-seeking know-it-alls, you mean?" Lucy smiled, and the muscles in Lou's back released. "Stubborn to a fault and prone to tunnel vision. They can overlook something obvious if they've got an idea in their head. And blindness can get them killed."

Lucy placed a hand on her hip and turned toward the large living room window. Her face was pallid in the orange light, and the dark circles exaggerated, looking puffier than usual.

Had she been crying?

Lou'd rather be shot than ask. But she'd try to bridge the distance anyway. "Are you..."

"What?"

"Are you guys fighting?" Then seeing her aunt's confusion, Lou added, "You seem... disgruntled."

Lucy sighed. "You're right. I'm being too negative. He is kind. Loyal. And very brave. He's definitely a man worth his salt."

"Is that so?" Lou forced a smile. *We'll see about that.*

22

King went to bed not long after Lou left. Only he didn't sleep. He lay on his bed, staring at the bubbly nodules of the popcorn ceiling, and thought of the long white skeleton bone protruding from the hay. It wasn't the bone that haunted him. It was the way Lou had rolled it under her boot like a soda can on the street.

Her face had been unreadable. As cold and impenetrable as the creek behind his great aunt's house in winter. When she pretended, when she smiled or adopted a lilting tone as she had with him in the alley to throw off the man following him and again at the picnic table with Paula Venetti, it had seemed as if she had thawed in these moments. But he knew now it was a lie. The real Lou was the one who'd rolled a dead woman's bone beneath her boot and said nothing.

And it made him uncomfortable that after hours with her and a full report from Lucy, King had discovered little more. Lou was the hardest read he'd ever encountered.

Was she sociopathic? Maybe psychopathic?

King couldn't tell. Did she honestly feel nothing? Or did she have the cop face to end all cop faces?

No wonder Lucy had been desperate enough to contact him. Though Lucy's belief this was a phase had been a mistake. This wasn't the kind of chip on the shoulder they could eradicate with some positive energy and hours of therapy. They should have started working on Lou when she was younger. *Much* younger. They'd waited too long. Whatever Lou was now, that was what she would always be. For better or worse.

He understood it. And he had no idea how he was going to break it to Lucy.

Lucy—a whole other box of questions. *Why now? Why him?*

He could smell a secret there too but hadn't yet figured out how to ask Lucy the truth. How to press her right. He needed a better hold on the thread if he hoped to unravel the mystery of Lucy Thorne.

Maybe he could develop a plan if only he'd get a good night's sleep. As he lay in his king-sized bed, staring at the ceiling, he couldn't list a single thing he wanted more. He wanted to sleep, but the *walls*. The moonlight hadn't done enough to make the room feel bigger. Too many pillows crowded his face. He shoved them away, and when this didn't work, he turned on the bedside lamp.

The bedroom walls seemed to move back an inch. Better.

Maybe it was that he lay on his back. In the dark under a collapsed building, King had lain in this position unable to move. Perhaps the claustrophobia would abate if he moved his body into a different position. The act alone defied his feeling of confinement.

With a great sigh, he turned over onto his side. His folders and papers lay in an unorganized pile beside the bed. The corners flapped in the draft caused by the fan whirling overhead, a high-pitched wind buzzing in his mind.

At least the shop was closed, and the goddamn skeleton was no longer screeching downstairs. Once, a gaggle of girls must have crossed the threshold, because as soon as the bony guard screamed, a choir of wails followed. For a full five seconds, it was hysteria before the squealing was swallowed up by nervous, fretful laughter.

It was clear Mel had decided to keep the damn thing.

A fly trap waved in the corner of the room before the open window. The ferns lining the balcony looked like silver-headed crones from his bed. He imagined counting the leaves on each tendril and his limbs relaxed. A welcome weight settled into his arms and legs, and they softened like butter left on the table after dinner, long into the night.

Almost, a voice thought eagerly. *Almost asleep...*

His breathing had just begun to slow when the blade pressed to his throat.

Lou resisted as along as she could, then she slipped. The pressure to do so had been mounting since she took King to the barn. Her internal compass wanted her to go somewhere, and it finally got its wish.

She crouched behind a sofa, her shadowed entry point, and listened. Someone was in the next room. The sound of a zipper unlatching its teeth caught her attention and then heavy objects bouncing off a mattress, the coils groaning.

Her heart sped up, and she pulled her gun. *Where am I?*

Slowly, she rose from behind the couch.

A hotel suite. The cream and rose furnishings. A window with the sliding curtains pulled aside.

An American city, but not one she recognized immediately. A Ferris wheel burned blue beside an interstate six or seven lanes wide. The blue Ferris wheel rang a bell. Before she worked it out in her mind, a door closed and someone began taking a piss.

She lifted her gun higher and crossed the room. On the other side of an archway was the bedroom. A suitcase was open on the bed. Suits lay on top of each other. A garment bag was unzipped, and slacks lay smoothed over the suitcase beside half a dozen shopping bags from high-end department stores. To the left of the bed the closed bathroom door drew her eye.

A line of light traced its frame. A toilet flushed. A sink ran.

The bathroom door flew open, and a man stood there. His hair fell into his eyes and across his cheekbones. Bright green eyes widened at the sight of her pointing a gun at him. She recognized those eyes immediately. She took him in, head to toe. The scruffy jaw. His bare chest and a tattoo snaking up one bicep. A crow and crossbones. Then again the beautiful eyes.

He said something in Italian.

Swore. In *Italian*.

She lifted the gun and fired.

The bullet bit the trim, tearing a chunk of wood away from the door frame and spitting it out onto the tile floor of the bathroom.

He flinched, pinching his eyes shut as wood chips pelted his face. But he pulled his own gun and fired two shots wildly.

Konstantine.

She understood her compass had taken her straight to him. The last Martinelli. The last thread to burn before her revenge was complete.

And here was her chance to finish him, while he was alone and defenseless.

Only two things happened at once.

First, the pull was on her again. Her inner alarm flared to life with its urgent throbbing. The same compass that had led her to Konstantine was now tugging her away.

Time to go, it said. *Time to go!*

The second thing that happened was she recognized Konstantine. She *knew* him.

She hadn't seen him in years, true. And he was a man now, his body thick and muscular, no longer the wiry limbs of a street rat. Only she hadn't known his name when they were children, when they met long before she'd killed her first man.

He'd grown up.

And she wasn't that girl anymore.

But this sharp recognition was enough to unmoor her, throw her understood and arranged world into chaos, and send all the important pieces careening across the floor of her mind.

She stumbled back into the dark living room into the thickest shadow coalescing in the corner of the chamber behind a sofa. Another bullet slammed into the wall beyond her head. She dove for the corner, slipping through the smallest of cracks.

Her heart hammered in her temples, giving the world an unbearable tilt. She expected the sanctity of her own closet. Somewhere to catch her breath before rounding back and finishing the man.

Only she wasn't in her closet. There would be no time for a costume or weapon change or a chance to wrap her mind around why the hell her compass took her to Konstantine at all. Why it had chosen him of the seven billion souls on the planet—then or now.

She brushed a wooden edifice six inches in front of her face. If this wasn't one of her closet's three walls, it was the side of King's entertainment armoire. Cherry wood, bright in a sliver of moonbeams.

A man cried out.

Another voice replied in a low and unfriendly tone.

King chuckled. "Go fuck yourself."

Lou tiptoed across the shadowed living room, skirting an industrial coffee table, and crept toward the bedroom door. It stood open. She pressed herself into the corner. She saw the overhead fan whirling and sheets the color of cream. King was on the floor with his hands tied behind his back. One of his eyes was swelling shut, a puffy purple bruise pinching the eyelids together.

Blood was bright in one corner of his mouth, and King kept flicking his tongue out to lick at the swollen, split lip.

The man with the blade stuck it under King's chin, forcing King to look up or have his throat sliced. It was the man from the alley.

She couldn't approach him without being seen because King had left his goddamn lamp on. *Who slept with a lamp on?*

You do, a voice teased.

Fuck this. Lou pulled the trigger. The bullet went right through one side of the man's head and out the other. Brains sprayed the wall and doused the white coverlet.

King froze, eyes wide and unseeing for several heartbeats. Then he turned and looked at her. "I guess he was right about only asking one more time."

She didn't laugh.

His shock dimmed when he saw her. "Are you all right?"

She was shaking. Not from fear like he assumed, but with anger. She'd been pulled into forced slips *twice*. Back to back, and then she'd put a bullet into a man's head without thinking, without taking them to her Alaskan lake. It was her first messy kill.

What the fuck is wrong with me?

Konstantine. That's what was wrong with her.

She'd woken in his bed nearly a decade ago, from the worst dreams about her father's death, and found him there. Cooing Italian. A face part wonder. Part desire. Part sympathy.

Why would her compass take her to Martinelli's son? Why would she go to him before she even decided on her path to revenge? And she didn't know who he was, at least not consciously.

You're Konstantine's bitch, Castle had said.

"Hey, Lou. Talk to me. Are you okay?" King asked again. His hands were still tied behind his back, but he was standing in front of her, grimacing down at her through his swollen eye.

"I fucked up."

He snorted. "You saved my ass."

"I don't shoot them on this side," she said through her teeth. She breathed. Focused on the floor under her feet. It wasn't actually tilting.

King frowned. He looked at the wall. "You couldn't have done it from over there. There's a wall in the way."

She touched her forehead, trying to find relief from the pressure building behind her eyes. Her right eye was thumping in her skull. "I don't mean this side of the room. I mean on this side of...oh god, whatever the fuck this is. I take them to a lake. I move them, alive to another place where I can leave them. No mess. No body. No crime."

"You have a dumping ground," he said. He puffed out his cheeks with an exaggerated exhale. "Of course, you do."

"I'll get rid of him," Lou said. It sounded pathetic to her. Like an apology. "I'll clean it up."

"Untie me, and I'll help. I know what they'll look for," he said as if he cleaned up crime scenes all the time.

She didn't refuse his help. She wanted this to be over as soon as possible so she could retreat to her St. Louis apartment and think. She needed to fucking think. There was too much bouncing around in her head as it was.

Lou pulled a blade from a forearm sheath and sliced through the zip cord binding King's wrists together.

King rubbed his wrists. "Thanks. After we clean this place up, we need to move Paula."

Lou arched an eyebrow. It was easier to do than form words.

King touched his swollen lip. "Because we're in deep shit."

23

Konstantine stood in the middle of the hotel with his heart racing. It was as if two hands had wrapped themselves around his neck and were squeezing. He couldn't draw enough air. Nor could he convince himself she was gone. So he stood there, frozen between the living room and bedroom, unable to move.

The gun trembled in his hands, the barrel jumping at the end of his sight.

The shadows didn't move.

His eyes roved the room as he went from switch to switch, turning on every light he could. The room filled with bright, cheery light.

She wasn't here. She wasn't.

Sweat trailed down the side of his face. The moisture on the back of his neck began to cool, and along with the queasiness in his guts, he felt ill.

Wood splinters from the bathroom's door frame stuck to his damp cheek like sawdust. It reminded him of the days he spent down by the harbor while men sanded the boats and bent soft woods into place. The air around the workmen had been thick with dust. The ocean blew it back from the harbor. So even if he kept his distance, he left with a sheen on his skin and clothes.

She'd gotten too close. And hadn't he just been thinking about her?

He'd been thinking about her almost nonstop for the last 24 hours. Ever since he'd arrived, he'd been playing scenarios in his mind on how such an encounter might go.

If only she knew my intentions, he had thought. *If only she could see and understand what I want.*

But he knew his chance would never come. She had no interest in hearing him speak. And yet, she'd recognized him. She'd hesitated. He was not mistaken about that. And she *missed.*

She never missed.

The moment he wet his lips they felt dry again. His whole mouth was dry.

Someone knocked at the door, and he fired two bullets into the wall.

"What the hell! Mr. Konstantine, are you all right in there?" a man called. Another sharp bang. "Mr. Konstantine?"

Konstantine went to the door and opened it.

Julio stood in a long white T-shirt which stretched to his knees, and sagging acid-washed jeans. The American's repulsive dress code wasn't enough to bring the world into sharp focus. He still felt as though he wavered on the edge of hysteria. All the adrenaline left him as it did when one was in a near collision. But he had no rearview mirror from which to gain reassurance. No method for looking over his shoulder and ensuring that the danger had in fact passed and he was in the clear.

"Julio?" he rasped.

Julio's eyebrows shot up at the gun. "You okay, boss? You look...like you need a drink."

"What are you doing here?"

"I told you I was coming." Julio slipped a bright yellow backpack off his shoulders. "I got information on your girl."

Konstantine kept glancing over his shoulder.

"Is—" Julio stopped and considered his question more carefully. "Is this a bad time?"

"No," Konstantine said, bringing his forearm up to wipe at his brow.

When Konstantine didn't move or open the door wider, Julio asked, "Should I come in?"

He could, but Konstantine didn't think he could stay in this suite. "Is the lobby well lit?"

"Like fucking Manhattan. Why?"

"Let's go downstairs. We'll order some drinks, and you can show me whatever you want to show me. I need..." Konstantine wiped his sweaty palms on his pants. "I need to get out of this room."

Julio slipped the pack on again. "Sure." Then his eyes fell to the gun. "But do you think you should be walking around with that hanging out? I mean, there's a lot of security."

"Yes, you're right."

Konstantine grabbed a shirt from the bed, his wallet, and his room key before rejoining Julio in the hall. His movements were rushed and jerky. But relief washed over him as he stood in the bright hallway, securing the gun under his shirt, tucked into the waistband of his pants.

If Julio had any other critiques about Konstantine's behavior or dress code, he said nothing. He waited for Konstantine to adjust himself before he led the way to the elevators.

Julio had been right about the lobby. Despite the late hour, it was as bright as midday. The bar, however, was swathed in shadows. Konstantine took a long look at the black bar and its black stools. Then he gave Julio a hundred-dollar bill and asked him to buy him a gin and tonic. Konstantine kept himself planted on a white leather seat in the center lobby. His back was to a wall, which was fine if the early evening was any preview to his lady's intentions.

Konstantine watched Julio go to the bar with his yellow backpack still hanging from one shoulder and order the drinks. A girl in black and white dress slacks and shirt combo came out and talked to Julio for a moment. She looked over at Konstantine when Julio pointed at the chairs along the wall and nodded. She said something too, her pouty little mouth bobbing open and closed, but Konstantine did not read lips.

It was hard not to think of anything but her.

She had come.

She had come, and he was not ready.

He thought he understood her and how she worked. She was cautious. She always surveyed her prey, stalked her prey before moving in. He had not, quite obviously, expected her to appear so late in the evening. And in the intimacy of his bedroom—like old times.

What struck him most: she seemed as surprised as he was by this encounter.

A moment of shock registered on her face, rendering her a decade younger in a single flash. One moment she was the merciless angel of death, with her sharp blade severing spines without conscience. Then their eyes met, and she'd become the girl again. Innocent and wrapped in the shadows of his bed, with the thinnest line of moonlight across a milk-white cheek. Troubled by the dreams in her dark heart.

He pushed back these thoughts as Julio crossed the lobby, bouncing the sack across his spine, adjusting its weight for better placement.

"The girl will bring our drinks," Julio said. He sat in the chair opposite Konstantine's, so close their knees touched. "I left the bill as a tab, is—"

"That's fine," Konstantine interrupted. The muscles in his back twitched. It didn't seem to matter how soft the chairs were designed, how much they encouraged lingering near the bar and consuming one's fill. He was uneasy. "What do you have for me?"

"I've been looking for your girl," he said, yanking his computer and a notebook out of his bag. For a common American thug, Konstantine thought he was rather organized. If not for the black teardrop tattoo on his face, and the ink up and down his arms, most of which was representative of the unskilled lines of prison art, he could be mistaken for a school boy. A nontraditional student returned to get a degree. In nursing, maybe. Or computer programming. "I started with the father like you said. Got her name."

Konstantine's heart hitched. He imagined what name she might have. Alessandra. Vivianne. Something unmistakably feminine but also feline. But less European he suspected. Emily perhaps.

"Louie Abigail Thorne."

"Louie?" Konstantine's heart flopped. "*Louie?*"

The sing-song word was too sweet. The hardest edge he could find when he turned the name over in his mind was a cowboy quality like Louis L'Amour.

"Louie?" he asked again. "Really?"

Julio shrugged. "Americans name their kids all kinds of weird shit. They name them after fruits and colors too."

Konstantine opened his hand to accept the paper Julio thrust at him. A copy of a birth announcement. Newsprint photocopied.

Julio recited the information from memory while Konstantine read. "Born to Jacob and Courtney Thorne on January 23, 1992."

More papers were passed over. Transcripts. More scraps pilfered from public records.

"She didn't do so good in school. Lots of her teachers made notes about her being 'distracted' and 'withdrawn.'" Julio snorted. "Like that's so bad. Teachers are the dumbest people I know. Too educated. Drop them in the desert, and they'd be dead tomorrow."

Konstantine was looking at a yellow sheet with the words *counselor evaluation* printed on the top. *Psychosis-neg. Depression-neg.* Then printed in a meticulous blocky script below, in a box marked *additional comments,* someone had written: *Displays anti-social behavior. Intelligence exemplary. Placement test suggested. Perhaps bored with coursework and children her own age.*

"Her aunt put her in one of those schools for gifted kids," Julio said, offering Konstantine more paper. "She did better in the gifted school."

Konstantine frowned at him. "Her aunt?"

"Yeah. Thorne had a sister. She took custody of your girl when her parents died."

"And after school?" he asked. He felt as if he could not get enough information on her. He wanted to know everything. He slid back a sheet and saw the photocopy of her driver's license. Sixteen years old. Eyes brown. Hair brown. Weight 130 pounds. Height 5'7.

What a bland description of such a magnificent creature he thought, taking something and rendering it to measurements and scientific specifications stripped the leaves from the tree. He realized Julio hadn't answered.

He looked up. The barmaid was putting their drinks on the table on top of two cardboard coasters with the hotel's logo. She gave him a grin and wink when she placed his gin and tonic on the coaster. "Will there be anything else?" she purred. When she leaned forward, her breasts filled his vision, giving them a swollen appearance.

He instinctually pulled the photocopies close to his chest, shielding them. "No thank you."

Her smile faltered.

"Thanks," Julio said, poking the lime slice down into the neck of his beer bottle with a stab of his finger.

The girl wandered off looking more than a little dejected.

"After school?" Konstantine asked again.

Julio pulled back his teeth in a hiss, either from the sour lime or the question. "That's it."

Konstantine's heart dropped an inch in his chest. "Nothing else?"

Julio shook his head, his lips pressed into a thin line. "After high school, she goes dark."

Konstantine wet his lips with the gin and tonic, drawing a steady breath. To be given so much and so little was infuriating. When he felt he could trust himself to speak, he said, "Nothing."

Julio wiped a hand across his brow. "I think she let her license lapse. Or she legally changed her name. So, she's not registered in the system. She doesn't have any bills in her name. No phone. No utilities. She's got a bank account and some money, but it's managed by a financial advisor. Her address is a P.O. box in Detroit."

"That doesn't mean anything." Konstantine grimaced. "She could get to any P.O. box anywhere in the world."

Julio went on. "Yeah. If what you say is true. And her bank transactions are limited. She doesn't have any credit cards. Either her bills are paid by the guy who manages her parents' estate, or she pays cash. Her bank records show ATM withdrawals, but they are all over. In the last two years, which was as far back as I could go, she hasn't made a withdrawal from the same ATM twice."

"Which bank?" Konstantine asked. The gin and tonic balanced on his knee was starting to melt through his pants. Julio told him the name of the bank and Konstantine snorted. "They have ATMs on every corner."

"She doesn't vote. She doesn't work, you know, for money."

"And she has no family," Konstantine said. "No way we can get to her."

Julio smiled. "She has the aunt. There's an Oak Park address on file. The aunt *does* vote and pays her taxes. And she's got a lengthy medical record."

Konstantine reviewed the file and considered this.

Konstantine didn't know if he wanted to threaten the aunt. At the rate he was going, Louie—*Louie*—he would have to adjust to this name

—would put a bullet in him quicker than he could ring the aunt's doorbell.

And he did not think he had the element of surprise any longer. Whatever surprise he had was used up in the hotel room this night. His next move would have to be quite bold to elicit the same luck. And yet, it'd be good to have leverage should she ever return.

He had to talk to her. Reason with her. He wanted something so small from her. Surely, if he asked the right way, she would give it to him. But how to approach her? How to present himself?

Perhaps it was best to follow through with the first part of his plan. If he could expose the lies about her father's murder, and clarify the Martinelli involvement in his death, perhaps it will get through to her better than bullying or coercion.

If he delivered the *real* man responsible for her father's death, maybe she will help him.

Konstantine turned the rocks glass in his hand before lifting it and taking a sip. He met Julio's eyes over the rim. "Let's talk about the senator."

24

King was on his hands and knees beside the bed, scrubbing carpet cleaner into the rug with an old, torn up St. Louis Cardinals T-shirt. He drew breaths in and out of his nose slowly. Combined with the back and forth scrubs, it was like a meditation—until the pain set in.

"I'm too old for this shit," he groaned. He leaned back and placed a soapy hand on his low back. His knees creaked, and sharp pains shot all the way up to his hips. Pulling himself to standing, with the help of his bed frame, required a Herculean effort.

It wasn't until he dragged a sponge across the wall to mop up his attacker's brains, he realized Mel had never come up to check on him. And he could not recall the surprising *crack-boom* of a gun going off. Had Lou used a suppressor? She must have.

Who fucking cares? a voice said. *You're awake at three a.m. scrubbing blood out of the carpet and wiping brains off the wall with a kitchen sponge. Is this how you wanted to spend your retirement?*

Spending time with a would-be mercenary?

Hunting for corpses in Oklahoma backcountry?

Being knocked around and threatened for information?

He was sure none of the above was healthy behavior for a man hoping to see his 70th birthday.

King ran the sponge under the tap in the bathroom again until the water ran clear. Little bits of bone hit the porcelain. Part of the skull cap. His stomach turned.

His bed thumped as it was lifted and dropped.

"What the...?" He stepped toward the dark bedroom, but before he could examine the scene, the knock on the door came.

"King, good lord, what are you doing in there?" Mel's voice was raspy with sleep.

"Fuck." King stuffed the carpet cleaner and the sponges under the sink and hobbled to the door, his knees still stiff from bending.

Mel pounded on the door again. "Don't make me use my key, Mr. King."

"I'm coming, I'm coming." He hurried through the living room and kitchen to the door. He plastered on a smile before he pulled open the door, but smiling made his mouth hurt, and his lip split anew.

"What the hell you be doing in here?" Mel was in a purple cotton bathrobe, eyes puffy. "I'm an old woman. You can't be hanging pictures and rocking the bed at 3:00 a.m., no siree."

"I'm sorry," King said and wiped his damp hands on his pajama pants. "I didn't mean to wake you. I—" He was already searching the Rolodex of his mind for a lie that would suit this occasion. But all he could think was *I need to move the fucking bed so mine isn't flush with Mel's. You can probably hear everything through the thin plaster.*

"Oh my god, what happened to your face?" Mel elbowed herself into the apartment, staring up at him with wide eyes. "Somebody beat your ass?"

King knew what lie he'd have to use then. There was only one for his predicament. "I was having a nightmare. I rolled out of bed and smashed my face on the nightstand." He made a face-to-palm gesture with his hand, and followed it with his best little boy shrug of disappointment. He thought it was excellent acting.

"No, you got your ass beat," she said. "I know an ass beating when I see one. And I'm not stupid, so don't try to fool me. Were you in the bar tonight?"

King groaned. "Come on, Mel. Not everyone is a goddamn alcoholic. Plenty of teetotalers get beat up. They fall out of bed and bash in their faces too."

Mel poked at his bruises with relentless fingers. He hissed and squirmed until she let go.

She sniffed. "What's that smell?"

"I don't smell anything," King said. And he didn't, but that didn't stop him from running a furious checklist of *possible* smells. Gunpowder. Blood. Brains.

Mel turned on the kitchen light, which revealed nothing more than the clean, unused kitchen. So, she turned on the living room light.

"I didn't know random inspections were part of our agreement," King said. His voice was an octave too high. "Do I need to say I don't consent to a search?"

She gave him a hard look, pulling her robe tight around her. "I heard a crazy sound. Sound*s,* and I smell something funky. Are you hiding something in here? Oh Lord, did you kill somebody up in my house?"

"No," King said, and he felt a muscle in his face begin to twitch even though it was the truth. *He* hadn't killed anyone.

But Mel didn't look convinced. And she was going into the bedroom.

"Hey!" King called out as she stepped into the room. "Stay out of there. I—"

His bed was in disarray. His sheets were crumpled and tossed about in a way that made one think of a pterodactyl trapped and thrashing with its great wings. The bed was also at an oblique angle. The footboard pointed toward the bathroom about ten more degrees than it did before King had answered the door. The nightstand too had been pulled away from the wall, its corner edge pointing into the room.

The rug was gone. Entirely *gone.*

Lou must have come back and yanked aside the furniture and taken the whole goddamn rug. There was a wet spot on the wall still drying, but there was no sign of blood or brain there. He knew if forensic scientists ever decided to come in and black light his walls, he would fail their test miserably, but he doubted Mel would even recognize the slight reflection on the wall as moisture, or imagine what sort of matter had been stuck there thirty minutes before.

King knew he'd never see his rug again.

"One hell of a nightmare," Mel said, her eyebrows arched, yet somehow more relaxed now.

"Oh you're not mad," he said with a huff. "Now that I'm not a drunk with a bed full of young, beautiful women."

"Let's clean you up," Mel said and went toward the bathroom.

"That's all right," King tried to say, and his voice hitched. The first aid kit was under the sink with the sponge and carpet cleaner.

Nosebleed, he decided. He would tell her he'd bled on the rug and had tried to clean it up with the cleaner. When it hadn't worked, he'd given up and thrown out the rug.

That was pretty good.

Mel stood in his bathroom, pointing at the closed toilet seat. "Sit."

"No, really, Mel. It's so late. I don't want to keep you up, babying me."

"Sit. Down." She gave him a look that made his testicles recede inside himself.

He turned off the bedroom light and then squeezed past her and took a seat on the closed toilet lid. His knees were forced against his chest, effectively pinning him between the tub and wall, with Mel blocking the exit.

She gave him a smile. "You already woke me up. You got me up here and your face looks like shit. I happen to know how to clean a face. So sit there and keep your mouth shut."

King looked up at her from the toilet. The lid held him but groaned. He was sure the plastic snaps keeping the lid in place would pop, and he would slide off into the floor with about as much grace as the pterodactyl that had destroyed his bedsheets.

She opened the door beneath the sink, and he expected to see the half bottle of cleaning solution and a wet sponge. But they were gone. The torn-up Cardinals T-shirt was gone too.

Mel pulled a bottle of peroxide from beneath the sink and took the white cap off the brown bottle.

"Cotton balls are in the cabinet," he offered.

She found them beside an oversized bottle of Tums.

"You've got yourself in some deep shit, Mr. King. And if you ever want to get off this toilet again, you're going to tell me what's going on."

King looked up into her dark eyes. Even in her already dark complexion, the dark circles were noticeable, a slight pink color to the purplish flesh, gave their own impression of a bad bruise.

He wanted to lie. His instinct was to deny everything. Lou was purging the apartment of evidence, perhaps this instant. After all, hadn't he seen a shadow move behind Mel twice already? Something dark darting across his blackened bedroom.

But when he opened his mouth to speak, Mel arched an eyebrow and cocked her head. It was a challenge to whatever he intended to say next as if she was prepared to dismiss his first story on principle.

And there was the matter of her safety. It had been her shop. Her apartment was in this same building. The man had come for King, but Mel had been close. Too close. And what would have happened if Mel had used her key to let herself in? Would the gunman have turned and put a bullet between her eyes, no questions asked? Would he have taken her hostage or used her against him?

He dropped his gaze. "I should move out."

Mel's arched eyebrow fell, knitting together with the other. "Excuse me?"

"The case I'm working—some men came looking for me," he said. "You could've come in here. You could've gotten shot. I can't have that on me."

She stopped cleaning up his face and her scowl deepened. "And how do you think I'll fare when they come looking for you and *don't* find you? Do you think a couple of pissed off thugs might not go across the hall and take it out on the first defenseless, old woman they find?"

"If you're old, then I've got one foot in the grave," King said.

"Two feet, I dare say," she replied and dampened a fresh cotton ball with peroxide. "And it's that girl's fault."

"Lou's got nothing to do with this," King said, feeling his anger uncoil inside him. Like a snake, it lifted its flared head.

"This trouble didn't show up until her auntie came asking for your help."

"Actually," he said. "The problems started when I accepted a case from Chaz Brasso."

Mel dabbed at the cut on his face. King would have bet good money that she was hurting him on purpose.

King hissed. "Easy there!"

"Are you a sixty-year-old man or a little boy," she wailed. "Sit still."

King gritted his teeth and looked up at her.

"What was in that folder you brought home the other night?" she asked.

King bat his eyes at her.

She exhaled. "I read the cards about this one. She's the angel of death, Mr. King."

"Don't start with the cards," King said. "It's hard to talk about something as ridiculous as cards after I got pistol whipped by—"

Mel slapped him upside his head. It wasn't vicious. But with his abused face, it hurt plenty. "Stupid cards. My Lord, show some respect. Don't get me started on *your* stupid. I've seen plenty stupid out of you for you to be insulting an old woman's beliefs. My views are as good as anybody's. Not one person on this rock knows what's going on. I *trust* the cards. I believe in them. They never lie to me. I might be too dumb or blind to see the message, but they don't lie, which is more than I can say for some ungrateful tenants around here."

King touched his tender scalp gingerly with his fingers. "Maybe. But you're wrong about Lou. She's been through a lot, and she's got issues. But she's not evil."

Mel placed a hand on her hip. "I never said the angel of death was evil. But she also isn't someone we want to be inviting to dinner."

She tossed the pink cotton balls into a wastebasket wedged between the toilet and wash basin.

He wasn't going to placate her with hollow reassurances. He hated the automated way some men did that to women. He could recall a night his mother had woken to the sound of broken glass. An intruder had busted out the back window, intending to sneak into the kitchen and steal everything that would fit into his pillowcase. His father had chased him away with a baseball bat and his big booming voice. *It's okay. Now, now. Don't be so worked up. They're gone. And they aren't coming back*, he'd told his inconsolable wife, patting her like a worried puppy.

Only they *had* come back when his father was out of town, and they'd cleaned out the whole house the second time. The room they didn't get to was the bedroom because she'd locked it. And when she heard them in the house, she'd pulled Robbie into the bedroom's bathroom with her and locked that door too before she called the police.

He remembered thinking his mother had been right to be scared.

Afraid kept a person cautious. Afraid kept you *alive*. And so, he wouldn't give Mel any sugar-coated bullshit.

"I'm sorry," he said, holding onto her forearm. "I didn't mean to bring this on you. When I told Brasso I'd take the case I—"

"You knew it was trouble," she said, her lips pursed. "Don't say otherwise, Mr. King."

"I wasn't looking to get anyone hurt."

"But that's the thing, isn't it? When you go looking for trouble, it's not yourself that gets hurt. It's the people who love you."

"I'll move out tomorrow," he said. And he meant it. He had no idea where he would go. But he would take his bullshit with him.

"You'll do no such thing," Mel said, closing the cap on the peroxide bottle. "You'll stay right here and be ready to clean up the mess you made!"

King frowned at her.

"The next time they come knocking, you better be here to blow their heads off."

"You can't possibly be okay with living next door to a guy who's got a big target on his back."

"Better to live next to you than with you." Mel gave him a small smile then. It wasn't a pleasant, loving smile. It was flattened out by her pity and remorse. "Don't make me beg. You know I can't afford for you to move out. And maybe I like having your ass around."

It was a damn sweet thing for her to say, in not so many words, that they were friends. And that she'd no sooner throw him to the dogs as she would throw herself.

He smiled. "This is the French Quarter. You'd have another tenant in no time. You can even raise the rent. They won't know any better."

"But then I'd have to trust someone new," Mel said. "I just don't have the energy for that."

I trust you.

A lightning bolt of recognition shot through King's mind, a searing hot stab of betrayal electrifying him. He swore and stamped his foot. "Ah, you fat *fucker*."

"Excuse me," Mel said, one hand on her chest. "Did a devil take hold of your tongue?"

"Mother*fucker*," he said again. He sucked in his belly and squeezed past her into the dark bedroom.

"Who?" Mel cried, coming up behind him. She bumped into his back when King made a sudden stop between the living room and kitchen.

Chaz stood in there, in the kitchen, front door open behind him.

"Hey Robbie," Chaz said over the black-eyed barrel of his gun. He centered his aim on King's chest. "Where's Chuck?"

25

Water ran over Lou's hands, staining the sink in her bathroom with pink droplets. She looked into the mirror and saw a spray of blood had begun to dry across her cheek.

Looking deep into her own eyes, she replayed parts of King's conversation with his landlady. She thought the woman had seen her. In one moment between snatching the rug out from under King's bed and mopping the last of the brains off the wall, her eyes had fixed on her, where she crouched down in the dark beside King's bed.

But the woman's gaze had slid right over her. And the way she'd spoken to King in the bathroom while she fixed him up had been part-fury, part-care. It made her think of Aunt Lucy.

It made her think of her first kill.

"Blood?" Aunt Lucy had said when she saw her. She stood up from the kitchen table in their Chicago apartment. The tea cup had jumped, knocking a few drops onto the black lacquer tabletop.

Louie was shaking from head to toe. Her body was soaking wet. Red droplets chilled her skin.

She'd just stood in the kitchen, dripping as her aunt ran her fingers all over Louie's body. She was searching for a wound, for some evidence

of the attack. When she found none, she turned Lou around and started
on the angular plane of her back.

"It's not my blood," Lou managed to spit out between chattering
teeth. "I-I'm okay."

Her aunt went still beside her. Her warm fingers withdrew. "What
happened?"

"I had to."

"Had to *what?*" Aunt Lucy had taken a step back. "Oh my god."

"He deserved it," Louie said, shivering harder. Her teeth chattered.

"I don't want to hear it."

"He—"

"Shut up!" It was the first time Aunt Lucy had screamed. It had
shocked Louie into silence. Tears threatened to spill over her cheeks as
she replayed Johnson gasping and choking on his own blood.

Aunt Lucy looked at the red on her hands. Her face flushing, she
turned and darted into the kitchen behind them. She scrubbed her
hands beneath the hot tap. Louie watched her, her heart pounding.

"He's the one who betrayed Dad. Johnson was the reason—"

"Don't tell me! I'm serious," Lucy hissed. "No names. No, no *details*.
Not another word!"

Louie chewed her lower lip, swallowing everything she wanted to say
about Gus Johnson. How she'd lied about going to a graduation party.
How instead, she'd spent hours in the basement of the public library
searching microfilms for news of her parents. How the moment she'd
seen Gus's face in the interview, she'd known he was guilty. He was the
one who had sold them out to the drug lords so he could save his skin.

Gus himself had admitted this in not so many words.

The way the traitor's mouth opened, the eyes rolling up and to the
left in preparation for his lie.

Louie hadn't let him get far. She'd pounced. He knocked her off
easily, outweighing her by more than two hundred pounds. He'd raised
his gun to shoot her.

All the rationalizations. All the excuses. All her justifications.

She wasn't sorry she'd buried her father's pocket knife into the crook
of his neck. She wasn't sorry he bled to death on the shore of Blood
Lake in La Loon. She didn't give a damn that Jabbers took care of
the rest.

But the way her aunt had finally looked at her, her fingers bone white from clutching her sink so hard, she *did* care about that.

Aunt Lucy had the appearance of serenity, if not for those fingers holding onto the sink as if any moment a tornado was going to rip the ceiling off and carry her away.

"I want you to take a bath," Aunt Lucy had said. Her voice was even and low, almost too low for Louie to hear. Now she was the one shaking.

"But—"

"Get in with your clothes on," Lucy said, ignoring the interjection. She didn't turn away from the kitchen window as if the very sight of Lou was unacceptable. "Take them off and leave them somewhere. But not on *this* side. Go to that place. Leave everything there."

"Aunt Lucy—"

"*Everything*," she said, refusing to be interrupted. "Your shoes, your underwear. *Everything*. If you used—something—leave it. Do you understand?"

She hadn't wanted to give up her father's pocketknife, the small blade she'd buried in the hilt of Gus Johnson's throat, but she also understood the danger in keeping it. A weapon, however sentimental, was evidence.

"Go on." Lucy had waved her toward the bathroom at the end of the hall. "Do it now."

Before Louie could protest, her aunt walked into the empty linen closet in their old Oak Park apartment and disappeared.

She didn't need to see it, to know her aunt had slipped.

The apartment had hummed with her absence.

Lou did as she was told.

She'd run a warm bath and then she'd climbed inside it, shoes and all.

It was three in the morning by the time her aunt returned. She wasn't sure where Lucy had gone. Her aunt had favorite places she liked to haunt just as Louie did. But Louie couldn't describe her immense relief when Lucy came back. That she'd come back at all—that had been something.

"Louie?" Lucy sat down on the edge the couch where Louie lay, pretending to sleep. The cushions creaked under her aunt's weight. She placed a hand on Louie's knee. Then as if she'd sensed the girl's reluctance to start a conversation, she squeezed the knee and said, "Talk to me."

Louie turned over. It was hard to look her in the eye, but Louie tried to hold her gaze. The grim lines around Aunt Lucy's mouth had smoothed over in the last few hours. And her brow was no longer pinched in anger. Now she looked sad. And perhaps a little scared.

"Did you take care of it?" Aunt Lucy whispered as if someone would overhear them.

Louie nodded.

"It was someone who—" Her voice broke. Her aunt looked up at the ceiling and sucked in a breath. Once she seemed composed, she tried again. "He was responsible for your parents' death."

Louie nodded. "The Martinellis got to him first, and so he sold out Dad to protect himself. He's probably the one who told all those lies about Dad too."

Her aunt nodded as if this confirmed her suspicions. "And are there others? People you plan to..." Her voice trailed off. "Don't tell me details. If I'm ever captured and tortured I can't say anything to incriminate you. I can't tell what I don't know," Aunt Lucy had said in jest. She smiled, and made it seem like a joke. Lou knew better.

And she knew the answer to her aunt's question. Even before she began her hunt, her search, she instinctually knew that the murder of her family was part of a large and intricate web. After the research into Gus Johnson and the Martinellis, the world changed. The world she was taught existed dissolved. A new, more menacing world reshaped around her. She saw the strings, the puppeteers, and all the figures working in the darkness, controlling what people did and didn't see on the mainstage.

And who better to understand this truth than her? No one needed to make Louie believe there were *in-between* places. She'd traversed these herself. And she knew that in the darkness your senses deceived you. You couldn't trust what you saw, what you felt, or heard—you could trust nothing but the compass inside you, the one you're born with—a force that tugged and urged and spoke inaudibly—and her compass said the work wasn't done.

Yes, there are others. Angelo Martinelli and his brothers. Maybe their father too. And anyone else who had a hand in it.

"Listen to me," Aunt Lucy said, fighting for Louie's attention. "This is very important."

Louie lay flat on her back and gazed up at the woman.

"I know you must be so angry. *I'm* angry." Lucy swallowed before going on. "When I think about your father, I'm filled with so many regrets. There are so many things I wish I'd said to him. And about a million things I would have done differently. I'll never get that chance. We must learn how to live with this, Louie. You and me."

Louie's throat tightened, and her eyes burned. She thought of her father, her last vision of him from the bottom of their swimming pool. His figure blurred and distant as she swam futilely toward him. If she had reached him—if she had pulled him into the water—

"If you are anything like me," Lucy went on. "You think you could have saved him."

"I could—"

"No," Aunt Lucy stopped her. "*No*, and that's my point. You couldn't have done anything differently."

"But—"

"I know you don't believe me now, but you'll see I'm right if you stop and take a minute to think about it." Lucy pressed her lips together, wet them, and then continued. "Your father would not have *let* you do anything differently."

Louie came up on her elbows.

"He pushed you into the pool, knowing you would escape. That's what he wanted. It was *his* choice. And he would sacrifice himself for you every time, no matter what you did differently. He made his choice, and we have to live with it."

"He deserves justice," Louie had said. *I deserve it.* "What else am I going to use my ability for? Why do I even have it?"

"Why?" Lucy repeated. Sadness pinched her brow. "Why do ET salamanders breathe through their skin? Why do tufted deer have fangs and eat meat? Creatures adapt to their environment. An evolutionary necessity here. A chromosome mutation there. *Why* you have it is to survive. And it's what your father wanted when he sacrificed himself to save you. He wanted you to survive."

He wanted you to survive.

Louie burst into tears. She wasn't sure why her aunt's words had affected her, but that small admonishment had cut deep. Her guilt soured.

"It's not too late to honor his wish," her aunt said, stroking Louie's hair and rocking her softly in her arms. "It's never too late to let it go. Promise me you'll try to let go, Louie."

But the image of Johnson's bloody lips was already burned into her mind. Louie knew it was too late to let go. Even at seventeen, she understood that when you're this deep, it's best to keep swimming or you'll drown. She'd survived her revenge. She'd taken out all the Martinellis who'd killed her parents one by one. And now there was only Konstantine left.

Konstantine.

Bright eyes. A man in a doorway.

The hot water scalded her hands to the color of raw meat and was now turning cold. She reached up and turned off the faucets, but she didn't move away from the sink.

But you'd gone to him before you'd ever thought about revenge, a voice reminded her. *Something else is happening here.*

She reached up and wiped the steam off the mirror, revealing her hard face.

Her compass whirled. Something was pulling at her again, urging her to step into the darkness and follow the current.

The one thing she trusted was betraying her.

And she did trust her compass. Even when she questioned La Loon and why she would ever be drawn to such a nightmarish place, she came to trust the result all the same. The universe—as her aunt would call it —knew her family would be betrayed, knew she would need such a place to do her work. Even as dangerous and violent as her first visit had been, it had been necessary.

And every jump ever since.

She trusted that voice. So why did she feel like she couldn't trust it now?

"No," she said to the woman in the mirror staring back at her. She wasn't going to let herself be pulled around and controlled. "*No.*"

The compass trembled, telling her it was time to go. There was somewhere she needed to be.

Master this, Lou-blue. Don't be its victim.

Her resolve solidified at the sound of her father's voice in her mind and the feel of his heavy hand on her scarred shoulder.

The compass wavered.

"I'm not a victim," she said, clutching the sink. She held firm to the world around her. "I say where I go."

26

King stared into the gun barrel, into the gaping black eye of Brasso's gun. "You little prick."

Brasso gave a good ol' boy shrug. "What can I say, Robbie? You've always been a little too eager to see action."

"You didn't want me to build a case against Ryanson. You wanted me to find Venetti for him."

"You've always been good at finding things. I knew if I set you on her trail she'd turn up sooner or later. But I must admit, this was a quick turnaround, even for you." Chaz's eyes flicked to Mel, and King stepped to shield her. "Did you get your pet psychic to read her cards or something? I'd like to see what other tricks she knows."

Mel huffed. "Why don't you come over here and *pet* me and see what happens."

King said nothing.

Chaz's smile widened. "You always liked them a little mean."

King was desperate to turn his head, to look over his shoulder into the dark and see if Lou was there. She would come. She *had* to come. And when she did, she was going to shove Brasso's gun so far up his ass the gunmetal would press against the back of his teeth.

King laughed then. The tight sound softened into a hearty chuckle. The damn thing was, once he started, he couldn't stop.

Brasso's brow creased. "What's so funny?"

He couldn't say how hard the humor had struck him. At 59 years old, he'd been hit with the realization, *I'm waiting for a girl to save me!* He couldn't say it. Nor could he make himself stop laughing. His belly began to ache.

Mel arched an eyebrow. "Mr. King, I'm not sure this is the appropriate time to get the giggles."

Brasso raised the gun. "If you don't stop laughing, I'm going to shoot you in the gut."

The little boy voice Brasso used to threaten him made him laugh harder. It had sounded too much like *if you don't give me back my train, I'm going to tell Mom!*

Brasso, face furious, pulled the trigger and put a bullet through a cabinet door. Something in the cabinet, a glass or bowl because he kept both there, ruptured. The door popped open with the force and glass was vomited out onto the stove and countertop. Glittering shards cascading over the countertop to the tiled floor.

King stopped laughing, sweat prickling the back of his neck. "You really want to do this?"

"It's not personal," Brasso said with another shrug. "It's business."

King arched his brows. "Whose business? Ryanson's?"

Brasso didn't answer.

"Did you set me up just to kill me?" King said.

"No. I sent Chuck to find out what you *weren't* telling me, and when he didn't come out, then I came to see what the hell happened."

"Chuck didn't come," King said. Mel shifted beside him.

Brasso snorted. "Your fucked-up face says otherwise. Where is he?"

"I want you to say it. Tell me you're working for Ryanson." King watched Brasso's face, searching each micro-movement for answers he knew the man wouldn't give verbally. "Or is it someone else?"

"That's your problem, Robbie," Brasso said. "You ask too many fucking questions. I should've known you wouldn't find the girl and hand her over. You'd have to ask fucking *questions*."

King thought he would pull the trigger then. His face tightened, and the gun centered on his forehead. And King had time to think about two sets of brains hitting the walls in one night when he saw her.

She appeared behind Brasso, raising a cast iron skillet over her head.

He kept his eyes on Chaz's, so the girl and the skillet remained in the soft focus. He hoped Mel was as unreadable as he was.

Piper brought the skillet down on Brasso's skull, and the man crumpled. The gun fell from his hand and didn't go off. But the clatter along the kitchen tile was as jarring.

Mel threw her hands in the air. "Sweet Jesus, Mary and Moses."

She placed his kitchen rug over the broken glass as if bloody feet were their priority.

"Is he dead?" Piper asked. She touched the hemp necklace around her throat. Her eyes were the size of half-dollars. "Oh my god, am I going to go to prison for killing a dude?"

King bent and pressed a finger to his throat. "He's not dead. And you won't go to prison."

King pulled out his cell phone and Lou's card. He punched in her pager number, and a robot confirmed his page. *Press # if this is an emergency*. King smashed the # with his thumb twice. The robot thanked him. He slipped the phone back into his pocket.

"What are you doing here?" Mel asked. She turned all her fury on Piper.

"Uh," she bit her lip. "I was going to give you this."

She tiptoed around Chaz's collapsed body and passed over a handful of printed pages to King. At a glance, it was the information he'd sent her looking for. Everything the internet could provide on Ryanson and his dealings.

He arched an eyebrow. "You always deliver info at 2:00 in the morning?"

Piper forced a smile.

King stuffed his hands into Brasso's pockets, searching for a phone. Keys. Anything useful. Clues that might let him know the true depth of this rabbit hole.

"Forget Piper." Mel turned her finger on him. "Who the hell laughs at a man pointing his gun at you?"

Piper snorted.

They both turned and looked at her.

"His *gun*," she said with a crooked smile. Then she frowned. "Never mind. Who knew getting shot at made people so *grumpy*?"

"Why were you here?" Mel and King demanded in unison.

Piper held her hands out in front of her in surrender. "Oh, my god. *Calme-toi!* Okay. I was outside creeping. I admit it."

"Why?"

"I was hoping I could bump into King's friend."

They blinked at her. King slipped a hand into Brasso's pockets. Anything. He needed anything to go on.

Piper sighed. "You know. The girl."

"Why would you want to *meet* her?" Mel's eyes were twice as large as normal.

Piper pursed her lips and tilted her head. "Really, Mel? You can't guess."

"It's two in the morning," King said.

"*Puh*-lease!" Piper cried. "The bars aren't even closed. But then I heard the gun go off and so I wanted to check on you."

"You'll get your wish." King pulled a green poker chip, a folded piece of paper, and a pen out of Brasso's pockets. "She'll be here any minute."

Piper pumped her fist in the air. "I knew it! Good things come to those who wait!"

27

Lou's watch buzzed on the island countertop. She leaped off the sofa and snatched it before the third buzzy chirp. A New Orleans number flashed on the screen followed by 911.

King. No one else in New Orleans had her number.

She took 911 to mean *guns*. She threw open a closet. Not *that* closet, and grabbed a shoulder holster. She put it on and holstered her twin Glocks, one on each side. She put a Beretta in the thigh holster.

She was about to duck into *that* closet when the watch buzzed again. She stopped, hand on the cool handle. This number was from San Diego. Also, a 911 page.

The internal compass was whirling, trying to decide which situation was more dire.

"Fuck," she said and threw herself into the dark. She pulled the closet closed behind her.

It was the second time that night she appeared at King's to find a body on the floor.

She stepped into the kitchen with her gun in her hand. Three faces watched her. The landlady was here in her bathrobe, one hand on her hip. Her eyes were narrow. She even shook her head. The girl, the blonde with dark eyebrows and wide, glittering eyes smiled at her. She gave a little wave. Lou humored her with a *hey*. Then her eyes met King's.

She looked from King to the body, to King again. "You're worse than me." She meant the body count. For the last several years she'd thought she was the only one who piled bodies the way others piled laundry.

"Paula isn't safe," King said by way of introduction.

"I know," she said and tapped the beeper tucked into her pocket. "She just paged me."

"Fuck," King said. "We have to go."

The landlady's voice went high. "What about *him*?"

"I need to question him," King said. He cut his eyes to Lou. No one had ever looked at her that way before. Part apology. Part desperation. His lips pursed with a question, but when he looked back at the blonde who was still smiling, the question died on his lips.

Lou took a breath before saying. "You want to save Venetti or question the man? Even I can't be two places at once, King."

King mulled it over. He ran his hands through his hair as if this would help him prioritize.

Lou looked at the girl again, because it was hard not to. She was *staring*. And when someone's gaze was that heavy, you couldn't ignore it.

"What?" Lou asked, scowling at her.

If the girl sensed Lou's irritation, she was not discouraged. "I'm Piper. I'm King's assistant."

The landlady muttered something under her breath.

The beeper buzzed again. Frantic vibration rattled Lou's wrist. It was as if Venetti herself were frantically shaking it. "King?"

"Fuck," he swore. He hissed his disappointment through clenched teeth. "Go without me. Move her somewhere safe and then come right back. I'll need your help with him."

"Bye," Piper said with a pout.

Lou was already stepping toward the closet cut into the bedroom wall. Only when she entered the closet, she stepped out of the world. It spun like a slot machine. Another time and place lining up in the dark.

She would worry about what to tell King's friends later. Then maybe they wouldn't see her at all. She was hidden by the wall. It would be easy to say she'd exited through the bedroom and leapt down off the balcony. Like a cat.

Lou stepped out of the dark into a park. She frowned.

A sidewalk stretched in both directions. Lined with street lamps made to look like antique lanterns on black posts. Her eyes skipped from orb to orb. But the tangerine-colored spotlights were empty, and the trees on either side of the red brick path were still. Not even a cool breeze disturbed the leaves.

A woman screamed. "Help me! Please, somebody, help me!"

A gun fired. Not the enormous *boom-blam* of a handgun. It was the compressed sharp torpedo of a bullet passing through a suppressor. The tree ten feet to Lou's right exploded in a spray of wood chips.

She dropped into a crouch, pulling her gun as she went down. The movement to her left drew her eye. Paula tore past her, running at full speed through the trees. Another bullet struck a tree, another explosion of wood splinters sprayed out into the night. Paula screamed again.

Lou pivoted on her heels toward the source of the bullets and spotted her target. A man, lean like a starving cat, kept shuffling forward. His arm was outstretched, moving in a slow arc as he tracked the woman running through the trees. He wore a baggy black T-shirt that stretched to his knees and dark jeans. His breath came in strangled pants. Tattoos snaked around both arms and up from beneath the collar of his shirt. His jaw clenched as he pulled the trigger again and again.

Paula howled.

Lou put a bullet in his knee. He screamed as blood bloomed on his right leg. His other knee buckled and he went down hard. The gun clattered against the red brick walkway as his palms hit the dirt, breaking his fall.

He moaned and cursed as blood poured from a hole above his knee. His eyes met hers across the walkway, and he snarled. *Snarled*, like a jungle cat in a zoo.

Lou put a bullet between his eyes and the snarl softened to an open, slack-jawed *O*. The eyes went unfocused, rolling up into the back of the shooter's skull at the same moment he fell back onto the grass, limp. She noted the tattoo on his arm, before she ran in the direction of Paula's screams.

She found the girl leaning against a tree, crying. Light cut across her face revealing dirt smudges and sweat gleaming. Her hands were covered in dirt, too. She must have fallen at least once when trying to escape.

Lou grabbed her, and Paula whirled, a large blade flashing in the moonlight. Lou caught her wrist and took the knife away.

"Easy," Lou said, releasing the other woman's hand before she broke it. "Easy does it."

As soon as Paula saw her, all the strength went out of the arms that had been resisting Lou and visible relief washed over her face.

"Thank god," Paula grabbed onto Lou's forearms. "I've been shot."

"Come on." Lou pocketed the knife so she would have her hands free to carry Paula.

Lou pulled her to her feet, and Paula cried out. It was the arm Lou had grabbed. Blood oozed from the deltoid, and because Paula wore a cut-off flannel with no sleeves, Lou could see right into the wound as she pulled the arm. The fleshy mouth puckered as the skin was stretched, pulpy tissue jutting in all directions around the gaping wound. It hadn't been a clean shot.

Lou's stomach hitched, but she didn't let go of the girl. She stepped left, away from the walkway lights and into the cover of the tree's shadows. In a heartbeat, they emerged from the closet of her aunt's Oak Park apartment.

The closet banged open, and Lou fell out into slivers of moonlight. She noted first the temperature change, the way the warm apartment differed from the cool night. Second, her aunt's surprised squeal.

"What in the world?" Lucy stood from the kitchen table and came forward, her mouth opening in surprise.

Lou had counted on this. Counted on the nocturnal habits of her aunt to work for them.

"Are you hurt?" Lucy demanded. Her fear had made her angry.

"I'm fine." Lou rotated her shoulders to alleviate the ache of supporting Paula's weight. "But she's been shot in the arm. Fix her up. She can't go to a hospital."

Lou handed Paula over as if she were nothing more than a bread basket. Paula didn't even protest. She went as easily from Lou's arm to Lucy's, as if forsaking one bit of flotsam for another in a turbulent sea.

Lucy eased her into the kitchen chair. "I'll get my kit."

Lou felt her pager buzz. King. No doubt he was wondering what the hell was going on.

"What have you gotten involved in *now?*" Lucy whispered as she shouldered through, her voice went high with panic. Again, twice in the same night, Lou found herself thinking of her first kill, of taking down Gus Johnson and all the blood that had been on her hands ever since.

"*You* got me in this," Lou snapped. Her eyes fell on the six or seven pill bottles beside Lucy's laptop on the kitchen table. Too many pill bottles. Lou couldn't see the names of the drugs because the type was too small.

Lucy placed a hand on her chest. "She's King's case."

Lou didn't offer an explanation. By way of avoidance, she pulled her gun, counted the bullets, and holstered again. She was searching for what to say. With an irritated hiss, she issued her last order. "Clean her up. Stay indoors. Keep the doors locked."

Her aunt's frown deepened. "Louie, this is too dangerous. God, why did I think I could trust him?"

Lou was already opening the empty linen closet, so much like the one she had back home. Aunt Lucy's closet smelled of lavender and cedar sachets. Lou's smelled of gunmetal and grease.

"Just keep your eyes and ears open." Lou paused with her hands on the linen door. She pulled the knife out of her pocket and shoved the handle toward Paula. "Don't hesitate."

28

Mel dragged a pleading Piper from the room, while King stood vigil over Brasso's unconscious body. Looking at the man turned King's stomach sour.

He tapped his service revolver against his thigh and sighed. "You ambitious fuck."

Because King had no doubt ambition was to blame for this. Brasso had become Ryanson's lap dog in exchange for money or promotions. Did he party on the same yacht the girls were thrown from? Expensive gifts? Luxuries above a DEA agent's pay grade? King tried to think back, searching every memory of his partner for clues. Suggestive conversations.

Brasso always had that *me first* way about him. He remembered a few luxury items. An Armani watch. A $1500 bracelet. But Brasso's first wife had been rich, the daughter of a man with a fashion empire.

King pried open the folded piece of paper he'd found in Brasso's pocket. It was a rectangular sheet of cream stationery, with *Hotel Monteleone* printed in elegant script across the top of the page.

Beneath it, in Brasso's scrawl, was a series of numbers and letters. FLR-CDG 815-1005. CDG-IAH 1040-205.

He also had a pen from Huang's carry-out and a green poker chip.

He slipped these items into his own pockets as Lou reappeared.

King's heart jolted as if kicked by a horse when he saw her. "You got shot?"

She frowned at him, looking down at herself as if seeing all the blood for the first time. She met his eyes. "Not mine."

Nausea rolled over him. "Venetti?"

"Shot in the shoulder. She'll live. Lucy is cleaning her up."

King flinched at the mention of Lucy.

Lou clenched and unclenched her fists. "Decide what to tell her before she murders you."

He ran a hand through his hair. There was nothing he could say to Lucy that wouldn't provoke her wrath. She'd expected him to rehabilitate Lou. Help her find a better way of slaking her bloodlust, not launch a death match against a senator and a corrupted DEA agent. "Let's hurry then. I want to solve this before she tears me limb from limb."

Lou frowned at the unconscious man. "I'll dump his body in La Loon."

King swallowed. "Okay."

To his surprise, he hadn't realized until this moment he might have to kill Brasso. He had no desire to kill his friend, even if the fucker had been about two seconds from putting a bullet in him.

But as soon as he'd said it, he knew she was right. Killing Brasso was a real possibility. What was the alternative? Turn him over to the authorities? Maybe. But his leverage against Brasso, an active serviceman, was limited.

It didn't help that he couldn't explain himself as well as he'd like. If he found himself in a media maelstrom, how would he explain how he found Venetti? How did he get to San Diego? He would start to look as suspicious as Brasso and twice as fast. And King saw the destruction of Jack Thorne firsthand. Being the good guy didn't immunize you against public opinion or the consequences of that public opinion.

King said, "I think he was staying at the Monteleone. I want to check his room."

Lou frowned. "Do you want to investigate or interrogate first?"

He hesitated.

She arched an eyebrow. "He isn't going to stay unconscious much longer."

She was right. Damn.

Lou's eyebrow arched higher as she watched him debate inside how to deal with his traitorous friend. "I have a place."

"What do you mean *a place?*"

"Somewhere to hold him where he won't be found and he can't escape."

A chill ran up King's spine. "No one should have a place like that."

She looked up at him through dark lashes. "I do."

"Fine," he said and bent to help lift the man. "We'll take him—"

She already had him up under the other arm, lifting. King tried not to gape at her. It was discrimination, he knew, to be surprised a woman was as strong as he was. And while he might not have controlled his gaping mouth as well as he could have, at least he had not said anything stupid like *how much can you lift?*

The fact that she'd pulled Brasso out of his arms and balanced him against her shoulder was testament enough. Brasso was 220 at least.

"Grab on to me," Lou said without any hint of strain in her voice. King reached out and placed one hand on her hip before realizing it was far too intimate, the feel of her taut core under his hand. He moved it up to her shoulder, inching his finger between her shoulder and Brasso's bicep.

She pulled him toward his armoire as if it wasn't there. He had a moment of disbelief when he thought she was going to crash right into the giant piece of furniture. It was dark. Maybe she didn't see it?

"Hey—" he began, but the word stuck in his throat. His stomach dropped, and he was riding down the impossibly high roller coaster again, his body caught in a slipstream.

Then the ground came, and his knees buckled, wobbling.

"Fucking hell," he groaned and stumbled away from her. "I'm never going to get used to that."

King let his eyes adjust to dim light. It was completely dark in this space. And it was a space. No more than eight feet by eight feet. And as King ran his hands along the wall, he knew it was made of metal. Ore, perhaps. The scent of rust was strong. There was no door. No window. No hinges of any kind. Lou had popped them right into a sealed box.

His panic rose. The walls seemed to move an inch closer to the center, ready to crush him flat. "Where are we?"

She didn't answer. She propped Brasso against a wall and a fan kicked on somewhere. King felt a stream of cool air pump into the sealed box, and he used the back of his bare hand to follow the stream. When he was right beneath it, he jumped, arms stretching up, groping for the vent, but he grabbed nothing.

"It's twelve feet up," Lou said.

"What kind of place is this?" he asked. The walls were moving in on him. He felt the familiar closing of his throat. Claustrophobia bit into the back of his neck.

"I'd tell you," she said, her hands clamping down on his arm. "But I'd have to kill you."

Another chill ran up his spine. He opened his mouth to say something funny, anything to lessen the tension squeezing his chest, but the rollercoaster drop came again. The world had been yanked out from under him, and he was falling through the dark.

His legs trembled when the ground reappeared.

Lou let go of his arm, and he wobbled even more.

"A little warning," he hissed. He ran a hand over his face, but closing his eyes intensified the dizziness. Despite the nauseated waves in his guts, relief swelled in his chest. No box. No crushing claustrophobia. He ran a palm over his sweaty face.

Lou looked as steady as a 9-to-5 job with an employer-matched 401K.

"Why doesn't it affect you like this?" he asked. He would've asked her any question right then if it meant pushing the walls of his world out.

Lou shrugged at the mouth of the alley. She stepped back into the light and looked up and down the street. "Lucy would say, 'Why would a bird get motion sick when it's flying?'"

"Call me a penguin then," King said and stepped into the light.

The Hotel Monteleone gleamed. The imposing white building loomed with its textured surface and grand flags hanging on either side of the shining entrance. It was in the Antebellum style and looked like a horse and carriage would pull up at any moment, Southern Belles stepping out in their glossy gowns, fans waving in their white-gloved hands.

"Do you know his room number?" she asked.

"No," he sighed. The night air cooled the sweat on the back of his neck. "But I've got these."

He put the poker chip, the folded stationery, and Huang carryout pen in her open hand.

She scowled at him. "What the hell am I supposed to do with this?"

King frowned. "Can't you use your *compass* to find out where these things came from?"

She snorted and shoved the objects back into his hand. "You're confusing me with your landlady. I'm not psychic. I don't touch objects to my forehead and see the future. I'll slip and see where it takes us."

"Then how does it work?"

"Here's your warning." She pulled him back into the alley.

This time, King managed to suck in a breath before the rollercoaster dropped, but he was no less wobbly when they appeared inside a hotel room.

Double beds in golden coverlets and gaudy curtains. Far too many ruffles for King's taste and the overkill was intensified by the pinstriped wallpaper. He suspected he would have appreciated the wallpaper, maybe even liked it, had the décor been more neutral.

"This is a grandma room," Lou said.

King scanned the room. A laptop sat on the cherry desk with curved feet. The cover had a DEA sticker on it they'd all received at an annual conference a few years back. He plopped into the desk chair, the wheels sliding under him.

He opened the laptop and saw the screensaver. Brasso was on a beach, reclining in a lounge chair, his pasty white arms looking too vulnerable in the blaring sun. A drink the color of sunrise sweat condensation in his right hand. He smiled behind enormous sunglasses and an oversized hat.

"Do you know his password?" Lou asked, her tone impatient. What? Wasn't he moving fast enough for her?

King huffed. "I have no idea. Wait. I can find out."

Lou unplugged the laptop and wrapped the power cord around it. Then she moved on to a black leather satchel, lying against the rolled arm of a chair. Papers jutted from several pockets, and from where he stood, King could see the tabs of manila folders, much like the one Brasso had given him, sticking out of the open mouth.

Lou threw the satchel over her shoulder. It was amazing, actually.

The way she came into the room, quickly identified what was important, and rushed on. God, it reminded him of Jack's hawk eyes.

"Why the rush?" he asked.

She gave him a look he knew well. It was a look his ex-wife had given him every time something came out of his mouth.

"He had friends. They could show up. Or your friend could already be awake."

All true but King thought it was something else too. Was it the light in the room? She was still, her movements calm in the shadows. But in the light, she couldn't move fast enough.

The black face of her pager flashed in the lamplight.

"Can you jump through your worm holes with technology without frying it?" After all, he'd had his cell phone in his pocket as he had slipped with Lou to San Diego the first time. He had not thought to ask or show concern until now.

She followed his gaze, glancing down at her wrist. "I've never had a problem with this."

"Isn't a computer a little more complex?"

"It's turned off. We'll be fine," she said with an air of irritation. "What else are we looking for?"

King wasn't sure. She tossed the satchel stuffed with the papers and laptop at him. It hit him in the chest, the corner of the laptop catching his ribs.

He harrumphed.

Because she wants her hands free, he realized. She can't get to her guns as quick as she liked, not bogged down by Brasso's things. The idea struck him again, the bizarre absurdity that he was traveling around with a young, beautiful woman whose primary concern was her weapon. Not having drinks with friends. No dancing or shopping, or any of the other strikingly feminine interests his wife had when he met her—at about Lou's age.

There was a sound in the hall. A cart on squeaky wheels rolled past the closed door. King and Lou both held their breath until the person whistling *Sunshine, My Sunshine* rolled right on by. King smelled boiled meat. Pot roast maybe. Or stew.

When she spoke again, her voice was much lower. "Are we done?"

He adjusted the computer against his chest. "Yeah. No. Check the safe." Something in his brain clicked into place. "If there's anything else, it'd be in there."

She went to a coat closet by the entrance and slid back the mirrored door. Wooden hangers hung waiting on a metal bar that ran the length of the closet. An iron sat in a cradle nailed to the wall. An extra pillow and blanket wrapped in protective plastic rested on the top shelf. The safe, a metal box the color of bullets, was open, the door wide. It was bare. Nothing but shadows inside.

"Let's go," King said. "Is Brasso going to be okay, if we go somewhere else first?"

He wasn't sure what the conditions for his cell were. Maybe they'd stuffed him in a furnace that would kick on and burn him to a crisp.

"He'll hold." She turned off the hotel lights and left King in pitch black darkness. He stood there, heart pounding, desperate for his eyes to readjust. A sliver of light from the Quarter poked through the side of the curtain, an inch between the fabric and the wall itself.

Then he felt her hand on his in the dark.

"Do you know where you want to go?" she whispered. Her mouth was hot on his face. "For the password?"

"Yeah," he managed, half-choking on the word. The walls moved in again.

The coaster dropped, and for a moment he thought he let go of the laptop in surprise. What would happen if he let go while they were in motion? Would the darkness gobble it up? Would the item fall into some space between one place and another, like coins between sofa cushions never to be seen again? Like the second sock that went into the dryer, but never came out again?

Then the ground was shaking. No, it was his legs shaking beneath him.

His eyes focused on an illuminated sign hanging above a doorway. It was the Saint Louis DEA office. The two-story brick building looked like any other municipal headquarters. Square. Practical.

"What the—" he started. He hadn't seen this building since he retired and it hadn't changed one bit with its boxy exterior and rows of windows. The staggered positions of the blinds. Some down. Some up. Some at half-mast. They gave the impression of a man not quite right in the head looking back at him.

"Isn't this where you wanted to go?" It didn't sound like a question.

"I thought Brasso had transferred to a Texas office. But if this is where your compass took us…" He couldn't question her sense of direction. She'd found the gaudy hotel room on the first try.

"Will anyone be in there?" Her eyes measured the plain brick façade. A breeze blew her hair into her face.

"Not yet, but some of the guys get here as early as four in the morning."

"What about cameras?" she asked, swiping at her eyes.

"Not where we're going. It's an office, not a pawn shop."

She pushed him back a step, beneath the thick limbs of an old oak tree, and the roller coaster took another hill. Then they were stepping out of a bathroom on the second floor. He knew this bathroom. It had been a year since he'd taken a piss in one of these bleached white urinals while looking at the off-white and teal alternating tiles. But he knew exactly where he was the moment he saw it.

The light flickered on as they stepped out of the stall. Lou pulled her gun.

"Motion-sensors." King pressed a palm against the top of her gun and pushing it down before she put a bullet in something. Can't be leaving a bullet behind in Headquarters. They could analyze it in the basement for fuck's sake and who knew what kind of trouble that would conjure. "It was part of the measurements enacted with last year's budgets. All the lights are motion-sensor. Presumably to cut down on electricity consumption."

She hissed. "I hate motion-sensor lights. Get whatever the hell you need and let's get out of here."

King took the lead, but before yanking open the handle, he grabbed a scratchy brown paper towel from the dispenser by the door. He used it to cover the handle as he yanked the door open. He doubted most of the unhygienic fucks he'd worked with had learned to wash their hands in the months since he'd left.

Propping the door open with a heel, he waited, tossed the brown towel toward a waste bin, and missed by a mile. Lou crossed in front of him, sweeping her gun over the hall. There was nothing in either direction. The lights overhead clicked on again, and he saw Lou's shoulders twitch. The hall smelled like a burnt burrito, the scent of someone abusing their microwave privileges. And the air was artificially cool from the overworked A/C.

"Hurry up," she said, squirming beside him. "We have to get out of here."

"Easy girl," he said. He led her right toward the door at the end of the hall. "We'll be quick."

King searched for little black globes protruding from the ceiling. There had been no cameras when he retired, but things could have changed.

His shoulders relaxed when he saw the smooth, white tiles above.

In the bright hallway fluorescents, the blood caked on Lou's skin and clothes was even more horrifying. Lou looked like a victim from a slasher movie, who had dragged herself out of some hellish pit toward safety after watching all her friends get hacked up. She had said it wasn't her blood, but no one would know it by looking at her.

Her demeanor was far more solid than any victim, though. In this movie of his mind, he wouldn't have been surprised if, at the end of the movie, it was revealed she had been the one who'd wielded the machete all along.

The door at the end of the hall was locked, but only until King fished some keys out of Brasso's satchel and started fitting them into the lock. The door popped open with the fifth key.

It creaked on its hinges as it swung inward. The office was dim, but the moment he saw it, he knew it was still Chaz's office. The desk was littered with sandwich wrappers and papers. Cardinals action figures were poised in a row at the front-most edge. Old paper cups with half-finished beverages were sweating rings onto computer printouts. The blinds behind the desk sat at half-mast, revealing the empty parking lot littered with symmetrical orange spotlights illuminating the pavement.

Across from the desk along the wall was a giant whiteboard. The last note scrawled in green sharpie was dated six days ago:

Brasso- Lieutenant wants to talk when you get back. Answer your phone, you fat cunt. -Stevens

So, he'd been out of the office for nearly a week. One week, hunting New Orleans, checking him out, baiting him with false cases and pulling his heartstrings for remembered glories.

The light started to flicker overhead as they stepped into the room.

Lou growled and slammed the butt of her gun into the plastic switch on the wall. Sparks shot out, and plastic pieces of the broken socket rained onto the floor.

King jumped back and swore.

Darkness fell over Brasso's office. The remaining light came from the orange spotlights outside.

"Jesus Christ. Was that necessary?"

"Yes," Lou said. The growl had not left her voice entirely. "I *hate* motion-sensors."

King took one look at her, the angry snarl marring her features, and let it drop. He wanted to argue that of all the rooms in the DEA head-quarters, perhaps light would be useful in here at least. He'd like to see where he was looking. But as his eyes readjusted to the darkness, he realized perhaps that wasn't true.

Generous light the color of daylilies spilled across Chaz's desk from the parking lot outside. He relied on it as he bent down and reached a hand underneath. A momentary fear seized him as he stuck his hand into the darkness. He thought a hand would reach out and grab him, yanking him off to some godforsaken place.

But no cold hand of death grabbed his. His arm disappeared as if painlessly amputated by the darkness. He reached up and felt the under-part of the desk, his fingers running over the gritty pressed board until his nails snagged on the corner of a piece of paper. He gingerly felt around the corners, memorizing the edges before using his thumbnail to separate the tape from the desk's underbelly. *Thank god*, he thought. He was lucky Brasso was a creature of habit.

He sat back in his old partner's desk chair and read the baby blue post-it aloud.

"booBiEs4Me," he said and snorted.

Lou arched an eyebrow.

King felt the heat rise in his face. He turned the post-it toward her so she could read it for herself.

"A mature guy," she said, nervously thumbing the safety of her gun on and off as she peered through the crack in the door down the lighted hallway. The lights flickered off to conserve energy now that no motion was detected. He could see something in her relax visibly as darkness overtook the building once more.

King removed the laptop from the backpack and powered it on. As soon as he was prompted, he entered the password from the sticky note.

"How did you know he would have his password taped under his desk?" Lou asked. Even her voice was softer now in the darkness. The strident irritation clipping her words had dissolved.

"We were partners for a long time," King said. He felt his throat tighten as if a beignet had gotten stuck halfway down and was threatening to either suffocate him or come back up. He swallowed again. *And he saved my life. Something about that really makes you pay attention to a person afterward.*

"How long?" Her voice dropped, soft.

"Fifteen years," he said. "He was my first."

"How romantic," Lou said.

He looked up and met her eyes, expecting derision or the bland sarcasm he'd been privy to before. But her face wasn't flat and unreadable. Her lips were turned up on one side. Sympathy.

"You were betrayed," she said, her face a perfect mask of seriousness.

He wanted to ask her what the hell she knew about betrayal. She was too young and didn't appear to have anyone in her life. She only trusted Lucy, and Lucy wouldn't squash a bug, on principle alone.

But then he thought of Gus Johnson. The way he'd acted in the days following Jack Thorne's death. Or hell, the way *he'd* acted in the days after Jack died.

"Louie," he asked softly. Darkness was intimate. You didn't shout in the dark. You whispered. You held holy deference as if you were in an inner sanctum. In the presence of some ancient primal force. A god, maybe. In this case a goddess. A goddess of the dark. "Did you kill Gus Johnson?"

"He betrayed my dad," Lou said, without hesitation. "He gave Martinelli our address."

"Jesus Christ," he said and ran a hand over his head. "You just confessed to murder."

"Did I? I don't believe I did." Lou asked with a hint of amusement in her voice. "I'm just stating facts."

He realized it was true. She had not filled in the gaps for him. She's said the exact thing she needed to say to let him know *of course* she'd killed him.

"All they ever found at his house was blood," King said. He remembered going to Johnson's house himself. He wasn't in homicide and had no business being there. But Kennedy was the lead on the case, and Kennedy had looked up to King since the academy. He knew Johnson was one of his old students and gave the older man his due.

He also knew the Johnson case was cold. Long dead in its grave. So dead, daisies were sprouting through the dirt annually. Unless King stumbled upon a bloody weapon or Lou confessed on tape, he had nothing that would reopen it.

And he found he didn't want to turn the girl in.

How the hell had she worked him over so thoroughly in such a short time?

"You wouldn't have been more than sixteen or seventeen when Gus... disappeared," he said, typing the password into the blinking white box. Then he waited for the main screen to load.

"Is that so?" She wasn't shutting him down exactly. The same humor was there, beneath the surface. He had nothing, and she knew it. She knew his best grab was nothing more than smoke and shadows.

"Was he your first kill?" King asked.

The smile on her lips flattened. She didn't answer. And in its way, it was an answer unto itself.

Yes, the voice said in the back of his mind. It had been her first kill. And if that was true then Lucy had truly tried to deal with this on her own, tried to rehabilitate the girl and keep her from going nuclear. She'd tried for a long time before caving and asking King for help. He did the math in his head because Gus had been dead for eight years.

But it also meant Lou had been out for eight years, hunting and destroying the Martinellis, and that was a lot of ammo to go through. A lot of bullets fired. King was under no delusions a person could be rehabilitated after that much killing.

She's too wild. King imagined himself breaking the news to Lucy. *I'm sorry.*

"What does the computer say?" Lou asked. She didn't look at him. Her gaze remained fixed on the hallway beyond the crack they'd left in the door.

King blinked, pulling himself back to the task at hand. The screen had several documents still up as if Chaz had been in the middle of something when he'd powered it down and walked away. Or he'd stepped away from the computer, and the screen had locked itself after minutes of inactivity.

It was information for two flights.

King opened the satchel and started searching for the scrap of paper he'd lifted from Brasso's pocket. He found the folded piece of stationary and read the numbers again: FLR-CDG 815-1005. CDG-IAH 1040-205.

He looked at the screen. Flight numbers.

"It looks like he was expecting someone," King said.

Lou came around the desk and peered over his shoulder at the laptop screen. "Who was on both flights?"

After minimizing two tabs, voila. Lists for each flight sat framed in the screen. "I'm the detective here."

"You're not a detective," she said. "You said so yourself."

"I'm the one with experience." He regretted saying it immediately. After all, if they were going to compare credentials, he knew how he'd size up in the body count. King only killed one man in his life, and it hadn't been intentional.

He stopped scribbling names. "There's only four passengers who were on both flights."

He showed her the list:

Sasha Drivemore
William Glass
Paolo Konstantine
Dominic Luliani

Her shoulders stiffened.

"See something?" He asked, his eyes running down the list again. None of the names meant anything to him.

"Yes."

After a full minute, he made an *out-with-it* gesture with his hand, waving it encouragingly in the air. "Secrets never made friends."

"Konstantine." Her face scrunched up as if she'd gotten a whiff of rotten meat. "He's Martinelli's son."

"Martinelli's son? I thought you killed all of Martinelli's sons?"

"There's one left."

"What the hell does Ryanson want with him?" King asked, more to himself than to anyone else.

A car door shut and they both froze.

King scrambled to his feet, closing the laptop and adjusting the leather satchel on his shoulder. He pivoted in the desk chair and peered out the window. A red Sedan sat parked beneath one of the orange halos.

A man in a brown suit with a green tie sauntered toward the building with a travel mug in his hand. King didn't recognize him. But at four in the morning, it was probably some young buck, recently hired, putting in the hours to get ahead.

King turned and stopped. He blinked twice, but the scene didn't change.

Lou was gone.

He was alone in the room, and down the hall, the motion-sensors began to click on.

29

K onstantine stepped off the sidewalk in front of his expensive hotel room and toward a black sedan pulling up to the curb. The car stopped, and he lifted the handle, but it didn't open. A man from the driver's seat exited the car and came around to open the door for him.

How strange American men are, Konstantine thought. The richer they become, the more they like to appear helpless. Unable to open their own doors or drive themselves. Cook for themselves. They evolved into entirely cerebral creatures who would do well to be plugged into giant computers, pumping their thoughts and decisions into a main-frame. Their bodies would remain motionless and out of the way while they exerted their real authority on the lives of others.

Konstantine forced a smile despite his desire to open and close his own door. *When in Rome.* "Thank you."

The driver dipped his head in acknowledgment.

Konstantine slid into the car. The temperature shift was shocking. One moment, he stood under the blanket of Texas heat. The next, he was in the car's refrigerated interior. The enclosure gave the impression of a grave. A large box deep in the earth and surrounded by crawling things on all sides.

Senator Ryanson smiled at him from across the seat. He wore a gray suit with a red tie. The suit made Konstantine think of small rabbits he had seen as a boy. Vulnerable things which could easily be squashed beneath the tire of a car in the city center if it had dared to dart across the cobblestone at the wrong moment.

"Mr. Konstantine," Ryanson said with a wry smile. It did not reach his eyes. "A pleasure."

The man reached across the seats and offered his hand. Konstantine knew the American custom and accepted it. The hand was frigid. A corpse's hand, fitting for the corpse box they sat in.

The car pulled away from the curb without instruction.

"I can give you twenty minutes of uninterrupted access to the HIA database," Ryanson said. Straight to business. "Will this be enough time to gather the intel we need?"

"Yes," Konstantine said. He did not care to elaborate. *More than enough to get what I want on you.*

"Once you link up," Ryanson said, the same false joviality puppeteering his features. "How long do we have before they know something is up?"

"It depends on the nature of their security," Konstantine said, his shoulders tensing against the leather seats. "The more security, the less time."

"As long as I'm on my party boat and celebrating by 6:00." Ryanson smiled again. This time, the smile was genuine. His eyes crinkled at the corners, and he shared a wide toothy grin with Konstantine before raising a rocks glass to his lips and drinking. Ice clinked against the rim, and Konstantine found himself staring at the water ring on the knee of his pants where he'd balanced the beverage.

"This is why I brought you here," Ryanson said with a grin. "Sponsored your visa, got you through customs. It was a small price to pay for such brilliance. You know we brought Einstein here too. Another political refugee."

And what about my brothers? What had you brought them here for?

He couldn't ask, of course. It was too soon to give up the game.

And the American was babbling again. Konstantine wanted to look out the window, watch the streets and buildings go by. He marveled at American architecture. It all seemed so new. So infantile. Malformed like a child's building blocks. In his country, they built with stone and rock. They prepared for war, having a long history and the basic comprehension it *would* come.

Even the newest buildings in his country had perhaps a century or more on these chapels made of glass and electricity. Where would the Americans hide when the war reached their shores? Not in these glass giants so easily brought down by their own vulnerability and gravity.

It was moments like this when Konstantine thought of his mother. She had done nothing wrong. She'd caved to Martinelli's affections because to rebuke him would mean her death. But what had it gotten her? A heartless end. Another man who'd wanted to hurt Martinelli but couldn't reach him, hurt her instead. Like a lion grabbing the weaker gazelle in the herd.

As of now, he knew of at least one other woman who'd lost her life this way.

Louie's mother.

"Not a very talkative man," the senator said, and he did not bother to hide his sneer. "You know, in America, we would call that rude."

"I prefer not to speak unless I can improve upon the silence," Konstantine said and offered his best disarming smile. *And you are talking enough for the both of us.*

The senator's sneer softened. "You'll enter the HIA with me under the pretense of my personal bodyguard. When I begin to speak to Fenner, I will leave you by the door. It's customary, a sign that I trust him as we do our cloak and dagger negotiations. It's all about the Mexico trade agreement. As much as you might want to be privy to *that* conversation, I think we both know you have something better to do."

Konstantine acknowledged him with a nod of his head. He thought, *I wonder how she will do it? Will she put a bullet between your eyes? Or will she use a blade? Slowly? Enjoy it?*

"The door to his inner office is to the right, and the door to the hallway is to the left. Take the office door instead of exiting and you can work your magic." Ryan fiddled with his cuff link again. "I'll spill my drink when it's time to go."

"It's like a spy movie." Konstantine smiled.

The congressman tilted his head and smiled back. "I thought it was a clever idea."

You're an imbecile. Elected by imbeciles who do not know how you work against them. She will see right through you. She'll know you for exactly what you are.

The congressman went on smiling. "Regardless, this computer is on the HIA server. You'll be able to do what you need to do from there."

"And after?" Konstantine asked with a grin to mirror the senator's.

The congressman's smile turned wolfish. "Then I will take you out on my boat to celebrate. Have you ever seen the Houston harbor at night?"

"No," Konstantine said.

"It's beautiful. Absolutely to die for."

30

Lou leaned against the cool tree trunk, clutching the bark as if it were a great log in a wide river. Her compass spun inside her. One part of her wanted to go back to King. She saw him in the upstairs window, in the fat bastard's office, a sliver of light across his face as he searched the hallway.

Another part of her wanted to go to Lucy. Aunt Lucy needed her. Was it Venetti? Or was some greater, more venomous danger on the move? She couldn't be sure. A third part of her pulled again toward Konstantine. At last she'd put the name to the face. And once she'd seen him, her compass forever marked his direction. When she listened through the darkness of her mind, she could smell him, the thick musk of his cologne and the pulse of his heart in the back of her head.

Stay, she commanded her shaking legs. *Don't be the victim, Lou-blue*, her father said. His voice echoed in her bones as if he was beside her, cooing encouragement into her ear. As if he'd never left her. *Master this*.

"I'm in charge," she said. All her life she'd been a slave to this greater current.

No more.

I say where we go. Get King. Then my apartment.

Lou let go of the trunk and plunged through reality's fabric. She reached out and grabbed the back of King's coat. He still had his face pressed to the crack of the door, searching the hallway for his chance to escape.

He sucked in a breath when she yanked him away from the door, but whatever he was about to say was swallowed up by the black ocean stretching between two fixed points in time and space. When they stepped out, they were in her closet. King's enormous body squished hers. The closet was too small. Grunting, she squeezed through the door. Fresh air hit her full in the face.

Lights from the buildings along the river danced across her apartment floor. While cabs raced down wide boulevards outside, she crossed the room and removed a painting that hung on the brick wall. A replica of Picasso's "Girl with a Mandolin." She'd always loved this picture since the first time she saw it with Aunt Lucy in the MOMA. It was a perfect representation of her being.

A girl, all broken up, but recognizable.

That's what happens to me when I slip through the darkness, she thought. She split into pieces, fed through the cracks and reassembled on the other side.

She propped the painting against her shin and pressed three bricks on the wall. A click rang out. The façade popped out. She peeled back the edge of the brick, revealing a gray steel safe set into the wall. Lou entered her six-number combination until the safe also clicked open. She shoved aside the extra guns and stacks of cash and grabbed a handful of glow sticks. She also grabbed one of the guns and extra ammo—the kind that exploded when it hit its target, leaving more shrapnel in the body than could be dug out.

She'd slipped it off a table at a gun show. The dealer, a man missing one of his front teeth, the other half-dissolved in blackened decay, hadn't even seen her do it. She was in and out of the shadows before he could ask her to show ID.

"I thought you lived in a hovel," King said. He *was* enormous. A wall of a man in her studio apartment, craning his neck to absorb the details. "I sort of pictured an abandoned warehouse, maybe a mattress in one corner and enough guns and explosives hanging around to take over New York."

He must have seen her glare.

"But this is nice. Real nice," he added.

His eyes roved over her counters, the bare island, and the unused stove. Lou didn't think she'd turned it on once since moving in two years ago.

And if she was honest with herself, she would have been fine with an abandoned warehouse. She'd only gotten this apartment, filled it with home goods and hung art on the walls, so that Lucy would stop begging her to get an address.

King opened a cabinet and found her six water glasses. Another had her four bowls and four plates. The third, a box of crackers and a bag of ground coffee. The other cabinets were bare.

"A man could live here." He pointed at the Picasso. "Men love to have naked boobs on their walls. Even artistic ones."

"I don't want to live with a man." She shoved the guns, ammo, and glow sticks into a canvas bag.

King frowned. "I wasn't suggesting you needed a man. I'm commenting on the gender neutrality of the apartment."

"Get in the closet." Lou tossed him the bag. He doubled over when the sack hit him square in the gut. "We're leaving."

King squeezed himself into the closet and looked ridiculous doing it. His shoulders were hunched up to his ears as she slid in, trying to find a niche for herself. The door wouldn't close on the first try.

"Suck in," she told him.

He snorted. "I am! It's the bag."

"Suck in *harder*."

"You need a bigger closet."

"You need to lose ten pounds."

"That's unfair!" King said, creating another inch or so by angling his body deeper into the corner. "If I said that to you, I'd be an asshole. That's sexism."

Lou managed to get the closet door to click shut and then they were moving, exploding out into the other side.

"Fuck," King said, bumping against the inside of the shipping container deep in Siberia. The cold of the container rushed in on them, raising the goosebumps on her arm.

Lou shoved her hand into the canvas sack, fingers searching until she felt the plastic tubing of one of the glow sticks. She snapped it in half and shook it. Neon orange light filled the shipping container. She handed the stick to King.

"What's this for?" King held the light over his head. From that angle, the tangerine glow illuminated the whole container. Chaz Brasso's dark liquid eyes blinked open in a slow, dazed sort of way.

She handed King three more glow sticks, keeping one for herself, and gave him the gun from the safe along with a full magazine. "Interrogate him. I'll be back."

"What?" he said, panic rising in his voice. "You can't leave me here."

"Lucy needs me," she said, closing the canvas sack and slipping her arms through. "Something is wrong."

His panic only deepened. "If you don't come back, I'll starve in some hole in the middle of fucking nowhere."

"A shipping container in Siberia," she informed him.

"A shipping container!" he exclaimed. "In fucking Siberia!"

"I'll be right back. Hide the stick under your shirt. Wrap your coat around it. Come on. I need a shadow."

When he didn't move, she plucked the transparent tube from his fingers and shoved it into his pocket. Then she was gone.

31

Lucy ran the once-white washcloth under her kitchen sink. Red ribbons of Paula's blood dripped down the back of her hand and into the metallic basin. She watched the blood swirling down the drain with all the intensity of an old crone reading entrails, looking for a way to save her village from an impending drought.

And she hurt like an old crone. The burning in her chest. The swollen and aching feet.

The blood made her think of Jack. Blood always made her think of Jack.

When he was dead, and Louie was missing, she'd gone to the morgue under the cover of night. She remembered how cold the place had been as if stepping into a meat locker. Except this time, the carcasses weren't hanging from the ceiling on hooks, waiting to be hauled down by some butcher in a stained white apron. This time, the flesh was tucked neatly away in drawers, like the kind one might pull open at the bottom of a stainless steel refrigerator to retrieve a soda or a beer.

Except one of these drawers had held her brother.

She'd pulled open the drawer and slid him out.

He was pale and naked on the silver slab. They had not done the autopsy yet, for which she was grateful. But his chest was still a mess.

Nine bullets had punctured the flesh, leaving behind nine puckered black holes. Some were misshapen, and Lucy imagined the morgue attendant inserting snipe-nose pliers into these wounds and digging out the bullets for the cops. They'd need them for their investigation, she was sure. If they intended to hunt the killer, that was. She had doubts. The way they smeared his name, his *good* name, she suspected the cops as much as the disgruntled drug dealers.

Lucy reached out and touched her brother's ghostly pale face. Tears spilled across her cheeks as she placed a hand on the unmoving chest. "I'll look after Louie." She'd promised him. "I'll do my damnedest to keep your baby alive."

She'd been certain, that night in the morgue, the killers who'd murdered her brother would be back for Lou. Much like the ancient Romans, after running through the soldiers with their swords, they dashed the babies' skulls against the hearth for good measure.

"I'll keep her safe," she said again.

I'm sorry, Jack. She thought now at her kitchen sink, watching the years stretch out between now and then. *I didn't do half of what I promised you.*

"Lucy?" Paula said.

The girl's voice pulled Lucy from the daydream of her dead brother. She looked down and saw that she'd wrung the washcloth until the water ran clear. Her knuckles were scalded red by the water still running.

She turned off the faucet. "I'm sorry, what?"

"Can I have another Coke? I don't know what's wrong with me, but I'm so thirsty."

"Sure. Bottom drawer." Lucy nodded at the fridge to her right.

Paula flashed a weak smile, either because her mood had not improved despite the passing danger, or because her swollen and purpling face didn't allow her to smile.

The stainless-steel drawer slid out, and a gust of chilled fog escaped into the kitchen. Instead of a drawer full of soda cans, Lucy saw Jack, chest full of black bullet holes.

She threw the rag in the sink. "Why don't you take some Tylenol with that?" she said. "Your face must hurt like hell."

Paula gave another weak smile as she popped the cap on the soda can. "I'd love some Tylenol. I'd even take something harder if you got it."

The girl's eyes slid to the line of orange prescription bottles lined up on Lucy's table.

"You wouldn't want those," Lucy said and flashed an embarrassed smile. "They're not for pain."

Lucy never made it to the bathroom.

When she stepped out of the kitchen and into the living room, three men stood there. Behind them, her apartment door stood open, revealing the dim hallway with a flickering bulb that the manager had promised to change no less than a hundred times and yet never found a chance to do it between fighting with his wife and the NASCAR races blaring on his television.

All thoughts about Tylenol for the girl left her.

Lucy took in the three men. How had they found her? How had they reached her so quickly? Lou had mentioned San Diego and a vegan drive-thru. But San Diego was a million miles away, and the men here couldn't possibly be the same ones trying to kill the girl.

"Lucy Thorne." The first man said, and he raised the pistol an inch in a sort of shrug. It wasn't a question.

So, she didn't answer.

"You wanna take a ride with us?"

"No," she said. It was a stupid thing to say, but it had come out of her mouth before she'd thought it through.

"Excuse me?" the first one said. His brow furrowed.

"No," she said, fighting to keep her voice even. "I don't want to take a ride with you."

The two men behind him laughed. It wasn't friendly rolling laughter. It was a short, harsh bark like a crocodile snapping at bait dangling two feet above muddy marsh waters.

"Even better," the one in front said and sucked at his teeth. Lucy's skin crawled at the sound. "I like it when they say *no*."

Would you *like to take a ride with us?* Only *you*. No mention of Paula. If they didn't even know about Paula in the kitchen, then this was something else.

Only they hadn't seemed that surprised to her.

A drawer opened and closed in the kitchen and at the same time three guns raised.

Lucy took a step back, her hand going to the hollow of her throat. Her mouth had opened in a dramatic O, but no sound was coming out. Instead, all the air was going in a great panicked gasp.

"Is somebody here with you?" the man in front asked. His furrowed brow had worsened, his lips practically snarling.

She was going to say no, but Paula Venetti stepped out of the kitchen then and bumped into her back. When the girl saw the men with the guns, she shrieked, and she didn't stop shrieking.

"Shut the fuck up!" The first one said, but Paula didn't seem capable of shutting up. Lucy had to turn and clasp a hand over the girl's mouth. Paula trembled in her arms.

They were visibly confused. Each man's brow furrowed. The one in front shuffled his feet. His gun dipped.

But it was the one in the back, the smallest of the men, who spoke. "What is she doing here?"

"I don't know," the front man admitted. "But we'll take her too."

"But Chaz just wanted the one."

"It doesn't matter. We're taking them both."

Go go go, Lucy thought, her mind kick-starting. Her initial shock and panic and the erroneous connection between Paula and these men cleared away. She wanted to protect Paula, and she wanted to warn Lou, tell her not to come back to her place because someone was hunting them. Someone knew about her Oak Park home, and she should stay far away.

And Chaz... that name rang a faint bell.

But there were only three ways out of this apartment. One was the front door, now guarded by three men with guns. The second was a two-story drop to the street below, by either jumping off her balcony or tumbling out of a window. Either would surely end in a great deal of physical damage. The men would find it easy to haul away her busted body. After all, how could she protect herself if she had broken legs or half her brains spilled across the pavement?

The third exit was the closet.

She was already counting out the steps in her head, *eight*, maybe less if she took long loping strides.

She could yank Paula back into the kitchen, but it wasn't dark enough in there. Unlike Lou, who could slip in the barest of shadows, Lucy required full darkness. Dark so black she could hold up her own hand and not see it.

She wasn't sure she could reach the closet before she got a bullet in the head. She couldn't get Paula in the closet with her. The girl would collapse on her shaking legs after the first step.

"What you looking at?" the man asked. His eyes went to the closet. "You got somebody else in there *too*?"

"No," Lucy said reflexively. She regretted the words the instant they left her lips.

The man's brow deepened. "Donnie, look in that closet."

Donnie sported a cleft lip. He looked at the leader for a minute as if he wasn't sure he'd heard him. When he gave him an angry look, he crossed the room toward the closet as if it were the fire exit in a burning building. Lucy became aware of a sharp pain and looked down to see four red fingernails biting into her arm.

She pried Paula's fingers off her flesh and held her hand. The four crescent-shaped impressions ached and burned, but this did not compare to the discomfort of her hammering heart, which had even surpassed her general unease.

The pressure in the room changed. Her ears popped. The man opened the door and peered into the closet.

"Where's the light switch?" he asked, uninterested in going deeper without light. "It's as black as an asshole in here."

Lucy didn't answer him. There was nothing to say. There was no switch. It was a linen closet that had had the shelves removed. She was sure if Donnie had reached up and touched the wall, all he would feel would be the even studs running horizontally, on which the shelves used to balance.

The thick outline of Donnie's body completely disappeared as he reached the back of the closet with his hand outstretched.

Lucy's ears popped again, and she thought she heard a sharp intake of breath.

"Donnie," the leader said.

Donnie didn't answer.

"Donnie!" he snapped. "Dude, what the fuck?"

But still, there was no answer.

The leader raised his gun. "What the fuck?" He punctuated each word with a jab of his gun, and Paula screamed in Lucy's ear, making her head split into two throbbing parts.

"I don't know," Lucy assured them, though she most certainly did, and the realization made her heart pound and ache with more panic. *Stay away*, she begged the inside of the dark closet. *Please god, Lou, stay away.*

Lucy held her hands up in front of her in the universal signal of surrender. She hoped that she would not get shot. Though if she was dead, perhaps that would be preferable than dealing with the difficult road ahead. A long and exhausting illness that was sure to strip her down piece by piece.

The leader considered the closet. His brows pinched together as if he was working on a challenge he had not encountered before. He was doing the math in his head, Lucy suspected. If he sent the other man into the closet, then it might be one against two, and while he had a gun, the odds were against him.

They need us alive, Lucy realized. Alive for some godawful reason. Torture. Or ransom. What did this Chaz want with them?

Chaz...Chaz... her mind searched for recognition but only conjured a body bag and the sight of flashing blue lights against a dark house.

"What's going on with the fucking closet?" he yelled. Confusion made him belligerent, as with most people.

Lucy raised her hands higher, she lowered her voice hoping she sounded calmer than she felt. "How the hell should I know? It's a closet."

"You've got somebody in there! Donnie!"

Donnie still didn't answer.

"Whoever the fuck is in there. If you don't fucking answer or send Donnie out, I'm going to put a bullet in these bitches' heads!" He pointed the gun at Paula who shrieked like someone had stuck her bare hand into a boiling pot.

I can't let them see you. I can't let them have you, Lucy thought, and even as her protective instincts rose, so did the obvious ridiculousness of her statement. *They have no idea what they are dealing with*, a darker voice said. She looked into the open closet, into the pitch black. She couldn't see Lou, but she could feel her there, on the other side of night.

She was one with the dark. More of a primordial force than a girl now, shrouded in a substance that they had mistakenly believed to be the absence of light.

But Lucy had always suspected that wasn't true. Naïve. Darkness was not the absence of light. It was its own substance. An organism that came in and occupied space like any other nocturnal creature in this world.

The gang leader had had enough of the game. He stormed across the room, gun raised, and shoved the barrel against Lucy's forehead.

That was his mistake.

The open closet door had been shielding him. Now his profile was in plain view.

He seemed to realize this a heartbeat after Lucy did. His eyes widened, and he whirled, gun raised.

Then his face disintegrated.

One minute, Lucy was struggling to keep herself between the gun and Paula. The next, half of his skull cap had been blown off. The ripe smell of meat, blood, and piss flooded her apartment.

She stared into glassy brown eyes with bloodshot threads running through the egg white orbs. She noted the acidic smell of his breath. Tobacco. The scar along one side of his jaw that came toward his mouth and pulled at the corner like a fish hook.

Then it was all meat and the white gleam of bone.

The other man who'd waited patiently in the doorway, as if his purpose was to block the only perceived exit from the apartment, jumped back. His mouth popped open in surprise.

Lou stepped out of the closet then, coming around the door with her gun up. The fat man with the oversized T-shirt turned toward her slowly.

He didn't get his gun up in time. Lou put two bullets in him. One in his throat and the other in his upper chest. His strong hand with its short fat fingers went up to his throat and clutched the wound. Blood spewed from between his fingers down over his hairy knuckles.

He started to raise his gun, but she shot him in the hand, and his mouth dropped open in a wordless cry. Only blood gurgled up.

Lucy had an overwhelming desire to cry then. Not because she'd witnessed three lives lost, but because of the absolute calm in Lou's face as she executed the task. She could have been turning on a television or checking her email. Or—god help her—doing something she truly *enjoyed*. Lucy was horrified to realize she'd seen this very expression on her own face when coming out of a deep and satisfying meditation.

Relief, she realized. When Lou killed, it gave her peace.

Lucy's heart was crushed in her chest. She couldn't move. She couldn't speak.

Louie met her aunt's eyes. Her cheeks flushed red. "I'm sorry you had to see that."

Lucy grabbed her and hugged her so hard, Lou groaned.

"Go somewhere safe." Lou wrapped her arms around the smaller woman. "Keep moving until this blows over."

Lucy hugged her harder.

"I'll clean this up." Lou's voice was low and steady.

She put her hands on Lou's cheeks. So hot. On her brow. Blood came off on her hands, but she didn't care. She kept running her hands down the girl's arms and body looking for wounds, looking for fresh blood pouring out of some bullet hole. Lou had always been a stoic child, hiding her pain and fear when they went to the doctor or when she hurt herself playing. Once, when she crashed into a concrete barrier on her bicycle, she'd split open her elbow and needed six stitches. Most children would cry. Louie only said *gross*.

She suspected that tendency to hide rather than show pain had only deepened with her experience.

"I'm okay."

"Are you sure?" she heard herself say. Her voice went high, grew strident. "Maybe you were shot, and you don't feel it. Maybe—"

Lou cut her off by squeezing her hand a little harder. Not enough to hurt Lucy, but enough to get her attention. "Keep moving. I am not sure how big their network is, so try not to draw attention to yourselves, and don't stay in one place too long."

"Too long!" Lucy felt the pulse rising in her temples. "What's too long?"

"A day," she said after a moment of careful consideration. "One night per place."

Lucy touched the hollow of her throat. She could feel her heart pounding against her fingertips there as if it were going to leap out of her throat and fall to the floor.

Jack, she thought. *Oh god, Jack, what have I done? I sent her to King thinking...what had I been thinking?*

By taking Lou to King, she had hoped to cure a problem, not inflate it. Show her that there was a life worth building for her out there in the world. One where isolation and running weren't necessary. But she also did it because...because—

You're dying. You did this to give yourself peace.

But Lucy felt the tears streaming down her cheeks and the uncomfortable way Lou shifted away from her as if those tears carried the plague.

"I'm sorry," Lucy said. "Oh, Louie. I'm so sorry."

Paula tugged on her arm.

"Yes," Lucy said. "We should go. But we need to pack clothes. We can't walk around with all this blood on us. We'll draw too much attention."

She was already picturing the dark YMCA showers in her mind. Both she and Paula could clean up without notice this late into the night. And once clean, move on to somewhere else. She had half a dozen vacation houses in her mind that stood empty this time of year. She wondered how she could package the idea to Paula, *an exciting tour of European closets!* An imaginary brochure read. And then how silly that seemed. She was exhausted, and her adrenaline had turned her mind on its head.

"I'll stay until you pack," Lou said.

And she did. She'd closed and locked the apartment door.

Lucy went into her bedroom and pulled a vintage suitcase from the top shelf of her closet, throwing in clothes, a toiletry bag, and cash into the hard case. Paula trailed her like a puppy at the heels, drawn to movement. By the time she'd returned to the intersection of her hallway and kitchen doorway, she found the apartment empty of bodies.

The blood and mess were still there, but the bodies and the guns were gone.

Lou stepped out of the closet, her hands and forearms slicked up to the elbow with blood. She saw Lucy staring and said, "I'll clean the rest. Don't worry."

Tears stung the back of Lucy's eyes again, and her throat threatened to collapse on itself.

Lucy reached up and cupped Lou's cheek. "Don't die."

First, her mind added. *Don't die* first.

Lucy Thorne didn't think she could bear it.

32

I 'll be twenty minutes. Tops," Ryanson said, and he was saying it loud enough for the men in the other room to hear, but his eyes flicked left, toward a door. "Wait here until I need you. If I need you."

Konstantine did not move or smile or acknowledge him in any way. He remained standing in a foyer of an apartment until the senator had disappeared into the other room and another male voice joined Ryanson's in salutation. Their footsteps echoed the way they did in grand cathedrals back home. *Because their temples are the temples of commerce,* he thought.

Then the sound of chairs creaking and bodies settling in. Briefcase latches released. Someone cleared their throat.

Konstantine stood in the foyer where a magnificent crystal chandelier bloomed overhead. There were three doors: the one they'd entered from, the one Ryanson had exited from, and the last—a dark door to his left.

He waited for a guard to come and check on him.

A man in a red suit and black tie peeked at Konstantine minutes later. Then the guard disappeared again.

He still didn't move, but his eyes slid to the closed door again. He estimated how many steps it would take to reach it. He reminded himself why he was doing this.

When they came for his father, they took his mother instead.

In the middle of the night, men filled their house. They bundled up his mother and pulled a black sack over her head. So he wasn't surprised when they did the same to him. Their hands and feet were tied.

The stairs, the corridor and even the street outside their apartment were all familiar. He'd traversed these spaces so often he could do it with his eyes closed. But once the men put him and his mother into the back of a car, the familiarity was gone.

They drove forever. Or perhaps it was only the night that made the drive seem endless.

Then the car stopped as suddenly as it had started. They waited. His mother tried to soothe him with reassurances. He didn't know what to say to reassure her.

Men were talking outside the car. They were shouting.

Then the doors were thrown open, and he was dragged out. He could smell the linden trees and the night air even through the sack. He heard his mother cry out as she was forced to kneel beside him.

The sacks were torn off.

The first thing he saw was the giant hole in front of him. It wasn't the perfect square usually dug for cemetery plots. It was crude and shallow, wider on the bottom and more narrow at top.

His father stood on the opposite side. He saw him clearly. His mother saw him too and at the sight of him, began to cry. She didn't beg for her life. She begged for Konstantine's.

Somehow Konstantine began to realize what was happening. This was a negotiation. They wanted something from senior Martinelli, and they were prepared to murder his lover and bastard son to get it.

Martinelli resisted, and they shot his mother. Konstantine remembered the look that passed over her face. She'd known death was coming but her mouth still opened in surprise. The sight of her pitching forward, nightgown billowing as she fell into the dark hole. Her gown seemed to glow in the bottom of the dark cradle, but her body had disappeared, swallowed by the shadows.

He did not remember what happened next. He didn't remember returning to Florence. Didn't remember being turned over to Padre Leo for safe keeping. He knew his grief had swallowed him, masticated him to bits and spit out another boy, months later.

None of that bothered him.

He had only one regret.

That he did not pay more attention to his mother's final moments. Consequently, he did not know where she was buried, didn't know how to honor her passing or make sure her bones were properly laid to rest. He could not honor her on her birthday, holidays, or the Day of the Dead.

Good women died at the hands of bad men.

He knew this was true.

But he could not accept his mother was alone in some Italian field, waiting to be found, waiting for a proper burial in a place where her son could visit often. He would make this possible as soon as he found her.

And he *would* find her. Lou would help him. Somehow he knew, Lou would reunite them at last.

When the guard peeked and disappeared for the second time, Konstantine darted for the office door. He reached it in eight steps.

It was an office. Unlit and silent. And completely and utterly dark as he slid the door closed behind him. But leaving it open was stupid. Anyone who walked by would know where he'd gone. But with the door closed, he had only the light from the computer to guide him.

He wasted no time rounding the desk and inserting his USB into the port. The laptop was already open, and three fish swam on the screen as if in an imaginary aquarium. Konstantine punched a series of buttons, and the password screen fell away. The air in this office was cool and the keys soft under his fingertips.

As he furiously typed, he imagined a series of bots marching out of the USB into the defenseless computer, sliding down these channels toward their battle stations.

He strained to hear the men talking. Listened for their booming voices vibrating through the walls, but heard nothing. For all he knew, they could be standing en mass outside the office door, ready to seize him, string him up and tear him limb from limb.

There was also the matter of the office itself. The *dark* office.

Konstantine's eyes kept slipping toward the thickest shadows in the corners of the room. Places where the walls seemed to breathe.

Any minute she would be there. She would appear, her face glowing in the darkness like Banquo's ghost come to choke him in his guilt.

But the shadows remained shadows. The darkness remained still.

And even if she did appear, he couldn't stop. He had to do this.

For his mother. And for Louie.

One did not approach a goddess empty-handed, begging for favor.

On the screen a green bar marking his progress filled. The task was done. He stepped out into the hallway, closed the door again without a sound, and assumed his same statuesque pose.

The guard checked him for a third time.

Konstantine's heart pounded in his ears so hard that he was certain if someone spoke to him, he wouldn't hear it.

As long as no one wanted to shake, he would be okay. If he had to unclasp his hands for any reason, they would certainly notice the tremor in his fingers or the dampness in his palms.

But it didn't matter.

It would be worth it as long as he could complete the job.

Of course, this would be the hardest part.

How to stay alive long enough to deliver the truth?

33

King traced the small container for the hundredth time. Flecks of rust had wiggled beneath his fingernails, and when he tried to dig them out with another short nail, they were only wedged deeper. Now a sharp edge bit into the tender flesh and a line of blood filled the crescent moons.

"My head is killing me," Brasso whined as he pulled himself into a sitting position. And he made a ruckus doing it. His boots boomed against the floor, heels scrapping. And something was wrong with his arm. It lay across his lap, limp as a dead fish. But King couldn't remember anything happening to his arm. Unless Lou had done it.

Brasso rubbed the back of his head. "Did you give me a concussion?"

"No." King's tongue felt swollen. Either he'd bitten it and hadn't realized it, or it was his fear choking him. "You were hit in the head with a cast iron skillet."

"Jesus," Brasso said and touched the back of his head. "I should sue you."

"If you get out of this container alive, you do that." King's heart floundered in his chest.

These walls held no exit. No seam he could pry open. Lou had called it a shipping container, but unless the communists had tried to conserve money by not installing a door, it was an iron coffin.

His mind began a running list of everything that could go wrong.

What if Lou died? What if she was mortally wounded enough to make a return trip impossible?

Would he starve to death? Would Lucy come looking for him?

An air vent kicked on and air smelling like basement pipes filtered into the space. The air, no matter how dank, helped. He remembered what he was supposed to be doing.

He turned to Brasso and aimed his pistol. "Why did you do it?"

"What a stupid question." Brasso snorted and rubbed at his nose. "Why does anyone do anything? For the money. For the perks. If you want to start a conversation with me, Robbie, make it a good one."

"How much did Ryanson pay you?"

Brasso grinned. "A fuck ton. So much you'd piss your panties if I told you."

"Your reputation is fucked," King said, "The moment I get back—"

"Oh come on, King, you're not going to out me."

"The hell I won't."

Brasso laughed. *Laughed.* "You won't. You know why?"

The walls were warping, moving in. This fucking orange light wasn't helping. It gave the room an off-kilter look.

"Because when I go down, I'll smear your name all through the mud with mine. I'll talk about how many cover-ups we did in our years together. I'll point my finger at you so hard you'll feel it up your ass."

The world shifted as if on a tilt. "They won't believe you."

Brasso laughed again. A great big belly laugh. "Oh, they'll believe. And you'll rot in a cell right beside me. And I'll sell out your old ass *again*, more specifically your asshole in this case, to the first young buck willing to give me a cigarette."

King punched him twice. The skin split across his knuckle bones before he caught himself.

He pushed back. He ran a hand through this hair and resumed pacing. He threw one last punch. "Son of a bitch."

Brasso touched his face tenderly and hissed. "Yeah, yeah. You knew what *I* was. Like I've always known what *you* are, Robbie boy. The sanctimonious pratt who wants a gold star for every shit he takes."

King was going to kill him long before Lou returned, he decided. He would do it now, except the only thing worse than rotting in this container, was rotting in this container *with a dead body*. Everything was worse with a dead body.

"Thinking about killing me?" Brasso huffed. Sweat beaded on the man's forehead.

King shot him a look.

"Oh come on. I can read you like a stop sign. You're too predictable. Make you a little angry, and you want to shoot first and ask questions later."

"I was trying to decide if I wanted to eat you alive or dead."

"Ah, so we *are* stuck," Brasso said, his face pinched. "York all over again?

Mention of the collapsed building where King spent two whole days made his back clench. He was going to vomit. If he didn't pull himself together, he was going to do more than vomit.

"How long?" King asked.

In the orange light, Brasso's face looked slick with oil and his eyes shrunken in their sockets. "Twelve fucking inches. Why? You want to blow me?"

King didn't even flinch. He'd heard this dirty mouth for decades. "How long have you been Ryanson's fuck boy?"

Brasso's shit-eating grin flattened to a thin line. "Do you want to know that, Robbie?"

"Why wouldn't I?"

"It might change the way you view our relationship," he said. "The wife never likes to hear about the other woman. How happy can she be to learn her happy marriage included thirty years of infidelity?"

King's stomach dropped. Not unlike the way it dropped when Lou pulled him through the thin fabric of time and space. But she had not returned. The only time he was falling through now was his own.

"How long?" he asked again, and he felt the muscles along his spine clench as if bracing for an impact.

Brasso pushed himself up even taller before falling back against the rusty wall. The walls gave a metallic pop that echoed through the container. "Do you remember the *talk* Bennigan gave me? I was gone for a whole day, and then I came back with my tail tucked."

For a minute, King didn't. He reached deep into the back of his mind but felt only cobwebs. A sensation of groping blind in the darkness. Then a lightning flash of recognition and his pulse kicked. "When I got shot."

Brasso was nodding. "You took a bullet and became a hero, and I got a goddamn lecture about not being where I was told to be...like a fucking five-year-old. Bad boy, little Chazzy. Mommie told you to come inside when the street lights came on, and you didn't listen and look what happened. *You* got a medal and were sent off to school the kiddies..."

And had the pleasure of meeting Jack Thorne.

"...and while you did your 90-day tour of Quantico, I was downgraded to a desk. Man, that rubbed my ass wrong."

King was waiting for the connection to be made.

Brasso wasn't done talking. "So when Ryanson rolled up on a white pony with a fuck ton of cash tied in a pretty bow, why would I say no? *No?* To more money than I'd ever make with the department? No to black-tie parties drowning in beautiful women who would blow their own fathers six ways to Sunday if you offered them one snort of coke, which by the way, is about as easy to come by in the DEA headquarters as an STD at Coachella."

King tried to count how many times drugs went missing between the bust itself and the evidence locker. Too many to count. But had he ever imagined that Brasso was palming the stuff himself? No.

"Over twenty years," King said. The shock was wearing off. After all, he knew it happened. How many cops or agents were in the pocket of this or that powerhouse? Most. Why? Because everything had a price. King knew full well that the price of his guilt was too high to be bought by anyone—but he wasn't naïve enough to believe that meant he had no price at all.

"Or maybe you think I should've said no to being fucking appreciated for my talents rather than kicked like a dog who pissed on the rug? You know what happened when I saved your life?"

King pressed his back against the metal wall as if to make the room wider.

"Nothing," Chaz said. "No medal. No slap on the ass. Just a that-a-boy, Chazzy. That-a-boy."

"If Ryanson wanted something overlooked, I took care of it. I pointed the hounds in another direction. Maybe evidence went missing.

Maybe witnesses did. Enough misdirection to keep them off Ryanson's ass."

"So you betrayed the men and women who worked with you, to protect a rich bastard?"

Brasso rolled his eyes. "And you wonder why no one invites you to the parties, Robbie."

King ran a sweaty palm through his hair. This was all connected somehow. He knew it. But the pieces just weren't quite lining up yet. King still had more questions than answers: why did Brasso choose him? He could have chosen any number of private investigators to find Venetti.

He chose him so he could use him. Maybe even do away with him. If he could betray one friend, why not another? After King had delivered Venetti, maybe he was earmarked for a watery grave of his very own.

"Do you remember Gus Johnson and Jack Thorne?" King finally asked.

Brasso stopped smiling. "What about them?"

It was a strange reaction. The way one reacts if you say *I have a snake in this bag.* If King were an interrogator, he'd lean into that, press harder, and see where it took him.

He was a shit interrogator, but he had to ask. "Right before he died, Jack was working a case. A *big* case."

Brasso's feral eyes didn't blink.

"This case was against a mayor. He thought this mayor was selling drugs and perhaps girls. He had bank records and a couple of witnesses. That case never saw the light of day because, *surprise surprise*, when Jack died, the bank records and witnesses and all the other bits of evidence disappeared. That was real curious, because even Jack's partner, Johnson, couldn't seem to find any of it. Or maybe he didn't look very hard."

King made a poof gesture with his left hand, the right still holding the gun, making wide circles in the air before him.

"Are you calling me unoriginal?" Brasso taunted.

King wasn't going to let himself be distracted. "Did you know that same mayor went on to become a senator?" King heard the tremor in his voice. Felt the gun rattling against his thigh. The orange light in the container made his head swim. *If I don't take a breath, I'm going to hyperventilate,* he realized. *Breathe.*

Brasso still said nothing.

"But we all know the Martinellis killed Jack Thorne," King said. And he got the reaction he wanted. Brasso *relaxed*. "And we even know that Gus Johnson was the one who gave his partner up. Told the Martinellis where to look, even though Thorne had taken all the necessary precautions to keep his home and family off the radar."

"So then why are you telling me all this?" Brasso wet his lips and then cautiously met King's eyes. "I know you loved the prick. Thorne. The only time you stopped praising your ass was to praise his. But what's that got to do with me?"

King grinned. But it was a hard, curdled expression that made the muscles in his face twitch. "Because the more I think about betrayal, particularly *your* brand of betrayal, the more I wonder who wanted to put an end to Thorne's digging. After all, it wouldn't have been hard to convince the Martinellis to do it if they already had revenge on their mind."

34

Lou stared at the blood-soaked carpet in her aunt's apartment and wondered where shit had gone wrong. She had a process. A clear-cut, no error approach to killing. Take them to her private Alaskan lake. Jump to La Loon. Kill them and leave their bodies for Jabbers.

No bullets. No casings. No gunpowder or evidence. No bodies. No blood. No witnesses, except maybe those from the point of abduction. But usually, she had enough counter-evidence to prove she was elsewhere. Enough improbability on her side to make people know she couldn't have been in both Milan and New York on the same night.

Therefore, Officer, you are mistaken. That person you're looking for only looks like me.

With a sigh, she knelt on the rug and sprayed carpet cleaner onto the darkest spot. Then she took the scrubber to it, moving her hand in stiff circles the way her mother had taught her.

Of course, Lou'd never even been questioned by the police regarding a missing person. The people she yanked off the streets were the vermin in the gutters. Why the hell would the police even look for them?

Yet here she was, in her *second* trashed apartment this evening, furiously scrubbing at another carpet. Why couldn't Lucy get a rug? Rugs were easier to dispose of.

She stared down at the wet spot. No blood. Someone could have spilled a cup of water and was letting the carpet air dry. The walls and everything else had been wiped down as well. She threw the carpet cleaner and scrubbers into a bag and vacuumed the place. She spent extra time on the wet spots, trying to make sure no soapy spots dried stiff.

She stood up an overturned chair and straightened a crooked picture of Aphrodite in a tree pose on her aunt's wall above the Indian print sofa.

If this whole murder-revenge thing ever goes sour, she thought, *I could open a cleaning business specializing in blood. Kill your bastard husband and need help disposing of his worthless corpse? Lou-Blue is there for you! 555-7687*

She grinned and stepped into the closet and closed the door behind her. When she opened the door again, she was in her St. Louis apartment. The door hit a boot with a worn rubber shoe and stopped. She had to squeeze herself through the crack in order to escape the cramped space. Pink dawn was starting to sprout on the horizon, but her work was far from done.

She still had the bodies.

Four bodies and a spattering of other evidence—sponges, a torn T-shirt used as a rag, two bottles of cleaner, and a handful of bullet casings —she'd get rid of these too.

She dropped the bag of evidence and wet rags beside a black boot. Then she stepped over all the legs between her and her bathroom.

A giant tub sat in the middle of the tiled room. It was a puckered, god-like mouth waiting for her.

Lou bent and turned on the faucet. Measuring the temperature with the back of one hand, she used the other to plunge the stopper into the steel drain at the bottom of the tub. The tub was made for two people and deep enough to reach a grown man's shoulders when filled.

Lou filled it.

Then she dragged the body of one of the men down the hall. Not for the first time tonight, Lou was grateful that her apartment had no carpeting of any kind, only hard floors that could easily be wiped clean.

She stepped into the water with her shoes on and hefted the man up into the tub with her. It was hard. Dragging dead bodies around always was. They went limp and completely unhelpful when they were dead. Gravity enters the bones of the dead in a way it can't with the living.

But once Lou got enough of the big figure onto the lip of the tub, the momentum of his corpse dropped him into the water. She cradled his bulk against her like a lover. Then she tried not to feel any panic regarding the fact that she was going to pull a dead body on top of her in a bathtub, and should her ability choose to fail her now, she would suffocate under the corpse crushing her.

She took a breath and submerged herself, the corpse still hugged against her chest.

Her gift didn't fail her.

She felt the bottom of the tub soften and fall away and then it was gone completely. She kicked her legs for the surface of the water and broke for air.

She let go of the corpse and watched it sink without her. She knew she should drag a least one of the bodies onto the shore for Jabbers, a sort of offering in honor of their working relationship. But she had three bodies left to go. It could wait. She dipped beneath the surface and let the lake take her again.

The tub bottom solidified beneath her, and she sat up, sucking in more air. Black hairs from the dead man floated on the surface, and Lou made a note to scrub and bleach the tub when she was done. She wasn't concerned about cleanliness. Lou never bathed in this tub. She used it only as a doorway. It took too much energy not to slip that the idea of soaking in a tub for an hour was ridiculous. Her mother had loved to do that, with wine and a book.

But Lou would be exhausted after five minutes.

That's what the shower with its glass doors in the far corner was for. And it sat beneath a bright, beveled window for extra measure.

Her boots squeaked against the slick floor as she held onto the tub for balance. Water sloshed over her knuckles. But despite the discomfort of wet clothes clinging, she pushed on.

She dumped two other bodies, the full trio who had lay siege to her aunt's apartment, in Blood Lake. With each return trip through the tub, the water was a little pinker than the trip before. La Loon water clung to her hair and clothes. The tub was as red as blood when she climbed into it for the last time, with the body of the man who had pistol-whipped King, demanding answers to Venetti's whereabouts.

When she broke the surface of Blood Lake, Lou didn't let go of the body this time. Instead, she lifeguard dragged this corpse toward the shore until the silty bottom rose at an angle beneath her like a partially submerged boat ramp. Each step elevated her out of the water.

Dragging a wet corpse was even harder than dragging a dry one.

She didn't even have the corpse out of the water when the leaves rustled. Something thrashed through the thick jungle foliage on her right. It would be here in twenty or thirty seconds.

The two moons hung in the purple sky and Blood Lake was still in the quiet evening.

Of course, it was always a quiet evening in La Loon. Every time Lou had visited this strange place, the sky was the same color, the moons hanging in the same position. She had no idea if some version of the sun rose and set on this place. Perhaps this part of Jabbers' world was like Alaska. For months at a time, everything traveled the sky in the exact angle.

Lou realized she didn't have her gun.

A black face broke through the trees and screeched. A mouth opened wide showing no less than four or five rows of long needle teeth the color of puss. A large white tongue lolled in its mouth, and the interior cheeks puffed, making Lou think of the cottonmouth snakes she'd seen as a child, hiking the woods with her father. Jabbers might be the same black-scaled, white-mouthed coloring of a cottonmouth, but she was no snake.

She had six legs with talons, curved nails that dug into the earth as she walked. Between the toes was webbing, no doubt useful in the lake spreading out behind her. But the talons made her think of gripping and digging in. Did she nest in the mountain range a mile in the distance? She imagined the beast waking in some cave each morning and climbing down to the water's edge, waiting for her offerings.

Jabbers darted forward, and Lou pulled her bowie knife. The beast stopped in its tracks and hissed, pulling itself up to its full height.

Lou took a step back away from the body, moving so that Jabbers could easily pounce on the corpse, as she'd seen her do many times before. Foxes hunted like that, jumped down on the frozen waters to get seal pups out from underneath the ice.

Only Lou wasn't sure it was necessary if the prey was dead, served on a proverbial platter. They weren't going to put up a fight. But then again, if one has spent a lifetime putting a napkin across their lap before eating, one doesn't stop because the menu changed.

Lou was clear of the corpse and lowered the knife.

Jabbers pounced, coming down on her forepaws with a playful air of a puppy seizing a toy from its master's hand.

Though no one in their right mind could look at Jabbers and see a playful puppy. She was too terrifying with her slit eyes and teeth and the way her body contracted from shoulders to rump with each movement. She was a solid mass of muscle.

Lou heard a splash and looked out over the lake.

Fins cut the water, darting one way then the other, like fish on the Discovery Channel evading predators. Only these fins were far too large to belong to fish, and she couldn't imagine anything as large as a killer whale traveling in formation, needing to protect themselves from predators.

Movement caught Lou's eye, and she whirled back toward Jabbers to find herself face to face with the beast.

Lou raised the knife instantly, but she was too slow. The blade touched the underside of Jabbers' chin, and when it did, a grumbling sound came from its throat. Lou's arm tensed, ready to plunge the blade up through the beast's jaw and into its brain—if its anatomy remotely resembled the creatures back home.

Fucking stupid, she thought. *Fucking stupid for taking my eyes off you. Why in the world would you munch on a corpse with fresh meat so close?* Water drying on the end of Lou's nose began to itch.

Lou could smell her—smell corpse meat on her breath as her growl deepened.

Then her hind legs folded and she sat down on her rump. The long white tongue came out of her mouth and lapped lazily at the blood drying on her muzzle.

Not growling. *Purring.* Purring like a goddamn cat.

Immediately her mind flashed with news stories meant to warm sappy souls. How lions came to love their masters, recognizing them, *hugging* them, jumping up and wrapping those large furry paws the size of a grown man's face around in a gentle embrace, even after years in the wild. How a tiger would not eat a goat that was put into its cage as a meal.

Lou had formed a shaky alliance with a creature straight from a child's worst nightmare, taming it with the corpses of her enemies.

But she had no illusions. She had a ragged scar on her shoulder that wouldn't let her make that mistake.

Lou took a step back into Blood Lake. Cool water lapped at her ankles, then the back of her calves. She held the knife out in front of her. Jabbers didn't mind. She lifted one taloned foot and began to gnaw at it, digging out the guts stuck in the webbing.

Lou dove beneath the water and wiggled herself out of her clothes. When she surfaced again, she was naked in the blood red water of her bathtub.

Her arms were shaking from overuse. Her head pounded with each heartbeat.

She pulled the plug and watched the water drain, leaving a pink ring in the tub. She bent beneath the faucet and rinsed her hair and body until the water ran clear. She smoothed a hand along the rim until all the pink droplets became white.

Jabbers' bright eyes and the smell of her corpse breath burned in her mind. That had been too damn close. Close and stupid. What was wrong with her? She'd never been this careless before. And Jabbers wasn't even her first mistake.

Konstantine.

She was still unable to explain the uninvited pull to visit Konstantine.

What do you want from him? She asked as she shivered, naked in the empty tub. *Your enemies are dead.*

Almost, her heart whispered. She paused with the comb in her hair. *Almost.*

35

Konstantine slid into the back of the sedan as the driver opened it. The A/C instantly began to cool the sweat on his neck as he took the seat opposite the doors, his weight against the partition. The small window was open, revealing an empty driver's seat. The senator followed him in, unbuttoning the jacket on his suit as he slid across the leather.

The door closed, and the car rocked gently to one side. The driver's shadow fell over them as he rounded the car, ready to reclaim the wheel.

Ryanson was clearly pleased. "That went well. Perfect. I can't wait to see what you've drummed up."

Konstantine handed over a USB indentical to the one hidden inside his boot.

"Any plans this evening?" The senator asked. His mood was bright and contagious. "A woman waiting maybe?"

Yes, Konstantine thought. And if she did not find him tonight, she would find him the next, or the one after that. She was waiting all right. Waiting to slit his throat. He had to decide, while he had a chance, what to say first. His first words may be his last. So what could he say that would stop her?

*Who **understands** you better?* They were born of the same crime-ridden and violent world. They'd both lost their mothers. They both wanted revenge.

Too presumptuous, he decided.

I dream about you.

Perhaps too intense.

I only want one thing.

Too demanding.

"I considered visiting downtown Austin," he said. *Where she was last seen hunting Castle.* Her hunting ground. "There is a bar there."

"That's a shame," Ryanson said. He made an exaggerated pout with his lips. "Can't I persuade you to come out with me instead? I have a beautiful boat. Congress doesn't reconvene until Monday, and my flight isn't until Sunday night. I can bring five girls to make you forget about the one you miss."

Konstantine forced a polite smile.

"Ten girls?"

"No, thank you."

"You know, I don't like double-crossers," the senator said.

Konstantine looked up from his lap and met the man's eyes. He noticed the shift in the man's tone, the change in the air's temperature.

"I have your man Julio in the trunk," the senator added. His eyes clung to Konstantine's, measuring him up.

Konstantine cocked his head. "Julio?"

"It took us a long time to crack him. Longer than I expected actually. He was very, *very* loyal to you."

Was. Konstantine's heart kicked his ribs, began thrashing in its cage.

"It's true that I planned to murder you both anyway. I don't like leaving trails," he said. Then his face brightened. "But when I found out who you were, hoo boy! You're a wanted man, Mr. Konstantine. Your father has—had—a lot of enemies. And Father Leo wasn't a favorite either. Unfortunately, you've inherited enemies on both sides."

Konstantine took inventory of the weapons on him. Two guns and a blade. Ryanson had the advantage of being by the door. And assuming the driver was loyal to him, he had a man at Konstantine's back. But he was still sure he could get to his guns before either of them moved.

"So I decided to have an auction. The highest bidder gets you and I'm spared the trouble of killing you myself. Win-win."

Konstantine's fingers brushed the butt of his gun the moment before a sharp pain pricked the side of his neck. He turned in his seat as the driver pulled his hand back through the partition. His fist clutched a syringe, the needle and a tube with the plunger completely depressed.

Konstantine reached up and touched his neck, felt a knot swelling under the skin. A drop of blood came away on his fingers.

He raised his hand up to strike out at the driver, but the partition slammed shut and his hands connected with the window weakly. All strength drained from his body, like water poured from a cup onto the floor.

"We'll keep it civil. Lots of guards. It'll be a bit of a sausage fest on the boat tonight, but I think it'll be fun nonetheless. Don't you?" Ryanson asked, leaning forward. He pulled a bottle of whiskey from the sideboard. He popped off the lid and poured the tea-colored liquid into a crystalline rocks glass. He cut it with water from the mini fridge. All his movements were slow and methodical as if he had no worry at all that Konstantine might reach out and attack him.

And he was right.

The backseat began to stretch and whirl around Konstantine. *I must not lose consciousness*, he told himself, as if his will could override the drugs coursing through his veins.

"You used me," Konstantine said and found he was smiling. Of course, he had been used. He couldn't even say that he didn't have it coming.

"No more than you used me," the man replied. It was *the man* because he could have been anyone now. The face and body blurred. A child's finger-painting done on a living room wall.

Konstantine's eyes couldn't focus on the light shooting through the windows. He was leaning forward. That much he knew because his face was inches above his knees. His body was a rock seeking a solid foundation in the jostling ride of the car.

"Close your eyes and when you open them, we'll be there. It'll be a party just for you." The voice elongated like a tape played in slow motion. The kind he used to have to rewind with his school pencils when the tape players ate the coffee-colored ribbons. He was such a tape now. Unraveled. Pulled apart.

The car hit a bump in the Texan road, and Konstantine was pitched forward. He was falling. Falling through the darkness. And he lost consciousness before he ever hit the ground.

36

King counted backward from one hundred. When Lou still didn't appear, he counted forward to one hundred. The numbers trick was something he'd picked up in therapy during his divorce. He had not sought treatment after the Channing incident. He was told to, and medical leave was forced upon him, but he couldn't go.

The therapist he *did* see, with her horn-rimmed glasses and bangs that fell into her eyes, had insisted that human emotion could only be felt for ninety seconds. So, anytime he felt overwhelmed with anger and grief, his best bet was to stop whatever he was doing and to count to a hundred slowly, keeping his breath slow and steady as he did it.

It turned out that this particular therapy technique was not very efficient when used in a fucking sealed Siberian transport container.

Big fucking surprise!

After counting to one hundred the first time, he didn't feel any less anxious than when he began. In fact, his anxiety grew like a black spider on the wall, larger and larger. The numbers seemed to be building toward something.

Something terrible.

"Can you sit down?" Brasso begged. "You're making me motion sick."

"The container isn't moving," King said through grit teeth. "You can't be motion sick."

"You're moving!" Brasso whined. "It's you moving that's making me sick."

King glanced at the thick orange rust coating his fingers, like a hand left too long in the Cheetos bag. It proved he had been tracing the inside of this container for a long time. Black lines ran up and down the wall where he'd completely rubbed off the rust. Breathing in these rusted particles was probably *wonderful* for the lungs too.

"What were you going to do with Venetti?" King asked.

"Not this again," Brasso begged. "Shoot me already."

No, he thought. *If I have to eat you, I'm going eat you fresh*, he'd decided. He'd already, in his mind at least, started calling the corner where Brasso leaned "the kitchen nook." And his eyes kept sliding to the opposite corner, which was slowly becoming the bathroom, as his bladder grew heavier and heavier beneath his belt. An uncomfortable burn formed inside his trousers.

"Answer me, or I'll shoot your foot," King insisted. He'd resumed pacing. Going from wall to wall helped. It reminded him of how much room he had.

"You know we were going to kill her and dump her in the bay. Don't play dumb."

King nodded absentmindedly. "What else?"

"I like daisies and when the girls touch my pee-pee. *Please* stop fucking *moving*."

Pressure rose suddenly between King's ears followed by a sharp *POP* as the pressure equalized. He turned and saw a girl form herself out of shadows, out of nothing.

"Get me the fuck out of here!"

The words exploded from King's mouth. Some wise, distant part of him noted, *I'm hysterical*.

Lou froze as if afraid to come closer to him. But then her hands were on him and—thank god in heaven—the shipping container dropped away. A clear, moonlit floor of his apartment rose to catch them. Only it wasn't moonlight. It was too purple.

King turned to his watch. 6:36.

Evening. He'd been in the shipping container all fucking day.

He had taken a lunging step toward her before he realized he'd done so.

She had already moved out of his reach.

"Don't you ever!" he bellowed. "Don't you ever leave me somewhere like that again!"

Lou's frown evened out.

"Do you hear me?" King said. He felt the cords on the side of his neck standing out. A vein in his forehead throbbed. "Don't. You. Ever."

He sucked in great gasps of air.

A panic attack. *I'm having a panic attack.*

He dropped to one knee.

Lou shifted uncomfortably. "Are you dying?"

He shook his head.

"Are you sure?" she asked.

He waved her off, pointing emphatically toward the bedroom. He made a motion with his hand hoping she understood. He sucked at charades.

She went into the bedroom. Drawers opened and slammed shut and then she returned with a red rescue inhaler. He swatted at it, knocking it into the floor before fumbling it up to his mouth. Pump. Inhale. Hold. Pump. Inhale. Hold. He breathed. Deep. Steady breaths.

He collapsed onto his ass, still clenching the inhaler in his fist.

The black spots and red sparks in front of his eyes began to disappear.

His palm holding the inhaler fell to his lap. The world came into focus. The throbbing headache didn't leave him, but the air was going in and out of his chest again.

He looked up, expecting to see her gone, but she stood there. Gun in her hand, watching him.

"You're hyperventilating," she said.

"You fucking think!"

"Use your inhaler."

"Where the fuck were you?" he asked when he felt like he could spare enough breath to ask a question. His lips were ridiculously dry. He reached up and wiped away congealed spit from the corners with his thumbs.

He was dehydrated and yet, ironically, had to piss like a racehorse. But getting off the floor was not an option.

"Men came after Lucy," she said in a steady voice, speaking the way one might to an enraged horse.

"What?" King said. The air was leaving him again.

"I took care of it," she said. "But it took a while. Lucy has carpet. No rugs."

"Lucy has carpet," he repeated. He was starting to see things now. The perfect steadiness in her hand. She wasn't thumbing the safety. And her clothes were clean and her hair was still wet from a shower, presumably.

"You're tired," he said. He snorted, absolutely surprised. "I thought you were like a fucking terminator. Send in a hundred bad guys, and you just say *I'll be back*."

She didn't smile. She didn't even shrug.

"Is Lucy okay?" His chest tightened again.

"She's on the move with Venetti. They'll keep moving until we finish this."

"Until we finish this," King said, his mouth was going dry again.

"Why do you keep repeating everything I'm saying?" Lou's brow scrunched up. "Are you sure you aren't having a stroke or—"

"You abandoned me in a *Siberian* shipping container and...and..." King searched for the next words.

"And he's claustrophobic," Mel said.

King turned and saw Mel standing in the archway between the living room and kitchen. Her eyes were lined in thick black makeup and golden bangles jingled on her wrist. How had she crept up on them without a sound?

Lou hadn't looked away from where King crouched on the floor with his inhaler. She'd known Mel had snuck in. Of course she did. The girl probably saw a whole spectrum of things that King couldn't imagine.

"What are you carrying on about, Mr. King?" Mel said. "I have customers downstairs. You can't be up here screaming and carrying on."

King ran a sweaty palm down his face. "I thought you wanted atmosphere."

Mel arched an eyebrow. "A screaming man upstairs isn't the kind of atmosphere I'm going for."

"Why are you claustrophobic?" Lou asked.

"He was buried alive for days. A whole building came down on him. Ain't that right, Mr. King?"

"You should have told me," Lou said.

"Yes, because you look like the type who is very sympathetic to weakness," King said.

Lou flinched, and King wished he could take the words back. He'd been scared and angry, but he was wrong to direct it at her. That's what pathetic men do. But it was worse than that.

Lou looked like hell. She was too young for the thick bags forming under her eyes. Dried blood had begun to flake off her skin.

"I'm sorry I yelled," King said. "You didn't know."

King looked to Mel, curious what she thought of this girl.

Mel crossed the room, palms turned over in welcome, like she was going to hug the girl. Lou was mortified. Her shoulders tensed, inching up toward her ears.

"You wouldn't know," Mel said. "But men are worse than children. They cry about all the wrong things. When they have a papercut or a cold, they act like the world has rolled over their legs and they'll never walk again. When they've been beaten half to death, they tell you not to fuss."

Sensing Lou's resistance to an embrace, Mel stopped short. Instead, she took Lou's shoulders in her palms and squeezed. Lou softened under the woman's grip.

"Priorities," Lou said with a pathetic smile.

"Speaking of priorities, you need sleep," Mel said. "It's written all over your face."

"We have a lot to do," Lou began. It was the opening line of an argument.

Mel's hand went to her hip, and her tone sharpened. The harsh, bird-like Melandra that King knew returned. "Aren't you tired of carrying around dead bodies?"

Lou's lips twitched with the hint of a smile.

"They can't be light," Mel pressed.

The smile widened.

Mel arched an eyebrow.

King wasn't sure if he should get up or stay on his knees. "You two do what you want. You're both grown." Mel gave first, throwing her hands up and turning toward the door. "Just keep it down, Mr. King. You're not the only one trying to do business here."

The door shut behind her. Then the wall behind the stove vibrated slightly as she descended the stairs back into the shop. The ghoul by the door screamed.

King pulled himself to standing. Gratefully, Lou did not try to help him. He felt enough like an invalid, old man as it was. "You can have my bed," he began.

But when he straightened he saw that she was already stretched long on his red leather couch, one arm folded under her head and the gun, still in her grip, resting across her navel.

I'll have to wait to tell her about Ryanson, he thought. Because his bones ached and his head throbbed and the air moving in and out of his mouth wasn't nearly as smooth as he needed it to be if he was going to go in guns blazing.

37

L ou couldn't sleep. The cold barrel of the gun was a reassuring weight on her belly, but every time she closed her eyes, she saw blood. She saw a man's head exploding. Jabbers bloody snout ripping an abdomen, guts erupting as if spring-loaded.

Her aunt's wide and tearful eyes as she surveyed the carnage in her apartment. The carnage that Lou had brought to her door.

Lou sat up, listening to the dark. She heard nothing. She'd already taken two steps toward the large cherry armoire before she realized what she was doing.

When she placed her foot down again, silk shirts brushed her cheeks and the smell of a man's cologne lingered. She reached out and found the doorframe, and then the closet's handle.

She pushed it open, peering out into the room. It was a child's bedroom, two twin beds with spaceship sheets. Her aunt and Paula slept. Paula snored as loud as her father had when she was a child. A deep rumbling rattle in her chest, her head tilted back and mouth slightly open in the moonlight spilling through the open window.

Her aunt was curled on her side, facing Paula. She was on top of the sheets, her shoes still on.

Ready to go, Lou thought, and a wave of sadness struck her full in the chest.

How could I be so stupid? How could I think that what I did would never come back to her?

Lucy stirred in her borrowed bed. Lou understood it was some empty vacation rental in an offseason. The world was surprisingly full of them, rooms waiting to be filled. Some more stocked than others. Time-share cabins and condos. Rentals or houses for sale. They could be found the world over.

I'll finish this, Lou thought, watching her aunt, so small and fragile, sleep the night away. *I'll make you safe again.*

She remembered all the prescription bottles lining the kitchen sill. A lot of bottles for a woman who thought love and tea leaves would cure all. Lou couldn't look at that truth yet, its significance. So she turned away and slipped back into the darkness.

When she stepped past the armoire into King's apartment, she couldn't bring herself to lay on the couch again.

She had better things to do. Like cut off Ryanson's hand and slap him across the face with it.

Before she realized it, Lou had paced herself right out of King's apartment into the stairwell. Only it wasn't a stairwell so much as an overlook. A railing created a partial hallway that ran waist high to the left. There was nothing right. When Lou looked over the railing, she saw only the store below.

The lights were on, and a girl was pulling the door closed and turning the lock.

Lou descended the steps as the girl picked up a broom propped against the wall. As she turned, she saw Lou and jumped. Her movement awakened the skeleton beside her, which also shrieked, a blood-curdling cry.

"God!" the girl said, stamping a foot. "I hate this thing." She bent and yanked the cord out of the wall.

Lou crossed the floor heading for the door. She would walk the block and cool off. Give King another hour or so of sleep before taking him into a firefight.

The girl stepped back into the wall, bumping her head.

Lou stopped advancing. "I'm not going to hurt you."

The girl's eyes doubled in size. "Oh, I'm not scared. I was—"

"Moving out of the way of someone holding a gun."

The girl frowned. "No. It's not like that."

Lou didn't move. She was unsure what to do with herself. Why was she even down here?

She saw King in her mind's eye. Saw him collapsing to his knees and holding his chest. He went down the way a man who was shot goes down. Like how her father went down.

There you go, stupid girl. Be honest with yourself at least.

He's not my father, she thought.

No. And you don't need him to go after Ryanson. So why are you still here?

The girl standing with her back pressed against the door seemed to wonder the same question. "Hey, are you okay?" she asked. "You don't look so good."

Lou holstered her gun for the first time all night. Her eyes blinking open as if she were coming out of a dream. "I should fix this."

"No, I mean you look good. You just look..." she searched for words. "Stressed maybe? Tired? Like what was the deal with the guy in the apartment? The one I clobbered?"

Go alone. If something happens to you, it's just you. Venetti, Aunt Lucy, and King—they need to stay out of it.

As if on cue the compass inside her whirled to life.

Go, go, go, it murmured, tugging at her insides. *Before it's too late.*

Lou had turned away and hurried toward the velvet curtain. Surely it would be dark enough back there to slip to her apartment first and then—

She threw back the curtain and found Mel bent over a table peering at cards in the candlelight. A chubby guy in his mid-twenties looked up with wide eyes.

"What the fuck?" His chin wobbled in surprise.

Lou didn't have time to look for another exit.

"I'm sorry," she said to Mel. Before slipping in plain sight of the landlady and her customer she added, "Tell him I couldn't wait."

38

Lou took only five minutes to suit up. Three compartments from her secret vault were emptied. She brought five guns and the corresponding clips. She strapped two knives into sown-in slips designed for their enclosure. At last, her father's bullet proof vest hugged her as tight as his arms ever had.

And then she stepped out of a closet and into...what? A toilet pressed against the back of her leg and she put her hand down on the porcelain surface of a sink. A tiny bathroom then. She listened to the thin door for voices but heard only the low rumble of an engine. A car on a distant street? No. The floor swayed under her, back and forth. The gentle rocking of a boat and the slapping sound of rough waters assailing the hull. The scent of salt was sharp, burning her nose.

Ryanson's boat then.

No doubt the same boat Venetti had leapt from with an oxygen tank in hand, her last-ditch attempt to save her life. The question: why did Lou appear here now? Was Ryanson dumping more bodies? Killing more girls? Making shadier deals with the parasites feeding on the world's underbelly?

Her heart skipped a beat. She had hoped she would walk in on Ryanson alone. The good little senator tucked in his bed. A hop, skip and jump to La Loon, and then it was dinner time for Jabbers.

She'd clearly packed for more.

At the very least, he wouldn't go easy. He thought too highly of himself to roll over. And Lou knew in a distant kind of way that she could just as easily die tonight. It happened when you didn't expect it. She'd known this since watching her father die through a watery prism.

She supposed it didn't matter what Ryanson was doing here. Her intentions were clear. So whatever she was walking into—

So be it.

She eased open the bathroom door.

It was a bedroom. A giant bed with a mirror hanging overhead and a mirrored headboard behind it. Overkill. To the right were stairs leading up to a door. And voices.

So more than one man. More than one threat.

She ascended the stairs as slowly as possible, one foot in front of the other, keeping a hand on the wall for balance. She would have to come out guns blazing, she knew. The deck would offer no cover, and if she intended not to have her head blown off straight away, she would have to use the door for protection.

But there was no time to fool with the hinges in the dark, popping the pins and creating a wooden shield that might prove as flimsy and pathetic as cardboard.

Keep low, she thought. The voice was her father's, and the sound of it made her heart constrict. She imagined him here behind her, the scent of him as he guided her. In her imagination, they were on the same team and about to bust a drug house. He was walking her through it. He had her back.

Duck down. Use the steps. Throw the door wide. Target. Shoot. Get as many as you can before the door closes. Track left to right, following the swing of the door.

She took a breath.

And threw open the door. She dropped as the door swung wide and banged against the opposite wall. All the guns came up. Five in all, from her vantage point. A man on the ground eye level with her was gagged and bound in front of a row of white leather benches, fluorescent in the light. A man with a power drill kneeled in front of him while Ryanson stood off to one side with a drink in hand, looking like a vodka advertisement, shades pushed up on his head and shirt billowing in the wind.

On the other side of this door stood two more in the moonlight. Their skin shone as if polished.

They didn't shoot. Neither did she.

As good as her father's advice had been, giving up her cover when she could gather intelligence instead—she couldn't pass it up. So she remained frozen. Not a single muscle in her body twitched.

"What the fuck, Ryanson? You got a haunted boat?" the man with the power drill asked.

"No wonder it came so cheap," Ryanson joked, but she could hear the terror in his voice. The strong tremor to his words despite his insinuation that he had paid anything less than six figures for his beautiful seabird.

"Go check it out, Rick."

Rick was walking toward her when the cabin door clicked shut. So she stepped back into the dark and drew her knife. The wall behind her softened, and fell away.

When she slipped through, she was on the deck, beneath the white benches Venetti had described. Lou surveyed the forest of feet. With one swipe, she cut through the boots of the man with the drill. He cried out as his Achilles' tendons snapped and he fell backward.

His back hit the deck hard, and he cried out again. The drill clattered across the deck.

Someone bent down and looked under the bench, and Lou put a bullet into his brain and a second into the next lookie-loo. *There are more than five*, she realized. Some must have been hidden by the door. But she couldn't count them properly now either. They were jumping up onto the benches, out of her line of sight, like a gaggle of teenage girls escaping a mouse.

The bench above vibrated and at the last moment, she realized someone was running along it, positioning themselves above her so they could shoot her through the fabric and wood barrier from above.

She pressed her back against the undercarriage and slipped. The inside of the cabin with Ryanson's gaudy mirrors and throne bed reformed around her. The man who'd come to investigate the door, Rick, was running up the stairs toward the commotion. She shot him in the back of the head, and he stiffened, falling straight back like a tree.

Timber, her dead father said, and Lou smiled.

A bullet shot through the window of the cabin and sliced through her upper arm.

Her lips pulled back in a hissing grimace. Without thinking, she shot blindly at the window and wasn't sure she'd hit the gunner until she heard the scream and the splash of a body going overboard.

The water. She could sink this boat and take the whole thing to La Loon.

Only she was sure that the boat was designed *not* to sink.

She hunkered in the corner. The corner was dark, a potential exit, but also good cover. She tried to breathe through the pain of being shot, gather herself, count in her head how many more men she thought she'd seen—reassess her situation before commencing round two.

They were shouting on deck. Someone had looked under the bench, found nothing, and now they were spooked.

It would buy her a couple of minutes if nothing else.

I need to bring you down, she thought, imagining the boat sinking into black watery depths. *How to bring you down.*

Her strategizing was interrupted by another round of bullets. Two hard knocks slammed into her vest, punching her into the wall. Then a third pierced her thigh and the knee folded under her weight.

39

King woke to Mel shaking him. "Get up you log! Get up! Get *up*!"

King wanted to remind her that he'd been shot at, beat up, and left in a Siberian shipping container all day. His chest still hurt from his attack and his throat was raw and burning.

It was hardly like he was a lazy bum.

Then his brain clicked on and registered the fact that Mel was the one shaking him awake in the dead of night. Not Lou.

King bolted upright so fast his forehead clipped her chin.

"Watch it!" she said, moving back.

"What's happening?"

"Your girl did a disappearing act, right in the middle of one of my readings. She said to tell you she was sorry but she couldn't wait. So I called your lady friend, and now there's a girl in my apartment and..."

"What?" King put one hand against his head. Then louder as if to shout over his blaring panic. "*What?*"

Lucy cupped King's bare foot in a strangely intimate gesture. It was as if she'd just appeared there, at the foot of his bed, materializing from the darkness as she did.

But her touch had a strong effect on him. King became hyper aware of the women beside him, of himself only in boxers with the chilly night air coming through the window, of the sweat drying in the fold of his neck.

"Lou went to kill Ryanson. Alone."

When King looked perplexed that Lucy knew the senator's name, she added, "Paula and I talked. She's in Mel's apartment."

"And this one!" Mel was pointing. "*This* one can disappear too."

Lucy gave a weak smile. "Secret's out, Robert. You have some explaining to do."

Mel touched her brow as if blessing herself. "You're going to sit down and tell me everything. At the very least, tell me what to say to Piper. She's inconsolable. She said all her unborn children are dying as we speak."

King pressed his fingers to his forehead hoping his brains would go back inside his skull.

Their excitement and dread, playfulness yet resignation, King tried to absorb it, understand it. His mind pushed through the mania of their combined emotions and tried to focus on what mattered.

Lou took off. Alone. And she's doing it without knowing the truth.

"We have to stop her." King swung his legs off the side of the bed. "Ryanson ordered the hit on Jack. He orchestrated everything. If she murders him, the truth dies with him."

Lucy blinked several times.

"We could clear Jack's name," King said again. He tugged at the jeans on the floor. They didn't come up until Mel stepped off them.

Lucy offered him a shirt. "Let's go."

King's head snapped up "You're not going. No vegetarian Buddhists allowed in the gunfight."

Lucy threw the offered shirt into his face. "And how exactly do you intend to get to Houston without me?"

King's heart kicked. Damn. She was right.

Guns. But Lucy would never take one. Mace, maybe. Handcuffs certainly. And a bullet proof vest for sure. He would have it all on her before they stepped out of this apartment.

King pulled on a boot and began lacing it. He glanced up at Mel, who still scrutinized him with an arched brow.

"If I come back in one piece, you and I will sit and have a nice long talk about all this," he told her.

Mel threw up her hands, and the gold bangles on her wrist jingled. "You're damn right we will. And what do I tell Piper?"

"Tell her not to underestimate Lou."

40

Konstantine fought against the grogginess saturating him. His limbs were heavy. His head felt as if it had doubled in size, rolling around on a neck that could no longer support it. The lights were too bright, and every sound struck him like a slap.

Then everything happened at once. The gunshots. The screaming. And suddenly a knife was in his hand.

He felt the blade brush his fingers. The edge sliced his finger open, and a stinging fire shot up his hand. It sobered him, pushed back the drug-induced fugue.

He managed to pick up the blade again, gingerly this time now that pain forced him to be cautious. And he began working the blade up and down on his bonds. It was an awkward, slow process and all the while he could only watch the other men on the deck.

He hoped she had left, escaped in the confusion. Half of the men were already dead.

When Ryanson caught Konstantine looking at him, he slid down onto the bench seat as if suddenly aware what a big dumb target he was, looming over the others. He sat with his knees folded against his chest, resembling a terrified boy. Konstantine thought he could reach Ryanson if he needed to—ten steps, maybe fifteen at most.

Konstantine's bonds snapped, and he darted to the nearest pistol lying on the deck, a few inches from a slack hand. He grabbed the gun and turned it on Ryanson. He would not be leaving this boat prematurely. Lou would have her father's executioner and the USB still hiding in his boot. He felt it, poking into the side of his heel and the knot in his chest released.

The cabin door burst open, and there she was, leaning heavy on the door.

Louie. She met his eyes but didn't see him.

There was too much blood.

Mio dio, he thought, *she's going to bleed out.*

Her right thigh was soaked with blood. It dripped like rain onto the top step. He could not tell if the femoral or the aorta were slit. Perhaps both. She had only minutes.

The last of Ryanson's men stepped in front of her, and she blew them away like a child blowing dandelion seeds. Konstantine had never seen someone shoot so fast, with such precision, even in her weakened state.

She shot all the men huddled at the boat entrance in a small circular movement, pulling the trigger six times. Six bullets. Six bodies hit the deck. Then she pulled another gun with her other hand, and the body count doubled. Naturally ambidextrous or practiced, he couldn't tell.

When she pulled the third gun, she didn't shoot. Her eyes fluttered, and she slumped forward onto her hands. She dropped her gun.

The last two men, apart from Ryanson and himself, came around the corner.

She doesn't see them.

Konstantine put a bullet into each before aiming on Ryanson again. The two dead men fell at her feet as if prostrating to a queen.

In one fell swoop, she'd killed them all. *All of them,* except for Konstantine's minor two-body contribution. Traveling in and out in that way of hers.

Ryanson collapsed on the bench, surveying the carnage. He looked bewildered, unbelieving at the number of bodies on the boat deck. The blood that seemed to run from all directions, this way and that way depending upon the tilt of the sea.

Lou frowned at the dead men too. She looked from Ryanson to

Konstantine, confusion screwing up her face, as if she'd forgotten what she'd come here for and was trying to remember.

Then she looked up and met his eyes. Her eyes focused despite the blood loss, and she saw him for the first time.

She recognized him. And lifted her gun to aim.

41

The boat rocked under Lou, unsteady, and her pounding headache didn't help. She was nauseated. But it was more than that. She'd felt this before—an alarming level of blood pouring warm down the inside of her thigh. If she didn't get the hell out of there and pump herself with a couple of pints of O-neg, she was going to become a permanent fixture in Ryanson's graveyard. Or she could jump overboard, sending herself to La Loon. A final offering for her faithful companion.

That was how it should be.

Ever since the creature had bitten her, shaken her, thrown her into the lake to die—they were one. They'd exchanged blood. The power of this arcane rite bound them together. Somehow this ravenous creature was her. It was a manifestation of her spirit. Her soul. Her shadow. It thirsted for blood the way she did. It knew only peace when she killed.

Horseshit, her father said.

His voice sharpened her mind, bringing her back from the edge of delirium.

She had to focus. She was almost done here. She just had to be strong for a few minutes more.

Bodies fell at her feet. *Forget them. Focus*, she said again. *Find Ryanson. Put a bullet in his brain.*

But it wasn't Ryanson who held her attention. It was Paolo Konstantine. A busted lip and bruised cheek made him more handsome than ever. And the fact that she found him attractive when she was bleeding to death pissed her off more.

"Konstantine," she said, her gun trained on his face. She wanted him to confirm it. Declare himself.

"Yes," he said in accented English. It was the kind of stupidly sexy accent that women went to movies and got all wet over. Her desire to shoot him increased tenfold. "And you're Louie. Louie Thorne."

And then like that, she had a third reason to shoot him.

Yet the gun trembled in her hand. Sparks danced in her vision, and she thought *goddamn, I'm going to black out.*

She was going to black out with the image of a teenage boy, with big beautiful cow eyes smiling down at her, purring Italian at her with a face full of tenderness. The first kind male face she'd seen since her father had died.

You need to elevate your leg, her father said. His heavy hand was on her back, and the weight of it was pushing her down.

"You need to elevate your leg." Her father's voice changed. Deepened. No, not her father. King. She was still on the deck of the boat, an arm's length from the cabin door.

"I heard you the first time," she said. Someone prodded the wound in her leg. She screamed.

"That looks horrible."

Lucy and King's faces solidified. They were both armored to the hilt. They had the sharpness of reality, unlike the warped delirium rolling her. Had Lucy entered from the dark cabin as she did? It didn't matter. She had to stop her mind from wandering.

Stay here, she commanded herself. *Don't you fucking black out.*

"We need a hospital," King said, prodding the leg again.

"She won't go to a hospital," Lucy warned. "She hates them. I'll have to pump her myself."

"Hates hospitals?"

"The light," Lou murmured. "All the light."

Speaking helped. It grounded her to a time and place outside her head. In the dark of her mind, the world was timeless, unformed. Everything existed all at once.

Lou seemed to realize that she was about to be transported, about to be taken away from her kill, and she raised her gun, centering it on Konstantine. His hands went up.

"What the hell are you going to kill him for?" King asked.

"He's the *new* Martinelli," she said. Her vision danced again.

"I'm Paolo Konstantine," he said. "It's true that Martinelli was my father, but he did not give me his name or a minute of his life."

"You're a criminal."

"You're the one holding the gun," he said with a soft smile.

The Glock shook in Lou's hand. *Why you? Why do I keep coming back to you?*

"Ryanson ordered the hit," King said behind her. But the hand on her shoulder was Lucy's. "It was Ryanson who wanted your father dead."

"Wait, what?" Ryanson said. He sat up straighter on his bench seat, making everyone aware of him again.

Lou turned her gun from Konstantine to Ryanson.

"I got the confession out of Brasso. He's the reason your dad's name got smeared all through the papers. And the reason he got shot and killed. The Martinellis were just the hired dogs."

Lou pushed herself up, forced herself to look at Ryanson. "It's a lie. I don't know what these crazy people are trying to tell you, but it's—"

He didn't finish before Lou was on him. She seized him with both hands and shoved. They tumbled into the black water. Hitting the water hurt. Everything hurt.

But Lou knew that if she was going to die, so be it.

She'd find enough strength inside herself for this.

When she broke the surface on Blood Lake, Ryanson was screaming.

Her limbs shook, threatening to fail. Her breath was labored, coming in pants.

But she wasn't looking at the half-drowned man she dragged toward shore. Her eyes were fixed on the beast waiting for them. She sat on her haunches like a poised cat, some ancient goddess prepared to accept the offering.

In ankle deep water, the senator finally stopped screaming. Seeing Jabbers had rendered him speechless.

"You like to have others do your dirty work for you," she said into the man's ear. She shoved him forward. Retribution rose to meet him. "So do I."

EPILOGUE

King put his dollar bills on the counter in exchange for a coffee and a plate of beignets. Then he shuffled from the service counter to the table beneath the green Café du Monde umbrella. Lucy sat at one of the tables in the July heat, eating pralines from a white parchment bag and sucking the caramel chocolate off her fingers. She grinned when he spotted her.

Her beauty was enough to kill him.

"Is this seat taken?" he asked, surprised, but happy to see her. She'd been absent in the two weeks since Ryanson's death. He assumed she was taking care of Louie because he hadn't seen her either. In his heart of hearts, he hoped this meeting meant there was more to their relationship. That perhaps they wouldn't disappear now that the case was over. Thorne women were hard to pin down.

But he also knew this might be goodbye. So he'd better say his piece while he had the chance.

"Please." She grinned and nodded toward the opposite chair. "A girl hates to eat alone."

"Not all girls," he said.

Lucy's smile softened. "Louie will come around. Give her time."

King squeezed himself into the chair. He put his coffee and fried donuts soaked in oil and powdered sugar on the table. They ate and let silence build between them. Fading sunlight sparkled across her face and the gray in her hair shined. He loved her more for those few gray strands.

"How long?" he asked.

She turned toward him smiling as if he'd said the magic words that she'd been waiting for. She waved a hand for him to go on.

King sighed, mustering the courage to say what he feared most. "I don't think it's a coincidence that you sought me out now. So how long?"

"That's the question, isn't it? Unfortunately, the doctors don't know. No one knows."

"Is it bad?" he asked. He'd stopped breathing.

"It's metastasized from my breasts to my bones," she said, sucking the chocolate off her thumb. "I've got anywhere from three months to twenty years."

He scowled, his appetite rapidly leaving him. "Weren't they even a little specific?"

She plucked another praline from the white parchment bag and studied it. King could smell the sugar from here. The sweet richness of the chocolate. "Most survive two or three years once their cancer metastasizes. Twenty-five percent can make it more than five years, and some hit the ten or twenty-year mark."

"You'll beat this," he said. It was a heartfelt wish as much as it was a declaration.

She spared him a weak smile. "We'll see. But I didn't come here to talk about being sick, Robert. I wanted to thank you for helping me with Louie."

He laughed. It was bitter. "You wanted me to be a positive role model. I think we can both agree I failed. Miserably."

She tilted her head. "You are a good man. I'm the one who needs work."

He barked a laugh. "How so?"

When she looked up at him through dark lashes, his heart fluttered. She said, "There's an idea in Buddhism that says nothing in this world is good or bad. It is only our thoughts that make it so. This is as true for cancer as it is for wayward nieces."

"It's good wisdom."

"Is that so?" she said, grinning. "If only I could remember it."

She reached across the table and stole his coffee, sipping it with a mischievous smirk.

He'd never buy her coffee again if she always promised to drink from his cup like this. Despite her coquettish flirtations, the truth unsettled him. Metastasized breast cancer. His grandmother had died of that, and it had not been pretty. It was a long, hard road out of that hell. And he wasn't sure he had the strength to watch her suffer like that.

"I see this as a win anyway," she said, her tone light. "I don't think you realize how withdrawn Lou was when I came to you. One case with you and something has changed. If not in her, then in me."

"Really?"

"I have *hope*."

"Hope for what?" he asked, stealing his coffee back. He turned the cup so he could press his lips to the place she'd just pressed hers.

"That she'll find happiness. And if not happiness, then contentment. Peace."

"Then she is normal," King said, touching his foot to hers under the table. "Happiness and peace—that's what we're all searching for."

After a moment of surveying his empty beignet plate he said, "So can I go with you?"

Lucy arched an eyebrow. "To death? This isn't Romeo and Juliet, Robert."

He smiled, but it was a sad smile. "To the doctor. I'm sure you've got appointments and treatments." His face flushed. "I'm not saying you need me and maybe you don't even want me there..."

Lucy took his hand and squeezed it. "You're the sweetest man alive. Do you know that?"

Lou stood over Konstantine's sleeping body with a gun in her hand. He was bare-chested and laying on top of his sheets. Italy slept outside the window behind her.

She stood there and watched him, unsure for the first time in her life of what she wanted to do.

"How old were you?" Konstantine asked. His lashes fluttered open, and he turned his head to look at her. "The first time?"

She didn't even need to ask what he meant. She traced his lips with her eyes, full and pretty like a girl's mouth. She wanted to sock him in it, see the tender flesh split and bleed. Then maybe she would kiss it.

"I think you were fourteen or fifteen," he said, smiling. "Am I right?"

"Your English is better." She still wasn't putting her full weight on her leg, but she didn't need to. Her shoulders, elbows, and hands worked. She didn't need her leg to pull the trigger and wipe the last trace of Martinelli off the face of the world.

He came up on one elbow and patted the empty bed beside him. "Would you like to lie down? For old time's sake?"

She raised the gun.

He jutted out his lower lip in an exaggerated pout. "Or are you here to put a bullet in my head?"

You're a Martinelli. You're a criminal. I want to kill you—But each statement sounded more pathetic than the last.

Instead, she said, "He never claimed you."

"No. To him, I was not his son. He only spared my life for the sake of his pride."

"Do you hate him?"

Konstantine looked away, and Lou's gaze slid to his neck. She watched the muscle move as he swallowed. Saw the throat jump with his words. "I hate what he did to my mother. She was a wonderful woman. She didn't deserve to be discarded that way."

Silence swelled between them. Finally, he looked at her again. "Do you hate your father?"

"No," Lou said too quickly. She caught herself and in a controlled voice said, "Not at all."

Konstantine nodded. "I am sorry for what Angelo did."

Her finger twitched on the trigger. "Why did you go after Ryanson?"

Konstantine looked at the barrel for a moment and then he reached out, slowly, and pulled the gun forward, pressing it under his chin. If she pulled the trigger, it would blow off the top of his skull. Easily.

"I understand drive," he said. His eyes never left hers. "I know how hard it is to stop before a thing is done. If you need this, take it."

Lou pressed the barrel against his chin so hard it would bruise.

She waited. She waited for the rage to fill her up. To roll her like a wave and pull her down with it. But the fury never came.

Then he was talking again. And she was listening.

"When I saw you on the boat, dropping one man after another, I almost laughed."

She arched an eyebrow. "Do you find murder amusing?"

He snorted. "No. But Ryanson had called the gathering an auction. Once he realized I was after him, he was going to sell me to the highest bidder. As a Martinelli and as a Ravenger, there were many bidders. But there you were, killing them all. It was...poetic. If I belong to anyone it's you. Of course, you should win any auction for my life."

She shifted her weight. The gun grew heavy.

"I am not your enemy," he said. "I believe we are drawn together for a reason. You came to me when you were dreaming. Did you dream of killing me?"

No. Her heart hammered. But the gun remained perfectly steady against his chin. She'd dreamed of feeling whole again. Dreamed of having someone who understood her as surely as her father did. Someone as steady and immovable as that mountain of a man. Someone to replace what had been taken from her.

And she still needed it—something to replace the revenge.

Her gaze bore into his, but she found no deception. She saw only dark eyes as deep as nighttime waters. An escape. Possibility.

"I wanted you to know the truth of Ryanson." He didn't push her gun away. Didn't try to pull her close. He laid there, belly up and vulnerable as he spoke. "I couldn't return your father to you, but I could give you the truth."

"The truth died with Ryanson."

Konstantine grinned. "Did it? We live in a new age, Louie. *Now* the truth cannot die."

Her battle-drum heartbeat, relentless. The gun came alive in her palm again.

"What do you want in return?" she asked. Because nothing was without price, no matter how pretty the packaging.

"My mother," he said. His eyes shone. "I want to bring her home."

. . .

KING HAD NEVER SEEN THE SHOP SO BUSY. IT WAS LIKE A RAVE. Sweaty bodies were crammed in on one another. The place was alive with the excited chatter of amateur ghost hunters. News of Lou's disappearing act had spread through the quarter like a gasoline fire. Melandra's money problems disappeared in the rearview just as fast. And however heartbroken Piper might have been over Lou's disinterest, she seemed as chatty as ever. She showed a customer with a green Mohawk a voodoo candle with a wick where its penis should be. Piper said something and the girl laughed riotously.

All around the mood had improved.

King himself was there as crowd control, one enormous body to remind all others to behave. It was pretty much the only gig he had since Venetti was saved and the senator dispatched. Without Brasso, no one else was turning up to offer him the chase of a lifetime.

He wasn't complaining.

There was so much commotion in the shop he probably wouldn't have seen Lou if the movement hadn't caught his eye. He looked up and saw her on the landing outside his apartment. She didn't wave. Didn't call out *hello*. She stood there in front of his apartment door waiting to be acknowledged.

King shuffled her way.

Mel touched his arm as he pushed past. She followed his gaze. "You going up to talk to her? Tell her that I'll give her $100 for every night that she does her ghost trick for me. If she says no, negotiate. I'm willing to go up to $500, but good Lord, don't offer her that unless you *have* to."

"I'm not sure she's interested in performing carnival tricks on demand."

Mel slapped his shoulder then shoved him in the direction of the staircase. "It doesn't hurt to ask! Tell her I'll be up until closing if she wants to stop by and negotiate. Anytime! Anytime is fine by me!"

King climbed the stairs to his loft and wasn't surprised to see that Lou no longer stood on the landing. He found her on the couch instead, scanning the first page of the *Louisiana Times. Hero Agent's Honor Restored*, the headline read. A picture of Jack smiling, two thumbs up filled the top half of the page.

"I was wondering when you'd turn up," King said. "Can I offer you a Coke? A beer?"

"Lucy wouldn't shut up until I came to see you," Lou said.

They were talking then. Good. He wondered if Lou knew about the cancer. If she didn't, she would soon enough, one way or the other.

King leaned against the doorway, looking down on her. "She's your aunt. She loves you. Though why she thinks you should waste your time on this old fool is beyond me."

Lou gave him a weak smile. "Maybe she feels pity for both of us."

King snorted, got a Coke for himself and returned to the living room. He sat beside her on the sofa with an empty cushion between them. They said nothing.

"What *did* you do with Brasso?" King asked, taking another sip of his Coke.

Lou smiled. "Who?"

King ran a hand over his face. "You *left* him there?"

"I gave him a one-way trip to La Loon."

King's eyes fell on the scarred shoulder in the moonlight. "That's the place where you keep your pet Jabberwocky." He was having a hard time understanding such a place existed. And even if seeing was believing, he thought he'd be okay if this one remained fantasy.

"And Venetti?"

"Enjoying her new life as a hotel manager in the Keys. But if you repeat that, I'll have to kill you."

He had no doubts she would kill him, if she wanted to.

He shook his head. "You know, when you jumped overboard with Ryanson, I thought that was it. The truth would die with him. No one was going to know what really happened to your dad."

Lou stilled on the sofa beside him.

"But lo and behold, your father is a hero again." King tried to read her face but saw nothing she wouldn't let him see. "Did you have anything to do with that?" he asked.

She didn't answer but her shoulders relaxed. The hard lines on her face softened. She looked ten years younger. How much youth was she hiding under Kevlar and bad dreams?

"All right, all right," he conceded. "Keep your secrets. But what will you do now? Your father is avenged. You've killed a lot of bad guys. The ones that are left are running like rats. You must be bored stiff."

"I'll think of something." She grinned and the resemblance to Jack struck him, a bittersweet blow to the heart.

"In that case, kid, come back anytime you want. I'm always looking for trouble."

ACKNOWLEDGMENTS

Always so many people to thank...First and foremost, my wife, Kim. Her enthusiasm for my stories is the biggest encouragement. Many of the ideas my readers read and enjoy—they can thank her for their existence. If she had been even a little negative or dismissive, I would have put that story aside and moved on to something else.

Thank you to my Horsemen: Kathrine Pendleton, Angela Roquet, and Monica La Porta—*especially* Monica—who let me rely on her native Italian skills to give Konstantine some authenticity. You give every story the critical eye it deserves and because of that, you make the books better—and me a better writer. I hope I'm doing the same for you.

Thank you to the horde of volunteer proofreaders who are always eager to jump in line for ARCs. We all know I'm a one-woman show here, and I rely on the generosity of those who are willing to help without compensation—except for my unending gratitude and an honorable mention here on the acknowledgments page. So this time around, thank you to Claudette Bouchard, CC Ryburn, Andrea Cook, Rachel Menzies, Rebecca Shannon, Ashley Ferguson, Misty Neal, Joe Thomas, Rhonda Green Barron, Ben Rathert, Leslie Church, Shelly Burrows, Sharon Stogner, Lisa Morris, Julie Evans, Evonne Hutton, Ashley Owen, Kerri Krauter, Amy Chadbourne Brown, and Wendy Nelson.

Thank you to The Cover Collection for the first edition cover. And Christian Bentulan for the second edition cover. They're both beautiful. And thank you to Hollie Jackson, who narrated the audiobook.

Thank you to every blogger—professional or amateur—who shined light on my work and anyone who talked about it to family or friends. Thank you for every review. *Every* review counts. It may seem trivial to you, the time it took to write your review, but it increases my discoverability and potential audience. You're vouching for me. You're giving my work a spotlight. And that is **priceless**.

I also want to thank all the Jesse fans who read this. I began my publishing journey with *Dying for a Living*—a first novel that I wrote at the tender age of 25... and many of you have been with me ever since. When I announced that I was writing a new non-Jesse series, you were overwhelmingly positive about it. You were willing to follow me into uncharted waters. And that feels pretty damn good. Really, *really* good. I thank you for it a thousand times over.

Thank you to every person who took the time to say hello on Facebook, Twitter, Wattpad, or Instagram. To everyone who took the time to write me a sweet, thoughtful email or send along fanmail. You guys are remarkably good at sensing when I've hit a rough patch in the writing. More than once, your kind words pushed me back into the saddle.

UNDER THE BONES

SHADOWS IN THE WATER BOOK 2

This one is for Josephine,
the best of writing companions.
Rest in peace, my sweet girl.

1

The blood loss was slowing him down. Darkness pooled in the corners of his eyes and he was certain at any moment, he would black out. The three bullets in his body shifted, burning in their punched-out sockets.

The toes of his leather boots scraped along the stone floor, but he kept moving. Crooked corridor after corridor, he tried to find his way out of this winding place. This palace of shadows.

It was sacrilege to die in Padre Leo's church. His old mentor had entrusted his empire to Konstantine to protect, to ensure his legacy. Not die at the hands of the first gunslinger to breach its walls.

Konstantine's knees weakened and he pitched forward. His right shoulder clipped an unforgiving wall. Pain shot through his side and stole the breath from his lungs. He crumpled to his hands and knees, the shock of impact ringing through his bones. Blood ran down his arm from the knife wound in his left shoulder. More dripped directly onto the stone from the puncture in his gut. It splattered against the corridor's floor in a soothing *pit-pat-pit-pat* that made him think of summer rain.

Not here, he thought. He wasn't sure if he was begging or praying. It didn't matter. *Not here.*

"Konstantine!" a cheerful voice called out. "Are you leaving us so soon?"

Cruel laughter echoes through the darkness. It sounded as though it was everywhere at once. Behind him. Ahead. Above and below. The sound of a hungry beast in pursuit, nearly on top of him.

"Behold your fearless leader, Ravengers," the voice went on. That omniscient, all-encompassing orator. "This pathetic boy you worship, he is nothing. Nobody."

Konstantine spat blood onto the floor, and pulled himself up to standing. His desperate fingers scraped the wall. But he was moving again and the white-hot pain sharpened his mind.

Where was his gun? He needed his gun.

"Did you really think your man Enzo could hold us back? Or the others you sent after him? *Nothing* can hold me back, Konstantine. The Ravengers belong to me. Your life belongs to me."

"No," Konstantine replied. Then his chest tightened again and he could say no more.

"No?" A hard kick to his ribs made Konstantine gasp, the leg coming seemingly from nowhere.

Konstantine dropped onto his left side, his head connecting with the sharp corner of a wooden pew. Even as red sparks exploded in front of his eyes and his vision swam, he knew where he was now. He'd made it through the bowels of the church up to the nave. There was only the center aisle and then the door that would let him out of this place.

Only a few feet more...

Yet the world was shaking. No, *he* was shaking. From blood loss and coursing pain. His body would go into complete shock at any moment.

"No?" Nico teased again. His voice hissed directly into Konstantine's ear now. "Surely you knew this was how you would die. Surely you knew I would be the one."

Konstantine supposed he did know he would die like this. On his back, his guts pumped full of gunmetal. His flesh singed with ash.

But he had always hoped it would be *her* on the other end. *Her* hands that drew his soul from his body.

My life belongs to you—if anybody. Louie Thorne. My goddess of death.

He began to laugh then, hysteria washing over him. The men beat him harder for it until all that remained was the darkness, the pain, and one clear invitation.

If you still want to kill me, Louie, amore mio, you'd better hurry, he thought. *Before it's too late.*

2

Lou lifted the orange pill bottle from the windowsill and turned it in light. She set it down, selected another, her thumb picking at the edge of a peeling label. The entire ledge was covered with these white-capped bottles like little plastic soldiers in formation.

Waiting for orders. Waiting to die.

Her hand shot out and slapped them from their sill in one furious swipe. Some bounced off the counter and spun on the kitchen floor. Others clanked into the sink.

When her petty strike wasn't enough to release the rage bubbling inside her, she curled her left hand into a fist and put it through the window.

For a moment, nothing. Then pain bloomed across her knuckles. Her whole face grew hot and she could feel her pulse spread through her chest down into her fingertips. A six-inch shard of glass protruded between her third and middle fingers. She gripped the shard and pulled. Blood spurted into the kitchen sink, splashing onto the demolished windowpane and a couple of pill bottles. Her heart rate returned to a slow, steady calm as she watched her blood coalesce into red pearls.

When she felt in control of herself again, she thought, *better clean this up before Lucy comes home.*

Her second thought, *Lucy is never coming home.*

Aunt Lucy couldn't care less about a broken window or a lost security deposit. The blood in the sink or the glass shards in the garbage disposal. Nor the pills on the floor.

She would leave NOLA Cancer Center in an urn. And that would be the end of it.

Without her aunt, she'd have no reason to pretend anymore. No one to convince that she was still human with a human heart.

Lou turned on the tap and rinsed her bloody hand until the pierced flesh looked as pale as a corpse's. Bloodless.

Why am I even here?

She wrapped her hand in a dish towel and stood in the kitchen entryway. She surveyed the apartment. There sat the sofa with its afghan, where Lou had done most of her homework until graduating eight years ago. There sat the wooden rocker holding her aunt's meditation pillow, where Lucy herself liked to sit in the evenings with a glass of iced tea in her hand, no matter the temperature outside.

True, she'd replaced the rug recently. But the pictures were all the same, and the coffee table with its scuffed legs was the same. And the sparse second bedroom at the end of the hallway still looked the way it did the last night Lou slept in it. The last night she called this place home.

The only thing that had changed was the damn pill bottles. So many damned pills bottles.

Lou didn't need to pack any of this up. She could make King do it. She could hire someone. There were whole companies that specialized in bubble wrap and cardboard boxes.

She had no reason to be here. Yet here she was.

This was your home. The only home you had after I died.

It was Jack's voice. Her father's steady tone unmistakable.

And she's the only family you have left.

Jack's ghost was never far these days. She knew her aunt's would join him soon enough. A menagerie of spirits to keep her company through the long days and nights stretching before her.

Lou pulled open a kitchen drawer and grabbed a second blue hand towel from the top of the pile. She rewrapped her bleeding hand and cast one more look at the busted window and scattered bottles before stepping into the pantry and closing the door.

For a moment, she only stood in the dark. Breathing. Her eyes slid unseeing over boxes of macaroni and cheese and instant rice that would never be eaten.

Lucy hadn't been able to use the pantry for slipping. The cold, thin light wedging itself through the cracks was enough to keep her pinned to this side of the world. Her aunt had needed complete pitch to slip through the thin places.

It wasn't the same for Lou. The light seeping between the trim and door didn't hold her back. Nor the light spilling across the floor. As Lou stared at a bag of potato chips, sealed closed with its red clip, the world thinned anyway.

It shifted beneath her. Softened. Already the slot machine handle had been pulled, and a new time and place was lining up in the dark for her.

She thought of the mess of broken glass, blood, and destroyed hand towels she was leaving behind.

Later. She would deal with that later.

You can't run from this, her father's ghost chided.

Not running. Hunting. Two hours and it would be full dark.

This one promise of violence loosened a growing knot in her back. Some women dream of slipping out of their heels and having a nice glass of wine at the end of the day. Lou dreamed of the smell of gunsmoke and the itching feel of blood drying on her hands.

She knew peace only when staring into the wide whites of a man's unseeing eyes. When she knew their heart beat out its last rhythm to the sound of her gunfire.

She slipped.

The pantry and Aunt Lucy's Chicago apartment fell away. An ambulance siren was replaced mid-wail by whooshing water in pipes. A steam engine honked in the distance. An announcer from Busch stadium called out a play.

Her towel wrapped hand pushed open the closet. The orange rays of a late afternoon stretched across her studio's bare floor. In the enormous picture window, an unobstructed view of the Mississippi river. Lou watched the water shimmer, the great red wheel churning on the back of a steamboat, a tourist vessel that seemed to float up and down the river 365 days a year. Ant-sized people wandered the boardwalk. Dogs chased the pigeons. Children splashed in a fountain. A couple paused to share a kiss.

Where were they going? Home? To their families? To warm dinners waiting or their nightly television shows?

Could she have been one of those people—if her life had started out differently? If her parents hadn't been murdered when she was a twelve. If she hadn't been born with such a terrifying and extraordinary gift...

Did it even matter?

Every body she dropped took her farther away from the life her parents and aunt had imagined for her—even if she never had the chance to imagine such a life for herself.

Lou unwrapped her bloody hand and inspected the puncture between her knuckles. The bleeding had stopped, a clump of dried blood crusted there. She tossed the towel onto her bed.

Sunlight from the adjacent buildings sparked in her eyes. While cabs honked down wide boulevards below, she crossed the room and removed a painting that hung on the brick wall. A replica of Picasso's "Girl with a Mandolin."

She remembered the first time she'd seen the painting in the MOMA, with her aunt standing beside her.

I love this painting, her aunt had said, a floral dress swaying softly along her thighs as she came up onto her toes for a closer look. *Isn't she intriguing?*

Lou hadn't been intrigued. She'd known only clear comprehension, convinced the painting was the closest thing to herself she'd ever see represented. Not because of the mandolin. In no world would Lou pick up an instrument—her only melody was gunfire—but the fragmentation, *that* was something she understood.

This is what happens to me when I slip through the darkness. Lou was split into pieces, fed through the cracks and reassembled on the other side. She kept the painting to remind her of who she *really* was—not the woman Jack or Lucy wanted her to be. They saw nothing more than pieces, assembled in the shape of a woman. A familiar image the mind constructed when confronted by the unknown.

Not the truth.

Lou knew the truth.

That if someone opened her up, they would find only darkness inside. That it was the emptiness—all the space between—that made her what she was.

Lou lifted the painting from the wall and propped it against her leg. She pressed three bricks and the façade clicked. Her thumb worked under the edge, prying it free to expose a steel safe set into the wall. Lou entered her six-number combination until the safe opened itself. She took the two Browning pistols from the top of the cash and the extra magazines.

She considered tonight's possible targets. Henry deVanti—a pimp in Atlanta who specialized in sex trafficking young girls from South Africa. Ricky Flint— a heroin dealer in New York who beat his wife and kids. Or maybe Freddie Calzone, a coyote in So-Cal who took the money from poor Mexican women dreaming of a better life, before raping them and leaving them to die in the desert, either killed by militia or captured by ICE.

So many men in the world that she wanted to see at the other end of her gun.

Once the safe was resealed and the painting back in place, she stood in her apartment with a pistol in each hand.

Her eyes roved over her counters, the bare island, and the unused stove. The mattress shoved under the large windows, the place in the apartment offering the most sunlight, and a safeguard against slipping in her sleep.

Every item she saw. The plum throw pillows. The slate gray sleeper sofa. The glass coffee table. The art deco lamp—every piece of it was Lucy's doing. It was Lucy who had begged her to get an address. To stop roving from vacant home to vacant home. Lucy who kept trying to tie her to this time, this place. Lucy...her last tether to this world. And when it's cut—

Lou looked at the pistol in each hand. The extra ammo clipped to the belt around her hips.

The compass inside her whirled to life. That internal intuition that dictated where she slipped and when. More instinctive animal than logic.

Go, go, go, it howled. *Before it's too late.*

She resisted. Her aunt may want her to visit, to hash out their last argument again, but Lou wanted none of it. Not the arguing. Not the disagreement. Not the relentless bright light of the hospital, the least safe place in the world as far she was concerned.

Lucy wanted peace. No more violence. Lou couldn't give her that.

But it wasn't her aunt on the other end of this tug. No sense of that benevolent, Buddhist essence.

There was darkness on the other end of the wire. The promise of violence.

Lou didn't like to think about her compass as having an intelligence of its own. Doing so forced her to consider an uncomfortable truth: she wasn't as in control of her ability as she wanted to be.

As a child, this was apparent. Every slip was accidental and seemingly unprovoked.

As an adult, she'd convinced herself she'd grown into it. *She* chose her locations and moved where she wanted. But she knew a lie when she heard it. And she'd been forced to confront this uncomfortable truth in June, when Konstantine, the bastard son of her sworn enemy, came crashing back into her life.

Konstantine.

She recognized the dark energy now. Konstantine was in trouble.

Go, go, go, the pull begged again. *No more time.*

Hadn't she warned him the last time they spoke that he'd better hope he never saw her face again?

He must be very desperate then.

And ready to pay the price.

3

More guns, the better. Lou removed Monet's "Waterlilies" which hung to the right of the Picasso, and opened the much larger safe behind it. She grabbed a shoulder holster from its metal shelf. She put it on and holstered her twin Glocks, one on each side. Then twin Berettas on each hip. And she kept one Browning at the small of her back and more ammo at the belt.

Safe closed, picture in place, she stepped into the closet. It was midnight in Florence, if that was where she would find him. The cover of darkness would be on her side.

Even with the three walls bare, her converted linen closet wasn't large. Her back pressed against the wall as she pictured Konstantine in her mind. Those infuriating brown eyes. The perpetual pout of his lips.

The world shifted. The steamboat's horn was cut short as the world thinned. Lou felt herself falling through the darkness, the wall at her back disappearing.

A stone floor rushed up to meet her, unyielding as it pressed the guns into her palms.

She stared at her pale hands on the stone, reorienting herself. The gash between her knuckles began to bleed again. No matter. She felt nothing. She turned her attention to the laughter. Cruel and deep. The rolling purr of Italian echoed off the walls.

She was in a church. Some ancient construction that smelled of crushed bone dust and the souls it was built on.

Flesh struck flesh. A foot or fist connected with the meat of another man.

Someone groaned.

She inched forward slowly, between the pews toward the center aisle and the sound of violence, until the clear outline of leather clad feet could be seen in the swimming candlelight.

Konstantine was on his back in the center aisle. At least three circles of blood had bloomed through his shirt, small bullet holes torn in the fabric. And when he rolled away from the kicking feet, a dangerously deep cut spread on the side of his neck, revealing far too much corded muscle beneath.

They were going to kill him, whoever these men were.

Probably crime lords like Konstantine himself. Rivals perhaps? Old enemies?

A man pulled a gun from his waist and pointed it into Konstantine's face.

Konstantine said something in Italian that she didn't understand. *A presto, amico mio.*

Lou was in a crouch, a Beretta in her hand, before she'd fully decided she wanted Konstantine to live. She pulled the trigger. One shot and the side of a man's head ruptured. The skull cap lifted like a divot from a golf swing, up into the air while the body itself hit the ground. Brains spilled into the center aisle, cereal sloshing from the rim of a dropped bowl.

The man closest to her turned immediately. Their eyes met over the church pews between them.

He fired, but she'd already rolled beneath the pew and slipped, falling through the stone floor and reemerging behind a pillar on the opposite side of the church, with all four backs to her.

Konstantine's enemy found her again, easily and his second bullet bit into the stone column three inches from her head. Dirt and grit sprayed across her face, coating her lips with salty earth.

A third shot hit her square in the chest, knocking her back. Even with the vest, it stung. A fourth bullet grazed her upper arm. It burned.

The bastard was a fast shot.

But she was faster, already falling through the shadows and rising up between two pews behind the man's right shoulder.

Her re-entry wasn't clean and he must've heard it, the pew shifting under her sudden weight. He was halfway to turning toward her when she fired. The bullet slid along the side of his face, grazing the cheek and cutting through the flesh beneath the eye. A curtain of blood now cloaked that half of his face.

He rolled out of sight, seeking shelter in the opposite pews. She emptied the Beretta into the wood, splinters flying into the air like confetti on New Year's Eve.

The Beretta clicked, empty.

She pulled the Browning without stopping to reload. Two of the hiding men popped up from between the pews.

A round was already chambered and she dropped the second man with a bullet between the eyes. He hadn't even hit the floor when she put a bullet in the third's throat. Blood spurted between his fingers as he tried to compress the wound.

It didn't save him. He sank to his knees and bled out in seconds. His own puddle meeting Konstantine's halfway.

Only two men were left of the original five. Konstantine's *amico mio* and the man closely watching his back.

Three more rapid fire shots hit her chest like three hard punches. She fell, but her back never hit the ground. The shadows swallowed her up, spitting her out on the right side of the large wooden doors. There was Konstantine, still lying in a heap in the center aisle, breath labored. If she didn't move this along, he wouldn't make it.

At least the men had forgotten about Konstantine. She proved to be very distracting.

Amico mio scanned each dark corner, eyes wide. One hand pressed a torn purple cloth to his face, soaking up the blood she'd drawn.

A purple cloth. The mark of a Ravenger.

Was he in Konstantine's own gang? Or had he simply taken the cloth from someone?

Questions she didn't have time to think about. *Amico mio* was on to her. He wasn't inching toward the row where she'd fallen. His eyes were searching the room, ready for her to appear anywhere.

His comrade bent down to examine the space between the pews.

When he rose, she blew out his brains with a double tap from the Browning.

Amico mio was already turning toward her when she stepped from the darkness.

Their eyes locked as both guns raised. She emptied the clip into his chest. He got off two more rounds into her vest. He fell backwards over the pew behind him, Italian leather boots pointing skyward before his head cracked against the stone floor on the other side.

She waited for him to rise. To pop up and seek revenge like the villain in a horror story. But the church was quiet. The scent of blood and sweat bloomed bright in the cool air.

She holstered the guns and knelt beside Konstantine.

His eyes fluttered, seeming to see her for the first time. He murmured, "*La mia dea. La mia regina oscura.*"

"You're welcome." She grabbed the bloody lapel of his shredded clothes and pulled him through the night.

4

R obert maneuvered his enormous body down the crowded corridor of NOLA's Cancer Center, a white paper bag of beignets clutched in his right hand. He flashed polite smiles at every nurse he passed, most recognizing him and returning the smile. They were a perpetual carousel of movement, in and out of rooms like drones in the hive.

Georgette, a blonde beauty queen of a nurse, stepped out of Room 716, carefully closing the door behind her. She brightened when she saw him. "Good morning, Mr. King."

"How's she doing?" Robert asked, reaching up to smooth his hair out of his face. It didn't matter that he saw Lucy every day, that there were a million things on her ailing mind besides his misplaced hair. He stood as nervous outside her hospital room as he had on their first date. Back when he was still a seasoned DEA agent and she the head-turning sister of his brightest mentee.

Something flashed in Georgette's eyes before she could mask it. She tried to hide it by picking at a clump of mascara tangled in her lashes. The black smearing across her thumb.

But the damage was done.

It wasn't Georgette's fault. King had decades of interrogation experience. It was all about the microexpressions, those hints of real emotion laid bare before a formal façade could conceal them. He didn't need her to tell him this was a bad day and it would be best to lower his expectations before stepping into the room. The flash of sadness that pinched her face told him so.

But Georgette's painted red lips projected only kindness. "She'll be happy to see you."

Robert thanked her and stepped inside the room.

The woman confined to the bed was rail thin. It was as if the breast cancer that had started in her chest before moving into her bones was liquefying her from the inside out. Only a husk remained, like the cicada husks he'd found as a child. The shape of the insect remained intact, but paper thin, and vulnerable to disintegration under the slightest touch.

"Hey baby," he said, quietly closing the door behind him.

For a terrible moment, only silence filled the room.

She was dead.

She'd left this world while he'd stood in the hall with the nurse. She'd slipped right out from under him, the way a few dealers had slipped right out the back door of their haunts as he'd kicked down the front.

Then Lucy turned toward him, repositioning her head on the white pillow.

"Why hello, Robert." Her voice was as dry as sandpaper.

The fist crushing his heart relented. He drew a breath.

He came to her bedside and eased himself into the plastic chair. Not an easy task given his size. He'd lost weight in the last three months since their reunion, but his nights in the gym had bulked him up.

Exercise. Hospital visits. Paperwork. And endless cups of black coffee filled his days now.

It wasn't the retirement he'd envisioned. He wasn't complaining. Only marveling at how even the most well planned, diligently laid tracks were rendered useless in the course of a life. Life, like water, cut its own path.

He sat the oil-soaked paper bag on the attached hospital tray. Then tore the white paper to reveal the beignets.

"I had Millie make these fresh for you," he said, sucking the powdered sugar from his thumb.

He reached into his duster and pulled out the card. Everyone at the café had signed it. Red, blue and black inks competed for each available inch of the cardstock. A watercolor tree painted on the outside, and a corny message—*Get well soon. We're all "rooting" for you*—was scrawled in calligraphy within.

He propped the cardstock tent on the table beside the beignets. "They miss you."

"I miss them too," Lucy said, her voice weak and dry. She didn't try to pick up the card. The first bad sign. She only turned her head slightly to regard it.

"It's a good thing that this room isn't darker. Or else I might fall right into the donut fryer." She tried to laugh and fell into coughing instead.

Robert had wondered. When the illness got bad enough that Lucy couldn't stay away from machines and medical supervision, he had worried how this could work. Lucy had tried to explain that her gift— what Lou called *slipping*—wasn't the same. She had never slipped by water for example. And unlike Lou who seemed to step through the thinnest shadows, even this dimly lit room was enough to hold Lucy and her failing body in place—no matter how desperate her desire to leave it may be.

Face red and chest rattling, Lucy tried to prop herself up. The plastic tubing running to her arms and nostrils trembled as her body shook with the effort. A vein stood out on the woman's face.

"Easy there," he said. He put a hand under each arm—god, when had she become so light—and lifted, easing her onto the pillows.

Then she reached for the large plastic cup and red bendy straw. He beat her to it, angling it between her cracked lips. She'd aged twenty years overnight. He was sure part of it was the hair loss, which made her face look older. And the black circles beneath her eyes amplified their sunken look.

Lucy stopped drinking, following his gaze to the inside of her arms, to the bruises he couldn't help but scowl at.

"It's fine," she said.

"It doesn't look fine. What did they do? Let the new kids practice on you?"

He scowled at the new IV.

She rolled her eyes up to meet his. "The nurses say I'm dehydrated. When you're dehydrated, the veins constrict."

Her iron was already low. Surely that didn't help.

"It's all right," she assured him again in that quiet voice. The ice shifted in the cup.

He settled back into his seat.

"How's Lou?" she asked, those blue eyes searching his.

King didn't know. He hadn't had a proper conversation with Louie Thorne for months. He could see her plainly in his mind. He'd climbed the stairs to his loft and had found her on his red sofa. He remembered how he had sat beside her with an empty cushion between them, saying nothing for a long time. The way her scarred shoulder had looked in the moonlight, not unlike a burn scar except for the ring of deep punctures forming, what could be mistaken for a shark bite. But it hadn't been a shark that had gotten ahold of her. King knew that much, though he hadn't dared to ask more.

King tried to keep his voice level despite the anger rising. "She still hasn't come to see you?"

"Don't be mad at her," Lucy chided, flashing those big blue eyes. "She's probably the only reason I'm still alive."

He frowned. "You mean you aren't living for the beignets?"

He got the grin he was fishing for. True enough it had been Lou who'd saved her, not him. When Lucy collapsed four weeks ago, Lou had been there in a heartbeat. Emerging from the darkness as if from thin air. She'd scooped the woman up and taken her straight to the hospital without hesitation, even though King knew Lou would rather bleed to death—had almost bled to death—than step foot inside a hospital. It was something about all the harsh, unforgiving light. A perpetual daytime.

Yet when the moment of reckoning came, she'd done it without the slightest pause. It seemed that before Lucy's body had fully rest on the floor, Louie had been there, scooping her up into her arms and disappearing through the dark with her.

Lucy seemed eternally grateful for this salvation. King's gratitude had limits.

The straw slurped at the bottom of the cup. Lucy shook it gently to shift the ice around. "She can't fight her way out of this."

King twisted off the white cap from the plastic water bottle and refilled her cup.

Lucy went on. "There is no killer to hunt. No one to point her gun at. She knows death, but not like this. This is different. Do you understand?"

King wasn't sure he did, but he didn't interrupt. Strength was coming back to Lucy's voice and he liked to hear it. He wanted her to keep talking. And he wanted her to drink more water.

"When I die, Jack, she won't have anyone to blame. Then what will she do?"

Jack.

All the medication they had her on at times made her fuzzy around the edges. As long as she kept breathing, he didn't care what they pumped her with—or what she called him.

It was more than that. The drugs kept her from the worst of the pain, which he knew despite all her calm reassurances, was bad.

"I'll look after her," he said, angling the straw toward her cracked lips again. He would bring Chapstick next time. And maybe some sunflowers to brighten the room. "I promise I'll keep her out of trouble."

They were supposed to have six months at least. That's what the doctors said in the beginning. But it was all moving so quickly now.

Lucy's eyes fluttered and King took the cup from her hand before she could drop it. He pulled a small pad of paper from his front pocket and a ballpoint pen. In black ink he wrote:

Chapstick
Gatorade
Maybe Ensure
Flowers

He listened to her steady breath, certain she'd dropped off to sleep.

But then she spoke. "You'll have your work cut out for you, Jack. She's as smart as you are, and twice as stubborn."

Her mouth dropped open a few minutes later, and the real snoring began.

King didn't mind.

He had his paperback and enough cash in his pocket to wander down to the cafeteria if he got hungry. Change for vending machine coffee or a Coke if he got thirsty.

There was nowhere else in the world he'd rather be.

It was enough to be with her.

He only regretted not searching for her sooner. He should have tracked her down long before she'd turned up in his apartment three months ago, begging for the favor that had sent his life careening off the tracks.

He should have forgiven her sooner, too.

Forgiven her for disappearing. Forgiven her for dropping him like a summer fling so she could assume the mantle of guardian to a pre-teen Lou.

He'd been angry, sure. But it'd taken him a long time to realize he was only angry at himself. Angry mostly for not going after her.

How many years they would've had together if he'd only gone after her.

More time with Lucy. With Lou. He could've steered the girl toward a better life. Gotten her into legal work or the DEA. Done right by her like Jack would have wanted.

Coulda, woulda, shoulda. Useless.

All that wasted time—and he would never get it back.

They'd had only two good months together before her illness had taken this turn. Two months of picnics in Jackson Square. Long nights in his bed with the French doors open and jazz music filtering in from the streets below. The sweat drying on their bare skin. Two months of pralines and red bean jambalaya and coffee on the balcony in the early morning light, her cool hand in his.

Then the collapse. Lou's rescue. A two-day coma to stabilize her.

He leaned across the hospital bed and brushed the damp bangs off her forehead. He listened to the machines click on and off, measuring her heartrate, her breathing and whatever else it deemed necessary.

He plucked a beignet off the white paper and ate it. He sucked the sugar from his fingers but it was already souring in his mouth.

In the beginning, when the weight had begun to drop off and her bones became as light as a bird's, he'd managed to get her to eat as many as six beignets in a single go. Then only four. Three. A bite. And this week—none at all.

They were running out of time.

Lucy. King. And Lou.

They were *all* running out of time.

5

L ou dropped Konstantine on the floor of her apartment. She left him there, crossing to her back bathroom where she opened the cabinet and removed her kit. A tin box the size of a laundry basket. It had plastic shelves within, army green. The top row held tweezers and twine, needles and iodine in its square compartments. The second row, rubbing alcohol and gauze of every conceivable shape and size. Wraps and cotton. Surgical scissors and clamps. Fire for cauterizing. A small bottle of whiskey. A mouthguard and bit of leather for biting down. A belt for slowing circulation.

She carried the box into the living room with a handful of old, faded and stained towels, their edges frayed. She rolled the man onto his side and put two towels beneath him to protect her floors. Then she pulled him up long enough to get the shirt over his head. With his cheek to hers, she could smell him. Blood and gunsmoke and beneath that... something that belonged only to Konstantine.

She let go and his head hit the hardwood floor too hard. He didn't complain.

She inspected the wounds. The deep cut in the neck. Four bullet holes—not three—in the torso. Two knife wounds in the back. He'd lost a lot of blood, but she could help with that. She, like Aunt Lucy, was O negative. If it came to it, she had the tubing for a transfusion in the bottom of the kit.

But she would begin with sanitizing the cuts, then digging the bullets out. She dragged the lamp over and angled it, giving her a bright, unobstructed view of the work ahead of her. Then she filled a plastic white bucket with warm water.

She settled down beside him to begin, her knees pressed against his ribs.

With alcohol and iodine, she disinfected the wounds. She pried open the scorched flesh, checking for debris. She inserted the locking tweezers into the first bullet hole, feeling it scrape against metal. A sensation she felt in her teeth. She opened the tweezers wider, spreading the wound until the metal slid around either side and clamped down.

With a sucking sound, she plucked the bullet free and dropped it into the pan beside her utensils.

Konstantine's eyes flew open, followed by a stream of Italian curses. "Abbi pietà di me!"

His eyes fluttered and she hoped he would drop back into sleep. But as she grabbed the second bullet. He was awake and cursing again. She moved fast, dropping the second bullet into the pan beside the first.

His hand seized her wrist when she inserted the tweezers into the third hole. He rolled those brown eyes up to meet hers. He was fully awake now, panting. He clutched her wrist hard enough to bruise it, but her face remained placid.

She slowly arched a brow. "Do you want me to leave it in?"

His nostrils flared, eyes dilated. A sheen of sweat stood out on his brow. "Be quick."

She plucked the third bullet out as he opened and closed his other fist. The bloodied knuckles went white, filled with color, only to go white again with each clenching motion.

She moved onto the fourth hole without pause. This bullet must have been blocking an artery rather than sitting squarely in muscle. Once plucked, blood ran like rivulets across his abdomen, following the lines of his muscles. He groaned, releasing her wrist as the tweezers hit the pan.

Too much blood. She grabbed the metal rod no wider than the face of a dime. She plugged it into the wall socket beside her bed and the heating element immediately began to glow.

"What are you—?" Konstantine began.

"You'll bleed to death if I don't."

"If you don't *what?*"

She stuck the white-hot rod into the oozing bullet hole and straight out again. The blood smoked and hissed.

Konstantine howled and kicked the floor with his boots. Lucky for him she'd already moved the rod away or he'd have cauterized more than the bullet wound.

She wet a towel in the bucket of warm water and raked it over his skin, trying to see what was left to be done. She let her left hand rest on his stomach, the towel pressed beneath it as she inspected each wound in turn. That gash where his neck and shoulder met would certainly need stitches.

He came up onto his elbows, trying to inspect it for himself. "I'm fine."

"Lie down."

"No more. I'm *fine.*"

"Lie down or I'll put you down."

He didn't. He placed a hand over hers. The sweat on his face shone.

Lou met his gaze, weighing it with her own.

"Please," he said, squeezing her hand.

She threw a right hook across the man's jaw. He dropped, the elbows folding out from underneath him.

She shook out her fist before breaking open one of the nylon suture packets.

"I don't have a way to anesthetize you and I don't want to listen to you cry anymore."

You don't have to explain. He can't even hear you.

She took a breath and pushed the needle through his flesh, deep enough to close the wound in his neck without popping through the skin. When metal peeked through the other side, she tugged the black string through in small jerky movements until there was enough blood to make the string glide slick.

She stitched the bullet holes and the ugly cut in the side of his neck. Then she added the rough gauze pinning it into place with masking tape. The water in the bucket was pink by the time she finished. Stained, bloody rags bobbed on its surface.

Confident she'd repaired the worst of it, she pressed her fingers to his pulse and found it rapid. His breath wasn't shallow. No blue tint to the lips or fingernails. His skin was warm to the touch. He might need that transfusion yet.

The urge to bend forward and lick the blood and salt from his skin swirled in her mind. She ran a finger across his jaw where she'd struck him. The line of it already darkening with the promise of a bruise.

You need fucking therapy, her exasperated aunt had cried once. Lou snorted at the memory.

She sat back on her heels and stared at the unconscious man. She rolled him onto his side to check his back.

If she had wanted to kill him, why stitch him up? Why stare at his body, searching for signs of hypovolemic shock? Why give him blood from her own veins if only to kill him later?

You know why, her father said.

If she was being honest with herself, she did know.

It was what had happened one night a month after her fourteenth birthday. She'd slipped in her sleep, unbidden, to the bedroom of an Italian boy.

Why him?

Of all the boys and all the bedrooms in the whole wide world, why had she appeared in his?

She had theories.

Their shared hatred for Martinelli had been enough. The man responsible for killing Lou's father was the same man who ruined and betrayed Konstantine's mother.

But was that really all of it?

Two dark-hearted children drawn to each other because they hated the same man? But Lou hadn't known Martinelli was behind the kill yet. So this theory was shit.

As well as a second theory that he could slip too. That perhaps they were drawn together out of that commonality. But if he could slip, he would have saved his own life tonight. Used it to cement his power with the Ravengers. So that wasn't it either.

And why should she care about the *why* anyhow? Konstantine was a street rat, like any other piece of gang trash that she wiped from the world. Worse, he was a *leader* of the trash heap. He was the puppeteer and she wanted to cut his strings.

And she could. Right now. While he was laying on her apartment floor with the Martinelli crest on his ring finger. A gold ring bearing an ornate capital M and two dragons chasing one another head-to-tail around the letter.

He's an enemy. I should be putting a bullet in his head, not draining my veins for him.

She pulled her reloaded Beretta and pressed it against the temple of the sleeping man. The cool trigger thrummed beneath her finger. The slightest pressure would be all it took to spray his brains across the floor.

He didn't stir. He didn't open his eyes, his soft breath fogging the wooden floor beneath his mouth.

I'm not your enemy, he'd said to her once.

Was that true? Or the sort of lie that a man like Konstantine relied on?

It felt as though they'd reached some agreement in their last encounter. He'd delivered the information needed to clear her father's name, and restore him to hero status. And she'd helped him find his mother's unmarked grave. Helped him unbury her and carry her back home.

But he was still the son of the man who had her father killed. He was still one of the crime lords she was trying to wipe from the face of the earth.

It didn't matter how he'd looked the night they dug up his mother. The glow of his relaxed and pensive face as they'd stepped from his dark apartment into the Italian countryside to find the night alive around them with insect song, summer in full swing, and the heat so thick it was like trying to breathe with a blanket over her face.

Yet she remembered how the sweat on his neck and back had shone in the moonlight, every muscle shifting as they dug their spades again and again into the dirt. The look in his eyes when the spade hit bone— when he knelt and uncovered what remained of her with gentle hands.

Lou lowered the gun from his head.

Nothing needed to be decided now. Others waited. Henry deVanti. Ricky Flint. Freddie Calzone.

She would start there. And if those three men weren't enough to slake her bloodthirst tonight, Konstantine would still be here.

He wasn't going anywhere. There was nowhere in this world he could go that she couldn't find him.

HER OWN WOUNDS CLEANED, AND GUNS AND AMMO REPLENISHED, Lou stepped into the emptied linen closet once more. She planned to start on the East Coast, where the sun was below the horizon, and work her way west. Henry deVanti in Atlanta or Ricky Flint in New York— either would do. And hopefully by the time she was done with them, sunset would have made its way to San Diego.

Surprise me, she told that inner compass. Henry or Ricky, it made no difference to her.

The thin veil between this side of the world and the other began to give, sliding out from under her. Her hand shot out and touched the grainy wood of the closet's opposite wall. She held this space.

The sounds materialized first. A taxi laying on its horn. Someone shouting in a harsh New York accent. Voices speaking Chinese excitedly. Tourists arguing over prices while a tired child cried.

She stepped out of the closet into the streets of New York's China-town. The scent of fried noodles and fish hit her nose. The red gates at the end of the avenue were spotlighted, twin dragons ready for a fight. The street itself illuminated with paper lanterns suspended on string.

So where was Ricky?

She scanned the crowd, checking each face in turn. She spotted him on a metal stool outside Mr. Wang's Noodle Shop, a walkup window where any passerby could stop for a quick bite. Ricky with his black baseball cap turned backwards slurped fat noodles into his mouth. His motorcycle boots with bright brass buckles kicked out arrogantly into the walkway, so that pedestrians had to maneuver around his extended legs in order to continue down the street. A mother scowled, angling her large stroller around Ricky's legs first, and then a grate spewing foul air.

A subway car screeched somewhere out of sight.

Lou leaned against the wall, her guns hidden beneath her leather jacket. She pretended to look at her phone, no doubt resembling any number of women her age all up and down New York's streets. Few would've noticed her occasional glance over the top of her screen at the man slapping cash onto Mr. Wang's counter before entering the wave of nighttime bodies.

He worked a toothpick in his mouth as he walked past Lou up the sidewalk.

She fell into step behind him, noting how he moved, which side he favored. If his gait was short or long. His pants loose or tight. Buckles or straps that could be pulled or wrapped around a throat. Bulges where a gun might sit, or the hint of a sheathed knife.

She enjoyed this part of it almost as much as the kill itself. Measuring her prey. Sizing them up. She always knew a great deal about her targets *long* before she put her hands on them.

When he started down the steps of the subway tunnel, she followed. She kept the same pace and distance. When he slapped his commuter card to the turnstile's sensor, she paused to glance at a magazine stand, pretending to give a damn about a European prince and his impending marriage, a celebrity's new baby. Someone's bout in rehab.

When he moved toward the northbound platform, she put the magazine down and stepped between two ticket-dispensing machines, and out onto the platform. She hovered there, at the very edge where the darkness met the stairwell.

This put her in front of Ricky.

No matter. She calmly walked forward, spacing herself evenly away from everyone else as the others had done. The train came. Everyone got on. Ricky worked his way to another car while she stood near the door between a pregnant woman reading a romance novel and a black man with a purple mohawk and gauged earrings wide enough to hook a finger through.

She hovered, not daring to raise her hand to the handles overhead, lest someone see how much heat she was packing under her leather.

When Ricky exited four stops later, she let him go. Making her way to the back of the car as a new throng of passengers wedged themselves aboard. A gaggle of drunk girls cackled loudly, everyone a similar shade of blonde, eyes painted black. They were her age and yet she couldn't have felt more different from these candy-coated creatures than if she'd been born with a second head.

Lou slipped through the shadows connecting the two cars and found herself in Central Park.

A small stream babbled off to her right. A dog and its master trotted by, white reflectors bouncing in the darkness.

She spotted Ricky a few feet away, smoking a cigarette and talking to a Latina woman with hair as red as the dress stretched tight over her comically large breasts. When she turned away from him, he grabbed her wrist and brought his open palm across her face.

Lou's hand was on her gun before she thought about it. She was going to put a hole through that hand. She caught herself, reigning in her thirst.

She would have him, but there was a process. A fool-proof procedure and she wouldn't throw that away just because he'd pissed her off.

Be careful, Jack said. And he'd said as much when he was alive. *When you're angry, that's when you have to be careful.*

They'd been doing dishes together. He was wet up to his elbows and she was drying plates. She'd been complaining about her mother, no doubt. And Jack told her the story of Bernie Jensen, a young agent who got himself shot twice in the face because he couldn't control his temper.

Anger is powerful, he'd told her. *That's why you have to be very careful when it's on you.*

When it's *on* you.

He'd made it sound like a beast that could seize you in the dark if you were caught unaware. She'd had quite the education in anger before his death, and much more after. And she had to agree with him. It *was* a beast in the dark and sometimes you didn't know it was on you until the teeth were quite deep.

Her eyes scanned the park. Most had vacated this area in the coming nightfall. Just as well.

When Ricky's hand connected with the side of the woman's face a second time, Lou slipped up right beside him.

She grabbed the back of his neck and pulled, yanking him clean off his boots, away from New York and what remained of his life.

Central Park was replaced with an isolated lake thick with midnight fog.

Once the fresh air hit her, she let him tumble to the sandy bank.

One of his hands, the one that had slapped the woman, hit the water's edge. The place didn't smell like pine as her Alaskan retreat did, but of dense forest all the same. Trees she'd never smelled in the U.S. mingled with the evergreens. Linden perhaps. Maybe scotch broom.

Lucy would know.

Her chest clenched.

The frogs fell silent, the croaking chorus stalling at Ricky's splashing. But the rest of the night remained alive with sound. Something screeched in the darkness overhead. Nighthawks or an owl searching for a meal. Crickets continued to sing. She breathed deep. The only shame was the cloudy sky blocking out the stars.

This wasn't her favorite lake. But this little plot of remote Nova Scotia wilderness was priceless in its own way. It was harder to find water like this far from human eyes and the industrialized world. The perfect entry point to her alien dumping ground.

Ricky's boots slid in the dirt as he regained his balance. He reached behind his back for the .357 he kept there. Then his face pinched with predictable confusion. They always reached for their guns like this, only to find she'd already relieved them of it.

Lou pointed the pistol at his face.

This was her process. A clear-cut, no error approach to killing. Take them to the water's edge. Somewhere dark. Somewhere remote. Slip through the waters to La Loon, that otherworldly destination unknowable to any but herself and her victims. Kill them and leave their bodies for the beast who prowled its shores.

No bullets. No casings. No gunpowder or evidence. No bodies. No blood. No witnesses, except maybe those from the point of abduction—like the prostitute turned drug mule who no doubt stood in Central Park right now, trying to wrap her head around Ricky's disappearance.

"Get in the water," she said.

He didn't. Instead, he lunged toward her, hands out to grab the gun.

No sense of self-preservation then. She shot his hand. The one he'd used to slap the woman in Central Park. It stopped him in his tracks. He turned, howling, crushing his wounded hand protectively against his body. This did nothing to staunch the blood. It ran down his front, soaking his shirt.

"Get in the water."

"Fuck you!" His whole arm shook as he cradled his bleeding hand against his chest.

She shot him in the shoulder, four inches above his heart. He cried out, collapsing to one knee.

"If I have to ask you again, Ricky. I'm going to shoot you in the face."

And she would. She didn't like talking and if she had to, she wouldn't waste the energy on a man like this.

The furious man stumbled to his feet. He considered diving for the gun again. She saw the desire written all over his face. One smile from her lips, a silent *I dare you* convinced him otherwise.

Instead he dove for the water. His leather jacket slapped at the surface. The image of it reminded her of Angelo Martinelli, the night she killed him. He'd swam away from her too, his jacket also floating on the water's surface.

She stooped to pick up the two bullet casings before tucking his gun into her waistband and diving into the water after him.

When he saw her coming, he turned to face her, probably believing he had the upper hand now. This only excited her. Her pulse jumped in her throat. She caught up to him in a few, long strokes, her hands seizing wet fabric of his jeans beneath the water.

He grabbed a handful of her hair. Pain bloomed through her skull. No matter. She had her arms and legs around him. A python's grip as she pulled him down.

And down.

Until the nighttime waters turned red, became a different lake in a different place. Then she pushed off his body and launched herself up.

She broke the surface first. The red patina stretched out endlessly before her. The white mountains in the distance. The strange yellow sky overhead holding not one, but two swollen moons. A black forest with short trees and heart-shaped leaves. Incongruous colors that were so different than those of her home world.

La Loon.

No matter what waterway she entered in her world—be it a river, an ocean, a bathtub—La Loon with its eternal dusk was the only destination.

Ricky surfaced behind her, screaming. He kicked and flailed in the water, no doubt drawing every predator within a mile to its shore.

She swam toward the beach in slow, controlled movements. Not panicked. Not like prey. Each easy stroke was an act of self-control. And should she find herself jerked under by some creature, that was what her knife was for.

But she wasn't attacked. The silty bottom rose beneath her like a partially submerged boat ramp. Each step elevated her out of the water until she reached the shore. She stood there dripping wet, watching Ricky flail in the water.

"What the fuck? What the fuck?" He paddled tight circles. He seemed unwilling to swim toward the shore. Instead he gaped at the moons, at the water, at the mountains.

Had she looked so bewildered the first time she'd fallen through and broke the surface of Blood Lake? No doubt. But she'd been a child.

"Keep screaming and you'll be eaten," she called to him, enjoying his wide panicked eyes. She could put a bullet in him here, spray his brains across the water's surface. Watch the little creatures bob up to gobble the bits the way fish often did in their tanks. And even if she did nothing, he would exhaust himself soon enough. He couldn't tread water for long in that leather coat and boots.

Something flashed in her periphery and she pulled her bowie knife without pause.

A monstrous black face broke through the trees and screeched. A mouth opened wide showing no less than four or five rows of long teeth the color of puss. A large white tongue lolled in its mouth, and the interior cheeks puffed, which always made Lou think of the cottonmouth snakes she'd seen as a child, hiking the woods with her father.

The first time she'd seen this creature it had tried to eat her. Bit clean through her shoulder and tore the muscles there. She'd survived only because she'd fallen backward into the water, the creature still astride her.

Since then, they'd reached an understanding. This beast might have the same black-scaled, white-mouthed coloring of a cottonmouth, but she was no snake.

She had six legs with talons, curved nails that dug into the earth as she walked. Between the toes was webbing, no doubt useful in the lake spreading out before her.

"You could eat him," Lou told the creature. "But I don't think he's going to come out."

She lowered the knife.

"Come up here, Ricky. Someone wants to meet you. Don't be an asshole."

Ricky, who'd been gaping at the mountains, pivoted toward shore and saw the beast. Nothing short of abject terror seized him. Screaming as if he were being boiled alive, he paddled with all his might away from the shore, toward those white mountains in the distance.

As if he'd ever reach it.

With an excited purr, the scaly creature slid off the bank into the water after him. Her long, graceful body skimmed the surface, the contracting muscles propelling her forward in a smooth glide.

I guess she does look like a snake, Lou thought, grinning.

"Don't run, Ricky," she called out. "You'll only excite her."

6

Nico stood bare-chested in front of the bathroom mirror. Splattered blood had dried into his chest hair, matting the coarse strands together. He met his eyes, a dark amber and took a deep breath. For good measure, he wrapped his hand around the sink basin. With his other, he slipped a thin blade into the puckered wound below his left collarbone.

Metal scraped metal.

Gritting his teeth, he dug deep then flicked upward, dislodging the bullet from its hole. It hit the basin with a fresh splatter of bright blood. It rolled toward the drain, resting on top of the silver grate.

Her eyes burned in his mind. That slender neck he wanted to wrap his hand around.

So she was real.

He'd heard the stories.

Before he'd moved against Konstantine, he'd learned all he could about his "brother." He'd heard of the woman. But he hadn't believed she was real. That Konstantine was stupid enough to devote himself to a woman—of course. He was soft the way his father had been soft.

But it had been the way the Ravengers spoke of her, as if she wasn't really a woman at all.

She's a ghost. A strega. A demon.

Konstantine sold his soul to her and she made him invincible.

Tutte cazzate. Nico didn't believe a word of it. Men could be superstitious fools.

They made her immortal. Untouchable. A creature who couldn't be reasoned with or bought. Coerced or demurred.

She comes for your soul and she eats it.

That he believed.

He'd seen her with his own eyes. Her stare had been cold and unforgiving. There was no woman on the planet who had that look about her. Like she would have blown out his brains and licked the skull cap clean.

But he saw the truth tonight—along with the horror.

Not only was she a monster, but the beautiful beast did, for whatever reason, serve Konstantine.

He had a monster—but she wasn't immortal.

She hadn't used teeth and claws to tear his men apart. She'd used guns. And he'd seen the way she fell back when he put a bullet in her chest. The vest saved her life. And how lucky he'd been wearing one himself.

No, she wasn't immortal. She was only a very dangerous woman with a very powerful gift.

A knock came at the door.

"Sì?" Nico said.

"The men are restless, sir."

They would be. Their master has disappeared and while he was certain he held most of the dissenters at bay with his own small army, he had to bring order. He needed to calm them, push them into line.

"Gather them in the nave. I'll be out in a moment."

The footsteps trailed away.

He thought of the bright bathroom with its blessed light, and the twisting, dim corridors that stood between him and the nave.

He met the wide dark eyes of the man in the mirror. He laughed. One firefight, and he'd become terrified of shadows.

That wouldn't do.

This empire was his birthright. And his chance to seize it was at hand. He wouldn't let a *thousand* bloodthirsty she-demons keep him from it.

He ran a hand over his shaved head, fingering the new cut she'd given him.

He straightened, running a wet cloth over his bloodied chest. He stuffed the bullet wound with a wad of cotton, no time for suturing now, and pulled on his bloodied shirt.

Let them see the damage.

The blood crusted under his fingernails and the cut across his face, where her bullet had kissed the bone. The oozing sockets.

Let them see that he was ready to pay any price.

Reloading his guns, he slipped them into their holsters. Every movement made his lungs constrict with pain. No matter. He could lick his wounds when he was alone. Now was not the time for it.

He stepped out of the bathroom into the darkness. His heart sped up, his eyes darting to the corners, ready for any movement beside his father's old bookshelves, the fireplace where the hearth burned. Flame flickered across the desk and chairs, the stone floors. The shadows danced, seemingly alive.

He didn't linger.

He stepped through the great wooden doors and found his personal guard waiting at attention.

They fell into step behind him as he took the lead, up the stairwell to the church above.

Voices murmured through the open space.

The pews had been righted, but wooden splinters sat clinging to the red carpet of the center aisle.

When they saw him, all their eyes fixed on him. The conversation died.

"Where is Konstantine?" someone called.

Nico's right guard put a bullet between that man's eyes. Brains splattered onto the men closest to him as the body hit the floor like a sack of flour. A mist of blood hung in air where his head had been.

Nico waited for the commotion to settle, for the men to stop cowering in the pews like scared children. Then he spoke.

"You've heard the stories about his *strega*," Nico said. "She came to claim him. Spirited him away earlier tonight. I don't think he will be back."

He saw the hate in their eyes. There was a great deal of loyalty to that traitorous bastard. This didn't matter. He would win them over in time. For now, he would settle for obedience. And if they wouldn't obey, well, he had a plan for that too.

Uneasiness shifted through the masses. The soft murmuring began again.

"And why would you want him?" Nico asked. "She preys on you. She's plucked so many of our own men from the streets and he has done nothing to protect you. He *lets* her take your lives, sacrifices you like little children to a hungry demon."

Every eye was fixed upon him.

"Is that what you want? To fear the darkness? To live each day, dreading the coming night?"

Murmurs of dissent rose.

"I can offer you more. And why shouldn't I be the one?" he said. "*My* father, our beloved Padre wanted to name me his successor, but he feared Konstantine and the strega."

Some outrage burst from the pews. The guard on his left raised their guns but Nico waved them down.

"You don't believe me? You think Padre preferred that traitor to his own flesh and blood? Does that sound like the Padre you knew?"

Confusion rippled through the crowd.

"Konstantine is not who you think he is. He uses you only as a means to an end and will betray you, if you give him the chance. He is a Martinelli. Old World power. And we do not need him."

Someone cheered. A few clapped.

Most sat silent.

Maybe he hadn't sold the idea, but he had sowed the seeds of doubt. That was well enough. The rest would come in time. When he dumped the bodies of Konstantine and his strega at their feet, they would have no choice but to bow to their new king.

7

L ou stared down at the man in her bed. A man. In her bed. The idea itself made her itch for her gun. She supposed it was only fair. Hadn't she slipped into his bed all those nights ago?

She had tried leaving Konstantine on the floor but the pressure from the hardwood made his wounds seep. She considered dumping him on the couch, but if he bled on it, she would be forced to scrub at the purple suede, more effort than she was willing to invest.

The bed at least was soft enough to cradle his wounds without pulling them open, and also easier to clean. Sheets could be washed—or burned—much easier than couch cushions.

And she'd be lying to herself if she said she wasn't curious.

Is this what it had been like for him?

When he woke one night twelve years ago to find a girl in his bed?

She tried to imagine herself as that girl. Her hair had been long, nearly to her waist. His room had been full of moonlight, as her apartment was now.

How long had he stood there, thighs pressed to the side of the mattress staring down at her? That's what she remembered seeing when she woke up.

A looming boy, his hand reaching toward her cheek. When his fingers had brushed her, she'd shot up, realizing she wasn't dreaming.

Despite the extra lights, all their precautions, she'd slipped in her sleep anyway.

She remembered how he'd stepped back when she'd gasped. Held up his hands in apologetic reassurance. The soft Italian rolling like a song from between his lips. Such an innocent boyish face. And he was a boy then. None of the sharp angles and battered flesh he was now. He'd grown just as hard over the years as she had.

And what had she thought the first time she'd seen Konstantine the man?

She thought her compass was only bringing her to another target. Another hit. She expected another quick, efficient kill.

But when the bathroom door had finally opened, there he was. His hair in his eyes. Green eyes widened at the sight of her pointed gun. She'd recognized those eyes immediately. Even before she registered the scruffy jaw. His bare chest and a tattoo snaking up one bicep. A crow and crossbones tattoo that now shone in the moonlight from her open window. As he lay turned away from her, his back swelling with each rhythmic breath.

Why *him*? Why did her compass keep throwing them together?

"I can't stay here," she said. As if he were awake and needed her excuse.

She grabbed the Browning off the coverlet and stepped into the closet before he could wake to the sound of her voice.

At first she only stood in the dark, slapping the gun against her thigh. *Anywhere*, she told the darkness. *Take me anywhere.*

Instead of directing the compass as she often did, following some predetermined pull, she let go.

She let go and fell backwards through the dark.

Cold tile pressed into her back. A metal bar running the length of one wall appeared under her sweaty palm.

A strip of light spilled from the space between door and jamb, cutting across a porcelain toilet.

A bathroom then. Another bathroom. So often Lou's world felt as if were made up of bathrooms and closets. Like stop signs on every corner. A common thoroughfare.

"Louie?" a voice called.

Her heart faltered in her chest, her empty hand tightening on the metal bar. And she knew in that instant where she'd gone.

More betrayal. Could her compass even be trusted at all anymore? This is what she got for loosening her grip on its reins. For being stupid enough to trust the wild horse galloping within her.

"Lou?"

She stepped into the doorway and stopped breathing.

Lucy lay in the hospital bed. Her blue eyes shone wide in her gaunt face. The clear breathing tube in her nose matched the tubes running from her bruised left arm. Machines clicked on and off. That smell...that *horrible* smell. Acrid and sour.

Not coming from her aunt exactly, but the hospital itself. As if it were a living, breathing creature and they were huddled in its bowels, soaking in its stench.

It took her a moment to recognize it as the scent of death. It was so unlike the death she knew. Violent death that bloomed like night jasmine, opening its petals to the full moon. That scent was fruit dashed against the kitchen floor. Fragrant decay burst open.

This was a death she didn't know. Seeing the different side of someone you thought you knew well. Shocking and in its own way, more terrifying than anything she'd faced on the other side of her gun.

"Please don't go," Lucy said. Her voice cracking with the effort.

She tried to sit up.

"Stop. Just stop," Lou begged her. "Let me help you."

This seemed to settle the woman. Lou lifted her gently, flinching at her aunt's hiss of pain. This close she could smell the scalp. The medicine oozing from the pores in her skin.

Lucy's hand clamped onto hers. It was so cold. As cold as any number of the corpses she'd heaped onto the shores of La Loon.

"It's so good to see you," Lucy said, her breath labored.

Lou couldn't return the compliment. Not because she didn't have tremendous bittersweet love for the woman dying before her, but because her aunt looked horrible. There was nothing nice about what she was seeing. She was death personified. A mummy that someone had dressed up as her aunt.

"Has King been keeping you company?" Lou asked.

The idea that her aunt could've been alone in this bed, trapped in this place...

"He comes every day." Her blue eyes searched Lou's face. "You have blood on you."

"It's not mine."

Her aunt gurgled. Choking. Then Lou realized it was laughter.

"What a relief," her aunt said with a wry smile.

Lou wanted to sit down. Her shaking legs threatening to buckle under her.

Her aunt's hand tightened on her own, probably mistaking the movement for an early departure. "I'm sorry I got sick."

"Don't say that. It isn't like you could help it."

Lucy's soft smile vanished. "I want you to promise me something."

Here it is, Lou thought. *The command to stop killing. The final bargain between us.*

She missed their old arguments. When her aunt began with gentle encouragement, before devolving to guilt-tripping and outright demands. At least then they'd been on equal ground. This was like fighting a child. Like pointing her gun at a dog in the street.

"Don't blame yourself for this."

Her words stole the breath from Lou's lungs.

"I know it will be hard, but there is no one to blame for this."

Lou's throat tightened in on itself. She hoped her face didn't betray her.

Lucy raised a shaking hand and touched Lou's cheek.

"You have so much strength, Lou blue. You need to turn it *out* instead of turning it on yourself. Promise me you'll try."

"I don't know what you're asking for." She was fairly certain she'd turned all her abilities against the world. Every time she plucked a man from the streets, soaked her hands with his blood—wasn't that what she was doing?

Lucy's hand seized her own. "Use your gift to *protect*, not punish. You could help so many. All I ask is that you try. *Promise me* you'll try."

"I—" Lou began, but she didn't finish.

The door to Lucy's hospital room began to slide open and Lou only caught sight of the barest hint of blue scrub pants. She tore herself from her aunt's grip and bolted. She dove into the bathroom's darkness and through to the other side.

8

Konstantine's eyes fluttered open. Sunlight cut into his vision, whitewashing the world. When he turned his head to escape it, all the air left him. There she sat, on a sofa the color of a king's cloak. Eight or nine guns were spread on the table before her, their shapes flashed prismatic onto the floor beneath. He watched her clean and inspect their chambers, the sunlight radiant on her skin.

So it hadn't been a fever dream. She had truly pulled him from Nico's merciless grip.

But the idea was as strange as seeing her here in full daylight, his creature of shadow.

He rolled onto his side and groaned. Pain flashed red behind his eyelids. Sharp pricks all the way to his toes.

"Bust another stitch and I'll let you bleed to death," she said, looking into the barrel of a .357. His gun, he realized. "I'm tired of stitching you up."

"Are you cleaning my gun for me?"

"My gun, you mean?" It sounded like a joke, but she wasn't smiling.

He sat up, inspecting the gauze taped to his chest and neck. What he could see was pink, soaked through with blood. She'd left the blood crusted across his knuckles, the few good hits he'd gotten in.

Nico.

Konstantine had known there would be opposition to his rule. When Padre Leo had taken him into his study beneath the church and made his wishes clear, the old man had said as much himself.

He hadn't expected it to come from his own men, those who'd known and loved Padre as long as he had, who'd known his wishes. But they'd known Nico too. All of them boys, having the run of the church and the Florentine streets—Konstantine should have guessed what would happen if they were forced to choose sides.

"Problems with the wife?" Lou asked. Her voice pulled him from his memories.

Her face was placid and unreadable.

"I don't have a wife." If he wanted anyone in the world to know he was available for such a union, it would be this creature. Though he couldn't imagine marrying Louie Thorne any more than he could imagine transforming into a crow and flying into the sunset. This woman, with an arsenal laid before her, that cold and unwavering glare—his *wife*?

He began laughing and instantly regretted it. His ribs throbbed as if a knife was wedged between each one.

"A boyfriend then," Lou said, inserting the magazine into the clean gun and picking up another.

"Nico Agostino would sooner drown me in the Arno river than kiss me," he said, daring to look at her again. Had he been permitted to simply gaze at her like this before?

He supposed he hadn't had the luxury since the night she appeared in his bed, a mantle of black hair flowing around her. But her hair wasn't black, was it? It looked so in the moonlight, as rich as crow feathers. But in the sun, he realized it was actually a radiant brown, warm hues of red underneath. And her face wasn't alabaster. A Michelangelo come to life. Pale, yes. But a hint of freckles across her cheeks.

"I'm just trying to understand how one of the most powerful crime lords in the world was able to get jumped. In his own house."

"We grew up together, Nico and I," he said. It was hard to speak with his chest as bruised as it was. The wounds made it tight. "As boys we had the same friends. We all entered Padre's gang around the same time." *Francesco. Matteo. Vincenzo. Calzone.* And how many more? "They helped him."

"No honor amongst thieves," she said.

Thinking of the betrayal hurt more than he expected. He tried to think of anything else.

Anything.

Fortunately, here was the most beautiful distraction.

So different was his goddess by day, that if he'd seen her on the streets, would he have recognized her?

"Did you kill him?"

"Your boyfriend?" she asked. "I emptied my clip into his chest, but I'm pretty sure he had a vest on."

"You didn't check?"

Her cold stare met his. Ah, there was his death goddess. His Kali come to dance on his stone cold corpse. "If I'd wasted time checking on him, you'd be dead."

She had let a kill slide in order to scrape him off the church floor? Abandoned a thrill to save his life? A fortnight ago he would have sworn it impossible. *I wonder if she herself understands the significance.*

She was still watching him, eyes narrowed. "Would you rather be dead? Because I can fix that."

She chambered a bullet.

"No. I'm...surprised."

She put the gun on the table and twisted the cloth between her fists. "That makes two of us. Who knew the great Konstantine would call for help."

"I didn't."

"You *did*. I—" Her teeth clenched. She swallowed whatever she'd meant to say next.

"Is that how it works?" he asked, unable to hide his curiosity. "You can feel people call to you and you simply go to them?"

It was clear the question unnerved her.

"I don't come like a dog."

"I didn't call you," he said, sitting up on his elbows.

This admission only seemed to trouble her more.

"I didn't call you the first night you fell into my bed either," he added, his voice tight. Pain ricocheted through his body. Every movement hurt. It felt as if he'd been lifted and slammed against the church's stone floor a hundred times.

She stood from the sofa suddenly and stepped into the adjacent hall. A cabinet opened. A tin lid clattered to the floor. A tap ran, splashing water into a basin.

She reappeared with a wet rag and a bundle of gauze.

Instead of kneeling before him, tenderly wiping at his wounds as he desperately hoped she might, she threw the rag into his face. Its wet body hit home, blotting out the world. A heartbeat later, the plastic wrapped gauze hit his chest.

"You're bleeding again," she said. "Better wipe it up or you'll be sleeping in it."

She was right. The white gauze covering one of the bullet holes, one about six inches below his left nipple had blossomed red. A geranium in the afternoon sun. He carefully worked a nail under the curling tape and wiped the cloth across his bare skin.

She scowled. "Don't wipe it. *Press.*"

He rolled his eyes up to meet hers. "I have done this before."

"And you've got ugly scars to prove it."

"They aren't ugly."

She cocked another gun. "They're *hideous.*"

He caught a hint of a smile before she stood and walked away from him toward the kitchen. Then he seemed to see the apartment for the first time. The regal sofa the color of bruised fruit, yes. But also the large windows and mattress on the floor. Four pieces of art on the brick wall running the length of the apartment. The wood floors and an island with a gray marble top. A kitchen that looked as though it belonged in a museum—untouched. Her apartment was only a little larger than his own.

"Is this where you live?" he asked. He didn't say *you brought me back to your place?* But he was certain the astonishment was clear enough.

"I don't usually perform minor surgeries in dark alleys. Even for ungrateful men who *call* for my help."

"I didn't call you," he insisted. Then his mind betrayed him with a pristine memory.

If you still want to kill me, Louie, my love, you'd better come now.

"Not exactly," he amended.

She stood there with a glass of water. Eyebrow raised.

"I only thought, 'if you want to kill me, you'll miss your chance if you didn't come.'"

Her long ponytail rested over her shoulder, her face the same unreadable mask it always was. But he thought he saw something in the eyes.

"How considerate," she said finally, putting the glass on the table out of reach.

"May I have a drink of water?" he asked.

She pushed the glass toward him. He tried not to flinch at the sound of it scraping across the surface. He was fairly certain she did it to rouse him. To provoke him to anger.

He only said, "Grazie."

When he opened his mouth to sip, his jaw clicked. Fresh pain welling up with another memory.

"You hit me," he marveled.

"You wouldn't stop crying."

"I was *not* crying."

"Maybe not with Nico. But with me, you wouldn't shut up." She picked up another gun from the coffee table, meeting his eyes over its barrel.

Was this affectionate teasing? *Dio mio,* how he had dreamed of this. When he laid in his bedroom, surveying the starlight on his ceiling, he'd imagined what it would be like to hear her voice. To speak with her. To feel her smooth skin under his hands, her legs and body wrapped around him.

Yet the moment was tainted by Nico's snarling face. His promise to undo all that Padre had built. A legacy he had trusted to Konstantine with his last breath.

He couldn't let that happen.

"I will need your help to bring him down," Konstantine said, setting the water glass on table.

"Again—not a dog."

"And I would never treat you as such."

Her face pinched, her gaze sliding up and away at a memory. Was he asking for too much?

"I'm only asking you to do what you would do anyway," he said. "Take down a dangerous man who would hurt so many. Restore order."

"Is that what you do, Konstantine? Keep order in the criminal world? How is Nico any different than you?" She removed the magazine from a gun, pressing her thumb against the top bullet. His body softened at the sound of his name.

He wanted her to say it again. And again. He wanted her to moan it.

"Why should I care about your petty turf wars? If you kill each other, it's less work for me."

"Do you really think we are all the same?" he asked her. He didn't hide his offense. "Is there a line in the sand for you? With all the narcos and crime lords and bastard sons of thieves on one side and who then is on the other? You?"

She leveled him with an unmoving glare.

It occurred to him that she might be nervous. All the guns between them, the incessant unloading, cleaning, reloading—did he make her nervous? He was wounded, vulnerable. But so was she in full daylight. And he was here.

Where was *here*? He sat up on his elbow and gazed out the large windows. There lay an unadulterated view of the shining river. A steamboat like something out of a Mark Twain novel, floated on the water. Tourists ambled up and down the cobbled river walk and to the right, a tall, sweeping arch, shining like a fish in the sunlight. He'd seen this structure in movies and on postcards. The Arch.

St. Louis.

But the part that stuck in his mind was the apartment facing a river like his own. Were they really so similar? Or was he a romantic fool?

For all he knew she brought men here all the time. Any man she wanted.

Fire surged up his neck into his face. He would sever the fingers of any man who'd touched her. He'd draw his knife right across those knuckle bones, feel the blade scrape the joints, then *crack*.

He released his anger with a laugh, falling back onto the pillow and covered his face with his hands.

Forget Nico. This creature would drive him mad long before that fight came.

"What's so funny?"

He groaned. "Me."

The bed smelled of her. God help him. He was swimming in her scent. He put the pillow over his face and breathed.

Something poked through the pillowcase, catching the corner of his eye. His finger traced its outline. A tag? No. This was thicker, and larger. He slid his hand into the cotton casing and plucked the object free.

A photograph came away in his hand. The edges were curling in on themselves. Perhaps for being so poorly preserved inside a pillowcase instead of in a frame where it should be.

In the picture, a large man smiled up at him. His eyes were haloed by dark hair, the same color as Lou's, wet and falling into his eyes. But the eyes themselves were different. She must have her mother's eyes.

When Konstantine registered the massive arm around Louie, a girl then even younger than when they first met, he realized who he was looking at.

It was her father, Jack Thorne. He saw the resemblance now. But his gaze kept sliding to the girl tucked into the crook of her father's big arm, one ear pressed to his chest, a front tooth missing.

A child. To imagine such a creature was once a child.

And as if by premonition, Konstantine imagined another girl this age in ten or fifteen years, looking like Louie, but with Konstantine's green eyes.

The photo disappeared from his hand as if by magic. And Konstantine turned in time to see Lou slip the plucked photograph into the back pocket of her cargo pants.

"Touch my things again and I'll dump you on Nico's step, hog-tied with a ribbon pinned to your ass."

"I'm sorry," he said. Because for all his jokes and banter, her father was no laughing matter. He knew this was one untouchable part of her. A bone that had been broken long ago and reset poorly. If he prodded this carelessly, she would end him. This he understood. It was like the wound he carried for his mother.

Go watch your movie, amore di mamma. A cool hand brushing through his hair.

This was a day for memories it seemed. A day for ghosts.

Silence stretched between them. The light from the large windows turned orange with afternoon.

"At least we understand each other," she said, finally, settling onto the sofa across from him again.

"We do?" Konstantine turned toward her. Every inch of him ached, but for now, it was enough just to look at her, watch her body move as her scent cocooned him.

"If anyone is going to kill you, Konstantine," she said with a delicious grin. "It's going to be me."

9

Nico crossed the plaza enshrining the Duomo and headed south, toward Konstantine's apartment. The crisp September air slid along his shaved scalp, prickling his skin. The scent of food wafting through restaurant windows and petrol burning from engines surrounded him.

Florence.

He'd been born and raised in this ancient city, before his traitorous father exiled him. But it had changed in the ten years since he'd left.

He loved Florence. With its cobblestoned town center and statues as old as civilization itself. Loved the stone walls, bridges, and ancient churches. Loved the river cutting through it as pigeons the color of sheet rock perched on buildings. Loved how one could turn a corner and suddenly be staring at a fountain built centuries before.

It was an old city built on the corpses of men. Bones fertilized the earth beneath his feet. Kingdoms rose, flourished, and fell here. Some of those kings had even been banished, like himself, only to return and dance on the corpses of their enemies.

And Nico would dance.

He thought of his father. Of his last night in this city before he'd been shackled and thrown into the back of a truck.

He'd been seized from his own bed. Gagged, shackled, and dragged through the street. He rode in the back of a squat car, bouncing on the cobblestones in the early morning mist. When the brakes squealed at the water's edge, for a terrifying moment, he thought they were hefting him into the river. Surely the shackles would have pulled him down, pinning him to the bottom of the Arno's dark floor.

He was certain it was a rival gang. Enemies that had found his home in the night and had moved against him.

But when the tailgate dropped, and he saw his own father—he knew the truth.

He was to be the sacrificial lamb.

And why? Because his father's friend Giovanni lost a daughter. Bella had been caught in the crossfire of a petty bust, taking a bullet from Nico's own gun, and now he would be thrown to the dogs for it. As if it was meant as a personal offense.

What story did his father tell himself? An exiled child in exchange for a dead one? That he was saving Nico's life from Giovanni's retribution? He probably painted the betrayal as mercy.

Lies.

The truth was Nico had always been ambitious. He wanted the Ravengers for himself. He thought he'd hidden this desire to usurp his father well enough. But looking into those pale eyes in the morning mist, that unforgiving face in the light—he knew he'd done a poor job of it.

His father, the great *Padre,* or *Father Leo* to every street rat in the city, had the power to placate Giovanni.

A thousand men in the city would've answered his every beck and call. If only he'd raised his hand or voice to rally them. Instead, he'd used the first transgression brought against Nico as an excuse to be rid of him. If it had been Konstantine who'd slain the girl, there would've been no hesitation. Padre would've moved Heaven and Earth for his bright boy.

But Nico was not Konstantine.

I know why you're really doing this! He'd shouted through the gag as three men dragged him from the truck bed and tossed him into the back of the waiting truck, the coarse straw pushing through his night shirt. *I know why!*

Nico was the only real threat to Padre's empire and his heir. For if given much more time, Nico would've risen up and seized his father's throne. He was what the Ravengers needed. To be the most feared crime family not only in Italy, but the world.

His father had grown weak and indulgent in his old age. It wasn't only that he'd sheltered all the brats in the city. Or his soft ways with women. It was that he viewed his work as something other than what it was. *This is an opportunity to shelter the forgotten. To offer discarded souls a way out of the gutter. Out of the dark.*

Bullshit!

They sold drugs! They governed the underworld. The cities they built were meant for those like themselves. Souls without a future. Souls with no way out but down. His father spoke of revolution, of freeing the people. And Konstantine was infected by the same blindness.

Nico was the only one who could see the world clearly. Some were meant to live beneath the boots of others. There was no shame in that. The notion of equality and freedom for all—*grow up, brother.* There was no place for idealism in their world.

Nico had thought all of this as the truck shifted and swayed. There was only one salvation on that terrible night. The truck and pre-dawn exile meant his father hadn't had it in him to kill him outright.

That was his mistake.

Because if he'd lived long enough, Nico would have put a bullet between his eyes.

After the exile. After the ten long years in a work yard where he toiled and sweat and endured endless humiliations until news of his father's death reached him.

And he knew he couldn't wait any longer. The time had come.

At the edge of the Ponte Vecchio, Nico paused to look out over the water. The camp felt like a lifetime ago. His father, a mere dream.

And maybe this was not even the same city. For now the sun shimmered on the surface, like pebbles tumbling in a stream. Tourists clustered around the shops and gelaterie. A beggar woman lay prostrated, face down with her open palms cupped in offering.

Nico put a euro note into her outstretched hands. He knew what it was to be hungry and to have nothing but your own will to sustain you. It had been his hate for his father that had kept him breathing all those years in the labor camp. Konstantine was *nothing* in the face of that hatred. The will.

He'd survived hell. He'd rallied the others in the camp and overthrew their guards. They killed every single one of them, stole every gun, every ounce of supplies. They'd traveled the treacherous miles between the camp and Florence, hard weeks of living hand to mouth, stealing for food, sleeping where they could.

What obstacle did Konstantine pose compared to what he'd already overcome?

How would it have hurt him to know that for months his old friends had sent word to Nico, letting him know Padre was dead, that he should come home. That they would help him reclaim what was rightfully his?

He remembered the look on Konstantine's face when Calzone and Vincent pulled their guns on him, and Nico stepped victorious from the shadows.

He would replay that memory for years to come, wringing every ounce of joy from it.

Nico crossed through a portico into the apartment's atrium and courtyard. He passed beneath the rounded archway and ascended the old stone steps, noting each number beside the apartment door. The attic then. Overlooking a lush courtyard and fountain on one side and the Arno itself on the other. He paused to admire the carved cherub, his delicate mouth spitting water while his fingers poised above the strings of a lyre.

He turned the key in the large metal lock and heard it release.

He could've sent anyone for this mission, but he'd wanted to see for himself. How better to know his enemy than to see where he slept, where he dreamed?

Nico stepped into the cool apartment and hit the light. He pulled the curtain, revealing the courtyard below, giving the room even more light by which to see. A large chair in one corner and a desk with a computer in the other. A red and brown rug covered the length of the room.

He went up the stairs to find the loft. A rumpled bed. The compressed pillows. He opened the double doors on a balcony and the glory of the shining Arno river. Someone was cooking in an adjacent apartment, rich spices and sweet cream wafted through the open window, carried on the cool river breeze.

He opened drawers, looked in closets. The closet lights were already on. And strangely, when he tried to turn them off, it seemed the bulbs had been screwed into a socket in such a way that the lights couldn't be turned off. A quirk of an old apartment perhaps?

He found a collection of shoes. Some Italian leather. Some American. Two leather jackets and an abundance of black shirts and several pairs of sunglasses. A toothbrush on the sink. A single bottle of soap in the shower stall. Cologne on the bedside table.

Downstairs he searched again. Pencils and pens and paper in the desk. The laptop itself which was password protected. Some novels in both English and Italian.

He unplugged the laptop from the wall and wrapped the cord around it. This was likely his only find.

A giant oil painting of a man with a sword raised high hung on the wall. Is this how he saw himself? Konstantine The Great? A warrior astride his horse? More like a joke of a man. A stolen horse.

He'd stood sneering at the painting until he heard a small sound behind him. A shoe scuffing on stone.

"Konstantine!" A boy called out. "I'm back. We've—"

The boy's voice froze in his throat, his Adam's apple bobbing as he swallowed the rest of his sentence down. He took one look at Nico standing the middle of the apartment and bolted.

He didn't get far. Nico seized the back of his jacket and hauled him into the apartment, kicking the door closed. He slammed the boy against it, eliciting a cry.

Nico's hand pressed over the kid's mouth, the same moment he tossed the laptop toward the chair. It landed squarely on top of the rose-colored cushion and bounced. Good enough. Nico needed his free hand to pull his blade and press it to the kid's throat.

The boy's body went perfectly still.

"Where did you come from?" Nico asked. Because he'd laid siege to this city in the last 48 hours. Surely this boy had learned of the change of power.

"Prato," the boy said, without hesitation. Good. Perhaps Nico wouldn't have to kill him.

"And what were you doing in Prato?"

"Where's Konstantine?"

"Dead." *Or he soon will be.*

The boy's shoulders softened against the door.

"*What* were you were doing in Prato?"

The boy swallowed. The knife pricked the skin.

"He wanted me to check on something."

"Check what?" Nico pressed the blade against his throat. Blood trickled down, soaking the collar of his t-shirt.

This terrified the boy into silence. His eyes going as wide as cow's before the steel bolt penetrated its head. He released the pressure only enough to encourage speech.

"He's having a room built there."

"Go on."

The boy looked horrified for a moment, as if he wasn't sure exactly how he would go on.

"It's—it's just a room, signore," he said, sweat beading along his hairline, matting his bangs to his forehead. "In an old winery outside of town. It's in the basement."

He believed him. After all, if Konstantine was smart, he would've chosen the boy for his ignorance. If he himself were commissioning a room for some dark purpose, would he tell anyone what it was for? As a safe for his fortune or a bunker against one's enemies? No. He suspected that secret would stay quite close to his chest. As close as this terrified boy with his panting breath stood now.

He released the kid. "What purpose do you *think* the room is intended for?"

Visible relief washed over his face as he stood and tugged his shirt and jacket back into place. "I can't imagine. It's a strange room."

"Describe it to me."

"It's padded. Floor to ceiling. Not even a ceiling really. It's only lights up there. Every inch. Too high to reach. The lights do not turn off and it makes the room so bright. It hurts my eyes."

The lights do not turn off.

Like the closet in the apartment.

What a mad man you were, Konstantine, Nico thought.

"He sent you to check on this project of his?"

"Yes." He used the collar of his shirt to mop up the blood from his throat, crushing the cotton against his slender throat.

"And what was the message you came to deliver today?" Nico asked, wiping the boy's blood on his pants.

"It's ready."

10

When King stepped into the hospital room with a cup of coffee and a wrapped po'boy sandwich, he knew something had changed. Lucy was sitting up in bed. Nurse Naomi, King's favorite of all the caregivers at the center, was beside her. Naomi was a lovely woman with dreads tied at the base of her neck. The woman spoon-fed Lucy a steaming bowl of soup, in slow, patient offerings.

"Good morning, ladies," he said, sliding the door shut behind them. "Looks like I'm in time for lunch."

The nurse spared him a small smile. "Good morning, Mr. King. Miss Lucy and I were talking about my niece Cassandra. She's getting married at St. Thomas parish this weekend."

"Congratulations," King said, pulling up the chair on the opposite bedside. "I hope the weather holds for you."

Lucy turned her face away, her features pinching closed. Naomi and King exchanged a look.

Naomi set the bowl down on the side table. "You tired? We can pick this up later."

"Leave the bowl and we can try in a little while," King said.

Lucy didn't speak until Naomi had excused herself, slipping unobtrusively from the room. Then seemingly to the wall she said, "Weddings are lovely."

King unwrapped his sandwich. The smell of fried shrimp, vinegar, and BBQ sauce wafted up to greet him.

Her face pinched again.

"Is this smell bothering you?" he asked, wondering if he'd made a mistake in bringing it. He'd given up on the beignets. If he was sick, dying from the cancer eating away at his bones, would he want someone trying to force feed him donuts every other day? Probably not.

She didn't seem to hear him. "I'm so nauseous today."

"Is it the smell?" he asked again. No food at all then. That's where they were now. His heart sank even as she shook her head no.

He was torn between his own hunger and trying to read unspoken cues.

"I'd always hoped that I'd see Lou get married."

King snorted. "Imagine the domestic disputes over drawers left open or socks on the floor."

It was either eat the sandwich quickly or throw it away. King dared to take a bite.

Lucy turned and smiled at him then. "We could get married."

King coughed, choking on the po'boy. It wasn't what she'd said. It was the clear eyes and sweet smile. Perfect lucidity. This wasn't the drugs talking.

"What's wrong, Robert?" she asked with a broad grin. "Not the marrying kind?"

If there was a woman in the world that he would dare to love again, to give himself completely to, it was Lucy Thorne. But he'd already done that. Not on paper. But what did that matter?

"I didn't think you'd have me," he said, cracking open a water bottle and washing down the shrimp stuck in this throat.

"Don't I already have you?"

"Yes." He wiped at his fingers with a flimsy paper napkin.

She turned away then. "I'm a fool to expect more than I've already received."

He snatched her hand. "Not a fool."

She laughed, a tired, dried out sound. He offered her the water but she turned her face away.

Her blue eyes measured him. She wanted a real answer.

And what could he say to her? As she lay in this hospital bed, her body turned against her. And so young. She would never see her fiftieth birthday. He had already seen ten years that she wouldn't. And why should he get the extra time? What in the world was he doing with his life that was so damn grand? She was a thousand times worthier of a long life than most of the bastards who got one.

She had every right to feel like the world had jilted her. He couldn't count on one hand all that it had taken from her.

Her brother. Her health and sometimes her mind. Twenty or more years of life that she could've spent seeing Lou become the amazing woman she dreamed she would be. Her chance to guard and guide the young woman. Any hope of fulfilling her promise to Jack.

And what about his own selfish wants? He would've given his testicles for twenty more years with her. Hell, for ten.

"Can you imagine the wedding? In my condition?" she said, more to herself than to him. "I should be grateful I had one more good summer with you. It was a great summer, wasn't it?"

"The best."

He was certain she was drawing deep on some Buddhist bullshit. Non-attachment. Gratitude. Something to lessen the fact that she was too young to be dying, yet still had the audacity to dream. And why shouldn't she, damnit?

He squeezed her hand. "If you're serious, and if you'll have me, I will marry you. Big wedding and all."

Lucy smiled. "Lou might even come."

"I'd make sure of it. Say the word and I'll make it happen."

"The word," she whispered, and her eyes fluttered closed, a smile tucked sweetly into the corner of her lips.

With his car parked in the alley behind him, King stood on the curb outside Melandra's Fortunes and Fixes and watched the world go by. On the worst days, like this one, when Lucy was as ill as he'd ever seen her, the world felt like a dream. It floated past him like clumped debris in a river.

When the nurses had tried to get Lucy up and walking, the screaming had frightened him so badly they'd asked him to leave.

How long do I have? he'd asked the doctor before getting into his car and coming home.

It's so hard to tell. She's still having good days. The best we can do is keep her comfortable.

Good days, but not as many King knew. How long could she last now that the pain made it impossible for her own bones to support her?

And what happened when they couldn't make her comfortable anymore? How could he watch her suffer, knowing he could do nothing for her?

The world came into focus again. A breeze from Lake Pontchartrain cutting across St. Peter.

The first thing his eyes registered was a group of Asian tourists across the street, talking rapidly as they read a map. Filipino maybe.

"What are you looking for?" he called out to them, switching the briefcase from his left fist to his right, feeling the weight of the world again.

A short man with thick black hair said, "St. Louis Cathedral."

King pointed them toward Royal Street, with instructions to follow the long and winding road until it opened up on the square and grand white cathedral they were looking for.

They thanked him, and disappeared down the adjacent street, leaving King on the sidewalk.

A small brass band a block up played bluegrass music.

He breathed deep, caught the scent of fried pralines. Could the world really go on without her?

It had to. It had no choice.

He would never say this to Lucy, knowing it would hurt her feelings more than help her. But when he returned home after long mornings in the NOLA Cancer Center, sometimes he stood on the street corner, or on his balcony above and breathed. Cajun spice, fresh air. Hell, even the scent of booze or vomit was more pleasant than the hospital stench.

The French quarter smelled like life. No matter how boozy, or marijuana-ridden that scent became in the hours between midnight and dawn, he welcomed it as he welcomed the ruthless heart beating in his chest.

And it was more than that.

He could no sooner stop pulling air into his lungs than the world could stop spinning.

His heart, like the world, was slave to its own momentum.

When he spent three days in the rubble of a collapsed building, King had been sure he would die then and there, his organs crushed beneath tons of poured concrete and metal beams. For a long time, that moment was his Big Bang. The cataclysmic remains that he carried with him through the gravity of the day.

Now the low-ceilings of the cancer center were what he dreamed of. His fear of Lucy's impending death and his own claustrophobia had entered his psyche and mixed somehow. Lucy's death would unmoor him again.

Already his nightmares stretched the cancer center corridors to funhouse lengths. Pressed the ceilings down on him from above and Lucy's screaming filtering through the space that remained. On most nights, he had to transverse the darkness to find her. To claw his way through the rubble to rescue her trapped body.

None of this would stop him from visiting her of course.

Not the claustrophobia. Not the anxiety.

No number of sleepless nights or nightmares. But he would be lying to himself if he didn't admit that standing here on the open bustling street, so full of life and vibrancy, was better than the center. He was freer here. The air came easier.

And he didn't think she would hold that against him.

"You drunk or something?"

King pried his eyes open and followed the voice up. Piper stood poised on a metal ladder, hanging cobwebs from the Melandra's Fortunes and Fixes sign. She wore baggy jeans and a black Star Wars t-shirt with its iconic yellow script. Chucks on her feet. Her bleached hair was braided into a side ponytail, revealing the silver cuffs on her ears. Her hemp necklace with its glass beads caught and reflected the sunlight across the metal sign.

"No," he said, with a smile. "Do I look drunk?"

"You're standing there sniffing the air. It's freaking weird. You high?"

"Maybe I'm happy to be alive."

"You almost get hit by a car? Someone clipped me on my bike the other day. Monsters."

"What are you doing up there?" He gestured toward the cobweb and lights in her hands.

"Mel wants this Halloween shit up today."

"It's September."

Piper rolled her eyes. "I'm thinking she's hoping to draw the Halloween crowd early."

The central streets of the French quarter were enough like a perpetual Halloween party as it was. It didn't have to be Mardi Gras or any other holiday to see masked revelers crawling the streets.

"Have you ever planned a wedding?" King asked her.

Piper wobbled on the ladder. "Do I look like I've planned a wedding?"

"Maybe you have a sister—"

"Only child—"

"Or your mother—"

"My mother has been married four times, but she's more the week-end-in-Vegas kind of bride. Why? Who's getting married?" Genuine concerned scrunched her features. Her eyes were painted to resemble an Egyptian cat's. Strangely, he thought it suited her, her features striking him as kittenish, even on makeup-free days.

"I think I am," he said. He placed one hand on the metal post, cane height and topped with a horse's head. This was his ritual, of checking his feet before stepping into Melandra's shop. If the city decided to remove these historical markers of old tie-up posts, used for horses in the last century, he wasn't sure his old body would know how to proceed. The pointed ears pressed into his palm as he struggled to balance himself, scrapping the bottom of his shoes against the curb.

"You *think* you are? You going to propose to Lucy?" Piper teased, the tension leaving her face as she wrapped a fresh coil of eerie purple lights along the sign's post before pivoting toward the black iron railings of his balcony.

"Hey, hang those from inside. You'll fall leaning over like that." His heart ratcheted at her precarious position. "Who did you think I meant?"

Piper hesitated, pretending to fiddle with a knot. "I don't know. Maybe Lou was engaged or something."

King grinned and Piper saw it. She burst out laughing. "Right. Okay. Glad to know I have a chance."

He didn't think she had a chance with Lou at all—and wondered if he was cruel for thinking so. Was he fool enough to think he knew anything about Louie Thorne's interests? Apart from slaughtering drug lords, of course.

King watched Piper work against the backdrop of the building, fire engine red with hunter green shutters. The oversized windows overlooked both Royal and St. Peter streets. Ferns lined the balcony. Something about the ladder made him uneasy. *A goose on my grave,* he thought.

"You know if you had a case for me to work on, I wouldn't be up here fooling with these damn lights," Piper grumbled.

"I'm waiting on my license to arrive." It was a lie. King had already completed the forty-hour training course and sat for the licensing exam. He'd paid the agency fees and submitted all the paperwork with his fingerprint cards. He'd been certified weeks ago, updated his concealed carry permit, and even informed many of his old colleagues across America that he was in the business again.

Most congratulated him on finding something worth his skill and time in his retirement and promised to send work his way soon. A few affectionately teased him, calling him *Uncle Robbie,* a jab against cops who didn't know how to exit the force.

What had stopped his burgeoning new career in its track had been Lucy. When Lucy turned the corner and her move to the cancer center became permanent, King had stopped answering emails. He respectfully turned down offers from the local precinct and pulled his ad from the *Times-Picayune*. He even turned down his side gig of adjuncting for LSU —teaching Intro to Criminology courses as needed. He told them this fall semester was impossible and likely the spring too.

Lucy was his concern now. And Lou.

"It's fine," Piper said with a huff. "I'm making great progress in my apprenticeship. I've only got ten hours left before I'm a certified tarot reader."

"That's great." Though King had no idea who certified fortune tellers.

"But hunting criminals is more fun and tarot is more of a side gig. So...you know." Piper wagged her eyebrows at him.

"I'll let you know if anything changes," he assured her, before stepping around the ladder and into the shop.

The skeleton by the door shrieked, vibrating the hairs inside his ears. He took a breath, slowly unclenched his fist and stared around the shop.

The store was smoky with incense. Patchouli and jasmine today. Despite the open door and late breeze, a visible cloud hung in the air, haloing the bookshelves and trinket displays full of sugar skulls, candles, statues of saints, and porcelain figurines. Beside the wall of talismans hung the purple curtain. He could hear Mel's soft voice muffled by the thick curtain, the tone dramatic and grave. Whoever was having their fortune read in that candlelit nook wasn't receiving good news.

No one else was in the shop.

He took the stairs up to the landing above, veering left to his apartment. If he kept walking around to the other side, he'd be met with an identical door leading into Mel's own apartment, a mirror image of his own.

But he worked his key into the deadbolt first, then the lower knob.

His red leather sofa against the left wall and his beast of a coffee table that looked like a floating door salvaged from a shipwreck, bolted onto wooden feet. His collection of mismatched cardboard rounds were stacked nicely in one corner of the table, each he had stolen from local bars.

He remembered how worried he'd been about Lucy seeing those. That she'd think him a drunk. Or a pothead for the 8th of weed he kept inside his Bob Dylan vinyl with a pack of rolling papers. He hadn't smoked in months. Or drank more than a beer or two for that matter. Part of it was the drug test required for the P.I. license. The other part was simply time. He couldn't show up at Lucy's bedside smelling like weed or a distillery and there wasn't a day he didn't visit her.

He supposed that even without the illness, he would've cleaned up for her, if for anyone. He only wished the twilight of her life hadn't been the reason.

King plopped onto the sofa and opened the briefcase.

Document after printed document lay sandwiched on top of each other. He pulled them out, examined each one. Beneath the stack, he fished out the yellow legal pad and began a new list. It was the sixth or seventh such list on this page. But each that had come before it had been crossed out, with little side notes marked.

All the print-outs had a single thing in common. Lou Thorne. They either bore an image of her face or description of her person. He'd been scouring every public and private database he could for news of her. Files or suspicious reports. He was doing this for Lucy, he told himself. Or sometimes he told himself that he was doing it for Jack. Rarely was he able to convince himself that all the hunting, the searching, was for Lou herself.

Because while she may be the direct beneficiary of his efforts, he couldn't seem to believe that she really *needed* him. They could send a hundred men, maybe a thousand. And King suspected that she might very well kill them all.

Scouring reports for her name, silently deleting files and photos, all of it was for someone's benefit. He just wasn't sure whose.

He canvassed the disappearances until an incident caught his eye.

A man was reported missing in New York three days ago. His girl-friend, who looked like a clown with magenta eyeshadow and fuchsia Lycra pants in the photo, said that a woman fitting Lou's description had come around looking for him the day before.

Two known drug mules, brothers in Dallas were reported missing by their mother. She said they'd gone to the park across the street to meet up with their friends, but never came home. The last thing she saw was her boys talking to a young woman in a leather jacket and sunglasses—despite the late hour. In the report, the mother openly admitted to wondering if the woman was a prostitute, saying quote *knowing my boys, I wouldn't have been surprised.*

Senator Thompson of New York never reached his benefit gala in the city. The last person to see him alive was the limo driver. Russel Postma swore that Senator Thompson had gotten into the limo alone. He'd asked Postma for silence while he reviewed his notes for the speech he was to give somewhere between dessert and coffee. Postma obliged, rolling up the partition and turning off the radio. They were two miles from the banquet hall when he heard Thompson shout. By the time he pulled the limo over and rolled down the partition, he found the senator gone. The notecards strewn across the leather seat. He was certain that the senator hadn't exited the vehicle. He simply disappeared.

After reading the new reports and interviews, King had a list of five new sources to investigate. Nothing that mentioned Lou by name, no. But each disappearance had an unmistakable *Lou*-ness about it.

King's hand paused in scribbling a name when the sudden urge to look up overtook him.

There she was.

"Fuck!" King threw the notebook and sheets of computer paper briskly into the case, slamming down the lid once, twice, before managing to get the gold clips settled into place.

"Am I interrupting something?" she asked. He couldn't see her eyes behind the mirrored sunglasses, but her voice was flat, uninterested. Only the arched eyebrow gave away her amusement.

"I have *two* doors." He wiped his hands down his face. "You could knock. On *either* one of them."

"I'll come back." She slid her hands into her leather jacket and turned away.

"No," he barked, perhaps too earnestly because she shifted her weight. He sucked in a breath and tried to relax. "No, I need to talk to you."

A deep crease settled between her eyes.

"How's Lucy?" she asked.

King was about to launch into his lecture. The prepared speech that began with *you would know if you'd visit her your damn self!*

"She looked like shit when I saw her," Lou added.

King's prepared defense fell out of his head. Everything he'd meant to say, about her hunting, about Lucy's dying wish for a wedding, even a half-hearted plea to say hello to Piper or Mel—all of it vanished.

"You saw Lucy?" he said, staring at her. He wished she'd take off the sunglasses. "When?"

As if reading his mind, she pushed them up onto her head. "Last night."

A million responses danced on the tip of his tongue.

Would it kill you to spend more time with her? She raised you! And as hard as you might be trying to kill yourself, she's actually *dying.*

This is your last chance, kid. Don't fuck up like I did.

He exhaled all his unspoken grievances and fell back against the couch. He put his large hands on his knees because he didn't know what else to do with them.

This wasn't really about what Lou did or didn't do.

This was about figuring out where the two of them stood—Louie and him. And where they'd go from here, once Lucy was gone.

Once Lucy was gone.

His heart clenched. "How've you been?"

He was surprised by the gentleness in his tone. And he wasn't the only one. First her eyebrow arched higher, then she said, "No complaints."

No complaints? Your last remaining family member has one foot in the grave and you have no complaints?

He opened and closed his fist compulsively. Looking for something else benign to say. Something. Anything. He wanted to keep her here, keep her talking.

This had to work. For Lucy's sake, he *had* to make this work.

But *god*, did he want a reaction out of her. He wanted Lou to scream. To cry. Hell, he'd settle for having her pull a gun on him.

But she gave him nothing. Every muscle in her body was the calm patina of a lake in the early evening. Not a ripple in sight. And no matter how many rocks he threw into it, he couldn't change her any more than the stars in the sky.

God, Lucy, how did you do it?

King was suddenly grateful he'd never had kids of his own.

Lou said, "How was Lucy when you saw her?"

He said finally, squeezing his knees. "In a lot of pain. There was a bit of an emergency this morning and they sent me away. She was stable when I left, but..."

Lou wasn't stupid. With her life, absolutely. But in her head—not at all. There was nothing King could tell her that she likely didn't already understand herself. Not about Lucy's health or her time left in this world.

He wanted to ask *why did you finally visit?* He considered how to frame this. "It's good to see you, kid."

There. Concern. He'd nailed it.

"Did you drop in to say hi?" he asked. "You could've called."

"I needed to get out of my apartment."

Irritation bit at the back of his neck. Was that really all? She finally gracing them with her presence because she was a little stir crazy. No, wait. That didn't compute. King knew for a fact that she left her apartment all the time.

"What are you saying?" he asked.

"My apartment is crowded."

"Why? Who's in it?"

"Paolo Konstantine." She gave him one of her measuring sideways glances. "Martinelli's bastard son. He runs the Ravengers. Or he did."

The name spun King's mind in a different direction. "Martinelli? The man who had your old man killed?"

Paolo Konstantine. He remembered hearing the name for the first time from Lou herself. What had she called him? *He's the new Martinelli.*

That's right. She'd been bleeding to death on Ryanson's boat deck.

He remembered Konstantine now. Remembered his hands going up in surrender when Lou turned her gun on him. A handsome man. Dark hair. Green eyes. He looked as tough as Lou, with that crow and crossbones tattoo on his bicep, the hungry look in his eye.

What the hell are you going to kill him for? King had asked.

He's the new Martinelli.

That was when King had told her the truth. That Ryanson had ordered the hit on her father. But surely that wasn't enough to change her opinion of the crime lord's son. This bit of truth was enough to befriend him rather than put a bullet in his brain? No way. She hunted those bastards. She didn't play sleepover with them.

There was quite the distance between revenge and taking a man home...wasn't there?

He gave Lou a good hard look.

She had new wounds. The first two knuckles on her left hand were faded purple. Repeated blunt trauma. She had a cut on her chin. Hard to tell if it had been a bullet or a blade. And her upper arm had been grazed. But none of this told him why Paolo Konstantine was in her apartment.

"Are you bringing the strays home now?" he asked, trying to find his footing again in the conversation.

"He was bleeding to death. I thought about dumping him on the ER floor," she said with a shrug. "But I didn't know if he had a record and if that would've been like throwing him to the sharks. And he'd blacked out, so I couldn't ask."

"What happened?"

She smiled. "Someone kicked his ass."

"Who?"

"From what he's said, it sounds like there's been a hostile takeover of his little gang. Nico Agostino is in charge of the Ravengers now."

"Who the hell is that?"

"Nico is Padre Leo's biological son. Leo built the Ravengers, then left it to Konstantine when he died."

King felt like he was watching an Italian soap opera. A drama surrounding infamous crime families. Only he'd missed six or seven episodes and now couldn't remember who was who and all the Italian stallions looked alike.

"So Padre chose Konstantine over the son, Nick—"

"Nico."

"—Nico. And he's butthurt about it."

"It doesn't sound like Nico was ever an option. He killed someone's daughter and was banished to a labor camp in Russia. He broke out as soon as he heard his father died and came back to reclaim the Ravengers."

"Konstantine told you all this?"

"Parts of it. I did some digging. Asked around."

Asking around meant breaking fingers and slitting throats.

"Why are you telling me all of this?" King asked, draping one arm across the back of the sofa.

"I want to kill him," she said.

"Nico or Konstantine."

She smiled again. "Maybe both."

King snorted. "I don't think you're asking my permission."

As if she needed it.

"I'm looking for the right time. And I want you to let me know when that is." She shifted and King saw the butt of the Beretta tucked against her ribs.

She bent and snapped up his briefcase.

Before he could process what was happening, she had it open, a collection of papers in one fist, the yellow legal pad with his lists on the other.

He opened his mouth to defend himself, but she was already speaking.

"Yeah, like this," she said, meeting his eyes over the legal pad.

He hesitated. "Like what?"

"Listen to the wires," she told him. "If Nico makes any moves, over-reaches, or if you get the sense that he's planning to strike, let me know."

King's pulse leapt in this throat. "Strike against who? You?"

"I shot him a couple of times," she said. "I don't think he's dead. When you shoot people and don't kill them, they tend to be pissy about it."

"Did you spare him on purpose?" he asked, unable to imagine her missing any target.

She tossed the papers back into the briefcase's gaping mouth. "I was distracted."

Distracted. What in God's name could distract her?

"Is Nico a superhuman mutant or something?"

"It doesn't matter." She slid her shades down over her face again. "It won't happen again."

He sensed the shift, her imminent departure and shot up from the sofa. His knees popped from the effort and his back groaned.

There was still so much to tell her. About Lucy. About their plans for Lou once Lucy was gone. Things that he and Lucy had discussed about her future.

But she didn't wait for him. She'd already disappeared through the shadow of his large armoire, leaving him alone in his apartment with his pile of paperwork.

"Next time then," he said to the darkness.

If they had a next time.

11

Konstantine woke to full darkness, heart hammering. He sat up, looking around the unfamiliar apartment. Then he saw the purple sofa, two feminine throw pillows tucked into each corner. Lights from the river dancing across the brick walls. No. That was the pool. Steam rose into the chilled night. Lights shimmered beneath its surface, casting a glow against the *No Lifeguard on Duty* sign fixed to the surrounding gate.

A luxurious studio with a heated pool. Wasn't she living the life?

But the apartment itself sat dark.

He rolled out of the bed. Or he tried. Every muscle in his body groaned. His stitched up bullet wounds, yes. But also the muscles that had been tenderized by Italian leather boots.

He placed his feet on the cold wooden floor and hissed.

He ran a hand over his chest, as if to reassure himself that it was intact. Then with much effort, he pulled himself to standing. Bones creaked. Tendons popped. He was that man from the children's story, who'd fallen asleep beneath a tree and woke a hundred years later. Or at least he felt as if he'd aged a hundred years in one night.

He turned on a lamp, pulling the metal cord hanging from the bulb beneath the shade. He stood there, listening to the night bustle around him. One of the windows was open, and a light breeze blew through, rattling the horizontal slats.

The air licked the feverish sweat from his skin. The moonlit sheets fluttered. Outside, a train whistled and huge iron wheels screeched against their rails. Horns blared even at this hour.

It was as loud as his Florentine apartment. Even the river seemed the same, the water's surface shimmering with collected moonbeams.

His .357 sat on the glass coffee table.

He lifted it from the glass top, inspected it, and found it to be loaded.

Beside it, another present. A brown bag held a burger and fries, the paper so soaked with grease that it sagged from the weight of the burger. Cheap American food. Back home, under no circumstances would he ever eat such garbage. But he was far from home and his stomach grumbled the moment he peeled back the plastic wrapping and the scent of cooked meat struck him.

Yet he ate it with relish, sucking the salt off his fingers the way a marooned man sucks water from the stream. He would've eaten two more burgers and another five fistfuls of fries had they been in the bag.

His hunger sated for now, only his curiosity remained. He opened the closet closest to the couch but found it empty. Three bare walls no wider than the door itself, and a carefully swept square of wooden floor serving as its bottom. He scraped at the notches in the wall with his bloody nails, noting the places where shelves had once been.

No light above, only smooth plaster.

He closed the door, releasing its brassy handle.

He found the two safes behind the paintings and could guess at their contents. All manner of destruction no doubt. Perhaps cash. He didn't think passports or documentation would be in there. After all, hadn't he searched for such items himself and come up short?

She was a ghost in the modern world, no license. No credit history.

Not counting the brief blip in the news which had surfaced when her father's story surged to the surface again in June, there'd been no mention of her. The news hadn't even had a recent picture. They'd relied on one over a decade old.

Reporters no doubt wanted to interview the daughter of a man who'd been exonerated of treason fourteen years after his death. Her interview would have been prime time. Her account of surviving the murder, only to have her father slandered after—living with that cruelty all those years. The American public loved emotional drama. They would have sopped hers up like a biscuit through gravy on a dinner plate.

If Lou had been an emotional woman.

And if her privacy had been threatened by the reemerging interest in an old story, he supposed he'd have himself to blame. Hadn't he fed the evidence himself to the public? He'd provided the clips and conversations between Jack's partner Brasso and Senator Ryanson. Proof of the money that had changed hands. Photos of their conversations. Counterbait that had perhaps deterred the press from looking too hard at a fallen hero's daughter.

For now.

The manhunt for both Ryanson and Brasso went national. And of course, the press only amplified when neither could be found. That had been Lou's doing—no doubt she disposed of the bodies in that untraceable way of hers. A secret she kept close to her Kevlar vest.

He'd almost seen that dumping ground himself.

He touched the notch under his chin, the place where she'd pressed her gun.

I'm not your enemy, he'd said. *I believe we are drawn together for a reason. You came to me when you were dreaming. Did you dream of killing me?*

He'd been trying to reason with her as her gun had remained perfectly steady against his chin. She'd only regarded him with those placid, unreadable eyes.

But she hadn't killed him. She'd done as he wished and taken him to his mother's grave.

When he closed his eyes, Konstantine could still hear his mother begging for his life as his father stared down at her in a shadowed Italian field.

He's your son, Fernando. Ti prego. Abbi pieta', Fernando.

Konstantine would never forget the *POP* of the gun. Her mouth opening in a surprised *O*. The sight of her pitching forward, nightgown billowing, into the dark hole. Her gown seemed to glow in the bottom of the dark cradle, but her body had disappeared, swallowed by grave dirt.

Grief swallowed him whole in that moment and when he came to his senses again, seemingly months later, he hadn't known where they'd been. A field, yes. But there were a thousand fields near Florence. His mother could've been in any one of them.

He would've never found her without Lou's help. He owed her everything. Would give her anything.

You lie to yourself, he thought, chiding himself inwardly.

I want to give her everything. I also want to take everything from her.

His fingers caught on a something. His memories broke through the surface of his mind.

Konstantine ran his hand over the kitchen island again, his fingers tracing its cool surface until he found it. Beneath the counter was a small metal latch that could be undone with the flick of his finger. He looked nervously at the closed closet door behind him, wondering how much time he had to investigate with impudence before the lioness returned.

He flicked the latch and the side of the island popped away from its frame. Not the side of a counter, but a secret door.

He opened it wider and discovered stairs descending into the dark.

Heart hammering, he took them one at a time, his bare feet gripping the wooden steps cautiously. The hem of his jeans scrapped over their surface.

Cold air licked up his bare chest. Something brushed his face. He mistook it for a cobweb, but quickly realized it was much too thick. Pawing the space above his head he found the string. He pulled it and light spilled across the room.

Konstantine's breath stuck in his throat.

Cristo!

Shelves lined three of the four walls. The one accommodating the stairs was the only bare space. Every other inch was given over to her arsenal. For there was no other word for it. Guns, large and small were crammed into every available inch. But not only firearms. Switch blades —a whole shoe box full of them—and throwing knives. Then a machete the size of Konstantine's arm, shoulder to wrist. Grenades. Tear gas. A flame thrower with four exchangeable tanks fit into a backpack. Full body armor that would have fit her form like a glove.

She could lay siege to a fortress. To a kingdom.

He loved her.

His desire for her rose so suddenly that its crushing throb pulsed between his legs.

He ran his finger over a throwing blade, so sharp it pricked his fingertip at the slightest touch. He sucked the blood from it until the finger went numb.

He wanted to fuck her down here. Right against this wall, her back shoved into the concrete cinder blocks. Or maybe on the floor, her astride him, his back ground into the dusty floor until her knees were rubbed raw.

He turned off the light and dragged himself up the stairs.

He half expected to find her standing at the top. Perhaps she'd slit his throat and kick him down the stairs, retrieving his desiccated corpse in a week or two, whenever the rot began to bother her.

But the apartment was quiet. Nothing moved.

He stood there, watching the moonlight on the river until the heat drained from his head and the only throbbing that remained was in his pricked finger.

There was nothing else to search. He noted the lack of personalization. No photos of family, apart from the one he'd found in her pillow. There wasn't a television or a bookcase—though he did see a small stack of paperbacks under the end table, wedged between the sofa, bed, and wall.

Apart from the central area including kitchen, living room, and bedroom, there were two doors. One on the right side of the hallway had shelves above for towels and a four-drawer dresser below.

A second door sat at the end of the short hallway.

It was a large bathroom.

A small-tiled mosaic in blues and golds stretched beneath a sink, clawfoot tub and shower stall. The tub itself looked most inviting. And Konstantine's jaunt up and down those hidden steps had left him light-headed.

A bath would help the ache in his muscles.

He bent over the porcelain rim and turned the silver faucets. Warm, but not too hot, he filled the tub. He tore the worn gauze from his body and tossed it into the trash bin in the corner, right of the sink. He noted the only piece of furniture in the room. A white cabinet sat against the far wall beneath a window only large enough for a cat to squeeze through. He opened the cabinet and found a tin box the size of a laundry basket.

It looked like a medic's kit. Something a soldier would use on the battlefield, a moving surgical unit. He suspected he was looking at the reason he was alive.

He'd clean himself up again after the bath, suspecting that now he was awake, Lou would no longer play nursemaid.

With the water close to the brim, he closed the faucets. Removing his bloodied jeans and black briefs, he eased himself into the tub, careful to hold the edge should a muscle choose this moment to give beneath him.

The heat bit deep, working its way into his muscles with its ruthless fingers.

He grabbed a washcloth from the shelf above the tub and soaked it in the water. He used the bar of soap, with an emblem of a bird punched into its soft skin, to lather the rag. It smelled like her. The scent was enough to send his mind careening toward desire.

A door creaked open. Konstantine didn't think it was the front door. He leaned forward in the tub in time to see the closet door shutting. A holster full of weapons, and two knives clattered to the wooden floor, where the hallway and central living area met.

Then she was standing naked before him, wet from head to toe. Her nipples were hard and goosebumps stood out along her arms and legs. Her dark hair stuck to her cheeks. Droplets dripping onto the mosaic tile at her feet.

He began to harden.

He leaned over the tub's edge to hide it. He would think of anything, *anything* to soften it. His own mother's soft brunette hair. Padre Leo coughing blood into a white napkin.

As long as he didn't look directly at her nipples, and the gooseflesh on her thighs, he thought he'd be all right.

Her eyes. He would only look at her eyes.

But her eyes were on his crotch.

This is it, his mind said, ever hopeful. *She will climb into the tub, slide those beautiful milk white thighs on either side of my body and pull me inside her.*

The erection throbbed painfully.

"Do you know how many dead bodies have been in that tub?" she asked.

Then her gaze flicked away, the perfect mask of disinterest.

He burst into laughter so hard his stomach ached. "Signora. That one look could have destroyed me."

"I'll try harder next time." She shut herself into the shower, and turned on the faucet.

With her body hidden away by the frosted glass, reason returned. His mind turned to more practical concerns. He glanced at the weapons, wet, lying outside the closet door again. "Did you just emerge from your closet, naked?"

No answer.

"Is that something you do often?"

Still no reply. Instead he was forced to watch her through the frosted glass as he half-heartedly soaped his arms and legs.

You do this to yourself. He could get out of the tub, and go into the other room. He could...wait.

"Would you happen to have a man's clothes?" he asked her. He would put on his filthy rags again if he had to, but it didn't hurt to ask.

If she said *yes, I have a whole drawer of man's clothes* that would cure him of his erection. He was certain jealousy and blind rage would likely replace it.

The water turned off. He braced himself for her reappearance, another confrontation with her nipples and the slender tuck of dark hair between her legs.

But only a hand emerged between the glass to seize the towel from its hook. When she did emerge, her body was blessedly concealed beneath the gray cotton. Only the suggestive curves of her hips and the bare outline of breast poked through.

"You used all the hot water."

"I'm sorry."

But she didn't seem to hear him. She'd stepped out of the bathroom and reentered the closet, it's handle clicking closed behind her.

She appeared a moment later clutching a fistful of clothing in her hand. She dropped it on the floor just inside the bathroom doorway. "I don't know men's sizes."

"Thank you," he called. But she'd already closed the bathroom door, separating them the only way she could in her small studio.

A drawer opened and closed. The sounds of her dressing herself.

He stood from the bath, toweling the water from his body using a towel of the same soft gray cotton.

He pulled on the clothes. The shirt fit well, snug across his shoulders and stomach. It was the color of crushed violets. The black jeans were loose with a wad of black wool stuffed in the pocket, which Konstantine recognized as socks. The underwear, black briefs. He paused then, uncomfortable with the idea of wearing another man's underwear.

While he was certain she'd stolen these clothes from some drawer in some bedroom, and the clothes did smell like detergent...well, he supposed beggars couldn't be choosers.

The pants were a hint too long and too wide. He rolled up the bottoms once, and cinched the waist with the leather belt she'd provided. Good enough.

By the time he'd dressed himself, he'd found she'd done the same.

She stood in the living room in tight jeans that looked poured onto her thick legs, hanging low on the curve of her hips. Her shirt was white, a black tank top or sports bra showing underneath. Her wet hair had been brushed back away from her face.

"You need to leave," she said.

"If it's about the hot water—"

One glance silenced him.

"I want you to help me," he said, hoping that if he made his intentions clear, the thrill of the chase and kill would be enough to pique her interest.

"Of course you did," she said, rolling her eyes up to meet his. "You want your gang back."

He didn't like the word, but nodded. "I do."

She ejected a clip, checked it, reinserted it into the gun. "You have people you trust."

"Yes."

"Then you need to ask for their help."

"We could speak to them together."

Her glare could have boiled the flesh from his bones. "You're confusing me with someone else. I pulled you out of a bad situation. I let you heal up here so you wouldn't be arrested or assassinated in a hospital. That's it. We aren't friends. We aren't business partners. And we don't *talk* to people. *Together.*"

He looked away. He grabbed at the threads unravelling before him. He thought sleeping in her bed, staying in her home had changed something. But now this sudden pushback.

The watch on her wrist buzzed, its black face lighting green. She rotated the face toward her and his gaze slid down the curve of her neck, tracing its collarbones.

The visual feast was lost when she grabbed a leather jacket off the sofa arm and slipped her arms through.

"I'll drop you off wherever you want when I get back. There's food in the fridge."

Drop him. Like a body in the Arno river.

She stepped into the closet and was gone.

12

S he lingered in the closet, heart hammering. Her face and chest were unbearably warm. What the fuck was wrong with her? Konstantine swore in Italian and then her bed groaned as a heavy body collapsed onto it. No doubt he thought he was alone.

She should've put a bullet between his eyes instead of picking him off the church floor. Why had she done it? She didn't save crime lords. She rid the world of them. *But he's different. He salvaged your father's name.*

It was true that Konstantine had supplied the evidence to clear her father's name. In exchange, Lou had carried him to his mother's unmarked grave. Waited for him to uncover her remains as the moonlight beat down on their backs and the insects sang their nightly chorus.

She wondered what he'd done with her bones—as that was all that was left of her after so many years in the bare earth.

He'd given her what was left of her father. And she'd given him what remained of his mother.

They were even. She owed him nothing. So why was she fetching him clothes and food and letting him sleep in her bed?

Forget about it, she warned herself. She was about to work a job. She didn't need her mind wandering on its own. She needed to be absolutely focused or she'd get herself killed. Just like her father. But she saw

Konstantine's black hair, wet and curling around his hard face, the hungry look in his green eyes.

Fuck this. She gave herself over to the darkness, feeling the wall at her back go soft, and the warm air replaced by a fresh breeze.

Lou's hand found purchase on the rough bark of an oak tree. A mourning dove on an electric wire cooed at her entrance. A light breeze ruffled the grass in the park, which had been recently mowed. She could see it, saw it sticking to her black boots as she settled all her weight in this time and place.

A woman sat alone on a swing twenty feet away. Her back was to Lou, dyed auburn hair cascading, stark against a black wool coat. The swing creaked as the woman swayed back and forth, her boots trailing through the wood chips and sand beneath her.

Plastic tubing coiled and unfurled like caterpillars, yellow and green between the swings and adjacent fence. Lou scoped the area. The chain-link fence on all sides. The quiet houses settling beyond. The cars parked on the street with empty windows. Dogs barked somewhere on her left. Maybe a block over. Then understood why when the mail truck rumbled past.

Now certain they were alone, Lou crossed the playground. When the woman didn't look up at her approach, Lou intentionally stepped on a twig. Her black boot snapping it in half where it lay, no doubt blown down by the last storm.

The woman named Benji turned and fixed her wide brown eyes on Lou. "Shit. You scared me. You got my page?"

Obviously, Lou thought. But she didn't say it. She'd come to accept that people repeat the obvious all the time. In fact, it made up the majority of her conversations. And the quickest way to glean the information she wanted, was to let the babble run its course. If she pointed out what was useless, people became defensive. Or they stalled and stammered, weighing every word before uttering it until the conversation twisted in on itself like an ouroboros eating its own tail, stretching the conversation painfully toward infinity.

"You told me to page you if Jason got out of jail," she said.

I know what I told you. "So he's out?"

"Yeah." She worked the cell phone back and forth between her palms nervously. Its bejeweled case sparkled, casting diamond shapes across her skinny jeans. "He came to my house last night, with flowers. Said he'd changed."

Lou was struck by her long nails. Ridiculously long, at least a full inch beyond their fingertips, and the color of maraschino cherries. How could she do anything with those? "Do you know if he's talking to Camry again?"

"He's with him now. I saw his mom's car in the driveway on my way here. His girlfriend Teena says they went down to the beach."

Lou didn't need to know where Jason was. She only needed him out of jail. If she could put the two of them together—Jason and Camry—it would confirm Camry as the supplier. And if she plucked Miami's major supplier off the streets, well that would be a great day.

Lou glanced at the darkening horizon and realized she'd lost an hour jumping from St. Louis to Miami.

A white Cadillac rolled by blasting a Spanish pop song through its open windows. It hit the speed bump beside the park too fast and popped up comically.

"The restraining order is shit. Ain't no body gonna enforce it," Benji said. Her black makeup looked a day old, smudged around her eyes. You promised you'd get rid of him."

"I will," Lou said, feeling the Beretta shift against her ribs.

The woman loosened a breath from her chest. "I need him out of our lives."

Our lives. Lou had forgotten about the kid. A little girl, four or five years old. She'd seen her sleeping beneath a My Little Pony coverlet one night, as Lou had stood in the dark of her bedroom, listening to Benji and Jason scream at each other in the other room.

The girl had woken to the sound of Jason's fist connecting with her mother's stomach. Her eyes were as wide-set and brown as her mother's. But she'd gotten a thick head of curly hair from someone else. Not Jason. Maybe Benji didn't even know who the father was herself.

"Are you—" the girl began, but Lou had put a finger to her lips. The girl sat up in bed, but said nothing.

Then they'd both hovered in the dark, listening to her mother cry against the backdrop of Family Feud.

"I hate it when they fight," the little girl had said.

"They'll stop," Lou assured her, tucking her into the pony sheets.

"When?" Her eyes were black marbles in the thin light through the curtains.

"Soon," Lou had promised.

But she couldn't take credit for Jason's disappearance one week later. It was the cops that had pulled him from the little girl's life.

"He's being good now," Benji said, brushing her auburn hair back from her face. "But in a week or two, he'll be back to his old shit again."

"He'll be gone soon," Lou said, her eyes scanning the street again.

She imagined it was something her father would say. She pictured Jack Thorne, six feet of solid muscle in his full DEA SWAT gear, storming into Benji's home and arresting Jason. Slamming the scrawny man to the kitchen floor, twisting his arms up behind his back and cuffing them.

If he'd seen the little girl what would he say? *He can't hurt you now.*

Something meant to reassure her.

And there was something about her own path—how even though Jack had been removed from her world twelve years ago—somehow she ended up here. Chasing men like Camry Sanderson. Following the leads up the chain of command. Was her work so very different than her father's? He hunted with the full force of the law at his back, true. But Lou didn't need any of that.

But if he'd lived, would she be on the other side? In a vest? Part of a team?

Or was she always meant to do this her way?

She thought so. And how would Jack have felt about that? Sometimes she wondered if his death might have been a gift, a way to preserve his perfection for all of her days. If he had lived, there was the chance they would've grown apart as he'd grown apart from Lucy.

She couldn't imagine he would've approved of her methods.

He cleared the streets of drugs by arresting the men, obeying due process, only taking their lives if necessary. She plucked them from the earth. Judge, jury and executioner. Her father had only fired his gun a dozen times during his tenure on the force. She'd lost count before she was twenty.

Not executioner, not always, she thought. Sometimes, Lou gave that job to Jabbers.

Is that why Konstantine wanted her? Because she was ruthless and unforgiving as he was?

She hadn't needed to see his erection to know he'd wanted her.

She'd known from the moment she'd seen his face on the deck of Ryanson's boat. The blind desire that had consumed him even as she shot down man after man around them.

It didn't matter what he wanted. It mattered what she thought of him.

And there was the rub.

Her mind couldn't reconcile Konstantine the crime boss with Konstantine the Italian boy. Or Konstantine the man who so lovingly dusted soil from his mother's moonlit bones.

Or even the Konstantine she'd stood over with a gun in her hand, weeks after killing her father's murderer. Konstantine had been bare-chested and laying on top of his sheets. Italy asleep outside the window behind her. She'd stood there and watched him, unsure for the first time in her life of what she wanted to do.

All she knew that she wanted was to hit him in his pretty mouth with her pistol.

But she hadn't.

I understand drive. I know how hard it is to stop before a thing is done. If you need this, take it.

But she hadn't needed to kill him. The rage that usually filled her, rolled her like a wave never came as she'd held the gun to his head. For the men walking the streets, polluting the lives of those around them. *Yes.* Without effort.

She held no hate for Konstantine.

You came to me when you were dreaming. Did you dream of killing me?

No. She'd dreamed of having someone who understood her like her father did. Someone as steady and immovable. Someone to replace what had been taken from her.

What sappy pathetic bullshit was that? *What the hell is wrong with me?*

Konstantine was probably asking himself the same thing. She saw his mortification when he'd bent over the side of the tub to hide his erection.

Another car rolled by the park slowly. Men hung through the open window shouting obscenities. She realized the men from the stopped car were shouting at her.

Movement in the corner of her eye drew her attention. One hung from the driver's window, his other hand on the wheel.

"Hi Mami!" he called, dragging a thick tongue over his golden grill. His voice was distorted by the bass rattling the car. "You wanna show me what's under that leather coat, baby?"

"Sure." Lou pulled the Beretta in one fluid extension of her arm and shot the car. Three clean bullet holes punched through the back fender and the red Camaro dashed forward, hitting the first speed bump so hard it popped up. A chorus of male voices howled inside, mixing with the excessive bass rattling its tinted windows. A loose hubcap spun off the back wheel. Its tires squealed as it disappeared around a corner.

"Jesus Christ!" Benji screamed, clutching her red hair in each fist. "You could've killed someone."

"Hardly." She'd clipped the very back of the car. If someone had been in the trunk, she supposed, then yes. They were dead.

But people didn't usually ride around with living people in their trunk. So she hoped the odds were with her.

Lou had the decency to reholster the gun and flash an expression that could've been mistaken for apologetic. Probably.

"I have to go. Page me if anything changes."

"But when are you going to pick him up?" Benji stood from the swing, as Lou marched across the park toward the large tree. It would look like she left out the back gate.

"Soon," Lou called over her shoulder. "And you better leave now."

"Why?"

"Because those guys will come back." As soon as they pulled their frightened heads out of their asses.

She paused only long enough to make sure Benji was obediently jogging out of the park. The chain-link gate swung shut behind her, and heading east, she walked in the opposite direction of the cat callers.

With Benji out of sight, Lou slipped through the shade of the tree, thinking of her closet.

She hadn't wanted to wear body armor when meeting with the woman. Something about guns and ammo and looking like a warrior put women like Benji on edge. They wanted her to solve their problems, yes.

Ride in on a white horse, certainly. But they wanted her to also look like a woman while she did it.

Her converted linen closet manifested around her and she placed one hand on the door, ready to push it open.

But then her bed creaked, shifting under the weight of a restless body.

Right.

For a moment she'd forgotten about Konstantine's claim on her apartment. Even though he'd nearly died and was in no shape to confront his enemy, she suddenly wanted to pitch him from her second-floor window into the pool below.

With a feeble attempt to suppress her irritation, she pressed her shoulders against the closet wall again and sighed through the dark.

Unfinished wood materialized beneath her feet. Cold air licked up the side of her face. She reached up and pulled the string on the light-bulb suspended overhead.

A room came into focus around her. It smelled of sawdust. She'd built it herself two months ago, after her first encounter with Konstantine. She'd done a pretty good job of it, though a couple nails were crooked in places and one of the shelves slanted at an angle.

But she doubted anyone but her would notice it. It was what sat on the shelves that would hold their eye.

She surveyed her secret stock pile. She didn't need the guns, the blades, or flamethrower for a stakeout. Grenades and tear gas were certainly overkill. She needed some good body armor and enough fire-power in case unexpected trouble arose.

She reached for her father's adjustable vest.

Despite the abuse it had taken in the last few years, it looked much like it had when she first took it from her parents' home a few days after they'd been murdered.

In addition to the vest and some of her father's flannel shirts, she took his cut-resistant Kevlar sleeves which had to be resized later, but she'd found someone to do it.

The ones she used now slid over her black sweat-licking shirt and cut-resistant forearm guards.

Her father had worn it at the biggest size, the straps stretched fully extended. She wore it at the smallest, with the Velcro overlapping. Before she grew up and found a use for her father's vest, she would wear it on the nights she couldn't sleep. She'd put it on, tighten the straps, and crush it against her just to remember what it had felt like to have his arms around her. To be so completely engulfed in his strong arms and to feel safe.

Body armor on, cut resistant sleeves slid over each pale forearm, she checked her guns and ammo.

Good enough.

She exchanged her leather jacket for a larger Kevlar jacket preferred by bikers. Something large enough to fit over the vest.

The planks of her apartment creaked above. Konstantine was up and moving around now.

All the more reason to get going.

She pulled the string, extinguishing the lightbulb. For a moment she stood in the dark, hearing his feet gently slap the wood above. But then the dark softened, faded into the background and another piece of the world rushed up to replace it.

The smell of fish hit her first. Overpowering to the point of nausea. And then behind that, the ocean and breeze.

She emerged from the shadows and peered out. She was up high. On the second level of an enormous building, suspended on a wooden platform. It seemed as she was the only one up here, the wooden walkways bare in each direction. She peered over the railing and saw the concrete floor below.

A warehouse? A man lifted enormous fish out of a wooden cart and threw them onto a conveyor belt.

She was in the fish market, not far from the beach.

The whole place reeked of fish left in the sun. Another man with sweat shining between his shoulder blades and the back of his neck sprayed a hose on the concrete floor, washing the remnants of guts toward the drain.

In another corner, Lou spotted Cam. He was the only blond in the sea of black-haired workers, most likely illegal immigrants who'd hit the Miami shore looking for a better life. Cam spoke low, but animatedly, chopping his open palm with this other hand, emphasizing some point to the man in front of him. Lou took him to be the foreman. He was in a dress shirt and loafers, not the gut-smeared work clothes of the men handling the fish.

Jason hovered a few paces back, leaning against a wooden post, aiming for casual but failing. His shifty gaze darted from Cam to the fish cart to the workers too quickly. When he uncrossed and crossed his ankles, Lou saw the silhouette of a gun.

They weren't the only ones watching the workers.

An audience of seagulls had perched on the rafters, chattering away wildly as the man continued to hose down the fish guts. Lou suspected the gulls had infiltrated through the hole in the roof, a jagged mouth opened on blue sky in the southern corner of the building, facing the ocean. One more hurricane and surely this place would be lifted off its stilts and washed out to sea.

Oblivious to his audience, Cam stood in a tank top that reached nearly to his knees, his hairy pits flashing every time he raised his arms to point his finger at the man in front of him.

They were fighting, but Lou was too far away to hear about what. She stepped into an adjacent shadow, trying to get a good look at the man, hoping that maybe this was the contact she was looking for. The next link in the chain. Or at the very least, a new lead should this one fall through.

She placed her foot on the next plank, heard the wood groan and crack.

The planks gave way under her weight, splinters tugging at her jacket as she crashed through, pulling down half the dilapidated walkway with her. She threw her arms out instinctively, trying to seize anything to stop her fall. A scrap of wood, a hanging beam. But her hands found only air.

The concrete floor rushed up to meet her.

13

King spread the glossy magazines on the white coverlet. He angled the magazine's shiny faces so Lucy could see what was advertised in each. Dresses. Cakes. Honeymoon vacations with bikini-clad women strolling on pristine white beaches, shielding their eyes from the sun with their hands. Marriage wasn't a billion-dollar industry for nothing. "Where do you want to start?"

With a shaking hand, she groped each magazine. Her moist fingers stuck to the pages even as she tried to push them aside. She settled on a thick catalogue advertising wedding dresses. The brunette on the cover was someone King recognized. A model for a makeup commercial or something. Or facewash. He couldn't be sure.

It was Lucy's own scent that had made him think of soap.

Someone had washed her hair for her, so she smelled of lilacs. King was betting on Naomi. And he also noticed the pillow. A large cushion with some sort of Tibetan design of spirals in rich orange, mauves, and gold.

"Where did you get that?" he asked, scratching at the beading along one seam.

Lucy paused in her flipping to follow King's gaze. "I woke up and it was here." Her eyes flicked to the foot of her bed.

"You don't know where it came from?"

"Oh, I do. It's mine. It's my meditation cushion. And there's this."

She turned and pointed at something King had missed upon entering the room with his magazines and jumbo coffee. A little wooden Buddha. Fat and happy, his hands over his head in a victorious pose. And in his upturned hands, some sort of cup, filled.

She pressed her thumb to Buddha's round belly. "Lou must've brought them from my apartment."

"That was nice of her." He said no more, but he thought plenty. *Why didn't she stay? Why didn't she tell you she loved you? Offer to sit with you for a while? Why did she have to come like a thief in the night?* He wondered if the visit was like the one she'd paid him a couple of days before. Another way to avoid whatever was going on in her apartment.

"I like this one," Lucy said. She turned the magazine so King could see. A plunging neckline in Art Deco style. A mermaid fit, or so description read. As if King knew dresses any better than he knew daytime soap operas.

"Too bad I don't have the cleavage to hold it up," she said, turning the page.

"What are you talking about!" He took the magazine and flipped back to the page, finding the dismissed dress. "It would be gorgeous on you."

He earmarked the page, creasing it between his thumb and forefinger.

She smiled. "You're sweet, Robert."

Her smile warmed him to his toes.

"What about flowers?" he asked, fishing for another magazine. "You need a bouquet."

"Do I?" she said with a laugh.

"Knowing you, you'll probably want something seasonal." If not, she might refuse flowers outright. He remembered the five-minute lecture she'd given him about commercially grown flowers the first time he'd gifted her with some red roses wrapped in cellophane.

She lay against the pillow, breathing hard as if flipping through magazines was proving too strenuous. "Sunflowers are in season. Lilies. Mums. Dah-dahlias."

"What color?" he asked, scribbling in the margins beside the mermaid dress.

"Fall colors. Red or burnt sienna. Robert—" she rasped.

The wheeze made him look up, alarm bells sounding in his head.

"You don't have to do all this. There's no point," she whispered.

"No point?"

She placed a clammy hand on his. "I know you love me. That's more than enough."

He scoffed, hoping it hid the fear welling up inside him. "I'm doing this for the rich inheritance."

She smiled, but didn't laugh. Her breath remained too high in her throat. Should he call someone?

"What flower will you pin to your suit?" she asked. "A sunflower is too large."

"I'll get a daisy or something like it. There's that yellow daisy with the black center. I've forgotten the name."

"A black-eyed Susan."

Awful name, he thought. "Or maybe I'll wear *only* a sunflower. Strategically placed. We can have one of those naked yoga weddings."

She laughed, but it devolved into coughing. He held the water out for her, helping her to sit up straighter.

The sight made his chest ache. The hateful voice he'd been carrying all morning rose up, volume to the max. *This is stupid. This is pointless. She's barely more than a bag of bones. She'd break the second you tried to push a ring onto her finger. This isn't what she wants.*

The voice had started as he'd walked through the French quarter that morning. From the moment he'd stopped into the corner market across from his apartment and scoured the magazine racks for *Bridal Boutique, Bridal Monthly. Brides-R-Us, The White Dress,* and every wedding magazine he could find, this relentless voice ragged him.

But it had been worth it when she took the first magazine from the pile, her shaking hand flipping open the first cover. The way she'd smiled. The strength in her voice as she patiently answered each of his questions. The laughter.

Stupid or not, she was enjoying herself. And even if the walls caved in on her tomorrow, squeezing the last breath from her chest, he wanted her to die excited about *something.*

Anything. No matter how stupid, commercial, or pointless. Anything to make these last moments the best they could be.

"This one's all about dresses," he says, seizing The White Dress from the slick pile. "Are you *sure* you want a mermaid dress?"

Red-faced but breathing, she motioned toward the slick pile. "I want to look at the cakes."

"Now we're talking."

King had purchased *two* magazines that focused on cake and food. It was true that he was thinner now than when he'd first seen her months ago, but he still loved food, as he always had. He'd lost nearly twenty pounds over the summer they spent together, walking the Tuileries Gardens, West bank and Eifel Tower together. Seeing the inside of an Egyptian pyramid by flashlight. The Parthenon and Coliseum.

She had a bucket list as well as anyone.

So they jumped naked into the Mediterranean. Kneeled in the temples of Kyoto. Dove the Great Barrier Reef on a clear day where the sea turtles and clown fish could be seen easily.

They'd worked on checking them off one by one, together. Saving tremendously on airfare and lodging. Sandwiching in as many excursions as she had the stamina for between her chemo treatments. Some days her spirit and body held up fine. Other nights, they agreed that movie and popcorn was better. But it was mostly King who had eaten the popcorn and watched the movie, while Lucy slept in the crook of his arm.

He worried that while all the walking and activity was great for him, maybe it had worn her out quicker. Would she have had more time if she'd rested? If she hadn't tried to push herself to squeeze the most out of the days she had left?

He wondered what his life might be like when she was gone...

He'd drank quite a bit before she'd came back into his life. Now, he drank no more than three drinks in one go. He wondered if it would come back—the weight and the drinking—once she was gone. *We hold so much of ourselves back for the ones we love.*

Without her...Once she's gone...

Don't think of that.

King wished he wasn't so big, so that he could lay beside her in the hospital bed, look at the magazines side by side. He would have to satisfy himself with turning the page, as she pointed out cake stands and decorations that worked well with a fall theme. A croquembouche.

"Do you think this was produced sustainably," she said, and pointed at a wooden pedestal on which a cake sat. Globs of chocolate icing decorated with orange and red leaves across three layers.

Her face pinched suddenly, and her hand tightened on the corners of the magazine.

"Are you okay?" he asked. His heart hammered in his chest, his stomach filling up with acrid bile.

She closed the magazine, eyes clamped shut. "I'm tired."

He pulled the magazine from her limp hands and gathered them up, placing in a neat pile next the wooden Buddha on the little table.

"We can pick this up another time." He shook the styrofoam cup, rattling the ice. "Do you want more ice?"

She didn't answer.

"Lucy?"

She finally opened her eyes. They were bright with pain and fear. He pressed the call button before she even asked. Nurses entered a moment later. King stepped out of the way, clutching the cup of ice in his right hand, so they could fuss over her. Check the IV and the drugs.

Before they had to ask, he excused himself. He was too large to stand there gawking while others frantically worked. And it was just as well. The reality was his old claustrophobia had risen up to meet him. When Lucy had opened her blue eyes and revealed all her fear and pain, the walls of the hospital room had slid in closer. Four, maybe five inches. Even the ceiling seemed to press down from above. The air which had felt too cool one moment before, was suddenly hot. Way too hot. And instead of holding him up, the chair in which he sat seemed to pull him down.

He could never predict when his claustrophobia might arise. Often at night, he lay in his king-sized bed, staring at the ceiling. In those moments, he begged for sleep but the walls crept close. He would shove his pillows away. Open the French doors leading out to the covered balcony so a cool breeze could flow through his apartment. But often even the air and the moonlight weren't enough to relieve the mounting suffocation clawing at his chest and neck.

Only when he'd turned on the light did the walls of his bedroom seem to move back an inch.

Lying in the ruins of a collapsed building would do that to a man.

Eleven DEA agents had gone into a building for drugs and a mob boss, and only King had come out alive. He'd been standing beneath a set of stairs when the bomb went off, bringing down the Westside brownstone they were searching. Brick after brick crashed down around him, until he was pinned under the rubble. Four days he laid in the dark, trying to breathe, trying to stay alive.

Somehow he managed to keep breathing. He might have been pulled from the wreckage with all ten fingers and toes, but he hadn't escaped the rubble completely unscathed. His only company, the compressing darkness, was always with him now. And sometimes it liked to remind King that it was so.

King sank down into the plastic chair outside the hospital room. It was white and reminded him of an egg, whose shell had been emptied and cleaned before being placed on four metal legs.

He listened to the machines rattling in the room. To the rapid fire instructions spat between them.

He wondered if he should call Lou. Then decided against it. Two more nurses and a doctor rushed past him into Lucy's room.

The phone in his pocket buzzed. "Christ."

He fished the phone from his pocket, swearing as he worked his fingers into his coat pocket, getting seemingly stuck on corners that didn't exist.

He didn't recognize the number right away, but answered it. If he had been home, in the quiet calm of his apartment above Mel's shop, he would have let it go to voicemail. But any distraction, even a telemarketer, was welcome against the frantic commotion in the room behind him.

"King," he said.

"Robbie!" a deep vibrato greeted him. The kind of voice that rumbled up from the chest rather than from the nose or throat.

King knew it instantly. "Sampson? How the hell are you?"

"I've been better, honestly. How are you?"

King tried not to listen to the hushed whispers echoing through the open door.

"I've been better too. What's going on?"

King heard the click of keys and knew that Sampson was typing something. "I heard you'd opened your own private practice. Is that true?"

"I did. But something came up and it's on hold at the moment."

You'll have plenty of free time soon, a hateful voice hissed. King shoved the snake beneath the water of his mind. *Enough to turn right back into the fat, alcoholic you were.*

"Just as well," Sampson went on. "In four months, I'll be leaving the force myself."

"Got retirement plans? A houseboat in the Bahamas?"

The man laughed heartily. "I do love me some lime in the coconut. But no, no plans. Why, you looking for a partner? I wouldn't mind some investigative work. It's gotta be more interesting than Sudoku."

A nurse came out of Lucy's room, jogging right past him without a word. She cut into an adjacent room and reemerged with a box of some kind.

"You there?"

"Yeah, I'm here," King mumbled. But he was aware, if distantly, the way his mouth hung open, his eyes fixated on the nurse.

"If this is a bad time, I can call you back." Sampson's voice was so distant yet King saw him in his mind's eye. An ex-boxer like himself but they both had bellies now. Sampson as dark as he was fair. But a kinder, gentler man King had never known.

"There's nothing I can do unfortunately," King said. "So you might as well tell me why you called. Distract me."

King was certain that whatever Sampson might need, it wasn't post-retirement work.

"I called for a couple of reasons. First, you should watch your back."

"Who wants to kill me now?" King chuckled, but the sound was hollow. He was pantomiming a conversation. He was relieved to find he could still do it when necessary.

"We don't know. But 24 of our agents have disappeared this week."

"Field agents?"

"Yeah. And some undercover. It's not unheard of for undercovers to go dark, but the ones we've confirmed missed their check-ins. We wouldn't think anything of it except—"

"—except 24 is a lot."

"In 48 hours."

King whistled. "That is mighty damn suspicious."

Sampson agreed. "We don't know if this has anything to do with Brasso's disappearance. We haven't made a connection yet."

Brasso. King knew exactly where *he* was. After a brief stint of forced isolation in a Siberian shipping container, he'd received free one-way passage to La Loon, courtesy of Louie Thorne.

Just thinking of Brasso made King's jaw jump.

He may have saved King from the wreckage of a collapsed building, but apparently that hadn't been enough to inoculate him against betrayal. Brasso almost put a bullet in King himself—if Lou had given him the chance.

King heard a chair squeak through the line and wondered if he'd missed something Sampson had said. He tried to imagine the other man in the hustle and bustle of the St. Louis Headquarters.

The last time he'd visited that building was three months ago, with Lou in tow. They'd slipped right through the shadow of an oak tree up into Brasso's office, trying to get a sense of how deep the man's betrayal ran.

Where was Sampson in the building? In one of the cloistered offices? Or was he on the main floor, in the thick of it. An office with a closed door, he suspected, given the silence on the other end. That wouldn't have been possible if he'd been in the center of the fury that consumed the floor.

And the office itself? Sampson had been a military man and as neat as they come. No doubt all the trash was in the waste bin. The surface of the desk clear of everything but a computer and maybe a coffee cup. Behind him on a windowsill, a few pictures of his two grown kids and wife.

Doreen would've added something nice to the place. A rug. Maybe a plant.

"I want you to keep your eyes open," Sampson said, offering King solid ground again.

"I'm not a field agent anymore, Sammy," King pointed out, hoping to recover the thread of the conversation he may have dropped. "No one is going to come looking for me."

That was a damned lie. He'd done away with that illusion when his very own partner offered him a case—only with the intention of dumping his chained body in the river for the fishes to nibble on. And he hadn't cut Lou from his life, and with that one, who knew what the hell would come knocking.

"Keep your eyes and ears open," Sampson said.

"You said you called about a couple of things. What else?"

Silence stretched on the phone.

"Did I lose you?" King asked, his heart tapping out a strange rhythm. *Danger*, it said. *Danger*.

"Nothing serious," Sampson said, and King knew it for the bold-faced lie that it was. "But I'd like to tell you in-person. You free on Friday?"

14

Lou managed to get her body into an upright position before her boots hit the fish cart. Her momentum was more than the dead weight of the fish. Like a seesaw, her end went down and the fish went up. But the motion was enough to cushion the worst of her fall, absorbing her momentum. If she'd crashed through the landing a foot or so to the right or left, it would've been a different story.

She stumbled back a step with the shifting cart beneath her boots, knees shaking. Her balance was compromised. The back of her ankles hit the lip of the cart. This was enough to buck her off the other side.

She hit hard.

The unforgiving concrete floor bit her elbow. It sang, sharp pain ricocheting up the funny bone into her neck. She rolled under the conveyor belt, seeking shelter in its shadow. Before she slipped two fat tuna slapped against the floor an inch from her face. Their watery eyes wide-open, mouth parted in a pantomime of surprise. The tail slapping concrete splashed water into her face.

She recovered in the darkness of a closet. She didn't know what closet, and she didn't care as she ran her hands over her wet face. She reeked of fish. Her face. Her hands. Her clothes were wet too, no doubt from when she'd tried to break her own fall. She wiped at her cargo pants and snatched a shirt off a hanger above her to dab at her face.

She pat herself down, checking to make sure all the working parts were present and accounted for.

Only the elbow throbbed. It was a hell of a time to realize that this Kevlar jacket didn't have reinforced elbows like her leather jacket did. But the pain was tolerable. She could work with that.

Splinters in her hair and the reeking scent of fish clinging to her, she would have to push that aside. She still had her guns and her bullets. And if she was lucky, her target.

The closet door creaked open, slowly spilling light into the space. Her entrance must've been louder than she'd thought.

Lou pressed deeper into the darkness, and right out the other side. No doubt the closet would be searched and some tenant confused and frightened. She probably cost someone a decent night's sleep.

She was back in the fish house a moment later.

A man screamed. Too close. So close her ears rang with it. She turned just as Jason, wide-eyed reached for the gun tucked into the back of his jeans. She'd appeared right beside him without meaning to. What had he been doing? Squatting in a dark corner while everyone else tried to solve the mystery of the falling woman?

Before he could get his gun up, Lou grabbed his elbow, pushing down to lock his hands at his side, making it impossible to pull the weapon at that angle. She freed her own Beretta and yanked him through the dark.

A heartbeat later, her boots hit the dirt beside her Nova Scotian paradise. It was dark.

"What—" Jason began, his wide fearful eyes sliding from her face to the lake.

She didn't have time to play with him, especially since he wasn't the man she wanted. She wanted Cam.

She put the Beretta under his chin, watched his eyes double in size and pulled the trigger. The silencer kept the report from ricocheting through her head, splitting her ear drums. But the sudden explosion of brains and blood was unpleasant. The smell was gamey to her, like a deer skinned and gutted, ready for processing.

His body dropped like a sack of concrete and she released his elbow. One look at the crumpled body and a cursory glance at the endless wilderness to ensure she hadn't been seen, and she was off again, squeezing herself back through the darkness.

She emerged on the upper level of the fish house. She cursed her compass and the darkness. Hadn't they learned their lesson? Were they looking for a second dramatic entrance?

The gulls certainly hadn't. Squawking, they took flight in a flurry of white and gray, causing a whirlwind of feathers and bird shit to rain down on the commotion below.

All eyes turned skyward, but the birds offered surprisingly good cover. After all, no one wanted their face pointing upward as shit and feathers rained down.

She spotted Cam immediately. He had his pistol out and pointed upward, a phone pressed to his ear. No matter who he was calling, it was likely in Lou's best interest that she end that call.

Lou had a chance to press herself into the corner of the upper loft, finding darkness again and slipping down to shadow cast by the processing machinery to his right.

What she hadn't realized was that the foreman had his back.

She registered the gun only a second before it went off. She moved, but not enough. It tore through the side of the Kevlar jacket, no doubt skimming the vest beneath. A second bullet bit into her upper arm. She didn't have time to consider if the artery there had been severed before he was taking aim again. The third bullet hit her square in the gut. It was like a fist to the stomach, knocking her back into the machine. The vest absorbed the bullet, but it hurt like hell. A big, ugly bruise would sit purple over the bone tomorrow.

She swore, fury rising in her like a pissed off snake.

Cam, startled by the chaos was raising his own gun. His face a twin expression of the defiant and frightened foreman beside him.

Lou came to depend on the fact that men rarely aimed for a woman's face, at least straightaway. But they would eventually, when enough bullets to the torso didn't seem to slow her down.

If she didn't do something, she would lose her brains all over this machine.

She seized both the foreman and Cam by their shirts and yanked them toward her. An overzealous tug that sent both men crashing into her, pulled off their feet in surprise. The three of them slammed into the side of the machine. Its metal duct popped and creaked. Lou felt the force of it ripple through her back and set fire to her wounds. She pinched her eyes shut for an instant against her burning arm. But the darkness swallowed the groan bubbling up between her lips.

As it opened its mouth and swallowed the trio, she wondered what would happen to the men if she were to let go in this infinite dark. Would they simply cease to exist? Or exist forever? Perhaps reaching for her, grabbing at her like phantoms each time she tried to pass through the in-between.

The world opened again and she hit the dirt on her hands and knees. Panting.

Lou was losing blood from the arm. The Kevlar was sticking to her skin. But she couldn't tell if it was a superficial blood loss, or if the artery had indeed been sliced. One was a flesh wound. The other could end her life.

With two men against her, she couldn't stop to remove the jacket and inspect the wound. She could only hazard a guess. She was losing blood and her arm was going numb. Neither sign was good.

She couldn't keep both men alive—and herself. The first thing she did was take Jason's gun from the dewy grass three inches from his hand and put two bullets in the back of the foreman's head before he could recover from the slip. The shock of the sudden night and calm pool stretching out before him had been distraction enough. He hadn't even seen the bullet coming.

He fell beside Jason, another heap of gore.

Cam still had his gun.

"Fucking shit!" His mind was obviously divided. It didn't look like he could decide if it was better to stare at the two bodies on the ground between them, or to keep his gaze trained on Lou. A third factor snatched at his mind too—the sudden and bewildering change in scenery always baffled her prey.

Lou trained her Beretta on the man. He took a step back, the heel of his combat boots catching on Jason's limp, outstretched hand. He stumbled and fell. His ass hit the cold, hard ground.

It reminded her instantly of Castle, one of Konstantine's mules who she'd brought to a similar lake.

But this man wasn't the squabbling, squealer that Castle had been. He was ready for her. At last, Cam seemed to realize he had a gun too and lifted it, pointing the gun's black eye right between her own.

She slipped through the shadows and reappeared behind him under the cover of the giant oak. A swift kick to the back pitched him forward onto his hands and knees. His face inches from the two bodies. She went to pull the other gun with her left hand and found she couldn't. It was cold and limp at her side.

Bad news.

Cam vomited onto the bodies. A pile of brains inches from your face will do that. She let his stomach run its course, taking the precious moment to run her own inventory. Darkness crowded in on the corners of her vision and the cold in her arm was spreading toward her chest.

She'd better make this quick. She pressed her gun to the back of Cam's head.

"Who do you deal to?" she said. Her voice was as cold and flat as ever.

"Fuck you."

She pressed the barrel of the gun to his right shoulder, wedging it between the shoulder blade and spine. She pulled the trigger.

The bullet blasted through the shoulder muscle, beneath the clavicle and hit the foreman's skull cap on the other side. Something was spit into the water. Bone fragments possibly. Or a chunk of brain.

Cam howled.

He rolled sideways, instead of on top of the bodies. The bullets weren't a particularly large caliber. She suspected she could get as many as five in him before the cause was lost. Especially if she stuck to the outer fringe of the extremities. Fingers. Toes. The meat of the upper arm and thigh, assuming she didn't hit any arteries. He wouldn't talk if he bled out.

Lou spoke over the howling and cursing. "Your shipments come through Miami's ports. You process them and hand them over to *who?*"

"Fuck you!"

Lou's teeth began to chatter. She clenched her teeth to stop it which only caused her whole jaw to tremble. She shot Cam both in the right arm and the right foot. "It'll be three bullets next t-time."

Embarrassed by the chattering teeth, she pressed the barrel to the side of his face.

"This one will be in your cheek."

"Fallon!" he screamed. "Bruno Fallon."

"W-who else?" Because she knew he had two distributors that took in the Miami port shipments.

"What the—"

She shot the gun into the air and he bleated like a sheep.

"Paulie Kraninski! Bruno Fallon and Paulie Kraninski."

"Where d-do they send it?" A tremble in her left arm joined the tremble in her jaw. She lowered the gun. She hoped he thought her lenient rather than suspect the truth. She couldn't hold up the gun anymore. All feeling had gone out of that side of her body.

Hurry Lou-blue, her father warned. *You'll black out in two minutes. Three tops. Get somewhere safe.*

"Kran sends his shit up through Atlanta. And Fallon through Dallas."

"Thank you," she whispered.

And then shot him through the head.

"Thank you?" she murmured to herself. She laughed, a bewildered, off-kilter sound.

It was hard to drag the men into the water with one hand. And she didn't want to make multiple trips. So there was a stupidly comic moment when she had three men in the water, but was trying to get a hold of each while they slid beneath the surface.

But she managed to pull them beneath the nighttime waters and find blood-red water rushing in.

When she broke the surface of Blood Lake, Lou found she couldn't hold all three men. She released two of the water-soaked corpses and lifeguard dragged the third toward the shore.

Dragging a wet corpse was even harder than dragging a dry one.

She didn't even have the corpse out of the water when the leaves rustled. Something thrashed through the thick jungle foliage on her right. It would be here in seconds.

She dropped the body, which turned out to be Jason's, onto the soggy shore and surveyed the nightmare landscape.

The two moons hung in the purple sky and apart from the ripples she'd created swimming to shore, Blood Lake was still in the quiet evening.

Of course, it was always a quiet evening in La Loon. Every time Lou had visited this strange place, the sky was the same color, the moons hanging in the same position. She had no idea if some version of the sun rose and set on this place. She often wondered if this part of Jabbers' world was like Alaska. For months at a time, everything traveled the sky in the exact same arc.

The beast emerged through the trees liquid fast. Her lithe, black body contracting and expanding, like an enormous cottonmouth snake. But she was no snake. Not with her body as big as an elephant's, her six legs, and taloned feet. Nor with the terrifying mouth that opened and released a blood-curdling screech. The air vibrated with its assault.

Jabbers darted forward, and once upon a time Lou would have pulled her knife or her gun then, anything to remind the creature that she wasn't prey. The mangled scar tissue on her shoulder showed just how indiscriminate the beast was when it came to fresh meat.

But Jabbers only bounded past her, playfully pouncing on Jason's limp body the way a fox pounces outside a rabbit hole.

Dizziness overtook Lou. The world tilted and she went down, her knees hitting the soggy earth at the water's edge. Her hands hit the mud.

She wasn't sure if it was the exertion of dragging the men, or if the seeping bullet wound itself—*I must've hit the artery after all*—but now she understood she'd overdone it.

Bloody water lapping at her backside and hips. She struggled to breathe.

A large black head rubbed against the side of her face. It struck Lou as very cat-like gesture. The way felines will rub their heads against a leg.

Another nudge, harder this time and then the sound of sniffing. Nostrils as large as a dragon's, inhaling the scent of Lou's bloody arm. A tongue the color of vanilla ice cream licked the wound, blood smearing across its surface like strawberry syrup.

In this way, apart from the deceiving black fabric she wore, Lou realized just how much blood she was losing. And how incredibly appealing a fresh kill must be compared to the soggy corpse several feet down the bank.

She'd been stupid to lower her guard. Stupid to think that her own bleeding body on the shore wasn't enough to tempt the beast. She should pull her gun. She could protect herself but her limbs were so heavy and darkness crowded in on the edges of her vision.

And the beast was fast.

Another hard nudge and Lou hit the water with her back, sinking. Blood red water overtook her.

And then she was through the other side. Breaking through the starlit waters a galaxy away.

She dragged herself to shore, feeling the breath tighten in her chest as if a belt were being pulled tight against it. She couldn't seem to get enough air into her lungs. Or blood into the heart.

What just happened?

Had the beast really shoved her back into the water? And she hadn't crawled in after her. Hadn't gobbled her up like a wonton in some sweet and sour soup.

If not to eat her, why?

She couldn't follow this train of thought very far. Her mind blurred at the edges and her arms shook violently as she hauled her torso onto the blood-soaked grass where bits of brain and remnants of skull dried in the lakeside grass.

She'd have to clean that later. If there was a later.

There was only the briefest experience of grass. Of cold earth and the scent of dirt. But it was quickly replaced by wooden walls and a hard, flat stone against Lou's back.

No, not stone. Wood. A wooden wall, wooden bench. A closet? What kind of closet has a bench?

All she could do was sit in the dark, breathing. She wondered if she would die like this. Would someone open a closet and find her rotting corpse. She hoped it wasn't a child.

"You may begin whenever you are ready," a man said.

Lou caught the scent of his aftershave.

"Begin what?" she croaked. It was hard to speak. She realized straight ahead was a curtain, not a wall like the panels surrounding her. But the box itself was too dark to make out more. Except there was a voice coming through a small hatchwork window, the pattern too intricate to reveal who was on the other side.

"Is this your first time?"

"My first?"

"It isn't a problem. You simply begin by saying 'forgive me father, for I have sinned. And then tell me what you did wrong.'"

"There's no such thing as sin," Lou said into the dark, her eyes flut-tering closed.

The man laughed. "There is no evil in your world?"

"More than average, I think."

"If you have nothing to confess—"

"Confess," she whispered, her voice rasping. Then she realized where she was. Her mother Courtney had been an ex-Catholic. And while Lou had only gone to the stone church in their hometown on Christmas and Easter, she knew about confession.

She asked the compass for somewhere safe. Somewhere quiet. And this is where it brought her. Like the universe was offering her a chance to ask forgiveness before she departed this world.

She smiled, laying her head back against the unforgiving wood.

The priest misinterpreted her swelling silence.

"Sometimes it is difficult to know where to begin. Maybe we simply feel that something is wrong or—"

"I know what's wrong," she managed. All feeling left her hand and the gun slipped from her fingers and clattered to the floor of the confes-sional. "I'm bleeding to death."

"What?" The priest's alarm was instant.

But Lou couldn't worry about that now. Her body was so cold that she couldn't move her fingers or her arms. Nor could she break her fall as she pitched forward, careening through the curtain.

15

Nico entered the large warehouse, his bootsteps reverberating up to the high ceilings. His men, because who was left was *his* now, stood against the walls, out of the way of center floor.

Eight men sat on their knees with black sacks over their heads, their hands tied behind their backs sat center stage. Nico had learned this technique from his captors in Russia. In the work camp, they used all manner of intimidation to lord over the men kept there. They stripped them naked, whipped them, starved them, blocked out their vision with blindfolds. Restrained them with ropes or suspended them in the air. It might seem counter intuitive, but Nico understood there was something especially cruel about blindfolding. The darkness heightened the fear.

It was warfare of the mind. No one could torture a man like the mind itself could. And the blindfold was only the first step in unleashing that tethered mind. Without the outer world to distract it, the mind turned on itself.

So he was not surprised that two of the eight men were openly weeping as they sat on their knees, head hung.

Only three were perfectly still, listening and waiting as their training had instructed. The other three were near hyperventilation. The sacks over their faces compressed and expanded with each panicked breath. Nico wouldn't let them suffer for long.

He crossed the large space to the man standing in its center. A camera tripod set up before him. This man, Jonathan, wasn't one of the ones that Nico trusted implicitly. There were several such men, hanging around in the dark of this warehouse two kilometers outside of Florence, further down the bend in the Arno than Ponte Vecchio.

Nico had killed those who were openly loyal to Martinelli's bastard. He'd put a bullet between every pair of eyes. But the silence was contagious. Quickly, they'd stopped fighting him and fell in line. That was how it should be. But Nico was certain that was for the sake of their own lives or families, and not out of any true loyalty to Nico.

If he was lucky, Konstantine was dead now. Bled to death in the arms of the bitch who tried to save him. Nico had pumped enough bullets in his guts to have done the job. And if not, that knife in the back should've done the job. But Nico had lived in the labor camps a long time. He understood that some men were simply harder to kill. And he was open to the possibility that Konstantine was such a man. And perhaps also the bitch.

If they lived, and if Konstantine intended to return with his dog to reclaim the Ravengers, he had a plan for that too.

"When are we going live?" Nico asked the cameraman. He repressed the urge to put his thumb to his mouth and chew on the meat of it. It was a habit from childhood and one that had always risen with his nervousness. But this was no time to show weakness.

All eyes followed him around the room, assessing him. After all, if one mutiny could be pulled off, so could another. If any heart in this warehouse had such ambitions, Nico's assault might be encouraging rather than a deterrent.

The man paused, drawing on this thick cigar. "Six minutes before the broadcast is up and running."

"And you're going to seize their stations. I want this live."

The cameraman only nodded, silver smoke pouring out of his nostrils the way smoke pours from the mouth of a dragon.

"Everyone into position!" he shouted over the soft conversation that had steadily grown with his back turned. Eight men from the wall crossed the concrete floor and came to stand behind the black-sacked captives.

"Four minutes," the cameraman murmured, fidgeting with the black machine on top of his tripod.

"Ready?" Nico shouted again and the men standing behind the kneelers lifted their blades, showing that they were in fact in position and ready. No doubt the men kneeling expected a bullet between the eyes. A quick executioner death given the positions in which they were forced. But Nico had a flair for the dramatic. And he wanted his message to the agencies that would hunt them to be very clear.

If this move didn't rid him of his enemies, and convert the rest to allies, he wasn't sure what would.

"Ninety seconds."

The man removed the lens cap from the machine and adjusted it. Once satisfied with the camera's setup, he plugged a small microphone into the side of the machine before passing it over to Nico.

"More light, please!" he called up to the rafters. And until that moment, Nico had forgotten about the men up there, working the spotlights that set their little stage.

Bright light filtered down on the kneeling men. It looked like a Broadway play ready to begin.

"Very good," the cameraman said. He adjusted the lens one more time. "Sixty seconds."

He pulled the cigar from his mouth, and wiping its burning end across the bottom of his boot, left a smear of gray ash in its tread. He tucked the fat roll behind his large ear and leaned down into the camera.

Waiting.

Nico tried to still the hammering of his heart. Nico struggled to tell the difference between fear and excitement, but he suspected this one was the latter. He needed only make sure it was not mistaken in his voice.

"Ten, nine, eight, seven..."

The cameraman held up his hand, showing all five fingers. Then four, then three...

The men at the corners of the room froze.

Then the cameraman was holding up only a fist, which he lowered, and Nico understood it was now his time to speak into the microphone poised before his dry lips.

"For years, the Americans have waged war against us. They call it the

War on Drugs. But we know better. This is the war on poverty. The war against those who dare to rise above their circumstances. Those who want to feed their families, warm their homes, send their children to good schools. The system abandoned them, so they created a new system—and were punished for it. You blame drugs for destroying families, destroying lives. But it is your own greed. Your own unwillingness to invest in the people around you...That is what is destroying the world."

Nico wet his lips, took a breath. He motioned for the men to remove the black sacks from the kneeling man's heads.

"You send your dogs after us. But we are not afraid."

Nico waved his hand, the signal. And eight pale throats were stretched like sheets before the knives slid across them. A red mouth split open on each, blood bubbling up and over. The men squawked like chickens in the hen house.

"We will tolerate your tyranny no longer." Nico put his mouth close to the microphone. He spoke in the clearest English he could, enunciating each word carefully. "I am Paolo Konstantine. You will hear from me again, very soon."

16

King sat on the balcony overlooking Royal Street. The ferns lining his patio waved in a gentle breeze. The sweat on the back of his neck chilled and offered some relief from the heat of the day. A trash truck beeped as it backed up toward the alley to seize a dumpster there.

He'd tried working inside, preferring the air conditioning and overhead fans to the mugginess of the day. But the walls wouldn't let up. The heat spiked. It was like trying to breathe with a blanket over his face. Opening the balcony doors to let in the breeze hadn't been enough to loosen the crushing hold the walls had on his heart yet. He understood it wasn't really the heat of the day wearing him down.

Every time he thought of Lucy, of the scare they'd had the morning before, it felt as if a fist squeezed his heart. He'd managed to linger in the hospital for hours, a parade of nurses and four different doctors, six trips from the room to perform this or that test. All of it had yielded only a "stable" condition.

The doctor told him vaguely about spiking compounds in the blood and stresses to her heart. Nothing which really meant anything to King except, of course, the three things he already knew.

One: Lucy was dying.

Two: They were running out of time.

Three: There wasn't a damn thing he could do about it.

He carried this heavy reality with him as he moved his workspace out onto the balcony. The sunlight, the people, the elevation, and open space, all of it helped. A little.

At least he'd salvaged most of the afternoon. He'd removed six more marks against Lou from the databases he'd swept. Three that were her handiwork without question, known drug mules plucked from a park in New York, a subway stop in Boston, and outside a corner store in Detroit. And three that *might* have been Lou. He worried he was abusing his privilege. Was keeping his friend's daughter safe—Lucy's niece—away from the public eye really enough reason to destroy evidence? It wasn't evidence of a crime *exactly*. A couple keystrokes here and a video deleted there. Any threads that could lead back to her if someone decided to start digging.

And what if someone caught on to what he was doing? The dummy IP addresses he used to crack the system would defer suspicion only to a certain extent. If anyone was remotely as skilled as he was—and he wasn't even top shelf talent—they could find him easy enough. Then what?

You know what, he thought. Lou would put a bullet in the unfortunate soul and call it a day.

Sneakers on his kitchen floor caught his ear.

"Okay," Piper called out. She walked out onto the balcony with a glass pitcher of Mel's sweet tea in her right fist and two glasses stacked on one another in the other. "Two glasses of sweet tea as requested."

She put the pitcher on the outdoor table and flipped the glasses over. She poured them each a tall glass, making sure one of the lemon wedges slopped out into King's glass.

"Thanks, kid," he said, squinting at her through the sunshine.

"It's the least I could do. Thanks for covering for me earlier." Piper gave him a sheepish grin. "Mel would've killed me."

King had opened the storeroom, looking for the register tape Mel had asked for and had come upon Piper in the passionate embrace of another girl. This one had a high, sideways ponytail of black curls spilling down over one shoulder.

The girl was ready to laugh. King saw the embarrassed grin and barely repressed giggles threatening to erupt from her. Piper must've seen it too, because she'd clamped one hand over the girl's mouth. King could only stare at Piper's ruddy red nose and swollen lips for a moment, before reaching over and plucking a white roll of register tape off the storeroom shelf.

He'd closed the door without saying a word, replacing the tape while Mel continued giving her tarot reading behind the velvet curtain, none the wiser.

"I doubt she would've killed you," King said, taking a deep drink of the tea. Ice clinked against his front teeth until he pulled his upper lip down to shield them. "A lecture maybe."

"She hates it when I use the stockroom as a make-out closet."

King barked a laugh. "I didn't realize this was a common occurrence."

"Only if there's no one in the store." Piper gave another sheepish grin.

"Mel will appreciate that you put the customers first." He balanced the cool glass against his knee.

Piper didn't seem to hear. At least, she'd already turned to her laptop in front of her, a large archaic machine that probably cost her no more than a couple hundred bucks from a local pawn shop. The laptop's fan sounded as if it were about to take off, simply lift the laptop off the table and fly it away over the Quarter's streets.

"So what am I looking up first?" Piper asked.

King had been covering Mel's expenses by giving Piper grunt work through the summer and into the fall. Most of it was reading news stories for suspicious activity. Anything on the drug trade or border control. Politicians suspected of any connections. Missing persons. But that was before he realized he could crack the DEA's and FBI's private servers.

Piper took a deep drink of her tea, crunching ice between her teeth. "Come on. What has our girl gotten into lately?"

King snorted. *Our girl.*

"I want you to find out who carries mermaid wedding dresses in town. Probably a size six or eight. He pulled the magazine that Lucy had flipped through from his bag at his feet and handed it over to Piper, opening it up to the dog-eared page.

"You're going to marry her!" Piper exclaimed, taking the magazine. It fell open across the keyboard of her laptop, right to the earmarked dress page.

"If she'll have me," King said.

Piper's face screwed up. "You're going to marry, *Lou?*"

"No!" King shouted, perhaps too forcefully. "I'm talking about Lucy."

Piper put a hand over her heart, her silver rings catching the sunlight. Prismatic light danced on the tabletop. "Whew. My goddess. Okay. Right."

King wasn't sure how to take this. Did Piper think he was too old for Lou? He would've agreed with her there. But any other disqualification would've hurt.

"Would you be sad if Lou got married?" King asked, teasing her.

"Uh, yeah. You know she's my dream girl."

"You seemed to be doing just fine in the storeroom earlier."

"Vanessa? Oh, we're friends."

King snorted, the sound of it echoing in his tea glass. "I'd hate to see how you treat your enemies."

King wouldn't ask the wildly inappropriate question *how many women have you slept with Piper?* He tried to do the math in his head. How many women had he seen around the shop this year alone? A dozen at least, since January. And he'd seen her in Jackson Square a few times, kissing one girl or another in passing as he left Café du Monde with his sack of beignets and coffee.

Had she really slept with them all?

"You have a lot of friends," King said, cautiously, as Piper continued to clack away at the keyboard, scribbling names of dress shops in town on the top of the yellow legal pad he'd given her. The black ink pressed hard into the page.

Piper shrugged. "I'm good company."

That could mean a hundred things, he supposed. And he had seen a core group of the girls over and over again. Return customers were usually pleased customers.

Customers.

"Do they pay you?" he asked.

Piper's mouth fell open. "Hey! Just because I'm capitalizing on my youth and good looks doesn't mean I'm a prostitute, man. Geez."

"It's none of my business."

"Damn right. And what have you got against prostitutes? Whatever a woman wants to do with her body is her business."

"Of course it is," he said, offering no protest. And feeling like he'd just stepped in a massive pile of dog shit, added, "And I like prostitutes."

Piper's eyebrows shot up. "TMI, man."

"They are great sources of information."

She pulled out her cell phone and started dialing the first number on her list. King could hear the ringing across the table.

"Hi, yeah. Can you tell me if you carry any mermaids? What color?" Piper's lips turned down. She looked at King and then seemed to think better of it. "Uh...one sec."

She frowned at the dress in the magazine. She squinted at the fine print below the model, describing the dress. "Uh, cream maybe. Yeah, no. Not white. What sizes are available?"

Piper leaned back in her chair, waiting for the woman to check the colors they had available.

"What are you supposed to be doing?" she asked him, turning the cell phone up so that the mouthpiece was pointed toward the sky over her head.

He was supposed to be scanning the databases for more evidence of Lou's hunt. "I don't know. I can't focus today."

Piper looked ready to say something but she pivoted the phone over her mouth again and began to speak to the shopkeeper again. "Yep. Ready." She grabbed the pen, scrawling notes. "Awesome. How much?" Her eyes bulged, and she whistled. "And the other two?"

More scribbling.

He watched her write and wondered if he was a fool. Of course he was. What use did dresses and flowers and all that have now? Lucy might not even see the end of the week. And she was bone tired and in so much pain. Why would King drag her from her bed, put her in a dress and make her play some part? This was his own desperation shining through, as if marrying her will tie her to this world—and to him.

But she'd been so happy looking through the magazines, talking about cake. It had been the brightest he'd seen her eyes in weeks. Maybe clinging to the hope this would make her happy did make him a fool.

But frankly, he didn't know what else to do with himself between now and visiting hours.

King turned on his own laptop.

"Yeah, thanks for your time." Piper terminated the call and started dialing the second number on her list.

When she finished, he'd have her start on the flowers. He would do the cake and food himself. He wondered if Café du Monde could do a croquembouche out of beignets. A small one. What else...

A photographer?

His dark screen finally lit with his welcome page. A search engine that compiled the daily news. He was halfway through typing *New Orleans Wedding Photographers* when the banner changed to the bright red *Breaking News!*

He clicked it without thinking and saw a face he recognized.

Paolo Konstantine. Martinelli's bastard son stared back at him from the screen.

A polished news anchor with swept blond hair spoke to the camera. King expanded the video with a double click of his mouse. "Authorities say they have identified the man responsible for the on-camera slaughter of eight federal agents. While the man's face is never seen on camera..."

King sat back in his chair, watching the blonde rewrite a story worthy of the news. Sensationalism at its best. But now that he'd seen it, he couldn't take it back. He googled Konstantine, and found that the man's face was the leading story on over twenty online news sites, with more and more updates pouring in. *Trending* with an upward arrow appeared by his name.

And he'd thought Lou had problems before...

"Did you hear what I said?" Piper asked, tapping her pen against the legal pad.

King reluctantly pulled himself from his thoughts. "Sorry."

"I said I've got over twenty dresses here. Should I stop now or call the other three shops?"

"Twenty is plenty," he said. He fished his wallet out of his back pocket and offered Piper the plastic card. "Why don't you take one of your lady friends dress shopping. Pick one about Lucy's size and shape."

"The dress?"

"The girl," he said.

"Nah," Piper said, plucking the plastic from between his fingers. "I can't take someone wedding dress shopping. It sends the wrong message."

"How will you know how they fit?"

Piper tore the dress from the magazine and folded it into eighths before slipping it into her own Teenage Turtle wallet with King's credit card. "I'll try it on myself."

"Try to keep it under $2500. And if in doubt, get it a little larger rather than smaller. We can always tailor it down, not the other way around," he said, as Piper saluted and started down the fire escape on the side of the balcony. He had no idea why she liked to climb up and down that thing so much. King's back and shoulders ached just looking at it.

He returned his interest to the computer screen and Konstantine's face. A myriad of portraits from every conceivable angle. The internet darling, a forward facing death glare.

King wondered if his efforts to protect Lou might prove pointless after all.

There were some things you couldn't prepare for.

17

Lou's eyes flew open. She sat up in bed. Bed. Lou turned toward the skyline and saw it was night. The pool shone two stories below, its spotlights ominous in the dark. The sparkling water seeming to beckon unwary swimmers into its depth. Someone had replaced the petunias with mums in the patio planters and cut back the creeping morning glory entwined with the No Lifeguard On Duty sign.

Stretching out beyond the pool and its walled garden was the St. Louis skyline. The arch cut the sky with a delicate whoosh. Lights shimmered like candles from distant windows.

Ice clinked in a glass.

She turned and saw Konstantine sitting on her sofa. His arm draped lazily across the back of it, a chilled glass of water perched on top of his thigh.

He watched her with a guarded expression. "Dare I ask what happened to you?"

Memories bobbed up from the inky depths of her mind. Benji on a park swing. A wooden walkway collapsing beneath her. The scream of gulls. Cam on his knees in front of her, hate screwing up his snarling face.

"I'm not sure," she said. And she wasn't. She didn't have the whole story anyway. She vaguely recalled the melodious voice of a priest in the confession box. And all her strength leaving her at once. But then what?

"You appeared here about four hours ago," he said, those liquid eyes remaining unreadable. "Were you in a hospital?"

She frowned. "Hospital?"

He pointed at her. No. At the wrist resting on her coverlet. Encircling the small, bird-like bones was a white hospital bracelet. *Boston University Hospital.* The new bracelet wasn't the only change. Her Kevlar jacket, father's vest, and every gun were gone. Even her underwear. She had only the scrubs, the hospital bracelet and the gauze covering her upper left arm.

"Fuck," she swore. "Did I look like this when I showed up?"

"I haven't touched you. You appeared in the bed, as you are now. If I hadn't been sitting here, I would have thought you'd come home and put yourself to bed."

She noted the novel open and face down on the sofa cushion beside him. He was more than halfway through. Of course, she had no television, laptop or radio in the apartment. What else could he do with his time except perhaps plot his revenge against Nico.

"The priest must've called 911," she muttered, throwing back the cover and placing her feet on the cool wooden floor.

His face at last revealed emotion. His right eyebrow hiking itself up onto his forehead. "You were with a priest?"

"I must've slipped back after the surgery," she added. She clearly wore enough gauze to suggest medical intervention. And she doubted she slipped away while on an operating table. All the bright lights shining down on her would have made it impossible. But the moment they took her back to her room to rest? Turned down the lights and adjusted the IVs? No doubt.

And at least they hadn't known who she was. *Jane Doe* was printed in place of where a name should be on the bracelet.

She stood, and a wave of dizziness seized her. She swayed on her feet.

And then he was there. His arms under hers.

"Where are you trying to go?" he asked. The heat from his breath was on her face.

"I need my vest," she said. She hoped the priest had had the good sense to remove most of the armor before the paramedics arrived. He would've had to if he'd tried to staunch the wound until help arrived.

"It will have to wait."

"My father's vest—"

"You won't ever wear it again if you're dead," he said.

She froze against him. Her limbs were like sacks of wet sand. Absolutely useless. It was the relentless gravity of the room that wouldn't let go of her.

"You're bleeding," he said softly into her hair. She realized how rigid his body was against hers. And the breath between his lips was thin and strained.

He smelled like her soap.

She pulled away from him under the pretense of inspecting her arm. She stood there in the center of the apartment, her back to him. She lifted the scrub sleeve to inspect the wound, but found only gauze soaked through with bright red blood. "This is why I can't wear white."

He laughed. A short chuckle in his throat. "I can't imagine it's your color."

She frowned. "I love white t-shirts."

She wanted to say more. About how clean a white t-shirt felt. More than that. It had also been her father's favorite. He seemed to have only two outfits in her memory. The black t-shirt beneath his adjustable vest. Black cargo pants and boots. Or a white t-shirt and jeans, which he wore on the weekends when he helped her mother around the house. Cutting the lawn. Pulling weeds. Repairing a fence.

She squeezed her eyes shut against the memory of him.

Since the truth had come out in June, and the story of Brasso's betrayal splashed every paper and magazine for a week at least, it had been easier to think of him. A cold stone settled in the pit of her stomach the night he died, and it hadn't loosened for the fourteen years that followed. Until the world knew again what she'd always known. Jack Thorne was a good man who didn't deserve what happened to him. The truth brought her peace.

But sometimes, when she wasn't expecting it—like this very moment —a memory would emerge, bright and beautiful and it would suck all the air from her body.

Those moments were hard and she suspected that as long as she lived, she would have them.

She preferred this to the alternative—to forgetting the face of her father.

She often stared at the photo of her father, now safely hidden beneath the kitchen utensil tray, and retraced the lines of his face. His strong jaw with the scar in the chin that Lucy said came from a motorbike accident when he was fifteen.

He hit a stump and went clear over the handlebars!

Those bushy brows and scruffy cheeks. She'd gladly give up an hour to this practice of remembering, if it meant he wouldn't become a shadowy figure in her mind.

Lou pushed back thoughts of her father and turned her attention again to the gauze on her skin. It was easy to remove once she worked her nail beneath. It was too soaked through to adhere to her skin properly. No matter. She'd use her own kit to replace it. She'd obviously popped a stitch or something.

She turned toward the window to get a better look at the wound in the light.

Konstantine whistled.

She understood why.

Her arm was black and blue and swollen from shoulder to elbow.

The bullet hadn't nicked the artery as she'd feared but had split the flesh in her upper arm completely, no doubt giving the look of a hotdog that had been sliced down the center, exposing the vulnerable inner meat within. They would've had to use a few internal sutures to close the gaping wound. Those would dissolve out of sight without her ever seeing them. But the tight sutures snaking across the surface of her bicep were seeping blood.

Crimson bubbled up between the black nylon and she could see that one stitch in the middle had popped and frayed. Its snapped end sticking up from the puckered flesh. What had she done to snap it, she had no idea. Lay on it maybe, add too much pressure to the arm. It would have had to be a significant force.

She understood why she'd bled so much now. This was a nasty flesh wound that would scar horribly.

"You need to rest your arm," Konstantine said, interrupting her assessment. "Do you have a sling?"

She leveled a cold stare at his face.

He held his hands up in surrender. "I'm not a doctor."

"If you want to play doctor, get my kit," she said. It wasn't until these words were out of her mouth that she realized their implication. If Konstantine had taken them perversely, she didn't know because he'd already walked out of the room, his back to her as he walked down the hall.

He appeared carrying her large box of medical supplies.

She sat on the edge of the bed, elbows resting on her knees as he placed the kit beside her right leg.

He popped off the lid, revealing the topmost tray of silver tools, packets of medicinal cream and bandages.

She pointed at what she needed. "Those pliers, the peroxide and the gauze."

He fished each item out with deft fingers. She noted the bruises on the back of his hands had faded from the purple to yellow.

She handed him the old bloody gauze and took the peroxide. "There are old towels under the second tray."

He handed her a faded green scrap of cloth, which she pressed against her arm, just under the wound. It was hard to clean up this particular part of her arm. It wasn't on her dominant side, which helped. But it seemed impossible to hold the cloth under the wound and pour the peroxide at the same time.

"I'll do it," he said and he already had the white cap off the brown bottle and was kneeling over her.

Cold liquid hit the wound and burned like hell. The fizz and pop of the solution pricked her ears. But she'd felt worse. The burn was little more than irritating and she knew to save her real annoyance for what was to come.

"There's a lighter in the second tray. Top left."

He hesitated, but only until she gave him another cold stare. Then he was handing over the orange lighter.

"I want you to pinch the two snapped lines together long enough for me to light them."

He didn't move.

"If you pinch the nylon together so that some of it sits above the pliers, I can melt it back together. This will prevent it from pulling at the wound. Grab the pliers too."

She watched him rummage through the trays. The light from the window fell across his neck and jaw. She realized she was staring and turned away.

The wound was ugly.

"Here, pinch them together."

He hesitated.

"You'll have to come closer than that," she said, calmly. Her voice was utterly emotionless. And it remained so even as he had to scoot forward, placing himself between her legs.

She swallowed. "I'll squeeze the wound together and you clamp the wires."

"Okay," he said, licking his lips.

She added the slightest pressure to either side of the wound where the nylon had snapped, and the wound gaped open.

When the wires were overlapping, he clamped them together. His eyes were very green in the light and fixed in concentration on her arm. She caught herself staring at his full mouth, the scruff around his lips. She wanted to rake her fingernails over it. Maybe bite his lower lip hard enough to make it bleed.

Instead she said, "Hold it. Twist the ends together if you can."

He did as she struck the metal on the lighter with her thumb until the orange-yellow frame sprung up.

She lit the ends and watched them evaporate in a puff of smoke.

When he removed the pliers, the black nylon lay fused over her skin once more. But when she bent to pick up the towel from the floor beside her left foot, she heard the slight *pop* and saw a fresh trickle of blood spring down her left forearm, rolling along the crease in her arm. The wound looked like a bloody mouth, opening to speak.

"Or not," she said. Damn. She had no choice but to restitch it.

She sighed and motioned for the box. He leaned over her right leg, his abdomen pressing into her thigh. It sent a deep clenching thrill up the inside of her leg, centering below her navel.

"Skaggs black?" he asked. And he turned toward her, making her glaringly aware of how close their faces were. And she knew he knew it too. Despite his calm mask and uninterested expression, she could see the pulse jumping in his throat.

"That will do," she said, hoping her own throat wasn't betraying her. And if it was, so what of it?

I could fuck him, she thought. She wanted to. But here, in her own apartment in her own bed, with someone who knew her name and her history...

It was a sobering effect, the light that removed all shadows. The desire died away almost instantly. Her back straightened as she accepted the little paper packet.

She tore open the white packet and tapped its contents out onto the back of her scrubs, using the top of her right thigh as a sort of table. A curved needle was already attached to the black nylon. And the string was coated in antimicrobial agents, or so said the packaging. So no need to worry about using the peroxide again.

"Do you need anesthesia or—" he began.

She inserted the needle through her skin before he could finish. It was Konstantine, not herself, that hissed, rocking back onto his heels.

"Cazzo," he said.

Lou didn't know much Italian, but knew this was a swear of one kind or another.

"You can look away if you're squeamish," she told him.

He didn't. Instead he said, "What the hell happened?"

"I was shot."

"How?"

"A bullet ejected from a gun and I happened to be in its way."

Whatever he wanted to say next, he dropped it.

She glanced past him at the green digital clock on her stove. It was nearly one in the morning. "After I'm done you can go to bed."

He laughed but understood a dismissal when he heard it. He repacked her kit and carried it out of the room, leaving only the bit of gauze and tape she needed to redress the wound. With his exit, he took that wall of heat and her hyperawareness of his body in relation to hers. It was as if someone had opened the window and let the night breeze wash in over her.

When he returned he said, "How do you get those supplies? Some of them are for doctors only."

"I take them from medical supply stores or pharmacies." How many times had she slipped into some dark supply storeroom at night, stuffing her bag with gauze, tape, needles and bottles of disinfectant.

"You're a thief?" he asked. He smiled as if amused.

"I leave cash on the counter." *Usually*.

Unless she knew that pharmacy was owned by a mob, which sometimes she targeted, or if the pharmaceutical company was Satan incarnate. Then she took without care.

She stood and crossed to the kitchen. Tossing the suture needle into the trash underneath, she washed her hands in the sink and added the gauze Konstantine had left aside for her.

"Go to sleep," she told him. "You're healing."

She motioned to her bed.

He shook his head. "You're more wounded than I am now. You take the bed."

She didn't want to tell him she couldn't. That the pillows, sheets and all of it smelled like him. That the idea of sleeping in the apartment where he also slept—freely, of her own will—was like agreeing to something.

But he'd already tucked a cushion under his head and turned away from her, offering the long plane of his back in the light from the window.

And the fact remained that she did need rest.

It wasn't only the pain wracking her body. Now that the danger had passed, her body ached. Every muscle had grown stiff and unforgiving. *Dragging three corpses across worlds will do that do you...*

And there was the fact that Lucy was on her radar.

The compass inside her whirred softly, a tug urging her to go and visit the woman again. It wasn't the firehouse alarm that had woken her weeks ago. The night Lucy's health turned a corner, Lou hadn't been fully awake before she found herself kneeling down and scooping her aunt off the floor.

A hop-skip-and-jump away and she'd delivered the woman to the hospital she'd never visit for herself.

The woman. Already her mind was taking steps to distance herself from the inevitable. As if Lucy wasn't the one who'd wrapped her arms around her the night her parents died. As if reducing her to nothing, to no one, could lessen this blow.

It was Lucy who had assured her that her parents were gone—irrevocably gone—but that she wasn't alone.

I can never replace what you've lost, her aunt had said. How strange she had seemed at first. This hippie with bleached hair in a long flowing skirt and arms as defined as any man's. *But I can give you a home and love you and help you in a way they couldn't.*

She had meant slipping of course. Not only the fact that she was now offering Lou room and board and an alternative to six years in the foster care system.

But she couldn't see Lucy now. Not looking the way she did, shot and bleeding. It would only upset her. Make her worry.

She pulled back the covers and slid between the sheets. She leaned across the mattress and felt the plastic slats of the blinds. With restless fingers, she pried them apart, one by one, welcoming more and more light into the bed.

It had been a while since she'd tried to sleep in this bed at night. It was easier to sleep from dawn until the late afternoon, when the sunlight was strongest. She could fall into deep slumber then, without any fear that dreams of the men she hunted may deliver her to their bedrooms.

But it was more than that.

Her nighttime habits had also taken over, hadn't they? It was easier to hunt by night. Under the cover of nightfall, stalking her prey was almost too easy. It was when she tried to do it during daylight hours. When they themselves may be more alert, but also the shadows against her. Shadows she could work, true. And it was only the light against dark that projected them. And yet, night was her natural ally. She didn't need a shadow when she was hunting under the cover of night. The world itself had become a shadow for her.

She let her back soften into the mattress, welcoming the support against her aching body. But she found a spot she could lay in.

She didn't think she could sleep though. Not only because a man lay less than two feet from her, his skin wrapped in the moonlight. The back of his neck a tuft of black hair.

But she had to try. Fighting sleep would only make healing harder.

"How did you survive?" Konstantine asked.

His voice was far too intimate in the darkness. Not full volume, but enough above a whisper to be clear.

"I slipped into a confessional. I guess the priest took pity on me and called an ambulance." *And I'll take pity on him if he still has my father's vest.*

"Not tonight," Konstantine said, turning over on the sofa. The coils creaked beneath him. His eyes shone like onyx in the dark. "The night Angelo came to your house, how did you survive?"

In her mind, Lou heard the quick *blat-blat-blat* of gunfire. Saw the strobe lights flash in the window and knew her mother was dead. Saw the side gate fly open and a ghostly hand shoving aside a lilac bush. Petals the colors of bruises rained down on the lawn. That glimpse of the phantom illuminated by the motion lights before her father lifted her off the ground and threw her into the water knowing it would save her.

Her back arched instinctively. Fourteen years separated that moment and this one, but she still felt the cold water knocking the air out of her, before sucking her down, enclosing her limbs like tendrils of seaweed. That unforgettable image of her father turning and running away, his white shirt an ethereal haze, he himself a target drawing the gunfire away from her.

"We were talking in the backyard when they came," she said. "He threw me into the pool."

"Ah, yes. Like in the bay when you took Ryanson. Your father knew you could exit through the water?"

"Yes."

"What happened when you came back?" If he had looked too interested. If he had come up onto his elbow, turned this into some slumber party share time, she would have shut down.

But he'd closed his eyes.

Dark lashes spread across his cheeks and serene light shined on his skin.

She wouldn't give him all of it.

Wouldn't recount for him what it was like rising out of Blood Lake with the full weight of her terror on her shoulders. Wouldn't tell him how she'd hidden on that strange shore until her terror of the place overtook her and then she tried to go home.

But it hadn't been their pool she'd crawled out of. It had been a river. And then a bathtub that had been left to fill while its owner stepped out of the room for a book or glass of wine. Then it had at last been a pool, but not hers. Rather an Olympic pool in a closed gym. She cried herself hoarse on the shallow steps, the eerie glow of the water not frightening her as it always had.

She had a new fear. And it had eclipsed her world.

Finally, she made it home to find the house crawling with officers and not one of them was her father. They'd wrapped her in a beach towel and sat her on the front step with a glass of water she never touched.

She understood now that her blind panic was partly to blame. And also the idea of defying her father. He had wanted her away, wanted her safe. Her compass wanted this also. Both of these factors stacked against her. And so when it came time to return—a third strike. She had been aiming for her parents. Trying to let the compass take her to the arms she wanted most.

But they weren't there anymore. That connection had been severed.

A tether snapped.

"Why does Nico want to kill you?" she asked. She wanted the conversation to steer away from her now. Far away.

His eyes opened again, and light reflected in those ink-black pools. "Padre warned me this would happen. Nico was jealous of me since we were boys. When we were children he would hit me, push me around and Padre always put a stop to it. He never did that for other boys. I think that only made Nico hate me more. One day he broke my hand with a hammer."

She said nothing.

"Padre tied him to a post in the courtyard behind the church and beat him for it. He made everyone watch. I'm certain we've been enemies since."

"Padre must have known he was fueling the rivalry."

He was silent for a while. Finally he said, "Whenever Padre had a problem, he would ask me what I thought even though my suggestions were often ridiculous. For example, he once asked me how could he bring in something very large through the city without anyone seeing it. And I told him to put it inside an elephant."

He smiled to himself.

"This was ridiculous, of course," he added. "Padre and all the other men had laughed. But then his face lit up and he cried, 'Madonna Santa!' He used the statues in the parade to hide the guns. They were carried through the streets right to his church and no one knew the difference. He always listened to me. Encouraged my ideas."

"I imagine intelligence is hard to come by in the criminal world," she said.

He didn't laugh. She noticed.

Finally he said, "I would argue that intelligence is very common is the criminal world. We must know your rules well enough to break them. And we must know the minds of men, so we can control them."

Silence hung in the air for a long time.

"There is a blanket in the closet," she said, before turning away.

18

Lou woke before Konstantine. It wasn't dawn. She had at least an hour or two of night on her side. The pain in her arm made it hard to sleep. It wasn't only the pain keeping her awake.

She hadn't slept so near a man, not since she was a child. When her mother was away on their annual sisters-only vacation, when they left their husbands and children at home and retreated to somewhere tropical—once the Virgin Islands, another time, an all-inclusive resort in Mexico—she would sleep with her father then.

She would climb up onto their elevated four-poster bed with much difficulty and he would let her watch television while he did paperwork that he hadn't finished on this or that case during the day. She would wake hours later, to find the popcorn bowl moved, and she herself tucked into her side of the king-sized bed, while he snored softly beside her.

It was too vulnerable, sleeping beside someone. Sex was easier.

From time to time, she found men while hunting. Never the men she hunted. Someone who was simply in the right place at the right time. Someone who walked up to her, and said hello while she tracked this or that man. Someone who'd smiled the right way. Someone who'd noticed her in a world where she moved mostly unnoticed.

She'd let them take her back to their place. But she didn't tolerate wine, conversation, or any of the tactics that they seemed to think she needed. They gave her names. Numbers. She gave them nothing.

She'd never seen a man more than once. Never taken them back to her apartment. And sure as hell had never brought them food. She couldn't imagine lying down beside them, and closing her eyes. There was always the chance a knife would slice her throat or a gun would be pressed to the side of her head. So no, she hadn't slept beside a man since Jack Thorne died.

Yet here he was. Konstantine. His chest rising and falling with each relaxed breath. His cheek on her pillow.

Of all the men in the world...

It's done, her father said. *If it's done, no point in worrying it like a bone. You're only punishing yourself twice.*

She slid from her bed and grabbed her black boots. Still wearing her scrubs, she stepped inside the closet and closed the door behind her.

The first stop was a thrift store. She exchanged the scrubs for camo pants and Ramones t-shirt. A black hoodie befitting the chilly September night. A black sports bra with one of its cups missing, the other easily removed. Socks for her feet which she laced her boots over. Had she come during business hours, this ensemble would have cost her $13. She took a twenty from the pocket in her boot and put it on the counter.

The first thing she did to every pair of boots she bought was sew an inner pocket into the tongue. Something tight enough to hold a few compressed bills without them slipping loose.

When she needed two hands for guns, purses or backpacks were impossible. Even fishing money from a bra was too much trouble, often shifting and disappearing in this or that corner of the fabric.

She wasn't fit to see the priest, but hopefully she wouldn't see him. Get in, get out. Avoid the formalities.

She stepped out of the parking lot light spilling from a display window of the thrift store and into a changing room outfitted with a thin black curtain. When she emerged, she was in what looked like a ticket booth. Did churches have ticket booths?

She supposed this one did. And a cash register. But the room was locked, so unless she wanted to bust the handle, she was forced to slip again. This time she emerged behind a great stone pillar reaching up to the tremendous ceiling above.

A prism of color danced across the blood-colored carpet running between the pews toward a suspended figure of Christ on the cross. She stepped into the light and looked up. A stained-glass ceiling spraying reds, blues and yellows. Emerald greens and the white wings of an angel. Mary holding a child, as the angels bore her on high. The first light of dawn.

"Can I help you?" a voice called.

A man approached her.

He wore the black clothes and white collar of a priest. He was bald on top and what was left covered the flesh from his ears down.

He stopped three feet from her and confusion seized his face. "It's you!" he said. With part terror and part excitement.

"Are you the one who found me?" she asked, shifting in her boots as the socks she'd hastily pulled on began to slide down. They were too small. A small price to pay for keeping Konstantine asleep and avoiding more slumber party chitchat.

"Yes," he said. He raised a shaking hand as if to touch her face and then froze, dropping it. "How did you survive?"

She realized now what she'd forgotten. Her sunglasses which she saw perfectly in her mind's eye on the glass coffee table back home.

If she had been wearing them, he likely wouldn't have seen the hard, uncompromising glare that met him when he'd reached out to touch her. She knew her gaze was hard. She'd heard more than one person comment on the way she seemed to look through them. Benji had said that when she smiled it didn't reach her eyes. Lucy had said much the same. *I feel like you smile only to please me, Louie. Never because you're happy.*

When conversation was unavoidable, it was best if she wore sunglasses.

"Thank you," she said and smiled, hoping that at least some of it crossed the plains of her cheeks and achieved a facsimile of sincerity. "But you have something of mine."

It was part question, part hope.

And it was enough to kick the priest into motion. "Oh yes! I have it all. I'm so glad you came back because, heaven help me, I honestly didn't know what to do with all of it. Follow me."

The two of them, utterly alone at this hour, moved silently through the dim church.

She didn't ask why he was the only one here. She had no right to question why the good father couldn't sleep at night.

At the end of a short stone hallway, he pulled a collection of keys from his wrist.

A loud clanking sound released and he pushed the door wide, flipping a switch on the wall. It illuminated a small office. A desk that was very tidy but also quite full of books and papers in need of reviewing.

The priest went around the side of the desk and bent under it, slowly retrieving one thing or another from the darkness beneath.

Her holster. The guns. Blades lined up one after another on the tabletop.

Then at last, the vest.

Something in Lou's chest loosened when she saw it. Though blood soaked as it was.

"Thank you," she said. "For keeping it safe."

Then she wasted no time slipping the weapons into place where she could. The priest stood silent, watching her every movement as if she were an elegant dancer on stage.

"You really are just a girl, aren't you?" His mouth hung in wonder. "Forgive me, young woman."

"What did you think I was?" She put her arms through the holster, moving quite slowly with the left arm as to not pop another stitch while the flesh was swollen tight.

"I'm sending an angel ahead of you to guard you along the way and to bring you to the place I have prepared."

Lou froze. *The place I have prepared.* She thought of La Loon instantly. That nightmare standing between her world and what?

"Exodus 23:20."

"I don't know the Bible," Lou said, checking to make sure everything was secure. The knives in their holsters and the guns in theirs. Not the vest though. She would simply have to put it on or carry it. And there would be no walking around in public tonight. As every piece of metal she wore stood in plain sight.

"Angels," he said. "I'm speaking of angels."

She searched his face. But there was no teasing there.

She gestured at the guns, the knives. "Do I look like an angel?"

"Angels are the warriors of God. And you simply appeared."

Irritation nipped at the back of her neck. "I'm not an angel."

His face screwed up with genuine concern. "Why?"

"I have too much to answer for."

"Don't forget this." He handed her something she'd forgotten she'd been wearing. Her German watch. The international pager that Lucy had given her several birthdays ago, under the pretense that she should be able to reach her niece if she needed her.

She clicked the small button on the side of the device and its digital face blinked to life. Four pages. One from Benji, a thank you no doubt. And three from King.

"I have to go," she told the priest. One page from King would have been enough. Three...

"Godspeed," he said, his eyes wide with wonder. "I hope we meet again."

Careful what you wish for. Lou stepped into the corner of his room and pressed her back into the shadow.

A dramatic exit, she knew, that would only fuel his superstitions. But it was rare that Louie had a chance to enjoy herself.

19

K ing looked at the cell phone in his hand again and sighed. Would paging her a fourth time really matter? If she didn't answer the first three pages, it was either because she wouldn't or couldn't. If the first reason, it pissed him off. But that voice in the back of his head was quick to point out the ridiculousness. *She owes you nothing. She isn't going to come running just because you've given her a page, Robbie.* Maybe there were women in the world who responded that way, but he understood Lou Thorne wasn't the kind to come at his beck and call.

If she wasn't answering because she couldn't—well, that was a whole other bag of shit.

He squeezed his eyes shut and exhaled slowly. "At least have the decency to die after we put her in the ground."

"I'm trying," a woman said.

King looked up from his socked white feet and met the eyes of Lou Thorne. She stood armored, clutching a vest in her fist. He recognized it was one of the old, outdated vests they used in the DEA SWAT teams. He wondered if that was Jack's vest, the one that had never ended up in inventory after his service weapon and all other equipment had been reclaimed.

"Coming or going?" he asked.

She glanced at the vest in her hand and seemed to note the guns and knives for the first time. "I'm not hunting tonight."

Hunting. King laughed. "This is your usual evening attire, is it? I guess I will cancel that Macy's gift card for your birthday then."

This was meant as a joke, but she wasn't laughing. She seemed only interested in getting him back on track. "You paged."

Right to it then. King ran a hand through his hair. "Do you, by chance, still have Paolo Konstantine stowed away in your apartment?"

There. The smallest twitch in her arm and a stiffening of her neck.

Before she could put a bullet in him, he added, "It was a guess. I haven't been snooping."

Her shoulders didn't relax. "Good guess."

That's a yes then. "I'll hazard another guess that you haven't seen the news in the last 48 hours."

She frowned. "What's happened?"

He sank onto his red leather sofa and used the remote control to turn off the fan overhead. She propped the vest against the side of his coffee table and took a seat on the cushion beside him as he powered up his laptop.

The page he'd viewed last was still up and running, so he simply refreshed the page and then clicked the arrow that restarted the newscast.

She watched it without speaking. When it was over and the screen was dark again, she said, "Is there more?"

"Not public, no."

"What's un-public?" she asked.

It took him three tries to get onto the DEA server. They were changing things up then. A televised beheading can do that. King could crack it, but admittedly, they were making it harder. He filed this warning in the back of his mind, along with the idea that he should change his IPs more frequently and then found what he was looking for.

He hesitated for a moment before playing this death tape. Then he realized how ridiculous he was being. Trying to shield Lou Thorne from the sight of slaughter was like trying to prepare a carcass out of the tiger's sight, lest he disturb its tender sensibilities. There was nothing on this tape she hadn't seen with her own eyes—or caused for that matter.

He pushed play.

And watched as eight men forced onto their knees had their throats slit for the camera. He turned away from the screen and watched her reaction for the last line: "I am Paolo Konstantine. You will hear from me again, very soon."

He saw what he wanted, loosing a breath he hadn't realized he was holding. "It's not Konstantine on the tape is it?"

"It's Nico Agostino," she said. "I told you there's a turf war over the Ravengers."

King didn't recognize the name. He grabbed the yellow legal pad off the coffee table and scribbled. He didn't have it in him to ask her how she spelled it. Augustino?

She glanced at his page. "You spelled it wrong."

And corrected him.

King tried to recall what he knew of the Ravengers and the man who ruled them. The last time King had seen Konstantine in the flesh, he was tied up on Ryanson' boat, about to be drilled to death by another gang member.

What interesting friends you have, he thought but he didn't speak. She seemed deep in her own thoughts.

When he couldn't stand the silence, he said, "It looks like Agostino wants to remove Konstantine from the field completely, not just from the drug trade."

She was cold beside him. No warmth radiating from her. A chill ran down his spine.

"It looks like it," she said.

"I can't believe you missed."

She leveled him with a frosty stare.

He raised his hands in surrender. "I'm sure it couldn't have been helped."

She gestured toward the screen. "What does this mean for Konstantine?"

"Three of those agents were British Intelligence, but the other five were ours. So I suspect that the great US of A will be rushing in, guns blazing soon."

"Konstantine will have to stay out of sight until his name is cleared."

King laughed. "Do you think they'll just let him go? A drug lord?

Once they realize he isn't the man they want, I'm sure they'll find something else to arrest him for."

She considered this.

King swallowed all the comments he knew were uncalled for. *What would your father think of you shacking up with a drug lord?* First of all, it wasn't King's business what Lou did or didn't do with any man in her life, and two, he knew better than to bring up Jack Thorne. He glanced at the vest propped against his coffee table.

"What about me?" she asked, meeting his gaze directly.

The strange question startled him out of his thoughts. "What about you?"

"Has my name turned up?"

"No," he said, perhaps too quickly.

Her gaze hardened.

"I've been watching and listening to the wire," he said, trying to infuse his voice with indifferent calm again. But it wasn't working. Throwing the ball back into her court would be better. "Did you end up in a hospital by chance?"

She blinked. The briefest fluttering of eyelids.

"I wondered if that was you. Unnamed woman brought in for several gunshot wounds. Which arm was it?"

He reached out to brush her left arm, but she was already up and across the room, standing in the center with the vest in her hand.

"I'm sorry," he said, hoping he hadn't gone too far. Now was not the time to push her away. "Is that why you're taking the night off?"

"I'll be ready when it's time to take out Nico."

Anger, surprisingly furious, rose in him suddenly. "So are you going to take on half the world to protect Konstantine with only one of your arms in decent shape? That sounds *brilliant*. See where that gets you."

He expected her to storm off then. Like a scolded teenager, slamming the door as she went. But instead her hard gaze seemed to soften into something like curiosity.

"How's Lucy?" she asked.

So that was how she was going to play it?

"You would know if you visited her."

"Sure thing, grandpa."

"I'm marrying her."

Lou laughed. "A lot of good that will do you."

"She needs something to look forward to. Something to hold on to."

Her laugh cut short. "Wedding dresses or cakes or any of that bullshit? That's what you think women hold on to."

"Some women."

"Says the divorced man who's been single for at least the last ten years."

"At least I'm spending time with her! At least I'm soaking up every second I have with her before she's gone from the face of the earth! And when she is, all you'll have left is your regret."

Lou moved the vest to the other hand. And for a horrible minute King thought it was so she could pull her gun and put a bullet between his eyes.

But she didn't. She was adjusting for the pain, some wound, old or new, was her giving her grief.

"Congrats on your engagement."

She delivered this with all the enthusiasm of someone declaring their imminent death. Then she was gone.

20

Nico sat in the front row pew of his father's church, San Augusto al Monte. He stared up at the figure of Christ, with the tears upon his face for all the misery of the world. Or perhaps it was not Christ he regarded with his upturned face. But the face of his own father. A face of misery, despair.

It wasn't Nico's father who had built this church. That was done by friars in the 1400s. But he himself had commandeered it from the mob boss with whom he'd apprenticed. Padre told him stories of Bellini when Nico was a little boy and how much Padre had learned from the hard man—*what to do right and what to do better*.

As a boy, Nico had no doubts that he would inherit his father's empire. He was secure in his father's love. That was until Konstantine arrived. He remembered the day everything changed, standing on the stone steps of the church beside his father. Padre had a package for Konstantine, no more than eight or nine years old, to carry across town.

I can do it, Papa, Nico had said. He was four years older than the boy. Surely at thirteen he was more capable than the green-eyed brat in his American sneakers.

No, his father had said. *I need someone clever for this.*

Had Konstantine heard these words, Nico would have likely attacked him on the street before the kid could get any ideas. But he was already running down the street through a cloud of pigeons, the brown paper package tucked under his arm. His father had spoken to him and him alone.

Who is clever now, Papa?

The life Padre Leo built for more than forty years had been seized by the very son he cast out. His legacy business turned over to the hands he wanted most never to touch it. How would God have felt, if Adam had returned triumphant to reclaim the Garden of Eden?

Of course, perhaps it would be easier to forgive the seizure of a mere garden.

Unless it was also worth more than three billion dollars.

The casinos, the firearms, heroin fields in Afghanistan. The cocaine pumping into Europe. A network of thousands of loyal men and women the world over. And all of it run by a single man. Paolo Konstantine. Every protocol, every decision, run by him first. As if he were their god.

Reclaiming his father's life work was only the beginning. Once he repaid those few who dared to elevate him to his rightful place, he would be unstoppable. Whole markets had been left untouched and Nico was going to change that.

Humans. Sexual exploitation. An untapped market that Konstantine nor his father dared to harness. People were a commodity that could push the Ravengers' three billion to eight billion or higher. Look at the Russians. Worth nearly ten billion and why? How did the Americans put it?

Sex sells.

And why not? People were so easy to acquire. So many displaced from their countries every day. War, famine or drought—a dozen reasons. It was no trouble at all to make them disappear, especially the children and women.

Narcotics had to be grown or manufactured. They took time. But people? They could turn a profit almost immediately. And their shelf-life was better. A drug offered only a single use. Put black tar in the veins or powder up the nose and that was it. More had to be ordered, made, shipped.

But one woman could be used over and over and over again. All night, every night for years. She could bring in twice as much revenue if a businessman like Nico spread her right. And she could be shipped too—anywhere to fill the demand. A whorehouse in Atlanta. In Budapest.

Perhaps Konstantine, not his father, had seen the possibilities. Or they hadn't had the stomach for such an enterprise, but Nico was stronger and smarter. He would expand the Ravengers holdings in all the ways these two pathetic men couldn't.

The steps across the stone floor echoed behind him. He cocked his head slightly, turning at the hint of danger. But it was only Gigi. A lanky boy of fourteen. Nico sat up at the sight of him, excited.

"Did you find what I asked for?" Nico said, leaning back against the pew.

The boy slung the black backpack off his shoulders and squat down on the floor to scrounge through it. "Yeah. Can we talk here?"

He blinked up at Nico from his place on the floor. Nico swept the church, eyes peering into every shadowed corner. But his orders had been followed. No one had approached him today as he sought guidance from his father in the nave. Perhaps they would have worried more if they'd known what was in his fevered heart. That he hadn't in fact been seeking Padre Leo's approval at all but had been basking in the self-righteous pleasure of knowing he'd accomplished the very thing that his father denied him.

The plan he fulfilled after ten long years of dreaming in the work camp. *He* manifested this moment. And he knew it. Every time the bullwhip was brought down across his back and his blood spilled on Russian soil. Every time a boot slid between his ribs or a fist made his ears ring, he'd thought of his father, thought of the moment he would pull this empire out from beneath him. His only regret was that he hadn't been able to do it looking in the old man's eyes.

But Konstantine was a lovely consolation prize. Seeing him fall, in some ways, would be even sweeter.

"I found these," the boy said.

"Yes," Nico said, placing an arm along the back of the wooden pew. "What do you have for me?"

The boy pulled out a paper folder with two pockets, one on each side. He removed a jumble of photographs with trembling hands, and handed them over to Nico. Pointing over the top of the photo as he shuffled through.

"He has a whole collection of photographs, just of her."

"Seems obsessive," Nico noted. But he understood why. It wasn't only that the woman was beautiful, it was her strange talent. What was it about the darkness that made you want to look closer? "When were these taken?"

The boy took the top photo and flipped it over, showing the date stamped on the back. "Most of them are dated about three months ago. But some are even older. I think he started his collection years ago."

Nico looked at him expectantly.

The boy cleared his throat. "I ran these photos to find the matching face. There were no names but Konstantine wrote something on the back."

Nico turned the photograph over and read Konstantine's small script "Lou. It's a man's name. Perhaps it isn't for her."

"Is it true what they are saying about her?"

Nico regarded the boy's round face. It was still a boy's face in every regard, even if his voice had changed. Soft round cheeks and eyes. No hint of facial hair.

"What do they say?"

"She captures men like a spider and eats them."

Nico smiled. The boy had the good sense to look embarrassed.

"Yeah, I don't believe that," the boy said, pulling himself up as if to make himself taller. "I think she's like a ninja or something. She saved Konstantine's life. Twice now."

Nico gave him a hard glare and the boy fell silent, his eyes downcast.

Nico then regarded the photos dreamily. The woman clad in black standing in a shadowed bar, her hair pulled up off her neck, exposing a tender stretch of flesh. He could slit that pretty throat easily. He needed only a way to pin her dark wings to the floor long enough to do it.

He thought of the strange room that Konstantine built outside of town and smiled. *Had that been your intention, brother? To betray her? Trap her and bleed her dry? Or perhaps only to keep her all to yourself...*

If the woman was his only remaining ally, Nico could fix that. Once she knew what he was, and his intentions for her, she would turn on him. Then perhaps he wouldn't even have to put the bullet between his eyes himself.

That had been his mistake after all.

He should have simply shot Konstantine in the head while he could. When he saw Konstantine, he would kill him quickly. If the woman didn't beat him to it.

"That is all," he said to the boy. The boy hesitated for a moment, clearly expecting payment. But one wolfish glance from Nico sent him running from the church without another word.

Now what to do about the woman. Nico looked at the granulated image of the woman watching someone else. A man perhaps. It was hard to tell, even though the unwavering gaze, a hunter's gaze, was easy enough to recognize.

No matter what his father said, he was no fool. He knew that assets and allies would be what carried him through—carried his vision to completion.

Nico had a long, hard road ahead of him. It seemed a waste to destroy a creature so unique and valuable.

If only he could turn her against Konstantine. If only he could offer her what no one else could. He would simply have to figure out what her desire was. People were easy like that. Particularly women. Special talents and bloodthirst aside, she was a woman.

An offer she couldn't refuse, he mused. And a reason to turn against Konstantine so that she wouldn't stand between Nico and what needed to be done.

He settled against the pew, his shoulder blades rubbing against the cold wood. He looked defiantly into the face of the weeping Christ. The tears of a father who could only watch his wayward children and wait.

The bright image of the padded room flashed unbidden in Nico's mind. With all its bright, unwavering light.

Yes, that was how he would do it. How he would change her mind and make her see the truth of it.

A dog, no matter who was master, still loved the hunt.

She could be trained like any other.

21

K onstantine heard the door to the closet click closed. He turned onto his side. Her blankets were bright with moon-light, tousled but empty. He rolled onto his back with a sigh, the sofa springs creaking. He placed one hand beneath his head.

The ceiling above collected long shadows from the room.

His body ached, but he had healed most of his wounds in the last few days, hidden here in her apartment. He should be grateful for her sanctuary. He seriously doubted she'd ever offered such a place to a man before. To women, perhaps. He'd followed her movements closely leading up to their encounter in June and since. Never too close to be noticed. But he was curious.

He wanted to know everything about this woman, how she lived her life, how she supported herself.

As foolish as it sounded, he wanted her. His urge to woo her was like any urge to woo a woman. But he understood that dinners, flowers, and myriad of attention and declarations would be not only ridiculous, but were likely to be met with a blade to the throat.

And simply showing her his erection—even if unintentional—hadn't worked in his favor either. He had his eye open for the opportunity, certainly, but was unsure what the opportunity might look like.

So he'd taken to watching her instead. To get a sense of anyone, one must look at what they do with their time. What they cared about.

She enjoyed slaughtering men. But that would hardly make a fitting gift. Gifting a lioness with a pig when she could bring home the gazelle was insulting. But what else did she love?

The aunt, to be sure. And also the retired DEA agent in New Orleans who lived above some occult shop in the French quarter. But most of her time was given over to hunting mules.

To his surprise, it had a symmetry. A rhythm that suited her.

She didn't go for the highest men in charge, those who would be simply replaced with another power-hungry mind. She went for the workers. The reliable soldiers who got the work done. Those on whom the bosses relied to exert the will—those, who if missing, brought production lines and shipments to a grinding halt.

It was brilliant.

Many of her targets were his own men and she had cost him more than enough trouble and money. But he was not her only target. She seemed to target all the drug cartels indiscriminately. And the Ravengers were far from the only one in business.

True she once focused solely on the Martinellis and their intricate connections. But since his brothers and father were dead, it seemed her only ambition was to undo their influence brick by brick.

For that reason it had been easy to step in and offer a bargain to his late father's cousin, a partnership that had merged the Martinelli empires with Padre Leo's Ravengers. This was what Padre Leo himself had wanted—though he had had no idea of Lou Thorne's part in this acquisition. How she had all but gutted the operation from the inside out, so that by the time Konstantine arrived on cousin Giuliani's step, the deal was done.

And by appearing as an ally he had prevented a bloody takeover between their two tribes. He let Giuliani Russo run his cartel and Konstantine focused on the Ravengers.

What Lou knew of this arrangement, he had no idea.

Her time seemed mostly focused on dismantling the Mexican cartels in the last month or so. It was their drug lords she purged from the streets. And with their sixty percent market share on America's unquenchable demand, Konstantine couldn't be upset by that.

And what if what she desired was the Ravengers? If in exchange for her body and soul, he must give her the 3.3 billion dollar empire, lock and key?

Could he betray Padre Leo? A man who'd protected him and entrusted him to look after his legacy in exchange for the woman he desired?

He wasn't sure.

And he feared that day, that decision, may be rounding on him sooner than he'd like.

Yet he couldn't handle her the way he would any problem—decisively and directly.

To do so surely meant chasing her back into the shadows, and away from him. He didn't think she was interested in business alliances.

If she carried her father's ideology in her own mind, she meant to undo the entire drug trade. Including his own. And if that was what it took to have her...

He sighed into the empty apartment, looking at the future with unease.

A flash of light caught his eye. He sat up on his elbows, searching for the source.

It was the island cabinet. The light shining through the trim would've been impossible to see, if he hadn't been lying in the dark.

The light clicked off and Konstantine repressed the urge to feign sleep.

A moment later, the closet door popped open and she strode inside. Her boots moving soundlessly across the wooden floor. *La mia leonessa. No wonder the men never hear you coming.*

She entered the kitchen and pulled a glass down from a cabinet shelf. He listened to the faucet run. The filling glass caught the moonlight from the windows.

He wondered what it would be like. To have a home with this woman. To hear her moving about it in this way, dressing, showering, cooking...knowing that she belonged to him.

He would settle for belonging to her.

What a pathetic romantic you are, he chided himself.

She stared down at him, water glass in her hand, the side of her leg pressing into the sofa.

He met her gaze from the flat of his back, silently praying she would sit on the end of the sofa. That she would put a hand on his thigh. Or better yet, put down the glass and climb on top of him completely, letting the weight of her body sink onto his.

She only stood there. "Nico fucking hates you."

He laughed, surprised to hear such a filthy word from such a pretty mouth. "I'm aware, mia cara."

"Are you *aware* he beheaded eight agents on live television and gave you all the credit?" she asked with an arched brow. "You're on the news."

His laughter died. He swung his legs off the sofa, throwing himself onto his feet. "*Vaffanculo*! I need to make some calls."

She took a long drink of the water, her eyebrow arching.

"Please," he added. "If you are not currently engaged."

She finished her water and put the glass on the coffee table.

She went to the picture hanging on the wall and removed it. Konstantine was unsure if he should act surprised, indifferent, or sorry.

Apparently a reaction was unnecessary. "You've been snooping."

"My apologies," he said, and hope she noted the sincerity in his voice. "I was bored."

She snorted. "And the most interesting thing you found?"

"An armory where your cookware should be."

She stiffened. "You think women should be cooks."

"And men. We are all responsible for feeding ourselves, aren't we?"

The safe popped open and she removed three magazines and two pistols. She put the ammo in the pockets of her black cargo pants and then the gun in the waistband of the small of her back.

"Are you eyeing the guns or my cash?" she asked as she closed the safe and put the picture back in place. "You have plenty of both."

Did she know how much he had at his disposal? Cash and assets? "You think I'm rich?"

"Oh, you have a few billion," she said, flicking her eyes up to meet his. "Likely more if those casinos you built in Singapore take off soon."

She stepped past him to the closet, leaving the door open.

He only looked at her. How had she come by that information? He wondered. It wasn't printed anywhere. Only his accountants knew those numbers. The men who looked at the proverbial books. He ran an imaginary list through his mind and wondered who might have gone missing or had an arm twisted.

Of course, it was fair play. He'd been learning all he could about her, too.

She holstered one of the guns. Konstantine assumed the other pistol was for him, but she kept it.

"Can I have a gun?" he asked.

"No."

"Don't trust me with a gun?"

"No one touches my guns."

"At least it isn't personal."

"Are you coming?" she asked, beckoning him into the waiting closet. "I thought this was urgent."

He slid into the dark beside her. Chest to chest, he could feel the heat from her body radiating over his skin. She turned her head to reach for the door and something brushed his cheek. Hair? He wanted to lean in, and make sure. Find her lips in the darkness and press her back against the wall of the closet. He was sure she could brace her knees against the wood as he entered her.

"Where are the people you need to call? What city?" Her breath was hot on his face. Intimate. Voices in the dark always were.

"New York," he said, squeezing the words out, feeling the fire in his face and the desire throbbing below his belt.

With his body pressed full frontal against hers, it was almost too much. He could feel the erection forming. The building pulse. And if he didn't shift himself away to create space, she was surely going to notice it as well.

But it wasn't Konstantine that leaned in close. She pressed her body against his, pinning him against the wall. He wanted to reach out, wrap his arms around her, take a fistful of her hair, but she'd pinned his arms in place with the weight of her. He shouldn't have been surprised by how strong she was. He'd seen her lift and drop men twice his size with ease. But feeling her uncompromising grip on him was different.

An edge of panic entered his mind.

Then they were falling backwards through space. He felt as if a rug had been yanked out from under him. The momentary panic grew. The sensation of weightlessness followed by compression in his head.

Then the world was beneath them again.

At some point, her hand had snaked around his hip, holding him in place. Again the urge to wrap his fists up in her hair rose. But before reason could be overruled, she released him and stepped out of the closet into a dim bedroom.

Two double beds side by side, a nightstand between. A desk with stationery. Not a bedroom exactly. The name of a chain hotel printed across the top of the stationery. He heard a metal *clank-clack* and realized she was locking the door no doubt leading to a hallway.

"Hurry," she said, nodding toward the phone. "Local calls are free."

"We are in New York?"

"Yes. Be sure to dial 1 or you'll confuse the desk clerk. This room isn't checked out."

Konstantine picked up the beige phone and pressed the key to connect him to the outside world. The dial tone greeted him.

"I'll come back," she said.

And when he turned to ask her where she intended to go, the closet door was already closing behind her.

Just as well. He would feel strange conducting business under her watchful eye.

He dialed his friends in New York.

He'd already considered which men he would contact when this happened. After all, Konstantine had been expecting this. Not Nico necessarily. But bloody succession was always possible when the leader of a crime faction died. Padre Leo had prepared him for this moment. And now Konstantine had to wonder if part of that preparation was against Nico himself.

Keeping secrets from me, Padre?

Mario Ricci picked up on the third ring. His New York accent was comically thick. "Who the hell is this?"

The unknown number calling his personal emergency line no doubt had startled the man.

"Ciao, Mario," Konstantine said, nervously twining his fingers up in the phone's cord.

"Konstantine!" the man said with a relieved sigh. "I wondered if I was gonna be hearin' from you. I was starting to think you were dead."

"No, amico mio. Not yet." Konstantine wet his lips, his eyes falling on the cheap hotel print across the room. A photocopy of a boat sailing down river beneath a soft blue sky. "No doubt you know why I'm calling."

"Oh yeah," said the man with a dry chuckle. "Your pretty face is all over the news right now. Congrats my friend, you're a celebrity."

"In our business, that isn't such a good thing."

"Tell me about it. So what's the plan?"

"I will handle the press," he said. "I need your help with something else."

"A trip to Florence to kick Agostino's ass, maybe?"

Konstantine laughed. "Word does travel fast."

"Especially when you got two ears and an asshole pressed to the ground."

"I can offer you two million in exchange for your men and time, Ricci."

"Aww, that's sweet," Ricci said and Konstantine heard the refusal coming. His pulse quickened.

"But you don't need to do that. Padre already cut a check for 2.5 million if I helped you."

So you did expect this Padre. And the old man had set up protections. Konstantine's throat tightened at the news. That a man such as Padre would ever pay him such kindness. A man who had owed him nothing.

"Padre is very trusting to cut you a check so early," Konstantine said. "And you're a good man for admitting you received it."

Ricci laughed, a hearty chuckle that no doubt jostled the man's large belly. "Yeah, well, I don't know about *trusting*. He cut Tommy Romano 3.5 million to put a bullet in my head if I *didn't* help you or if I didn't fess up to the money. And you know that chump bastard's been looking for a reason since I married his ex-wife."

He didn't know. But now he did.

"Besides this seems to be the day for calling in favors. When it rains, it pours," Ricci went on. Konstantine heard the flint of lighter strike once, twice, and then the sharp inhale. A cigarette or a cigar.

"What do you mean?"

"You ain't heard? Conway's distribution chain is fucked. Two of his guys disappeared down in Miami and there's a warehouse in the fishing district that had forty three bullets—43—pried out of the walls and machines. A fucking mess. The Cubans were going on about a devil coming to claim souls, but Conway thinks it was Hendrix fucking with him. I swear those two are gonna kill each other before the year is out. Anyway, he's got nobody at the docks so Conway asked me to send a couple of my guys down until they can get it sorted. Untile then, a ton of cocaine is just sitting in the gulf."

Konstantine thought of Lou, naked, stepping from the closet. The heart-stopping sight of her wet hair stuck to her cheek. Konstantine suspected he knew what might have happened in the fish house.

Ricci coughed. "So when you want to move against Agostino?"

"When can you be ready?"

"Tomorrow? I'll call my guys at the jetway and get us some birds to put in the air. I don't know what Tommy Romano's got, but I know he's bringing something smart. Can you hold off that long? They's huntin' you pretty hard."

"I can until tomorrow."

"Good. Meet me at the Charlie's tomorrow at 1:00. And don't get caught on the way here."

Konstantine thanked him and ended the phone call. Six million to secure his succession. And no doubt more, tucked away with this or that hand in case Konstantine had needed the help. The list that Padre had made him memorize in the event of an emergency...it hadn't been so random after all. The men and women selected were those who Padre knew and trusted best from decades of working together, but they were also hands that he'd deliberately greased.

You are still looking out for me, Padre. Grazie.

Melancholy crushed his chest.

"You sure you can trust them?" Lou asked. He looked up to see her leaning against the wall. He wasn't sure how long she had been there, watching and listening.

"Padre trusted them, and that is enough for me."

He expected her to laugh at that, but she didn't. Then he remembered the aunt and the New Orleans ex-cop. Perhaps Lou knew something of inheriting help herself.

"Are violent successions really so common in your world?" she asked.

Konstantine stood, his bones creaking. "We even have a name for it.

Dispute resolution. And yes, in addition to forming alliances, it's good money."

"Is it only about money for you?" she asked.

Her face was dangerously calm.

He smiled. "No. There are some things I want more."

22

King had just put in the order for his beignet croquembouche, assured by the manager that it could be ready in 48 hours when the cellphone in his pocket went off. At that moment, the world stopped and began spinning in reverse.

He didn't remember running back to his apartment, getting in his car or racing to the cancer center. He became somewhat aware of himself halfway down the hallway to Lucy's room, pushing through the swarm of nurses and patients.

When he reached her room, his heart faltered.

It was empty.

"Mr. King," a voice said.

He turned and found Naomi standing there. Her braids pulled behind her head and secured with a tie. For a horrible moment, he felt the walls closing in on him, felt his lungs compress, threatening to explode. *She's trying to figure out how to tell me Lucy is dead Lucy is dead Lucy is dea—*

"She just got out of surgery," she said quietly.

"Is she—" His breath was tightening in his chest. He should've brought his damned inhaler.

"Her heart is having a real hard time with it all, but the surgery went fine," Naomi said, taking his two pale hands in her dark ones and squeezing them hard. Too hard. But enough to bring him back to his own body and this time and place. The walls moved back. He drew his first real breath. "They might keep her up there tonight, have more eyes on her."

"Can I visit?"

"Not until they're sure she's stable. I'm sorry."

"When will they know if she's stable?" he asked, grateful for her cool hands. It kept him steady in a room that started to spin around him.

"An hour, maybe two."

"I'll wait."

She gave his hands another squeeze. "I'll come find you in the cafeteria if I hear something."

He thanked her. Walking toward the cafeteria was a much calmer affair than his entrance had been.

When he got there, and smelled the food wafting from the hot bar, his stomach turned. But he walked up to the counter and ordered a large black coffee, served to him in a paper cup too thin to protect his hand from the heat. He removed his cell phone from his pocket and laid it on the tabletop beside the steaming cup.

Then he did nothing. He was unaware of any thoughts trailing through his mind.

In their place seemed to be a general anxiety. A low-grade buzz that filled every bit of space in his mind and allowed for no other ideas to materialize.

He stared into the inky black of his coffee for who knew how long, looking at a reflection he didn't recognize. The hollowed-out eyes with deep purple bags beneath. A part of his mind understood it was his own reflection, but still more disbelieved it.

He reached into the pocket of his black duster and found his wallet. His fingers fished out the white card with a number printed on the back. He almost had it memorized now, but didn't trust himself not to screw it up while his mind was a million miles away. Robotically, he punched the number for the fifth time in the last 24 hours and pressed the # key to designate this was an emergency.

Lou may hate hospitals, but she would come. She had to come.

The coffee was cold when she showed up, sliding into the booth seat opposite of him. Her eyes hidden behind mirrored sunglasses and her leather jacket sat evenly on her shoulders. He couldn't tell if she was packing, but suspected so. If her arm was a wreck from her run-in the other night, there was no evidence of it. She moved as if no part of her body ailed her, which was a hell of a lot more than King could say for himself. Half the time he walked bent slightly at the waist, because his low back was so stiff.

Even if his heart wasn't collapsing in his chest, the ache in every joint would ail him.

"Is she dead?" Lou asked as last. He hadn't realized until she'd spoken that he had been silent for several minutes, looking into his black coffee without acknowledging her arrival.

"She's in critical care," he said. His voice cracked. He took a sip of coffee, cold and disgusting, but enough to wet his pipes. "Her heart is giving out under the strain of...of everything."

"Have they let you see her?"

"No."

"I'll take you," she said, her palms pressing flat to the table.

"No," he said, perhaps too quickly. "They don't want us in the way. I'm sure they have their reasons. We'd only prevent them from doing their job."

"Which is what?" Lou asked. He searched her face for cruelty or sarcasm. But it was only his own eyes staring back at him in the reflection.

"Keeping her alive as long as they can."

"Maybe she doesn't want to be alive anymore."

King's hands curled into fists. The blood red knuckled turned white. "That's not for you to decide."

Lou looked ready to speak. But then her lips flattened. Finally she said, "Konstantine is about to move against Agostino. He's working with the Ricci family."

King knew the name. They'd tried to nab the Riccis in the 70s. All the good it did them. They were slick snakes.

"Did you know they have a name for it? Dispute resolution."

"Yeah," he said. "That's how the old, powerful families stay in power. And they rely on the alliances of other groups to maintain that power."

"Who knew thugs were so aristocratic," she said.

"Don't you think this is the wrong time?" he asked.

"For what?"

"To be running off to Italy for a gunfight. You should be here. You should be with her."

"I offered to take you there and you said no."

"Can't you holster your bullshit long enough to tell her goodbye! Properly!"

He was screaming. Sweat slid down the side of his face.

Lou was perfectly impassive in the face of his anger. She only said, "Are you looking to join her? When is the last time you took your blood pressure medicine?"

He'd actually been removed from the medicine after the last checkup. The doctor had been pleased with his weight loss and new exercise routine.

"What do you want from me, King?" she said. Not petulance. Again that utter calm which in its own way was more infuriating than if she'd yell at him. Slap him across the face. Anything. Show any damn emotion.

"I want you to stay with her! I want you to show her you give a damn! That woman raised you, kept you out of foster care and now she's *dying*, and you can't even take the time to make sure she doesn't die alone."

He expected her to leave then. To get up, walk through the lunch room and disappear around some dark corner.

Instead she said, "You've made a lot of assumptions."

"Fucking hell." He fell back against the booth's back.

"Maybe she doesn't want me to see her like that. Doesn't want me to remember her that way."

His breath hitched. "You need to do what's right! You need to make this easy for her!"

"Easy for her or easy for you?"

And at this she did rise and exit the booth. He watched her go, her long lean steps and the jacket shifting over her shoulders as she went.

23

After a bowl of ramen in a busy Tokyo street annex, Lou spent the early hours of the day walking the streets of Paris. She stood outside a macron shop and saw the little wafers made of almond paste. It was too early to buy Lucy a half-dozen to enjoy with a cup of Earl Grey. And knowing King, he'd been trying to shove food down her throat for days.

He's figuring out how to let her go. Just like you.

Lou shook these thoughts from her head as she wandered past Notre Dame, over Pont Neuf. A batobus slid silently down the river, its lights casting shadows along the flanking cobblestone banks. She stepped up behind a stone pillar and out onto the streets of London. She hadn't intentionally chosen such a place. But the mere thought of Lucy had brought her here.

She remembered a ninth grade social studies report, where she was expected to write about the history of a city of her choice. Lou had chosen London because it was the birthplace of so many books and writers she loved—even more so after her parents' death, when there were days that felt as if books were all that she had left. Any world was better than the shattered world in which she lived.

At the first mention of the report, Lucy had been delighted.

Well let's go see it, Lucy said and the next thing Lou knew, she was stepping out of her aunt's cramped Oak Park linen closet and into Piccadilly Circus, with the red double decker buses and funny black taxi cabs whirring by.

Lucy had always been able to surprise her like that.

In the beginning, Lou was certain that her ability to travel through the dark or water was a curse. Something to mitigate and endure. But Lucy had been the first to show her the magic of it. The power of it. The freedom.

There isn't a place in this world you can't go, Louie, her aunt had told her in those early days. *You just have to know where you want to be.*

"You gave me this freedom," she murmured. Her chest compressed painfully.

A boy pushing a bike with a flat tire clipped Lou, setting her wounded arm on fire.

"Sorry, love. I didn't see you there." He flinched at her cold expression. "You all right?"

Rather than answer him, she headed toward the National Gallery, to the other side of Nelson's Column.

"Sorry!" he shouted after her.

The bright pain faded to a steady throb, to an unpleasant heat. She refused to take off the jacket and inspect the wound. Not only because of the guns it hid, but because of the muggy, damp quality to the early morning air. One press of her watch told her it was only 4:30 in the morning. Most of the shops were not yet open, and the world was mostly quiet in the early dark. A few people were hurrying across town trying to make their jobs. Or those catching early flights or trains out of the city.

Such as the mother marching past the gallery steps with her red roller bag in tow as well as two children, a boy and a girl, with matching suitcases. The girl gave Lou a long, hard, fearless look. And Lou couldn't suppress a smile in the face of that defiant chin.

When she could no longer feel her fingers, and knew no more calm could be gathered by wandering, Lou bled into the building's shadow and emerged from the corner of a hospital room.

A machine clicked and beeped. The sound of something being pressurized and released in turn.

Her aunt seemed to know the moment that she'd entered. Her eyes fluttering open and her head turning toward her with much effort.

"Hi, Lou-blue," the old woman croaked. And she did look quite old now. Her blue eyes brighter than Louie could ever recall seeing them, as if the last of her light had gathered there.

"Hi," Lou managed. Though the smell of the place was already pressing in on her. The smell, in its way more offensive than any blood or brain matter sprayed on her. In its way a perversion.

"I miss you," Lucy said.

Lou would often say nothing to this sort of remark, but it seemed cruel now. "I miss you too." And she found that once she said it, it was true. She missed the woman her aunt was. The caustic wit. The benevolent goddess energy, always visibly straining to accept some new horror that Lou had committed. Her patience. Her reassuring presence.

"I just went to London and Paris," Lou told her. "Our old haunts."

"I miss traveling," Lucy said with a dry-lipped smile.

Lou saw too much of the bones in her face. She considered sitting but there were no chairs in this room. This wasn't a room that welcomed visitors. So they'd come that far then. It was time.

"If you could go anywhere in the world right now—" Lou began. But she didn't have to finish.

"Somewhere warm. I'm always so cold now. No matter how many extra blankets they pile on me, I'm always cold."

Lou slipped her cold London-chilled hand into her aunt's and found that it must be true. Somehow the frail grip was icy.

"Maui maybe," her aunt mumbled, pinching her eyes closed.

"How long do you have?" Lou asked, hoping her voice wouldn't betray her. But her heart hammered hard in her chest. She could feel it pressing against the bottom of her throat, making her voice thin.

Death, which had always been so familiar to her, was a stranger again. Someone she didn't know knocked on the door. The death she knew was a firecracker. A whirling dervish. Fast, violent, and quick. This death was larger. It slid into a room, took up all the available space. It wouldn't leave. It ate up the heat and joy. It lingered like a revolting grease smeared on the mind that if touched, you were reminded of it all over again.

"On the machines?" she asked. "Oh we could stretch this on for a while, I think. Maybe weeks."

"Off the machine?" Lou asked.

Lucy met her eyes, considered her face with a mix of hope and fear. "A few hours at best."

"Maui's sunset is in an hour," Lou said. She counted the machines in the room. Counted the tubes running from her aunt's paper-thin skin. And when she was done assessing the situation, she caught her aunt staring.

"Yes." She searched Lou's face, looking almost as if it weren't real. "Yes, take me to see the sunset."

Lou, as carefully as possible, unhooked each cord and tube and machine tying her aunt to this place. Then she crossed the room and turned off the light.

In pitch blackness, there was a terrifying moment when she thought she'd touch Lucy and find her already dead. Or already gone. Maybe slipping away accidentally, leaving Lou to search the world for her.

The silence of the room without the monitor was deafening.

But then a bony hand seized her forearm with surprising strength and tried to pull herself up.

"Don't," Lou commanded. "Let me."

She threw back all the blankets but one and slipped her good arm under the woman's knees. Frail arms went around her neck and then they were through.

The first thing Lou heard was the chatter of birds, a raucous in the trees. A few fell silent at their shocking arrival, but then went right on with their conversation as if to say *oh it's only you?*

Lou stepped out of the woods with Lucy in her arms. She was heartbreakingly light as Lou's boots sank in the sand. But Lou kept them both upright as she carried her down the strip of beach to the water's edge. She placed her on the sand a foot from the waves, so the water could only reach her toes, but climb no higher.

Lucy laughed with delight. "Oh yes. This is so much better. We should've come sooner."

Lou stood over her awkwardly as Lucy removed her socks.

"A hospital in no place to die. Sit with me, Lou."

Lou obeyed, plopping down onto the sand beside her. She was confident that they wouldn't be disturbed. Not only because they were the only souls for as far as the eye could see. But this was a private beach belonging to a billionaire. And he was at a Geneva technology convention or so said all the papers. If someone did come to ruin her aunt's last few moments in this world—Lou would handle it.

Her aunt took a deep breath and inhaled. The wind from the ocean blowing back the hair from her face. For a long time they said nothing. They only looked out over the western horizon at the sun dipping lower with each breath. Waves crashed on the sand enveloping them. Eventually Lou had to take off her boots and roll up the end of her cargo pants so that they wouldn't soak through with salt water. These were her best boots. She wanted them dry if and when she faced Nico.

Lou glanced at her aunt once or twice from the corner of her eye, wondering if the woman would drop off at any moment. And Lucy noticed.

Smiling, she said, "No, I'm not dead yet."

Lou snorted.

"I'd forgotten how beautiful the world can be," Lucy said, her hospital blanket whipping around her.

Lou realized suddenly that she wore only a paper gown under it. "Are you cold?"

"No. The sand is nice and warm. It's like sitting on a loaf of freshly baked bread straight from the oven. Mmmm."

Lou drew circles in the sand between her legs. She found it easier to focus on the sand than on the woman beside her.

Finally Lucy said, "I've often thought of this moment. The moment of death is a big deal in Buddhism, you know. How your mental state is at the moment you pass will impact your future life."

Lou didn't interrupt her.

"So I had all of this planned bullshit I was going to say to you. Things I thought that would help us both let go. I was going to apologize if I gave you the impression that I wanted you to be anything other than what you are. And I was going to find a way to help you and Robert not be so angry. Because of course anger and guilt are part of it."

She thought of King's twisted, grieved face in the cafeteria earlier.

"And now?" Lou asked, throat tight.

"Now..." She turned and looked at Lou's face with intense regard. She reached up and cupped her cheeks. "Now I only want you to know that you're loved, Louie. You've always been loved. And I hope that I see you again. In the next life."

Tears were pulled from her eyes by the relentless wind rolling off the ocean. Lucy wiped them away with her thumbs.

"I just—" Lou began but her voice broke. "Thank you."

Lucy smiled but said nothing.

"You taught me not to be afraid of slipping, and you taught me how to listen to my compass. I hope—I just hope you don't regret what I chose to do with it."

Lucy brushed the hair back from Lou's face. "You helped me too. Before you, it was only me."

The sunset bled from orange to pink, their hands clasped.

"I know you will find your way. I really do believe that," Lucy said, squeezing her hands. "You should believe it too."

Lou put her arms around her aunt, and kissed her bald, scarf-wrapped head.

"What do you want to come back as?" Lou asked, pulling away and untangling herself from the embrace.

"What?"

"You believe in reincarnation, don't you?"

"Oh, yes." She thought for a moment. "Something that can fly. I've always loved cardinals."

Lou laughed. "They don't live very long."

"You're right. So perhaps a cardinal, then a crow. Before making my way back to human again."

"A man or woman?"

Lucy snorted. "A woman of course."

They watched what was left of the light dip lower behind the horizon, that false line implying there was an end to it all.

They knew better.

24

A hand squeezed King's shoulder, waking him with a start. The cold coffee shook with the movement, rippling its black syrup surface. Lou stood there, looking down at him in her mirrored sunglasses. But her jacket was gone. And her shoes. Her pants were rolled up to the mid-shin, with sand clinging to her feet and toes. He stared at this, bewildered.

"Hurry up," Lou said as if they'd been in the middle of something.

"Where the hell have you been?" he asked, rubbing his eyes. "Fiji?"

"With Lucy, come on."

King's heart took off like a rabbit, kicking hard in its fear. To echo this was the pounding of feet. He looked across the cafeteria in time to see four or five white coats rush by.

"We need to move," Lou said and looked ready to haul King out of the booth if he didn't move himself.

"What the hell have you done!" he screamed.

And then Lou did haul him from the booth, pulling him toward the shadow where the walls met.

His rage built, ready to release its fury on her, but then the world tilted. The rollercoaster dropped and that squeezing sensation forced all thought from his mind and air from his lungs.

A orange-pink world rushed up to meet them.

Birds of every conceivable color darted in the branches above, chattering as loudly as any pack of monkeys. Through the canopy of thick foliage, thin sunbeams hit the forest floor.

The temperature shift was enormous. The cool, humid air that held New Orleans in its grip was replaced with the balmy warmth King always associated with beaches.

And sure enough, when Lou pushed back the low branches, she revealed a gorgeous beach. Pale, clean sand and aquamarine waters tinged with the orange of sunset. For a moment, King could only stand there, marveling at the beauty of white crests rolling gently onto the dusky shore. They had only a few minutes left of sunset he was sure. For a moment he'd forgotten why he was so angry, so alarmed, until he saw a small figure wrapped in the cancer center's pink blanket. Then it came rushing back.

He crossed the beach in no time at all, coming down onto his knees beside her.

"We have to get you back to the hospital," he said. His voice was strained, strident.

"This is where she wants to be," Lou said.

"She's confused!" King screamed. He pounded a fist into the sand. "Half the time she calls me Jack! She doesn't know what she's saying."

"Robert," Lucy said calmly. "Look at me."

King blinked.

"Look at me," she said again, reaching a hand up to cup his cheek and force him to meet her eyes.

King obliged her.

"I don't want to die in a hospital bed."

He desperately searched her eyes for the glaze of pain. That look of confusion that often overtook her when her veins were full of the medications keeping her alive and comfortable.

"One hour on this beach is worth a hundred days in that room," she said, running a thumb over his shaven cheek.

"What happens when it gets cold and dark," he said finally, transitioning from his knees to his butt in the sand.

"Lou will get us more blankets. Build us a fire. Roast me a marshmallow," Lucy said, with a broad smile. "I'd love a roasted marshmallow. And a good beer."

Lou stood up, brushing much of the sand off her feet before forcing them back into her boots. Then she marched back into the woods, leaving them alone.

"You can't eat that stuff," King said, doubtfully. "I've been trying to feed you crap for weeks."

Lucy shrugged, her blue eyes bright in the sunset. "Maybe I want to be alone with a handsome man."

He leaned in and kissed her then, but he had no illusions about where this was going. The last thing this woman needed was his weight on top of her. But it seemed enough to hold her in the crook of his arm and place kisses on her scarved head.

He wanted to ask about the wedding. Tell her about the dress that Piper found and the croquembouche that had been ordered. But all of that seemed so ridiculous now as she sat curled up at his side.

"Are you sure you don't want to go back?" he asked.

She squeezed his hand. It was a weak grip. "I've had enough of that place. I want to die breathing fresh air."

King said nothing else on the subject. Instead he only took off his long duster and threw it over her shoulders, adding another layer to the blanket around her. The last of the sun gave way to twilight.

"She will be okay," Lucy said finally. She squeezed his hand again. "And you will be too."

"You have a lot of faith in me."

"In both of you."

King's heart hurt. "And if I fail? What if she's dead before she's thirty?"

"Ah, well the best of us die young, I suppose," she said. And he knew she was only trying to lighten the subject. She was right to do it. Now wasn't the time to speak of death. Or reminding her of all that she wouldn't get to see.

She searched his face as these thoughts rolled him like ocean waves.

"Nothing is good nor bad," she said. Her words had a strange lyric quality to them. He was sure she was reciting something. "It is only the mind that makes it so."

"More Buddhist bullshit?" he asked. He hated how the anger clipped his words. But he wasn't sure he could hide it any better than he was.

"It's okay to be angry," she told him. She cupped his face and ran a thumb over each of his cheeks again. "But I have no regrets, Robert. I'm glad I came back for you."

The words unleashed a stream from him. "I'm sorry I didn't come to you sooner. I had every excuse. I could've said I wanted to see how you and the kid were doing. I could've—"

She covered his mouth with hers. He relaxed into the kiss, trying to enjoy it. It was hard. Part of it was the smell. Though they'd brought her out of the hospital and into the world, she smelled of death. That acrid medicinal taste clung to her dry lips. And that scent filled him with terror. Irrational, claustrophobic terror. But he willed himself to remain in place and to kiss this woman.

When she pulled back she smiled. "Do you remember that time I made you go to Yuri's naked hot yoga class with me?"

"As if I'll ever forget. I've never been asked to put my face so close to my own junk before."

She laughed. "And you fell!"

"Because I looked ahead at the woman in front of me doing that moon pose..."

"Half moon."

"It wasn't her moon I was looking at."

Lucy laughed. When was the last time he'd heard her laugh like this? Maybe the fresh air was better for her.

He went on, hoping to milk this drop of joy for all it was worth. "It's a shame you weren't ahead of me. I would've liked to seen you from that angle. I feel bad for the guy who was behind me."

They fell into laughter then. And it felt good. It felt so good that those remnants of anger receded. He was sure they would appear again soon, rising up some dark and ugly night to remind him of all his regrets. But for now, Lucy was in his arms. She was laughing, and the night had bloomed beautiful around them.

Lou seemed determined to keep herself busy. King was vaguely aware of her comings and goings as they continued to sit, watching the sky darken. But her deliveries were endless. She brought new meaning to the idea *move heaven and earth for you.*

Though heaven and earth in this instance was a pile of wood for the fire. Kindling and a striker. A pile of blankets that she arranged for Lucy beside it, making a pallet big enough for the two of them—Lou herself got a low beach chair.

And she didn't stop there. She showed up with a large pizza and a six-pack of beer. Pillows, which King recognized as those she'd brought to the hospital room. When it was all said and done, it was quite the beach party. The only thing they were missing was someone on guitar.

Lou used a bottle opener to pop off the cap from a frosty bottle.

"Soft Parade!" Lucy cried softly, with a bright smile, accepting the bottle from her niece. The firelight danced in her eyes. "I love this beer. Perfect for a warm night like this. Have you ever had it, Robert?"

King admitted that he had not.

He watched the women talk, reminiscing about ridiculous times, about good times. Lou followed her lead, smiling at all the right moments though from time to time, King caught a glimpse of hollow distance in that gaze.

No one spoke of death. Of dying. King himself added to the conversation where he could, adding his own adventures with Lucy to the proverbial pyre.

Lou continued to deliver wood and feed the fire well into the night.

"Do you have any regrets," Lou asked her aunt, throwing another log onto the fire. This one was wrapped in yellow twine and King wondered who she'd stolen if from and if he cared.

"You'd love it if I gave you a kill list," Lucy laughed. The words were delivered sweetly, no hint of anger or cruelty. And King could tell that Louie was relieved by this. "But no. I have only one regret. I'm sorry that I didn't marry you, Robert."

She placed a hand on his knee and squeezed it. She snuggled deeper into the crook of his arm.

Without a word, Lou rose from her chair and disappeared through the woods. King wondered if it was to give them a bit of time alone. If she'd read some signal in Lucy's tone, or if the affection going between them had simply left her uncomfortable.

But a moment later, she reappeared.

Lou emerged from the forest edge with a man in tow. For a wretched moment, King thought *Konstantine. Lord help us, she's brought Konstantine here.*

But when the man stepped into the firelight, it wasn't the Italian at all. This man was much older and stately in his black robes.

The priest looked nervously from Lou to the couple cuddled together by the fire. "She tells me that you would like to be married?"

25

K onstantine was restless. He stared out at the river, counting how many ferry crossings the old-fashioned boat made, overloaded with tourists and the occasional starburst flash of a camera sparking from the opposite bank. Families wandered up and down the boardwalk, one child holding a bright red balloon that bounced and bobbed as she skipped between her parents.

He knew he should feel only gratitude. Her apartment, however small, was his sanctuary. Nico had nearly killed him. No matter what counter measures had been necessary, Konstantine would have had to hide until he was strong enough to retaliate.

And what better place? No one knew this place or this woman. Not really. He'd circulated and encouraged overblown tales meant to keep his men alert and in awe of their supposed alliance. But none knew her name or her real identity. Unless...

If Nico was smart, he would go through Konstantine's possessions, leaving no mattress or safe unturned. Given enough time, and he had been given enough time, he would likely find the photos. That was a possibility—and a threat.

All the information his old servant Julio has drummed up on her, in his initial quest to learn her identity—birth certificates, news reports regarding the murder of her parents, and school records—he'd burned it all.

But he hadn't had it in him to burn the photographs.

On the nights when he craved her so badly, sometimes sitting at his desk in his dark alcove, a glass of Chianti at hand, he would thumb through the photographs. No matter how grainy, the sight of her was enough to put his mind at ease.

Or if she did something to anger him...

When she killed his best port liaison in Jersey, for example. He'd received the call the next morning that four distributors had gotten nervous and rescinded their shipments when Wallie Rambo never answered their calls nor gave them the information for the drop point.

Some of the men thought Wallie had bailed. After all, he had quite a few gambling debts and had angered a local card shark.

But Konstantine knew who had plucked him from the dark, and it was no card shark.

It cost quite a bit of money and time to reconfigure the distribution line to his liking. Good, trustworthy men were hard to find in this business. And despite his penchant for gambling, Rambo was reliable, and did as he was told.

In those moments when he found his anger and frustration rise, he need only look at the photographs, see the strong outline of her determined jaw and remember who she was. What she really was to him.

Their destiny was so much bigger than either of their minor schemes.

Her gift had brought her to him, long before she could have known who he was. No matter what else they were doing in this world, they were tied together for a greater purpose.

Konstantine understood this.

And Padre Leo had taught him patience. Some things cannot be rushed.

Look at this great cathedral, Padre had said. Konstantine could still see Padre's black pants and a black dress shirt that was open at the collar, a gold chain at his neck.

They'd been decorating the church for Christmas and Padre had pulled Konstantine aside from the other boys when he heard him complaining about how long the work was taking. It felt as if they'd been decorating for days, and just when Konstantine thought they were done, another heap of red ribbons or garlands would appear.

She is beautiful, isn't she?

As a boy Konstantine knew nothing of beauty. But he'd loved the high ceilings. The magic of a mosaic that had lasted centuries.

It took six hundred years for this church to become as you see it, Padre had said. *Remember that.*

You cannot rush greatness. You must be patient. You must build it brick by brick—

A sharp sound yanked Konstantine from his memories. He turned away from the window, expecting the closet to open. But it didn't. Then he heard a sound that he would recognize anywhere.

A fist connecting. And it came from that secret room beneath the kitchen island.

He was across the apartment before thinking. Then he had the latch flicked open and was descending the stairs.

Lou must not have heard him as her fist repeatedly connected with the wooden post over and over again.

He seized her wrist mid-swing and she redirected easily.

But he'd expected this. He'd seen enough rage in violent men to know how they reacted if you dared interrupt them.

What he hadn't been expecting was the momentum. Though he'd seized her other wrist, deflecting the blow, her forward movement had thrown them both into the wall at the bottom of the stairs. They stood beneath the halo of lamplight. He held her wrists so she wouldn't strike him.

To his surprise, she let him.

With each breath her body grew softer against his, until she was simply leaning against him. He was pinned against the wall under the weight of her.

She looked so slight and no more than 5'7 or maybe 5'8. But she was solid muscle and he supposed that made up the weight. Or maybe it was something in that gift of hers. Perhaps gravity was different for this one.

He loosened his grip on her wrists cautiously.

"What happened?" he breathed into her hair.

At first she didn't speak. And he considered that she might not answer him at all.

Then she said, "She was sick for a long time and didn't tell me."

He understood then. He'd known about the aunt's illness. Tracking her had been easy compared to the woman now leaning all her weight against him. Lucy Thorne wasn't a ghost. She had as many public records as anyone, including some private ones, which Konstantine had accessed with ease.

He thought of Padre, of how again it seemed like this woman's life echoed and intersected his own. Padre too had hidden his illness until nothing could be done but say goodbye.

Konstantine turned her wrist so he could inspect the damage. The knuckles were split and bloody, but on a whole, it looked all right. He wondered how often she might have rages like this, and how conditioned her hands must be as a result.

"Did you get to say goodbye?" he asked softly, running one thumb over the back of her hand.

She nodded.

"Good," he said, finding his voice dangerously calm. He was hiding his own emotions well enough. He hoped. When he felt more in control of himself, he said, "We should clean this up."

She mounted the stairs without a word, taking all that heat and weight of the moment with her. Konstantine turned off the light behind them.

She was already sitting on the edge of her bed, the kit open before her, cleaning the wound by the time he latched the island door closed.

He knelt before her and helped her wrap the hand carefully. Then it was done.

As soon as he fastened the lid back onto the box, she pulled him into the bed with her.

She rolled him onto his back easily, her legs sliding down on either side of his waist. It felt even more delicious than he'd always imagined it would. Her muscles shifting. Her heat.

She wanted him. He could see it in her eyes, a look of hunger as easy to identify as his own. But it wasn't tender. It bordered fury.

His eyes slid over her body, his hands on each of her hips. He wanted his hands to be right here when she slid herself down onto him. He had only to undress her first. He reached for the hem of her shirt but she slammed his wrists back into the mattress, pinning them on either side of his head.

He was fine with this. He would give every ounce of control to this woman, if she wanted it. Whatever she needed to trust him.

But when he met her eyes again, tears stood out in the lashes.

He bucked her forward with his hips and flipped her over. She hit her side, then her back, until he was rolling her away from him.

Her tight body pressed into that perfect seat of his lap and his arms went around her.

He lay still behind her, holding her against him as snug as that vest she wore so often. "If you need to take care of—"

"—it's done," she said. Despite her tears, her voice remained perfectly steady.

"It's dangerous to fight when you aren't yourself," he said.

Her power and abilities would be his greatest ally in the fight against Nico and his army, but he wouldn't want her to truly endanger herself. He knew firsthand that pain in the heart and mind were more crippling than pain in one's body.

She remained motionless in his arms. So warm. He thought of kissing her neck. Her hair. Of sliding the hand on her abdomen down to find that place where her legs met.

He didn't.

You must build it, brick by brick.

"With so many bastards in one place," she said, her neck luminous in the moonlight pouring over his shoulder. Her breath hot on his arm. "I'll be more *myself* than you can stand."

26

Lou rose from the bed without making a sound. Konstantine never woke. He'd fallen asleep where she'd left him, on his back in her bed. Lou however couldn't sleep. Not because she didn't understand what was happening between them, but because she wasn't sure she had enough sense left to be cautious. She'd almost slept with him. And she would have if not for the sudden, bright memory of Lucy's dying face flashing across the screen of her mind.

Her bony hand cupping her cheek. *Forgive me, Louie.*

The last thing she would ever say.

By now, no doubt, they'd found her body in the hospital room where she'd returned her. She'd placed the body back into an empty bed just after sunrise Hawaii time, and pressed the call button. She didn't wait to see who would come, or if this was even the correct room.

What they would think of the sand, of the smell of smoke in the dead woman's hair, and her lack of shoes...Lou didn't know. She took the blankets and departed, certain King would fill in the gaps sooner or later.

He'd insisted on being returned to his apartment where he could change and wash the smell of smoke from his hair and errant sand from his body. He thought if it looked as if they had both been to the beach, it might've been enough for them to push an inquiry, even if there was no way they could prove anything.

So shower first, and then he would return to the hospital, prepared to receive the news he already knew was coming.

She suspected that it was possible he could've been tied up at the cancer center for a while with some kind of bureaucratic bullshit. But he should be at his apartment by now.

Lou stepped into her converted linen closet and let her compass whirl in the dark, searching for King.

When it locked onto him, and the walls melted away, she wasn't greeted by his familiar red couch or beast of an armoire. Not by his king-sized bed nor his tiny bathroom.

It wasn't his apartment at all.

She emerged from the shadows onto the street. A woman screamed, immediately falling into giggles, one hand on her chest.

"Christ," she said, her voice high. "I didn't see you."

She wobbled past Lou with her plastic cup, her heels unsteady beneath her.

She read the street sign, the corner of St. Peter and Bourbon. She took one look at the neon bar sign, noted the thudding bass blaring through the open door, vibrating her chest, and knew exactly where King was.

The doorman motioned her forward. She didn't bother. Rounding a corner, she took the alley in. Alley to the bathroom. Bathroom into the bar itself.

It was easy to spot King.

Mostly because he was such a massive man. Also because he was making a fool of himself.

A man beside him was talking shit and King had turned on his stool to eye him with a wrathful gaze. Before Lou could even cross the dim bar and reach him, the basket of pickle chips had been overturned, and the first punch thrown.

A brown beer bottle was knocked over, pouring frothy booze over the lip of the wooden bar.

She reached him in four long strides, stepping between him and the other man. It was a man in a leather jacket with his fingers wrapped in fingerless studded leather gloves.

He was at least a hundred pounds lighter than King. He was built like a soccer player. Tall, thin.

When Lou stepped between them, she gave King her back. She'd hoped that at least he wouldn't hit her.

When the biker threw his second punch, Lou was there to intercept it. She deflected it with her rotating wrist and struck the man in his throat. His eyes bulged, both hands going to his neck.

Before his anger overrode his surprise, she gave him a swift kick in the knee to think about. He toppled.

Lou turned, ready to haul King from the bar and was greeted with a fist. She moved at the last moment, sparing her face from the wild hook. But because she'd stepped back, she'd put her wounded shoulder right in the path of his blow.

Her arm sang. Furious, waves of pain radiating up her arm, she seized him with her good arm and yanked him from the bar. She didn't head toward the exit, but rather the bathrooms. As piss-scented and filthy as they were, they were far darker than the streets.

King howled the whole time. Hellbent on defending his honor.

"What the hell did you do that for?" he screamed. "I was fine. I was handling it fine."

He no doubt had more to say but the slip swallowed his words whole.

When they appeared in his apartment, the first thing King did was fall to his hands and knees and puke onto his rug.

The acrid scent of sour vomit and booze bloomed in the room. Lou opened the balcony door, hoping the breeze would overcome it. Watching him sit back on his heels, his eyes glazed, she realized how drunk he was. Quite. And a man his size didn't get drunk like that quickly.

"Did you go back to the hospital?" she asked.

"No," he shouted. She wasn't sure if this was on purpose or if he had no idea how loud his voice was.

"Why?"

"Because I didn't have my car," he said, even louder. "I didn't have a car. It's still in the parking lot. I drove to the center yesterday. And it's still there."

"So you went to the bar instead? Because it was walking distance?"

"So what if I did? What if I *fuck*-ing did!"

No doubt he'd been drinking all day. He smelled like it. He looked like it. What time did bars in the French quarter open? She had no idea. But she was sure that he'd been there when someone unlocked the door.

Drunk revelers stumbled through the streets, their laughter rising up through the window, mingling with the whine of a violin.

King seemed to regard the vomit on the rug as if he wasn't sure how it'd gotten there. Then he threw up onto the carpet again.

"What the hell is all this?" Mel appeared in the kitchen, closing the door to the apartment behind her. "What is he going on about?"

"He's drunk," Lou said.

"I'm not drunk," King said.

"The hell you aren't. And in my house!"

Mel saw the vomit and wrinkled her nose. "What in the world would Miss Lucy think of you carrying on like this?"

King laughed. Laughed, maniacally until the rolling laughter gave over to tears and he covered his face with his hands.

"The hell," Mel murmured. She looked to Lou, hoping for answers. Lou noted her fortune teller get-up. The long purple skirt. The scarf tied around her head and gold bangles on her wrist. The deep kohl lining each eye.

"Lucy is dead," Lou said, finding the words foreign on her tongue. Her grief made the words heavy and unreal in her mouth.

Melandra's rage softened. "I see now."

Lou couldn't bear to look at the concerned face. "I'll go get his car."

"No need," Mel said, going to the freezer and fetching a frozen bag of peas. "I'll send Piper to get it. Can you help me get him onto the couch?"

Lou lifted him and plopped him on the sofa.

Mel looked a little surprised. "Thanks." She placed the peas over the worst part of King's swelling face.

Lou couldn't stay here. Not with the scent of vomit, not with Mel's concerned, mournful face. She turned to leave, and a bony hand caught her wrist.

Her instinct was to swing. To throw a fist into whatever wanted to pull her back into the misery. But she'd already done that to Konstantine tonight. Now having seen King do the same, it left a taste in her mouth. If she'd looked half as ridiculous as he had, she'd never lose control again.

"You going to be all right?" Mel asked. The hold on her wrist loosened. "Is there anything you need?"

Yes. She wanted to choke the life out of a man. Any bottom-feeding scumbag would do.

"I'll be fine," she said and turned before Mel could see her grimace.

Mel let her go. "I'll look out for Mr. King. Take care of yourself."

Lou gave some sort of noncommittal nod, only somewhat aware of the room around her. Already her thirst, her desire had risen up in her. Her nerves seemed to thrum with it. Every fiber in her being begging for some kind of release from the anguish plucking at her nerves. The whine filling her mind like razorblades on guitar strings.

She stepped into the shadows of the armoire and out again. She wasn't sure where the darkness would take her. Where she wanted to go. She only knew she couldn't be near King and all his anguish. And she sure as hell couldn't be go back to her apartment to face Konstantine and all his desire.

People with their fucking feelings. She didn't even want to deal with her own.

No, she needed a distraction. A nice, dangerous distraction that would take up all the space in her mind.

A kitchen materialized from nothing.

A gleaming surface held pots and pans. Dishes ready to be served. She expected people in little white uniforms, familiar chef's attire to appear any moment. Instead the prep table was lined with white bricks. Rows and rows of white bricks wrapped in clear plastic.

Then she heard the male voices. The angry arguing. She crossed the grimy tile of the kitchen, checking the gun at her side. She marched right down the center aisle. *Reckless*, her mind breathed, as it searched for nonexistent shadows.

She pulled the gun with her bad arm and it burned.

Reckless.

Still she marched forward.

And then there they were, two men arguing so fiercely amongst themselves that neither of them saw her. At first.

"This isn't enough!" the one screamed, his broad back to her. His bomber jacket bouncing with exaggerated fury. "Where's the rest of it?"

"Tony, I fuckin' told you. This is all he gave me. Call him and ask him yourself. This is all there is."

"But I paid for twice as much, at least. If there's no dope then give me my fucking money back!"

The bomber jacket shoved the shorter man. By pushing him out of the line of view, it revealed him for who he was. A squat Asian man, maybe no more than 5'5, 5'4. His eyes wide at the sudden push. But his new angle gave him a full view of Lou, approaching from behind.

"Don't be looking like a scared little bitch, Po. You aren't going to fool me with shit again. Looking behind me, trying to get me to turn and then when I turn around, you fucking bolt like a pony at the track. No way. Fool me once and all that shit."

Tony pulled his gun and pointed it at the man named, Po.

"But—" Po began.

Lou seized Tony by the back of his leather jacket with her free hand, her good hand, and with the butt of her gun, opened the freezer. Po stood stunned, and unmoving as Lou dragged the howling man into the freezing dark. The cold didn't last.

His knees hit the dirt.

Lou wasn't sure if they always toppled like this because she released them so abruptly after the slip, or if slipping through the dark was such a dizzying affair. King had complained about it once, but she herself had no problem emerging from the dark on her own two feet, head clear, and the night calm around her. Unless of course she'd been shot, or was dying. She supposed that was true.

But she hadn't even put a scratch on Tony. Yet.

She should change that.

Her right hook crashed into the side of the man's face. Her knuckles slid along the jaw bone finally connecting with the mouth. The lip split over the teeth. It swelled instantly, blood pooling in the crack.

She waited. She stood there waiting for him to retaliate. She *wanted* him to retaliate.

Not in my name, Lou. Lucy's plea rang through her mind the second before Tony's fist connected with her gut, winding her. She went down on one knee.

His leg rose, and she knew he meant to kick her in the face.

She let herself fall. Fall through the dark and appear three feet behind him in a moonlit patch that seemed made for her.

His foot connected with earth with more force than he'd expected and he was pitched forward. His arms waved comically trying to reestablish control. She kicked him in the tailbone, and he cried out. His back arched furiously as he threw back his head and howled his pain.

Why do you pick fights? Lucy asked.

It was the aunt she remembered best in her mind's eye. No more than 42 maybe. Lou was fourteen and halfway through her first year in a new school.

There are better ways to deal with your anger, Lucy told her after she picked her up from school on the principal's orders and walked her down to the city bus stop. They did public transport to and from school at Lucy's insistence. *No slipping in school.*

Apparently, kneeing a guy during gym was also forbidden.

"He slapped my ass."

"Language."

"He *assaulted* me," Lou had said. "Be glad all I did was knee him."

Lucy's silence after that had weighed on her. Gave her mind such a wild and menacing playground within which to dream up the possible insults she must be composing for her niece in her mind. Lou had braced herself for her rejection. For her cold regard. But on the bus, halfway to their Oak Park apartment Lucy said, "Fighting isn't an appropriate way to dispel your anger."

"Don't start up about yoga again."

"No, not yoga," Lucy agreed. "I have something else in mind."

The next day she'd dropped Lou off at an aikido dojo on Chicago's east side and Lou took to it like a bird to the air.

But all the training in the world hadn't seemed to prepare her for this. For the moment when her life was thrown into the pool again.

She was drowning.

She was falling through and there was no one to pull her out.

Nowhere to go but down.

And now, thinking of her aunt's calm face, the fight left Lou. Her heart sank to irretrievable depths and with the last of her fury, she seized Tony by the back of his neck and hauled him up. She threw him into the lake with one great shove. He hit the water the way Lou must've hit the water that June night her father saved her life. Mouth open in surprise. Arms out as if to break a fall. An ugly splash that had winded her.

She marched through the water after him. And just as his head surfaced, she was on him.

She wrapped her legs around his body and pulled him down, squeezing the way an octopus with its many tentacles must squeeze its prey before pulling the food to its beak for rendering.

The water warmed. Turned the color of blood.

And then there they were on the other side.

Tony's reaction was one she'd seen a hundred times. Blind, abject terror. He flailed in the water. He screamed at the terrible landscape. He followed her to shore howling, as if she were his salvation instead of the person who'd condemned him to die in this place.

Then the familiar screech she'd come to expect broke open the sky.

The beast bounded around her, circling her twice and swiping at her stomach with its head as if in greeting. Then she chased after Tony the way a puppy chased after his master. But when she caught him, the sounds that emitted from his mouth couldn't be mistaken for play.

Lou sank onto the embankment, and put her face in her hands. She wiped the water away, and smoothed her hair back from her face. She'd lost her sunglasses. It was hard to give a shit about sunglasses when Lucy was dead.

She breathed, head between her knees. When the world stopped spinning, she shrugged off the leather jacket to give her burning arm a good look. It was swollen, the flesh pinched red between the black wire. But it was not bleeding, not oozing puss.

She heard Jabbers behind her but didn't bother to turn. "Fucking eat me. Put me out of my misery."

She wouldn't.

The beast had saved her life by shoving her into the water before she'd blacked out. Lou understood that now. She'd known it was smart, possessing an intelligence of some kind. But now she suspected the walking nightmare had even more than she imagined.

It understood that she came and went by the water. And it understood that somehow, on the other side, there was a possibility that she could heal.

It sniffed Lou's wounded arm, and sneezed.

Lou cringed, using the water to rinse the wound. "Hope you don't have some horrible tropical disease in your snot."

The monster sat on its haunches beside her. Its white tongue licked the blood from its snout before chewing the guts from the webbing in its feet.

Then it slid into the water, paddling a circle before diving underneath. Lou only watched, catching her breath, taking in the eternal twilight and double moons.

Seemingly tired of water play, the beast crawled onto the shore again, once more taking a seat beside her, reclining on all fours and licking what could only be called forearms.

Lou reached out and touched the cool, damp flesh. The beast made a sound, not unlike purring.

"Who needs retail therapy, when I've got you," Lou said, patting that reptilian snout.

And then, just as she had on the night her father died, Lou cried herself hoarse on the banks of La Loon.

27

King woke on his red sofa, staring up at a long patch of sunlight across his ceiling. At first all he could taste was the burning, citrus taste of booze, like maybe salt and lime had been left in his mouth all night to putrefy. He smacked his lips a few times and found the moisture gone.

He sat up and the world spun. His arm shot out and grabbed the first thing he could find—which turned out to be his enormous coffee table. He held its smooth surface with a weak grip until the room stopped spinning and came into focus again. The large armoire in the corner, cherry wood that looked especially red in the light pouring through the open balcony. Sunshine glittering across his white bedspread in the adjacent bedroom. The quiet kitchen with a water glass sitting half full beside the silver basin.

A leather jacket on a hanger, hanging from the trim above his bedroom door. Its hook was placed so that the weight kept it steady despite the slight swing in the breeze.

Lou was sitting his armchair. Beside her rest his record player on its stand and a stack of vinyls leaning against it. Their fraying cardboard edges reminded him how old, how vulnerable they were. His eyes slid to the Bob Dylan vinyl where he kept his weed and a half-used pack of rolling papers.

Seeing Lou in the chair, flipping through one of the bridal magazines that had no doubt been on his coffee table, and those records—all of it brought Lucy to mind.

Had it really been only three months since she'd walked into his life again?

Three months since she'd stretched on his red leather sofa, an icy glass of sweet tea balanced on her bare knee. Her body had been ethereal in the moonlight sparkling through the open balcony door. It was as if she'd never left him if he overlooked the longer hair. What would he give to rewind those three months and start all over again? And how much more, to go back twelve years, when he'd let her leave and hadn't even tried to stop her.

A wave of sadness slammed into his chest. A fist seized his heart and squeezed.

He wiped at his eyes with balled fists. Doing so made his knuckles burn, reminding him of the split flesh from the night before.

"Are you still drunk?" Lou asked, closing the bridal magazine and tossing it to the floor with disgust. He saw she was sporting her own bloodied knuckles.

What a pair we make, he thought.

"No," King croaked. "Unfortunately. I hope to change that very soon."

"Your landlady will kill you if you do," she said. Her mirrored sunglasses were up on her head and she regarded him with Jack's unflinching eyes. But the glasses looked different. Maybe she got a second pair.

"Is that your jacket?" he asked, pointing at his bedroom door. It hung from a hanger balanced precipitously on the top of the frame.

"It got wet," she said, as if this explained everything.

Then more of the room came into focus. The dried vomit on the rug. His bloody knuckles which burned as he flexed and balled his hands in turn.

Dead. Lucy was dead.

She'd died in his arms on a beach in Maui. And as fucking romantic as that sounded, it didn't spare him an ounce of the grief.

Then he was crying. *Really* crying, his whole body convulsing. He hadn't cried like this when his parents died, nor his beloved grandfather.

Not even Jack, whose death had hurt his heart in a way none had before.

Before he knew it, Lou was pressing his red rescue inhaler into one of his hands, pushing against the knuckles until he unballed his fist and accepted it.

She was shoving a bottle of Jack into the other.

He laughed, a strangled, humorless sound, when he saw it. "Where the hell did this come from?"

She didn't seem to hear him. She was fishing his cell phone from the kitchen island and handing it to him. "Your phone has gone off several times. You've got messages."

King put down the bottle of Jack on the coffee table and accepted the phone.

He did have messages, so many that his screen looked like an emergency. Red flags blaring at him from several icons.

He listened to each one in turn, informing Lou of its contents.

"Piper got my car and parked it in the alley."

"They found Lucy and want to know if I want to see her before they send her to the morgue." His voice cracked and broke on that last one.

The last voicemail was from Sampson informing him that he would be visiting him today at approximately eleven. His tone was grave.

King squinted at the green clock on his stove. 10:53. "Shit."

The fire escape rattled the same moment as Melandra blew into the apartment. "Mr. King, get up. There's a cop looking for you."

Before he could process this, Lou had crossed the room, snatched her leather jacket from the hanger and disappeared into his bedroom.

"What did he look like?" King asked. But he didn't need her answer. In the same instance, one finely clad leg stepped onto his balcony followed by another. The spit-shone black shoes. The uncreased navy blue dress pants. A nice cotton, collared shirt tucked into the pants. A gray mustache trimmed and clean.

Sampson hadn't aged a day since King saw him last.

"What did I tell you?" Melandra started before Sampson could even cross through the open balcony. One hand was on her hip, the other pointed a fierce finger at the man's face. "I will call the law on you, do you hear me? I want to see your damn warrant!"

Sampson held both hands out in front of him, palms out in surrender. Or they would've been, if the left hadn't been clutching a manila folder.

"Mel, it's all right," King said. He would've said this even if it wasn't. He was desperate for some quiet with the throbbing headache splitting his brains in half. It was the headache, no doubt. But crying hadn't helped. "Sampson and I are friends. And we had an appointment."

Without missing a beat Sampson said, "We do."

With no target, Mel threw up her hands in exasperation. And perhaps that would have been the end of it had she not spotted the bottle of Jack on King's coffee table.

She yelped and snatched it up with one clawed fist. "No, sir!" She shook the bottle at him, brown liquid sloshing against its sides until it was King's turn to hold up his hands in surrender.

"It was from...a gift," he quickly corrected, dropping Lou's name from the sentence. "I didn't drink any."

Something flashed in her eyes and King suspected she knew what he'd meant to say, but she arched her brow all the same. "Who gives half-drunk bottles as gifts, King, I can't say."

But she took the bottle and left him alone with Sampson.

"A spirited woman," Sampson said, in obvious admiration.

And King laughed at the unintentional pun. Because surely he hadn't meant Mel's penchant for cards and conversing with the dead. Instead he said, "You have no idea."

Sampson glanced around the apartment. "Nice place you have here, Robert."

"Thank you. But I don't think you came all the way from St. Louis to compliment my paint job. What's going on?"

"I needed to talk to you," he began.

"Obviously."

"And it wasn't something that should've happened over the phone." Sampson regarded him with dark eyes. "Lest it be admissible in a court of law."

King's heart stopped on a dime. When he recovered he said, "I would offer you a drink, but I'm afraid Mel took it away. Water?"

"No, thank you."

Sampson took a seat in the leather chair that Lou had just vacated.

"If we are talking court, do I need to ask you to lift your shirt for a wire?" King asked solemnly.

Sampson didn't even look offended. He untucked his nice collared shirt and showed his tight brown belly. Swaths of gray hair covered his chest, but no wire.

"Who is investigating me?" King asked.

"I am."

"Are you serious?"

"As of this morning," he said and tapped the folder against his leg.

"May I ask what *for*?"

"We know that you signed onto the server and accessed unpublished information."

King's heart sank. Now he *really* wished that Mel had left the bottle behind.

"Though looking at you, I can hardly believe it," Sampson said, ramrod straight from the leather chair. He'd always had impeccable posture from years of band followed by a military career, he'd once told King.

"Why do you say that?" King asked, wondering if he should lawyer up. And if so, with whom? Someone expensive no doubt.

"Robert, you look like hell."

"I've had a rough 24 hours," King said, lying back against the cushions.

"How rough."

"My wife died."

My wife.

"I'm sorry. I didn't realize you were married."

"It wasn't finalized," he admitted. "She'd been sick in the hospital. There was a priest but no marriage certificate. I'm not sure it would hold in court." King knew he was rambling. But focusing on the bull-shit details that didn't matter felt better than looking too closely at the raw reality. Lucy was gone. Lucy was gone and she wasn't coming back.

Tears stung his eyes.

"None of that matters if you loved her."

"I do. I did." His voice cracked.

Sampson said nothing. Puzzlement danced across his face. King saw his conflict, his desire to push forward with his business in coming here, warring against the decency of not kicking a man while he was down.

King wanted him gone. And if the man had flown from St. Louis to talk to him, he wasn't leaving until he'd done what he'd come to do.

"How bad is it?" King asked.

"That's what I came to ask you," Sampson said.

King said nothing.

"I can see now that this isn't a good time, and I'm real sorry about that," Sampson began. "But you've got to talk to me. Tell me what is going on."

"I needed some information," King said.

"About Paolo Konstantine?"

"Just an old man's curiosity," King insisted. "Go on and call me an uncle, but it's not like I was using it maliciously."

"What does Louie Thorne have to do with all this?"

The mention of her name made King's blood freeze in his veins. Had he really been so careless? He thought he'd done a good job of entering and exiting the server using different IPs and encrypted lines. Whatever emotion played across his face Sampson must've seen it.

"Isn't she Jack's daughter?"

Of course he made the connection. Because Sampson knew Jack too. Knew how much the grunt had meant to King when he was flying high in the St. Louis unit, in the peak of their glory days before his murder and the slander of his good name had brought everything crashing down around them.

And hadn't it been Sampson himself who had testified on King's behalf, vouching that no matter what Jack may have done, no matter how many connections formed with the Martinelli cartel, King was innocent of all wrong doing.

"To help you along," Sampson said, his face somewhere between masked and sympathetic. "I'll tell you what I did. I compiled every search conducted on our server in the last ninety days and what I found was a whole lot of people were checking on the name Louie Thorne. Or sometimes Lou Thorne and once in a while Lucy Thorne, who turns out, is Jack's sister and a woman you've been visiting at the New Orleans Cancer Center nearly every day over a month. And I take it she's the wife you are referring to?"

King tried to control his exhale.

"What's going on, Robbie?" Now Sampson's face was genuine concern. "What are you doing? Is this for your P.I. business?"

"If I told you," King said, running a hand over his weathered face. "You wouldn't believe me."

When had he gotten so damn old? His head ached. His back and neck ached. His hand knuckles were the color of a split plum.

"Try me," Sampson said. "Because I've been tasked with detailing every suspicious log-in for the last ninety days and I need to have a good damn excuse for this. The department is on high alert over this Konstantine mess. There's a real possibility that innocent people like yourself will get caught in the crossfire if we aren't careful. They want to cover their asses and they want to blame someone. You know how it goes. And this is suspicious as hell, so give me something you can float on here or you're going down with the ship."

King looked up and saw Lou leaning in the doorway of his bedroom.

Shock ran through his body and his surprised jolt must have alarmed Sampson as well. He was on his feet, holding the manila folder down at his side as his right hand snaked toward the small of his back. So he was packing. Weren't they all these days...

King had thought she'd left. That she'd simply taken the leather jacket she now wore and had slipped through some shadowed corner of his bedroom, or perhaps from beneath his bed. But here she was, mirrored sunglasses and all.

"Won't you introduce us?" she said.

King finally found his voice. "I don't believe you've met Jack's daughter, Lou. Lou this is Sampson. He worked with your old man back in St. Louis."

Sampson couldn't contain his surprise. And King understood full and well. The creature standing before him was like something out of the jungle. Her entire leather-clad presence from head-to-toe. No wonder she blended with the underworld so well. She looked cut from the same cloth. And for anyone who'd hunted danger in the dark, they knew dangerous when they saw it. When it stood before them, the urge to reach for the gun was high.

But Lou was offering her hand. She was saying hello.

Sampson found his voice at last. "It's nice to see you again. You're... all grown up."

King arched an eyebrow at the other man but Sampson didn't seem to notice. And he couldn't read Lou's eyes either behind those sunglasses.

Lou was speaking. "It's my fault that he keeps searching your database."

King's skin chilled. Sampson was a do-gooder. He stood on the right side of the law. And though that made him a trustworthy man, it didn't mean he could be trusted with the truth.

If Lou saw his panicked expression, she continued as if she hadn't.

"The Italian crime factions thought they won when my dad's name was publicly trashed," she said. "When he was exonerated, they became angry. They've made threats, tried to track me down. King knew they were looking into your servers. And he wanted to make sure there was nothing there that could lead them to me."

King was holding his breath. It was a damn good lie. It was a damn good lie because it wasn't exactly a lie at all. The criminals were trying to crack the server. He was sure they were pissed when Jack was elevated to hero status again. And no doubt more than one drug lord would love to know this woman's real name and how to find her.

Sampson was trying to detect a lie, King could see it in his searching expression. But he couldn't find one.

"They threaten you?" he asked, finally.

"Almost every day." Another truth. Sampson didn't need to know that those threats usually came delivered from fear, at knifepoint.

"Why haven't you reported it? You could have asked for protection?"

It took considerable control for King not to burst out laughing. Louie Thorne, in need of their protection?

"Do you think I can trust the DEA after what Brasso did to my father?" she said. "Then he takes off and you can't even find him."

Sampson was the first to avert his eyes.

"I see," he said finally.

"King was just trying to protect me."

More truth, though King wouldn't have been able to say it from his own lips without dipping the words in guilt first. He wanted to honor Jack and Lucy, but it wasn't enough.

He flexed his hand and saw fresh blood spring up between the malformed scabs. Sampson was looking at his busted hand too, no doubt drawing his own conclusions.

"I've got all I need. I'll leave you to your grief," Sampson said. "I'm sorry I came at such a bad time. And I'm sorry for your loss."

He hesitated at the balcony door. "King. One more thing?"

With much effort, King dragged himself from the sofa and followed Sampson out onto the balcony. He pulled the door shut behind them.

"*That's* Louie Thorne?" Sampson asked, his face overrun with disbelief.

King wasn't sure if this was a real question or verbal processing. "Yeah. Makes you feel old, doesn't it?"

"I remember her at the picnics. Quiet. Liked her books."

"Still quiet," King said, unsure where this was going.

"You've got to stop logging on," Sampson said. "They're in a frenzy over this Konstantine bullshit."

"All right." He held up his bloody knuckles. "I'm in need of a break anyway."

"And you should keep track of the threats," Sampson added. "In case this all ends up in court, you'll want proof that she's been threatened."

As if Louie Thorne would ever let it get that far. "It's good advice, Sammy."

He was staring at the closed balcony door. "Is she all right?"

"What do you mean?"

Sampson touched the side of his head and raised his eyebrows. "What happened to Jack, well, that'd mess up anybody. And she was there that night."

"Does she seem crazy to you?" King asked, genuinely curious. He wondered what the rest of the world saw when they looked at Lou.

"No," Sampson said, shaking his head. "No, she seems smart. Charming. But Ted Bundy had been charming too."

King laughed. The jab was too close not to strike him funny. "She's not eating people or fucking their corpses. I assure you."

But King was sure that Lou had surpassed Bundy's body count years ago.

"Well, look after her," Sampson said. He frowned at King. "And yourself, Robbie."

"I'm trying."

Sampson squeezed his shoulder and climbed onto the fire escape with the folder tucked under his arm. "I'll be in touch if anything develops with this."

"You know you can use the front door. Mel won't bite. Probably."

Sampson only laughed. "My momma didn't raise no fool."

King listened to the fire escape rattle with the large man's descent before he stepped back into the apartment and closed the balcony door.

"You're not being careful." Lou leaned against his bedroom door, watching him.

King snorted. It was all he could muster in the form of humor. His heart wasn't in it. His heart, in fact, was nowhere to be found. "Maybe that's why Lucy linked us up. She wanted you to babysit an old, stupid man."

Lucy. Just her name, the thought of her, as light as a dry corn husk in his arms. He pinched his eyes closed and pressed his thumbs into his temples.

This hurt. And it was going to hurt for a long time.

"You can't go on the server anymore," Lou said.

"No shit."

"There's another way. I don't know how it works, but I know he's good at it."

"Him who?"

"Sober up and I'll introduce you."

28

Konstantine tried not to pace the apartment. He had one hour before his rendezvous with Ricci. Tonight he would be back in Florence. Tonight he would face Nico and... what? Would he win? With Lou by his side, his victory was assured. He'd seen her on the boat with the senator, exacting her revenge. She'd dropped a man with every bullet. Nico's army would be nothing against her, especially with his borrowed New York army behind them.

And yet...

Something ate at his stomach. There was an unease inside him that he didn't trust.

God speaks to us when we listen, his mother had said. *But only when we listen.*

His mind turned over the possibilities. All the ways the plan could go sideways.

The closet door burst open with more force than he'd come to expect from Lou.

An enormous man emerged first, Lou bursting in after him. Konstantine froze beside the rumpled bed, composing himself. He knew his outward appearance was calm, dignified. He'd practiced it enough to know how the expression felt on his face even when he himself couldn't see it. But his heart hammered.

Lou turned her dark eyes on him, arching an eyebrow. "I see you're ready to go."

"We have one hour," he said, hoping she hadn't forgotten that he would need her to transport him. She seemed nonplussed by this news. He took this for affirmation that she hadn't lost track of time.

But then why was the cop here. *Ex-cop*, he thought. This man had gone through the police academy, served several years on the Minneapolis force before being promoted to detective. Ten years later he applied for and was accepted by the Drug Enforcement Agency and began his career in St. Louis. He left the city only once, when an injury sidelined him and it was during that teaching exile he met Louie's father.

He'd been married once before for eight years, was a decorated hero, a minor boxing champion in his 20s. And he had liked to drink.

That was all Konstantine knew of the man standing before him.

He gave the man a once over, appraising him as politely as possible and concluded that whatever else might be true, the drinking was not such a thing of the past.

He looked rough.

Though his hair was recently washed and slicked back from his face. His eyes were dark with circles beneath and he had the posture of an old man. No, a *defeated* man. Even when he saw Konstantine and tried to pull himself up to his full height, it didn't quite leave him.

Perhaps it wasn't the drinking or the age. Perhaps, Konstantine realized, what he was looking at was grief.

"Robert King," the man said and extended his hand.

"Paolo Konstantine," he said and accepted the shake. Neither man tried to overpower the other or squeeze too hard.

For a moment, neither of them knew what to do with their bodies. They hovered as Lou disappeared down the hall to the bathroom and emerged changed. Fresh black cargo pants and a new black shirt. Her feet were bare on the wood floor and her hair pulled back to reveal her neck, keeping all strands from her face.

Konstantine couldn't help but watch her move, admiring the shift and sway of her body. Whatever grief she felt for her dead aunt was tucked neatly away in a corner of her heart for now.

Konstantine knew King was watching him, watching Lou. "Lou says that you're good with computers."

"I have a bit of talent," he said.

Lou snorted as she opened the safe. She threw guns and ammo over her shoulder onto the bed. "Who knew Italian men were so modest."

"You're the one who gave the proof of Jack's innocence?" the large man said, slowly sinking onto the sofa.

"Yes." Konstantine mirrored him, taking a seat on the side of Lou's bed, far enough that a pistol wouldn't hit him in the face.

"I've been monitoring servers and databases, trying to erase anything that linked to Lou. But it looks like they're onto me. Is there a way to do it *without* being noticed?"

"Of course," Konstantine said. "I will be happy to show you."

"Can you get a computer in New York?" she asked.

"Ricci will give me whatever I need. I'm sure a laptop will be no problem. But if you intend to do this tutorial before—" He let his words hang in the air.

"If you're busy—" King started.

"Konstantine will probably die tonight," Lou said as casually as one says *we're expecting thunderstorms.* "It's now or never."

"All right," King said. "When do we leave?"

"Now," she said. "I'll take Konstantine first and then I'll be back for you."

King looked ready to object but she was already stepping into the closet. Konstantine didn't hesitate. It wasn't only the opportunity to step into the dark with this beautiful creature again, to feel her hard body against his, it was also his eagerness to begin. He'd felt like an eternity, not days had passed in that apartment.

He tried to relish it, every shift of muscle under his hand as he embraced her.

"Ready?" she asked and he knew her lips were quite close to his. Oh the temptation. But he was no fool.

The world shifted into view. They stepped out from under an overhang, some back-alley stoop with an added layer of shadow from the adjacent dumpster. She left Konstantine on this back stoop of Charlie's Chinese House and was gone again before he could thank her.

He rang the bell. A slot slid open revealing only black eyes. "Tell Ricci that his 1:00 is here."

The slot closed and Konstantine was left alone in the garbage-reeking alley for a moment to compose himself. He heard the hobbled steps of Ricci sound before the door opened on the round, joyous man.

"Hey! You're early! But it's all right, it's all right. Get in here!"

He ushered Konstantine in with a pat on his back.

"Who the hell are you?"

King stood awkwardly in the alley.

"He is with me," Konstantine said.

The two men exchanged looks as King gave a solemn smile.

"Is this guy okay?" Ricci asked. He'd lowered his voice for Konstantine's ears only. "I'm getting cop vibes."

King burped loudly and excused himself.

"Or maybe he's the town drunk," Ricci added.

"He is a cop, but he's one of my cops." He slapped Ricci's shoulder. "And he and I need to conduct a bit of business before we leave for Florence."

Ricci shrugged. "All right. You can use the Jade room until Buddy gives us the go. You remember Buddy? He's Karlene's boy. Anyway he runs the airfield, everything that goes in and out goes through Buddy now. So when he says we're clear to fly, then we'll take a little drive down to the airfield, and we're off."

Konstantine thanked him.

They followed Ricci through the kitchen and maze of hallways of Charlie's Chinese House. They passed the open door of an office and Konstantine paused.

"Can I borrow a computer?" Konstantine asked, gazing into what no doubt masqueraded as a restaurant manager's office. Wood paneling on all four walls and a great wooden desk. A tray with receipts stacked and a rubber band tying them all together like a fat roll of cash. A black box that looked like a walkie-talkie. But Konstantine wondered if it was a police scanner. Perhaps he had both squirreled away in there somewhere.

"Sure, sure."

Ricci stepped into the office and fished a key out of a ceramic tray on his desk. It looked like one of those misshapen creations that chil-

dren gave their parents from art class. He tried to remember how old
Ricci's daughters were now. Teenagers, perhaps? Maybe the eldest ready
for college. He couldn't recall.

The key opened a cabinet and after a brief search, the man found
what he was looking for.

Ricci handed over the laptop, wrapping the snake-like charger cord
around and around its square body. "It's a dummy. So if we gotta burn it
after, it's fine. Can I get you anything to drink or eat while you're
waiting?"

Konstantine was in fact starving despite his nerves. He told Ricci as
much. "I'll have Valerie bring something in for you guys. Go on and get
comfortable. I'll make sure nobody else bothers you while you do your
business."

The Jade room was probably named so for its emerald green wallpaper and the gold flourishes in Chinese design that ran vertically along
the walls. A large red table with carved dragon legs sat in the center of
the room, flanked by wooden pillars the same color.

He pulled out a chair and sat while King did the same.

"Tell me," Konstantine began. "Does...our mutual friend often leave
you alone with people you do not know?"

He wanted this to mean more than it did. That she trusted him not
to harm this man—whatever he was to her. Or perhaps she trusted the
man's ability to protect himself, should it come to it. Though one look
at his bloodshot eyes and purple circles told him that perhaps that was
not true. At least not today.

But again this only gave Konstantine hope. That maybe, with time,
she could grow to trust him.

"At least this isn't a Siberian shipping container," the man mumbled
taking in the emerald wallpaper and golden accents.

Konstantine didn't know what to think of this. He searched for
footing in the conversation.

"Did she say anything?" He hoped the question sounded casual. He
kept his gaze on the screen as he created the cloaking he would use to
show the old man a few tricks.

"She told me to stay with you until she got back. She's going to pop in
and check on—" Here he paused and looked around the room. Good. He

understood that they were being watched then. He wouldn't make the mistake of saying Lou's name or share any information that perhaps he didn't want a man like Ricci to know. He licked his lips and said, "She's scoping out the situation before you go in. So you know what to expect."

Useful. Very helpful.

Konstantine loosed a breath he didn't realize he'd been holding. "Right. Let's begin with whatever you did before."

"I used old passwords to access the servers. Sometimes I was able to guess the new ones."

"That's called social engineering," Konstantine said. "A SQL injection from a logless VPN would be better."

King only blinked at him.

"You know how to create dummy IP addresses, I assume."

"Yes. But they still knew it was me."

"That's because you can't truly be anonymous even if you are hiding behind someone else's IP. They will trace it back to you eventually. Instead I would use a paid, logless VPN. I can recommend a few, if you like?"

King said that he did and Konstantine told him how to contact the service and set it up.

"Once you have your logless VPN, then you can use SQL injections from your browser to access the host database. Then all the data stored there will be yours for the taking. I would suggest you take *all* of it, indiscriminately, rather than search for specific items, say, *names*, or anything that could form a pattern. You don't want anyone to know what you are looking at exactly, now do you? So take it all and go through it on a burner, offline, later."

King shook his head.

He handed the computer over to the man and let him try a few simple commands. He wasn't a complete luddite. Konstantine saw the knowledge and skills. But it was clear that the technology was advancing faster than perhaps this man had trained for. And maybe he didn't have the passion for the machines, like Konstantine did.

A young woman with a tray appeared burdened with chicken and pork covered in sauces, wontons and dumplings steamed, crab legs, heaping plates of rice and noodles. It was enough for a large family *and* the two men who sat there. Leaving plates, napkins, silverware, soda, and water, she departed the moment Konstantine thanked her.

King only stared at the feast. He looked like he would rather vomit on the food than put it in his mouth. "Will he be offended if—"

"Not at all," Konstantine interjected.

King drank deep of the soda on the table, but he left the food untouched.

He returned his attention to the computer, working to recreate what Konstantine had demonstrated with ease. He was getting a little faster with each pass. His face relaxed and eyes focused at least.

Konstantine ate a little bit of everything, hoping that it pleased his host that he did so. When King looked as though he was tired for now, Konstantine spared him.

"You know that none of this is necessary?" Konstantine said at last, as the man's practice was well underway.

King looked up, face pinched. He reached for the water pitcher and poured himself a full glass. Drank it down and filled it again, all while Konstantine continued on.

"I monitor all the intelligence databases. CIA, FBI, DEA, USSS, FPS, even the Coast Guard." He laughed. "And not just here. But Italian Interpol, most of the agencies in Europe and Russia too. China."

King's surprise couldn't be more evident. His mouth hung open.

Konstantine capitalized on the silence. "It would be nothing to protect the anonymity of our friend. I will continue to do so. Should something come up, I will handle it."

Then he seemed to recover himself at last, putting down his water glass, and scratched at his scruffy face with a yellowed thumbnail. "In your line of work, you must have business connections in every corner of the planet."

Konstantine said nothing, laying his fork against his demolished plate and taking another helping of the steamed dumplings.

"And you want to know who knows your business in each of those corners," King added. "Especially if business is going well."

"If business is going well," Konstantine countered, pointing with his fork. "There is no mention of me at all."

"Agostino changed that when he announced your name to every agency in the known world."

Konstantine smiled. "Perhaps. But my point is that it is no longer only my name that I keep an eye-out for."

King nodded, showing that he understood. "Then it doesn't matter if I can do any of this, does it?"

"If things go wrong tonight, perhaps very wrong, you will have to do the job."

"Hey, Mr. Konstantine, you get enough to eat?" Ricci stood in the doorway, his thumbs in his belt loops, pudgy belly hanging over the denim band.

"It was wonderful. You've been very hospitable, my friend," Konstantine said. "I will treat you even better the next time you come see me in Florence."

Ricci was pleased with this answer. "Good, good. I'm glad to hear it. If you're ready, we should head down to the airfield now. Buddy says we've got the hangar to ourselves and no prying eyes for the next 45 minutes."

Ricci looked at the man powering down and closing the laptop. Konstantine also considered him for a moment.

King caught the exchange and said, "She wanted me to stay with you."

"Come on then," Konstantine said. "We wouldn't want to disappoint her, would we?"

Ricci didn't ask who *she* might be and Konstantine knew he wouldn't. Ricci had lived to be the ripe old age of 68 for a reason. He was damn good at keeping his mouth shut and his eyes and ears open.

"I don't have my passport," King said, pushing back his chair. "Not on me."

Ricci laughed.

Konstantine smiled and slapped the man on the shoulder while coming around the table, leaving his half-demolished feast behind. "The way we are traveling, you will not need it."

29

Lou stood in her apartment, taking in afternoon light. She wanted a moment to clear her head before she went to Florence. Something about Konstantine and King together, the marriage of those two parts of her life—it had unnerved her. Don't overthink it, she warned herself. For all she knew Konstantine would die tonight, fighting in Padre Leo's church, the hallowed ground of the Ravengers.

San Augusto al Monte.

While so much about Paolo Konstantine confused and infuriated her, this she understood. Padre had been like a father to him. And he left this empire to his adopted son with the expectation that he would protect all that he'd built. Surely he felt some obligation to protect that legacy.

Her father had died too soon to leave her an empire, except of course the multi-million dollar life insurance policy meant to carry her through life.

What he'd left her was intangible. The drive. The thirst. He'd given his life for hers. If that was his gift, she'd been too careless.

Your life is your own to live, Jack said. Good answer.

The Mississippi River shimmered and the white seagulls dove and bobbed from above.

She checked her five guns and the corresponding clips again. Double-checked that she had enough ammo to fight her way out, should something go wrong. Two knives stuffed into sewn slips at each forearm and one more at her right thigh. And at last, her father's bullet proof vest snug over her chest.

This first glimpse was only to get a sense of what they were walking into. The layout of the church, how many men Nico had, his plan for attack. She'd gather the intel she could, sticking to the unobtrusive shadows. Then she'd get King, take him back to New Orleans before he had a chance to get hurt.

Konstantine could do what he wanted with the information that she found. It wouldn't alter her plans in the slightest.

Lou stepped into the closet, welcoming the familiar darkness. The compass whirled inside, lining up those two invisible slots in the machine that would move heaven and earth. When the darkness softened and Lou herself stepped through, she felt the shift. Another floor in another country rose up to meet her. Her hand finding not the opposite closet wall, but a cool stone pillar.

The church came into focus around her. The orderly pews and clean stone gave no impression of the firefight that had taken place here a few days before. She knew her own bullets had chipped away at these ancient facades.

It was so quiet. Too quiet.

She slipped through the shadows, taking in the church from different angles. Men were stationed, waiting in the wings for Konstantine no doubt. But there was no sign of the men that Lou recognized. Those who were in Konstantine's closest entourage. Had Nico killed them outright?

Nico was nowhere to be seen.

Two men standing near the image of the weeping Christ spoke in hushed, whispered Italian. But she understood what happened next.

One man lifted the purple cloth to reveal a mess of wires and jugs of fluorescent fluid.

A bomb.

Nico was going to blow up the church—no doubt when Konstantine was inside. It made perfect sense. If Nico harbored as much hate for his father's betrayal as Konstantine said, why wouldn't he want to bring down his father's empire, brick by literal brick?

And take out the clever golden boy while he was at it?

No doubt he would make a big show of it. Station enough men here to oppose Konstantine, to make him believe that Nico was hidden in the bowels of the church, a prize to be had if only Konstantine could fight his way through.

But if Nico wasn't here, where was he?

Lou pressed her back into the shadows of the stone pillar and let her compass shift and whirl. It clicked into place and she stepped through.

A padded floor rose up to meet her. She wobbled on her feet, her body caught off guard by the unsteady nature of the flooring. She dropped into a crouch to steady herself and gain a better understanding of her surroundings. Pitch black. Not an ounce of light from anywhere. She couldn't even see her hand in front of her face.

And this strange floor... it felt like linen. A thick material with something stuffed inside it, billowing it into a stiff pillow shape beneath her hands.

Then the lights turned on. Lights from every conceivable direction blared down on her like the light from a thousand suns. She moved to jump into the shadow, only to find there was no shadow. No seam, no crevice, no crack. So much light that she couldn't see any more than she could have seen in the darkness. She pulled her gun and shot wildly. The bullet connected with something, pinged off in an unseen direction.

Then she thought to shoot the lights. She would have to shoot out the lights. She raised her gun and aimed it at the sky.

An electrical current shot through her body. Her convulsing hand emptied the clip into the wall, not the ceiling. She crumpled onto the floor, unsure if she still held her gun or not.

It's in the floor, she thought. *There's a current in the floor.*

And then she thought nothing at all.

30

Every time King closed his eyes, he saw Lucy. He saw her sitting in a Café du Monde bistro chair, sucking praline chocolate off her thumb. He saw her walking beside him down Royal Street, her red sundress sliding across tan thighs. Her saw the sunlight sparking in her eyes.

The way she'd cupped his cheek and said, *I do*. The firelight dancing across her cheekbones.

He pinched the bridge of his nose and exhaled a ragged breath.

"Can I get you anything?"

King turned and saw a young man, maybe twenty, leaning toward his airplane seat, his face open and neutral.

"A coke," King said. "And some aspirin if you've got it."

The kid wandered away and King caught Konstantine's eye. The man sat opposite him, in an adjacent airplane seat.

King only vaguely noted his presence. He kept replaying the moments of Lucy's life on the screen of his mind. His only reprieve was his last conversation, when Naomi of the cancer center finally called to inform him of her passing. As if he didn't know.

There was no mention of the body's strange condition. No doubt Lucy was still covered in sand and her clothing reeked of campfire smoke. But why would they tell him that? Grieving family members were unpredictable. Explaining the strange discovery was an admission of guilt. They could face a lawsuit for wrongful conduct.

King was certain that whatever strange thoughts the attending physicians must've had over what they found in her room, they planned to keep those thoughts to themselves.

Nurse Naomi only said what all cancer center nurses were required to say. *She passed this morning. It was peaceful. We are sorry for your loss.*

"I'm sorry for your loss," Konstantine said, and the words echoed his own thoughts so closely that it jolted King from his mind and back into the airplane seat.

The small private jet held Konstantine and himself, a pilot, a body-guard that Ricci had given to Konstantine for this trip, and the boy who waited on them all. Another plane full of muscle, the loaned army, would meet them on the Italian airfield. He'd heard the men agree that the muscle and the weapons should travel separate, should either be seized.

"Thank you," King croaked. His throat felt abnormally tight and it burned. Speech seemed impossible.

Konstantine turned away, looking out the window.

"It seems very strange," he began, in his accented English. His hands were loosely clasped over his crossed knee. "After traveling as she does, to be moving so...slowly."

Konstantine looked at the silver watch on his wrist and frowned. "It's been six hours."

That explained the darkness outside the plane window and the fact that the plane carried them forward in time.

King leaned over the armrest and peered out into the impenetrable darkness, one red bulb flashing on the end of the wing, and found the suggestion of gray clouds. He knew the ocean must lay below them, but he didn't care. He didn't care about anything.

"Something may have happened. She has no other reason to leave you in my company so long. Not that I don't enjoy it," Konstantine added diplomatically.

"Perhaps she can't..." King realized what he was about to say. "Maybe she has a hard time catching flights."

Konstantine smiled. "She met Donatello Martinelli on a red eye. New York to Rome."

King hadn't known this. He knew about her careful destruction of

Konstantine's family—a family by blood, not bond—but didn't know the particulars of each kill. One was taken from prison, thought to have escaped. That he remembered because it had been all over the front page of every paper and nighttime news story.

"Do you think she ran into trouble?" King asked. At last the world was coming into focus around him. It was still raw with his grief.

The sounds were too bright. The light of the cabin was too bright. His own pain was too bright.

But he was here. He longed for the part that would come after. The hollowed-out numbness that would rise from the wake of the initial shock. The days he would lie in his bed and feel nothing but emptiness.

It would be a blessed release.

Konstantine smiled. "She's very capable."

"What do we do if we land and she still hasn't come back?"

It was easy sticking to the job, focusing on what needed to be done here and now. He had other thoughts about this man. About his connection to Lou. But in his limited mind all he could think of now was Lucy. The meteor of her death had left a crater-shaped hole where his heart should be.

Konstantine turned toward the window and considered the night. King watched the red light flash on and off on his face.

"You will stay with me as she asked," Konstantine said finally. "I assume you know how to use a gun."

"Of course." *The real trick will be not using it on myself.*

31

Nico knelt over the unconscious woman. The pure rubber in his boots—that which would protect him from the current in the floor should it come on again—found the padding springy, nearly pitching him off his feet and on top of her.

Not that it would have been an entirely unpleasant experience to land on top of that body.

"Strip her," he commanded. And the two men flanking him did as they were told. He didn't trust himself to do the task. Taking off her clothes seemed too intimate a gesture.

They made quick work of it, removing her guns, her armor, and the knives one by one from her slim body until only naked flesh remained.

"Her panties too?" one man asked.

"No," Nico said, perhaps too quickly. That thin swath of cotton was all that was holding his temptation back.

He knew it was in his power to take what he wanted of her. He'd seen the guards in the work camp do it any number of times to the women and the men. Women for pleasure, men for humiliation. Or perhaps pleasure as well. But the sight of the guards' pale, naked asses thrusting, muscles clenching while their pants sagged about the ankles —the way they carried on without regard for who was watching—it sickened Nico. He wouldn't have the men see him in such a way.

"Put the jacket on."

They rolled the woman onto her side. Her beautiful breasts lay on top of one another, her nipples the color of cinnamon. Thankfully the men maneuvered each of her arms into the canvas sleeves and then hid them from his sight.

"Should we bind her legs?"

"There's no need." Without her guns and weaponry, without her power to move like a ghost through this world, she was no threat to him. Under her flesh, under the bones, she was only a woman after all.

Nico dismissed them.

He sank onto his knees beside her aware of the risk. One of the men could turn traitorous. Flip the current on and knock him unconscious too.

They didn't dare.

He watched her chest rise and fall, her black lashes long against her freckled cheeks. Her pale lips were parted, offering the smallest hint of teeth.

He reached forward and brushed the hair back from her face.

Silky smooth.

How long had it been since he'd touched a woman? He couldn't remember. And it wasn't something he'd prioritized upon his return to Italy. He'd had only one ambition once he reached this city. He would see his father's legacy destroyed, his heir ruined. And all of that was going so well.

The world hunted Konstantine. His one advantage, this creature at Nico's feet, couldn't save him. And the surprise lying in wait for Konstantine...

It would rid him of his rival and what remained of his father's house.

Yes, it was all coming together just as he'd planned for all those, long, desperate years.

Despite the terror he'd known in that place, perhaps he should be grateful. For it had allowed him to plan with such painstaking detail, the perfect execution needed to win.

And now...all that remained was to decide what to do with his spoils.

His prisoner of war.

He could keep her in this room always. Visit her. Take from her all that he desired. Put a bullet between her eyes if at last her care became tedious. But that seemed such a waste of her talents.

No. He would win her over.

If such a man as Konstantine had been able to gain her loyalty—why couldn't he?

He was a thousand times the man Konstantine was. She would see that.

You will serve me. He stared at those soft, parted lips. He reached out and stroked her cold cheek. *You will give me the world.*

It was only a matter of time.

32

It was only twenty minutes from the jetway to San Augusto al Monte. But this was enough time for Konstantine to consider Louie's absence with growing dread. He kept remembering her naked, wet body, the way it had looked when she'd stepped from the linen closet into his line of sight, while he cowered in her bath.

She'd been bloody, her scars from every battle shining on her skin.

And when his mind didn't torture him with that glorious vision, he thought of her on the deck of Ryanson's boat, bleeding herself unconscious as King and her aunt tried to fend off death.

These weren't only memories. They were sharp reminders.

She was powerful, yes. The most capable creature he knew, certainly. But she was not immortal.

His heart hammered at the thought. *Mama*, he thought. *Proteggila.*

It was not the first time he'd prayed to his mother. And he knew it wouldn't be the last.

The armored transport van rolled to a stop outside of the church. From this quiet view of the piazza, all looked well. The pigeons bobbed along the cobblestones, pecking at the stones with curious beaks. Somewhere a dog barked and the distant sound of a Vespa cut through narrow alleys, no doubt traffic from the main road several blocks over.

At least the area was vacated. If it hadn't been, Konstantine was sure that the sight of twelve armored trucks rolling up outside the church would have been enough to encourage anyone to head home.

But as it was, it was nearly six in the morning. Traffic was minimal.

In his earpiece, the plan was rehearsed again with Konstantine breaking in only to confirm this or that detail. His ears were busy, but his eyes remained focused on the American in the seat across from him.

He watched the large man suit up. The driver was offering him a loaded Benelli and a vest. King was trying to shrug himself out of his black duster and roll up the sleeves of his collared shirt.

"You must stay in the van," Konstantine said without his thumb on the intercom, so that his voice would remain in this van only.

King didn't protest. Konstantine suspected that had this been anyone else, he would have faced a negotiation. But this man was here in the country illegally and running with a notorious gang. Perhaps he thought that this once, it was best to follow someone else's lead.

Yet Konstantine felt the need to reassure him. "The truck is armored. You will be safe inside it. I will come back as soon it's done."

"Sure."

Konstantine gave the order and black doors opened up and down the street. Men of every shape and color exiting the armored vans, guns drawn.

Then it was only the two of them. Konstantine hesitated.

"If she returns before I'm back," he began, but he wasn't sure how to finish.

"I think we both know she'll be jumping right into the fray," King said with a humorless laugh. "She has no interest in sitting in a van with the old guy."

Konstantine nodded, but this was not what he had meant to say.

He meant if she appeared, wounded or in need, King should call him. King should come into the firefight and get Konstantine as if the mouth of Hell itself had opened.

Konstantine only nodded and stepped away from the van, his own gun warming between his cupped palms. It was cool in the early Florentine morning. Moisture hung in the air and chilled his face and neck. He took a deep breath, gathering his focus and will.

The objective was to kill only Nico and Nico's armed guard, sparing as many of the Ravengers as possible.

But the guns were going off even before Konstantine walked up the stone steps and entered the church through its stone archway. In the slender nave, the temperature shift was ten degrees at least, and it took a moment for his eyes to adjust from the early dawn of the piazza to the candlelit walkways inside the church.

Three men moving in formation ahead of Konstantine were doing a good job of sweeping the area. Too good.

In the upper level, masked men stood guard, their guns pointed down at Konstantine and his men as they entered. Their Harlequin masks and black clothing made them vengeful gods.

They shot everything that moved, without assessing who was truly a foe. Konstantine wove through the pews, seeking protection behind the stone pillars from the flying bullets. But something was not right.

The bullets missed him by wide margins. None of the men who had entered with Konstantine had been shot yet, though gunfire was constant and more than one man stood in the eaves above, with pistols aimed down at them.

A man from the upper landing was shot, and stiff armed, tumbled over the stone bannister and crashed to the floor below. Konstantine went to the man to confirm his suspicion.

"Fuck." He knelt beside the broken body and saw the situation clearly for the first time.

The man was bound with duct tape only able to move enough to give the impression of being alive and in command of his own body. But the gun that Konstantine freed with a blade was not loaded.

Blood poured from the two bullet holes in the man's chest. He pulled back the masquerade mask and saw wide, fearful eyes. Fellini, one of his most loyal men. Konstantine used the tip of his blade to very carefully open the tape covering the man's mouth, the tape that bulged and concaved with each rapid breath.

He's going to die. He's going to die before I even get the tape off.

"I'm so sorry," Konstantine breathed, as he worked to remove the tape as carefully from the man's lips as possible. "Fellini, forgive me." He ripped off the tape, tearing the skin surrounding the mouth.

Of course Nico used his own men to distract him. He would have been a fool to sacrifice his loyal few.

He wasn't the fool Konstantine remembered from his boyhood. He would pay for that mistake now. How high the price was yet to be seen.

Finally the tape was free.

Fellini's breath came out in panicked puffs. His chest heaved and fell in short, sharp exhalations. He was trying to speak.

"Don't," Konstantine begged. "Don't speak. I'll send for the medic."

Into his microphone Konstantine gave the commands. "Stop shooting. It's only my own men who are here. Don't kill them. They are bound and gagged. Gather them up and bring them into the piazza. Send me Romero. I'm between the pews on the right of the nave."

"B-b," Fellini tried again.

"Shhh." He tried to soothe Fellini. "The medic is coming."

But Fellini wouldn't listen, or he perhaps he didn't know Konstantine had spoken at all.

"Bah, bah." The words wouldn't come. Blood bubbled up between his lips, painting them crimson.

Konstantine tried to shush him.

"*Bomb*," he said. His wide desperate eyes fixing on Konstantine's. "*Bomb*."

Konstantine's heart sputtered in his chest. His skin iced as all the blood rushed from the surface, seeking shelter in deeper cells.

A bomb.

"Bomb," Fellini choked out and then the light left his eyes.

Konstantine stood, running for the entry as he shouted. "Bomb! There's a bomb! Everybody out—"

The explosion rocked the cathedral and Konstantine was thrown forward by the force of it.

33

The textured surface of the floor came into focus first. For a moment, all Lou could do was look at the fibers, listening to her breath roll in and out of her nostrils. Then the strange black boots. They looked like the boots worn by an electrical crew and she understood why.

She sat up and noted each sore muscle, no doubt from the current which had coursed through her. Her vest and weapons had been removed and this pissed her off more than the fact that her pants, socks and shoes had been taken too. She couldn't be sure about her shirt, since the stiff canvas of the straitjacket sat close to her skin, but the feel of the harsh fabric against her nipples made her suspect it had been confiscated also.

The old familiar rage bubbled up inside her and she welcomed it. She hadn't felt something quite so seductive, so warm and inviting since Angelo Martinelli was alive, and the idea of killing him had driven her through every morning and night.

She was going to kill this man too. And she was going to enjoy it.

"Perchè stai sorridendo?" he asked. "Why do you smile?"

She didn't answer him. Instead she moved her arms slightly inside the jacket, feeling for weaknesses. It would have been easier to escape had she been awake when they'd laced it up. There was a trick to making one's arms and shoulders bigger in order to allow escape by mere compression of one's muscles. The same was true of handcuffs. But her arms had been relaxed when they wrapped her up. Unfortunately, this meant the fit was quite tight.

She looked into Nico's eyes. They were brown, muddy water, no doubt hiding vipers beneath. She saw where her bullet had grazed his face before, but otherwise he looked well. Damn.

"You must know that I'm Nico. But I don't know your name."

And she wasn't going to give it to him.

"I bet Konstantine knows your name."

A muscle in her face twitch involuntarily. He smiled.

"Cosa ti paga? If you protect him because he pays you, I can pay you more. Whatever the price, I will triple it."

Her tongue rolled over cracked lips. "He doesn't pay me."

He grinned with obvious surprise. "You have a beautiful voice."

She kept measuring the weaknesses in the canvas. If she weren't pinned in this room by the relentless light beating down from above, it would be easy. How many vertical, whirling blades there were in the world. She only needed one small cut in the fabric and she'd be on her way. She knew of a butcher shop in Austin, which hung its meat on hooks. One good snag. That was it.

But there were no shadows. The lights must have been placed just so. And no wonder all of her items were removed. She could have tried to hide beneath a pile of clothing under a body.

But no shadows were cast on the wall. And she realized it was because light came from the walls too. Perhaps from every angle, now that she thought about it.

This room had been designed to contain her. This was what she got for not confirming her kill.

"If it isn't for the money," Nico said, bending down to her level. Here a small shadow did form between his squat legs and the floor, but it must've been no larger than a book, and the palest gray.

Until the lights went off, she was stuck here.

"Do you love him?" Nico asked. "Are you bound to him by...?" He seemed to search for a word. "Affection? Feelings?"

She said nothing.

"He's not even your friend," he said. "It was only a matter of time before he betrayed you. He built this room. Why would he build this room if he didn't plan to keep you in it? Cage you like some animal?"

She knew her face gave him nothing and she was glad for it. Because inside, her heart pounded. The blood throbbing in her temples seemed to be leaking into her vision.

Konstantine held her wrists in the dark, forcing her to have mercy on her abused knuckles. His hot breath in her hair, sliding along her ear. *Did you get to say goodbye?*

Konstantine in her bed, pinned beneath her. How still he'd lain while her desire and grief rolled her like an ocean wave. The feel of his hard chest pressed against her back.

But it was Nico speaking now. "But I don't want to cage you. Think of what we could do together. Don't look at me like that! You don't think Konstantine had the same plans for you? You were only a means to an end."

Her anger crystalized in her chest.

Nico's smile turned wicked, lecherous as he let his eyes rove over her legs. "And what would happen to you when you grew bored of him? When he couldn't satisfy you?"

He inched closer to her.

"You need someone who understands thirst. Hunger. Who knows you can't lay in your own bed at night peacefully because of the hunger inside you."

He placed a calloused hand on her leg.

"Konstantine has had everything given to him, every moment of his life. My father let him want for *nothing*. He could never appreciate you."

Lou met his eyes and saw the wildness in them. *He's a little crazy. More than a little crazy.*

"I would," he said, lowering his voice and looking at her through dark lashes. He placed a sweaty hand on her bare thigh. "I would be a man worthy..."

She brought her leg up swiftly. Her knee connected with his chin. He rocked back on his heels, arms going out to break his fall.

The moment his back hit the padded floor, she was already standing over him. She brought her foot down on his face, splitting the nose like fruit dashed on the floor. Blood erupted from the crushed features, running over the cheekbones like water from a faucet. His rolled onto his side, spitting blood onto the floor in desperate gasping. She kicked him onto his back and collapsed onto him.

She had her legs on either side of his head, squeezing. His face, what part of the skin that wasn't covered in blood, turning purple as he suffocated.

"Is this what you wanted?" she asked him, squeezing harder, aware of his hot breath through her panties. Blood from his busted nose spread slick across her thighs. "Is this how you'll satisfy me?"

A door squeaked open only a second before half a dozen hands seized her, hauling her up and away from Nico. But she wouldn't let go. She squeezed harder and it took two men, then two men more, wedging their fingers between her blood-slicked thighs and his throat before they could pry her legs apart.

No doubt she'd find finger-shaped bruises along her inner thigh later.

She didn't care. She got in one more kick, this one clipping Nico's ear, before they'd safely pulled him from her reach.

She was dropped without ceremony onto the padded floor and Nico was ushered from the room before she could get off the flat of her back.

The moment her back slammed into the padded floor, her compass whirled to life.

Go, go, go.

Konstantine. King. Something had happened.

Go.

"I can't!" she screamed in frustration, knowing that these words meant nothing to the men around her. She wanted to punch someone, scream out her fury. But she was alone in the room, her arms bound and too much light to find relief. She turned and saw Nico's face framed in the door's small window. His face was a bloody mess and his eyes were murderous.

She would have flipped him the bird had her hands been free. She settled with an implied curtsy cut short when fresh electricity surged through the floor.

34

King didn't want to be left alone now. He'd never been the kind of man that needed company. He'd known men like that. Brasso, his ex-partner had been one. He wanted to lunch with the guys, party until the early hours, always with a woman or two under his arm, especially after his wife left him.

But King had always enjoyed his solitude. Until now.

Now every quiet moment was an invitation for his anger and regret. For blame.

Anger that Lucy, given all the lousy fucks in the world, was the one who had to die. Why not any of the worthless men on the planet? Murderers, pedophiles. Rapists.

Regret that he hadn't been in her life sooner, that he'd let twelve years slip by without so much as a fucking phone call. A phone call! How hard could a phone call have been? *Hey, how are you doing? How has life been treating you? I haven't fallen out of love with you. Let's get a coffee.*

He was only distantly aware of the gunfire in the church, the *rat-a-tat-tat* recognizable to anyone familiar with the sound.

King's mind was a million miles away. Back in his old St. Louis brownstone, four blocks from DEA headquarters where he used to walk to work each morning.

He'd already settled into his pajamas, a cold beer in hand and a Rams game on the tube, when Jack turned up on his doorstep in the rain, begging for his help.

He'd looked like a kicked puppy. *I need you to find my sister.*

He hadn't known about Lou's condition then, or even about Lucy herself. But the moment his eyes had fallen on her beautiful face as she stepped out of her Chicago apartment and threw her beautiful legs over the seat of a bicycle...

He should've never let go. *What a fucking fool I am.*

Don't do this to yourself, Robert. Lucy's voice was so bright and clear in his mind that his breath sputtered.

His face pinched and knew he would cry if he didn't pull himself back. Yet he was reaching toward that voice, leaning into it. Anything, no matter how painful, that promised a taste of Lucy Thorne.

The driver eying him in the rearview looked equally alarmed. Babysitting a weeping American man in an armored van wasn't what he'd signed up for.

An explosion rocketed through the church, vomiting stained glass and the wooden doors out onto the street. The van rocked up onto two tires, skidding along the street until it slammed into the adjacent building. The sound of crunching metal assailed King's ears.

It was compounded by the force of the blast.

Then the building was coming down. A slow motion free fall of the collapsing dome and pillars.

Car alarms went off. The dogs that had been merely barking earlier, now howled.

"Shit." King had his door open and was running across the street. The driver shouted Italian after him, but he didn't stop. He peered through the powder-white dust, trying to estimate where the entrance had been.

He supposed he should feel terrible, being delighted by the sudden tragedy. No doubt, someone had died in this blast.

But this was action. This was something to do with the mind that was slowly eating itself alive.

He shoved aside the rubble slowly, methodically. There was a way to do it, to make sure that it didn't collapse and crush any survivors beneath. He focused on the pieces light enough to move by hand. Those that would require a crane or machinery, he left in place.

King knew all about this strategy himself. Brasso had informed him in excruciating detail why it had taken them days to pull him from the destroyed building that'd nearly killed him.

But now he had a new, real fear. That Lou had been in this building. That Lou had been in the middle of the action, as she was wont to do, and had caught the bomb full on.

King couldn't bear it.

He couldn't let himself believe that less than one day after losing Lucy, he would lose Lou too. Lucy had given up years of her life, her home, her time and her heart trying to do right by that girl.

King wasn't going to let that sacrifice be in vain.

His large hands seized a piece of demolished stone and moved it carefully to the side, laying it on top of a more solid rock base.

He kept moving, painfully slow.

"Anyone under there?" he called. He shifted one stone. He was careful not to pull a stone that would compromise his own footing and send him sliding into the rubble himself. He knew firefighters suffocated under the ashen rubble when mistakes were made.

King caught sight of a hand. A bloody hand, with one of its fingers twisted backward, broken at the second knuckle.

He removed three more stones until a smoky white face appeared. The hair may have been dark once, but now it was coated in plaster dust and crumbled stone.

It was as if the man had been turned over in a mound of flour.

King didn't dare pull him from the rubble until only his feet remained hidden.

It wasn't Konstantine.

His eyes were glazed with shock and his limbs trembled.

"Was she in there?" King asked, seeing a thick trail of blood running down the man's head from his ear.

The man didn't answer. He continued to stand on top of the rubble, mumbling Italian to himself.

Others were beginning to emerge from the rubble. Not many. Perhaps only one percent of the men who had entered the building with Konstantine now had two limbs to stand on.

Another man was bleeding profusely from a wound in his throat.

One was coughing up dark blood onto a pile of stones. King

would've bet a thousand dollars he was hemorrhaging internally, and if
he didn't get to a hospital soon, he would die.

But King didn't care about any of them. He cared only about one
person now.

"Did anybody see a woman in there?" he called out. "Uh,
una femma?"

They didn't seem to understand him. He spoke louder, his voice strident with his growing panic. "Lots of guns? Shooting?" He pantomimed
the movement. "Anybody?"

"Chi? Di chi parli?"

"English, goddamn it! Speak *English*."

"She's not here."

King turned toward the voice and found Konstantine pulling himself
from the ashes. He beat the dust from his own clothes and turned to
spit on the ground.

"She's not?" King asked. Relief washed over him. *There is still time.
There is still time to make this right.*

"No." Konstantine beat the dust from his clothes. He looked like a
ghost of his former self, a starving phantom. "But I know where he
has her."

35

Nico stood outside the padded room and spit blood onto the concrete floor. His face hurt like hell. It wasn't only the broken nose that he'd been quick to reset, should it fuse crooked, it was his split lip. His swollen throat that hurt even to swallow. All of it.

He'd sent all his men away, told them that he wanted a minute alone with the bitch to teach her a lesson about respect. They'd hesitated, but only until he'd turned his hateful gaze on them. Then they seemed to have no problem leaving.

She'd come to consciousness much more quickly now.

And she sat in the middle of the room, regarding him with her unwavering eyes. She seemed like a snake, unblinking, unmoving, lying in wait for the perfect moment to strike.

Her unsettling gaze was only intensified by the blood smeared all over her thighs. The bottom of the straitjacket was also dyed bright crimson.

Nico's blood.

If only she had some on her mouth, then the look would be complete. A lunatic sitting in a padded cell, and waiting for her chance to escape.

He had tried to reason with her. Tried to appeal to the bloodthirst he saw so clearly in her eyes. But he knew that none of it mattered now.

She wouldn't serve him.

He was beginning to doubt that she had ever served Konstantine.

Perhaps their paths had simply crossed. Or perhaps they had been interested in the same end. It didn't matter. It didn't change the fact that Nico would have to kill her now.

He wouldn't make the mistake of getting close to her again. He only needed to be bitten once, so to speak, to understand the danger.

She hadn't needed her weapons or her armor to kill him. She hadn't even needed the use of her arms.

No.

He wouldn't challenge her. He would electrocute her into unconsciousness, using this red push button beside the reinforced metal door. And when she was out, he would go in and slit her throat.

He would watch the blood pour from her onto the padded floor, running along the creases where the cushions meet, as red as a Biblical river.

Such a waste, he thought. But it was better than the alternative. That he let her live only to find his own throat slit in an alley hours, days, or weeks from now.

His index finger went to the red button, hovered over it as he looked into those brown, unmoving eyes.

She smiled at him. Smiled as if she knew what he was about to do.

And he understood now why the men were so frightened of her. Why they called her Konstantine's *strega*.

He mashed the red button. Her back arched, body twisting. She was flung back, rolling on the padded floor, every muscle in contraction.

"Agostino! Agostino!" the men called. Feet pounded down the concrete hallway, running toward him.

He hesitated, looking away from her long enough to see what the commotion was about.

"Someone is here," they said. The youngest, a man with a buzzed haircut and beady eyes put his hands on his knees as if to catch his breath. He jabbed one thumb over his shoulder. "Someone is coming up the driveway."

Nico gave the unconscious woman one more look before turning away from the door.

Slitting her throat would have to wait.

Reluctantly he followed the messengers through the winding corridors, up the stairs to the atrium of the reception area. This had once been the main villa of this winery, no doubt overrun with tourists or wine enthusiasts. But no one had been here in a long time.

They'd found over two thousand dusty wine bottles in the cellar and moth-eaten furniture covered in white sheets. The sheets themselves were splattered with bird shit and inches of dust.

Sunlight spilled through the windows onto the portico.

Nico stepped out of the villa and onto the stone walk, giving himself a full view of the driveway. A kilometer and a half, maybe two out, he saw what had frightened the guards.

A line of armored trucks came single-file down the driveway, their tires spitting debris. Clouds of dust swirled up into the sky.

So the bomb hadn't ended Konstantine at all.

He was likely too cowardly to go into the church himself. It was probably his men that were killed in the blast. Just as well. He would enjoy ending Konstantine himself.

With his own bare hands.

He was certain he'd enjoy it even more than murdering the little lunatic downstairs.

"Tell everyone to suit up," he said to the silent guards. "Konstantine is coming."

36

The truck bumped along the country road, forcing the men to jostle back and forth on the opposite benches. Konstantine's eyes were trained on the passing countryside outside the truck's window. He kept opening and closing his fist, and then catching himself doing it, forced his hand motionless and flat against his leg.

If Nico hurts her, so much as bruises *her...*

He scanned the interior of the truck. Nine or ten men were in this van. Probably eighty in all, if he counted the entire 7-truck caravan. He couldn't be sure how many men Nico would have at his disposal, but he expected as many as a hundred. He would be a fool to have fewer than a hundred in the event that she was able to rise against him.

He would find one of three scenarios at the winery.

In the first scenario, all of the men are dead. He imagined bodies strewn in the portico, pools of blood beneath them. Maybe he would find them slumped on the stairways or sitting against the wall with their brains drying on the stucco.

If this was the situation, it meant Lou had saved herself. And no doubt, Konstantine would be dead before the sun reached high noon. She wouldn't wait for him to explain himself. She'd end him before the moon rose.

In the second scenario, he would fight his way through Nico and

Nico's men and save her from the padded room where he was no doubt holding her. And he would have a chance to explain what he'd done and why he'd done it.

In the third and final scenario, King would succeed in severing the power to the building and the lights would be turned off. In that momentary blackness, she would free herself, join them in the fight, and no doubt slaughter them all. Hopefully she would see King, know that it was Konstantine who'd come to save her—and that might buy his life.

He didn't expect gratitude. In fact, he expected a knife to the gut. But at least he would have a chance to explain himself in the latter two scenarios.

A chance to explain was the very best he could hope for now.

He sighed and ran a hand through his hair. He surveyed the men sitting knee-to-knee on the benches. The men faced each other on opposing benches, bulletproof glass windows framing the passing world beyond. Those who met his eyes politely looked away. The American cop didn't. But he wasn't truly seeing Konstantine either.

He wore his grief like a mask. The eyes fathoms deep and full of shifting shadows.

"Are you sure you can do this?" Konstantine asked.

King's eyes focused, light sparking in them. "Another gun wouldn't hurt."

"Of course. And I will send some of the men with you." He quickly added, "For cover."

He didn't want to insult the cop with words like for *your protection* or *in case you fuck up*.

He suspected the American wasn't fooled. He seemed to understand the implication clearly.

"My entrance will be the diversion you need. Stick to the plan and you should be fine."

"You don't think he will have someone guarding the box?" King asked, the purple bags under his eyes pronounced.

Konstantine forced a patient smile. "That's what the gun is for."

He hoped his façade of control remained intact. In reality, his nerves jumped and twitched beneath his skin. Sweat collected on the back of his neck. The interior of this truck was too hot. Too crowded. He wanted to open the back door and throw himself on the dirt road.

He remained in his seat, reviewing his plan for the thousandth time.

No doubt the power box providing electricity to the main house was guarded. And if Nico was aware of it, the generator as well. He hoped the man was oblivious to its existence, but in reality, the fact that he was here at the winery at all was evidence enough that he knew—and understood—Konstantine's investment in the place.

The winery lurched into view. A sprawling compound amongst the orchard rows. The green hills framed the ancient home beautifully. Sunlight shone on its sienna roof. He counted fourteen vehicles in the circle drive outside the exterior wall. Craning his neck, he looked out over the field to a structure in the distance.

"Once I get out, the truck will carry you out to the...workhouse," he said. He hesitated with the word *workhouse*, unsure if that was the best translation for the distant structure where the equipment and the generator were kept. The cop seemed to understand.

To his own men, the few they'd saved from the rubble of Padre Leo's desecrated church, he spoke Italian. "Tenetelo in vita se viene ucciso, dovete finire il lavoro. Tagliate il corrente."

He didn't expect the men to give their lives for some American they didn't know. But he wanted them to at least try to help him fulfill their mission. Though he wasn't sure any of these men knew how to disable the electricity.

The tires ground to a stop and the back doors to the truck swung open. They waited for open gunfire, for some retaliation. But they were only met with eerie silence. No bird song. No wind through the grass. It was the silence before the tempestuous storm tore off the roof. Dirt shifted as the other trucks pulled up beside them, mixing with those already parked.

All the men filed from the truck with the exception of the driver, King and the two men that would accompany him. Konstantine's boots hit the road and he turned back to the cop one more time. For now the open doors shielded him from any incoming fire, should they try to eliminate him before he even entered the portico.

"Remember you must disable the generator first," Konstantine said, unsure if he was saving, or damning his life with these instructions. *She will listen. She will understand. Dio mio,* he hoped so.

King only nodded and the doors to the van closed between them.

Konstantine hesitated, watching the van circle around the parked cars before pulling out of his sight, leaving a trail of dust in its wake, the only sign it had been there at all.

Konstantine adjusted the body armor, checking the fit across his chest.

I must look like Lou, he thought. His head to toe black clothing. Protective plating over his thighs and outer arms. The chest and groin protected as well. The six guns within arm's reach and a belt's worth of ammo.

He saw men on the upper terrace then. Guns pointed at him from all directions.

But calmly they crossed beneath the archway and through the courtyard. They moved through the portico.

Nico didn't let them get far.

He stepped from the shadows and out into the early morning light.

"Konstantine," he said. His grin was wolfish, his eyes. "You didn't get my message, did you?"

Several of the men, more and more of them emerging from the shadows, laughed at their master's teasing tone.

Konstantine saw he was outnumbered perhaps three to one. But Ricci's men were good at what they did. As well as those who'd remained loyal to Konstantine himself. He would have to hope it was enough. Or that they would get lucky.

Nico's gaze was malicious. Hungry. "You aren't wanted, my friend. How embarrassing that you keep trying to take something that doesn't belong to you."

Konstantine noted his swollen nose, the purple-black bruise spreading across his face. The way his eyes were nearly swollen shut.

He smiled despite the rage wrenching his insides. He gestured toward Nico's nose. "Looks like I'm not the only one trying to take something that doesn't belong to me."

Several of Ricci's men laughed and Nico's eyes caught fire.

Konstantine saw the shirt hanging from Nico's pocket and the world stopped on a dime. It was the shirt he'd last seen on Lou that morning. It was bloody and torn.

Nico followed his gaze and grinned when he realized what Konstantine was looking at.

He pulled the shirt from his back pocket and lifted it up to his face as if to smell it. It was for show. That busted nose wasn't smelling a damn thing. It enraged Konstantine all the same.

"What did you really come for, Konstantine?" Nico asked, eyes ablaze over the bloody, ravaged cotton. "The Ravengers? The woman? Or your pride?"

Konstantine pulled his gun in a single movement and before he'd even exhaled the air from his lungs, he fired.

37

A gunshot made King's head snap up. He pivoted on the bench, craning his neck so that he could see out the armored van's window. He saw nothing but the smattering of cars collected in the circle drive beside the villa. It was the sort of villa he'd expected to find in the Tuscan hills. Though he couldn't be sure they were in Tuscany at all. They'd been in Florence that morning, but in what direction they'd driven after the church had been brought down, he couldn't be sure.

Thinking of the van rocking on its heels in the blast, the sight of that stone façade crumbling—not out, as one might think—but in on itself. It had triggered him. It gave him sweaty palms, a shallow pant and knocking heart.

King could forget about his claustrophobia on most days, so it was always surprising when it reared up unexpectedly and seized him again. And here he was amongst all these unfamiliar faces…it wasn't the time to fall apart. No matter how much his fear rolled him, or his grief.

Lucy.

He saw her beautiful smile. The way she'd looked when she'd slipped her arms around his neck and came up onto her toes to kiss him. First his nose, then each cheek, before impatiently, he seized her mouth with his own.

That life seemed so far away. Like a vivid dream he'd had years ago, but could still remember with shocking detail. It shone in its strange way. And Lou...

Where the hell are you?

He didn't believe she was dead. Couldn't believe it. That she would leave this world at all was like seeing the sun gone from the sky. The Louie Thorne he knew wouldn't miss this firefight for anything in the world. She was hurt or detained somehow.

Had to be.

The truck bounced to a stop outside a large shed. The back door opened and King slid from the bench into the open air.

He saw the villa in the distance.

Something whistled past his head and slammed into the armored door.

A second bullet followed. It bit the metal five or six inches from his face.

"Shit!" He ducked and took cover on its other side while the men around him burst into action.

More bullets flew as King hurried toward the shed, his hands over his head as if that would stop a bullet.

When he reached the wooden door of the shed, he found it locked with a large chain and padlock. King pressed the eye of his gun against the chain and pulled the trigger. Part of the metal was blasted away but he still had the slow task of getting it unhooked from the chain and unfastening the door.

The firefight continued around him and he couldn't be sure from which direction the men were coming. Only that they must be on the other side of the van. Something heavy slammed into metal. There was a distinct *thump - POP* and King suspected it was a body hitting the armored plating.

If I don't get inside, I'm going to be next.

The last of the chain fell away and he pried open the door.

The dark was nearly complete, with only thin beams of light filtering through cracks in the dilapidated roof above. King kept moving, heading toward the back of the shed where Konstantine had been sure the generator waited.

King found it, a bulky black box in a corner, with only dirt beneath it and rough wooden walls on either side. He bent down, his fingers rushing to inspect the surface for a plug to pull or wire to disconnect— any hint at how it might be disabled.

He found a thick cable running from the back of the machine to the wall. Then the cable continued up the wall, disappearing behind the landing above.

He pulled the cable, trying to wiggle it from its socket.

Nothing.

Placing his boots on either side of the box, he pulled again, throwing all his weight into it.

The cord popped free with a spark.

The shed door bounced open and three men clambered inside. They weren't Konstantine's men.

Before they realized where he was and what he was doing, he began to climb. He used a wooden ladder to follow the wiring up the side of the shed's wall. He climbed quickly, pausing only when a bullet punched a hole beside his head, offering a bright pinhole of sunlight. Then he climbed even faster.

He didn't understand Italian and had no idea what they shouted. But with every bullet hole and new pinprick of light, the message was clear.

Then he was shot.

A bullet bit into the meat of his lower left side. Something in his back spasmed and he almost fell off the ladder. One hand released completely and for a moment he hung there, unsure if he would crash to the dirt below. Then more gunfire erupted and the shouts commenced. But they didn't seem to be directed at him any longer. Someone else had entered the fray and was drawing the fire away from him.

He resumed his climb and with much effort hauled himself onto the wooden platform above.

His back burned. The fire in his lower back spread in all directions, sucking the air from his lungs.

But he crawled forward, still following the electrical lines, hoping to find the place where they met some sort of circuit box. His shaking hands caught on the rough wooden floor. The dirt and grit dusted his palms. His chest constricted and he coughed.

His hands grasped blindly in the darkness until his fingers found cool metal and then a switch. He flipped it, or he thought he did.

His vision swam. His limbs were so heavy that he felt as if he were underwater, trying to swim toward a surface he would never reach.

Just as well, he thought. *It wasn't worth it without you.*

38

Nico saw the gun jump in Konstantine's hand. Then the bullet slammed into the vest hugging his chest. He stumbled back a step, but didn't fall. The sting was nothing compared to the joy he felt in seeing the hatred on Konstantine's face.

So calm, so collected. Padre's perfect bright boy.

A pleasant boy who made friends effortlessly with his easy manners. He was never rattled, never overcome by emotion. Nico had always known better. He might wear a mask for the men around him, but the woman was the key.

She would be his destruction. The gap in his armor where Nico could drive the blade home.

Both sides pulled their firearms and the shooting began.

Gunfire erupted in the courtyard. Nico had time to dive behind a partial wall for cover. Konstantine's eyes never left him. He dodged the crossfire and raging men to make his way closer. Nico followed his movements behind the lattice work, but it wasn't possible to get a clear shot from here.

He peeked around the corner, gun up. Konstantine fired at him immediately. His bullet bit into the stucco beyond his head, blasting a quarter-sized chunk of wall away. Nico fell back, rounded a corner and took off down the hallway. He would come around the other side, through the adjacent door and snare him from behind.

Nico turned a corner, expecting to find another hallway. Instead he caught a fist to the face.

He rocked back on his heels, his shoulder clipping the wall. A door behind him snapped open and they crashed into a kitchen. He staggered past the counter and stools. Nico tumbled, taking a stool down to the floor with him in a clatter.

He opened his eyes the second before his nose was seized. Pain exploded through his face and he screamed. Two fingers squeezing the wounded bridge forced water from his eyes.

"Brother," Konstantine climbed onto the man's chest. The light behind Konstantine's head burned like a halo, wrapping his face in shadow. It could be anyone delivering this vengeance. His own father. God.

Nico brought his knee up, felt it connect with its mark and Konstantine stiffened.

Nico gained the upper hand. He rolled on top of the other man, pinning him down with his own weight. His head bounced off the floor. Now Konstantine was on the flat of his back, his face spotlighted by the overhead bulb.

The gunfire and men shouting continued, but this was better.

He could take his time in here. Enjoy this revenge that was always owed to him.

How should he begin? In what ways could he hurt Konstantine the most, wring the most pleasure from this moment?

"I don't want you to worry about your woman." Nico laughed, pulling his blade. "She's cold now but any horse can be broken, if ridden hard enough."

Konstantine tried to buck him, his fury clear in his eyes. But Nico knew how to keep the other man down.

"Since your gang is mine now, and your woman..." He pressed his blade against Konstantine's face. "What is there left to take, Konstantine? Your pretty face? Your life?"

He drew the blade across Konstantine's cheek, splitting the flesh. He started at the chin and moved upward, toward the eye. Like unzipping a woman's dress.

Konstantine screamed.

Maybe Nico would take it. The eye. Keep it in a jar on his bedside, even after he disposed of this corpse. Something pleasant to look at, to assure him of his power, before he drifted off to sleep each night. The tip of the blade had just reached the cheekbone when the light overhead clicked off.

For a moment, Nico sat in the shadows, his blade hovering above Konstantine's eye.

Gunfire faltered and the house was filled with the sound of men running.

The light overhead clicked back on.

Konstantine laughed as blood welled from his cut face and painted half his face and ear red. "You lost power. Do you know what that means, amico mio?"

The cut opened and spread as he spoke, blood pouring into the eye and over the cheek.

Nico launched himself off Konstantine. He was down the corridor without looking back. Konstantine's cruel laughter trailed after him, but he barely noticed. He hooked a right, another left and reached the cellar stairs. He took the stone steps three and four at a time, his hands pressed against the cool wall for balance. Then he launched down the lit corridor. The lights flickered. The hallway darkened and then it came on again.

Something was wrong with the generator. That was why the overhead lights sputtered to life only to darken again. The flickering unnerved him. He expected the light to come on and reveal her there in the narrow hallway, standing before him as if from nowhere, a momentary phantom before she put a bullet between his eyes.

Or maybe she was still unconscious. Maybe she hadn't noticed the light had cut off at all and the generator would hold. He ran toward the door at the end of the hallway.

He had to know.

He had to confirm it with his own eyes. When he almost reached the metal door with its one viewing window, he slowed, his steps now cautious.

The lights stayed on.

He took a breath and cranked the large handle. The chamber door creaked loudly as it swung open to reveal the padded room. The room was lit again, but only partially.

Shattered glass sparkled like glitter on the floor, the ripped and bloody straitjacket lay in the center.

39

She was so angry, it took her three tries to get her pants buttoned. Her trembling hands missed the buttonhole with each furious swipe. But as soon as Lou had a black t-shirt over her head, she descended the stairs into her armory. It wasn't until she surveyed the shelves, counting gun after gun, that the calm finally began to return.

She chose each weapon with Nico Agostino's face blazing in the forefront of her mind.

Grenades went into her pockets.

She eyed the flamethrower lovingly, but had to be honest. It would limit her mobility. And with so many men crawling about that villa, she couldn't be hampered. So she stuck to what worked. Kevlar sleeves and a vest—though not her father's. And this loss only made her hatred burn hotter. As she loaded a new twin pair of Berettas and slipped them into hip holsters, she ran a list through her mind of all the little tortures she'd like to inflict on Nico.

A belt sat around her hips. She filled it with the bullets to be pumped from her gun.

She took a deep breath in the place that smelled of gunmetal and sawdust and the muscles in her back released. With more guns than hands, she felt like herself again.

Let him go, she warned herself. *Let him go for now.*

Her mind growled the way a dog would over a bone.

But if she thought too much about Nico, about his momentary seizure of her power, the rage would overtake her. It would claim the reins of her mind and set fire to all the control she'd carefully built there.

So she turned off her skittering thoughts. She gave her mind over to the dark, and shifted her compass to the foreground. It would be only instinct now. Instinct to carry her through the maze of this firefight and nothing more.

It had never failed her before.

Her armory dematerialized and in its place, a barn was built up around her. Or maybe this was a shed. The floor was dirt, the corners cluttered with unused machinery. At one end, twenty or thirty feet on her right, men clambered up a wooden ladder.

Lou didn't know what was so damned important on the landing above, what they were desperate to reach. She shot them anyway. The first, the one highest on the ladder, took a bullet to the back of his head and the force of it slammed his face forward into the rungs. The face-plant was followed by a limp, loosening of every muscle. When he fell, he took the two men from the lower rungs with him. He was dead before they hit the ground.

One man lay on top of the other, like turtles stacked on their backs, arms paddling air.

She shot the second man, who was trapped beneath the dead weight of the first, in his face. The gore exploded out the back of his head, and painted the face of the third. A crimson mask with wide, unblinking eyes.

Lou shot him too. Then a second, third and fourth bullet were pumped into their faces as if it mattered. The trigger clicked, empty.

Reload. She never took her eyes off the dead trio, waiting for even the smallest twitch.

She was done fucking around. If only she'd emptied her gun into Nico's face, she wouldn't have been locked inside that wretched room.

Blood dripped onto her outstretched hand. The droplet ran from knuckle to thumb. For a heartbeat, she thought it was from her kill. But gravity didn't work that way. She looked up and saw blood pooled on the landing above. It had seeped through the space between boards and was collecting like condensation.

The shadow where two shed walls met took her to the upper landing.

It reminded her of the fish house in Miami. And having learned a lesson there, she crept forward cautiously, wary of any loose planks.

King lay on his side, breath ragged. In one hand he held the end of a black cable. Lou understood now that it was King who'd freed her. When he cut the power, she'd been able to slip through the shadows to the butcher's shop in Austin. One rip in the canvas and she had the jacket off.

The smell of fresh air and dirt mixed with the scent of blood. An earthy, ancient scent.

"King." She knelt beside him. His skin was clammy and his pulse too quick. She pulled the cable from his weak grip. *He stayed with Konstantine like you told him to. And it saved your life.*

A surprising wave of affection washed over her. "King. I have some beignets for you."

He groaned.

She smirked. "Hang in there if you want those beignets."

A tarp hung over a wooden bannister. Lou slid it off the wooden post and threw it over King and herself. She pulled him through the dark beneath it, no doubt resembling a magician's disappearing trick.

Now you see them, now you don't.

They appeared outside a hospital somewhere in New Orleans—at least, that's what Lou had been aiming for.

It was raining. Fat droplets beat the parking lot stretching out before her, the sound of tires treading shallow streams.

"Excuse me," she said.

The man smoking beside the entrance jumped. "Holy shit!"

His violent trembling caused the cigarette between his fingers to jump and fall to the sidewalk. He wore a white lab coat over turquoise scrubs. *Dr. Jindal* the plastic tag said.

"He's been shot," she said. "Admit him."

"Where the hell—"

Lou pulled her Beretta and pointed it at the doctor. "Admit him. Now."

The doctor howled and disappeared through the automatic doors. Light spilled onto the paved walkway where Lou crouched, protected from the rain. The cool breeze wafting through the walkway pushed the hair back from her face and chilled her cheek. It had the first promise of winter in it, a hint of ice behind the clouds.

King's eyes seemed to rove the mulched beds and bushy plants lining the sidewalk. His breathing was too shallow. Lou slapped his cheek, hoping to bring focus to that distant gaze.

"I'll be back," she said.

She moved to stand, but his hand shot out and seized hers.

Now his eyes were perfectly clear. "Don't."

"I'm not done with Nico," she said, gently.

"Don't—"

"I'll be back," she promised. She reversed the grip easily and squeezed him hard, giving him something to feel beside the pain. "I'm not done with you either."

The sliding door opened and five personnel emerged. Two women in scrubs pushed a bed like the one Lucy spent the last weeks of her life in. A third held a long, plastic board that looked like a poorly designed sled. Neon orange with hand-holes lining each side. The fourth and fifth were the doctor who'd been smoking and an officer no doubt here to arrest Lou for pulling a gun.

A long plastic sled was laid onto the concrete beside King.

"1, 2, 3." They lifted him and placed him on the stretcher before transferring him to the white cot. Lou waited until he was pushed through the automated doors into the hospital, but she'd taken a step back toward the shadows.

The officer peered into the dark, trying to see the woman the doctor described.

A sharp flash of lightning illuminated the breezeway, defining the pillars and walkway, the east side of the hospital and its meticulous landscaping. A heartbeat later, thunder rolled.

But the officer didn't see anyone.

If there had been a woman, she was gone.

40

Lou stepped from the hospital breezeway, alive with cool, electric rain, into the heat of an Italian sunshine. She took a breath, adjusting to the shift, then put King behind her. She couldn't think of him now, not with an army of men to face and vengeance to be had.

A dusty room sheltered her. Forgotten furniture sat beneath white sheets. This part of the house was quiet. She slipped out into the hall, following the sound of gunfire. She moved the Beretta to the left hand and pulled the Browning with her right. Two hands, two guns. That was better.

She turned a corner and found two men beating the hell out of each other. They traded knee strikes to the guts, feral punches to the face. A tooth, knocked loose, sailed across the room and skidded to halt at her feet. She was almost sorry to interrupt the show.

Lou put a bullet in each before stepping over their dropped corpses.

Around the next corner—what a maze this compound was—she found men exchanging gunfire across balconies. They popped up and down over the railings like weasels, bullets spit back and forth over the heads of the men fighting in the portico below.

Lou shot two from behind and as the third was turning, put a bullet in his throat, severing his cry midstream. He slumped, glassy eyed against the bannister. Taking their place, Lou fired across and got two men on the opposite balcony right away. The third went down and stayed down. No matter. Lou stepped into the corner of one balcony and emerged from the corner of the other. She shot the hidden man from behind with ease.

It was very easy to shoot the other two remaining men. Their mouths came open in surprised *Os* as they turned to find her suddenly standing over them, guns in hand.

She surveyed the portico and counted no less than forty men exchanging fire. Bullets whistled through the air in all directions. Others relied on their fists or knives. More than one blade caught the sunlight and flashed it against the walls. One man had a lead pipe as long as his forearm, which he swung into the skull of another. That skull deflated like a basketball on impact.

But she didn't see Konstantine.

Someone darted out of an adjacent room and crossed the portico in a panicked stride. She recognized Nico by her handiwork. His busted nose had crusted over nicely with thick, black blood. She raised the gun but he'd already turned a corner and disappeared. Damn.

He hadn't seen her from her claimed balcony.

What would he think when he saw the ripped jacket on the floor? She'd thrown it there only to frighten him. A loud and clear, *I'm coming for you.*

She hoped it had scared the hell out of him.

Nico. He would be the dessert after the end of a good meal.

Sweeping the portico, checking one last time for Konstantine, she removed a grenade from her pocket and unpinned it. She tossed it into the densest cluster of men, bodies so entwined it was hard to tell which violent limb belonged to which body.

The grenade exploded. Throwing men, blood, and dust in all directions. One side of the villa gave way, cascading like a mudslide from roof to earth.

Lou stepped from the balcony down into the thick of it.

She moved through the dust cloud, using it as cover. As soon as a clear shape emerged from the chaos, she seized it. She put bullet through bone. Silenced screams with strikes to the throat. She had to reload twice, tossing aside empty magazines in a careless way she'd never dared to before.

On her fourth reload, the dust cleared and she met Konstantine's eyes.

He leaned against a doorway. A kitchen stood behind him, the barest hint of a gleaming work surface and white cabinets.

His face was destroyed, the meat of his cheek lay open, revealing muscle and bone beneath. Blood clung like a bandana over half his face, making his green eyes seem even brighter.

Fear reared up inside her, clogging her throat and nose, setting fire to her insides.

She raised her gun and aimed. A flicker of doubt flashed in Konstantine's eyes before she shifted her aim to the right and took out the two men coming at him.

Seeing him had stopped her, but she wasn't done. She remembered herself. Using the last of the dust to shield her, she moved methodically to shoot down the few men still struggling to escape the cloud. She gave herself over to the task, pulling the trigger whenever a target emerged. A vital organ. A skull. The side of an exposed throat—all the temptation she needed.

"Se seite con me!" Konstantine called out over the firefight. "Vattene prima che ti uccida!"

Men ran in every direction. They scurried like rats through the portico, out into the sunlight. Car doors slammed shut. Tires spun in the dirt.

Lou found the second grenade in her pocket.

Some of the men had regrouped in the east corner of the portico, they were working their way toward Konstantine. They became her new target. She pulled the pin and threw.

1...2...3...4...*BOOM.*

Dirt and brick and bodies were thrown into the air like confetti. The water main burst spewing a geyser ten feet into the air. A severed forearm with a serial number tattoo splattered against the walkway three feet from Lou.

The men who hadn't run at Konstantine's first warning, ran now.

All gunfire ceased, the cacophonous choir replaced with screams.

The spraying water settled the dust from this second explosion more quickly. Lou stood in the rain shower and turned in a slow circle, guns up.

Corpses lay heaped in nearly every corner of the portico, thrown about as carelessly as a child's toys. The water from the busted main ran red, washing away the spilled blood from the flagstones.

She was soaked from head to toe. But no one remained. Except Konstantine.

She turned her gun on him.

"Wait!" he said, lifting his hands in surrender.

Watching his deformed cheek flap with his efforts at speech disturbed her. But she didn't lower her gun. All that was left was the wreckage, the bodies and the unspoken words between them. She was too close to finishing this to quit now.

He licked blood from his lips. "You are angry about the room."

"A room without shadows that electrocutes me into compliance. What's there to be mad about?"

"I can explain."

She put a bullet into the wall beside his head.

He flinched. "My face hurts. Can we—"

She emptied the rest of the clip into the same wall. So much for saving bullets.

"I was afraid of you." He licked his lips and more blood smeared across his tongue. His teeth were red with it. "I want us to be allies. More than allies. But you are your father's daughter. Your father—"

She took a step toward him, jaw tight. The gun was trained on that piece of flesh sitting between his eyebrows.

Konstantine's eyes fluttered, but he kept his position. His voice was stronger now. His own anger rose up to meet hers. "Your father was a good man but he was a fool."

A cold fire burned through Lou's chest. The gun jumped at the end of her sight.

"The world isn't black and white. It isn't us and them. This side, that side. He was played by the system he served."

"And Padre Leo was the Pope. And your mother was a saint. "

He looked down at his feet. He took a slow breath, collecting himself before meeting her gaze again.

"We must be better. We can't see the world as they saw it."

"How is building a room like that *better*?"

"I never wanted to use it."

"It seems very functional for a room that was never supposed to be used. And that fucking straitjacket!"

"I didn't buy the jacket. That was Nico."

"Okay, just the padded room then. Got it."

Konstantine's breaths were ragged. "I began building the room when you tried to kill me in June. But it was only meant to keep you from hurting me. It was never designed to hurt you. The current in the floor was only if you refused to be reasoned with. If every attempt to speak was met with violence. If I'd wanted to hurt you, or kill you, I wouldn't have picked electricity and a padded room to do it."

"You built the room because you were afraid I wouldn't stop trying to kill you?"

Her rage rose and crested. Rose and crested and with each punishing wave her arm trembled. Her whole body shook.

"Yes. It may come as a surprise to you, but I don't *want* to be murdered."

Too bad. She wanted to kill him. She wanted to wrap her hands around his throat and squeeze the light out of those infuriating green eyes. And yet—and yet...

He could have killed her at any time. He could have killed her months ago on Ryanson's boat when she was nearly unconscious with blood loss. He could have killed her in her own damn apartment. There were a hundred opportunities over the last few days. And it wasn't like she didn't have enough guns lying around for him to manage it.

But he had never so much as pointed a gun at her. Could she say the same? No.

It was more than that.

Her father *had* been a fool. She'd thought so herself a thousand times. When she learned how Gus Johnson had sold him out. Chaz Brasso had ordered the hit. Both men from his own department. His so-called friends. He was a fool for not seeing how power hungry the men around him were.

And a fool about Lucy, the sister he abandoned until he needed her to save his own kid.

Thinking all of this felt like a betrayal. To love him, but to also see the fault in him...

It hurt.

Konstantine saw her struggle and lowered his voice, speaking gently. "I'd hoped to never use that room. That isn't what I want for us."

He straightened himself, pushing off the doorway that had held so much of his weight. He took a step toward her. "Whatever I may be to you—now, or later—I'm not your enemy."

Lou lowered her gun.

And a bullet slammed into her upper arm. The force of it knocked her to the ground, into the water. Fire ate through the meat of her arm into her shoulder joint. It set her whole left side ablaze.

Fucking bastard.

She was going to kill him.

She sat up, seeing the stream of blood pouring down her arm, mixing with the small flood still pooling from the ruptured water main.

But by the time she pulled her gun and trained it on the doorway where Konstantine had just stood, it was empty.

A gun went off again and a guttural scream full of animalistic rage rebounded through the portico.

Her eyes were drawn to a flurry of movement.

Konstantine and Nico were locked in battle. One, two, three rapid fire punches slammed into the side of Nico's face and he went to one knee. His gun fell from his hand and splashed in the water. And Konstantine was already lifting his foot to stomp him.

He rolled away and the boot came down in a puddle of water. Nico pulled a knife and slid it into the meat of Konstantine's calf.

He howled and pitched forward onto his hands and knees.

Right.

Konstantine couldn't have put a bullet in her arm from that angle. Nico must have emerged from the basement, spotted them talking and shot her. It's her own damn fault for letting Konstantine distract her, letting her anger get the best of her. If only she could've forgotten about the damned terror room for five minutes, she would've remembered the real threat.

No point in crying over fuckups. It was time to fix it.

Lou tore the belt off her pants and buckled it tight around her shoulder. It limited her movement, but it would also keep her from bleeding out.

Konstantine ripped the knife from his calf and buried it in Nico's shoulder. He used his good leg to kick Nico back into the adjacent wall. But he only rebounded, as if on a spring board.

Konstantine screamed. Nico had his thumb in one of Konstantine's old bullet wounds, probing deep. Fresh blood bubbled up around the thumb as Konstantine seized the wrist, trying to rip the hand away.

Arm secure, Lou was up and moving just as Nico twisted his grip and wrenched another scream from Konstantine's throat.

One hard kick to Nico's side sent him sprawling off of Konstantine. Lou had her hands around his neck, hauling him up before he'd fully landed.

Slipping to the balcony above, she kicked him once, twice. He coughed and spat blood onto the floor.

When he whipped the knife toward her own legs she jumped up in time to feel it catch the bottom of her boot. She twisted the wrist, took the knife and tossed it over the railing.

Then she hurled him over the railing after it.

He didn't even have time to scream before his body hit the wet stones of the portico.

Something cracked on impact. Lou peered over the railing to see the leg bent. From the knee, it twisted off at an unnatural angle.

But Nico wasn't giving up that easy. He tried to drag himself to sitting, slapping at the water as if to find his gun. Lou had relieved him of it on the balcony and left it there as she traveled down to the main level through the shadows.

Her boots now uneven on the bottom, sent ripples through the water.

Nico found the knife in the water.

Lou kicked it away.

He spotted a gun dropped by someone two or three feet to the right. He clawed for it. Until Lou brought her boot down and crushed the hand. Something snapped.

She pulled her own gun and trained it on his face.

"Konstantine!" Nico screamed, his face red, veins popping in fury. "We were supposed to be brothers! *Nostro padre lo voleva!*"

Konstantine dragged himself across the portico.

"He gave you everything." Nico's teeth chattered. "Everything that was mine! You owe me! At the very least you owe me my life!"

Lou arched an eyebrow. "You can lock him in a padded room. Since that's what you like to do to people who try to kill you."

Konstantine's stood hunched, his pained body folded in on itself. "No."

He trained the pistol at Nico's face and fired four times. The first bullet punched a hole clean through the skull. The other three only widening the first.

The gunshots echoed through the portico before being swallowed up by the rushing water.

For a long time neither of them said anything. They only stood over Nico's body and watched his blood darken the water around him.

Nico's eyes remained open, seeing nothing.

"So we're not enemies?" she said at last. She lifted her mangled boot and scowled at the scarred sole. *Bastard.*

"No." Konstantine fingered his wounded cheek, hissing. "But if you still want to kill me, please do it now. My face hurts. Unbearably."

"I'm not in the mood." She bent and seized Nico's collar, hefting his soaked body. He'd make a good meal for her six-legged friend. "Maybe next time."

EPILOGUE

King stepped out from beneath the green awning and into Jackson Square. He sipped his coffee and watched a man paint a Bob-Ross worthy landscape to a stop-clock, while a popular rock song blared from the boombox beside him. The cluster of bystanders hovered around him clapped on enthusiastically.

It's a beautiful day, Robert.

"Yes, it is," he said to Lucy. A woman walking her French bulldog gave him a wide berth and long sideways glance.

Crazy or not, everything reminded him of Lucy. Standing in the square, watching the street performers charm the tourists. The sight of a red balloon, released, floating up into the blue sky. The smell of pralines or jambalaya. Sunlight filtered through trees dancing on the pavement.

He plucked a fresh beignet from the bag and shook the excess powdered sugar off before plopping it into his mouth. He spotted Piper across the square at her army-green card table. She was reading the palm of a teenage girl, maybe seventeen, eighteen years old. Her black hair was pulled up in a messy bun on the top of her head and she laughed and blushed at whatever Piper said.

Piper caught sight of King and waved. He waved back.

He took his time down the narrow streets, walking east toward Melandra's. His leg was giving him grief.

The bullet that hit his lower left side and lodged in the meat had been removed cleanly, but not without cost. The nerves were damaged and his left leg remained weak. He couldn't walk without a limp now and a tingling sensation that ran up and down his entire left side.

He stayed on top of his physical therapy though. Walking. Stairs. Stretches. Anything to keep him from having a permanent limp. The doctor said he'd have full use of it again in eight or nine weeks. King suspected that full use would be similar to his full use of his shoulder. It would hurt him from time to time, but he didn't need daily Vicodin for it. Yet.

Only time would tell.

King stepped inside Melandra's Fortunes and Fixes, and breathed deep. It was morning glory and patchouli incense today. The air hung thick with it as several candles flickered from their pedestals. It was so nice entering the shop and not hearing the banshee wail of the skeleton that Mel used to keep by the door.

The storeroom opened and there was Mel, wearing her dark blue jeans and a black tank top.

"You're out and about," she said, obviously pleased. "How's the leg?"

He downplayed the pins and needles and incessant burning. "On the mend."

Mel snorted. "You better drink that tea I gave you."

King cringed at the thought of it. He'd tried one sip and found it tasted like dirt and crushed earthworms.

"Don't make that face," she said, eyebrows raised. "Drink it unless you want to walk with a cane."

"Canes can be cool. I can get one with a skull on top. Black maybe."

She rolled her eyes.

"You still coming over for dinner?" he asked. "I've got everything for the lasagna."

"I'll be over at 7:00," she said. "You better have the drag race show on for me."

King tipped his imaginary hat and started the slow climb up the steps to his apartment. He held the metal handrail and took them one at a time. He was breathing hard, sweat standing out on his brow by the time he reached his door.

It was dark and quiet when he entered.

He hesitated, listening to the ringing silence, expecting to find her there.

She wasn't.

Lou had checked on him twice in the three weeks since he returned from the hospital. He'd offered to give her Lucy's ashes, even though Lucy specified in her will that they were to go to King. Lou refused to accept them. So Lucy's urn remained on his enormous coffee table during the day, and on his bedside table each night.

He'd also tried to get Lou to talk about what had happened that day at the winery, but she'd brushed him off. She didn't seem eager to talk about Lucy or Konstantine.

She had promised to come back though, once they'd both healed, and help him get his P.I. business off the ground. He hadn't had a chance to tell her that the P.I. business would be a front for something else he had in mind. Another, perhaps better, way to help people.

But that conversation would come. If time was on their side.

King placed the sack of beignets on the kitchen island and opened the fridge. He gathered everything he needed for the lasagna from its shelves. The meat and cheeses. The sauce and peppers. He removed a pan from the drawer beneath the stove and threw the meat, chopped garlic and red onion into it. He stirred it while it browned. Once it was cooked and the danger of poisoning was behind him, he would make the layers in a casserole dish and hold it in the fridge until it was time to bake. Then he would take a long nap before Mel came over.

The kitchen already smelled like heaven when the phone rang.

"King."

"Robbie," a man said. "I heard you got shot."

When he recovered from his surprise, King spit out, "Flesh wound."

"Mm hmm," Sampson replied. A chair creaked on the other end. "That's what you said about your shoulder and you were in Quantico for months."

King added meat to the pan. "You calling to check on me, Sammy? Or do we need to have another chat?"

"No," he said. "No, that's all panned out."

King's hand faltered in the stirring. "Oh yeah?"

"Turns out that it wasn't even you who did the digging."

"Is that right?"

"According the data our IT guys pulled," Sampson said. "I just wanted you to know so you weren't worried. The department formally apologizes for accusing you of any wrongdoing."

"I didn't realize I *was* formally accused."

"All the same. I thought you'd like to know."

Silence hung in the phone before King choked out a "thank you."

"Dare I ask how you got shot?"

"Mugger. Here in the Quarter. They're getting bolder these days."

"Must be the recession," Sampson added. "Money makes desperate men."

King had fabricated that story as soon as his eyes had opened in the hospital room. He wasn't about to explain to a doctor and his staff that the bullet had come from a shootout in the Tuscan hills. Or they might've wheeled his bed right on down to the psych ward.

"You be careful out there, Robbie. You're attracting a lot of trouble these days."

King laughed, dumping the sauce from the jar into the sautéed meat and peppers. "It sure does seem to find me, doesn't it?"

KONSTANTINE KNEW SHE WAS THERE BEFORE HE STEPPED OUT OF HIS bathroom and into his bedroom. Something about the pressure in his apartment had changed. A sensation on the back of the neck, like being watched. Premonition or no, the sight of her body silhouetted in the big window, not three feet from his bed, squeezed the air from his chest.

Her lithe form was bathed in moonlight as she gazed out over the night river. So beautiful that he didn't want to turn on the light and ruin the magic of this moment.

She seemed transfixed by the shimmering waters, by starlight shining on buildings and cobblestone. A boat tread water noiselessly down the center of the Arno river, cutting waves.

He continued to towel his hair, aware he was bare from the chest up. He'd stepped from the shower and pulled on his sweatpants for sleep.

Had he known she would be here to greet him, maybe he would have left them on the hook behind the door.

"They call you the Executioner," he said softly, as if speaking too loudly might scare her away. "Not only in the Ravengers. Ricci tells me it's true the world over. You've become their boogeyman."

"A rumor you encourage, I'm sure." She spoke without turning around, her arms still crossed over her chest. He didn't mind. He appreciated the view from behind.

But finally she did turn and meet his gaze.

"The world stopped looking for you," she said. "One minute every agency in the world was hunting you, the next they're apologizing, calling it a mistake. Running a bullshit story about how a poor Italian farmer was martyred and his family's vineyard burned."

Konstantine smiled. "I needed an excuse for the pile of ash and rubble we left behind."

She turned away from him. He looked at the pale stretch of her neck and longed to kiss it. Those sharp collar bones. He was only a step away from wrapping his hand around her waist, and biting that little notch of bone.

Brick by brick.

"Do you own all the world agencies?" she asked. "Or just the right people in each?"

"Does it matter?" he asked. She had enough truth for now.

He could tell she was still trying to realign her compass. She hadn't completely given up her father's position on drugs and the drug trade. On men like himself. But she was starting to see it more clearly, the way good and evil were not so clearly aligned. Not in the world and not even within themselves.

He would never own her. Never tame her. And he didn't want to.

But he wanted her to understand. He would give her the time she needed.

"And here I thought you were just a rich boy."

He gazed at her slender neck again. The little space behind her ear that must be as soft as a flower petal. "I'm not without my weaknesses."

"Yeah, your scar is ugly," she said.

He laughed, surprised. "I was told that it needs to fully heal before any plastic surgery is done."

The doctors had accomplished what they could in spite of Nico's malice, but he'd cut the cheek deep. It had taken four surgeries already just to mend the muscles beneath and save Konstantine from a lopsided expression. He'd gotten lucky. The surgeon had done a good job of restoring him to his former glory, leaving only a jagged line from the bottom of Konstantine's eye to his chin.

"Don't," she said.

"Don't?" He stared at the river, side by side with her. Their shoulders brushed.

He couldn't name one feature of the landscape before him. It was only the heat from her shoulder, the shift of her hips he was aware of.

"You were too pretty before," she said. "Now your men might actually respect you."

He laughed. "There's a compliment in there somewhere."

"Not that you need your face to get what you want," she said. She was watching him again. He didn't dare meet those beautiful eyes, not while his knees felt weak.

"I have something for you." He was certain she was still pissed about the room, but he was determined to make it up to her, prove to her that he meant her no harm. "Before we burned down the villa, I found this."

He threw the towel on the back of the chair and crossed to the closet. He pressed on the top two corners of the wall, then the bottom two to release the false wood panel.

Behind it, he pulled out the bulletproof vest and offered it to her. "I had it repaired. The Kevlar was as thin as paper on the right side, along the ribs. The right knife or bullet would've punched right through. It isn't the best protection anymore, you know. They've upgraded this model about six times since your father was on the force. But it holds value to you so I thought you'd want to keep it. For luck."

She took it from his hands and turned it over, inspecting the extra layers that had been sewn in.

"Mario is very good. He kept the thin profile but added all this extra Kevlar here," he assured her, expecting her to be furious that the vest had been altered.

But then she found the white tag in the inside and the black scrawled *Thorne* across it. "He tells me that when you put it on, you won't even notice the—"

A hand seized the back of his neck and pulled him into a kiss. A hot mouth overtook his, forcing the lips apart with her tongue. Their bodies collided and all Konstantine could feel was every inch of her supple form against his. Full frontal. Thigh to thigh. Hip to hip. Her nipples brushing his.

One of her hands slid up into his damp hair while the other clutched her vest.

When he put his hands on her, he realized she hadn't brought a gun. She'd come to his dark bedroom, unarmed and now she was kissing him.

Damn patience.

Konstantine's arms slid under her thighs and lifted her off her feet. For a moment, all her weight sat on the cradle of his hips. He only made it three steps—only needed three steps—before he hit the side of the bed and collapsed. They went down, hitting the mattress like stones, her body pinned beneath his.

His mouth moved to find hers again but brushed only cool cotton. Her hard body was gone. Her heat evaporated.

He was left with only moonlit sheets and pillows.

He collapsed onto the mattress and laughed. He rolled onto his back and groaned at the ceiling. "I suppose I deserved that."

Fine. Let her go.

She wasn't the only one who enjoyed a hunt.

ACKNOWLEDGMENTS

It's always best to begin with the wife, Kim. Because really, she puts up with me more than anyone. And it's lucky for me that she happens to be such a great reader herself, and she is able to make wonderful suggestions every time. My books are better because of her, but more importantly, my life is worth living because she's in it.

My love goes to my sweet pug Josephine, who passed on while I was writing this book. This is the last book I will have written with her nestled beside me on my office couch. Her companionship will be sorely missed. And love to Charlemagne "Charley" the newest pug addition to the family, who kept my feet warm while I did the last read through.

Thank you to my critique group, The Four Horsemen of the Bookocalypse: Kathrine Pendleton, Angela Roquet, and Monica La Porta. You guys give every story the critical eye it deserves and because of that, you make the books better—and me a better writer. Let's ride!

Special shout-out to Diana Hutchings, nurse extraordinaire, for patiently answering my questions about gunshot wounds. Monica La Porta and Alison Carminke for their help with the Italian—giving Konstantine and Nico some authenticity. And the dozens of Street Team proofreaders who helped me catch those last minute errors. Any remaining mistakes are my own.

Thank you to my street team who are always eager to jump in line for ARCs. You guys are incredibly supportive and helpful about catching those last minute typos. If you're interested in joining my street team, and receiving advanced copies of my work, you can let me know at kory@korymshrum.com

Thank you to the incredibly talented Christian Bentulan for the beautiful cover.

Thank you to every person who took the time to say hello online. To everyone who took the time to write me a sweet, thoughtful email, Facebook or Twitter message, blog comment, or leave a review for this book. By doing so, you are letting me know that you enjoy my work and want it to continue.

And for me, that's a dream come true.

DANSE MACABRE

SHADOWS IN THE WATER BOOK 3

In Memoriam
for Arthur J. Fedor
1950-2014
Thank you for your wisdom and tender kindness.
Thank you for patiently pointing out the path.

PROLOGUE

Lou held tight to the top of the trucks as they plowed east through the winter night. Snow fell from the black sky, illuminated momentarily by headlights.

A bright moon loomed overhead.

Lou took a breath and faded through the frosty roof of the truck. When the world reformed around her, she was crouching between the two front seats and the men who occupied them.

She pulled her gun and put a bullet in the driver first. The truck careened, rumbling off into the frozen field.

The passenger was trying to grab the CB, but one shot splattered his brains across the window. The bullet passed straight through the head and into the wall of the truck. The hole whistled as air leaked through.

Lou shoved into the driver seat and wrenched open the door. She pushed the body out into the snow and slammed on the brakes. They screeched and squealed as it slid to a stop on the packed ice.

Then Lou was gone again, fading through the shadows into the next truck in the caravan. These men were as easy to dispatch at the first. But then the other trucks were stopping, brakes squealing. Men spilled into the night and ran toward Lou on either side of the caravan. She remained in her seat until the last moment.

Then she slid through the dark to the truck's underbelly. Her knee pressed into the cold snow as the men tore open the doors and wrenched out the bodies.

Lou spared a bullet for every leg she could target—five in all. Then she shifted through the dark again to the front of the next truck.

As the men scrambled, trying to find the source of the attack, Lou picked them off one by one until only she prevailed.

The caravan idled in the desolate road. No noise remained but the gentle hum of engines and the crunch of frosty grass beneath her boots. No witnesses saw the twenty murders, except the large, unblinking moon.

She opened the back of one of the trucks and peered into its belly. Pallets of heroin sat crammed in tight, each laden with plastic bricks.

She tossed in a grenade and slammed the door shut. She escaped to the next truck before its expected *Boom!* lifted all four wheels off the snow.

Then she did it again and again, watching as each truck was thrown flaming into the air before crashing down again. She felt the heat even from a safe distance.

She watched the drugs burn.

As the flames died to a lazy smolder, Lou searched the glowing moonlit fields. Silence rang in her ear. She counted the bodies heaped on the snow, their blood sprayed out behind each. It gave the impression that they had fallen from the sky, landing broken.

Something moved.

One hunched form dragged itself away from the wreckage. Lou closed the distance, white smoke fogging in front of her face.

It was a young man, shot and bleeding. The snow beneath him was black with it.

"Будьте добры!" he cried. On his back, he held his hands out in front of him like a shield. Bright crimson burned in his cheeks and his eyes shone in the moonlight. Snow collected in his blond hair.

"I don't speak Russian," she said, and pointed the eye of her Beretta.

"Please," he said again. "I didn't want this. My father—"

The shot rang out. He spoke no more.

1

TWO MONTHS LATER

L ou woke with a start. Bolting upright, she found herself on the edge of her mattress, her feet bare on the cool wooden floor. She stared at her blood-crusted arm, at her flaking skin without seeing it.

Instead she saw the boy on the snow. It had been the same dream for months. When she'd finally fall asleep, she'd find herself in the snowy night again. Every detail of the dream had felt real. The frost on the back of her neck and the warm blood steaming on her hands.

And it always ended the same way. From the flat of his back, he begged for his life. The moment before she shot him, he'd turn into her father. She pulled the trigger anyway.

It was the gunshot that sent her careening into wakefulness.

Her head hurt. Her upper back hurt. She rolled her neck and elicited a thunderous crack up each side.

She shouldn't have engaged that sixth attacker in the parking lot last night. Not in her condition.

She could still smell the beer on his breath as she'd wrenched his head back, staring into his wide, fearful eyes. But she hadn't pulled her gun, hadn't been able to.

What was the point?

Every night this week she'd roamed the streets. Sometimes she walked for hours through the most dangerous districts she knew. If anyone made the mistake of approaching her, she'd take them on.

Not with her gun. She'd slam her fist over and over into muscle and bone. She'd split skin—her own and theirs—until blood ran.

Yet she couldn't pull her gun.

The cold, quiet rage she needed to lift her Beretta from its holster never came, never overtook her the way some demon overtook its host before feeding.

She blamed Konstantine. And her aunt. Even King was far from innocent. They'd churned these waters. Now it was too murky to see where she stood.

Her father's vision of the world had been easier.

Here were the bad guys. Here were the good.

When she'd found the desire to pull her gun, her mind was the betrayer.

What if he has a child at home? What if she loves him? What if killing him breaks her the way Jack's death broke you?

Her mind had taunted her with these unanswerable questions and the man at the end of her Beretta's sight had run. He'd run from the bar parking lot into the darkness and she'd let him go, finding she could only watch him disappear.

The heat, the thirst to kill had left as quickly as it came.

The insomnia wasn't helping. How could one have a clear head with endless sleepless nights? When was the last time she'd slept? When was the last time she'd actually put her head on this pillow, closed her eyes, and let the exhaustion take her?

Sleep had eluded her since her aunt Lucy died. Three months of nothing more than power naps, and treating her body like a punching bag.

It's going to catch up to you, a familiar voice warned. It was her father. She didn't need advice from the dead.

They weren't telling her anything she didn't already know. She dragged her hand down her face, trying to get out from under the weight of this exhaustion.

A knock sounded through her apartment.

I'm dreaming, she thought. She regarded the front door as if she'd never seen it before.

Perhaps that was because in the six years she'd lived in this apartment *no one* had ever knocked on it. The only person who had even known the address was Aunt Lucy. This wasn't Christmas Eve. No ghostly visits scheduled.

A second knock tapped out its rhythm and her heart leapt to life in her chest. She was awake and someone was here.

Without thinking, Lou crossed her living room. She passed the sofa and glass coffee table, and stepped into her empty linen closet. Her back pressed into the bare wooden walls.

The darkness softened around her, falling away. She slipped through it.

Another set of walls formed around her. She pushed open the door and stepped into the empty apartment down the hallway. This kitchen reeked of pine-scented cleaner. Her bare feet padded silently across the cold floor. Once she reached the front door, slowly she cracked it enough to see her own door down the hallway.

It was a boy knocking.

He was eighteen maybe, with a courier bag slung over his shoulder and a bicycle helmet hanging in one hand. Shifting his weight, he sighed, clearly annoyed.

He rapped on her door for a third time before calling out. "I'm not a Mormon or anything, okay? And I don't want to sell you shit. I have this letter for you." He held the letter up to his face, squinting at the small print on the front of the envelope. "Ms. Thorne, I need you to sign for it."

Lou eased the apartment door closed.

As if you would have shot him anyway, a cruel voice chided. *You haven't shot so much as an empty can in months.*

The vacant pantry returned her to her own apartment. It took only a breath to slip through the darkness again and find her warmer home as she'd left it.

She placed her Beretta on the kitchen island as she crossed to the door. When she opened the door she found the hallway empty. The kid was halfway down the hall.

"Hey," she called out. "I'm here."

He looked relieved, even though he had to come back. "Thank *God.*

This building has a thousand steps and no freaking elevator. No offense, but I didn't want to come back."

She only regarded him, extending her hand for the letter.

"Oh right." He pulled a plastic blue ink pen from behind his ear. "I need you to sign this sheet."

She waited for him to pull the folded sheet of paper out of his coat pocket. She signed it against the door jamb, the grain pressing through the paper and making her letters wobble on the page.

"Thanks," the kid said, his thin lips pulling into a bright grin. "Here you go."

He handed over the envelope. It was cream, a nice thick paper with red lettering in the top right corner. Her name was printed in black ink, slanting forward.

Hammerstein, Holt and Locke Attorneys at Law it said in the return corner. And Lou was wondering if she was going to have to murder a band of lawyers tonight.

The kid was staring.

Lou followed his gaze to the Beretta on the kitchen island and then to the blood drying on both her arms. She didn't think it was the thick, black grime under her nails that had doubled the size of his eyes. She looked like she'd clawed her way out of hell.

Kill him, the cruel voice taunted. *You can't let him go. He could tell someone. He could bring them back here.*

"Anything else?" she asked him, searching his eyes for danger.

He shook his head vigorously. "Nah, we're cool."

He backed away.

You're making a mistake. He could end you tonight.

Yet Lou didn't move.

"H-happy New Year," the kid said and ducked through the door beneath the marked EXIT sign as if he expected her to give chase.

New year, she thought, closing and locking her front door.

A *BOOM, HISS* rose suddenly.

The first firework of the evening exploded in the sky, raining orange ribbons of light over the dark Mississippi river.

She turned the envelope over and slid a thumb under the flap.

2

King scrolled through his phone, checking his messages as he stood in line for coffee. He deleted the junk from his inbox and sorted the messages that required more attention than he could give right now into his priority folder.

They were two days from opening The Crescent City Detective Agency for public inquiries. Not that his desk wasn't already overflowing with opportunities, mostly freelance from his old contacts in law enforcement looking for help with the cases they were building.

"Robbie," a woman chimed.

King looked up from his phone and saw Suze, tall, blonde with a bright smile behind the Café du Monde checkout counter. Her apron was dusted with flour and powdered sugar. The lines by her eyes crinkled with her bittersweet smile. She reached her hand across the counter palm up in offering.

He took it and squeezed her hand. Granules of flour and sugar rubbed between their palms. She had strong hands. No doubt from making donuts every morning for twenty years.

"What are you doing behind the counter?" he asked. "Aren't owners supposed to have their feet propped up in front of the fire, watching the profits roll in?"

She laughed. "You've clearly never run a business, Robbie. Besides half my girls are out sick with the flu and the rest of us are pushing to close early."

"For New Year's?" he asked, slipping his phone into his pocket.

"Yes, though I'll be out cold before ten." She tapped her pen against the notepad. "You want your usual?"

"A large black coffee, yes."

"What about the beignets? Full order or half?"

He patted his flat stomach. "I'm getting the jump on my resolution."

Though in truth, King had cut back on the cream and sugar and all his sweets before October. And the last of his cravings had been cut short with Lucy's death.

Grief robbed him of his appetite. Among other things.

"How you holding up?" Suze asked, as if sensing his mind's dark shift.

"I'm fine," he said and wondered if he really was. Or if he'd only said this line so many times he was now able to deliver it convincingly. "The agency opens in two days."

"Congratulations," she said, pouring out the large coffee in one of their Styrofoam cups, a green logo stamped into its side. "It'll be good to keep your mind busy."

She handed over the coffee, but also a greasy sack of hot beignets despite his protests.

Suze refused to take them back. "Give them to the girls if you want, but take 'em."

He put his $10 bill on the counter, thanked her and walked away before she could give him change.

Once out of the protection of the overhead umbrella, the cold winter wind struck him across the cheeks, pulling water from his eyes. The line for coffee and donuts was so long now that it snaked out from beneath the green canopy and into the French Quarter surrounding it. The bodies, huddled for warmth, followed the wrought iron outline of the café's patio.

King felt the heat radiating from the sack of donuts in his cold fist as he crossed Jackson Square. He was about to turn onto Royal Street when a dirty bundle stirred at his feet.

A man emerged from under his threadbare blanket. He eyed the greasy white sack in King's fist enviously.

King held it toward him. "You like donuts?"

The dirty man nodded hesitantly as if he expected King to pull back the bag and laugh.

It hurt King to see it. "Here you go. They're yours. Where're your socks?"

He pointed at the man's bare feet.

"Ain't got any." The man opened the sack to peer inside. His fingers smeared dirt across the white paper. "Someone stole 'em while I was sleepin'."

"I'll fix that," King said. "You need anything else?"

The man seemed to consider the question seriously. "Nah. Just some thick socks."

"You be around here?" King asked, gesturing to the square.

"Yeah, for a bit."

With a nod, King turned down Royal Street, and ambled toward the St. Peter intersection. He sipped his coffee, feeling the warmth slide down his throat and fill his chest. He should've given the man the coffee too. The thought hadn't even occurred to him and now he felt shame for having overlooked the obvious.

It would've warmed him better. *I could've done better.*

Are you talking about Lucy or the homeless man? he asked himself.

A gaggle of girls in feathered masks fell out of a shop in front of him, squealing with laughter. They parted like water around him, reforming on the other side. He knew the Quarter would be full of revelers tonight. New Year's Eve always drew all sorts to the black hole known as Bourbon Street.

He supposed Piper had plans to go out. Why shouldn't she? She was only 23.

King would spend the evening on Melandra's couch, watching the ball drop in New York, assuming either of them could stay awake until midnight.

Women would hang from the balconies, flashing their breasts despite the chilly temperatures. Men would drink their weight in alcohol and puke on the sidewalks or the side of a building.

A shirtless man with half his body painted blue ran past him chanting the university's cheer.

Sometimes King wondered if he'd traded his retirement for a never-ending frat party.

He loved all the indulgent, frenetic energy of this place, but he could've found a nice condo in Florida. Or retired to the Philippines and stretched his dollars far enough to live like a king.

But he'd wanted to be here in the Quarter. He'd never be able to explain why he loved this place. It was rambunctious, touristy and at times violent. Yet that was part of its charm. It had a personality that matched King's own.

You've got a past life connection here, Melandra had told him. She'd flipped over a tarot card on her wooden coffee table one night. He'd had his hands deep in the popcorn bowl they shared while watching the latest episode of RuPaul's Drag Race.

It makes as much sense as anything else, he'd said, as he'd knocked back another Dr. Pepper.

Maybe you were buried here, she said. *Lots of bodies under these streets. Maybe one of them is yours.*

King had laughed at that. *We all knew I had trouble letting go, didn't we? Why are you here?*

I'm supposed to be here. Same as you. It doesn't make sense. One hurricane and it could all go again, but that's life. If not a hurricane, then something else. And this place...there's something special about it.

The truth was King didn't believe in energies or fate. Palmistry, tarot, past lives, none of it rang true to him. But he respected Melandra and her insights. More importantly, she was free to believe whatever the hell she wanted.

We all need something to get us through the night, he thought. Because sooner or later, no matter how far inland one goes, the storm will come.

King stopped outside Melandra's Fortunes and Fixes. He raised his boots and scraped them against the curb, leaning one hip into the horse-head post embedded in the cobblestone walk.

The smell of egg rolls wafted from the corner store across the street and King knew that Zeke had pulled a fresh batch from his deep fryers. No doubt he was banking on hungry drunks late into the night.

King's stomach rumbled. He might be cutting back on the sugar, and trying not to eat from stores that sold beer, cigarettes, lotto tickets, *and* food all in the same place, but damned if those egg rolls didn't smell good. He could practically feel the oil coating his lips.

King stepped through the door to Mel's shop and was greeted by a ghostly chime. The candlelit chandelier flickered and a hoarse whisper ricocheted overhead. The volume rose and fell, giving the impression of phantoms swooping down on one's head.

This latest attempt at spooky ambiance befitting an occult shop was a damn sight better than the shrieking skeleton she'd erected last year.

Every time someone had crossed the threshold, and the man-sized skeleton released its blood-curdling scream, it'd shaved a year off King's life. He'd take ghosts in the ceiling any day.

Melandra was behind the counter. She looked up in the middle of a card flip and grunted a hello as he wiped his feet on the industrial mat inside the door for good measure.

"I'm thinking Mexican for dinner. You interested?" she asked.

"Zeke's got egg rolls," he said, jabbing a finger at the convenience store across the street. "I think it'll have to be Chinese for me."

She scrunched her nose. "Your mistake. You know he doesn't clean those fryers."

King smacked his lips. "More flavor."

Voices rumbled low behind the thick purple curtain. This was the dark secluded nook where Melandra gave her readings. But if she was out here, it must be Piper playing fortune teller today.

"How's she doing?" he asked, placing his coffee on the glass counter.

"Not bad," Melandra said. "She gets $20 tips."

King arched an eyebrow. "Really?"

"She doesn't have what my grandmamie called *the sight*," she says with a shoulder shrug. The bangles on her dark wrist tinkling in response as she turned over another card. "But she has something about her."

"Another kind of psychic inclination perhaps?"

"She's good at reading people and she's learned all the cards and the spreads. She knows the lines in the palm and even took up the bit of Chinese face reading I know. If she takes what she learns and combines it with her own instincts, she'll do all right."

King pointed at the battered tarot cards in Mel's hand. "But you're not letting her use your deck."

"Hell, no," she said, frowning at him and shifting her weight to the other hip. "These cards are over a hundred years old. She can have them when I'm dead."

He took another sip of his coffee, pleased to find it cool enough to finally drink. "Are you sure you want to share her with me? If you need her here—"

Mel waved a hand. "She wants to work for you. I can't tell her no and anyway I've got a new hire starting Wednesday. She'll work the counter and Piper will schedule her own readings and appointments and close up for me after she's done with you. I'll cover the rest."

"Do you ever wonder how she manages to work twelve hours a day and still spend her nights in the bars with the ladies?" King asked. It was genuine curiosity.

"She's young, Mr. King. I don't think they start sleeping until at least 36."

"Unless they have kids," he said. "Then it's late fifties, I hear."

Piper pulled back the curtain and a young woman with red colored contact lens and a shaved patch above her ear stepped out.

"See you." The woman thanked her, waved to Mel and King and then stepped out of the shop.

"She tip you?" Mel asked, shuffling the cards.

Piper flashed the twenty dollar bill rolled up in one fist. "Sure did."

Mel nodded as if this was the right answer.

"I can tip you another $20 if you run an errand for me," King said.

Piper plucked her phone from her pocket and checked the time. "Yeah, I've got 45 minutes before my next appointment. What you do you need?"

"I've got some socks and a blanket I want you to run to a homeless guy in the square. He's got a red hoodie and tattoos on the back of his hands. It's too cold for him to be out there in bare feet."

"Sure," Piper said. "And I'll buy him a coffee."

"And will you pick up my takeout order from Mr. Chang's on the way back?" It wasn't fried egg rolls from the corner market at least. King thought that absolved him of the indulgence at least partially.

Piper didn't answer. She'd come up to the counter and leaned against it. She looked at the cards as Mel flipped each one over, forming a cross on the glass top.

Piper grinned. "Is she coming?"

Melandra cut her eyes to King. "Looks like it."

"Lou?" he asked, surprised.

"It's the Eight of Wands," Piper said, tapping a card on the tabletop. The silver band around her thumb glinted in the light. "Visitors. Movement."

"The agency opens in two days," he reminded them. "Let's hope visitors are coming."

"But it's not only the Eight of Wands," Piper insisted, tapping another card. "It's the Death card. Louie always shows up with the Death card."

"I wonder *why*." Melandra arched her eyebrows. "And who is this page of wands? That's what I want to know. I don't need no more troublemakers coming around here. And this one looks like a *pistol*."

As King stepped away, mounting the stairs to his apartment above, he couldn't turn his mind away from Lou. His heart leapt at the idea. Would she come back? Lou had checked on him twice after he returned from the hospital with a cleaned out gunshot wound and a limp that he still had on bad days.

He'd offered to give her Lucy's ashes, even though Lucy specified in her will that they were to go to King. Lou refused them.

She had promised to come back though, once they'd both healed, and help him get his P.I. business going. He hadn't had a chance to tell her that the P.I. business would be a front for something else he had in mind. Another, perhaps better, way to help people.

Now that the opening was upon them, maybe he would finally get his chance to tell her. Or perhaps he was getting ahead of himself. He knew she was grieving for Lucy, just as he was, and there was no rushing grief.

With his pockets full of the thickest socks he owned, and a blanket tucked under his arm, he descended the stairs and gave Piper forty bucks and the goods.

"Be back," she said and left them standing in the shop.

"Why are you giving me that look, Mel?"

"I like her," Mel said, but she sucked in a breath as if preparing to give negative feedback.

"Piper is a good girl," he said, leaning against the counter and taking up his coffee again.

"She is. But I'm talking about the other one."

"Lou?"

"I used to think she was a demon from hell, but I really do like her."

"What changed?"

"Lucy," Mel said, matter of fact. She watched King's face carefully, as if waiting to see how he would react to hearing the woman's name. "Once I realized how Lucy saw her, I understood."

How Lucy saw her.

"But if she's going to be coming around again, if she's going to be part of your business, I think we need to take precautions." Mel scooped all the cards together and began tapping them into a respectable stack again.

"Even if she weren't involved, you attract enough trouble all on your own, Mr. King. And you're going to start following criminals around, asking questions you shouldn't, going places you shouldn't. I don't need to tell you it's dangerous."

"Mel if you want me to move out—"

"Shut up. You know I don't. But I want us to take precautions. I have some ideas."

"I'm listening," King said, taking another sip of his bitter black coffee.

But when Mel opened her mouth a groaning sigh circled the room. The chandelier flickered overhead. They both turned to see a courier heading their way, his messenger bag hanging off one shoulder and bouncing against his leg.

"I've got a letter for Mr. Robert King," he said, rubbing his fuzzy glove across his red nose.

"That's me," King said, placing his coffee on his glass top.

The courier produced a sheet for him to sign before handing over a letter. Thick, nice paper with a red stamp in the upper right corner and his name written in slanted black ink on front of the envelope. *Hammerstein, Holt, and Locke Attorneys at Law.* King slid a thumb under the flap and pried open the envelope. Inside were two sheets of crisp folded paper.

"And this," the boy said, producing a padded mailer.

"Somebody suing you?" Melandra asked. She slipped her deck of cards into her pocket for safekeeping. "Well?"

King opened the mailer and saw two VHS tapes inside. Then he read the letter.

"I'm not being sued."

His whole body grew heavy.

"They're from Lucy."

K onstantine's team exited the armored vehicles and swept the area. Londoners crisscrossed the pavement, hurrying onto their destinations. Many, no doubt, were hungry for their dinners, their feet desperate to rest after a long day of walking and tube travel.

Five men entered the Victoria and Albert Museum. They looked similar. Their height and build nearly identical. Each with crow and crossbones tattoos on their biceps. Their eyes were green. Their hair a deep rich brown, easily mistaken for black.

Only one wore a gold ring on his pinkie with the elaborate Martinelli family crest.

The passersby who saw this group were so struck with their similarity, they were certain the men were either brothers or perhaps maybe cousins. One woman would have wagered they were quintuplets. The crowd of museum visitors parted for them, as they moved in formation, like birds.

These men ignored the small commotion. They continued on course to the second floor balcony, overlooking the sculpture gallery.

At the sight of them, Dmitri Petrov stepped from the shadows of the armory room and up to the railing overlooking the gallery. He was a tall man, six feet at least. His shoulders were wide and tapered down to a slim waist. Konstantine thought he had the build of a boxer, but with a perfect aquiline nose. His blue eyes were bright and piercing, his brow still Augustan, if the chin and jaw weak. His hair was thinning but still brown, no doubt dyed, given the wrinkles at the corner of the man's eyes.

Konstantine put him at late fifties, early sixties.

Dmitri surveyed each man in turn and then spotted the one who wore the Martinelli crest. He appreciated the red jewel and twin dragons snaking around a projected M.

This was the man Dmitri addressed.

"Thank you for taking time to meet with me," he said companionably, as if he hadn't all but demanded this meeting with Konstantine. "But when I learned we were both in London, I could hardly pass up the chance to introduce myself to the famed Konstantine Martinelli. Who else among us could have our faces on the news one moment and become poor Italian farmers the next."

Dmitri's men laughed as expected.

Konstantine smiled.

"I'm sure you could've gotten out of that mess."

Dmitri shrugged. "I prefer my anonymity. I know you are here to do business with my rival Gerstein. I don't know *why* you would refuse my Myanmar shipments in exchange for his subpar Afghani crop. But how do the Americans say? To each his own?"

Konstantine refused to do business with Dmitri not because of the quality of his product, but because his money was often funneled back into the theft and trade of women and children. And while Konstantine might deal drugs to every corner of the world, he would have no part in slavery.

"Surely you didn't ask me here to complain that I wasn't buying your products? Is business going poorly, Dmitri? Would you like some money?"

Dmitri's face twitched. "I don't care who you trade with, Konstantine. We are both businessmen. We know how this industry works. I wanted to discuss another matter with you."

He leaned against the railing, surveying the alabaster sculpture of David below. A picture of nonchalant indifference.

Dmitri followed his gaze to the large sculpture of the naked boy.

"Yes, it's beautiful, isn't it? It's a mere copy of the masterpiece you have back home, but let's not get distracted."

Dmitri's accent crawled along Konstantine's skin as he stood in the marble corridor. A group of tourists mounted the stairs but were pushed the other way by Dmitri's men. *This gallery is closed.*

"Is it true that you have a young woman in your employ?" Dmitri asked, absently picking at the cufflink on his sleeve. "A dangerous creature with a 100% kill rate?"

"You need workers?" He arched an eyebrow. "Surely you have plenty of men and women at your disposal. Your gang is one of the largest in the world, as I understand it."

Dmitri visibly puffed at this flattery. "It's true. And I have my best. But even my own ballerina has had one or two get away. Human error, I'm afraid, cannot be accounted for. But I hear your woman *never* fails."

"I don't know what you're talking about."

Dmitri let his eyebrows rise and fall. "Yes, if I had such a weapon in my arsenal, I would keep the secret quite close to the vest. Unless, of course, the other rumors are true. Then perhaps it isn't about weapons at all."

Konstantine said nothing.

"Are you really in love with her?"

He remained silent still.

"Don't be stingy, Konstantine. I don't want to *fuck* her. I want to employ her. I hear her talent is...unparalleled."

"I wouldn't believe every rumor you hear," the man wearing the Martinelli crest said. "I suppose you also believe she's half ghost. That she appears and disappears in the bedroom of naughty children."

"If only I could be so lucky. I've been *very* naughty this year." Dmitri laughed and so did his men. Their hard sneers turned Konstantine's stomach.

"Rumors all have a kernel of truth inside them," Dmitri said with a condescending smile. "Don't pretend she doesn't exist. I'll admit I've been unable to find a scrap of *real* information on her. I do have one lead. But I suspect my inability to track her is your doing. You're good at making people disappear, aren't you?"

"If such a woman did exist." He placed a steady hand on the cool bannister. "Do you really think she would work for you? For anyone?"

"I can be very persuasive."

Another round of cold, knowing laughs.

"Women can be hard to satisfy."

Dmitri laughed. "This is true. But everyone has desires. And fears. She's no different."

"Every man that has faced her has died."

Dmitri considered this for a long while. His blue eyes swept the sculpture gallery below the way a king might survey his subjects. His hands sat loosely in their gray pants pockets.

"If she is truly a free agent, then I suppose the responsibility is on me to find and woo her. Though I'd hoped you'd make the introduction." Dmitri turned and smiled at him. "*You're* still alive, Konstantine. And my sources are certain that you've had more contact with her than anyone. Perhaps if I want to meet her, I should take *you* hostage. Let's see if she'll come claim you as she did when Nico staged his pathetic little coup."

Konstantine's men visibly tensed, sensing the implied threat.

"But I'm not as careless as Nico," Dmitri said, those blue eyes frosting over.

Dmitri seized the man by the front shirt.

"That's enough," Konstantine said. He stepped forward, placing himself between his decoy and the Russian thug. "Are you threatening to hurt my men, Petrov?"

Dmitri loosened his grip on the other man's collar and looked to Konstantine as if seeing him for the first time. "Ah yes. That's better." He took a deep breath as if inhaling Konstantine. "This makes much more sense."

"Threaten to hurt my men again and I will—"

Dmitri held up a hand in surrender, stepping back. "No need for cloaks and daggers. You had only to introduce yourself properly."

"I wanted to see if you were a man with manners. I am disappointed."

Dmitri's face twitched again, but Konstantine didn't care. His proxy, the brave Stefano had fallen back in line with the other guards.

Dmitri's men stood on one side and Konstantine's on the other. Of course they had met in this public place so that no guns would fire, and no lives would be taken. Konstantine hoped they would continue to honor that code.

"Is everything your man said true?" Dmitri asked. "Is your woman a free agent?"

"I don't believe anyone claimed she belonged to me like a dog."

"Or a whore." Dmitri smiled at this and it iced the blood in Konstantine's veins. It was a knowing smile.

Konstantine realized he hadn't done a good job of casting doubt. Dmitri *knew* Lou was real, *wanted* her to be real. And wanting her to be real would've been enough to keep him hungry and on her trail.

Dmitri leaned forward and whispered in Konstantine's ear, almost companionably. "I will find her, Konstantine. And I will make her an offer she cannot refuse."

"And if she refuses?"

"I'll put her in the ground."

When Dmitri pulled back, Konstantine mustered his most wicked smile. The one he forced himself to wear when he did something truly evil. When he must enter the darkness in order to salvage the light devoured.

Dmitri's smile faltered.

"Good luck, amico mio," Konstantine said. "*Good luck.*"

4

Lou paced her apartment, her Browning tapping her thigh lightly as she passed her kitchen island. Once, twice...twenty times. Long after she lost count, she turned to the counter again and stared at the cream-colored letter open-faced on the marbled surface.

The dead shouldn't be able to write to the living.

Lou understood that Lucy had probably composed the letter in the early days of her illness. Perhaps back in May or June, once she learned the inevitable was coming.

The letter was no less haunting.

She'd read it three times through before placing it on the counter and backing away from it as if it were as dangerous as the creature prowling the shores of La Loon.

One line repeated in her head again and again. *There is a woman I want you to meet. You know how to find her.*

Please Lou. Please talk to her. At least once.

Lou did know how to find her. Her compass could do that difficult task on her behalf.

But who was this woman? Why did her aunt want her to meet some stranger months after her death? And worse still: *She knows who you are. What we can do. You can trust her.*

That would be enough to send Lou into a fury, into making her feel exposed and betrayed by the woman who raised her. But the simple *I trust her* tacked onto the letter lessened the blow.

Lucy was as terrible at trust as Lou herself. In some ways, worse. So *I trust her* was as powerful of an admission as Lou could ask for.

A mysterious woman that Lucy trusted. And that Lou must meet.

It sounded so simple. Then why did this dread well up inside her at the thought?

As if sensing this discord, the compass whirled to life inside her. The immediate tug. The whirling confusion only amplified Lou's fear.

But then she felt the dark, brooding energy at the end of the line and knew it wasn't some possession by a dead aunt. She wasn't being forced into a clandestine meeting with a stranger against her will.

It was Konstantine.

Konstantine—all gun smoke and leather—who was calling to her.

She had not heard from him since he'd returned her father's bullet-proof vest to her months ago. She hadn't seen him since he'd apologized for building a room that could imprison her, should she turn against him. It was three months since they'd forged an uneasy truce.

Was this simply the limitation of his patience? The longest he could go without seeing her?

No. It felt more...urgent.

Cursing, Lou pulled on her combat boots and laced them tight. She stepped into her converted linen closet.

She even brought a gun, though carrying it around was beginning to feel like a joke.

Her back pressed against the cool grain. Splinters scratched at her arms. She should sand down the walls. Maybe that's what she'd do with her next sleepless night.

For a moment, exhaustion pressed itself heavily against her mind.

She felt herself sliding toward it. Toward that inevitable collapse.

But instead she slipped sideways through the dark. It softened, opening to accept her.

When the world formed around her again, she stood in a shadowed apartment on the edge of the Arno river.

Konstantine paced between the wall and bed of his loft, looking as unsettled as she had moments before. He hadn't noticed her arrival. His head was bowed in deep concentration. His eyebrows were pulled together in tight focus.

She almost laughed. The earnestness was too much. Or she was what her aunt sometimes called punch drunk—when sleeplessness made the world all the more ridiculous.

Then he turned and looked at her. His hair was longer than when she'd seen it last and falling forward into his eyes.

"Louie," he said and a rush of relief and something else seized those hard features. "You came."

FOR A MOMENT KONSTANTINE COULD ONLY STARE AT HER. SHE DIDN'T look well. Dark circles spread under each eye. She was too thin. Some of that muscle definition he'd admired was lost.

She tapped the gun impatiently against her leg and the spell broke.

"This is how you dress in January?" he asked, wondering if perhaps she'd been somewhere warmer. Hunting criminals in the opium fields of Bogota perhaps?

"My apartment has better heating than yours," she said, glancing around his bedroom. "Apparently."

"Are you all right?" he asked. "Have you been sick?"

"I'm fine." It was a flat refusal to share more. Konstantine didn't want her to bolt so he dropped it.

"I'm sorry to call you like this," he said, finding his voice steady again.

He wondered where he should put his body. There was only the bed. That may seem too much like an invitation. So he sat down at the edge, and rested his forearms on his knees. "I wanted to warn you."

She didn't come to him, didn't sit on the bed beside him. She only stood there, staring with those dark eyes beneath thick, black lashes. There was none of that warm heat that had passed between them after surviving Nico's siege. She'd kissed him. He'd thought he was forgiven.

Perhaps this wasn't about him.

"Dmitri Petrov is..."

"I know who he is," she said.

Konstantine shrugged. A kind of acquiescence. "I saw him in

London two days ago. He made it clear he wants to meet you. I would say he is hunting you."

"To kill me?"

"No, actually," Konstantine said with a bitter laugh. "He said he wants to pay you."

She said nothing. What did she need to say? They both knew she would put Dmitri Petrov in the ground the moment he showed his face.

"He has no way of finding me," she said finally.

"I wouldn't be so sure," he said. "I delete every photo, every mention I cross, but it would be foolish to think I don't miss something from time to time. Though you have been...quiet this winter."

"How do you know what I've been doing?" she asked.

She stepped into the light. He saw then the dark lines beneath her eyes were even worse than he initially thought. The gun trembled in her hand almost imperceptibly. But he also saw the dried blood on both of her arms. And the bruises, far more bruises than Konstantine had ever seen on her. Was she using her fists instead of her guns?

"When is the last time you've slept?" he asked.

She said nothing.

"You need to be at your best if you plan to face him," Konstantine said.

"How do you *know* what I've been doing?" she insisted again, and he saw the gun shift in her hand.

"I keep an eye on you," he admitted.

"Why?"

He didn't know how to answer that. He knew the truth, but was equally certain she didn't want to hear it.

"*Why?*"

"We're...friends," he said.

"Are we?" she scoffed.

He forced a smile, but her words had stung like a slap across his cheek. A slap from his mother's own hand perhaps. He knew he deserved it. If he hadn't built that room of light, his archrival Nico would have never been able to capture her. Hurt her.

"Yes," he said and hoped his sincerity rang true. "You must be careful. The men you meet in the bars could be—"

Her eyebrows shot up. "Excuse me?"

"You owe me nothing," he was quick to add, wondering if she thought he would be possessive after *one* kiss.

"I'm aware," she said.

He pinched his brow. "I'm only saying you should be careful. He could plant anyone anywhere. The men you seduce for questioning—"

She laughed. It erupted from her in a way that made Konstantine's heart leap into his throat by the sudden richness. "The fuck, Konstantine."

"What?"

"You think I seduce men so I can *question* them?"

He would have said *yes*. But the way she was looking at him gave him pause. He knew she tracked men, tracked criminals, openly each night. He knew that sometimes this took her to dark bars or places where such men congregated, and that on more than one occasion, his own surveillance proved that she left these places with a man in tow.

She never took them to her apartment overlooking the St. Louis river. But she went home with them, yes. And he knew what she did with those men once the doors were closed and the lights were off.

"You're not questioning them," he said.

"No, Konstantine," she said, sarcasm thick. "I don't need to *fuck* a man to get information. If I fuck them, it's for the orgasm."

To hear the words from her own lips made his heart drop. Of course she didn't. She tortured and killed as well as he did.

"I don't sleep with the men I hunt," she added. "But sometimes, someone else might catch my eye."

His stomach was eating itself.

"I would never interfere in your...wishes," he began, understanding his error now. "But you must be careful. He will find a way to get to you when you're...vulnerable."

"Through the random men I hook up with?" she asked. She looked ready to burst into laughter.

She's exhausted, he realized. *Borderline delirious.*

"I would track the stationary people in your life. Perhaps King or that woman with the shop. Even the blond girl who works the counter. Anyone I could find."

The humor left her face. *At least she isn't completely gone.*

"He doesn't know about them. He can't put us together."

Konstantine stood, moving his body within reach of hers. He searched her eyes. "You need to sleep."

"I can't," she whispered.

"Take something."

She snorted.

"If you need—"

She bit back a laugh. "You can't *help* me, Konstantine."

But he wanted to.

"If you don't go to sleep, it will find you sooner or later."

He raised one hand, tentatively, slowly, as if expecting her to run away. When she didn't move back, he grasped her upper arm. Despite the leather jacket, a thrill ran through him. He wished he could take that delicate ear between his lips. But he saw now was not the time nor the place. But there was no reason she shouldn't know how he felt.

"Unlike the boys you find," he said. "I can accommodate the full violence of your affection."

For a moment she leaned toward him. His heart hammered. He thought he might have a chance to help her sleep after all.

But then she stepped away, back into the shadows and the enveloping darkness.

"Thanks for the warning," she said, and was gone.

5

King slipped his key into the lock of 777 Royal Street and it turned. The door stuck, but with a bump of his hip, it popped open. Light from the storefront window cast shadows across the polished wood floor.

It still smelled of lemon cleaner. Piper's friend—a twenty-year-old woman whom she'd recommended for the once-a-week cleaning—did a great job. Even the fan overhead shone, the wooden blades gleaming with polish.

King turned toward the window.

The gold-letter decal covered the glass storefront, partially obstructing the view of each passersby. The words *Crescent City Detective Agency* lie projected on the floor.

He adjusted the three cherry-red plastic chairs against the wall closest to the window, which would serve as a waiting area. A table sat against the opposite wall, clean and ready for the items he bounced in the sack by his side.

He put the grocery bag on the floor and pulled out the plastic coffee maker. Nothing fancy. But it would brew eight cups on command. He affixed the plastic lid, and inserted the plastic basket. In the little drawer beneath he put the new box of paper filters, a bag of coffee and two boxes of assorted tea.

In the mini-fridge, which had been plugged in by the maid per his request, he put a carton of cream and a box of baking soda, which he opened and tucked into the door.

He used the lower shelf of the cabinet for the pack of Styrofoam cups and a bag of sugar. There was a ceramic jar for the sugar, hunter green, but he would let Piper fill that later.

Lastly was the box of plastic spoons.

Not the best for the environment, King knew. He practically heard Lucy's chiding voice in the back of his head, insisting that he think of the planet.

"If we get quite a bit of foot traffic in here, I'll get them next time. I'll even throw in some biodegradable cups," he told the empty room.

After sitting at one desk, and then the other, King decided he wanted the one on the same side as the window and waiting area. Piper —or whoever else he brought in to help him do the legwork on a case— could have the desk on the same side as the door and coffee station.

Should his little agency take off—and here he let himself dream a little dream—he supposed there was room for more desks. There was enough open space between here and the wall without blocking any of the three doors. One door led to the bathroom. Its opposite led to a storage closet, and the third led up to an unused apartment.

It was an apartment he'd half expected to move into. He was as aware of the dangers of this work as Mel was, so it surprised him to hear that she wanted him to stay. He wouldn't have left her without a tenant of course, but she wouldn't hear it. She did, however, want to install a new alarm system and asked King to start looking for trained police dogs, maybe a retired one in need of a good home. He agreed on all counts. He only hoped they'd get the measures in place before the worst should happen.

King wasn't sure what to do with the extra apartment above yet. He could use it for extra storage he supposed. Or he could sublet it to help cover the costs of rent. But that was a problem for another day. Presently, he had more than enough to be getting on with.

He sat behind his desk and put his backpack on the floor. He reclined in his chair and admired the room. The clean-for-now desks and gleaming floors. The clock hanging on the wall above the coffee maker. It was ten to nine and Piper would be here soon.

But for now, this was his space.

There was something pleasant about finishing the preparations. The calm before the starting shot was fired.

King smiled, feeling the way his mouth resisted, rife with bittersweet melancholy.

He wished Lucy was here.

Lucy should *be here*.

If Lucy hadn't come to see him in June, would he even be here now? Or would he still be drinking his afternoons away in the French Quarter dives, listening to jazz late into the night, and spending his days catching up on this or that game while smoking weed?

That was the retirement he'd imagined. That was the one he'd told himself he wanted when he left the DEA, putting his St. Louis home on the market and driving to New Orleans with his belongings packed into his car.

The storage closet opened and King was jolted out of his musings. His chair rocked back and for a moment he thought he would topple and crack his head on the brick wall behind him.

At the last second he righted himself, his chair clattering loudly onto all fours.

Lou stood opposite his desk. Her hands in the pockets of her leather jacket. Her snug jeans tucked into black boots. Her eyes hidden behind mirrored sunglasses that made her look more like a patrolling state trooper than a young woman. Her dark hair had been left free, hanging past her shoulders

"Christ. You scared me," he exclaimed.

Lou looked around the office, taking in the desk, the open window. "This is a nice place."

Pride bubbled inside him. "Thanks."

King was able to slow his heart enough to regain control of it. "Did you just come through the storage closet?"

She nodded. "Is the rent high?"

King laughed. "Yeah, the Quarter isn't cheap. But I can write the expenses off on my taxes and I've got enough to fund it for at least the next twelve months. Hopefully, we can build a reputation by then."

"We," she said and settled into the desk opposite him. "There are no computers."

"No, we'll use our laptops, haul them in and out. We don't want to worry about a break in and having them stolen."

She didn't say anything. He wished she would take off her glasses so he could look into her eyes rather than seeing his old, wrinkled face reflected back at him.

"Actually I'm glad you came. I wanted to talk to you about your role here," he said.

She didn't look surprised to hear this.

"At first, mostly what we'll do is build up cases for law enforcement agencies. Or attorneys who are trying to build cases for their clients. I've also got some referrals out, and an old buddy of mine is calling the NOLA PD this morning to recommend us."

"I'm not a detective," she said.

"You won't have to handle any of the paperwork. And most of that is a cover for what I really want to do. You remember Senator Ryanson?"

"The man who hired your ex-partner to murder and frame my father?" she asked, flatly.

King noted that rhetorical questions meant to prepare a conversation were another way to make himself look stupid. He'd try to remember that in the future.

"We did great on that case." He said it as if he needed to convince her. It was true that she said she would help, but he didn't feel her commitment to the vision yet. Partly because he was aware that she owed him nothing. She was only here because of a promise she'd made her dying aunt.

"Political corruption is rampant," he said. "They have too much leverage in the present system to get justice for their crimes. So I'll do the legwork, confirm they are guilty, and then you can give them a one-way trip to La Loon."

"You're judge and jury. I'm executioner. Lucy wouldn't approve."

He leaned back in his seat and scratched his jaw. In the excitement of getting the office open that morning, he'd forgotten to shave. "No. She wouldn't. But she'll have to forgive us."

"She sent me a letter."

"Me too. And some VHS tapes that I'm supposed to give to you. I want to check that they're authentic before I hand them over."

Lou shifted uncomfortably. "What did the letter say?"

He didn't want to recount the affirmations of eternal love. He cleared his throat. "Mostly information of how she wanted her estate handled and instructions to give you the tapes once I make sure they weren't tampered with. What did yours say?"

"She wants me to meet someone."

"That's vague."

"A woman," Lou said. "Who knows about me."

"Oh," King said because he had no idea what the proper response was. "Are you okay?" He realized for the first time she seemed subdued today. "Everything been okay with you?"

Nothing.

"I haven't seen you in three months," he said by way of explanation, again feeling like he had no right to ask about her life. "You disappeared like that after Ryanson, too. Is that what you do? Make a big kill then lay low for three months? Is it, uh, part of your process or something?"

She hadn't been lying low. He didn't need her to say so. He saw the split skin on the back of her knuckles. And realized the slump in her shoulders might very well be exhaustion. But who was she hunting now? More crime lords like Paolo Konstantine?

"If you're worried I won't show up when you need me to—" she began.

"I'm not worried," he said, holding his palms up in surrender. "You've always been there when I needed you."

How could he say otherwise? She was the one who'd gotten him to the hospital when he'd been shot in the back. She was the one who swooped in and saved Lucy when she'd collapsed. Lou had an uncanny ability of being exactly where she was needed.

She pushed herself off the desk. "Who are you targeting first?"

"There's a mayor from California, Richard Sikes. I think he's in deep with a sex trafficking ring. Modern-day slavery. I'm going to do some checking up on him, find out if he really is helping to smuggle people in and out of LA and then I'll let you know."

"*And* you're also going to run cases for the DEA?" she asked.

King grinned. "I get bored easily."

She crossed to the window and looked out, watching people wander up and down Royal Street.

"There's a Russian mob boss looking for me. Dmitri Petrov. Keep your eyes open."

King frowned. "You think he's going to come here?"

"If they figure out my name, then they can find Lucy."

"Lucy is dead." Saying it was like a punch to his gut.

"But you're connected to her. And I'd follow that connection."

King understood what she meant. "I'll keep my eyes open for anyone new."

6

Daniella parked her car in the parking garage, two blocks from Melandra's Fortunes and Fixes. Scooting back the front seat of her Dodge Dart as far as she could, she opened her laptop. There was one file folder, simply labeled *Now*.

She cast a nervous glance over her shoulder, craning her neck in each direction of the parking garage to make sure she was alone. A man stood at the elevator waiting for his ride, nose close to the screen of his phone.

Satisfied, she double-clicked the folder embedded on her taskbar. Inside was a Scrivener file and collection of photos. She double-clicked on the first photo and it enlarged on her screen.

A young woman in a leather jacket and boots, dark jeans, and mirrored sunglasses walked beside the man twice her size. Broad-shouldered, slightly hunched, he was mid-gesture as he spoke. His weight leaned to one side. The man she'd been able to identify easily—Robert King, retired and decorated agent for the DEA's St. Louis unit. He now lived above an occult shop in the French Quarter of New Orleans.

It was the only person she'd been able to put with the woman. Her only lead. But if Daniella was worth her salt, she'd be able to find out the girl's identity.

Looking once again through the photos, spotting landmarks in the

Quarter for future investigation, Daniella closed and powered down the machine.

Pulling on her coat, she stepped into the garage and locked the laptop and suitcase in the trunk of her car. Then she walked east, two blocks to the job that awaited her.

Her cheeks were icy cold by the time she wiped her sneakers on the mat and pushed back the hood of her coat.

The earthy scent of incense consumed her, mixed with the sweet, cloying perfume of candles. Fake candles flickered electronically in an old-fashioned chandelier overhead. It looked like something from a Viking dining hall. Ghostly moans circled the room, sounding as if spirits of the undead raced overhead.

Dani felt eyes on her and turned to find a black woman, stepping out of a room and closing the door behind her. Gold bangles jingled on her wrists and two beautiful rings shone. One a wide flat onyx on her left hand and a purple amethyst sparked on her right. Her head was wrapped in a gorgeous crimson scarf, which she tugged for good measure.

"You must be Dani," she said, coming toward her. They met in the middle of the room beside a shelf of figurines and a basket of corn husk dolls. "I'm Melandra. You can call me Mel."

The woman's bangles tinkled again as she stretched her hand forward to shake Dani's. It made Dani think of the windchimes in her mother's garden on the other side of Lake Pontchartrain.

Dani plastered on her biggest grin. "Yes, ma'am."

"You're early."

Dani released a tight laugh. "My momma said that it was best to be early if you want to make a good impression."

"Intelligent woman."

Dani forced a smile. She could say many things about her mother, but this was neither the time nor the place.

Mel gestured toward the cash register. "This job is fairly straightforward. You need to be mindful of the counter at all times, which you can see from anywhere in the store except the stockroom." She pointed at the door she'd exited upon Dani's arrival. "And for that there's the chandelier." Mel mimicked its ghostly moan.

Dani favored her with a good-natured smile and polite laugh.

"You said you had cashier experience."

It was Dani's chance to recite one of her many practiced lies. "I do. I worked in a grocery store back in my hometown. Biggly Bounds."

"What a name."

And the obligatory follow-up lies, of course. "It was a local mom and pop store."

Melandra arched her eyebrows. "Then you know how to count change. I'll put the money in the register in the morning. And Piper or I will close it out at night. So you won't have to do anything else except the transactions during your shift."

"And if there are no customers?" Dani's eyes trailed up the stairs beside the storeroom. They led to the landing above, which no doubt would take her to the ex-agent's apartment. Though there were two doors—one on the left and one on the right.

"You won't need to go up there," Melandra said. "Those are our apartments."

Dani realized she'd been staring too long.

"That one is mine," Melandra said, pointing at the right side door. "And my friend Robert lives in the other. You'll meet him soon. He's in and out quite a bit."

"Cool," she said, aiming for indifference.

"To answer your question, when there are no customers I want you to tackle the to-do list. I'll always put it here by the register for you. There won't be anything too hard. It might be restocking, or stickering merchandise, or cleaning. Just do what you can when it's slow. If it's too busy, don't worry about it. Customers come first."

"It sounds easy enough," Dani said. Her voice stuck in her throat when she caught sight of herself in the mirror. Black nails, dark eyeliner and a rock t-shirt. She even wore ripped jeans. If her mother, the great Beverly Allendale saw her, she would *die*.

Mel was speaking again. "Let me show you the appointment book."

She bent beneath the glass case on which the cash register rested and pulled out a thick leather book. Dani was certain its ominous appearance was intentional. The cover looked like tan flesh crudely stitched together by a rough hand. The pages were stiff yellowed parchment.

As the woman with the painted eyes flipped through the pages to find the line where a customer must sign, Dani knew the patrons must find a thrill in it—signing their name in such a book. In fact, they likely enjoyed every detail of the shop. The ambiance was perfect for those looking to venture into the dark. From the low, sultry music and the clouds of incense hanging on the air, to the trinkets, charms and all the magic they promised.

"If someone comes in and wants a reading, put them down here and write what they want. Palm, tarot, tea leaves, past life regression, medium, ghost communication—there's a whole list here and the price. Be sure to tell them the price. Piper can only be scheduled for palm, tarot and tea leaves readings. Piper, PPT, got it?"

Dani nodded. "How will I know your available times?"

Melandra slipped the book back out of sight and then grabbed the notebook off the counter. "Here's the to-do list. But on the back—" She flipped the notebook over to reveal its cardboard backing. "Here's the weekly availability. It says on the price sheet how long each reading is and the price for each person. I charge more than Piper. But you can figure out the rest. It's not as complicated as it sounds."

"I'm a quick study."

Melandra smiled. "Good. Come around here and stand behind the register then, and see how it feels."

Dani obeyed.

She marveled again at her painted black nails and the silver rings on her own fingers. She kept forgetting what kind of girl she was supposed to be today...and every day, until she got what she came for.

Mel came around the counter and surveyed Dani there. She nodded as if satisfied with what she saw. "Any questions?"

"It's pretty straightforward."

"Perfect. I've got you here until four today, when Piper comes in."

The ghostly chime rang again and a young woman bounded across the mat. "Mel, King just said he saw Lou—" The girl's voice broke off mid-speech when she spotted Dani standing behind the register. She slowed her pace until she crested the last row of merchandise and found Mel standing there on the other side of the counter.

Mel arched an eyebrow curiously. "Yes?"

"Uh, I need to talk to you when you've got a second."

Mel pointed upstairs at her apartment. "I was about to make myself a cup of tea. You want to join me?"

"Sure. But then I've got to get back. King sent me for sandwiches and to...give you an update."

Dani forced a smile, hoping it made her look sweet, innocuous and at the very least, uninterested. When she thought perhaps the stare itself was too much, she slid her gaze down the to-do list. She tapped the ink pen against the pad as she pretended to read it.

"Piper, this is Dani," Mel said, clicking her manicured nails against glass.

"Hi," Piper said, reaching up to touch the cuff on her upper ear. A slight blush had pooled in her cheeks.

"Hi," Dani said. She returned the smile and offered her hand over the glass counter.

7

The darkness thinned around her, offering Lou safe passage. She slipped from one side of the world to another, pausing in the dark so the world could reform around her. And then there was light seeping through a crack between door and jamb. This room was much bigger than her converted linen closet, but that's all she noted at a cursory glance.

She eased open the door as a train of waiters with silver platters rushed by. The smell of meat, rich cream, and spices wafted in.

She must be in a restaurant, and a high-end one by the look of the waiters' attire. There would be no seizing and killing King's suspect politician here. But she could get close. Size him up. Take his measure. And then perhaps when he went to the restroom, an opportunity would present itself. She loved it when they went to the restroom.

A female waiter approached from the dining room, an empty tray tucked under her arm. Lou watched her get closer and closer through the slight crack in the door. Then as she was passing, Lou threw open the door and grabbed her. She made sure to clamp her hand hard over the woman's mouth so no cry would ring out when she pulled her into the dark.

Lou considered her options for rendering the server unconscious. Striking her seemed unfair. She'd done nothing wrong. Lou decided on a sleeper hold. It caused the woman to struggle more, writhing against the side of Lou's body. Her elbow connected with Lou's ribs. A nail scratched her cheek as she reached behind trying to find Lou's eyes.

Play nice, Lou thought. *Or I will kill you after all.*

As if you could came the cruel voice again.

Don't leave her unconscious and naked in a broom closet, her father warned. *What if someone found her?*

Her father, though dead, was usually right about these things. Not to mention he was much easier to listen to than her newest voice—that unforgiving critic. Lou did have a place she could hide an unconscious waitress for twenty minutes or so.

Taking a step back into deeper shadows, Lou slipped through the dark again. The smell of food and the clink of dishes was replaced by cold silence. The kind of silence that prevailed in winter. Desolate and never-ending.

Lou's boots scuffed the bare floor of the metal shipping container. She was pleased to see it was still there, unmolested and forgotten. Of course, she only knew it was in Siberia somewhere. It could be an abandoned warehouse full of them for all she knew. She'd never seen the outside. Only this eternally dark inner chamber.

Of course, this was not the same one she'd dumped Chaz Brasso, King's traitorous ex-partner. She owed the girl that much courtesy at least.

The girl had stopped writhing in the crook of Lou's elbow.

Gently, Lou lay her on the floor and checked her pulse. It beat strong.

Lou wasted no time in undressing her. Stripping her of all but her underwear and shoes. She worried the girl might get cold in here, but hoped she wouldn't be gone long enough for that to be an issue. Still, Lou left her own t-shirt and pants, both draped over her sleeping body before redressing herself.

The pants were too tight in the thighs and the shirt too loose in the chest. But they would do.

Then Lou slipped, finding herself in the restaurant once more. Here, it wasn't pitch black like the shipping container. Here at least, Lou could find the small plastic buttons on her shirt and the black vest. Here she could see enough to know she'd missed a corner of shirt and tucked it neatly into her pants.

She bent and picked up the tray and stepped out into the hallway.

She saw a smudge of rust on the pristine white arm of the shirt and hoped that was the only place the fabric had come into contact with the old shipping container. She dusted at the cotton gently and some of the red dust fell away. Most began to smear.

Pushing open the swinging silver door, Lou stepped into the hallway. She followed it to the end of the hallway and entered the restaurant, only to find it wasn't a restaurant exactly.

If she had to guess, she was in a country club. This room of the club had been set up for dinner, obvious with its round tables and white linens, lit centerpieces and low music.

Her eyes swept the room, looking for Sikes. She found him at a table with two other men, and a woman on his arm. Her dress sparkled like the centerpieces. Her eyes were thickly lined with eyeliner and her lips were the color of blood.

Lou circled. She weaved through the tables, pretending to inspect plates and water glasses as if she cared, all the while getting closer and closer to Sikes. Until she was right behind him, practically breathing down the back of his hairy neck. His hair held gray throughout. And the top of his hair was thinning to the point that Lou could see the gleaming flesh beneath, bright with scalp oil in the overhead light.

She could reach him in four steps. Maybe three.

"Excuse me," a woman said.

Lou turned toward the voice. A woman in a red cocktail dress waved Lou over to her table.

"These prawns are cold and they still have grit in them. Were they *even* washed?" Her petulant tone made Lou's teeth set on edge.

"I don't know," Lou said, her eyes scanning the room.

"Daphne," the man beside her said. He had thick white hair and deep-set eyes behind glasses.

"No—I'm sending this back," the woman insisted pushing the plate across the white tablecloth toward Lou. "I want the baked chicken."

"Okay," Lou said, lifting the plate.

As she forced a smile, her eyes scanned the room one more time. She saw not one but four pairs of eyes on her. All men. She suspected this was mild sexual interest at first. But one of the men caused her to look again.

When their eyes locked, he froze, his thumb pausing in the middle of a text. He looked like a deer ready to run.

Getting a good look at his face, committing it to memory—the bushy brow, almost Neanderthal in its forward thrust, the eyes set too close together and oversized mouth, pockmarked cheeks—she noted it all.

He lowered his phone slowly to hide it beneath the table, a damning gesture. Lou knew the hunt well enough to know when she'd been made. The man excused himself from his party and walked through an adjacent door. Lou considered following him.

"I'm hungry," the petulant woman whined. "Can I get my dinner *tonight* please? What are you waiting for?"

Sikes also rose from his table, excusing himself. He headed in the same direction as the man, through the same door.

"I'll change it now." Lou spoke absentmindedly as she followed Sikes out of the room.

"The kitchen is that way!" cried the woman behind her.

Lou didn't care. She placed the cold prawns in front of another, very confused woman who sat closest to the exit doors.

When Lou stepped into the hall, it was in time to see Sikes enter into the adjacent bathroom, through the barrier-free doorway marked *Men*. Further down the hall, the mystery man spoke rapidly into his cell phone. Then as if he felt the eyes on his back, he turned and looked directly at Lou.

She had a choice. Seize the man and end his call, follow whatever trail had sprung up there, or finish with Sikes.

He can wait, her father suggested.

You won't be able to kill him anyway, taunted the critic.

Lou took a breath and stepped into the men's restroom.

Sikes stood behind a urinal. He didn't even look up as Lou entered. She hit the light switch on the wall and he cried out in surprise.

It was easier to find him in the dark.

"Hello?" Sikes called. "Hello? Is anyone there?"

She inched toward him, hovering within arms' reach.

He has three boys, she was reminded. *Three children who will wake up in the night, heartsick for the father.*

You're no better than Angelo Martinelli.

Gritting her teeth, Lou seized Sikes by the back of the neck and wrenched him to his knees. He struggled but could do nothing. Her grip was ironclad.

"Please," Sikes whimpered. There was fear in his voice, fear that Lou could practically taste. "Whatever you want take it. My wallet is in my back pocket. I won't stop you."

Her hand flexed, tightening on the spinal column. But the rage didn't come. Lou had only the cold winter wind blowing through her, an endless night of snow.

Take him, she pleaded.

Finish it. Just finish it.

Lou slipped, leaving Sikes crying, but alive, on the bathroom floor.

8

Dani woke to a velvet paw tapping her lips and nose.

"*Meow.*"

When Dani didn't rise, the cat added pressure until she was fully standing on Dani's face.

"Meow. *Meow.*"

"Christ, Octavia. *What do you want?*"

The cat flopped over onto her back, and dragged her tail under Dani's nose. Batting it away, Dani caved, pulling herself up to sitting. She fumbled her phone off the white side table and checked the time. "It's not even eight you little monster!"

The bedroom door was partially cracked. The chair she'd wedged under the door to deter the cat from entering had clearly been faulty. They made it look so easy in the movies. *Stick a chair under the door and no one can enter.* Lies.

She would have to consider a different setup. Of course, knowing Octavia, she would find another way in. The blue British shorthair seemed to know her place in this arrangement and had no trouble affectionately reminding Dani that who was the servant here.

Dani climbed from the bed and took the cat with her, cradling her like a baby and looking into those deep gold eyes. "How could I neglect such a sweet princess? You're my little empress. The noodle-monkey of my heart."

The cat purred, obviously vindicated for the momentary lapse of neglect, and leaned into the hand scratching her fluffy cheek and erect ear.

Dani placed the cat on the island counter, something that would have sent her mother into hysterics, and fished a can of cat food from the cabinet above the stove. She opened the can and forked the minced meat—and heaven knew what else—into the small porcelain bowl.

"Wait, you'll cut your little face!" She begged the impatient cat who seemed ready to eat from the can. "Tavie, we aren't *savages*," Dani said in her best Beverly Allendale voice.

Dani loved to mimic her mother. Not only because the comic material was rich, but it was all she could do with her pent-up resentment. Her mother wasn't a bad person, if an entitled and overbearing one.

While it was certainly true that her mother had made her own money as the owner of a successful cosmetics company, she'd inherited nearly six million from her dead father while she was in college. And he'd gotten his money from his exiled sugar baron father, a man who'd escaped Cuba with his life when Fidel Castro took control of the country.

Dani's father's family had been from Honduras. When he was twenty he opened his own brokerage and by thirty-eight, when he married Daniella's mother, he'd amassed a small fortune himself.

She loved her parents and was immensely grateful for the financial security they'd given her, but they were too materialistic. They knew nothing about passion, or *compassion* for that matter. She'd tried to use the word *calling* with her mother once to explain her passion for stories and Beverly had only blinked at her, uncomprehending.

I suppose you really do take after my brother, Beverly had said once, standing in her dining room, pearls at her neck and hair in a perfect chiffon bun. *He also...wandered.*

True, it had been her Uncle Charles who'd opened her eyes to the hypocrisy of their world when he'd invited her to spend a summer with him in Zimbabwe. She was fifteen.

Her parents had only agreed to let her go because she'd sold them on the idea of her stellar college application. How great would it look to the Harvard Medical School reviewers that she'd spent three months apprenticing with a renowned doctor in Africa, she'd argued.

And they bought her ticket the next day.

Two years later Uncle Charles joined Doctors Without Borders in Gaza and died in an air raid with thirteen children.

Maybe that's why her parents only passive aggressively resisted her decision to study writing rather than medicine. But she never forgot what she'd learned in Africa. About income inequality. About how often the rich were very rich and the poor were very poor. But also about how small and limited her parents' worldview was. They believed things about the world that simply weren't true.

Once she got a job at The Herald, Beverly began saying *Daniella wants to be a journalist,* as if it were an amusing quirk, a hobby she would surrender for a respectable husband and children with time.

I don't want a husband or children. I want a Pulitzer.

God, I sound just like them, she thought as she poured water into the coffeemaker and started a fresh pot.

How many women out there dreamed of pursuing their passions but had to sacrifice those dreams in order to keep food on the table and predatory loan sharks at bay? Dani knew that the financial security her family afforded her was a rare privilege. The least she could do was not waste it on vapid pursuits.

Coffee ready, she filled her largest mug, and doctored it with a cake's worth of cream and sugar. She retrieved her laptop off her desk charger and climbed back into bed.

Now began her search.

Lou, Piper had said. Of course that could be anyone. Chances were the mystery woman whose identity she sought to establish wouldn't be named *Lou.* But Piper had broken off mid-sentence hadn't she? Maybe she was going to say Louise or Louann. Maybe it wasn't Lou at all. Maybe it was going to be Lucy or Lucille?

Or they could've been talking about someone else, her mind insisted.

But she had to trust her gut on this. If they had been talking about just anyone, would Piper have acted so secretive all of a sudden? Dani didn't think so.

She'd start with the obvious. Google. The idea was to do a simple search and try to make a connection to Robert King.

She took a sip of coffee—*what magic*—and waited for her browser to load. In the search box she typed Lou DEA.

The first page had four or five articles, mostly local St. Louis press, outlining the heroism of a young man named Louis Hartford. He was a DEA agent who found three hundred pounds of cocaine hidden in a barge on the Mississippi River.

She kept scrolling and was nine pages in when an article caught her eye.

Murdered DEA Agent Hero Not Traitor.

She double-clicked and began to read. She didn't even notice the fed Octavia jump onto her bed and begin to wash her ears in the early sunlight.

Dani slipped on her glasses and lifted the steaming coffee to her lips. She read, learning about Jack Thorne and his wife. How weeks before he was gunned down, he testified against a drug lord from a powerful family.

At first, the DEA thought Jack had worked with the crime family. However, new evidence proved he was innocent, and in fact, Senator Greg Ryanson and Lieutenant Chaz Brasso had been the moles. They were also responsible for Jack's murder—and both of them were still missing.

Only their daughter Louie Thorne survived.

Dani choked, spitting half of her coffee back into the mug.

A small photo of the girl sat in the bottom right of the article. It looked like a school photograph. *Twelve-year-old Louie Thorne, pictured above, is the sole survivor of the attack.*

Dani leaned forward. Yes, she could see it. The shape of the face and mouth at least. The nose. She'd only seen the woman at night or behind mirrored sunglasses so she wasn't one hundred percent sure. But she was damn suspicious.

Dani tossed the laptop onto the bed, eliciting an irritated flick of the ears from the cat. She hadn't noticed. She tore through the covers trying to locate her cell phone.

She found it halfway inside her pillowcase. She punched a number she now knew by heart.

"The Louisiana Herald, Frederick Barnes speaking."

"Freddie!" Dani hissed.

"Yes?"

"It's Dani. I have a question."

"Hey," he said. "How's your undercover sting going?"

"That's what I'm calling about. Does your brother still work in the NOLA PD?"

"Yeah, why?"

"I need someone to do an age progression on a photo. I've got a kid's photo and I want to know what she looks like now."

"He's in Pensacola on some *feelings* retreat until Monday. But I can ask him when he gets back."

Dani drew a steadying breath against her racing heart. "That'll do."

"Send me the pic and I'll pass it along."

"Done."

A nasal bark resonated in the background.

"Gotta go," Freddie said. "Baker's tossing around marching orders."

"Text me as soon as you hear something."

Dani tossed the phone onto the pillow and took up the laptop again. She stared into those flat, black eyes.

Louie Thorne, she thought as she saved the picture to her computer. *Is it really you?*

9

As Piper walked the French Quarter, she ran her to-do list through her head again. It was growing exponentially fast and she loved it. When the day stretched out before her, and she had nothing to do, a feeling of vast emptiness would wash over her. Almost like a stomachache, or finding herself alone in a club, her friends gone on without her.

This was better. Direction. Purpose. A list to accomplish so that when she laid her head down at the end of the day, she had something to account for. Something to hold onto so the sleep would come.

She checked her watch. It was rounding on two in the afternoon. Damn. She needed to drop off these supplies to Mel, check in with King once more and get home before three. If she didn't...

Piper picked up her pace, her sneakers scuffing the cobblestone as she rounded the corner onto St. Peter. She stepped into the shop and found the new girl behind the register, tapping her pen against the notepad.

"Hey," Piper said. "How's it going?"

The girl startled, seizing her notes and clutching them to her chest.

A ream of nervous laughter escaped her. "Oh my God. You scared me."

"Sorry," Piper said, setting the sack of supplies down behind the counter.

"It's okay. I've always been jumpy," she said, sliding the notebook into the pocket of her loose pants. "Probably makes you wonder why I'm working in an occult shop."

"What did you do before?" Piper asked.

"I was a dancer," she said.

"Cool," she said, wondering if that was code for stripper. Of course, it was rude to ask, so she didn't press it.

But Piper couldn't help her curiosity. The girl was cute. She was *more* than cute, Piper realized. It wasn't the tiny waist and flaring hips or considerable junk in the trunk. It was her face. Her skin was smooth, almost glowing. Her eyes lifted at the ends. Her lashes were thick. If she was four inches taller, Piper could picture her on the runway.

Stop ogling her. You don't have time for this.

Piper tried to get ahold of herself. "Do you know where Mel is? I need to give her this stuff."

Dani tucked her hair behind her ear and pointed at the thick purple curtain. "Back there, behind *the silken, sad, uncertain rustling of each purple curtain, thrilled me—filled me with fantastic terrors never felt before.*"

Piper wasn't sure how to react to this strange response.

"Poe," the other girl said, her face blushing. "The Raven."

"Oh! Yeah. I haven't read that since high school."

Piper couldn't wait any longer. She still had to check on her mom before returning to King.

"Can you make sure she gets this?" Piper pointed at the paper bag of supplies on the floor.

"Sure."

"Great. Thanks." Piper whirled, ready to run out of the shop.

"Hey, Piper?" Dani called. "I was wondering if you were free later. I'm new to the Big Easy and I don't really know the area or have any friends. Wow, that sounds so pathetic. I don't want to come off as this crazy, clingy person but—" She hesitated.

"It's cool," Piper said, familiar with the way women liked to have such admissions punctuated. A *go ahead* that green-lighted the conversation.

"It would be nice to spend some time with someone other than my cat and to learn a little bit about the area. Like where to buy weed?"

Piper laughed. "I have to close tonight."

"Right. No big deal. Maybe some other time then." Her hopeful face fell dramatically. Oh yeah, this one was trouble. Piper knew it by looking at her and the way her stomach jerked at that pitiful expression.

"But after we close, I can take you around if you want," she said. "And introduce you to Henry."

Her face blushed. "Oh I don't like men...I mean they're okay as friends, but.. uh..."

Piper laughed. "Henry sells weed. And has two boyfriends."

"Oh!" Her face blushed deeper. She covered her mouth with her hand and laughed even harder. "Oh, right. Okay. Yes. That would be awesome."

With a wave, Piper ducked out of the shop, checking her watch one more time and knowing she was cutting it close.

PIPER STEPPED OFF THE CORNER AND KEPT RUNNING. WINDING through the narrow side streets to the crowded row houses wedged at the end of the district. Old neglected houses that seemed to lean into one another, braced against the wind rolling off the canal.

A short house with a wooden porch and torn screen door lurched into view.

Piper took the steps two at a time and found the front door unlocked. Stupid, but not surprising. She only hoped she wasn't too late.

"Mom?" she called out, as she crossed the threshold into a smoky hallway. The house reeked of cigarettes and kerosene.

Piper glanced up the narrow staircase ahead, toward her bedroom. She wanted to get more of her clothes but it could wait. She checked her watch 2:54. Damn, she was out of time. "Mom?"

"Willy?" a raspy voice called.

Piper followed the voice into the living room.

The room was dark except for beams of sunlight piercing the haze. Cheap wool blankets hung over the windows to blot out the cold and the sun. In those stray beams, Piper saw cigarette smoke swirl in the air, not unlike the incense that hung in Mel's shop.

The kerosene heater glowed in the center of the room, casting a halo of warmth and light.

Her mother sat on the sunken sofa. "Willy?"

"No, Mom. It's Piper." She didn't enjoy being mistaken for her mother's latest boyfriend and supplier. "Listen. I've got to tell you something."

Piper knelt down in front of the woman. She sat on the edge of the ripped sofa, trying to light the cigarette in her mouth. It bobbed between quivering lips as unsteady as the hand.

"Here, let me," Piper said and took the plastic lighter and struck it with her right thumb, cupping the side of her mother's cigarette with her free hand.

Her skin smelled acrid. That trash was oozing out of her pores.

"Get me a beer."

"In a minute, Mom. Listen. I need you to know something. Are you listening?"

She searched the woman's face, trying to get a good look into her eyes.

Their gazes finally met and Piper was relieved to see they were clear. As she opened her mouth, the screen door slammed.

Damn.

"NayNay, where you at?"

The fridge door opened and closed, bottles rattling. Piper knew she should tell her mother now, but it might start shit—a violent episode that could last for hours—and she promised King she'd be back in forty minutes.

Willy Turner stepped into the living room. He was a squat man. A solid square of muscle about six inches taller than Piper. He liked to puff out his chest and rub his stomach as if he'd eaten a big meal. His sneer made Piper's insides turn.

"You got my stuff," her mother said, hopeful. The tremble in her hand ceased.

"Maybe I do, maybe I don't. What you gonna give me for it?"

Piper detested everything about this man. His gut, his leer, his weak chin and glassy eyes. The hair on the back of his fat knuckles. Worse than his gross, unkempt appearance was the way he treated her mother. It sickened her to see them in the same room together. At least her mother had not married him, like the last two, albeit briefly. Her father had been the second marriage and the longest. She wasn't sure what that said about their relationship. But one thing was for certain. To her mother, these men meant it was time to get high. Anything that Piper said to her now would go in one ear and out the other.

She squeezed her mom's knee and stood. "I'll see you later, Mom."

Willy moved to block Piper's path. "Where you running off to, lesbo?"

"Work."

"You work a lot, but I don't see you paying any of these goddamn bills," Willy said, still in her way.

"Come on, give it to me," her mom said, standing from the couch.

Willy took a step toward her. Piper considered standing her ground. She'd traded blows with worse. But her mind seemed fixated on the words she'd failed to say before he arrived and the fact that King was still waiting. And she didn't want to disappoint the one reliable man in her life.

Piper stepped back.

Grinning as if he'd won some battle, Willy shoulder checked her as he entered the room. "Yeah, I got your shit. But you've got to pay for it."

He stopped in front of her mother. With a sneer, he began to undo the top of his pants, eyes locked on Piper.

Her mother sat back down on the couch. Her eyes roving back and forth between the heroin in Willy's right hand and the zipper he worked to undo.

Piper darted through the doorway and out the front door without looking back.

Forget the clothes. She'd try another time.

10

Lou stood at the edge of the water and regarded the night. The Alaskan lake shimmered in the moonlight. A pack of coyotes yipped nearby. If they smelled her, they pressed on, enamored with the chase. She envied them.

She lifted a rock from the shore and tossed it into the water. A resonant *plunk* silenced the frogs and crickets for a few heartbeats, until they bravely rejoined the nightly chorus.

Inhaling deep, she took in the scent of cool pine and icy air. Every pant from her mouth was white smoke rising.

She had a decision to make. She could go to King, and give him the update on Sikes.

Or she could find that man from the country club. His face burned in her mind's eye.

She stepped out of the moonlight into the shade of an enormous pine. She caught the strong scent of its sap before the darkness softened around her. The solid earth beneath her gave way. The roar of a living night disappeared.

She would check on the waitress first, then the man.

Walls erected themselves on all sides.

A floral scent, almost overpowering, welcomed her. Lou found herself in the center of a living room. Sparse furnishings looking like a recreation of a Pier One catalogue. The plug-in emitting a false saccharin scent doubled as a night light.

The orange tabby on the counter hissed. Its ears pressed flat against its head.

The waitress still slept on the bohemian couch where Lou'd left her. Lou glanced at the woman dressed in her clothes and wondered if she should take them back. If she woke, it would be her only evidence that she'd been abducted. Was there anything that could be tested, that could reveal Lou's identity?

Why do you care? You never used to worry about that sort of thing.

"That's not true," she whispered, her eyes still fixed on the slumped, unconscious girl. She had been worried about Aunt Lucy, about anyone hurting her to get to Lou.

It was one thing to have her parents murdered by the mafia and to live with that loss. Another to know she was the cause of it.

And to know you cause it for others...

But she didn't have to worry anymore. She had no one left to lose.

Is that true? Lucy asked.

Lou saw a shadow in the corner of her eye and turned. The second cat settled onto the window ledge, watching her with its unwavering gaze.

"I'm leaving," she told them.

When she emerged from the shadows she was in the narrow alley between two brick buildings. She recognized the city's bar district. Most metropolitan areas had one or three.

Lou moved into the light, looking for the man.

But he wasn't in any queues to get into the bars. He wasn't loitering on the street, smoking with his friends. He wasn't even leaning against a wall texting his girl.

A sound just out of reach caused her to turn.

The tip of a knife buried itself into the brick building behind her. It's where her throat had been a moment before Lou sidestepped. She wrenched the blade free, but another man appeared. A thick chain clattered against the concrete. He lifted the chain overhead and swung.

She ducked.

It slapped the opposite brick wall and ricocheted back, clipping the man's jaw. He howled. Lou stepped under his arm and caught the elbow.

She pulled it down as her knee shot up, connecting with the forearm. Her elbow slammed into the back of the upper arm at the same time.

The familiar snap of bone breaking pulled a scream from the man's throat. His knife clattered to the alley below, skittering into the dark.

The chain slammed into the back of her legs. She pitched forward, hands and knees connecting with concrete.

She rolled and seized the chain when it came down again, pulling the man forward.

The other with his broken elbow was still whimpering, crawling toward the knife he'd lost. Lou kicked it out of range and grabbed the back of the other man's shirt.

He had no problem begging. "I'm just the messenger, man. Please."

"For who?" she asked. Noting that shadows at the end of the alleyway were shifting.

"Dmitri Petrov wants to talk to you."

"I'm not interested," she said.

Laughter erupted from the darkness. Lou stilled, adjusting her grip on the knife.

"Do you know *who* Dmitri Petrov is?" A man stepped into the light. His orange hair was pulled into a long pony behind his head, his matching goatee trembling as he laughed. "You can't say *no* to him, honey. So come on. Let's go."

She saw the five men in front clearly. But not the ones further into the darkness. She guessed perhaps another five. Maybe six stood back there.

"I don't work for anyone," she said.

They mistook this statement for some form of pleading. Emboldened, they stepped closer into the light. Twelve. One of the them was the thick-browed tattletale from the country club.

She pressed herself into the shadowed nook of the wall and slipped.

The alley faded and reformed around her as she materialized behind the men. For a moment she only regarded them, considering her options.

Pull his gun, her mind whispered. There in the waistband of a man's pants rested a .357.

Use it. It's not your gun.

You're only protecting yourself.

It's not protection if I can leave, she argued.

You're not a coward. You don't run away.

The man began to turn and she pulled the gun, flicking off the safety. Her hand warmed to the familiarity of it. Something sparked inside her. It wasn't her full fury. But it would get the job done.

She grabbed two of the men and pulled them from the alley to the lake in a single, swift movement. Two bullets and they collapsed to their knees. She was gone before they hit the earth.

When she reappeared, the gun went off.

A bullet ripped through the top of her leg, where the meat connects with the buttocks. She staggered, repositioned herself through the darkness and took three more men.

Her arms burned with the effort, but now a radiating pulse ran up her left side.

When she appeared the third time, the numbers had reduced from seven remaining men to only three.

"What's wrong?" she asked into the darkness. She was pleased to find her voice steady despite the throb in her leg. "Did I scare away your friends?"

"We aren't supposed to kill you," he said.

Her stomach turned, curdling like sour milk.

Not for protection. For fun. You're no better than them.

She slipped up beside the man closest to her, and buried the knife into the corner of his throat, where it met the collarbone.

He cried out and the man with the orange goatee trained his gun on Lou. He squeezed off two shots. But Lou pivoted her captive's body so he took both shots in the chest. He slumped dead in her arms.

He fired again, seeming to forget his boss's request. Lou shifted enough to take a bullet in the upper arm. He emptied the clip and Lou slit his throat.

You have to send a strong message, her father said. *Men like Dmitri don't back down.*

And you're a monster anyway. No need to pretend otherwise.

The last man slid down the brick wall as Lou cut open his shirt to reveal his bare chest.

She dipped the knife beneath flesh and began carving *N-O-T...*

. . .

DMITRI PETROV SAT IN A CHAIR BY THE FIRE, COMPOSING A RESPONSE to the Archbishop whom he employed. He was looking to the ceiling, trying to remember the English word for *срочность*, but it wouldn't come.

Lou stepped from a dark corner into the firelit room to the sight of forty armed men in full tactical gear. With her body thrumming, she was in no mood for another fight. Darkness pressed on the edge of her vision and a worrisome tremor had overtaken her shot leg, as well as the arms that had thrown around hundreds of pounds for the better part of twenty minutes.

But she stepped into the light, so that the man rising from the high back chair could see her clearly. Blood and all.

She dumped the body at his feet. It tumbled, sprawling open ungracefully.

The carved *Not Interested* in the man's chest danced in the firelight. A dark scrawl in the luminous flames.

She leveled Petrov with her glare, saw his mouth, hanging open as he beheld her, eyes sweeping from head to toe.

He said something in Russian that she didn't understand. But the men began lowering their guns.

He stepped forward, his hands lifting, for what purpose she didn't know. To embrace her? To offer her a seat? To beckon her forward? Perhaps he wanted to slit her throat.

She didn't care.

Before he could reach her, she was gone.

11

Konstantine heard a thump in his upstairs closet. He'd just sat down, a caffè latte steaming on his desk. He closed his laptop and took the gun lying beside it. He crossed his living room to the stairs. Cautiously, he ascended, gun up and at the ready.

When he reached the loft, he could smell the blood. Cold radiated toward him.

She stood in his bedroom, motionless.

Her hair was soaked through, sticking to her skin, making her flesh look all the more pale.

She turned toward him, her eyes glazed.

"Shit." He lowered the gun.

"Can you stitch a bullet hole?" she asked, her teeth chattering.

"You're going into shock." He placed his hands on her upper arms and found her skin nearly frozen.

"I was worried I'd pass out before I could dig it out. Can you do it?"

She sat on the edge of his bed, smearing his sheets. She must have understood his expression. "I'll remind you that you trashed my bed. Not so long ago."

Her voice was too weak. It sent his heart careening.

"You need to hurry," she whispered, lying back on his bed. Her wet hair fanning on the covers. "Start here."

She pointed at her left hip. She spread apart the fabric to show him not only a delicious curve of her hip, but also the oozing wound.

"You told me I—how did you put it—*sucked* at stitches?" he said, hoping that his light tone would mask his fear.

"Yeah, well, you've got some hideous scars," she said, her voice dreamy.

"May I?" he asked, touching the button of her pants.

She made a sound that could be mistaken for consent.

"Can I give you anything for the pain?"

She didn't answer.

"Louie?" He leaned over and found her breath low, and deep.

He had only a moment to think about the curve of her lips. The dark lashes spread over pale cheeks before cold, fearful reality pressed in on him.

His hand was slick with her blood. This was no time to steal kisses like some bold school boy. He undid the zipper of her pants and lifted her hips enough to pull them down her toned legs. He grabbed a handful of the corded muscle and turned her, inspecting the damage to her hip. Her skin was so cold. Too cold. As if there was no blood left in her.

If this was where she wanted him to start, this is where he would start. Though rivets of blood oozed from the hole in her upper arm.

"You're right. This is only fair," he said. Thinking of the night Nico pumped him full of gunmetal, slashed him with a knife not once, but twice. It had been Lou who had picked his nearly-dead body off the church floor, stitched him up and put him in her own bed for safe-keeping.

It looked like this was his chance to repay that debt.

He pulled a kit from under his bed. He'd assembled it after seeing hers in all its thoroughness. But whereas hers was metal, like an old-fashioned medic tin, his was plastic. It resembled a portable toolbox, not a medical accessory.

He popped the lid open and found the suture packs and gauze. He worked an old towel under her hip—not to save the sheets, as that was undoubtedly a lost cause—but to save the mattress as best he could.

With the towel beneath her, her long legs bare, he bent over to do the work.

And unlike Konstantine, who'd woken howling every time she'd inserted the prongs of her tweezers into a bullet hole, she slept through it all.

He worried that was a bad sign. But her lips were not blue. Color still filled her face and her pulse was slow and steady. Once the wound was clean, a neat black stitch sealing the hole, he slathered on the antiseptic ointment and taped a clean piece of gauze over it.

He wiped her legs down, removing the drying blood and searched for other wounds.

He caught himself lingering—cupping her calf with his hand, fingers trailing her inner thigh.

He took a deep breath for focus.

Then he looked to the gunshot wound in her arm. It seemed like the bullet itself had not stayed. He stitched this hole tight like the other, patched it, and then moved north.

Konstantine watched her sleep. Saw her chest rise and fall in its steady rhythm. He reached up and pulled the elastic band out of her hair, letting the soaked strands hang free.

What would she think, if she saw me here now? he thought. *Hovering like this.*

He had his suspicions. No doubt she believed he desired her for her body. As a means to slake his lust. That was what women like her, like his mother, had to be on guard against all of their lives. But Lou herself had even more to protect. Her dark gift. Its limitless potential. Weaker men would use her power. They yearned to wield her like a shield and sword.

Refusing to surrender to such men only invited violence.

How could he make it clear to her—how could he prove that what he felt when she was near him, could *never* be compared to their hunger?

How could he prove that he truly believed they were created for one another? That together, the possibilities of what they could accomplish were limitless.

It was more than that.

No one would understand her better. No one felt as protective of her freedom as he did. Nor did he believe anyone else could understand his own dark heart. They were good people who could do the bad things that must be done. They could stand before each other as the monsters they were and hide nothing.

And should their hearts turn like lost fire, they could protect each other—from themselves.

He began to laugh. "What a romantic you are, Konstantine."

He raked a hand down his face and sank onto the bed beside her.

These musings were useless. Worse than useless. *Ridiculous*. This woman did not need him and perhaps she did not even want him, though he had seen the look in her eyes more than once—and that damned kiss.

Or maybe she did need him. It was clear some war waged within her. She wasn't sleeping, wasn't eating. And he'd seen the surveillance tape from last week. She'd let her target run off into the night without firing a single shot.

"What worries you, my love?" he whispered. He longed for the day she would tell him, when he was the one she *wanted* to speak to.

With a clean warm rag, he wiped her face and neck of blood. Her wounds cleaned, he marveled at her countless crisscrossed scars. How much hot gunmetal had grazed this flesh before?

His phone rang. She didn't even stir.

He stopped and pulled the cell phone from his pocket.

It wasn't his personal line. The one where his closest, most reliable men could reach him if there was a problem.

It was the business line.

"Konstantine," he said, staring down at the sleeping woman, the rag cooling in his left hand.

"I thought she was simply good at what she does."

Konstantine knew the Russian accent, of course. But as much as he disliked the voice and the man to whom it belonged, he was glad he called.

"But she is a *savage*. She is...she is like the Baba Yaga from our fairytales."

Konstantine didn't think Louie was anything like a cannibalistic witch who ate children. But he said nothing.

"Or Kali perhaps," he said. "The goddess of destruction. A fiend dancing on the bones of her enemies. Truly. There is something about her...her *presence* that invokes old archetypes. She is more than a woman, isn't she?"

"You've seen her?" Konstantine asked, hoping to sound curious.

"She killed a dozen of my men and then dumped my most prized man, Roman, at my feet. He was carved up. It doesn't matter. She is worth one hundred of him, isn't she?"

Konstantine considered how to answer now. He could keep pretending, keep playing Petrov's game. Or he could push the truth to the surface, though it may escalate the situation exponentially.

He followed each scenario in his mind as far as he could take him, while silence stretched out on the phone.

"Are you still there?"

Konstantine looked to the woman sleeping in his bed, her body a map of scars and gauze.

Luck favors the bold. Or at least, it seemed to certainly favor Lou. And wasn't it her safety that he feared for?

Konstantine took a chance. "We both know you aren't looking to hire her, Mr. Petrov."

"When I met you—" the other man began, ready to defend the lie.

"I know what you said when we met," Konstantine replied, shifting nervously. He was glad the other man could not see it. "But since that introduction in the gallery, I've done a bit of research. I know about Alexei."

The silence thickened.

"She killed your son ten weeks ago," Konstantine said, pressing harder. "I find it hard to believe that you'd want to hire a woman who murdered your son."

Dawn began to purple behind his curtain. Konstantine crossed to the window and pulled back the thick drapes to reveal the Arno River. Its smooth flow sparkled in first light. Docile today, so unlike the tremor in his chest.

He wasn't afraid for himself. He was afraid for Louie.

When Petrov finally spoke, his voice was distant, almost dreamy. "I sent him to the warehouse that night. I shouldn't have sent him. He didn't want to go."

"I am sorry for your loss," Konstantine said, and he did mean this. He couldn't imagine what it was to lose a son. The loss of Padre Leo had hurt him almost as much as the loss of his mother. Konstantine knew that men, even men like Petrov could be wounded by such blows.

"You understand I have unfinished business with her," Petrov said.

"I do. But if you want to enjoy a long life, amico mio, I would leave her be."

"I don't believe I can," Petrov said, finally. "I really don't think I can."

12

Piper counted out the drawer, wrote the totals on the end-of-day slip and bagged all the cash in the plastic pouch. The new girl swept the floors and stopped to turn a few crooked candles so that their labels faced outward.

"You don't have to do that," Piper said, knowing the girl got off hours ago and Mel wouldn't pay her for the time she put in off the clock.

"I don't mind," she said. "It means we'll get out of here faster, right?"

Piper couldn't argue with that.

After locking the register and putting the money in the safe located at the back of the storage closet, Piper locked the shop and stepped out onto the street.

Dani bounced on the balls of her feet, her face both hopeful and nervous. "So, where to?"

"Henry has a performance at the Wild Cat. I told him we'd meet him there."

"Cool. Can we walk? I have a car but I don't like to drive it if I don't have to. Parking."

"Yeah." Piper pointed in the direction of Bourbon Street. "It's this way."

She took the lead and Dani fell into step beside her. She didn't miss the way the girl scooted in close as they walked, probably under the pretense of seeking warmth. The wind was brutal tonight.

Piper cupped her mouth with her hands and blew hot air onto her icy skin. "It's not much farther."

"Good," the girl said, teeth chattering. "I don't want to be a popsicle when I get there."

She let out a nervous laugh.

"So, where are you from?" Piper asked, weaving around a group of drunks clotting the sidewalk.

"Baton Rouge."

"Oh, I've been there. It's nice. You have family there?"

"Yep."

Piper let this line of inquiry drop. She knew information dodging when she heard it. Wasn't she an expert herself? How often did she deflect questions about her home life, her parents. Hell, even relationships.

"So Henry has *two* boyfriends?" Dani asked with a shy smile.

Piper laughed. "Yeah, but it isn't a secret. They're all consenting. I should've mentioned we're going to a gay bar though, in case you're—"

"No, no," Dani said, with a frantic little wave. "It's cool."

Piper waited for the usual response. *I have a cousin who is a gay.* Or *I've always wondered what it was like to kiss a girl.* Or sometimes *I had a girlfriend in college.*

This was where sexually flexible women often made their interest known. Dani had the look about her. The way she kept watching Piper in the corner of her eye.

But hooking up with the new girl was problematic for a lot of reasons, not the least of which to consider was Mel. If this soured and the girl used it as an excuse to bail, Mel would blame her for being short-handed.

You don't shit where you eat, she'd say, undoubtedly in a self-righteous tone. And Piper wouldn't know how to respond because she'd never understood that metaphor to begin with.

The Wild Cat with its bright flashing sign appeared ahead. A drag queen in six-inch heels and enough sequins to light up the night offered Piper a purple flyer.

"Hey P," came the gruff voice.

"Hey," she said. "Where's Henry?"

"I just sent him back to the dressing room. Yasmine is doing his makeup."

"He can do his own makeup," Piper said, reading the flyer at a glance. Half off Hurricanes and $1 shots until midnight.

Dominique roared. "You know he's angling for the D, honey."

"Aren't we all," Dani said, wedging herself into the conversation. Both Piper and Dominique spared her a glance before roaring with laughter.

"Good luck finding some in here, shorty." Dominique waved them through the dark door. "This isn't the sausage party you're looking for."

Dani latched onto Piper's arm as they stepped into the darkness, holding on as they moved into the technicolor light show consuming all.

The music wasn't too loud yet, which was good, but when the drag show started in twenty minutes, it would be impossible to hear anything.

Bodies pressed in from all directions. Glitter sparked in the twirling lights. And snippets of conversation reached them as they pushed through. It helped that Piper was tall enough to hold her ground, cutting a path to the bar. But Dani was at least three inches shorter.

Piper pulled her forward, putting Dani between her and the bar. "Here. You won't catch an elbow to the face."

"Thanks. I feel like every time I go to the bar, I leave with beer spilled in my hair and trampled feet."

"Baton Rouge has good bars?"

Dani nodded as she motioned for the bartender. "They do. I don't like to admit it, but I drank away most of my problems."

"Oh." Piper looked around the room. "If you want to go somewhere else—"

"I'm not an alcoholic. I mean, that's what an alcoholic would say, isn't it? I guess I should say that I'm not in AA or anything. I found other ways to deal with...my problems."

Again Piper felt that press of the unspoken between them. A conversation on the verge of happening. But Dani didn't divulge and Piper had been the listening ears for countless women. She knew when to keep her mouth shut.

"What was the special on the flyer?" Dani asked. "I need to be cheap until I get my first paycheck."

"I'll get your drink," Piper said. The words were out of her mouth before she could stop them. Even though she knew damned well that she should be counting her pennies, too. But she wanted to buy Dani's drink for the same reason she'd given that homeless guy—the man King had sent her to deliver socks and a blanket to—the two fives from her pocket.

Something inside her compelled her to do these things even when she knew she shouldn't. Even when she knew that the last thing she should do was shoot herself in the foot for the sake of another person—she couldn't seem to stop herself.

The bartender, Tyler, spotted Piper first. His eyebrows wagged conspiratorially as he saw her arms on either side of Dani. "Pipes! Where you been?"

"Working," Piper said.

"Right!" he said, reaching for the Johnny Walker on the shelf and pouring three shots. "You're a big shot detective now."

"A detective!" Dani said, half turning. "Seriously?"

Piper flashed Tyler a look. "Henry's been running his mouth, I see."

"Only when he doesn't have something in it, honey," Tyler said with a wink. "So is it true? Are you working for that detective or not?"

She didn't want to talk about this in front of Dani. She didn't want to talk about it in an open bar at all. It wasn't only the way it smacked of unprofessionalism, or the way the hair on the back of her neck seemed to stand up, a cold panic rising at the thought someone might hear. Not just someone but the *wrong* someone.

Hadn't King *only* sent her to warn Mel that some shady Russian might be hanging around, sending in spies, looking for ways to get the drop on them like King's traitorous ex-partner had?

She had to be smart. Careful. More importantly, she had to prove to King she wasn't a fuckup.

But it was also the acute awareness that this was serious fucking business. Unlike fortune telling and counseling depressed girls behind a purple curtain about their jagoff boyfriends—this was life or death.

She'd seen the scars on Lou's arms and the blood dried on her cheeks. Lou would never be the kind of woman to kill and tell.

And that made Piper want to be the sort of woman who wouldn't either.

"Honestly, I'm nothing more than a glorified errand girl," Piper said, turning the shot glass. "It's not like he tells me anything about the cases."

She shrugged, hoping to sell the indifference.

You need something more, she thought. *Really sell it.*

She added, "But it pays damn well to pick up his coffee filters and shit." With a laugh, she clinked her shot glass against the bartender's. In unison, they threw back the shot, grimacing.

Dani took her shot as an afterthought.

"One more," Piper said, throwing a $10 on the bartop.

He poured three more shots and pushed one toward Dani. "I haven't seen you in here before."

"I just moved here. Like yesterday actually. I'm Dani," she said.

"And you found Pipes. She's the best French Quarter tour guide. Where are you staying?"

"I'm subletting a place," she said, picking up her second shot and sniffing it. She wrinkled her nose in a way that made Piper's stomach drop. "Some Tulane kid didn't come back this semester and needed someone to pay the rent. I hope to find something better by July when the lease is up."

Tyler winked at Piper again. "Maybe you'll find yourself a nice lesbian to move in with. I hear they have U-Hauls on speed dial."

Piper shot him a death glare.

Dani laughed and threw back her second shot. "Where's the bathroom in this place?"

Both Piper and the bartender pointed toward the back of the bar, past the stage.

As soon as Dani was out of earshot, Piper leaned over the bar. "Dude, what the hell?"

"Come on, she's hot and clearly in the mood. And Valerie isn't here tonight. Or Claudia. Or any of the other girls I've seen you with."

"I just met this girl. And we work together."

"At the detective agency?"

"No, Mel's place."

"Right right."

"So she's off limits."

Tyler poured another shot and started pushing it across the bar. Piper fished out another $10.

He waved her off. "On the house."

"Why?"

"You'll need the fortitude for not sleeping with the hottest girl I've ever seen. And an 'off-limits' one at that." He laughed and clinked the glasses together. "Good luck, my friend."

Piper hovered with the shot by her lips. "Wait, how is more alcohol supposed to fortify me?"

"Right." He pretended to reach for the shot as if to take it back.

Piper threw it back with a mischievous grin. "In case you're right."

DANI PULLED HER PHONE FROM HER POCKET AS SHE WAITED IN LINE for the bathroom. She opened the unread text message that had buzzed when she'd stood at the bar.

Anything? Even her boss's texts seemed demanding.

No visual confirmation yet. But she'll show. Just a matter of time.

Get a pic for confirmation.

Will do.

Don't fuck this up.

Her face warmed. Asshole.

I won't.

She waited for several moments to make sure that Clyde was through harassing her. When nothing else pinged, she deleted the thread and slipped the locked phone back into her pocket.

No visual confirmation yet. That had been true enough. But she wondered why she'd held onto her new theory. Why not tell Clyde?

I think the woman you're looking for is Louie Thorne. The *Louie Thorne.*

What would Clyde have said if she'd told him? She hadn't seen Lou with her own eyes, but she was willing to bet all of her considerable inheritance that the age progression photo was going to match.

What had Clyde told her when he'd given her this job?

There's a girl, a little older than you, who is the witness in a big court case. But she bailed before they could get her testimony. The cops are going to pay us big if we can find out this girl's name, address, anything. But we have to be quick about it. We aren't the only ones they've made an offer to.

Why don't they have her name?

They've only got her face on some security footage. And that's when Clyde had given Dani the photographs now resting in a manila folder on her bed. *She was there and they want her eyewitness testimony.*

Why me? Dani had asked. She was flattered that her boss would trust her with this, but also suspicious. If it was such a big case, he'd certainly want the credit himself.

She's your age, maybe a bit older. She'll talk to you. If she sees me she'll take off running.

It made sense at the time. But Dani couldn't help but feel like Clyde might backstab her. Maybe he would swoop in at the last moment and steal her glory. No, not her glory, her *story*. Even now Dani was busy constructing theories about the mysterious woman.

Had Lou been lying low all her life? Then by pure chance, she witnessed another crime, and fearing exposure, had taken off to protect herself?

None of her theories felt quite right.

She thought of the other names she'd written down after spending the day reading every article about Jack Thorne's murder and exoneration that she could find.

Senator Greg Ryanson
Chaz Brasso
Robert King
Jack Thorne
The Martinelli Family

These men seemed connected in a web somehow, with Lou Thorne at its center. Dani just needed to make the connection and the story—the truth—would emerge.

An email pinged on her phone. She opened it as she inched closer to the bathroom, two women passing her on their way out.

Ms. Allendale,

Please find the articles you've requested attached. Thank you.

Jennifer Milton
St. Louis Public Library

Dani's heart knocked wildly in her chest as she opened the first attachment and scanned the article. Then her eyes froze on what she was looking for. *Sergeant Robert King pictured above with partner, Chaz Brasso.*

She stared at the grainy black and white images and tried to steady her breath.

King was Brasso's partner. That was one connection made. If Brasso betrayed Jack, does that mean King also betrayed him? Did Lou know that? The way she walked beside the detective in her photographs, Dani didn't think so. They didn't *look* like enemies. Dani was no expert on body language, but she was pretty good.

But who knew what was hidden under all that leather and those mirrored shades as they passed the infamous Café du Monde.

Or maybe Brasso had betrayed them both—King and Thorne. Was that the connection? Were they brought together by their hatred of the same man?

Dani stepped forward and bumped into the back of the woman in front of her, mistaking movement in the line.

"Sorry," she mumbled.

The girl still looked ready to toss her drink in Dani's face. Dani opened the other articles attached to the email and read them in rapid fire succession. And she replayed her memories.

King just said he saw Lou— Then she'd forced a smile once she realized Dani was listening.

Piper knew Lou.

Piper had seen her, talked with her.

And unlike Melandra or King who might sense her snooping a mile away, Dani suspected that Piper was not as well versed in deception.

Piper was the key that would turn the lock and get her closer to the detective and hopefully Lou too. The job at the occult shop was good enough reason to be near the apartments, and perhaps find a way into King's place. But she needed more than that.

She had to keep her eyes peeled. At any moment, her target could turn up and then she'd have her chance.

She had to be patient.

If this story was as big as she thought it was—so much bigger than even Clyde Baker suspected—it was worth the wait.

HENRY, DRESSED LIKE HIS IDOL CHER, BENT AT THE WAIST, AND flicked his long black hair over his shoulder. His cheekbones glittered in the spotlight as he danced to "Dark Lady", twirling the long train of his dress in one hand, the other pressed to his heart. His white stiletto boots tapped out a mirrored melody on the stage.

Piper watched all of this from the table she'd grabbed to the right of the stage. In the opposite chair sat Dani, nervously combing a strand of her hair between her fingers. Her eyes were fixed on Henry.

This one was hard to read, but not in the sexual attraction department. Piper had always had the ability to identify, almost immediately, if a girl was into her. But there was something else coming through too. Beneath the flirting, beneath the batting eyelashes and self-conscious desire, was something else—and Piper wished she could put her finger on it.

When Henry's number ended, he bowed and exited the stage to enthusiastic applause. Someone screamed, "You're beautiful bitch!"

The next thing Piper knew, glittery arms were sliding over her shoulders.

"You were amazing," she said, accepting the air kiss from the bejeweled drag queen.

"You really were!" beamed Dani. "Where did you learn to dance like that?"

"My mom," he said. "P, who's your new friend?"

"This is Dani. She works at Mel's shop."

"Cool. You want to be a tarot reader too?"

Dani laughed one of her shy giggles. "No. I restock the candles. Hey, you want a drink? I bet you are hella parched after a routine like that."

Henry tilted his head like a bird. "I like her P. Hell yeah I want a drink. Tell them to make me a Mai Tai."

"You can start a tab under my name," Piper told her.

Henry watched her slide through the crowd. Then he took Dani's empty seat facing Piper. "You're dating a cop?"

"What? No."

"That girl is a cop."

Piper scoffed. "Don't be stupid. She's our age. Shit, she might even be younger than me."

"Whatever man, I'm getting cop vibes. She's sniffing around for something. So if you want weed, I don't have any."

Piper decided not to tell him that was exactly why Dani wanted to meet him, and why she was probably buttering him up with free booze.

"And if you wanna buy weed for your detective friend, you better do it later."

Piper laughed for real now, her breath skimming the top of her drink. "King hasn't smoked weed in months. I'm pretty sure he's still got most of what I gave him last time."

"Anyway, watch that one." He kept his eyes on the girl at the bar, coming up on her toes to speak to Tyler.

Piper followed his gaze. "No. She might have secrets or whatever, but she's not a cop."

Henry arched a brow and tilted his head as if to say *if you say so.*

"How's your mom?" Henry said, squeezing her knee, dropping his tone.

"Same," she said.

"You need to get the fuck out of there. When Kevin moves out at the end of the month, I want you in that other room, sweetie."

"Half my clothes are already at your place."

"Yeah, well I want the rest of your shit there too. Most importantly *you.* You don't need to be in that hellhole anymore."

Piper wasn't sure she wanted to trade an addict mother and handsy boyfriend for *three* drama queens, but she admitted it would be an improvement.

Piper knew she should take the offer. At least for a month while she saved a bit more of her paycheck. She wanted to make sure she could cover the deposit, two months' rent and still have enough to furnish a place. She could get most of what she needed from the internet. She didn't need to live large or anything.

But she wanted this move to be permanent. She didn't want to end up back at her mom's in a month or two.

That's not the only reason, a small voice in her head chastised her. *You want that second bedroom because—*

She shook her head to clear it. "I appreciate you letting me hang at your place as much as you do. I don't want to abuse that."

Henry laughed. "Remember when I was hard up for Peter, so much so he had me blowing his coke-head ass behind the Jack 'n the Box?"

Piper failed to suppress a snort.

"Who picked my ass up at three in the morning when he left me there with a crack head?"

Piper pointed to herself.

"And who listened to me cry for six days over some fuckboy not worth the vomit on my shoes?"

"You'd never let someone vomit on your shoes."

Henry ignored this. "Who drove my ass all the way to Pensacola to visit my sister when her baby came two weeks early?"

"But it was your car."

"True. But it doesn't change the fact that you're good to a lot of people, P. Not just me. It's why you break half the hearts of these Quarter groupies and they don't even hate you for it. You're sweet as hell and you think you're an asshole. Let someone be there for you for once. I know you don't know what the fuck that looks like, but I'm gonna show your boney little ass."

She laughed so hard her nose burned. She still had tears in the corners of her eyes—realizing now she was more than a little buzzed from those back-to-back shots—when Dani showed up with three Mai Tais and a big smile.

"Did I miss the fun?"

"Naw, sweetie," Henry said flipping his wig over a shoulder and crossing, uncrossing his legs. "We're just gettin' started."

13

Lou woke under thick blankets. For a moment she only lay there, enjoying the cocoon of warmth. Then she had to move out of necessity. Several of her muscles were too stiff.

Her bare thighs rubbed against each other and her hands felt cool against her warm stomach. She sat up and the blanket fell away to reveal a lot of skin. She was naked except for her black sports bra and black panties—the only color one could wear to hide the countless blood stains she knew she must have.

The left side of her underwear, the side where she'd gotten shot, was stiff, the cotton no doubt saturated with dried blood.

At the end of the bed, over the wooden footboard lie her pants and shirt, now laundered.

She vaguely remembered Konstantine undressing her. She'd awakened, reached out into the dark and had found his hands cupping her feet. He'd replaced her wet socks with his thick, dry ones.

So you will sleep better, he'd said, or she thought he'd said.

It seemed that once sleep had finally found her, it hadn't wanted to let go.

Beside her clothes rested a breakfast tray. It was lacquered wood and featured a red Chinese dragon against a black background. Light filtered through the water glass, dancing with the shadows. She heard voices outside. A door opening and closing somewhere nearby.

"Good morning," a voice said. She turned and saw Konstantine in a striped sweater pushed up past the elbows, and dark jeans hanging at his hips. "How do you feel?"

"What time is it?" Her voice was thick and cracked with sleep.

"What day is it," he corrected. "You've been sleeping for 25 hours."

"Damn," she said.

"Please eat before you go." He gestured to the tray at her feet. "Two rolls with butter and jam. Uh, *fette biscottate*...I don't know the word in English. It is like...a cookie, but also like a bread. It's delicious. Try it. And the cherries too, they're sweet." He extended a steaming mug toward her and she accepted it. "This is a caffè latte."

She pulled the tray toward her, felt her arm tremble. She was weak but also hungry. When was the last time she'd been hungry like this? She pried apart one of the rolls and slathered on the butter and jam with the knife on the tray. She ate half of it before sipping the coffee. She relished the heat. He hadn't added sugar, only milk. It was lovely.

But it reminded her bitterly of the coffee her aunt used to deliver to her on mornings without warning. Her heart flopped in her chest. The texture of the bread thickened in her mouth, turning to paste.

"Petrov called me while you were asleep," he said.

His weight sank onto the foot of the bed, arm's length from the tray. She eyed him over the rim of the coffee mug.

"He mentioned your gift. Did you actually carve *not interested* into a man's chest?"

"Why are you smiling?" she asked.

"I never realized you had a sense of humor," he said, his smile widening.

"You think carving a man up is funny?"

He shrugged. "I can see your humor in it."

She reluctantly placed the mug on the tray. She needed the hand to pluck a cherry from the bowl. Her hunger had reacted to the food the way a parched throat reacts to water. Sleeping. Eating. Her body acted as though she hadn't done either in ages. Honestly, she couldn't remember the last time she had.

"I'm glad he understands English," she said before taking another bite. "I can't write in Russian."

Konstantine nudged the tray closer to her. "I need to tell you something."

She met his eyes.

"He doesn't want to employ you. I believe that was only a trick to get you to come closer with your guard down perhaps."

"What does he want?"

He hesitated, smoothing the coverlet under his hand. "You killed his son ten weeks ago. In a warehouse near the Kazakhstan border."

Lou saw the white expanse of an endless winter. She saw snow falling down from the black sky, illuminated only by the headlights pointing out into nothing.

She saw the bodies in the snow, their blood sprayed out behind them on the icy field.

"Not in a warehouse," she corrected, taking a sip of coffee. "I killed them after they loaded the trucks. They'd made it about eight miles east before I...started."

She remembered the white smoke fogging in front of her face as she surveyed her carnage. The caravan of trucks sat in the desolate road, their headlights illuminating the pavement before them. No signs of life for miles in either direction. No noise but the gentle hum of idling engines and the crunch of frosty grass beneath her boots. No witnesses to the twenty murders but the large, unblinking moon and innumerable stars. She could still see the blood freezing on the back of her hands.

Please, he'd begged. *Please I didn't want this. My father—*

"May I ask you something?" Konstantine spoke quietly. He picked at his dark jeans, at an imaginary string that was not there. She'd seen him do this once before, but she couldn't remember when or where.

She paused in her chewing and arched an eyebrow.

"Is last night the first time you've killed since Petrov's son?"

She only stared at him. Then she managed, "Why do you ask?"

"You weren't wearing your vest. You didn't have any guns. You clearly fought with them but you weren't prepared to."

Of course he would have noticed. She'd begged him to stitch her up after all. And she couldn't deny it. She hadn't been prepared. But how in the world could she explain that she hadn't had the heart to put on the vest since he returned it to her.

"If you don't like the insulation I added—" he began.

"There's nothing wrong with the vest," she said. "I just..." *God, what do I even say? That I don't know what I'm doing anymore? That none of it matters? Kill them or don't kill them. Die, don't die. It's all the same.*

"What happened that night?" he asked again.

Another question she couldn't answer. Was it that he'd begged for his life? Plenty of men had before, but that had done nothing to persuade her.

No.

It was that the moment she'd pulled the trigger, she'd seen her father lying there. Not Petrov's son, *her father,* on his back and bleeding. Her father on the other end of her gun.

"I don't know," she said. She lowered her coffee to the bed, feeling the warmth on her leg through the covers.

"But you were able to kill last night to protect yourself, at least." His words hung somewhere between an accusation and a question. Both held hope.

"If you intend to face Petrov, you *must* be at your best. Wear your vest. Take your guns. Eat. *Sleep.*"

For a moment she could only look at him. "Are you worried about me?"

"Always," he said. "But I am more worried you will go to him and he will be ready."

She shouldn't have asked that question. Now she was in a conversational corner that was more than uncomfortable. She knew all the platitudes that would follow in such a moment. *I'll be careful. Don't worry.*

But why should she say these things to him? She owed him nothing. More than that, much to her horror, she suspected that he knew better than to believe her empty promises.

"Don't you have work?" she asked, before putting the remainder of the roll in her mouth and picking up the coffee again.

"That's what's good about being the boss," he said with a smile. But it was forced now. He knew she was steering them away from intimate territory and he was not challenging her.

The muscles in her back relaxed.

"I can come and go as I please. I can even hide in my apartment for days if I see fit. They will either think I've taken up with a woman, or that I am hatching plans for world domination."

"Do you often keep women in your bed for days?" she asked.

"This is a first," he said with a half-hearted laugh. "But you are welcome to come again, whenever you need. You won't find another woman in it. I promise."

Another lengthy silence, their locked eyes steady.

Konstantine scooted closer to her. "Louie. Surely..."

She turned the coffee mug in her hand, trying to decide if she should put it down or disappear with it. She was reluctant to let it go before finishing. And while the bread was gone, there was still the *fette biscottate* and three cherries in a bowl.

"This is the last time I will say it," he said as she popped the last three cherries into her mouth, preparing to flee. "I want you. It is an open invitation that you can redeem anytime, with any conditions you need."

She stood from the bed, still holding the coffee mug and plucked the *fette biscottate* from the tray.

"Where are you going? If I've said—"

"I left a pile of bodies somewhere I shouldn't have," she said. It was true. But it was also an excuse.

Cool air licked her skin without the protection of the warm blankets. She considered the laundered clothes, but thought it stupid to put them on given what she was about to do.

"You want your clothes?" he asked, seeming to read her mind.

"I'll be back," she said.

Before he could say anything more, she stepped into the corner of the room and let the darkness take her.

She stepped out of her linen closet into her apartment, mostly naked. She held a cookie and a cup of coffee. She stood there in the center of her living room, unsure of what to do with herself.

Her apartment was warmer than his, so that helped. But her coffee was still cooling quickly.

Dipping the *fette biscottate* into the coffee made it all the better.

She finally settled on the stool at her kitchen island. But here was her aunt's letter.

More requests of her. More expectations. More unfinished business. More emotion threatening to undo her focus.

It would mean the world to me, if you would go see her, Lucy had written. *Just once. There is so much I wanted to tell you but never found the courage. But Ani has promised to explain for me. So please go, Lou. Please go for me. It's my last request.*

Lou turned the page over as if this would make it disappear.

She shoved the last of the *fette biscottate* into her mouth and washed it down with the remaining coffee. She dressed herself in clothes she didn't care much about.

She knew these two meetings were rushing toward her. Both with this mysterious woman and Dmitri Petrov—she'd see each soon.

Lou stepped out of the shadows of the enormous pine and into the encroaching darkness. She took a deep breath, inhaling the icy cold and tried to appreciate it. In a few weeks, the eternal night that she came to rely on would lighten and she would be back to her Nova Scotian wilderness.

But it could never replace this landscape. The light fog hanging over water. The reeds and cattails framing its tranquil edge. The gentle breeze that rippled the surface. The endless rolling plain that spread out in all directions, punctuated only by large, looming conifers.

She breathed deep. First the scent of pine sap and crisp, cool air. Then the stench of rotting flesh.

She bent and grabbed the cracked leather boot closest to her and dragged the corpse into the water after her, the way a child might drag her favorite blanket in her wake.

The water was freezing, raising the bumps along her arms and legs. Every muscle tightened when it reached her navel. But still she continued out into the dark water. When it reached her bra, she ducked her head down beneath the surface.

She tightened her grip on the boot as the water around her warmed. The ink black was replaced by light red. She took this as her cue to begin swimming to the surface. She broke into warm, twilight air a moment later, breathing deeply.

This wasn't the heaviest corpse she'd ever dragged to shore. After the forced rest and breakfast, she found the task easy enough. Every step took her out of the water onto the bank. She dropped the body at the water's edge and looked toward the forest. Black trees and heart-shaped leaves.

La Loon.

Its eternal twilight had not changed in her absence. The two moons still hung in its sky. The white mountains in the distance remained covered in a dream-like haze.

The forest was still deceptively quiet. No sign of Jabbers. Had she moved on in Lou's absence?

Lou left the corpse on the shore and entered the water again. Several trips she made like this. From one lake to another, dragging the weight of the men onto the shore.

As she surfaced in Alaska for the last time, she felt the tremor in her arms. It wasn't only the unforgiving cold. It was also the labor of the work. Her hunger had returned again and she was glad. She detested forcing herself to eat for strength alone when she didn't want to.

Her mind wasn't completely at ease, not by a long shot. But she did feel the shift in her. Last night's kills had brought her some momentary relief. It had restored some equilibrium in her that had been lost. As long as she didn't look at this victory too closely, she suspected it would hold. For now at least.

"After you," she said to the last corpse, hauling its leather clad body into the water. She thought of Konstantine's grin. *I see your humor in it.*

She was considering her options for food when the Alaska waters began to turn red. A New York slice. Ramen from her favorite Tokyo noodle shop. Or perhaps gnocchi from Prag—

Jaws snapped. Rows of needle-like teeth closed down on the corpse, pinning her hand in the fold of its leather jacket.

The monstrous creature, part crocodile, part orca, twisted its body and pulled Lou down into the deeper, colder water. She caught a glimpse of its long, serpentine body and the spiky plates, erect along its dorsal side.

It took three hard tugs to wrench herself free.

And then she was floating in the dark. Lungs burning. Aware that she was much farther down in Blood Lake than she'd ever been before. She was also certain she had to get the hell out of there.

But the water would not take her.

Alaska, Alaska, Alaska, she thought. The waters didn't darken. There was no pull toward her own world.

Fearing she could wait no longer, she surfaced as carefully as she could. Calmly, slowly, trying not to make herself seem panicky and prey-like, despite the thunderous hammer of her heart.

When she broke the surface she was too far from shore, or at least, farther than she'd ever been. She didn't pretend to understand the logic of this nightmare world, or why, whenever submerged in water, she was delivered here on a current of its own. But there were consistencies.

She always arrived in the same place, in the shallows, maybe only twenty yards from shore.

Since it was also from shallows she returned home, it dawned on her with horrible certainty that perhaps she couldn't travel from this far out. Head finally above water, she spotted Jabbers.

Bounding up and down from corpse to corpse, delighting in her options, she seemed like a kid in a candy shore. She tore off a boot and spat it on the ground, only to drag her long white tongue over the dead man's foot.

Lou splashed as she paddled toward her, her movements clumsy from the cold. Jabbers hearing the splash turned toward the sound.

Then the creature did something Lou had never seen before. The plates along her back rose up arching like hair on a cat's spine. She roared. Her white maw stretched wide and teeth gnashed.

For a moment, Lou feared she didn't recognize her. In the water, only her head was visible and it had been a while since she'd come to this place.

When Jabbers bounded into the water, she skimmed the surface like an anaconda, crossing to Lou in a few easy strides. The six legs and their webbed feet helped, no doubt.

"It's me," Lou said, spitting water out of her mouth. "It's just me."

She hoped Jabbers would recognize her voice. The creature had bitten her before. Fifteen years ago, when Jabbers was barely bigger than her ten-year-old self, she had pounced on her, and sunk her teeth into Lou's shoulder. She still bore the shark-bite scar today.

But Jabbers didn't grab her, drown her, or eat her. Jabbers *dived*.

Her body slid under Lou's, creating a new floor. It wasn't until Jabbers swam beneath her that Lou realized how massive the creature was. Lou floated above the creature's black, buoyed by its contracting body.

One hard push of the creature's tail and Lou was shoved up out of the water and thrown toward shore. At the same moment she saw those dorsal fins rise again on her left. Too close.

Jabbers surfaced snarling and lunged for those fins. Her talons sank into the pale dorsal flesh.

Lou hit the water, ten yards from shore and sank.

Her feet connected with the top of a flat, slick surface.

A car. The submerged car that Lou had brought to this world along with Angelo Martinelli—the bastard who emptied his gun into her father's chest and face.

It was still down there, would be down there forever perhaps.

Pushing hard, Lou bolted for the surface and broke air. This was her cue to swim. And swim hard.

She no longer bothered with trying not to look or sound like prey, she only swam as fast as she could manage, arm over ear until her knee scraped the silty floor and she knew it was shallow enough to stand.

In ankle-deep water, she whirled back, trying to catch the last of the battle.

Jabbers was on the surface, circling, her face under the water. Seemingly satisfied that the corpse-eating creature had retreated, she began to swim for shore.

Lou collapsed on the bank, putting some distance between herself and the nearest body, and awaited Jabbers' arrival. The creature hauled herself out of the water, muscles dripping. Its gaze was unwavering as it regarded Lou with yellow serpentine eyes.

"I'm sorry," Lou told the panting creature. She ran a hand down her soaked face, clearing it of water. "I guess a large haul gives it too much time to reach the shallows."

But even as she said it, she knew the monster who'd dragged her out into dangerous depths had been aiming for the corpse, not for her. It could have latched onto her as easily as the body she'd been pulling along.

Perhaps its vision was terrible and it worked on the smell of blood alone. That would explain its aim. Then later, perhaps it was the movement of her body, the splashing that had drawn it closer.

Or a second one just like it. She had seen a pod of crooked dorsal fins cutting waves on the lake before.

It didn't matter. Even if she didn't fully understand the danger, it was clear Jabbers did. Her reaction had been visceral and immediate. She'd come into the water to rescue Lou the way a mother screamed at her child for playing in the street.

Jabbers sat back on her haunches, licking her right middle paw furiously. Lou saw the blood running down her arm into the water.

She wasn't sure what she could do for it, or how make to make amends.

The indignant way the creature eyed her made her feel like an apology was necessary for being stupid enough to almost get herself killed.

But *I'm sorry* was her language. How could she apologize in a way this creature would understand?

Lou reached over and grabbed the cold bare ankle of the nearest man. "I brought you this."

The beast paused in her licking, her eyes widening, her black pupils dilating until no white remained. Lou took this for excitement or joy.

She shook the foot a little, the way one might initiate play with a dog and his toy.

The beast seized the foot, pulling it into her mouth.

"I'm sorry," she said again as bones cracked and snapped. It sounded like someone biting an ice cube in half. "I'll be more careful next time."

A sound like purring began to emit from her throat.

Lou was forgiven.

14

King read the article for a second time, rubbing his thumb on the touch pad to scroll down the page. Unfortunately, this didn't change the story. Richard Sikes reported a robbery in the Richland Hills Country Club two nights ago. He didn't see his attacker because they'd first turned off the bathroom lights. Another woman from the same club reported a waitress who'd acted strangely before following Sikes out of the dining hall.

King sat back in his chair and sighed, tapping his foot against the wood floor.

"What's wrong?" Piper asked, glancing up from her own furious typing.

"I need more coffee," he said.

Piper pointed at the pot. "You want me to make more, or will you drink that?"

"I'll drink it. We can't throw away perfectly good coffee."

"Okay, but if you finish it, start another. I need about three more cups to get through this afternoon."

King emptied the remainder of the carafe into his white mug. This did indeed polish off the pot. He pulled out the soaked, cold filter, dropped it into the adjacent trash can and fished a new coffee filter from the box. He pulled the gallon of water from the fridge and refilled the reservoir. All of this was done without thinking, his body going through the motions as his brain remained fixated on what he had just read. And reread.

Lou almost kidnapped and killed Richard Sikes before he'd finished gathering enough information to confirm his guilt.

Granted, King was 95% sure that the man was garbage. Not only because of the reports of domestic violence from his first two wives. Nor because of the three DUIs he'd received, one of which crippled the other driver for the remainder of his life. And forget that these offenses had been somehow mysteriously expunged from his public record. It was his connections to known sex offenders and pedophiles in the area that made King truly hate the man. That a man like that was walking, talking, eating and shitting, while Lucy Thorne was only ash in an urn.

Still, Lou had been too close.

I'll have to withhold the names going forward, he realized. *I'll only name a target once I'm damn sure justice will be served. Otherwise, there's no guarantee she won't hunt them anyway.*

What a slippery slope that is, Robert, Lucy said. His dead wife's voice in his mind made his stomach clench. Wife for only a few blessed hours on a Hawaiian beach, but *his* nonetheless. *How do you know you're helping? How do you know what this world needs?*

These were excellent questions that he didn't have answers to.

But he needed only to think of Jack Thorne to find his self-righteousness fortified. Jack, his best pupil and friend had been hunted and killed because he started asking questions about Senator Ryanson. His own partner, Chaz Brasso had set the dogs on Jack.

Ryanson had a good man killed and received no justice—except the justice Lou delivered him. The same was true of Brasso.

And King was too old not to know that Jack was probably one of a hundred such men. There were perhaps thousands of good men who had been wiped from this world prematurely by assholes who would do it again if the opportunity presented itself. All of this said nothing about the women and children, too.

"I'm tipping the scale," he muttered to himself as the last of the new coffee dripped into the carafe and he poured it into his mug.

"What's that?" Piper asked, looking up from her keyboard, her blue eyes bright.

"Nothing. Just an old man muttering to himself."

"I bet you're wishing you'd bought a beach house in the Caribbean," Piper said, misreading his vacant expression. "You're thinking, why am I shuffling all this paper and reading all these reports when I'm supposed to be retired?"

King snorted. "Retirement isn't all it's cracked up to be. Some of us are made to work. I suspect I won't stop until someone puts me in the grave."

Piper shuddered. "Why you got to make it sound so ominous, man?"

He pointed at the coffee. "Three sugars and a bunch of cream, right?"

"I like my dessert brewed, yes," she said, taking the cup. She took a sip and wrinkled her nose. "Blech. This is...coffee."

"As opposed to...?"

"Caramel. Mocha. Toffee. God, toffee would be so good right now."

"I'll let you pick out the coffee next time," he promised. "How are you doing on the Bronovitz case?"

"Good. I've got all the photos and info here." She tapped the manila file folder on her desk. "And I'm halfway through the Russells case. Though you said he needs at least three eyewitnesses for his court appearance."

"He does," King agreed, taking his coffee back to his desk and easing his sore behind into the wobbly chair. He wasn't used to sitting so much during the day and his bones had begun to protest.

"Yeah, so I've got to make a few more phone calls on that. The names he gave us as possible witnesses are bailing left and right." She scratched her nose. "If your friend robbed a 7-11 would you testify that he didn't do it?"

"*Allegedly* robbed a 7-11," King corrected before taking a sip of coffee. "And yes, if I thought he was innocent."

"Maybe that's the problem. Even if he didn't do it, his friends are thinking, 'That *sounds* like the John I know'."

King smiled. He liked seeing Piper like this. Fully engaged. She was having fun. "You like this stuff?"

She grinned, bashfully. Color rose in her cheeks. "It's pretty cool. I've got friends who babysit kids and wait tables. Which is perfectly fine, but I'm tracking criminals and building real life cases that will go to court. That is *amazing*."

King sipped his coffee. "I'm glad you like it. Hopefully if business keeps up, I can pay you more soon."

"$13 an hour is awesome," she said.

"It's not enough," he said, finding his opening to have a conversation he'd been dodging all day. "This job is much riskier than flipping burgers. If we stumble across the wrong guy, he could attack you or—"

"I'll be careful." She held up three fingers in a scout's salute. "I saw what went down with your partner. I was the one wielding the cast iron skillet, remember?"

He'd forgotten about that.

"I'll be careful," she said again. "I won't run my mouth or go looking for trouble. I promise. So don't fire me. If I keep up my twenty hours for Mel, and twenty hours for you—that's like $450 a week."

The color in her face deepened as if she realized that she was rambling.

"I'm saving up for an apartment," she said. "If you wonder why I'm going on about money. It's not for drugs or anything."

King put his mug on the desk and patted his pockets. "You know there's an apartment up there." He pointed at the ceiling. "I can rent it to you."

"How much?" she asked, sitting up taller.

"$800, plus another $100 for utilities. $150 if you take hour-long showers like Mel."

He knew damn well that a 600 sq. ft apartment in the Quarter ran at least $1500 plus utilities. He was giving her a hell of a deal. But he liked this kid and he wanted her to see her do well.

"Shut up." She laughed. "Is it gross or something?"

"No." He found the key and fished it out of his pocket. "Go see for yourself."

She practically leapt at the chance, all smiles as she snatched the key from his hand and ran to the back of the office.

"Other door," he said. "That one's a storage closet. And Lou's personal entrance apparently." Maybe he should put her name plate on the door. It would be like having a silent partner.

King didn't think Piper had heard that last bit. Her feet were already pounding up the stairs. Then he heard the floorboards creak overhead.

She came down ten minutes later and the jubilance was gone.

"You don't like it?" he asked.

"No, it's nice. Really nice, actually. I like the high ceilings and the big windows looking out back. The person on the opposite side has got some kind of rooftop garden with ferns and stuff. Anyway, it's pretty."

"Then what is it?"

She scratched the back of her head. "I was looking for something a little bigger. Maybe even two bedrooms."

For whom? he wondered.

"If you need an office or something, you can always use this space if you want," he said, searching her face for hints. "Just keep the doors locked after hours."

She nodded, but King knew that look. She was already a hundred miles away.

"If it's the price—"

"No," she said, forcing a smile. "No, you'd be giving me a hell of a deal and you know it. It's just…it's just the space."

The silence swelled between them.

"Well, think about it," he said. "I've got to pay the rent on this place either way, and if you take it that's $800-$900 less I have to think about every month."

"Yeah, I'm sure your DEA pension isn't much."

He didn't correct her. It was true enough, but he didn't live on his pension alone. He'd paid max into his retirement account, had had a separate IRA and investments. Assuming he died before he was 95, King would die a comfortable man.

"And I could look after this place," Piper added, working her bottom lip with her teeth.

"Yeah, that too," he said, taking the key back from her and slipping it into his pocket.

Again he saw the conflict dance across her face.

"If you decide you don't want to stay in the Quarter, that's okay too," he said. "I just thought you'd like to be close to work." *For all three of your jobs*, he thought. Mel was around the corner. Jackson Square, where she sometimes did extra card readings for cash was at the end of the street.

"I don't care what you do up there," he added, wondering if this was about a girl. "It would be your space like any other apartment. You pay for it, it's yours. No questions asked. I trust you."

Her face tightened and she looked ready to cry.

Then she *was* crying, tears spilling down her cheeks.

"Hey." He got around his desk and met her in the middle of the office space. He wrapped his arm awkwardly around her shoulder. "Hey, now. I don't care if you don't want the apartment, all right?"

"It's not the apartment," she said. "That was *so* nice of you. Everything I've found in the Quarter is like $2000 at least. I guess because it's in the safest part of the city."

King wasn't sure the French Quarter was the safest. It was the most heavily policed, certainly.

"And the apartment *is* nice. It's perfect. It's got everything I need. A kitchen, a bathroom and a big closet."

"It doesn't have a washer and dryer," he offered.

"It does," she said. "You've got to open the little closet behind the door." She cried harder and King found himself floating farther and farther from the shore of comprehension. If the apartment was perfect...why was she crying?

"What's going on?" he asked. He knew nothing about Piper's personal life, except for the friends and girls he'd seen her hanging around the Quarter with. Was there a recent break up?

Or was something more going on? He was sure there was.

Not only because he saw her trekking the streets all hours of the day and night, but also because no 23-year-old would willingly work fifty hours a week if she didn't have to. She'd mentioned once that she lived with her mother—that she had a house off of Canal.

Did she have a fight with her mom? Was she being thrown out for being gay? He'd heard something like forty percent of homeless kids were gay.

Piper didn't answer his inquiry, so he let it go. He wasn't going to make her open up if she didn't want to.

"If you need something from me—money. Time off. A drink—"

Piper laughed, wiping at the corner of her eyes.

"Let me know what you need, okay?"

She stepped out of his embrace, nodding, and wiping at her eyes. "You know, I think Dani is looking for a place."

"Who?"

"The girl Mel hired. If you want to get someone in there now—"

"I'm in no hurry. The apartment's yours if you want it. And if you move into another place, that's okay too." King settled back into his chair and reclined. "I won't be mad. Do what you need to do."

She nodded, sinking back into her chair, looking at her laptop without seeing it. Her face red and eyes shimmering.

King wasn't used to this version of Piper.

He was used to the happy-go-lucky version whose excessive cheerfulness and playful nature he now worried was a carefully constructed façade.

"I'm serious," he said, before picking up his coffee again. "If you need something, please tell me."

"I will," she said with a forced smile, eyes watering.

King wished he could believe her.

15

———————

King locked the door to the shop five past five that evening. The sun was setting, filling the storefront windows on the opposite side of the street with its amber fire. He double checked, making sure the landline, which Piper had a good laugh over—calling it *archaic*, a *relic*, and *last wonder of the ancient world*, in turn—routed all after-hours inquiries to his cell phone.

A group of black men with brass instruments slung over their shoulders had to step around him as he struggled to get the old-fashioned lock to work. Then the deadbolt turned twice and King sighed with relief.

He fell into step behind an Asian man holding two paper sacks of groceries, his neck wrapped in a thick navy scarf.

King first saw his stalker as he stepped from Royal Street into Jackson Square. He'd deliberately walked in the opposite direction of his apartment to see if his shadow would follow.

Purposefully relaxing his shoulders, King began to whistle a tune. The only one he could think of was *Time is On My Side*. It would do.

He saw the men with their instruments again. Now they were met with four more musicians, as they arranged themselves for the imminent concert.

King smiled, standing in the square. He kept his eyes on the men and gave every impression that he was an interested onlooker ready to enjoy the music. The air was thick with the scent of Cajun spice and King glanced at the gumbo shop, his mouth watering.

Dinner would have to wait.

He had to continue the show, giving his shadow time to catch up to him, enter the square and find him standing there.

King saw him hesitate at the intersection and then continue forward, melting into a throng of tourists filing out of the gumbo shop on the corner.

King listened to a song, tapping his foot before starting off in the direction of Café du Monde. He pretended to look into the shops as if he'd never seen these sugar skulls, statues of Papa Legba, rows and rows of plastic beads and every form of souvenir ever imagined—from magnets to shot glasses, to plaster figurines of ghosts.

But when he got to the café, he kept walking. He didn't want to run the chance that Suze might say hello and mark herself as a friend. He didn't know enough about his admirer to know what they might do to one of his *friends*. What kind of questions he might ask.

Instead King thought of Lou. The efficient way she'd handled a tail back in June. Brasso had sent two men to follow them and she'd skirted them easily.

Lou sure would be helpful now in getting a good look at the man five or six feet behind him. If Lou would come—

A hand shot out of the alley he was passing and yanked him into the dark.

He opened his mouth to cried out, but the world shifted.

It compressed horribly around him. The pressure removing all air from the world.

Then he was standing in his living room, Lou's fist releasing its hold on the lapel of his coat.

There was his red leather sofa. There was his enormous armoire with a TV nestled inside. His coffee table still looked like some Titanic flotsam, a floating door bolted onto legs.

"Christ," he said, bending at the waist to suck air.

"You called?" she asked.

"Did I?" he said, hoping the room would stop spinning. "My mistake."

"What's going on?" she asked.

He couldn't answer her. For several breaths he could only watch her black combat boots scuff along his wooden floors. He saw the smear of dirt across the toe of her boot and wondered where she'd come from. Her hair was wet like she'd just showered, and he caught the strong scent of soap.

"I was being followed," he said, squeezing his kneecaps in his palms. It seemed to help with the dizziness. "I wanted to get a good look at them."

"Like Brasso's scouts," she said, catching on.

"Yeah, like that. You have to take me back." He sucked a deep breath, already regretting what he was saying. He hated the way she traveled and knew it was because he was clearly not designed for it. "Come on, before he gets too far away."

"You want me to drop you in the alley?"

"Yeah."

"And what do you want me to do?"

"Watch me. I'll walk around for a bit, pick up some groceries or something, and just see who is tracking me."

He was about to ask for a moment, for one more chance to take a deep breath, but she was already hooking her arm through his.

The world compressed. The darkness flattened him on all sides. He couldn't expand his lungs, couldn't draw breath. He couldn't turn his head or get a sense of up or down or if he was any *place* at all.

But fortunately the world opened up again. He took a step back and bumped into the side of the building. His knuckles scraped cold brick.

He opened his mouth to reiterate his instructions, but the words caught in his throat.

She was gone. He stood alone in the dim light of the alley.

"Well then," he said to no one, and stepped out onto the street. "Let's try that again."

MOST OF THE BUILDINGS IN THE FRENCH QUARTER WERE LOW-SLUNG. Prowling the roof and terraces wasn't a bad option for tracking someone below. And while it helped that twilight was slowly covering the district, unfurling its nightly satin, artificial light was springing up to replace the missing day.

Lou found herself in a brick corner. A vent beside her face spewed warm air, scented with spun sugar. No doubt there was a chocolatier below, or perhaps someone who specialized in pralines. She crouched and crept to the edge of the roof, her chin pressed to the cold, concrete ledge.

A brass band trumpeted out a tune that Lou recognized, a remix of some current pop song she couldn't place. Laughter rose up from the swell below. A girl, particularly squealish, cackled like a lunatic, falling into the arms of her patient friend. They only laughed harder when the stacks of beads around their necks tangled and they had to gingerly separate them strand by strand.

She saw King cross the square, heading back toward the office. He paused adjacent to Café du Monde and pretended to watch a street artist paint a landscape. He threw a $20 into the man's hat and motioned for one of the 5x7 prints propped against the wrought iron fence behind him.

That's when Lou spotted the man who trailed him. He was short, maybe 5'7 or 5'8. He was on the stocky side, the bulk of him bulging under a gray coat. Half of his face was hidden by a black woolen scarf, frayed at the edges. But his eyes followed King. Even as he paused to inspect a rack of magnets, his eyes remained locked on the ex-DEA agent.

It wasn't subtle at all and smacked of amateurism. Could Petrov's men truly be so terrible? Maybe she had taken out his best two nights before.

As King moved along, a new painting tucked under this arm, so did the tail.

She left her position on the roof's edge and pressed herself into the nook of the building again. The shadows softened, opening to let her pass.

She slid through, her boots finding concrete. She hovered on the stoop, in the shadow of the dark doorway and watched King slide by. Four heartbeats later, his tail stepped into view. Her boots scraped the step as she reached out to seize the man.

His eyes doubled, then tripled in size, revealing the wide whites. She pulled him into the corner. For a moment, their bodies were flush against each other, and Lou felt the gun tucked into the pocket of his oversized coat press into her ribs.

She slid her hand into the pocket as she pulled him through the dark.

When the world reformed around her, it was the Alaskan nighttime. The muddy banks under her feet sank with her sudden weight. She wondered if it had suffered a hard rain in her absence. The banks were uncommonly soft.

The man slipped out of her grip. His shoes were too fancy. Polished urban loafers with slick bottoms. In this natural landscape, it offered him no traction.

"Oh shit, oh shit, oh shit." The words flew from his mouth, pouring like water from an overturned cup. "Oh my God. What the —what *the*—"

His arms went out wide to steady himself and after some comical flapping, or perhaps his settling weight helped to secure him in the mud, he steadied himself.

"Oh my God. Did you do this?" He looked to the lake, to the surrounding forest, to the high swollen moon. He turned on Lou. "Did you do this?"

She pointed the gun at the ground. The movement drew his eye and he began patting his own pockets.

"And you have my gun. Oh my God. This isn't happening."

She'd seen this level of hysteria before, the blatant disbelief and borderline shock that came from having one's feet firmly planted in one place one moment and finding oneself somewhere else the next. It was this bewilderment that often gave her the advantage.

But she didn't want to kill this man. Not yet.

"Where are we?" he asked. "Where the *fuck* are we?"

"Why were you following that man?" She didn't want to give him King's name in case he didn't know it.

His mouth fell open as he took her in from head to toe. "What man? I didn't see any man."

She raised the gun.

"Oh okay. That guy. I liked his jacket. I wanted to ask him where he bought it."

Lou fired a shot into the ground between the man's knees. Mud splattered up into the face.

"Oh my fucking God is that *blood*? Am I *bleeding*? Did you *shoot* me?"

"Did Petrov send you?" she asked.

"Who?" His scrunched up features. "Who the hell is Petrol?"

"Petrov."

"I don't know who that is."

She raised the gun and pointed it at the space between his two eyebrows.

"Whoa, whoa, whoa. Hey. I don't know what I said, but I'm sorry." He held his hands up in classic surrender, palms bright in the moonlight. "Okay, you asked why I was following King."

So he did know Robert's name.

"I was told you hung out with him. I sent her to get your story."

"Who is 'her'?"

"Dani—Daniella Allendale. She works for me."

"And who are you?"

"Clyde Baker. Editor-in-Chief at the *Louisiana Herald*. But I swear to God, I don't know anything about Peter, petrol, whoever you're talking about. I was looking for you. You're my story."

"You're a journalist," she said.

"Yeah, but listen. It was Dani who was snooping around. She requested an age progression photo of you as a kid. She didn't even tell me. I did *not* approve that. But everything crosses my desk so when it came through—"

"Why would a journalist be looking for me?" Even as she said it, a few theories surfaced, but none close to the one Baker explained.

"I don't think there's a journalist in this country who *doesn't* want to speak to you. You're Louie Thorne. *The* Louie Thorne. When that story broke about your father being a hero, every news outlet in the world wanted to interview you—as you probably know. But nobody could find you."

"You found me." She lowered the gun, her mind racing.

Clyde mistook this as interest. "I was thinking we could start with what it had been like growing up after your dad died, believing he'd betrayed them. Where you were when you learned he was innocent and what it felt like knowing he was a hero. We can even go back to the night your parents were killed. You can take us through what happened, what it had been like losing your father and your mother, what you remember if anything—"

Lou remembered everything.

That white flash of gunfire in her mother's bedroom.

She remembered how the crickets filling the hot June night with their song had fallen silent a second before the back gate was kicked open and Angelo Martinelli stormed into the yard. She remembered how cold the water had been when her back slapped the surface of the pool—when her father had lifted her and thrown her into the water, knowing it would save her.

Her father didn't sacrifice his life so she could be the center of some media circus.

Lou lifted the gun.

"Oh, God. Uh, Ms. Thorne. Listen. I wanted your story for the front page, but I don't want to die over it, okay? If it's between your exclusive and dying of heart failure in thirty years, I choose the heart failure, all right?"

I think he's telling the truth, her father said.

"I mean if you wanted to give us the story, we'd pay you whatever you want. All you have to agree to is the interview."

Lou was faced with the unfathomable reality that she had brought a man here, to her secret dumping ground. And not only a man, but a man who knew her name, knew her history, and who she worked with.

Even if she gave him a story, blew her privacy out of the water, she would have to answer the question of *how* they got here.

She saw the curiosity in his eyes. The way they kept flicking from her to the lake, to the pine forest.

The gun wavered in her hands.

"Please, please," he said, hands on the top of his head, as if this extra layer of bone would protect him from a shot. "I don't know how the fuck we got here and I don't need to know. Just take me back, okay? I'll pull my girl out of there. You'll never hear from us again. I swear to God, we'll disappear. I swear to *fucking* God."

She considered taking him to Konstantine. Considered dropping this man on his doorstep. *If you want to protect my identity, protect it now.*

But that felt like cheating. That felt like asking someone else to do her dirty work.

No. If she cared about her anonymity, if she wanted the freedom to travel this world unseen, this was her business. This was her responsibility.

She raised the gun again.

And there was King to think of. Piper and Melandra. No one would escape unscathed if her story dropped.

"Please!" Spittle flew from his lips, white flecks bright with moonlight even as the shadows hid all but his frightened eyes. "*Please!*"

She pulled the trigger.

16

Piper found the extra roll of register tape in a brown box on the top shelf. Carefully fitting the lid back into place, she jumped down to Dani's applause.

"My hero," Dani said, batting her eyelashes dramatically.

Piper snorted. "Let me show you how to put it in."

"*Please* do," Dani said, her tone going deep and sultry.

Piper's face heated. This sort of ruthless flirting was continuous over the last few days. Whenever Dani and Piper crossed paths and Mel was out of earshot, Dani laid it on thick.

Piper was certain this girl was no cop, no matter what sort of vibes Henry was getting from her. And vibes aside, they were in agreement about one thing: Dani was *very* beautiful. It wasn't only an assortment of symmetrical features, or her olive skin and dark eyes.

There was something else...

It might've had something to do with the way the girl leaned over Piper's shoulder, their sides pressed together, under the pretense of learning how to change the register tape. But Piper could feel her hot breath on her cheek and fought to concentrate on the task at hand.

She worked the plastic casing off the register and fished out the spool inside. She replaced the last of the paper with its dark purple stripe. She pressed the feed button when she was done, and fresh white paper came through the slot.

"Thanks," Dani said, giving another coquettish smile.

"No problem." Piper checked her watch again. It was almost six in the evening. She had to get a move on. The asshole got off work at eight tonight and Piper wanted plenty of time to talk to her mom without him there.

"I've got to run, but I'll be back at ten to lock up," she said, hoping that would give her enough time to run home, talk to her mom, get the last of her stuff and drop it off at Henry's before he went to dance at The Wild Cat.

"Hey," Dani said, coming around the corner.

Piper hesitated, noting the shift in tone.

"Listen, I don't want to be weird. And if you're not feeling it, just say so. I promise not to quit or be a crazy or anything like that."

Piper arched a brow, and then worrying that would be seen as too cynical, added a crooked grin. "Yes?"

"I like you," Dani blurted and then laughed, wringing her hands. "If you're open to the idea, I'd like to spend more time with you. We could do dinner or a movie, or whatever you want."

Piper hadn't been on a date in months. She had a few girls who booty-called her—three this week actually—but dating...

"You are talking about a date, right?" she asked. "Like an actual date?"

Dani laughed nervously, her cheeks filling with color. "If it's weird you can bring friends. We can make it a group thing. I don't care. If you've got someone our age who wants to hang or—"

"Okay," Piper said with a smile, feeling a tad light-headed. "Tonight I was going to read cards in the square. You can join me if you want. I'll be there for a few hours and then after we can—" *Can what?* her mind accused. "We can do whatever," she finished lamely.

Dani grinned. "Yeah. And then *whatever*." She shrugged one shoulder, mockingly.

Piper laughed again. "Okay, I *really* have to go. Sorry."

"It's cool." Dani waved her on. "See you tonight."

. . .

PIPER'S FEET FELT LIGHTER AS SHE TRAVERSED THE ROADS BETWEEN the streetcar stop and her mother's door. She kept replaying the way Dani had looked when she'd asked her out. The blush in her cheeks, the way she'd bitten her lips and laughed nervously.

All those good feelings fell away when the house came into view. The house she grew up in as a kid, back when her father had still been alive. They'd moved into this row house when she was three or four. She couldn't remember exactly. Her father had once told her that they'd lived in his mother's house before that, until she died and left them a little bit of money. The house went to an uncle she'd never met.

They'd used the money to buy this house because, as run-down as it was, it'd been clean and close to his job.

But then he died of lung cancer when she was fourteen. No doubt the three packs a day helped with that, and it became her mother's house. Only her mother didn't take care of it.

The air conditioner broke first, and then the upstairs plumbing. The windows needed to be replaced and the roof sagged. She knew her mother had missed the property tax payments more than once. It was only a matter of time before the government foreclosed on this place. No love lost.

The only thing worse than living in a decaying house was the men.

She knew well enough to stay the hell away from them. And none of them had lasted long, even the two her mother married on a whim. One annulment and one divorce later and it became clear that her mom chose men who liked to move on to other women with more to give.

But this latest man—Willy—he was four years and counting. It didn't look like he was going anywhere.

Piper aimed to change that.

The screen door slammed behind her as she stepped into the house. Black smoke rolled along the ceiling. "Mom? Shit. *Mom?*"

"In here," she heard.

Piper stepped into the kitchen and found the source of smoke. A pan on the stove had caught fire.

She grabbed the towel off the rack and seized the handle of the pan. Throwing the flaming disk into the sink. Then the towel caught and she threw the rest in to contain the blaze. She couldn't be sure if this was a grease fire or if food was burning. The flames were too high to see the source. So she grabbed the baking soda from the fridge and doused it.

"Christ, Mom," she said coughing. She opened the window. Freezing air wafted in, sucking up the smoke.

"You're lucky the fire alarm didn't sound. Someone could've called 911 on you."

"No batteries in the alarm," her mother said, pulling a fresh cigarette from her case. Her back remained to the flame as she sat hunched over the kitchen table. As if her kitchen hadn't almost burned down around her.

Damn, she's high. Nothing Piper could do about it. She needed to talk to her mom and now was the time. "What? I just changed the batteries."

Her mother cupped her hand over the cigarette. "I needed them for the remote."

"Wheel of Fortune isn't worth dying over, Mom."

"Somebody won $50,000 today and a trip to Montana. I'd like to go to Montana. I'd like to get the hell away from here."

Piper didn't take this opportunity to tell her mom that the contestant likely won that trip and money ages ago. No doubt her mother was watching reruns.

"You'd like to get away from here?" she asked instead.

"Who wouldn't? It's too cold. This neighborhood is shit and I can't pay half the bills here. My check don't cover it. This month I've got to catch up the electric. Then I'll be dead broke again for weeks."

"What if you *could* move?" Piper asked, fanning a second ratty dishtowel over the sink, trying to help dissipate the smoke.

Her mother's eyes lit up, her mouth pulling into a grin.

Hope lurched in Piper's chest.

"We could get out of this neighborhood and get a smaller, cheaper place. Something that didn't require upkeep. We'd have more money. Wouldn't you like that?"

"Lord knows I do. Just the three of us?"

Piper's heart flopped. "No, Mom. Just me and you."

Her mother pursed her lips and drew deeply on the cigarette, the cherry burning bright. "I am tired of his ass."

"Then get away from him. *Mom*, get away from him. I'll help you."

"It ain't that easy," she said, grinding her half-finished cigarette into the glass ashtray. "I can't pay for this house by myself. I know you help, but Willy does more than his share too. But houses got more than bills. They got water heaters, plumbing, furnaces and shit like that."

None of which had received any attention from her mother in years, but she said nothing.

"We can sell it," Piper said. "And that's why the apartment is a great idea. Nothing to fix up. No extra bills."

"But this was your daddy's house," she said, smashing her cigarette against the kitchen table, six inches from the ashtray.

"He wouldn't care," Piper said. "He'd want you to have the money." *And to get clean.*

Piper often wondered if her mother started using drugs because her father died or if her father had simply done a good job of hiding it from his daughter.

Piper came to the kitchen table and sank down into the chair. For a moment, her mother only regarded her with one of those glassy, distant stares.

"You're so pretty," her mom said, patting her cheek with a shaking hand. "My beautiful girl. You're the best thing I ever did."

"Mom, I've got an apartment," Piper said, comfortable with this small lie. Because come payday tomorrow, she would have enough to put the deposit on a two-bedroom she'd found north of the French Quarter. Nothing fancy. Not nearly as charming as the apartment above the detective agency. But it was quiet and clean and roomy enough for the two of them.

"I can afford to cover it all by myself. You can sell the house, pay off your debts. Your whole check will be yours. You don't have to worry about anything."

Her mother searched her face, her eyes round with sadness. "You don't want to live here with me?"

"I can't, Mom," she said, looking at the back of her hands. She turned the silver ring on her thumb self-consciously. "I can't live with these men you bring around. I'm sorry."

Her mother opened her cigarette case and tapped out a fresh one. Piper produced a lighter from her pocket and lit it for her.

"But I want you to live with me. It's a cleaner, safer place. But you've got to agree to leave Willy behind, Momma. He can't come. It's only us."

"The house—"

"We'll deal with the house together. But right now—" *We've got to get you clean.* "We need to focus on taking care of ourselves."

Her mother drew deep on the filter, the white paper burning brighter in the dim kitchen.

"It's a nice apartment?"

Piper sat up straighter. "Two bedrooms. You'd have your own room overlooking a park. And it's on the second floor in a better neighborhood. It's even got radiator heat in there and a big bathroom. It's got a tub you can soak in."

"I do like baths," her mother said, with a wistful smile. "We don't get hot water in the upstairs bath no more."

"I know," Piper said. "But these taps are nice and hot."

"But no Willy?"

"No Willy," Piper said. *And no dope.*

"If I go with you, then I won't be able to get my fix no more," she said. She looked Piper dead in the eye. The gaze cleared.

Piper's heart skipped a beat. She hadn't wanted to have this part of the conversation yet, fearing it would push her mother in the wrong direction.

But her mother seemed to see the truth on her face. "You don't just want me to leave, Willy. You want me to get clean."

"I worry about you. I don't want to come home and find you dead one day with a needle in your arm. If you don't get clean, that's exactly what's going to happen."

No one said anything for a long time. Piper stood up to close the window. All but a thin haze of smoke had escaped into the blustery night. She checked the time. It was already almost 7:30. She had twenty minutes to get out of this place and she hadn't even made it upstairs to pack up.

Piper leaned against the sink, looking at her mother's frail bent back. She wasn't sure what else she could say, should say, to convince her this was what was for the best.

Then her mother spoke. "I don't want to live like this. I don't like waking up in the morning feeling sick. I don't like the way Willy talks to me, or the things he makes me do."

Piper bit down on her anger.

"But I don't want to be out on the streets either. This has been my home for twenty years."

"I can take care of you, Mom," she said quietly, reclaiming her seat at the table. "I won't let you rot in the streets."

"It's a nice apartment?"

Piper crossed to the kitchen table and took her hand. "It's great. You'll love it."

"And you'll be there?" her mother asked.

"I'll be there."

"And all $700 of my check will be mine?"

Piper smiled. "I don't need it. I can pay for that apartment and all our food and stuff with my jobs. You can focus on getting better. I want you to get healthy again."

Her mother squeezed her hands, her smile bright and infectious. "When do we move?"

17

After an uneventful drop on the shores of La Loon, Lou stepped out of her linen closet into her bright apartment. The sunshine on the river sparkled through the high window, splitting Lou's head in two. She drew the shade, turning a coin over and over her knuckles.

It was a coin she'd taken from the reporter's pocket.

She placed it on the counter, using it to pin down one corner of that annoying letter, and stripped naked. Her wet clothes hit the floor with a soaked *plop* as she stepped out of them.

This would be her second shower for the day. She'd wash her hair again. Lake water from some other world, not to mention what might have come off the dead reporter she'd hauled to the other side—none of which she wanted drying in her hair.

She turned on the shower, turned it all the way to hot and stepped into the stream.

His face flashed repeatedly in her mind. His wide eyes, his pleading.

She stayed in the stall, the hot water burning her skin raw until it turned cold on her.

Then she stepped out, grabbed a towel and went to the hall closet to dress.

In the kitchen, the coin glinted on the island.

She picked it up, turning it in the light. It was a half dollar. She turned it over and over in her hands as if she could divine the truth from it.

Did I kill an innocent man...?

There was one way to find out.

The coin cut into the palm of her hand. She was holding it too tight. Then the darkness gave her passage.

When she pushed open the door, she found herself in a tin cup of an apartment. A beat up sofa the color of shit sat in one corner. A boxy TV sat on an overturned milk crate. A coffee table with nicks gouged out of every leg rested between the two. On the opposite wall, a fridge and a single counter sat with a sink. The only other door opened onto a bathroom with a toilet and shower stall. There was no room to turn around.

She supposed if the window shade had been open and the room brighter, she would have entered through there.

On the sofa, beneath a standard pillow, was a laptop. Lou took it, following the cord to the wall and unplugging it. She wrapped it around the device.

Nothing else was worth taking. Not the handful of dishes nor the hot plate. A sad collection of utensils and a vacuum with dust on it sat in a corner beside the front door.

No pictures. She couldn't even figure out where he kept his clothes until she found the three large totes in what could've been a coat closet. There was some cash in these totes, but she didn't take it.

She stepped back into the shadows and slipped.

She expected to push open the door and find herself in her own apartment.

Instead, she stepped into Konstantine's bedroom. The bedroom was empty and the bed made. She put the laptop on the foot of the bed and crossed to the window. She opened it to find the river awash in sunset. People marched up and down the street, some engaged in rapid conversation. Some eating gelato despite the frigid night closing in on them. One girl's lips looked nearly blue as she laughed.

An old couple with shopping bags between them, pulled their coats tighter and marched on, a slow processional toward the river crossing.

Leaving the laptop on the bed, she went downstairs. This room was spacious with a tiled floor, uneven in its old world charm.

A desk sat in the corner, with a large painting hanging on the wall behind it. A fern hung from the ceiling, reminding her also of the ferns that lined King's balcony.

Past the desk was the kitchen.

She pulled back the curtain beside the front door and saw a court-yard below. She spotted a few apartment doors on either side and, on the far right, an archway connecting with the street.

She laid down on the sofa and closed her eyes.

Voices echoed outside the door, slowly pulling her to consciousness. A lock clanked, a door popped open and then Konstantine stepped into the apartment with a young boy on his heels. No more than twelve or thirteen.

Lou, still reclining on the sofa, sat up.

The boy spoke to Konstantine in rapid, excited Italian. Konstantine replied as quickly, pushing the boy out the door and locking it again despite his protests.

"Are you hurt?" he said, obviously surprised to see her.

"No," she said, realizing how this must look. She'd appeared in his house without an invitation. She'd checked it out and went to sleep on his couch. It was almost like a fairytale where the girl got eaten by the bear at the end.

He removed his coat, showing a tight sweater underneath. It was a charming blue. The color of the Mediterranean sea. He pushed the sleeves up past his elbows, showing a hint of the tattoos that snaked up both sides.

"Are you all right?" he asked.

She sat up, placing her boots on the floor. "I killed a journalist."

"Petrov sent him?"

"No. He was...just a journalist."

Konstantine's eyebrows arched in surprise. "Did you kill him acci-dentally?"

"No," she said. "Then I stole his computer."

Konstantine sat down beside her on the sofa. "Could you start from the beginning and perhaps tell me the whole story?"

Lou did. She began with King's call to the moment she put a bullet in the journalist and dragged him to La Loon, spending *no* time in the shallows this round. She recounted going to his apartment after disposing of his body and finding the laptop.

She pulled the coin from his pocket. "And I took this." She handed it over as if it was the last piece of business.

"He knew your name," he said.

"Yes," she said. "The undercover journalist that Mel hired must know my name too."

"Are you going to kill her?"

She said nothing.

Konstantine leaned back against the sofa, turning the half dollar in the light. "If he knew who you were and wanted to reveal your identity, nothing can be done."

"King, Melandra, Piper all know who I am and I haven't killed them."

"Yes, but they are your friends. What reason does a starving journalist have to protect you?"

She said nothing.

"Do you blame yourself?" he asked, surprise lighting his face. When she didn't answer he added, "If anyone is to blame for this man's death, it's me. I'm the one who published your father's story. My proof sent reporters looking for you. You were only protecting yourself."

"What am I protecting exactly?" she whispered, her eyes fixed on the back of her hands.

"Your freedom. If the world knows you, your face, your name, you will not be free any longer. That is why I remove every shred of evidence. I want you to be free to do as you wish."

"Why?" She turned toward him, pivoting at the hip, her arm stretched over the back of the couch.

"Can you not guess?" he asked, meeting her gaze. He smiled, but she saw the hint of nervousness at the edge of his mouth.

It wasn't only the way his hair fell at his cheekbones or that rich green of his eyes. Nor were the full lips that she wanted to drag her thumb across completely undoing her.

Had she found him in a bar, had he casually met her eyes in a dark room, she would've approached him and asked the same question: *take me back to your place?*

She would have gone home with him and satisfied that hunger. It wasn't so unlike her lust for hunting, because wasn't this hunting in its own right? And the desire to hunt had left her, at least for now. This hunger was all she had left.

KONSTANTINE SEARCHED THOSE RICH BROWN EYES, TRACING THE outline of her lips and wishing desperately he knew what she was thinking. He also wished he could close this small distance and kiss her. If she were any other woman, he would. But he knew Lou too well. He knew that if he tried to take the control from her, put her in a subservient position, she'd only disappear again.

Hadn't he learned that lesson last time?

He would wait it out. Only he didn't have to wait.

She threw a leg over his lap and straddled him. He felt the delicious heat of her sex as she settled her weight against him, pelvis to pelvis. He inhaled a sharp breath, scenting the side of her throat.

She slid her fingers into his thick hair and pulled his head back so that he had no choice but to look into her eyes. He was already looking, his hunger darkening to match her own.

His patience had limits. He lifted up, finding her mouth with his. A furious collision of flesh.

He wanted to flip her onto her back, wondered if she could tell by the gentle, anxious shift in his hips as he warred with himself. Again he exerted control, making sure this was what she wanted, how she wanted it.

What restraint you have, he mused.

A caress of her tongue against his, as languid as a cat's, obliterated all thoughts from his head.

Her tongue probed deeper, eliciting a groan from his throat. He was hardening, but the erection had nowhere to go. Between the tightness of his pants and the weight of her against him. This seemed to only intensify the throbbing.

He dared to wrap his arms around her, slipping his hands up the back of her shirt. Fingers trailed bare flesh. He crushed her against him, feeling every taut muscle contract.

The hand in his hair—vibrated.

She withdrew and it took considerable effort on his behalf to loosen his hold on her as she pulled away. She turned her wrist over and read the watch. The face was lit green, but he couldn't read the numbers at this angle.

"What's wrong?" he asked, his voice thick.

"King paged me."

He pulled her toward him again putting her within reach of another kiss. He tilted his chin up, hungry to taste her.

She resisted.

With a sigh, he withdrew his arms and fell back against the sofa. "All right. Go. The only person more prone to trouble than you is that man. And he is not nearly as capable of taking care of himself as you are."

Was that a smile touching the corners of her lips?

"Do you want me to hack the computer while you're away? Perhaps the journalist knew much more than he said. Or sent the information to another source."

And God knows I will need something to distract myself.

"It's on your bed," she said as she pulled her heat and weight from his body.

He watched her mount the stairs, voluptuous hips giving over to thick, strong legs to only combat boots. Then he listened to three, four, five steps.

Silence.

He remained against the sofa, grappling with his desire and disappointment.

When we are defeated, we must take the long view, Padre Leo had told him. *Will we see this to the end? No matter where it takes us?*

Yes, Konstantine thought. As long as he had air in his lungs, and the blood pumped in his veins, he wanted to see this through—no matter how tragic the end.

He found the laptop on his coverlet and opened the black case. She'd been kind enough to bring the power adapter. All the better.

This was more than enough for him to start.

18

D ani watched Piper count out the drawer and wrap the money in rubber bands. She pretended to dust a shelf for the third time.

"We still hanging out tonight?" she asked, hoping she sounded casual.

"I'm still going to the square if you want to come. But Henry asked me to drive him home after his show."

Dani's disappointment was genuine. There was clearly no invitation for her to join them. She gave it her best shot anyway. "You have a car? If not, I can take you."

"He does. But he'll be too wasted to drive himself and I'm crashing at his place tonight. I couldn't tell him no."

That would make it too easy for me, Dani thought. She frowned, searching for another opening. "Do you *mind* if I still come to the square? I've always been interested in that sort of stuff. It's why I'm working here, actually."

She gestured at the shop with the yellow feather duster in her hand. She reached up to tug one of her braids. She was starting to get used to the black polish. She might keep wearing it, even if it would make her mother's head roll.

Piper tucked the money into the bag and zipped it closed. "Sure. You can help me set up the table. It's easier with two people."

Piper ducked into the storeroom closet. Dani glanced around the shop to make sure she hadn't forgotten anything. Her phone and wallet were in her bag. Her coat rested on the stool behind the register.

The safe in the stockroom beeped as Piper entered the code to unlock it. A few heartbeats later she reemerged with her coat and backpack in hand. "Ready?"

Dani grabbed her coat and bag, tucking the feather duster into a cubby to the left of the register. "Yep."

Dani stepped out onto the street first, taking in that first bite of frigid air. The hair rose on the back of her neck. She burrowed her chin in her collar.

"How long have you been doing readings in the square?" Dani asked.

Piper inserted her key into the lock and turned it three times before pressing on the handle to make sure it was bolted tight.

"About three years," she said. "I've got some regulars."

"Fancy," Dani said, batting her lashes. "Why don't they come see you at the shop?"

"Cheaper. The readings in the square are by donation only. You can't set a price. But plenty of people pay."

"That's cool that they keep coming back to you."

"Yeah," she said, adjusting the pack on her back. She passed a shop window and the light caught in her eyes. Dani thought her beautiful.

"It's sort of like being a hair dresser."

Dani laughed. "How?"

"If you give a good haircut, people come back. They tell their friends that you're good and so they come see you too."

"Are most of the readers in the square fakes?"

Piper shrugged. "Not necessarily *fakes*. But people want good readings."

They stepped off the Royal Street curb into Jackson Square. A quartet with two cellos and two violins played a maudlin tune under the cathedral's lights.

"My table is in here," Piper said, pointing at a shop across the street. *Jim's Jambalaya.*

"You know Jim?" she asked, pointing at the sign.

"I do," she said with a smile. "And I give him $25 a night to rent out one of his card tables. He has poker in there on Thursdays if that's your thing."

Piper turned to her suddenly and grabbed Dani's shoulders. She stepped close enough to her that Dani could smell the cherry lip balm on her mouth.

Is she going to kiss me?

But Piper didn't kiss her. She only moved her over to a spot four or five paces from the large pine tree.

"Stay here," she said. "*Right* here."

Dani laughed. "*O*-kay."

"Don't move," she said, backing away. Piper ducked into the shop, the smell of Cajun spices wafting out behind her as the door swung closed.

Dani glanced around the square. There were couples arm in arm watching the quartet. A few people danced, swaying and clapping their hands. A queue had formed in front of the café. A few artists stood on the stone walkway, smoking and chatting. Someone dressed like the tin man remained frozen on his soapbox, playing the part of living statue for tips.

Then there were the other tarot readers. Some carried in tables. Others were already set up and reading. One woman taped a cardboard sign, like something made at a high-school bake sale, to the front of her table. *Palm and Tarot readings by Catherine the Great,* it said. And beneath that *I was Cleopatra too.*

Piper reappeared holding a table a tad too large for her arm span.

"Okay, I'll hold it open like this and if you can crawl underneath and fix the latch that would be awesome."

Dani heard her mother's voice in her ear instantly. *On your hands and knees on this filthy street, Daniella Vivianne!*

The stone was cold against her hand as she peered under the table. But now full dark was on them and she couldn't see.

"One sec," she said, fishing her phone out of her bag and using the flashlight to locate the small latch Piper insisted existed. At last she flicked it into place. "There. Got it."

Piper lifted and placed the table on all fours. Then she pressed the top gently to ensure that it was latched. "Thanks!"

But then she was running into the jambalaya shop again, only to return with four metal folding chairs. Two balanced on each arm. It reminded Dani of the way she liked to carry in her groceries, all in one trip. Broken arms or bust.

"He lets you take chairs too?" she asked. She rushed to take half of Piper's burden.

She held them as Piper unfolded two chairs on each side of the table. "For $5 each."

"Ouch! That's $45," Dani said. "Let me give you some money."

Piper waved her off. "It's okay. It's a convenience fee. It would suck to haul all that out here every night I want to work, and I'll make it back anyway."

She grinned and again Dani was struck again by how cute she was. *It's that smile,* she thought.

Their breath puffed white in front of their faces as laughter and music drifted through the square. Dani wished she'd brought gloves, and took to warming her hands between her thighs.

From her backpack, which Piper tucked between her legs, she brought out a cigar box. It was reinforced cardboard painted with blue-birds. Dani hadn't seen one of those in ages, not since her father quit smoking decades ago.

She flipped it open and pulled out a folded white cloth and threw it over the table. Then she tented a cardboard sign that simply said *Tarot and Palm by Piper.*

Dani laughed. "Way to sell yourself."

Piper snorted, cutting her eyes to Catherine the Great. "I don't want to overdo it."

It wasn't ten minutes before a young woman with dreadlocks and a punk rock boyfriend sat down in the opposite chairs.

Dani realized pretty quickly why Piper was so good at this. Not only because she was able to offer real advice to these people—*you've lost a friend recently and you feel like that might be your fault*—but she was a good listener.

When someone would open up or offer personal information, Piper would only hold their hands, look them in the eye and listen. It was powerful.

You're worried you'll regret this decision, but I think you'll regret not acting more.

You don't think you can do this, but you can.

You will reconcile.

You're scared about starting over, but this is the best move for you.

You might feel alone now, but you've got a lot of love coming into your life. Keep your eyes open. You'll see it.

And when the reading was over, they'd toss their $5, $10, or $20 bills into Piper's cigar box and bid her farewell with relieved smiles on their faces.

Dani filled the intermissions with small conversation.

"Do you go to school?" Dani asked.

"I was at UNO last year but I had to quit. Well, not quit exactly, but take some time off. I want to go back. I hope I can this fall."

"Needed a break?" Dani asked.

Piper breathed hot air into her cupped hands. "My mom...got sick. She needed help with the bills, so I needed to work more. I don't have time for school right now."

"Sorry." *What different worlds we live in.* "Will she be okay?"

"I hope so," Piper said, forcing a smile and effectively ending the conversation.

Another couple sat down in the folding chairs, drawing Piper away entirely.

The purpose of this outing was to build familiarity. She wanted Piper to feel comfortable with her. She needed to build rapport and trust. Only then would she be able to ask intrusive questions without blowing her cover.

Besides, this was the last place Dani saw Lou. In a photograph, true, but it was enough to hang out here and see if she turned up.

Piper prattled on beside her while Dani's eyes scanned the streets under the guise of people watching.

For hours, Piper's cigar box filled and waned. She was smart to roll up most of the cash and tuck it into a pocket between readings. The moon set behind the low-slung buildings, leaving them only the artificial light.

The crowd of tourists and drunks thinned. Leaner, hungrier-looking figures took their place.

"I think that's it for tonight," Piper said, as if sensing the shift herself. She gathered up the cards and tapped them into a stack. She pulled out the donations, counted the bills and rearranged them by value. Then she tucked the cards and the money into a separate box for safekeeping. It was smaller than the cigar box, and had some intricate design on the face, which Dani couldn't see well in the dark.

There were at least three hundred dollars in there. Dani wanted to warn her it was dangerous to be out here in a place like this with that kind of money. Someone could've been watching. Someone could mug her. Desperate drug addicts, or just some asshole itching for a fight might decide she looked like prey.

Anything could happen in a place like this.

But then Piper took the cash from her pocket and what was left in the cigar box and locked it into a metal lockbox. Then she tucked the entire bundle under a roll of clean clothes at the bottom of her bag. She did all of this bent over, keeping the money carefully out of sight.

She's not stupid. She's being far more careful than I expected her to be.

Dani found her heart racing, watching Piper pack up for the night. There was something about this girl. It wasn't only her adorable laugh, her witty quips or the way she went the extra mile to get that smile. There was something...savvy about her. It was so different than the polished, artificial glamour of her parents, of the people she knew from her private high school and extended network.

Nothing about Piper smacked of elitism. She wasn't charming the way her mother was to a room full of executives. She was smart and real.

Genuine, she thought. *That was the word.* Piper was genuine. It was a quality Dani didn't think existed.

Dani kept stealing glances at the girl's face as she helped her fold up the tablecloth. Piper tucked her toothbrush into the corner of her mouth while she rearranged the contents of the bag, situating everything just so.

So she didn't stay with Henry all the time, only a night here and there. Dani wondered why. Maybe her mother was in the hospital? Maybe she had nowhere to go.

Piper zipped up the bag and shouldered it. "Can you help me break down this table?"

"Sure." Dani found the hinge underneath and flicked it. The table tented in the middle and the girls were able to fold it in half.

Then they carried the chairs into the shop first. Dani relished the restaurant's heat against her frozen cheeks and the tips of her ears. Reluctantly, they returned for the table.

"I got it." Piper jogged across the square with the table in tow and ducked back into the jambalaya shop for the last time.

She emerged a moment later adjusting the backpack straps over her shoulders.

"So you're off to see Henry?" Dani asked. Her feet were starting to freeze in her sneakers. She stamped them to encourage warmth.

"Yeah. You can come for the show if you want."

"No. I need sleep," Dani said, not wanting to seem too desperate. And there was the other issue. She was beginning to like Piper. *Really* like her. And that made deceiving her feel wrong.

Piper snorted. "Yeah, I have a hard time falling asleep after going there. I think it's the music that hypes you up."

Don't do it, she thought.

The urge was rising up inside her nonetheless.

Don't complicate this.

Piper rubbed her nose. "Do you live near here? I have time to walk you to your car if—"

Without thinking, she came up onto her toes and kissed Piper. Their warm lips collided. It was a delicious reprieve from the frosty night. Dani didn't want to stop, but she pulled back first.

Piper's cheeks had reddened, bright even in the dim street lamp. Then her brilliant smile emerged.

"I'll see you tomorrow," Dani said, managing a smile before turning and running off into the dark.

19
<hr/>

King paced his living room. Ten steps toward the enormous armoire in the corner, twenty steps toward his checkered kitchen tile. Then back toward the balcony door and armoire again. His feet seemed to wear grooves into the wooden floor.

He didn't want to page Lou a third time with the *911* directive. This wasn't an emergency. But his anxiety sure as hell was rising with every moment he didn't hear from her.

When he'd asked her to follow his tail, he'd expected her to watch from a distance. He'd cut a lazy path through the French Quarter, giving her plenty of time to get a good look at the man who'd followed him.

But on Royal Street, while he himself was deciding whether or not to turn a block early or to head back to his own apartment, he'd heard the sharp intake of breath. The muffled cry.

King turned in time to see the man pulled into a shadowed doorway and disappear.

Under the pretense of confusion, should anyone on the street look out the window and see him, he'd calmly walked back the way he came and frowned at the doorway. He inspected its empty corners even though he knew what had happened. The unmiraculous details of a worn wooden door could tell him nothing.

King returned his cell phone to his pocket, removed it again, only to stare at the screen.

"You rang?" a voice called.

King turned to find Lou leaning casually against his bedroom door, her hands in the pockets of her leather jacket, her mirrored sunglasses pushed up to rest on top of her head. He thought her face looked a little red, especially around the mouth. Perhaps even swollen.

Maybe the other guy got a punch off before she—what? God, *killed* him?

"Are you okay?" he asked.

She gave a noncommittal shrug. "Why did you page me?"

"I wanted to know what the hell happened back there."

With this request aside, he became aware of his bulking size taking up most of the living room. He crossed to the refrigerator and opened it. "Can I offer you a drink?"

She agreed to a soda and settled onto the red leather sofa beside him.

"I asked him some questions."

"And?"

"He's dead," she said.

"His answers must've been wrong," he said, twisting the top of his root beer.

"He was a senior editor at the Louisiana Herald," she said.

"What the hell did a reporter want from me?" he asked. He could think of a few reasons, but none that required a man to follow him. Most journalists simply interviewed him if they needed information on a case.

"He was looking for me," she said, finally cracking open the lid on her soda. "He thought he could find me through you."

"Oh." That answered some questions and begged many more. "What did he want you for?"

She opened her arms as if to present herself. "I'm Louie Thorne. Daughter of Jack Thorne, slain hero."

"No," King said. "Damn. I thought we'd killed all those leads."

Except for the rumors that she lived in an asylum, of course. King had left those stories, mostly in small publications around the country. Why not indulge in a little misdirection?

"You and Konstantine both," she said. There was something in the way she said his name that made King look at her.

"How in the world did they tie you to me?" he asked.

"I think Daniella had something to do with that."

"Who?"

"The girl Mel hired. She's an undercover journalist. Also for the Herald." Lou took a long drink on her soda.

"Shit." King fell back against the sofa. "She looks young as hell."

"She's probably my age."

He didn't argue. Piper was also her age, if a hair younger. But how could King explain that it seemed as if centuries stretched between Piper and herself? That in no world could he look into Piper's eyes and Lou's eyes and say they were of the same mind.

"Do you think she knows anything?" King asked.

"I don't know."

Another strange tone that left him searching her face. "You can't kill her."

"I can't?" Lou asked, her head cocked like a bird's. "True it'll be my first woman but—"

"No, I mean she's a kid."

"I've killed dealers who were younger," she said, turning the drink in her hands.

"You can scare her," he insisted.

"Maybe she doesn't scare so easily."

"I think she has a thing for Piper," he said. This was mere conjecture. Coming out of his apartment he'd caught the look that the girls exchanged before he'd put his full weight on the stairs and made his presence known. "Maybe Piper can get her to understand—"

"Or she's using Piper to get information."

"Fuck." He wasn't sure what else to say. He tried to remember the last time he'd seen Piper.

"The journalist isn't my only problem."

"Our only problem," he corrected her.

She regarded him for several long seconds.

"We are a team," he said, wondering if she misunderstood. "Your problems are my problems."

"You need to be careful," she said.

"If I—"

"Not from me," she said, turning the soda again. The can caught and reflected the light from the overhead fan. "Petrov doesn't want to hire me. He wants to kill me."

"That escalated quickly."

"Apparently it was the plan all along. He wants revenge for his son, Alexei."

"I assume you killed Alexei?"

She took a drink, denying nothing.

King sighed. "If a journalist can tie us together, I guess a rich Russian mob boss can do the same."

"Revenge is dangerous," Lou said.

King suppressed a laugh. "You would know."

"If he were still trying to buy my loyalty, he might have gone easy on you. Only broken a leg or a finger. Or maybe he'd cut something off."

King snorted. "This is going *easy* on someone?"

Lou didn't seem to hear him. "But if he wants revenge, then he wants to hurt me. He will kill you."

King considered this.

"There was nothing that would have stopped me from killing Angelo Martinelli," she said quietly, placing her unfinished soda on the coffee table. "His ten-year-old son could've been standing between us and I still would've put a bullet in his head."

"You don't mean that."

But her face said she did.

"Don't put yourself between us," Lou said. She stood suddenly and he was worried she would disappear on the spot.

"Hey," he said. "Before you go, I have to give you something."

She hesitated in the center of the living room.

King crossed to his bedroom, and found the dresser. In the third drawer, beneath a stack of folded shirts, he found the padded mailer. He pulled it out, checked to see the two tapes were still there and also the letters inside.

Lou stood at the balcony door, looking out when he returned.

"These checked out. I was able to authenticate them, so this isn't a trap."

"How?" she asked, accepting the mailer with both hands.

"This tape," he said, pointing at one of the VHS tapes poking through the opening in the top. "This is the one Jack gave me to deliver to Lucy when I found her. It's just how I remember it."

She nodded, regarding the tapes with an unreadable expression. "And the other?"

"It's also your dad," he said, watching her face carefully. "But he's talking to you."

She reached up and pulled her sunglasses down over her eyes. She said nothing.

"Can I ask for one more favor?" he said, shifting to release pain from his tight hip. "Will you go check on Piper? I'm worried about her."

He thought she was going to refuse him. She looked like she wanted to.

"She might be spilling everything to that journalist. Can you just check on her please?"

"Okay," she said. "After I drop these off."

"I don't know how you're going to play them? Who even has VHS anymore? Turns out Mel has one, if you need it."

"I'll figure it out."

When she disappeared, King thought the knot in his chest would loosen. After all, she'd taken all her intensity with her and he'd done his job delivering the tapes.

But instead his anxiety had only increased.

He wasn't sure if it was Lucy's letter—*she deserves to know*—or if it was the promise of violence at the hands of Dmitri Petrov.

Both would have fallout. He supposed the real question was, were they ready?

Mel had echoed his concerns. But the alarm company couldn't come until Monday. And his messages with his friends in the canine community had yet to get back to him.

He'd loaded his guns and kept them close. Mel had done the same.

But real preparations would take time. Maybe time they didn't have.

20

Piper stepped off the concrete porch and shook the landlady's hand one more time, offering effusive gratitude.

The tiny woman with a hunched spine and coke-bottle glasses shuffled away from her, heading down the street toward her own home at the end of the block.

Piper watched her as she left, regarding the puff of wiry, white hair crowning her oversized coat.

It cost Piper a considerable chunk of her savings, but the apartment was now hers. The landlady wanted to take one more look at the contract, update it, and then Piper was to come by their office Monday morning, only three short days away. In the meantime, she could be safe in knowing that no one else would swoop in and steal this amazing find.

A large two-bedroom apartment with heat, water, and trash included. It overlooked a courtyard, its paving stones framing a single tree. While the apartment was quite close to the street, Piper didn't mind a bit of traffic noise. It was clean. It wasn't too far from work and best of all—it was hers.

Mom will like it here. It was the perfect place for them to put all of the past behind them and get her well again. Piper would take care of the bills and her mother could focus on her health. Money would be tight and maybe Piper couldn't return to school in September, but by next January—anything was possible.

This will work. This has *to work.*

Piper couldn't spend any more of her waking hours wondering whether or not she would come home and find her mother dead on the living room floor. Or another unexplainable black eye. Or, heaven forbid, her mother announced she intended to marry Willy, and make him her fifth husband.

Running back toward the bus stop, Piper felt better than she had in a long time. Things were looking up. She still had money in the bank, though admittedly not as much as she'd like. But she had more coming in from the jobs she loved.

Crossing Canal Street, white breath puffed in front of her face as she looked both ways. She wanted to pop into the shop and check on Mel before heading by her mom's place to deliver the good news. Stomping her feet on the mat, Piper stepped into Fortunes and Fixes to the flickering moan of the haunted chandelier.

Dani was behind the counter, bending down to retrieve a brown paper bag. She wrapped one of the Papa Legba figurines carefully in several rolls of newsprint then slid it into the bag.

"There you go," she chirped, smiling broadly at the young woman on the opposite side, a small kid hanging off her leg.

Piper waved at the child and she bashfully hid her face in her mother's coat.

"Come on," the mom said, drawing her away from the counter. "No, don't touch."

"Hey," Dani said, leaning over the glass table. "I thought you weren't coming by for a few more hours."

"I wanted to see if Mel needed anything. Sometimes she runs out of stuff before the end of the day but can't go get it herself, so..."

Dani jabbed a thumb at the curtain. "She's back there."

Piper's eyes took inventory of Dani's body—the curve of her neck, her hip bones, and the bare stretch of skin between her cut-off shirt and high-waisted pants.

Dani's smile widened. "You okay? You look...excited maybe?"

"I put down a deposit on an apartment today, so I'm pretty pumped."

"Congrats. They're hard to find around here. Or at least the good ones are."

"Yeah, and this one is perfect."

"Is it your first place on your own?"

"Yeah." Piper wasn't sure how much she should elaborate. "I mean, my mom is going to move in with me."

"Oh. That's nice. You'll be able to take care of her."

"That's the idea," Piper said.

"It's sweet of you to take your mom like that."

Piper's face warmed. "She's my responsibility."

Dani's face pinched curiously. It was as if she didn't understand the words coming out of Piper's mouth.

"What?"

Dani forced a quick smile. "Nothing."

Piper became aware of Mel's low voice droning behind the curtain as Dani closed the distance between them.

Piper licked her lips, also aware that her heart was hitching in her chest. "I guess Mel's busy. I'll have to check in later."

"We could go into the storeroom and see if anything's missing ourselves," Dani offered.

Her face was so close to Piper's now that she could feel her breath on her moist lips and smell the perfume along the side of her neck.

"A quick look," Piper said, her voice cracking in the middle.

Dani took her hand and pulled her toward the storeroom. Piper's heart was pounding so hard she thought her head might explode. They closed the door behind them but didn't turn on the light. For a moment, Piper stood in the dark, feeling nothing but the stagnant air of the place and the slight scent of cardboard boxes.

Then a cool hand trailed up her arm to the back of her neck. It was joined by its twin on the other side of her face as she was pulled forward. Hot, sticky lips found her. This was when Piper realized that Dani favored some kind of fruity lip gloss. She'd been wearing it for both kisses now. Not that Piper cared. Instead she sucked the lower lip between her teeth and removed the candy-coating with her tongue.

"All night I kept thinking about that kiss," Dani said. "I couldn't wait to do it again."

Dani laughed. A low, guttural sound that skittered across Piper's bones. Her breath tightened in her chest the same moment Dani's hands slid through her hair.

The kisses grew hungry, deep and fever pitched.

Piper stepped forward, pushing Dani back. They hit a wall and a cough of surprise escaped her.

"You seem to know your way around a storeroom," Dani whispered, the humor coating each word.

Dani had no idea how true that was. Usually Piper was the one who suggested the storeroom make-outs, but Dani didn't need to know that. No girl wanted to know something like that.

Piper slid one hand over Dani's bare stomach, until her fingers brushed the edge of a bra.

Denied, she thought, almost laughing. *Unless we storm the gates.*

A haunting moan echoed through the dark. But it wasn't from Dani. It was from the damned motion-censor chandelier.

"Damn," Piper said, pressing her cool hand on the girl's warm stomach. "You better get out there or Mel will lose her shit."

"Not until you tell me when we're having dinner."

"Tonight."

"You promise?" Her voice was breathy and Piper could feel her pulse jumping under her hand.

"I swear. Meet me here at close. Give me thirty minutes and that's it."

"Okay," she managed.

One more furious kiss and then Dani pushed open the storeroom door, pausing long enough to give Piper a wicked wink.

Piper stood in the dark, heart pounding for a full minute. Once she felt like most of the blood had drained from her face, she opened the storeroom door to find Mel on the lowest step, heading up to her apartment.

"Oh, you're here," she said, turning back. "I've got a shopping list for you. Come on up and get it."

Piper didn't dare look at Dani behind the counter lest she give the game away.

. . .

PIPER WAS STILL HEADY WITH KISSES WHEN SHE REACHED HER mother's street. She warmed her hands in her pockets, her chin tucked into the thick collar of her scarf.

She wasn't in a hurry because the asshole would be at work for at least two more hours. She had plenty of time to get in there, tell her mom the news and establish their moving-day plan.

Then Piper could—hopefully—get the last load of her stuff out of her upstairs bedroom. That would give her plenty of time to deliver Mel's order, close up shop, and spend the rest of the night with Dani—probably in Dani's sublet, given her current living situation.

She smiled into her scarf, mounting the three-step stoop with the sack of McDonald's in her right fist.

She opened the front door and stepped into the warm hallway. The glow of the kerosene heater danced on the wall.

"Mom," she called out. "I got you a Big Mac."

Nothing.

"Mom?" The silence sent a chill down the back of her neck, pooling in her stomach.

Oh God, it's happened. She's dead. It's happened, she's dead.

She stepped into the living room and saw Willy in the patched armchair, a rifle over his lap.

Her mother was on the sofa, seemingly unconscious.

"The fuck—" she said. "Why the hell do you have a gun?"

"Why the hell are you trying to secret her away like a fucking wetback."

Piper had no answer for this. She was staring at her mother, desperate to see her chest rise and fall.

"What did you give her?" Piper crouched down and pressed a finger to her throat. The pulse was there. Shallow and fast, but it was there.

"What she asked for."

"Do you care about her at all?" Piper asked. "Do you even give two fucks about her?"

He sneered. "I give a lot of fucks."

Piper's stomach turned.

He stood, tucking the rifle over one shoulder. "Do *you* give a shit about her? You're the one who can't spend five minutes in this house."

Because of you.

"Don't be coming around here with your self-righteous bullshit, princess. I know you think you're better than us, but you're nothing but a goddamn dyke."

Piper had never wanted to hit someone so much in her life, but she was no fool. He could take her easily. And while it wouldn't kill her to get her ass kicked, it would bring consequences she didn't want to deal with, from Mel and King for starters.

If she wanted to help her mom—and that's all she wanted—she had to keep it together. She couldn't let this trash-talking asshole get the best of her.

"Seriously, what's with the gun?"

"I was planning to use it if you tried anything stupid."

"Like?"

"Move her out of this house. Pack up any of our shit."

There was nothing in this house that belonged to him except his clothes and a few toiletries in the bathroom. Instead of pointing this out, Piper tried to find a way to control the conversation. Keep it from escalating. She didn't want her brains blown out by the likes of Willy Turner.

"She needs help."

He laughed. His rat face sneering. "Help? Do you think she *wants* to get better? Tell me you're not so stupid."

"You're the one that gets her high. You give her the drugs. You're going to kill her."

"Is that what you think?"

"Yes!" Piper screamed, her restraint flying out of the window. "*Yes, Willy*, that's what I think!"

"What the hell is going on here?" Her mother groaned and sat up. She pressed the heel of her hand to her forehead. "Why's everybody yelling?"

The relief at seeing her mother awake and speaking loosened some of the panic squeezing her chest.

"She doesn't want to quit doping," he said.

"Of course she does. No one wants to be sick. Mom, tell him."

Her mom said nothing.

"You mean to tell me, you thought she was just gonna get clean. That she'd get away from this house and that would magically cure her fucked-up head?"

Tears stung Piper's eyes.

"She was a druggie long before I came along. She was a druggie her whole damned life."

"Mom," Piper said, calmly. "Mom, get up. We're leaving."

"She isn't going anywhere."

"She's getting the hell away from you. You're the problem. I can't leave her here with you a minute longer."

"Because you think I'm the reason she's like that."

"You bring the drugs." Even as she said it, the accusation felt weak. Like every time she said it, it felt less true.

She blamed him for so much more. For the way he spoke to her, to her mother. The way he stole from them, and cashed her check. The way he degraded her a thousand ways each and every day. But Piper didn't want this to spiral out of control. And the situation already had that fever pitch feel to it.

It was a dangerous energy that some arguments had. Long, unproductive battles that left everyone spent and nothing resolved.

"I bring the drugs that she *asks* for," he said. "If it wasn't me, she'd find some other dealer to keep her high. I'm not the problem."

"Yes, you are! Mom, we're leaving!"

Piper grabbed the woman by the upper arm, knowing in some wiser part of her mind this wasn't going to work. Where in the world could she take her? To a clinic? To the hospital? The apartment wasn't hers until Monday.

But she couldn't leave her mother here. She just couldn't.

But there was another hand on her, wrenching her away from her mother. One hard shove and Piper stumbled. The back of her legs hit the end of a coffee table and she fell back, slamming into it with the full force. The flimsy pressed board collapsed under her weight and momentum.

Groaning, Piper rolled onto her side to see black combat boots stepping out of the hallway closet.

A milk-white figure, black hair, leather jacket, and eyes hidden behind mirrored sunglasses that reflected the flames of the kerosene heater. An icy hand reached down and pulled her to her feet. Piper only had a second to register that she hadn't actually brained herself on the coffee table. Lou was really here.

Lou was in her mother's living room, staring at Willy like he was a cockroach she wanted to cream under the heel of her boot.

Willy, having no sense of self-preservation, sauntered toward her. He reached for his rifle, turning the gun toward her.

Lou twisted the barrel and something snapped. Willy screamed. He cradled his hand as if she'd broken it in half. Maybe she had.

Now Lou lifted the butt of the gun and brought it down swiftly across Willy's face. He collapsed like a sack of bricks to the living room floor.

Piper surged forward. "No, no, no, no."

Lou hesitated.

"You can't kill him." Piper felt like she had to say it, as ridiculously obvious as it sounded. "You can't."

"I wasn't going to." Lou tucked the rifle against her shoulder. Her posture relaxed.

"Mom, come on," Piper said.

"What did you do to Willy?"

"Forget Willy, Mom. Come on! Let's go."

"I'm not going anywhere."

"Mom—"

"No!"

"Mom!"

Her mother wrenched herself away and regarded Piper as if she'd never seen her before. That's when Piper knew she'd lost. Her mom wasn't coming.

"Get in the closet," Lou told her. And though on any other occasion Piper would have rather crawled into a sewer than that cobwebby mess of a closet, she obeyed without pause.

Lou leaned the shotgun against the wall and stepped in after her, slipping one hand around Piper's waist.

"Do you want her to come with us?" Lou asked.

Piper thought of her mother's face. The way she'd stepped toward

Willy, not her when the moment mattered. Her mother made her choice.

"No," Piper said, her voice cracking. "Get me out of here."

"Take a breath," Lou said in the dark, her cheek radiating cold against Piper's. "And think of where you want to go."

Piper closed her eyes and made a wish.

21

L ou held Piper close as she stepped through the dark. She wasn't sure what she'd expected to find and could only guess where Piper might have wanted to seek refuge.

Then a bar formed around them and she was suddenly glad she'd left the rifle behind before they'd slipped. She'd had a momentary concern that he would kill Piper's mother with it. After all, the number one threat to a woman's life was having a partner. But Lou put that fear aside the moment she saw the hurt and betrayal in Piper's eyes. Her mother didn't warrant Lou's protection.

This bar was quieter than most bars. It was also scarcely populated. There was plenty of room to step from the thick shadows of the bathroom hallway into the main room. Piper plowed toward the bar, stomping almost comically.

"A hurricane, please," she said, slapping the bartop. "I have a whole lot of feelings to suppress!"

The bartender acknowledged her order before she put her head down on her folded arms, the way children put their heads down on their desks at school.

The bartender arched an eyebrow and gave Lou a look. "A Cherry Coke. Three cherries," she ordered. "On the same tab as hers."

The bartender left to fill their order and Lou stood awkwardly between two stools, watching over the sobbing girl.

For a moment, she wasn't sure if she should sit on the stool or if she should keep standing. She didn't want to leave before delivering King's messages and she couldn't leave Piper here.

Lou regarded the dark room and its patrons suspiciously but no one showed her the least bit of interest. The girl with her head down on bar sobbing drew a few looks, but those gazes slid away as soon as they locked eyes with Lou.

The bartender arrived with the drinks. "If she's already drunk—"

Piper's head shot up and she seized the drink from the bartender's grip. "Don't send it back! You already made it. And sad and drunk isn't the same thing, buddy."

She threw her head back and drank half of the hurricane in one go.

When the bartender lingered, Lou pushed the sunglasses up on her head and shared one of her coldest glares. "She's having a hard day."

The bartender put the Coke on the bar and left.

"I'm *so* stupid." Piper ran her nose across the sleeve of her sweater. "Why did I think she could change? Why did I think she *wanted* to change? I mean, *I* could never live like that."

She tipped the hurricane glass back a second time and Lou decided to sink onto the barstool beside her after all.

"I'm sick of it. I'm so sick of wondering about whether or not she kills herself with freaking drugs, or someone kills her *for* drugs, or hell, just someone hurting her. I'm tired of it. I don't even know why I bother. If she doesn't care enough about herself to get out of that shit, why should I care?"

Lou sipped her Cherry Coke and said nothing.

Her mind had already picked up the threads of Piper's thoughts and had begun to careen off on their own.

Who was to blame here? The drugs or the addict? Was Piper's mother another victim of a trade that exploited her weakness? Or was she to blame for her own actions?

Once upon a time, this answer would've been easy for Lou. The traders and dealers, they were the monsters. Women like Piper's mother were the victims.

But now... It wasn't so easy.

Lou's certainty had grown threadbare. Now good men—the politicians and police sworn to protect and serve—could be as destructive to a person's life and freedom as the men who loaded heroin onto a shipping liner bound for America. The dealers, who simply wanted to keep their bellies full and bills paid, were no longer murderous fiends but only trapped in a cycle that gave them no other opportunities.

Then there were men like Konstantine—*When the hell did it become so complicated?*

At least that much she knew. Senator Ryanson, Chaz Brasso, and Gus Johnson were the start of it. When she began to uncover the truth, her view began to shift. Konstantine only drove the wedge in deeper until she was forced to realize she wanted easy answers to complex problems—and finally understood there were none.

Piper remained oblivious to her inner struggle. "Does she even know what it's like? Does she even give a shit that I can't sleep half the time because I'm worried I'm going to get a call that she's dead? That she overdosed or burned the house down or was found in the fucking canal?"

Lou took another drink of her Coke and offered no false platitudes to the girl crying beside her. She said only, "She's your mother."

"She doesn't act like it!"

Again Lou found herself wondering if her father had lived to see her become a teenager, if their views would have diverged with time. Would they have fought the way that he and Lucy used to fight? Would he have loved her if she'd grown to disagree with him at every turn?

She didn't need to hear her dead father's voice in her mind to know that answer. Yes. His guilt for rejecting Lucy's truth and power would have kept him close to her side, kept him forgiving, even if affection hadn't been enough.

Guilt, after all, was a powerful motivator.

"She has as much right as anyone to ruin her life," Piper said, tipping the glass onto its edge, rolling the rim around and around on the bartop precariously. "But I don't have to watch it."

"No," Lou agreed. "You have your own life to ruin."

Piper gave her a wan smile, clearly unsure as to whether or not Lou was joking or being cruel at her expense. Lou forced one of the corners of her lips up into a crooked smile in order to remove all doubt.

"God, Henry was right. Mom's incapable of change."

Lou made no reply. The conversation was a one-woman show. And Lou was certain that Piper could give herself better counsel than Lou could.

"The real question, is can I do it? Can I start putting myself first? Stop enabling her. Stop trying to protect her. Stop trying to insist that she get better because it's not going to happen, or if it does, it's not because of anything *I* do."

Piper ran her hands down her face and sniffled. Then she waved to the bartender. "Another please?"

He looked ready to refuse her until Lou caught his eye. Then he had the second drink mixed before Lou slid her sunglasses back down over her eyes.

"God, I don't know. I'm probably as much of an addict as she is. Addicted to her bullshit."

When she finished the second hurricane, she seemed aware that Lou was still standing there.

"You're a good listener. Probably because you don't speak." Her words had taken on an audible slur.

Lou shrugged.

"I'm going to lose the deposit," Piper groaned. She ran a hand down her face again. "It's fine. That little old lady probably needs it more than I do. But man, I feel stupid for thinking my mom would actually come live with me."

"You love your mother." It seemed like something Lucy would say.

"Yeah, but she shouldn't have a free pass to treat me like shit just because she's my mom."

"No," Lou agreed.

Piper didn't seem to notice. "But I was like, 'she's sick,' 'she needs help,' and so I wasn't mad about it you know, no matter how fucked it was. Oh God, I'm whining now. Can I be any more pathetic?"

"I like listening to you speak," Lou said. And she was surprised to find it was true. There was a cheerful cadence to her voice that Lou hadn't noticed before. It was more than that. Lou found the act of speaking laborious, and tedious. Lou admired how this girl made it seem effortless, and borderline *fun*.

Piper looked as shocked by this praise as Lou was. "Yeah okay. So, I guess all I'm saying is that I don't know why I thought she would change. That if I got her away from those dudes she might actually give a shit about her life. Obviously I'm stupid."

"You aren't stupid. Most of the women who deal with addicts feel the way you do. I've seen a lot of it."

"You're being so nice to me," Piper said. She turned and regarded Lou in the low, barroom light. Even in the darkness, Lou could see the tears sparking in her eyes. "Did you just kill a bunch of assholes or something?"

"Only one," she said. "Actually, I'm..."

She wasn't sure how to finish the sentence. One of the good things about Lucy—the best thing actually—was the way she'd been able to read Lou. She knew what her niece felt and wanted even when Lou herself seemed unable to articulate her needs.

Lou didn't know how to tell Piper what was wrong.

She didn't know how to crack open this sense of unease in her chest whenever she thought of Konstantine. Of Petrov. Of her inability to lift a gun as easily as she had before Lucy died. All of that sat on top of the look in the boy's eyes just before she'd pulled the trigger.

"I have a lot on my mind," Lou said finally, turning the sweating glass between her palms, feeling the condensation chill her skin.

Then Piper seemed to realize that Lou had appeared in her mother's house for no apparent reason. "Why did you come get me?"

"King sent me."

"Oh, God, is he okay?"

"He's fine. But he wanted me to tell you something."

Lou wasn't sure if she should deliver another blow so soon.

Piper laughed, her cheeks full of color. "You've got a strong Matrix vibe right now. *There's something I need to tell you, Neo.* Did that whole leather badass look take practice or do you come by it naturally?"

Lou wasn't sure how to respond.

"Okay, I might be a little drunk." Piper tipped her drink toward her, clearly surprised to find it empty again so soon. "What did King want with me? I'm dying of suspense here. Give me a hint. What's it about?"

"The girl Melandra hired."

Piper choked on a piece of ice. "Oh man. *No.*"

Lou wasn't sure how to interpret this. "She's a journalist."

Piper frowned. "What story did she want?"

"Mine," Lou said.

Piper put her drink on the bartop and covered her face with her hands again. "God, I'm wrong about people left and right these days."

Lou put an arm around the girl's shoulder and squeezed. She had no idea if this was helping or hurting. The girl said something that Lou couldn't understand into the crook of her elbow.

"I'm sorry?"

She lifted her tear-stained face and shimmering eyes. "I said I'm probably wrong about you too."

Before Lou understood what was happening, Piper leaned off the edge of her barstool and pressed her lips to Lou's. Her lips were thick, moist, and parted Lou's so easily that she had a tongue in her mouth before she understood fully how it'd gotten there.

One moment it was simply, warm salty lips and then their absence. When Piper pulled away, she left tears cooling on Lou's cheeks.

Piper's eyes doubled in size. "Wow. That was like putting a gun in my mouth."

Lou had no idea how to interpret that.

"Sorry if that wasn't consensual, but I had to know. If this isn't going to happen, I'm gonna get that into my head right now. Along with all the other shit I need to sort out."

Lou regarded her round face and big blue eyes. "You like me."

Piper snorted. "Uh, worship. Adore. Obsess might be more accurate. But the kiss test has never failed me. Unfortunately, the data simply doesn't lie."

"I don't know what you mean," Lou admitted, turning her drink between her palms.

"If I'm trying to figure out how I feel about someone, I kiss them," Piper said with a shrug. Wiping at her eyes, she reached for her drink. "And no offense, but I can tell you're way too much for me."

"From a kiss?"

"Oh yeah. They are *very* informative."

"And mine said—"

"To forget about it. And you know what, I think I'm right. I need it basic at the moment. Nice and calm. I'll get a dog. Maybe some hummus. You know what I'm saying?"

Lou looked for any part of the conversation to grab onto. But her mind was still running the kiss on replay. The look in Piper's eyes when she'd pulled back, red cheeked and beaming.

"Lucy made good hummus," Lou said.

"Do not tell me that you, Lady of Darkness, can make fresh hummus. I will lose my shit."

"No," Lou said and found herself smiling. "But I like it."

Piper grinned too. "Well, first time I make some fresh hummus in my new place—wherever the hell that turns out to be—you have to come over and eat it. Promise? And wow, that sounded way dirtier than I meant it to."

But Lou was smiling.

"Listen," Piper said, scratching the back of her neck. "I don't want to be too forward here."

"More forward than a kiss?" Lou asked, eyebrow arched.

Piper snorted. "Right. Uh, I'm trying to say thanks for listening to me."

"You're welcome."

"Ah, no, don't do that."

"Do what?"

"That perfunctory, I've said thanks, you say you're welcome and then we just push it aside to never see the light of day again. You were a good listener and you were there when I needed you. So if you ever need the same—an ear or a shoulder or any other body part you might be thinking of right now—then let me know. I've got them. All the parts."

"Why?" Lou asked, a strange creeping chill nuzzling the back of her neck.

"I'm pretty sure all the parts come standard," Piper said with a smile. "I kid! Why?"

Piper searched for the answer in her hurricane glass.

"Because we're friends. And I promise to be your actual friend. This isn't some slutty trick to sleep with you in case you're wondering."

Lou must've looked as dumbfounded as she felt. The Cherry Coke halfway to her mouth was returned to the bartop undrunk.

Piper laughed. "What's wrong with your face? Haven't you had a friend before?"

Lou took too long to answer.

"Holy shit!" Piper said, sitting up on her barstool excitedly. "Louie Thorne, I'm going to be your first friend? This is amazing. Oh my God, this is almost as good as sleeping with you. Uh, no it's not. What am I saying? Shhhh, Piper, shhhh..."

Lou pushed the remainder of the drink out of Piper's reach. "I don't need friends."

"Everyone needs friends," Piper mused. "Who can we count on to have our backs should sexy journalists or freaking Russians try to probe our butts?"

"You're thinking of aliens."

Piper didn't seem to hear. "We need people we can count on to protect us."

"We have to protect ourselves." Lou was thinking of the man she shot.

"We can't always protect ourselves."

Piper stretched for the last of her hurricane and Lou inched it farther away.

"See," Piper said, regaining her balance on the stool. "You're already a good friend. I *have* had too much to drink. And I'm gonna be your friend, too. You wait and see. One day you're gonna need this."

Piper gestured to her whole body with a swipe of her hand.

"And I'm gonna be there to give it to you." She threw down enough cash to cover their drinks. "Okay, I'm done crying. Let's handle this shit."

Lou had to admit, she liked this one. She wore her vulnerability on her sleeve, which made Lou uneasy, but beneath that, Lou saw the steel. She saw how Piper drew it like a blade, when she was ready.

"I hate to test our friendship so soon, but can I ask for one more favor?" Piper bit her lip, giving Lou a sheepish smile. "Can you do your sneaky sneaky thing one more time for me? I need to get the last of my crap from my mom's house to my friend Henry's. After that, you can leave me there. He doesn't live that far from the shop."

Lou offered her hand and the girl took it before she pulled her into the dark.

22
———

Dani leaned against the handlebar to balance herself on the shifting streetcar. Checking the map again, she confirmed she had two more stops before reaching her apartment. It didn't matter she'd been here for years. There was something comforting about looking at the map and finding reassurance that she hadn't missed her stop.

The same was true of messages. She checked her email messages on her phone for the third time and found nothing. No news, no updates. It was strange to not hear from Clyde at least once a day. Her boss was the ultimate micromanager, and he'd been worse on this story than any other. So she was more than a little concerned by the lack of reply.

The only time he offered radio silence like this was when he himself was deep in a story. Considering how lazy he was, she could remember only twice that this had happened in her years at The Herald.

He'd better not be scooping hers. That's all she had to say about it. She should've realized the age progression photo would've crossed his desk first, but no matter. He didn't know half of what she knew.

But she needed his approval to draft this interview teaser. Dani was certain that the teaser was all she needed to secure talks with both Robert King and the elusive Louie Thorne. Once they saw the photo of them together, Dani would have the chance to suggest she knew far more than she did. Hopefully they would fill in the gaps, as often happened in these interviews.

The angle of her article emphasized their working relationship. A father's mentor and hero's daughter unite in his honor. She even had possible titles: *Honoring Jack Thorne – How His Only Child Keeps His Memory Alive*. Or maybe *When Bad Cops Are To Blame: Louie Thorne's Story*. She didn't love the second title, but it could work with the right image. And it would be a perfect jumping off point for Jack's murder and subsequent slander. Everyone loved a story about destroyed faith rekindled only by a renewed purpose. *That* was the story Dani wanted to tell.

Plus, with the rise of anti-cop sentiment on the airwaves these days, this would expand on an already viable market. Not to mention the novelty of an exclusive interview with lots of clickbait to be had.

Dani just needed Clyde to return her damned calls and get this ball rolling.

And to think *he* was the one who'd doubted *her*.

Of course, she resented this assessment. She didn't believe a woman had to be an asshole to chase a story. Direct, yes. Persistent, absolutely. But no one needed to be as slimy and underhanded as Clyde Baker himself.

She hoped this was her chance to prove she could do the job and do it well. That of all the journalists he could've sent out—her by far the youngest—that he'd made the right choice.

If she wrote the article well enough and slapped her pretty name on it, that would be vindication enough. Her work would speak for itself.

Hell, maybe she'd even win a Pulitzer for this story. *Don't get ahead of yourself girl.*

But a Pulitzer before 25 would be pretty cool.

She called Clyde one more time and again it went straight to his voicemail. *Come on, man. You want this story or not?*

The streetcar chimed and Dani leapt down onto her street, the convenience of living right off the stop not lost to her. It was cheaper to leave her car in its free space than to park it in the Quarter every day.

Rent was ridiculous this close to the Quarter, but she liked her little place, nestled between the grand mansions of Saint Charles Avenue and the Garden District and a stone's throw from the Quarter.

Maybe she could run the article *without* Clyde's approval. When the article turned out to be a major success, he couldn't possibly fire her. Or if he did, his loss. What news agency wouldn't want the rising young star who'd managed to snag the interview of a lifetime?

Then maybe her parents would get off her back about going into business.

Of course, one danger weighed on her mind.

She couldn't decide whether or not to tell Piper about the article before its publication.

If she didn't tell Piper beforehand, it would no doubt destroy the spark between them. If she *did*, Piper might warn Lou or King and try to prevent her from getting the story in the first place.

She liked Piper. A lot. But she wasn't about to let the chance of a lifetime be trashed by anyone. No matter how good they kissed.

Of course, that was easier said than done. On one hand, she had her financial freedom, career ambitions, and so much more to consider. But she also believed in serendipity. She knew people came into her life for a reason. From the moment she saw Piper walk into the shop, that adorable pep in her step and bright, easygoing smile, Dani knew there was more there. She'd felt it.

She wasn't a romantic. But she did believe in an order to the universe and she trusted her gut. Her gut said she had some business left with Piper. She only hoped that business had a happy ending.

Dani fished her apartment keys out of her pocket, flipping the keys along the ring until she found the red one that unlocked the front door to her building.

She turned the lock and stepped into the narrow lobby lined with mailboxes. She checked her mail with the second of four keys. Nothing but some Bed, Bath and Beyond coupons and an ad for the local animal shelter soliciting donations. Last, a BOGO offer for a large one-topping pizza. This she kept and tossed the rest into the recycle bin.

She took the stairs two at a time, dreaming of a hot shower and a fresh cup of coffee. Her apartment was on the second floor.

Using the third of four keys—the fourth for The Herald's front door —she entered her apartment.

She expected to find Octavia at the door, begging to be fed. She might be the cutest cat in the world, but she was *quite* the drama queen.

But Octavia didn't come running and meowing per usual. In fact, her entire apartment was quiet and dark. She tried to flip the switch, but nothing happened. A dead *click click click* as she turned the switch on and off and on again.

Dani saw a shadow in the corner of her living room and turned at the same moment a hand slammed into her throat. Her neck spasmed and all sound died.

Then she was lifted into the air and slammed so hard onto the floor of her apartment, all the remaining air left her. Red and white stars sparked in her vision where her head bounced against the floor. She clawed at the massive hand, which felt as large as her head. But it didn't relent.

Get a good look. Get a good look at the him! Her brain screamed.

Some confident, rational part of her was thinking ahead. It was focused on surviving this. That part of her considered the assault trial that would follow and how best to deliver the retribution she deserved.

She pried her eyes open. Something hissed, a long, terrible wheezing, followed by a suffocating burn. Cold liquid hit her eyes and nose. Her lips. Her tongue swiped at the corner and tasted the pepper.

She wanted to be angry, infuriated, that someone would dare to pepper spray her in her own apartment. But the acrid smell stuffed her nose with thick cotton. Her eyes swelled shut and would not open. She couldn't draw a breath.

Her lungs burned as they failed to draw the air they desperately needed. She kicked out, hoping to strike the attacker somewhere vital. But no matter how hard she kicked, her legs connected without effect. Darkness pressed in harder until darkness was all that was left.

Dani woke. Her throat hurt so badly that every time she swallowed it spasmed.

She tried to move her aching body and couldn't. Her wrists were tied behind her, latched to the wooden chair that creaked under her weight. A large strap of some kind pinned her back to the chair. Not only could she not move her torso, arms or hands, but her legs also resisted her commands. Every time she tried to lift a leg, something bit into the skin of her ankles.

She tried to open her eyes, but the sting hadn't left her.

Cold water slammed into her face and chest. She gasped in surprise and found she could breathe at last. The creak of a bucket handle was her only warning before a second splash slammed into her body. A rough towel scraped across her eyes, feeling like sandpaper on an open wound.

She jerked away.

"Good morning," a voice said. It had a thick accent that Dani didn't recognize. European maybe. Not British or Australian, both of which she knew, and definitely not Spanish or Italian, both of which she spoke.

She pried her eyes open slowly and tried to focus. It was her worst nightmare.

A dark nondescript room. Herself in the center, tied to a chair, spotlighted as if for spectators. Large hulking forms hid in the darkness. Men had abducted her and taken her to an unknown location.

God, this is bad.

A man stepped into the light giving Dani a good look. He was tall, muscular and ghostly pale with bright blue eyes. He was bald, the barest hint of gray bristles prickled his scalp. He smiled, which wrinkled the corners of his eyes. But it was a cold stare. One that struck terror in Dani's core.

"Good morning," she said, almost compulsively. As if this was the start of a perfectly civil conversation.

"Good morning," he replied. "My name is Dmitri. And you are Daniella Allendale?"

"That depends." Her throat ached with every word. No doubt whoever had choked her unconscious had bruised her vocal chords. "Do you want to hurt Daniella Allendale?"

"*That depends*," he said with another cold smile.

If they knew her name, then they wanted something specific from her. Rape? Murder? Ransom? She needed more information if she hoped to navigate this and get out alive.

But it was hard to think when her heart skittered in her chest and her eyes were so puffy she couldn't open them more than the barest slit. "Listen, I don't know what this is about, but I haven't taken money from anyone, or done anything that warrants being kidnapped and tied to a chair."

"Bad things happen to good people," Dmitri said, plainly.

"They don't have to," Dani said. "If everyone plays nice."

Another wicked smile that poured cold water through her bones.

"Will you *play nice* with me?" Dmitri asked.

She hoped this wasn't going in some sexual direction. She already knew these men were violent, and probably had no problem killing her and dumping her lifeless body in the canal, but she hoped she wasn't going to be raped and beaten until her heart stopped.

"What do you want from me?"

"You seem like a smart girl. You answer my questions and perhaps we can reach an understanding."

"I'm listening."

"Where is your boss?"

Dani hesitated. "Clyde?"

"Yes. Mr. Clyde Baker."

Fucking Clyde. "I don't know. He texted me a few days ago and asked about the story I'm working on, but since then he hasn't responded to my calls or texts."

Dmitri turned and peered over his right shoulder. Dani saw the second man for the first time.

A man as wide as he was tall—quite tall—and solid muscle held her phone in his hand. She recognized the Rage Against the Machine cell phone cover and the Jolly Roger flag charm.

She knew better than to complain that they'd taken her phone and were simply riffling through it. One must limit their requests when strapped to a chair.

After scrolling for several seconds, Mr. Thick Neck nodded.

"You're an honest girl. Good," Dmitri said, smiling at her. "So tell me, is it true you were investigating a young woman?"

"Yes. Louie Thorne."

"Louie Thorne," he repeated. "She wears a leather jacket and sunglasses. She spends time with a detective."

"Yes, that's her," Dani insisted. If it was Louie Thorne they wanted then it was Louie Thorne they'd have. After all, she would be far more capable of surviving this shitshow than Dani herself.

"Louie Thorne," he said again, as if he'd never heard the name before. "Why does the name sound familiar to me?"

"Her father was murdered by Angelo Martinelli. Turns out he was only following the orders of Chaz Brasso. And the man who owned him was Senator Greg Ryanson. It was big in the news."

"Martinelli," Dmitri said. He turned and smiled at the men behind him. "*Martinelli.*"

The murmurs grew. With horror, Dani realized at least five or six men were back there, hiding in the darkness. These numbers didn't bode well for her.

"Yes, yes. I see now." Dmitri was nodding to himself. "But that makes Konstantine even more interesting, does it not? Why not put him in the grave with the others?"

Dani recognized the name. Wasn't a man named Konstantine in the news a few months ago? He turned out to be a poor Italian farmer falsely accused of beheading US agents.

"Who's Konstantine?" she asked. The stupid words were out of her mouth before she caught herself. Showing curiosity of any kind was a recipe for a bullet between the eyes and a shallow grave.

Dmitri's patronizing smile said as much. "The bastard son of Fernando Martinelli. Do you know him?"

She shook her head.

"No, you wouldn't. That's a story for another time. What else did you learn about Louie Thorne?"

Dani wracked her mind for anything non-public, anything that would be useful to these goons.

"When her parents were killed she was adopted by her aunt Lucy Thorne."

Dmitri's eyebrows arched hopefully. "Is the aunt still alive?"

"She died last year of cancer. Now she works with the detective, Robert King."

"Robert King," he said. "Yes, I know about him. He was also a DEA agent."

Dani nodded.

He leaned in, smiling. The shadows across his face seemed to brighten the teeth, enlarging them and making the grin all the more wolfish.

"Clever girl. You took an undercover job in order to learn more about these people."

"I did."

"Where did you insert yourself?"

"Melandra's Fortunes and Fixes," she said. "Melandra is his landlady. He lives in the apartment above the shop."

"And Lou is seen with him often?"

"Yes."

"If we were to go to this shop now, would we run into Louie Thorne perhaps?"

She hesitated. *If you go to the shop now, you'll run into Piper.*

Dmitri walked around her chair, disappearing from her periphery. "You have beautiful, delicate fingers, Miss Allendale. Do you use these to write your stories?"

Instinctively, she closed her hands into fists.

Until a cool grip pried them open.

"No," she breathed. Her pulse quickened in her throat, pounding so hard all thought was obliterated.

"No, you don't use these for writing? You must be even more talented than you look."

The men in the dark laughed. Her index finger was pulled away from the rest of the hand.

"I haven't seen her in the shop," Dani said. "I haven't seen Lou Thorne anywhere. I swear."

"But she is seen with the people who live there, and work there, correct?"

She sucked in a sharp breath, blood pulsing in her temples.

"Please," she breathed. "I don't know where she is."

"I don't believe you," he sighed into her ear.

That was when the real pain began.

23

_____

Lou opened the padded mailer and removed one of the VHS tapes. She put it on the marble top of her kitchen island, then removed the other, placing them side by side. Even after all these years, she recognized the handwriting. These black letters on the white label were undeniably her father's.

For Lucy, one label said.

For Lou-blue, read the other.

Lou-blue. Her heart clenched in her chest. She saw her father's face in her mind, complete with his scruffy jaw and confident smile. The last time he'd called her that was the night he died. He pressed her hands to his jaw and forced her to look into his moonlit eyes. *Louie, Louiiii. Oh baby. Do you trust me?*

That stupid cover song from the '60s that he loved so much. And she suspected it was the real reason for her name. She'd been told it was after her aunt and after her mother's grandfather Louis. But she only had to hear the way he came alive to that song to formulate another theory.

Lou gathered both tapes up in one fist and crossed to the closet. She stepped in, shut the door, and breathed in the dark.

She waited for her compass to offer direction. She knew what she needed was rare but she would find one.

The darkness thinned. The firm wooden wall of the closet softened. The world dissolved around her and she moved through it.

Musty, stagnant air greeted her. Dust tickled her nose as she entered the room.

Not a room, a pawn shop, recognizable by the rows and rows of electronics sitting on moonlit shelves. Some were coated with dust. Lou inched toward the front of the store and looked out at the quiet street. A few lazy cars rolled by, one with a missing taillight, another riding on a donut spare. A car slammed on its brakes to spare a darting cat. Then the street was dark again.

In reverse letters, Lou saw *Hillsboro Pawn* stuck to the window with opening hours listed below. She checked her special German watch and found that she would be undisturbed for many hours, assuming the owner was at home snug in their own bed.

Lou searched the dust-covered shelves for what she needed. She saw game systems and laptops and electronics far too modern for her task.

But behind the counter, she found what she was looking for. A surveillance camera reviewed the gravel lot behind the pawn shop as well as the storefront and street. Three raccoons took turns diving into the oversized dumpster, reviewing its contents with greedy hands.

Beneath the television was a VCR.

She pressed eject, and a tape slid from its rectangular mouth. The screen went to static, or the ant race, as Aunt Lucy liked to call it.

Lou considered the two tapes in her hand. She decided to watch the one given to King first. She knew its history at least, that he'd been instructed to deliver it to Lucy on behalf of her father, years after their estrangement.

For some reason, Lou felt an aversion to watching the other tape— the one addressed to her.

The idea that her father might have something to say to her after all these years...

She settled into the dusty computer chair and pressed play.

For a moment it was only an office. Her father's home office as she remembered it, back in the Tudor house they shared before Angelo Martinelli spilled his brains across their patio.

A photo of Lou and her father at the beach was taped to the wall. Lou, seven or eight, was tucked under his massive arm. Lou still had that photograph in her apartment, hidden in her pillowcase. Beside that was a photo of her mother in a rose garden, her smile bright and practiced.

She wore a yellow halter dress and lipstick as red as the rose pressed to her cheek.

It hurt Lou to see it.

Beyond the mostly clear desk and curtained window rested a baseball mitt with a worn ball inside. He'd played on his work league, but also threw the ball around with Lou in the evenings when the weather was warm enough.

Her father appeared on the screen, coming around the camera—it must be some sort of tripod setup then—and took an empty seat in front of the desk. Lou's heart lurched. He was younger than she remembered, or perhaps it was only that she'd grown.

He ran a hand through his hair and seemed as though he was trying to compose himself.

"Hi Lucy," he managed at last. "If you're watching this, then you've met my friend, Robert. We work together at the DEA. I asked him to find you because I didn't think I could find you myself." He laughed. "I didn't think you'd *let* me find you. I've been trying for about a year now and you aren't returning my calls. I deserve it after how I treated you. I'm sure you'd prefer that I let this go. But the truth is I can't. I need your help."

He looked down at his hands, then reached up to scratch his jaw. Lou had forgotten how often he did that when he wasn't sure what to say, either to Lou herself or often her mother.

"It's about Louie, my daughter."

He licked his lips and stared into the camera as if expecting it to respond.

"She's like you, Lucy. Not with shadows, at least not that I've seen. Her..." He searched the back of his hands again. "*Gift,* if that's what we should call it, seems to be tied to water. She goes into it and disappears. It's been...hard on us."

He leaned back in the chair, resigned. "Forget about us. She's scared, Lucy. She doesn't understand what's happening to her. She can't control it. And I don't know how to help her. I know your gifts are different, but I feel like they must come from the same place. You don't owe me this.

You don't owe me anything and I have no right to ask for your help after the things I said to you at Gram's funeral."

He looked directly into the camera and Lou was shocked to see the tears standing in the corners of his eyes.

"I don't expect you to forgive me for the way I treated you. I know it's bullshit to be asking for your help now after everything. But this is my kid. I'd do anything for her and she needs help."

He sighed and fell back against the chair.

"Do you still believe in karma? You used to talk about that a lot. Well, it's my karma that I should have a kid like this after what I did to you."

His face reddened. "You have no idea how hard it is feeling like I can't protect her. I can't even help her. I'm *scared* for her, Lucy."

He wiped at the corners of his mouth, pulling his lips into an exaggerated O.

"You don't have to see me. You don't even have to talk to me. But please, *please* I'm begging you. Talk to her. I don't want her to feel alone like you did. I know I'm part of the reason you felt so alone and I'm sorry for that. But I'm begging. I'll do anything you want. Anything in the world. Just help her. *Please* help her."

Another long stare at his rough knuckles. Then he favored the camera with a weak smile. "I love you, Lucy. And I hope you can forgive me."

Her father rose from the chair and after a close-up of his arm and his white shirt, the camera cut.

Static burbled on the screen for the five seconds while Lou sat there, thinking, remembering.

More than a decade separated that night and this one, but Lou thought she knew the rest.

Lucy had responded and promised to help. She'd heard that much from King, the messenger who'd been sent to deliver the tape to her aunt, and from her aunt's own mouth.

But no sooner did Jack work up the courage to tell Lou that help was on the way, he was killed.

Lou removed the tape from the deck and put it beside the other. She considered the unwatched tape, curiosity rising in her. Was this second tape made before or after the plea to Lucy? There was only one way to find out.

Lou lifted this second tape to the rectangular mouth of the VCR. She hesitated before inserting the new tape. She pressed play.

Another introduction of a blank desk before Jack appeared, settling into his seat as he had before. However, this Jack wasn't in his white shirt and pajamas. This Jack still wore his bulletproof vest and badge.

"Hi Lou-blue," he said, offering the camera a weak smile.

"If you're watching this, that means I'm dead. Isn't that how these videos start?" He smiled at his own joke. But the smile didn't stick. It faltered first at the edges and then disappeared altogether.

"No parent wants to leave a video like this behind for his kid, but if I do end up dying, you deserve some answers. I don't want you living your whole life with questions. So, I'm going to tell you what I know now, while I can."

He leaned back in his seat.

"I asked the law office to deliver this to you when you're eighteen. So if you're eighteen now, you're probably heading off to college this fall." He straightened with pride. "Maybe you've got friends or boyfriends. I hope you still love books." He grinned. "I bet you do."

That's about the only thing you've gotten right so far, she thought.

Again the humor didn't stick. "I want to apologize for not being there for you, Lou-blue. For every birthday I missed. Graduation—"

Which I spent burying a knife in the throat of your traitorous ex-partner Gus.

"When you get married or have kids of your own—"

"Slow down now," she grumbled.

"I wanted to be there for all of it. And if you're watching this, that means I wasn't. I won't be. I'm sorry."

He ran his palms down the front of his pants.

"I'm making this video in case I'm murdered."

Lou's heart sputtered in her chest.

"I've gotten a lot of death threats over this case. They're mostly from the Martinelli clan but a few are from unknown sources. I hope it's bravado, but I know men like this. Sometimes revenge killings are a matter of honor and they won't stop until they're done."

He ran a hand through his hair.

"In the event that I am killed, I hope you and your mother aren't hurt. If you are, I can only hope you'll forgive me. It isn't that I value my job over your safety. I hope you don't think that. But this guy has got to be stopped."

And he was stopped, she thought. *The night I visited him in prison...*

"If I'm killed," he went on. "Please don't be angry. You might be angry at me for a long time, or maybe you want to hurt the people who hurt me. But please don't."

Her temples throbbed.

"That isn't the life I want for you, Lou. You're smart. You love books. Maybe you'll be a teacher or a scientist or hell, maybe you'll be an astronaut."

His face lit up. It hurt Lou to see it.

"But don't be a cop. Stay out of law enforcement. Don't go looking for revenge. What happened to me was my fault, and I would never forgive myself if I knew it led you down this path after I died. I don't know how you'll do it. But I hope you'll learn to forgive me."

"I love you. I love you more than anything in this world. No matter where your life takes you, I hope you know that. No matter who you are today, I'm proud of you. There's nothing you could do to change that."

He looked toward the ceiling with tears in his eyes. For a long time, there was only silence.

"Man, I want to see you grow up."

Lou heard the clatter of keys and the sound of a door popping open.

"Jack?" a woman called out.

Lou's heart skipped a beat at the sound of her mother's voice. It was every bit as imperious and high-minded as she remembered.

His face twisted in surprise as he half lifted from his seat. He dabbed at his eyes, blinking rapidly.

"We're back. Hurry up before it melts," she called out.

"Dad? Where are you?" This was a small, mousey voice that Lou didn't recognize at all.

The office door opened and there she stood. Lou herself holding a cardboard carrier with two sundaes nestled in the cups. Lou walked up to her father's side and showed him the treats, leaning into his leg with childish interest. She couldn't have been more than eleven.

Her father looked frozen in his seat, obviously plastering on a bright smile for her benefit.

"Are you crying?" Lou asked, hesitating out of reach.

"Allergies," her father said, turning up the wattage on his smile.

"Oh." Lou didn't look convinced. "Do you want the strawberry sundae or the hot fudge sundae?"

She remembered this night now. It was two, maybe three weeks before her parents were killed. She'd just started summer vacation and it was already hotter than it should've been for June in St. Louis. The ice cream was for her A in English.

"Which has whip?" her father asked.

"Strawberry."

"Strawberry for me then," he said.

Lou turned and looked at the camera. She bent down and looked into the eye of it like a curious bird. Her shoulder length hair fell forward like a curtain. "What are you doing? Are you making a movie?"

"I am."

"Can I watch it?"

"Maybe," he said. Jack stood from the chair, strawberry sundae in hand and reached for the camera's kill switch. "When you're older."

The static sprang up again. For a full minute, she let it run, unsure of what to do with herself. She barely remembered this life. Seeing it now was like seeing it as a show she'd loved once as a child and no longer remembered clearly.

You made this tape weeks before you died, she thought, falling back against her own seat. *You knew you'd be killed and you did nothing to protect yourself. Enter witness protection. Move your family. Nothing.*

Anger, fresh and bright rose up inside her as static buzzed on the screen.

You could be alive if you'd done something.

"Lou," a voice said.

The video flickered to life again. In the frame sat her aunt, as she'd looked the summer before she died. Lou looked around the pawn shop wearily, wondering if this was a ghost. Some kind of monster in the machine.

But it was her aunt's face, sure enough. Having just seen her father's face, she now realized how similar they were. Anyone would've guessed they were siblings. It also explained why sometimes Lou was mistaken for Lucy's daughter.

Aunt Lucy sat in her Chicago apartment, in her favorite rocker with the African quilt slung over one side. But she was already sick. Her face held that yellowed pallor and the cheeks had already begun to sink too deep.

"What you've just seen is the tape that the lawyers sent me on your eighteenth birthday. I watched it and decided not to give it to you. Now before you go and piss on my ashes, let me explain."

It was as if the dead woman had known that Lou's finger hovered over the eject button.

"This tape arrived eight months after Gus Johnson. I knew you were dealing with—your loss the only way you knew how. I thought the last thing you needed to hear after killing someone was your dead father telling you that he didn't approve of vengeance. So I held off. Rejection of any kind wasn't what you needed. I stand by that decision. But now here I am reaping my own karma for that. Because *I'm* dying and now I've got to make my own confession."

Aunt Lucy sighed.

"If you've learned anything from watching these videos, I hope it's that old people are fools." She laughed. It was a dry, raspy sound. "We do what we think is right and hope others can live with the consequences. I don't know what else to say Louie. Forgive us both. I went to the lawyers, today actually, and gave them two letters. When you read yours it's going to make a request that you go see my friend Ani. I hope you will. Ani really helped me—"

The sound of breaking glass caused Lou to lean back in her seat. She ejected the tape and returned the screen to its surveillance position, by inserting the original tape again and pressing the start button.

Two men were crashing through the front, with crowbars and pillow-cases thrown over their shoulders.

She didn't mind. She welcomed the distraction.

True, she couldn't kill them. Killing the journalist had seemed to deepen her rut rather than shake her out of it.

But it didn't mean she couldn't blow off a little steam. She'd even do it one handed, for a challenge.

Lou stacked her tapes on top of the other. Then she stepped into the shop, in full view of the men.

"Hi," she said. "Can I help you?"

They pulled their guns on her, taking aim at the woman in the shadows. Their mistake.

24

Konstantine tapped coffee grounds into the portafilter and pressed the switch. The machine hummed with the promise of fresh espresso if Konstantine's patience could only hold out for a few minutes longer.

It was nearly one in the morning. But since he'd cracked the pathetic encryption on the dead man's computer, his curiosity wouldn't allow him to sleep.

The honk of a Vespa reached him as some fool flew past the building too fast, engine motoring.

And at this hour, he glowered.

The machine clicked and Konstantine retrieved his espresso cup from the serving tray, carrying it over to his desk.

The computer sat open, waiting for his instruction. He examined the deleted files he'd recovered, dumping the information onto an external hard drive as he went. Later he would upload it to his private server, once he was certain no spyware remained.

He'd recovered photos of Louie and a few of King as well. In several, Louie fought in a dark parking lot, surrounded by at least six men in the haze of a granulated security camera. Her eyes shone reflective as a fox's as she moved around them easily. They resembled a hyena pack, hungry and circling. They stood no chance.

And yet she hadn't killed one of them. She'd beat them senseless and had let them return a few blows. This only solidified his theory that she was not hunting. Her last confirmed kill had been Dmitri Petrov's son. Had something happened that night? Or was this runoff from her aunt's death?

He thought of his own mother's death. For months that followed, he'd had no appetite. Not for food, nor company. Nothing in life could reach him. It was as if part of his soul had passed through the veil with her.

If that was happening to Lou now, it would explain this reluctance to kill.

He squinted at the photograph. *Dio mio. She hadn't even brought her gun.*

His pulse quickened even though he knew she was safe. She'd been in his apartment hours before, hadn't she? This photo was dated weeks ago.

Yet it wasn't entirely irrational to fear for her safety.

It was true he'd seen her in action himself, watched as she laid waste to every man on Ryanson's boat. One bullet, one body dropped as they scrambled to keep her in their sights.

Then she'd destroyed an entire villa full of Nico's men, bringing it down around them as easily as a child tumbles down her tower of blocks.

She was more than capable, so why should he be afraid for her?

Because he'd also stitched her wounds closed. He'd seen her blood awash on that wet boat deck, saw her bleed unconscious.

She was fast, strong, a predator. But she was not immortal.

Not immortal, not immortal... his mind taunted him at every turn.

She was also the girl who'd appeared in his bed over a decade ago, lost and mourning her father. He still saw the tears gleaming on her cheeks as she cried her way through nightmares.

She was that girl too.

He only hoped Petrov didn't know it.

"We all have our limitations," he murmured to himself, looking at the photos' metadata.

He searched the computer for a linked email account and found two that were password protected. One held mostly junk mail and typical correspondences with staff of The Herald. But the second email—

He opened the encrypted message coming from an indeterminate source.

1:15 EST was all it said.

Konstantine reviewed the call log from the man's phone bill, which he'd already downloaded in hopes of finding a connection. Had he been wise, Petrov would've sent a man in person to speak with Baker. Somewhere private like his home, where security footage wouldn't be a problem.

But maybe even Dmitri Petrov was careless from time to time.

Konstantine cross-referenced the date and time on the email to a number in Baker's call log. These computers made it too easy, syncing phone and all devices to a single hub.

Konstantine smiled, recognizing the number.

It was the same number that Petrov used to call him, the night a wounded Lou Thorne recovered in his bed.

As the path through this wilderness widened, Konstantine decided another espresso would do him fine.

After four shots and six hours of intense investigation, Konstantine had a decent profile of the dead man. He'd pulled everything from Clyde's employment records, credit score, educational background, past living arrangements, phone and email records—even his social media accounts.

The man who emerged was a man of many debts and two failed marriages. The second bankrupted him. He had two daughters, eleven and twelve, and a corgi named Trundle that went with the second ex-wife. Behind the mediocre GPA at the University of New Orleans and a decent record for the 100 meter dash, lay a man who loved to gamble. He also had an arrest record for possession of cocaine, but that was thrown out in court.

Why had Petrov approached this man? It was possible that he'd owed Petrov's bookies some cash or had a connection to one of his dealers. It was possible they'd decided to call on him in hopes of learning Lou's identity.

But why *this* man? That was the question.

Was that Konstantine's doing? Had he failed to delete some pertinent photo before Petrov's bots—of which Konstantine knew he had a legion—had captured it? He'd already found half a dozen annoying bots in the system this week. Bots whose sole purpose was to take a photograph—like the one of Lou he now reviewed—and duplicate it over and *over* until it flooded the wires.

Perhaps it was more than his own programs could handle. Perhaps one or two had fallen through.

He drained his espresso cup and ran a hand down his face.

Now was not the time to worry about his inadequacies. Whatever was done was done. The photos told a story of their own. Petrov had been looking for Louie from nearly the moment she killed his son and found a connection to New Orleans.

But he didn't think Petrov knew Louie's name, her history, or her connection to Konstantine. What he did know was that Melandra completed a W-4 for a young woman who also worked at The Herald. He didn't believe that was a coincidence. Not only because their social security numbers were identical, but because it would've been easier for Baker to send a proxy to investigate Lou than to follow her himself. Any mediocre search would've returned his name.

If the girl was placed, that means Dmitri was in New Orleans, or he would be soon. Konstantine was sure of it.

He opened his desk drawer and pulled out a cell phone, one he used in discreet situations like this. He considered his options. There were only a few men he would call in this situation, those he trusted. *Who is closest to New Orleans?* he wondered. Or better, *who could get there first?*

He dialed the number. A man answered. "Eh, yah. What can I do for you?"

Konstantine told him what he wanted and what he was willing to pay for it.

The other man whistled. "I can't imagine anyone would turn you down for that price, especially in The Big Easy economy. Momma needs a new levee."

"These men are not from New Orleans," Konstantine said. He did his best to make the situation crystal clear.

The man sniffed. "In that case, what if they expect more?"

"Pay it," Konstantine said, his eyes sliding to the gray photo of Lou, to her empty hands inviting death. "Whatever they want."

The man whistled again, this trill even longer and louder than the first. "And what about me? Will you cut me a blank check too?"

Konstantine named a figure.

"I'm happy with that."

"*I* will be happy if you accomplish what I need you to," Konstantine said.

"I've never disappointed you before," the man said, followed by an expectant silence.

Konstantine smiled. "No, you haven't." He hoped he sounded light-hearted.

"I'll call you back in a few hours with an update."

"Good." Konstantine ended the call without saying goodbye, putting the cell phone back in the drawer and closing it.

He stood, stretched and made his way upstairs. He pulled off his shirt and reached into the dresser for another. He pulled it down over his head as he entered into the bathroom and turned on the light. He brushed his teeth, washed his face and prepared to fall into bed. He was ready at last to welcome the exhaustion.

Except when he reentered the bedroom, he found Lou Thorne sitting on the edge of his queen-sized bed.

Her mirrored sunglasses were pushed up onto her head to reveal her beautiful dark eyes.

"How long have you been here?" he asked.

"My father knew they wanted to kill him. He stayed and prosecuted the Martinellis anyway."

Konstantine leaned against the bathroom doorframe. "Would you have stepped down? Even if it meant endangering your family?"

She considered him for a moment. "I would've hidden them somewhere first."

Konstantine gestured as if to say *there you go*. "You are your father's daughter. But smarter."

"I'm surprised," she admitted, placing one hand on the coverlet. The other rested on her thigh. Again he noted the lack of vest and guns. His uneasiness grew. "I always thought he was..."

"Caught unaware?" Konstantine asked. He loved this American expression and the comic image it conjured in his mind.

"Yes. It made him seem more...innocent."

Konstantine crossed to the other side of the bed. He lay on top of the covers, his back against the headboard. He expected her to get up and walk away from him. Perhaps she'd lean against the opposite wall or disappear altogether.

Instead she pivoted toward him, one leg still on the floor, and regarded him over her shoulder.

"You know who is *not* innocent," he said, hoping he seemed indifferent. Too eager was far from *cool*.

She regarded him with those dark eyes, saying nothing.

"Mr. Clyde Baker worked for Petrov."

"That's what his computer said?"

"It seems Petrov approached him, asking him to get more information on you. Clyde tracked you to King, and then sent one of his employees undercover. It makes sense. If Petrov warned him about your penchant for killing, he would be foolish to get too close to you. But when Petrov pressed him for an update, he was forced to follow King himself. That's when you picked him up."

"I knew Baker sent the girl. I didn't realize he was working for Petrov," she said. "Do you think the girl works for Petrov too?"

"No," Konstantine said, lacing his fingers over his lap. "I think Baker was using her. A means to an end." Another expression he enjoyed.

She seemed to consider this. Whether this weighed in the young journalist's favor or not, Konstantine couldn't be sure.

"Petrov must be in New Orleans," he whispered.

"He was in LA when I saw him. His men were going to take me to him."

"He knows about King. He'll be there soon."

He wanted to bite her lower lip hard enough to make it bleed, but she seemed to be listening to something in the distance.

"They're safe for now," she murmured.

"Does that mean you are unoccupied for the moment?" He reached for her mouth, desperate to steal a kiss or recommence what they'd begun earlier, but she pulled back, out of reach.

She hooked a thumb through the buckle of her belt and freed the leather strap. His heart jolted in his chest. Two tugs and her belt slid free. The sight of it sliding from its hooks made his palms sweat. His body became one thunderous pulse of anticipation.

Is this happening? he asked himself. *Is this really happening?*

All thoughts left his mind as she took his right hand in hers. She forced it over his head, aligning it with the wooden post holding up the headboard. It took her only seconds to bind his right wrist to the right post.

He smelled her hair cascading over his face. He was desperate to reach up and find her throat with his lips.

She slid her hand over his abdomen and tugged on the belt around his waist. Two more sharp tugs and the second belt was freed. Another breath and she'd fixed his remaining hand to the left post.

His body thrummed under her touch. His stomach churned at the realization, he was fully extended. He licked his lips nervously, trying not to squirm. He wanted to look calm, collected, even if everything inside him writhed.

Her boots hit the wooden floor. *Clop, clop.* She shrugged her shoulders out of the leather jacket and tossed it over the foot of the bed. She removed the sunglasses from her hair and tucked them into a pocket.

His mind was a chorus of *more, more, more, more.*

He wanted more of her skin, more of her body against his.

But she was still mostly dressed when she climbed on top of him. Her thighs clenched either side of his body. The pressure stirred his own desire, amplifying the undercurrent of fear he already felt.

This is a test, he thought. *She wants to see if I can truly surrender control. If I truly trust her.*

As if to verify this speculation, Lou reached behind her. The glint of metal flashed in the moonlight. A knife pulled from a hidden sheath. He recognized his blade in her hand and laughed. He was surprised that she'd known it was there.

But of course she'd known. Perhaps she knew where every weapon in this room was hidden.

She leaned over him, her loose hair tickling his face.

The tip of the knife dragged over his shirt, feather light.

He considered protesting, weighing his love of this soft, comfortable t-shirt against his desire for whatever might come next. He swallowed his protests as she drew a T through the delicate fabric. One slash from arm to arm. Then one down the front, following the plane of his abdomen.

She ran a cool hand over his torso and the shirt fell away.

What precision, he wondered, if she could cut the cotton off his skin but not cut the skin itself.

But then he saw the blood well up, and felt the light sting. Cool air sliding over his bare chest, she leaned down, her exhalations warm on his skin.

She dragged a tongue over the cut, rolling her eyes up to meet his.

He hardened, seeing those full lips bent low.

"Can we even the score?" he asked, hearing his throat click. "A shirt for a shirt. Pants for pants."

He thought he saw a smile quirk the corner of her lips. "No."

She fingered the button, undoing it with little more than a snap. Then two cool hands were running down his bare thighs, and over each kneecap, before circling under to the sensitive flesh beneath. His pants hit the floor.

She took the blade and put it between his lips, blunt edge against his tongue.

"Bite down," she said. He did.

Then she bit down. First on his hip bone, little more than a nip. Then harder on his quad. A little harder still on his inner thigh. Each press of her teeth caused him to throb more.

When he thought he would cry out and let the knife fall from his lips to the pillow, she would soften. She would kiss instead of bite. She would lick instead of tear.

Then she took him into her mouth all the way down to the hilt. He moaned, the blade vibrated between his teeth. She reached up and seized the hilt of the blade.

"If this falls out, I stop," she said.

He bit down harder.

Then she laid his world to waste.

25

King heard a rattle outside his window and muted the television. He leaned forward, looking through the balcony door into the dark.

Someone was on the fire escape. He slipped one hand under his sofa and found the .357 hidden there. Wrapping his hand around the textured handle he crept across the living room. Sweat cooled on the back of his neck and sprang up on his palms, making the gun feel precarious in his grip. He tucked himself into the corner of the room so he would have a clear shot of whoever appeared.

A figure emerged at the top of the escape.

King was ready. He could get an easy shot from here and stop Petrov's men in their tracks.

"Oh shit!" A girl squeaked. She toppled from the top of the ladder onto King's balcony with a crash. Her legs flopped out behind her like an afterthought, taking out one of his balcony chairs.

She moaned, cursing and clutching her head.

King opened the balcony door. "Piper?"

"Shhh!" She hissed, trying to stand but only wobbling on her two unsteady legs. "Don't let Mel hear you."

King checked the time. It was nine. The shop would close in one hour. "She's still downstairs. Why are you crawling around in the dark. You could've broken your neck."

"I need your help," Piper said, taking the outstretched hand he offered. "Undrunk me."

"Excuse me?" But then he smelled the alcohol, rolling off her in a putrid wave. "Christ. What did you have?"

"Three hurricanes?" she asked, as if to confirm it with him.

"*Three?*" Two hurricanes would've sent King well on his way, and he was quadruple her body mass.

"I'm supposed to close and you know if Mel sees me like this she's gonna lose her *fish*."

King laughed. "What makes you think I can help you? There's nothing to do but wait it out."

"Don't lie to me. I've seen you waltz in here pretending to be sober with that glassy look in your eye." She did a comic imitation of King *waltzing*.

King hadn't drank like that in months, but he couldn't deny the accusations. Before Lucy had reappeared with a mission to save her wayward niece, King spent his evenings—hell, most of his *days*—patroning the French Quarter bars, despite his landlady's strict policy on drinking.

"*Please*, pretty, pretty, *please*." Piper batted her lashes and begged with crossed fingers.

A wave of affection washed over King. "Get in here."

He shut the balcony door behind her.

"It's dangerous to be drinking like that by yourself. What if someone took advantage of you?"

"I wasn't alone," Piper said, shuffling into the apartment. The line she cut across the living room was far from straight. "I was with our ninja friend."

"Lou?" He couldn't hide his surprise. "Where is she now?"

"I don't know. She helped me move some stuff then she left me at Henry's. I slept for a while but then my alarm went off for work and I'm still drunk. I thought I'd be better with some sleep."

He opened his kitchen cabinets looking for food. He settled on a box of mac and cheese. "I can't believe you climbed up the fire escape. You could've broken your neck."

"*Mel* would've broken my neck if I'd walked through the front door. I'd rather face a fire escape than an angry *Melandra the Magnificent* any day."

King laughed. He filled a pot with water, and put it on the burner to build a boil. "You need to drink water. Here."

He filled her a glass from the tap and passed it over to her.

"Go sit down. I'll make you some food."

Piper obediently took her water glass to the sofa and sank into the enormous leather cushions.

Once the pot boiled and he got the noodles going, King fetched a washcloth from the bathroom cabinet. Three passes under the cold tap before he wrung it out and offered it to the pink-cheeked girl.

"God, you're good at this," she said, pressing the cloth to her face.

Her relief and audible sigh made him smile. "I used to drink. A lot."

"I'm profiting from your practice then," she said, groaning into the cloth. It fluttered with each exhalation.

"It's not like you to get trashed," King said. *Or to cry in the office when I offer you a place to live.*

She folded the cloth and pressed it over her forehead, still balancing the half-drunk water on one knee. He regarded her bloodshot eyes and ruddy cheeks. He was willing to bet half his pension that she'd been crying tonight too. Hard. And for a while. It was only a mystery if the crying had started before or after the first hurricane.

"Lou told me about Dani being an undercover journalist."

"And that set you off?" he asked, surprised. He thought the girls liked each other, but he would've never guessed it had progressed this far so quickly.

"No. I mean, it's *upsetting*. But no. I guess she's doing her job. Not *that* job—" Piper pointed in the direction of Fortunes and Fixes. "Her *liar* job."

"When is she working? Here?"

"Now." Piper tried to get the washcloth to stay on her forehead without lying down, but she couldn't seem to tilt her head back far enough. "I'm thinking about confronting her after I close up. We're supposed to have dinner."

"Or you could try to find out what she knows," he said, remembering the noodles. He returned to the kitchen. "Pretend you're a double agent."

"I *could*." She groaned, dabbing at her face and neck.

"How's the apartment search going?"

"I still need one. I mean, I could keep the apartment I put a deposit on, but it seems stupid to pay for a bedroom I don't need. Henry won't move in with me. It's too far from the bar."

She rubbed a hand under her nose and sniffed.

"You don't need two bedrooms now?" he asked.

She shook her head, downing the last of the water. King refilled it for her, motioning for her to keep going.

"No. And your apartment *is* nicer but now I can't afford it. It's gonna take me a while to get another deposit together and—"

"It's yours," King said. He took the water glass from her, afraid she was about to spill it all over his leather sofa, and put it on one of barroom coasters. This one from O'Brien's. "I don't need a deposit. If you punch a hole in the wall, I'll take it out of your check."

"Why would you do that for me?" Her face screwed up with fresh tears. "Look at me."

He smiled. "I see you. And the apartment is yours. You can move in as soon as you need to."

She put her head on her knees and cried. King offered her a pat on the back before getting up to check on the macaroni one last time.

The knot in his chest relaxed. He didn't know what was going on in Piper's life, but he was glad she'd be close. Like Melandra, it gave him peace knowing she was safe.

With the noodles cooked, he added the cheese sauce and stirred. The bowl was steaming when he stuck a fork in it and carried it into the living room.

"Eat up," he said. "Hopefully this will suck up most of the alcohol."

She took the bowl of mac and cheese from his hands and stared into it.

"You want bacon bits?" he asked, trying to read her puzzled expression. "Salt and pepper?"

"Bathroom," she said.

He pointed through his bedroom to the right. She sat the bowl down on the coffee table and bolted in that direction. Seconds later he heard pronounced heaving amplified by the acoustics of a toilet bowl.

"That'll help you along," he said. Not with the tears and whatever she was dealing with, but at this rate, she'd sail straight from drunk into hungover.

The toilet flushed and Piper reappeared, wiping the side of her mouth with toilet paper.

"You want a Dr. Pepper?" He motioned to his mouth. "For the taste?"

"Oh God, yes."

King pulled a cold soda from the fridge and cracked it open. He handed it over to her. She drank half the can in one go before picking up the mac and cheese again.

"Thanks for taking care of me," she said, dragging a sleeve under her nose.

He shrugged. "I'm paying my karmic debt. I can't count how many friends have doctored me up after one too many. Once I got so drunk that I puked all over myself. My friends came to the hotel where I was at, picked me up, stripped me down, and pushed me into the shower. They even redressed me before dumping me at home."

"Good friends," Piper said, throwing the Dr. Pepper back for a second time.

They were good friends, but King knew he'd had a problem and always would. He only hoped his love and promise to Lucy was enough to keep that propensity at bay.

"I already feel better." Piper returned to the couch and picked up the macaroni and cheese. "God, I'm actually hungry. How is that possible?"

Her eyes had cleared. But her cheeks were still too red.

"Go on. Eat up," he said. He got a Dr. Pepper for himself then settled on the sofa beside her, facing her with one arm draped over the back of the couch. She was cross-legged, shoveling oversized bites into her mouth.

"This is really good. It's like gourmet. You didn't buy this at the dollar store."

He snorted. "You're still drunk."

He drank his soda, replaying in his head the case file he'd been reading before Piper crashed onto the balcony. His mind also drifted to

Lou. It was interesting that she'd taken Piper to a bar, even for a few drinks. It seemed so normal.

Piper belched. Then laughed. "Sorry."

King shrugged. "You'd have to do better than that to startle me."

"I hear a challenge." With the mac eaten, her speech was almost normal now. She'd gone from looking very drunk to looking very tired. If she were lucky, Mel wouldn't notice.

"Do you care if I wash up in your bathroom? I need to swish some toothpaste and wash my face."

"Have at it."

She placed the empty bowl on the coffee table. When she stood up, she took a couple of uneven steps, but mostly she looked okay.

He took her bowl to the sink, soaped a sponge and washed it. When he turned off the water, the tap still ran in the other room.

He decided against a second soda so late in the evening. He was already having trouble dropping off these days. He didn't need another setback. He decided instead on water. Maybe he would finish off the mac. A nice heavy meal might help him along.

Piper returned to the living room looking fresh-faced. "I saw some eyedrops in your cabinet. I used them. Hope that's okay."

"They're probably expired." He'd bought it for when he smoked weed, which was even longer ago than his last drunken escapade.

"Can I ask you something?" she said. She checked her watch before sitting on the edge of the couch again.

"Shoot."

"When you were a DEA agent, you probably saw a lot of drug addicts, right?"

He settled onto the sofa, wondering if they were going to get to it at last, the heart of the issue. "Yeah. I knew some. And I'm not innocent myself."

He didn't point out that half guys he knew in the DEA were addicted to something, blow or something milder. It wasn't uncommon that evidence disappeared from the locker.

"Right, so how often do you think addicts get clean?" she asked. "Like 80% of the time? 75%?"

"You mean quit their drug altogether and never take it up again or get hooked on something else? I guess it depends on the drug," he said.

It did, but this was also his attempt to get more information. Fortunately Piper didn't seem to notice.

"Let's just say it's heroin," Piper said, shrugging her shoulders indifferently. "If someone was addicted to heroin for ten years, maybe longer, and then they wanted to get clean, what are the chances that they'd actually do it?"

King's heart fell. "Your mom?"

Piper reached for her Dr. Pepper, picking at the tab with her finger. "Yeah. I think she started up when my dad died, but it could've been before that. Hell, maybe she's been doing it her whole life."

"And she told you she wanted to get clean?" he asked.

She plucked the tab again. And again.

"When someone is hooked on something hard like that, they need a lot of help."

"I tried to get her out of that house. Maybe if—"

"She'd need a lot more help than a move, sweetie," he said gently. "She'd need even more than a strong resolve to quit."

Her shoulders sagged. She seemed fixated on the seam of her jeans, scratching it with a black nail. "I thought she just needed a change."

"She does. But for it to stick, she's got to be the one to make the change. She'd have to be committed. And when she screwed up, because everyone does, she'd have to be committed enough to *recommit*. Get what I'm saying?"

Piper threw back the rest of the soda and put the empty can on the coffee table.

"Hey," King said, seeing the tears pool in the corner of her eyes. "Hey, look at me."

Piper met his gaze, her lip trembling.

"Her illness doesn't have anything to do with you."

She nodded, but King wasn't going to give up this easy. He wanted her to hear him, *really* hear what he had to say.

"But it was dumb, right?" she asked. "I was stupid for thinking I could shake her out of it." She ran her hands down her face.

"People get addicted for all kinds of reasons. You didn't drive your mother to addiction and her inability to get out of it isn't on you either."

"But if I can get her enough help—"

"She has to help herself," he interjected. "This is her battle, not yours."

"It's hard not to feel like..." She bit her lip, meeting King's eyes with her watery gaze. The profound, wounded sorrow there hurt King. "I'm failing her. Or I'm not strong enough to pull her out of it."

"Don't take that on," King said. "This isn't about you."

She nodded her head, forcing herself to smile at him. But King worried she wasn't actually hearing the words. The voice inside her own head was likely four times louder than his.

"Come here," he said. He stood, opened his arms and a laughing Piper fell into them.

Laughter, he realized, was her default. It was how she dealt with the world. It was how she beat back the waters drowning her.

"You're enough to change for. She isn't ready to change," he said again, planting a kiss on the top of her head. "I'll tell you every time I see you from here until hell freezes over if I have to. Addiction is about the addicts."

"That guilt though, man," she said, pulling back. More laughter.

"I know," he said. "But you're going to get through this."

She nodded, but her face was crumpling again.

A sharp knock on the door silenced them both.

"Come in," King called, already knowing who those tinkling bangles belonged to. Piper squeezed him harder.

"It's okay," he whispered. "You've been crying."

Mel entered. "Well, I've got one no-show and the other is late!"

Then her eyes fell on Piper.

"Oh," she said, coming to stand before them. The three of them formed a triangle in King's large living room. "What's going on here?"

"Piper's having a rough night," he said.

"I see that," Melandra looked her up and down.

"I was going to come down in a minute," Piper said, sheepishly. "I was trying to clean up my face."

"Okay," Mel said. "Is this about your mom?"

Piper's lip trembled. "God, did everyone know?"

"Know what?" Mel asked.

"It's fine. I just need a minute. I don't want to freak out the customers." She laughed.

"No, it's all right," Melandra said, giving Piper's ponytail an affectionate tug. "I'll close up tonight."

"No, I—"

Mel waved her away. "It's fine. I don't have any readings. But this doesn't tell me why the other one is a no-show. Dani never came for her shift."

"She's an undercover reporter," Piper said, looking more than relieved to have the attention directed from her to Dani.

Mel snorted. "Of course she is. Who was she reporting on?" She gave King an appraising look, eyebrow arching. You?"

"Lou," he said.

Mel's eyebrows shot up. "You can explain that to me later."

"I'll make it up to you, Mel," Piper said, her voice thick.

"No need." Mel ran a thumb over her cheek, clearing a tear.

The shop moaned, the ghostly howl reverberating up to them from below.

"I better get out there," Mel said. "These candles ain't gonna sell themselves."

She sashayed out of the apartment and closed the door behind her.

"See," King said. "She had no—"

The door to the apartment swung open again. Mel rushed inside, slamming the door shut behind her. King reached for his .357 without thinking.

"They're not customers," Mel said, chest heaving and wide-eyed. "I think they're here for us."

K onstantine awoke naked, on his back, his uncovered chest cold. One of his wrists was still bound to the bed. He took the blade from underneath his pillow and cut the strap, freeing his second wrist. He turned on his side to find Lou stretched long beside him. She'd given him her back.

He traced the dip of her waist and flare of her hip with his eyes. He longed to reach out and touch her skin but he didn't want to wake her.

In his mind, he replayed the moment of his climax, when she latched onto him and wouldn't let go. The gentle scrape of her teeth had sent him careening out of his mind.

He'd pulled so hard that he snapped one wooden post on his bed, ripping the leather strap free. When she'd commanded that he put his hand behind his head and keep it there, he'd obeyed, but he would be lying if he said it hadn't taken every ounce of his considerable self-control not to wrap his fingers in her hair.

He rolled toward her, wishing to wrap a hand around her hip bone before the magic of their moment ended. A moment Konstantine understood may never come again. She had never revisited her lovers before. His snooping had told him as much. There was also the possibility that perhaps now she'd had a taste of him, she didn't *want* more.

After all, she had not let him touch her. She'd remained fully clothed yet had stripped him bare. He'd submitted entirely to her will and yet she'd given him...nothing.

Pleasure. Absolutely.

More pleasure than he'd ever received from so beautiful a mouth. But it had simply been a release, on her terms. She hadn't offered herself in anyway. She'd given him no chance to perform. This saddened and worried him with its implications.

His phone buzzed. He slipped from the bed, pulled on silk pajama pants and retrieved the cell phone from the bedside table.

Si sta muovendo. He is on the move.

He needed to make a phone call. But first...

Unable to contain himself any longer, he slid into the bed and placed one hand on the cool plane of her back. He traced a shoulder blade, her spine, his fingers sliding over her hips.

She turned toward him.

Except she wasn't aroused. The hungry, predatorial gaze she'd fixed on him earlier was replaced now with a cold regard. His hand froze.

Her gaze slid away and he realized she was listening to something.

Then he heard it too. The shuffle of footfall. The creak of a wooden step at the base of the stairs.

Lou reached down and pulled the covers over their bodies. With one arm, she pulled him against her. Her thigh slid between his own as her arms went around him. Her breath was hot on his ear and neck.

Then the world shifted.

LOU WOKE THE MOMENT KONSTANTINE GRABBED THE KNIFE. HAD HE shifted toward her, rather than away, she would have snapped his neck. But only a heartbeat later, he was sawing clumsily at the leather strap binding him to the bed.

She hadn't meant to fall asleep beside him. Not that it was their first time sleeping side by side, but she thought it suggested a certain intimacy. She didn't want him to get the wrong idea.

When he slipped from the bed to check his phone, a sound caught her attention. Downstairs.

The front door creaked open and she detected the muffled scuff of boots on a stone floor.

She strained, listening harder. Three, maybe four men had entered the apartment. They brought the cold morning air with them. The frosty air traveled up the stairs and licked the side of Lou's face, since she was closest to the landing.

Konstantine slid a hand around her waist.

She turned, and saw immediately he meant to speak. He had the look that men get when they wanted more of her. Sex, of course, but also answers to their questions: *Who are you? What's your name? Can I see you again?*

Konstantine already knew these simple answers. So what did he want from her?

She placed a hand over his mouth before he spoke. Let the assailants think he was asleep.

Then he cocked his head and his eyes slid toward the stairs.

So his senses weren't totally useless, she thought, though a hair slower than her own.

She reached down and grabbed the top of the cover bunched at her knees. She pulled it up and over her head, positioning Konstantine so that they lay face-to-face, her knee between his. She wrapped her hand around the blade, the one she'd made him hold between his teeth. It would have a very different job now.

She shrouded them in darkness, holding tight so that they could both bleed through. Konstantine piggybacked on her own talent.

The warm bed gave way to cold stone.

She felt him stiffen, his body wedged between mattress and floor. It was harder for him to be beneath the bed. It gave her a momentary appreciation of her compact frame. Sometimes hiding under beds was simply useful. Konstantine slid to one side and gave them both room enough to move.

She rolled away from him, positioning herself as first line of defense. She wrapped her hand around the handle until the grip felt good.

Lou caught a glimpse of a jaw and throat before the torso appeared, black-clad. Then legs, and boots with a thick rubber sole.

A phone rang and Konstantine stiffened behind her.

The last man coming up the stairs hesitated, eye-level.

He peered into the dark under the bed.

He saw the blade, she thought. *It must've caught the light.*

He raised his gun, pointing it at her.

Lou launched herself out from underneath the bed and plunged the knife through the slats in the railing. The blade struck home, slipping into the man's left eye socket and scraping bone.

He howled. The man wrenched himself away, the blade still buried deep in the socket. He missed a step and crashed backwards out of sight. Something shattered at the base of the stairs but Lou had no time to worry about that collision. Already she was rolling onto her back, looking for the other two attackers.

She heard boots scuff stone.

But before they appeared the mattress exploded suddenly, popping upward away from its frame. This made it easier to stand and Lou was on her feet in two heartbeats. Someone cried out as Konstantine shoved the mattress against the wall, slamming that man into the plaster behind it. Konstantine produced a gun and fired two shots through the mattress into the man.

The half-suffocated man returned three reflexive shots, ejecting cotton and fluff into the bedroom. It was like snow falling down around them.

Konstantine hissed, pulling back.

He brought the mattress with him, exposing a third would-be assassin. Lou kicked him hard and he sailed into the bathroom, lost his balance, and fell. The back of his head knocked against the toilet seat.

Konstantine was over him, firing a shot into his unconscious face before Lou fully recovered.

Lou went downstairs to find it empty. The front door to the apartment stood open, revealing the entryway and part of the courtyard below. But if there had been a fourth man, he had fled at the sound of fighting above.

She crossed to the open door. She shut it, locked it, and peered out the curtained window. She saw no one.

At the base of the stairs was the man she'd stabbed in the eye. His ankle was bent in the wrong direction and he lay on a pile of glass. Lou couldn't tell what it was he'd landed on. A sculpture perhaps? Some piece of art? Whatever it was, it would never be whole again. The shards shimmering in the first specks of morning light were too small to reassemble, even with glue and a steady hand.

She checked this man's pulse. Nothing. She was unsure if the blood loss or fall had finished what she'd started. It didn't matter.

Mounting the stairs, she half expected to get attacked herself. But no one was left. There was a dead man on the floor of the bathroom and another slumped against the wall.

Then there was Konstantine himself. He stood in his bedroom, fingers inspecting his left hip.

He was naked, head-to-toe. The right buttocks and thigh was bright red with his blood, as if a broad stroke of a paintbrush had licked up the side of his leg.

She had the sudden urge to lick him clean and taste the blood herself.

He met her gaze. "I'm fine."

"I can see that."

"It only grazed me."

"You'll live," she agreed, eyebrow arched. She wasn't sure what else he wanted from her. There was an anger in his voice she hadn't expected.

She wasn't sure if his irritation was the result of the flesh wound, or if he was angry to have had his bedroom so carelessly destroyed.

He flipped the mattress back into place.

"What?" she asked.

"You aren't killing," he said. No, he accused her.

"The man at the base of the stairs would disagree. And Clyde Baker I'm sure."

Konstantine waved his hand. "You know what I mean. You aren't wearing your vest or your guns and you aren't even trying."

He pointed at the man in the bathroom as if the sprawling corpse were evidence.

"Whatever you want to say, say it," she said. She had no patience for feelings or games.

He bent and lifted a plastic case from the floor. He popped open the lid and began riffling through its contents with impatient fingers. But she saw the transformation happen slowly. He composed himself.

"How do you intend to kill Petrov without a gun?" he asked. His voice was even now, almost devoid of emotion.

She had no answer for this.

He wet gauze with antiseptic and began wiping at the wound. She hated to see him do it. He was only widening the cut. It was stupid but she wasn't going to help him. Not now.

"Come on," he said, his face practically sneering. "Petrov wants to kill you. How do you intend to stay alive?"

She thought of the boy again. The way he looked with his back in the snow. The bright crimson in his cheeks, his eyes shining in the moonlight.

Please, he'd said. *Whatever my father's done, that's not me.*

Is that what he'd said?

Lou felt her mind couldn't be trusted. It seemed to embellish the scene with more detail every time she revisited it.

This time he looked even younger than possible. His face was as round as a boy's face with no hint of facial hair.

She knew this was a lie. She knew this was a trick her mind played on her. This didn't matter. What mattered was *why*? What was her mind trying to tell her?

She didn't have time to consider the possibilities because at that moment, the compass inside her whirled to life, throbbing with shrill alarm.

King. Piper. Mel. Three different pulls, but magnified because they called to her from the same place. Desperate pleading threefold—it was the most compelling cry for help she'd ever received.

"I have to go. They need me," she said.

"Yes, Petrov is making his move," Konstantine agreed. He snapped his supply box shut and bent to retrieve his pants from the floor.

Lou moved toward his closet.

"Wait," he cried out. He grabbed her wrist before she could fade.

She tore herself from his grip.

"Please don't go unprepared," he begged. "He *will* be ready for you."

She thought of her own arsenal. Of the small hidden chamber beneath her kitchen island and all the guns and grenades she kept there. A flamethrower and pipe bombs, not to mention enough artillery for a small war.

None of it would help her. She needed that familiar fire. The right-eous rage that would well up and overtake her, carrying her through the battle. But her fire was as cold as a snowcapped mountain. Just as silent and desolate.

"I want to come with you," he said, and pulled a shirt down over his head. "Especially if you aren't—well."

"I'm not sick."

"I can still help," he insisted. "I need to make one phone call. Maybe two."

The pleading cry in her chest deepened. She felt their fear. All three of them were very, *very* afraid. Fear was usually the precursor to pain. They didn't have much time.

"You have one minute," she said. "Then I'm leaving with or without you."

27

"Russians?" Piper asked, and swallowed the vomit rising up the back of her throat. She realized her decision to drink three hurricanes on the night of her impending murder was the worst decision of her life. Man, she was *stupid*.

Mel locked the door, before pulling a chair over to wedge under the handle. "How should I know? But I don't need to be psychic to see they came to hurt somebody."

King pulled the .357 and held it up, pointing at the ceiling.

"Wow," Piper said, trying to steady herself by widening her stance. "That's serious."

"Let's go down the fire escape," King said.

Piper gave him a pleading look.

"You got up here," he said. "You can get down too."

She couldn't argue with that. Of course her urge to puke on herself was much stronger now than it had been before the adrenaline spike. The idea that she was going to have to fight her way out of this wasn't helping her nerves one bit.

"Or we could call the police?" Piper said with a shrug. "They might skedaddle?"

Something slammed into the front door of King's apartment. The chair bounced. The frame bucked in place. A crack split the white plaster above the frame, raining dust onto the kitchen floor.

"No time!" King hissed. "*Go.*"

Piper fumbled with the balcony door latch before she managed to get it open. She inhaled cold winter air. It cleared her head.

"Go!" King shouted again but she thought he was talking to Mel, who seemed unwilling to leave his side. She'd taken up a kitchen knife.

Leaning over the balcony railing, Piper eyed the fire escape suspiciously. She placed one hand on the cold metal and shifted her weight so she could throw her leg over the ledge.

But it began vibrating.

The iron bar in her grip shook and rattled against her palm. Piper wondered if it was some trick of her inebriated mind. It wasn't until the man looked up, his pale face full of moonlight, that she realized someone was climbing up the fire escape. The vibration she felt in her palm was his ascent.

Terror sparked through her. And she vomited.

Her stomach convulsed once, twice, and ejected all its burning contents onto the climber.

He screamed. The fire escape rattled louder than ever and Piper was fairly certain he'd crashed to the pavement below.

Had she killed him? That drop was no joke. *Oh man, death by vomit. What a way to go.*

If they were lucky, the climber cracked his head open on the pavement and cleared their path to escape. The cold bar in her grip was still. She dared to peer over the side again.

In the dim light, she barely noted the dumpster opposite the alley and the pale outline of a door leading into another shop.

Then the rung was vibrating again, the cold bar warming. Another pale face turned up toward the moonlight, grimacing at her.

"If you fucking puke on me," he said, calling up to her in accented English. "I will slit your throat."

Piper grabbed one of King's patio chairs and threw it over the side of the balcony. It connected with the man square in the face and he fell back off the railing, but didn't lose his grip entirely. One hand still gripped the ladder tightly. He resumed his climb, muttering a lot of words that Piper didn't understand. She was fairly certain she understood the meaning though. He was probably promising her a slow, painful death.

"In that case, I've got nothing to lose," she said, and grabbed the second chair. She pitched it over the ledge into the dark.

The man cried out, wailing during his descent as the chair clattered in the alleyway.

But then a third man mounted the escape.

"Man, you guys are like a barrel of monkeys," she groaned, abandoning her post.

She pried open the balcony door and wedged herself into the warm apartment. "There are more of them on the fire escape and you're out of patio chairs."

Whatever thought she meant to say next evaporated. King and Mel were not holding the door closed. In fact, the door had been kicked inward off its hinges and lay in the middle of the kitchen floor. A spray of wooden shards littered the tile.

A man with a bleeding forearm had a gun to Mel's head. Beside him, another intruder had his gun pointed at King.

Upon Piper's entry, a third man pulled his gun and pointed it at her.

"Whoa," she said, taking a step back.

"*Now* it's impossible to sacrifice yourself and save *both* of them," the man said, apparently speaking to King.

"This is *twice* that I've had a gun held to my head in this kitchen," Mel grumbled.

"Toss it to me," the man instructed. His blood dripped onto the white checkered tiles. Mel must have slashed him good with the knife at least once.

"No," Piper said, when King thumbed on his safety and lowered the gun.

"Be quiet," King said.

And while being quiet was the last thing Piper wanted to do now with so many guns in the room, she obeyed.

The balcony door snapped open behind her. She hadn't even fully turned around before a swift kick in the back of the leg dropped her. Her knees hit the floor, throbbing. She didn't need to know who was behind her. The stench of vomit was sickening. She was going to puke again.

King was the second to hit his knees as his hands were wrenched behind his head.

"Call for help," King said.

"Call for help and we will kill you," the man holding Mel said.

But King was still looking at Piper, his gaze boring into hers.

Then she understood. He wanted her to think of Lou.

Seeming to sense her thoughts King turned those desperate eyes on Mel.

"All of us," he said. "*Now.*"

Piper thought she saw a flicker in Mel's expression, some sort of knowing comprehension. Then the man behind her threw her to the ground. Her bangles clattered against the tile and the scarf around her head loosened, falling free.

"Tape their mouths shut," he said.

Lou...Lou...Lou...Come on. We need you.

The familiar stretch and rip of duct tape sounded somewhere behind her before a rough hand squeezed her mouth so hard her jaw ached. The tape was slapped over her puckered lips.

King was next before the roll was tossed to Mel's captor. He pulled her head back by her hair and slapped the metallic strip over her mouth.

Piper hated this, every single second of it. They were the good guys. And King and Mel were the nicest people in the world. They didn't deserve this. None of them deserved to die.

Lou, we need you.

Piper braced herself for what she knew was next.

It was only two breaths before a sharp strike connected with the back of her neck. A jolt of electric pain rocketed down her spine and the darkness rose up to meet her.

KING WOKE FIRST. HE SUSPECTED IT WAS THE MURDEROUS THROBBING of his dead leg that woke him. The bullet that tore through his lower back three months ago made its lingering presence known. Never mind the months of physical therapy and the hard-fought healing behind him. A wound like that, no matter how old, couldn't tolerate hours on a concrete floor.

If it had been hours. King wasn't sure.

His eyes fluttered open once, noting only distant, nebulous light. Then again as his mind fought for consciousness. Objects swam in and out of his vision. It wasn't unlike shaking off the mantle of a particularly thick sleep.

But then the light brightened. The shapes sharpened. He pushed himself up to sitting and took in the room. A concrete floor made bright by an overhead light. Red tool boxes lined one wall. Overhead he saw four strange platforms.

It took him several moments of considerable staring before he realized what he was looking at. The strange pivots overhead were the platforms that would launch a car into the air for an oil change. They were in a garage. The stench of oil and grease made sense now.

The concrete floor stretched long and unbroken between pillars. It wasn't a quick lube place then. No one was running around down below. There were four bays, each capped with a white metallic door that no doubt rolled up to let the vehicles in.

Fitting, he thought, knowing they would tune up on him sooner or later.

But he preferred that to the alternative. Should this go south faster than it already had, he didn't know what he would do. He couldn't watch Mel and Piper endure the violence.

If that happened...

A metal chair scraped across the concrete floor. The wretched screeching split his head in two. Both Mel and Piper stirred on the floor beside him. Mel was closest on his left side, Piper beside her.

With each ragged breath, the tape over his mouth swelled and sunk against his lips.

At least the girls were alive and untouched for the moment. King had that much to be thankful for.

Footsteps came into view. Thick brown boots stopped shy of his own. He expected that boot to pull back and swing, kicking him in the face. But instead strong arms seized him and hauled him up to the post. His back was forced against the cold metal. He searched the edges with his hands, looking for a sharp place to rub the tape against, but the pole was smooth all the way around.

He groaned.

"You want to talk?" the man asked, stooping down to peer into King's face. "Dmitri, I think this one wants to talk."

King wasn't sure the accents were Russian. Ukrainian perhaps, or a different sort of Slavic language. But he couldn't be sure. It had been a long time since he'd heard anything of the sort. Back in the 90s he'd been assigned to a KGB case for a while, but that had been a lifetime ago.

"Robert King," the man named Dmitri said, pulling up the metal chair. He dragged the legs across the concrete floor, emitting a screech that made King's flesh crawl.

And he wasn't the only one. Piper and Mel came to full consciousness this time, no doubt roused by this godawful sound. When Piper pushed herself up onto her knees, King saw another body beyond hers. A slumped lump of girl. The blonde hair was matted to her swollen face. The blood in it stopped King's breath cold.

"Are you the same Robert King I've been hearing about?"

King flicked his eyes to the metallic tape covering his mouth.

Dmitri laughed before he dipped his head in acquiescence. "My apologies."

He looked into King's eyes as he grasped the edge of the tape. This close King could smell his cologne. There was too much of it. It reminded him of the aftershave his grandfather used to splash on in the mornings before taking off to spend ten hours in the butcher shop.

He's going to enjoy this, King thought. *He likes to see others in pain.*

King's mouth burned as the tape ripped free. Heat and blood rushed to the area, warming it. His lips swelled, feeling raw against his probing tongue.

"Yes," King said. "I'm Robert King. Though it's a common enough name."

"You worked in the Drug Enforcement Agency."

"I did."

"You spent years *dedicated* to destroying my business."

King said nothing. He cut his eyes to Mel and Piper, hoping they were okay. They were sitting up now, their backs against the cinder blocks serving as one wall of the garage.

"How much *trouble* you've caused me." Dmitri bent, slipping a hand under his chair. When he pulled it into the light, the Smith and Wesson

SD40 sat snug in his grip. "I should put a bullet in you for that reason alone. I love shooting DEA agents actually. I enjoy watching the surprise that crosses their face as they die."

King still said nothing. Irritation flickered in Dmitri's eyes.

"Is it true you knew Jack Thorne?"

"Yes." King was hard at work training his captor. When he asked King a valid question, he received an answer. Cooperation. When he taunted and threatened, he got nothing. He hoped the dynamic would hold. They only needed to keep him talking until Lou arrived.

She would end this. He was counting on it.

"And is it true that Angelo Martinelli was the one who pulled the trigger and took his life?"

"Yes."

"And she was there?"

"She who?"

"His daughter, Louie."

"Yes."

"But Angelo was working on his father's orders," Dmitri said.

"He was working on Chaz Brasso's orders, who in turn was taking his orders from someone else."

Dmitri arched both brows before nodding. "You see, that's the problem with you Americans. You blame everyone else for your problems when it's almost always a fox in your own house." He tapped the gun against his leg. That unblinking eye bored into King's until he shifted an inch to the left, removing himself from its line of sight.

"A man took her father's life and now she takes the lives of men?"

"Yes."

He fell back against the chair. "And how many must she have to be satisfied? How many lives do you think Jack Thorne is worth?"

"To her?" King asked. He wanted to keep Dmitri's attention trained on him. He could do nothing for Dani, who might already be dead. Her body was so still and lifeless. But he had Piper and Mel to think of. They needed him to do this right.

"Then there is no reason why I shouldn't kill every single one of you," he said quietly, retraining the gun on King. "You see, she took someone from me. My son."

Piper shifted nervously in his periphery.

Don't move, he thought. *Don't remind him that you're here.*

"She took from me and I should take from her. In her world, that's justice, isn't it?"

King had no answer for this.

"And that's the problem. It never ends. When will the dance end? Her *danse macabre*."

No one spoke.

Dmitri leaned forward, closing the distance between their faces. "And if I were to tell her this, when she comes for you, do you think she'll listen to me?"

"How do you know she'll come?" King asked, staring into those ice blue eyes.

Dmitri pressed the gun barrel against his jaw, so hard that it made King's mandible creak. "Pray she does."

28

Lou flipped the latch on her kitchen island, and the side separated from its base, revealing stairs. Konstantine followed her down into the inner chamber, reaching overhead to pull the string and flood the room with light. Wooden steps gave way to a sawdust floor and three walls of weaponry. The shelves were built of unfinished wood, but on them an arsenal fit for a king. The room smelled of lumber.

"Take what you need," she said, as Konstantine seemed to be waiting for permission. She liked him more for that.

He wasted no time. He pulled down one of the vests from its hook on the wall. Then he chose a pair of Browning pistols and a matching holster. He disregarded the blades, Kevlar, and flash bombs. But his eyes lingered on the grenades.

She surveyed her options too.

He saw her hesitate, and pulled her father's vest from its hook. He thrust it at her.

She could only look at it.

"Put it on," he insisted.

She took the vest and peeled back the collar to see the word *Thorne* scrawled in black ink on the tag.

"Why won't you wear it?" he asked.

Sawdust shifted under her boots. "Why should I?"

"In case you're shot."

"No," she said and tossed the vest back at him. "*Why?* Why should I?"

He tightened the Velcro across his chest, his face pinched in confusion. "I don't understand."

She wanted to rip the guns from the shelves. She wanted to tear this place apart.

"They kill me or I kill them. It doesn't matter."

I don't have a reason to be here.

His jaw clenched shut. He thrust the vest at her again. "It matters to the people who are waiting for you."

In her mind, she saw Piper first, her puffy red eyes and quivering lip. Then she saw King on his hands and knees, a cut in the side of his head bleeding. She saw Melandra's dark and accusing eyes.

Maybe she didn't deserve to be here. Maybe she'd served her purpose when she dragged Ryanson's corpse onto the shores of La Loon and Nico was an afterthought. But it didn't change the fact that she'd avenged her father and there was no reason for continuing like this. She had no family to live for. She had no reason to go on. What she'd set out to do was done. All the men she'd wanted dead *were* dead.

That's why she'd seen her father's face in place of the boy's. *That's* why her thirst and hunger refused to rise in her. It was done. *She* was done.

But that left Dmitri.

Her father had failed and it got him and his wife killed. Lou would not make the same mistake. She was the reason Dmitri was in New Orleans. She would face him. She would finish him so that he didn't hurt the others. And then...

Game over.

"They're waiting for you," Konstantine said again, as if hoping to pull her out of her inner turmoil.

She slipped on hip holsters and her twin Berettas, but she took nothing else. She left her father's vest on its hook.

That isn't the life I want for you, Lou.

Then you shouldn't have died, she thought.

In addition to the second vest and her Browning pistols, Konstantine took a belt of grenades thrown over one shoulder. He eyed her flamethrower with longing.

"Take it if you want it," she said and mounted the stairs. "But let's go."

Konstantine squeezed her shoulder. "Your friends are counting on you."

Friends.

She saw Piper's brilliant smile, heard her shy laugh. *Louie Thorne, I'm going to be your first friend.*

Inside her living room, Lou looked at the moonlit river once more. She watched a bird land gracefully on its surface before tucking its wings in tight.

A foghorn blared in the distance.

She wondered if she would ever see this place again and stepped inside her closet. She pressed her back against the wooden wall, making room for Konstantine.

He slid inside, taking up the remaining space. She felt his warm breath on her neck as his steady hand went around her waist.

"I'll handle Petrov and his men," she said and pulled the door closed. "I want you to focus on getting them out."

"You could try to get them out one at a time before he notices."

"No," she said. "The second he sees me move one, he'll kill another."

"They won't die," he whispered. "I promise."

I'll be right here, her father had said the night he died.

How easily promises were broken.

Konstantine's warm hand cupped her cheek. He ran a thumb over her skin. But whatever he meant to say or do next was eaten by the darkness as Lou pulled them through to the other side.

29

Piper felt like death. No, she felt like death scraped off hot pavement, put in a blender, and then declared disgusting, thrown through the garbage disposal for another whirl. She wasn't sure if it was the alcohol or the hit to the back of the skull, but her head throbbed in a way it never had before. If she saw some pink brain goo slosh out onto the cold concrete floor right now, she wouldn't even be surprised.

The room around her spun. Light smeared across her vision, red starbursts sparking every time she tried to lift her head.

I'm going to be—she turned and puked expecting it to splash onto the concrete floor.

Only she didn't have much left, which was good because it had nowhere to go. It hit the back of the duct tape and she was forced to swallow it back down.

Nose burning, she groaned. Somehow she got herself up into a sitting position. Then the spinning only intensified, so she leaned back against the cold wall and breathed. Christ. She probably had a concussion. *Or you got too drunk you freaking idiot.*

The room stopped spinning.

The woman beside her stirred. Piper thought it was Mel on her left but now that her vision was clearing, she saw Mel lay on her right. On her left was someone else.

She leaned forward, trying to get a better look at the woman's face and realized the woman wasn't wearing Mel's red scarf. That was *blood*. So much blood that it had matted her hair to her head.

She moaned through the tape.

A badly beaten Dani lay motionless on the floor. In addition to the blood-soaked hair, her face was purple. The eyes were crusted shut.

They've killed her, she thought. *Oh my God, they've killed her.*

"You're awake."

Piper turned toward the voice and found a man, maybe in his fifties, looking at her with mild interest. She wasn't sure if she should curse him or piss herself. Her emotions were vacillating somewhere in between.

"If I take off the tape, will you tell me your name?" he asked, pivoting in his chair. He'd been facing King a moment before.

She nodded.

He bent forward and tore the tape from her mouth. Moistened by her vomit, it came off easily.

First order of business, she wiped her mouth on her sleeve. God, what she would've given for a huge glass of water.

"Piper," she said. Only after the name was out of her mouth did she wonder if it was a bad idea to give her real name to a man like this. He looked like the sort of guy who would kill her whole family while they slept, or at the very least a beloved dog.

"Piper, do you know this woman?" He gestured toward Dani.

She suppressed the urge say, *Yes, you fucking monster*. It wasn't that she didn't want to spit in this asshole's face. If she were alone with him, maybe she would. Henry often accused her of having a self-destructive streak and no sense of self-preservation.

Piper disagreed. But she definitely didn't want to give this guy a reason to hurt King or Mel.

"She's your journalist," Piper said, trying to moisten her tacky lips.

The man arched his eyebrows. "*My* journalist?"

"She's working for you to get information on us."

"You're mistaken," he said, lacing his fingers in his lap. "I didn't hire this woman."

Panic seized Piper's chest. Her heart beat wildly. If Dani was innocent, that meant that she had no reason to be angry with her or feel betrayed. Or maybe Piper was missing some key part of the story here.

"Her boss sent her to get a story on a young woman, yes," he agreed. "But she had no idea why."

"Oh," Piper said. So Dani *was* using her to get information and there was still plenty of reason to feel betrayed. "Then why did you hurt her?"

"I want to know all there is to know about Louie Thorne. And she was reluctant to tell me."

Piper appreciated Dani's grit. Not many people could resist torture by some fiend, but her heart fell at the sound of Lou's name. So this guy did know something. But how much?

"What do *you* know about Louie?" he asked.

"Nothing," Piper said.

The man's eyes darkened, cutting to Dani's beaten body. "Do you want to look like that?"

"No," Piper said. *But I will if it means protecting Lou from you.*

"Then tell me what you know."

Piper searched the room. She saw men on the edge of shadows. She wasn't sure how many lingered, but she knew they were there. Likely blocking all exits and ready to put a bullet or knife in her at the first opportunity. Or worse...keep her alive for other things.

She would have to be smart about this. She knew Lou would come. She needed to buy her time. "It isn't that I don't *want* to tell you, Mister..."

"Dmitri."

"Mr. Dmitri, it's just that I don't know what to say. Lou is such a private person."

He regarded her as if trying to discern a lie.

"I saw them in the bar together tonight," a man said from the darkness. He inched forward, exposing the tips of his steel-toe boots. But the majority of his face remained hidden. She didn't recognize him. In fact, none of them looked like the guy she vomited on. Had they changed guard?

"Yes," Piper said. "But plenty of people have drinking buddies. It doesn't mean they know each other."

"They kissed."

Piper looked at the man standing on the edge of shadows. "*Really?*"

Petrov's clenching fist stole her attention. "Do you know where she lives?"

Piper looked nervously at that clenched hand. "Not here in New Orleans."

"Where she works?"

"I don't think she does."

"Whether or not she fucks Konstantine—"

Piper flinched. "I hope not."

It was true that kissing Lou had felt like putting a pistol in her mouth. It was exciting and made her stomach drop in the way a forty-foot free fall might have. But while Lou hadn't seemed disgusted by the kiss, she also hadn't swooned. Her face had remained placid, unreadable.

The connection wasn't running both ways.

Even if Lou could be cajoled into some mutually satisfying sex, was that what Lou needed?

Have you ever had a friend?

Piper didn't think so.

After all, she didn't think a girl could watch her parents get killed and spend the remainder of her life cutting up criminals because she felt loved and needed. Nothing about Lou said vulnerable or broken. Anyone could see that Lou Thorne was a force. But Piper would've bet a thousand dollars that Louie also had some major issues.

Don't we all, Piper thought, her mother's face flashing in her mind.

"You are thinking a great deal," Petrov said. He stood and dragged the chair closer to her. The scraping sound set Piper's teeth on edge.

"Yeah," Piper admitted. There was no point in pretending otherwise. "*Who* is Konstantine?"

His lips pulled into a sneer. "You must know more than this woman." Petrov pointed to Dani.

"Well, I didn't know she was running around with some guy named Konstantine."

Petrov grabbed Piper by the hair and dragged her into the center of the room.

King's and Mel's outcries were immediate and visceral.

He dropped her in the center of the floor. This close the man smelled like aftershave and something else. Something acrid. But she also caught the scent of her own vomit.

When she felt his ice cold fingers on hers, her heart rocketed. The throbbing killed her head. The pain obliterated all thought, as it seemed a hammer slammed repeatedly against the inside of her skull. *Elves pushing out* her mother always called it. Some desperate bastard in there was trying escape.

The tape binding her wrists popped free. Piper knew it was too good to be true that this guy was just going to let her go.

His ice cold hand remained clasped around hers, pulling it around in front of her.

"You have lovely, delicate little fingers."

Oh man. Piper had seen the movies. She knew where this was going.

"Do you make music with these hands?" Petrov asked. His blue eyes, as icy as his fingers, bore into hers.

"No," she said. She'd had maybe ten lessons on the piano as a child and played in a recital *When the Saints Go Marching In*. She'd been mediocre at best. And she'd taken that guitar class in her first year of college before dropping out, but she couldn't remember more than a few lines of a couple of songs.

She suspected the calluses on this Russian's fingers were from music. Or did he get calluses from murdering people? She'd have to check Lou's hand next time she had a chance—if she had a chance.

Petrov separated her index finger from the rest. "I think I'll take this one for my collection. It's a beautiful finger."

"No," King said. Not only King. His gruff man voice had been layered with another, higher, feminine voice.

Piper turned and saw Mel wide-eyed and pleading. Her nostrils flared with each panicked inhalation. It was Mel's and King's fear combined, more than her own, that pushed her over the edge into full-blown panic.

She heard a click and turned back to Petrov in time to see blade glinting in the light. It was a simple switchblade perhaps six inches long.

Piper tried to yank her hand back.

Petrov wouldn't let go. "I think I'll take this one too."

He straightened her middle finger pressing it into the side of the first.

"No, no, *no*." Piper squirmed. "Please. *Please* don't."

"No?" Petrov asked, his smile humorous. "You have eight others.

Surely you won't miss two? And they will look so nice with the others. I have a whole drawer, you see. A drawer full of beautiful lady fingers. I've been collecting them since 1998."

Piper wanted to throw up again. Her stomach turned again and she was certain that if she did puke on this guy, he would definitely cut her fingers off. Then he would do a lot worse.

She could get out of this. She could survive it. She only needed a plan.

Mel's and King's insistent begging only made it harder to think. And Petrov seemed to like it. He took pleasure in knowing that hurting her in turn hurt them too.

She saw his pleasure and something inside her cracked. Her fear was lost in a crashing wave of anger.

"You're a piece of shit," Piper said and shoved him back onto his heels.

The world stopped on a dime. Petrov's eyes opened wide in surprise.

"You like hurting people," she went on. "How fucked up is that?"

"You tell me." He grabbed her hand, twisting the wrist hard enough to make her scream. Then he seized the two fingers he wanted and aligned the knife with the base of her middle digit.

"Wait, wait, wait!" Piper wailed, squirming. Pain shot through her fingers. She wondered if she was willing to break them to get them away.

Petrov didn't seem to hear her. He pressed the blade to the side of Piper's skin. Red bloomed.

Her mind devolved into a nonsensical cry. *This is it, this is it, this is it.*

She took a deep breath and prepared herself for what was about to happen.

Until a leather boot shot out of nowhere and slammed into the side of Petrov's head. The man buckled and crashed onto the floor.

Piper stared at the boot uncomprehending. Then the leg. Then the gun. And finally the woman who stood where Petrov had been only a moment before.

Of all the times she'd been thrilled beyond measure to see Louie Thorne's face, none of them compared to this moment.

"Good timing," Piper said, and her body shook with relief.

30

"You okay?" Lou asked, her voice pitched low.

"Yeah."

Lou watched Petrov drag himself up to his feet, righting the overturned chair. Lou stole a glance at the girl and saw she still held her hand, but blood was running down the finger, pooling in the creases. "Are you sure?"

Piper looked down at her hand and saw the blood. "Oh shit."

Konstantine snapped the bonds on Melandra's wrists. In one fluid movement, the woman had her scarf off her head and was wrapping Piper's fingers tight.

"Here," she said, forcing Piper to cooperate. "Here, let me see it."

Konstantine turned to King next.

"Louie Abigail Thorne," Dmitri said, on his feet again. He pulled his shirt down in the front. "You grace us with your presence. Is that all it took? Kidnapping your friends in order to have a little conversation?"

"Did you try the phone?" she asked.

Anger flashed in his eyes.

"Get them out of here," Konstantine said. She didn't need to turn her head to know he spoke to King. Lou wanted to keep both of her eyes trained on the man in front of her. She didn't see a gun. But his men were flanking him now, putting themselves on his side of the room. King, Konstantine, Mel and Piper on hers.

Because they are *mine,* she thought. Whether or not she liked it, she was responsible for the lives in this room.

Maybe not the journalist on the floor. Lou barely recognized the girl under the pulverized flesh. Black and blue bruises so deep Lou wondered if she would ever wake up again.

"Did you do that?" Lou asked, gesturing to the unconscious girl. The cold, familiar fury was unfurling inside her. The same fury that had filled her chest when she'd put the gun to Angelo Martinelli's head. Then Nico's. That fury was her most faithful companion.

Dmitri seemed to see the shift in her. Whether he realized it or not, he took a wary step back.

"Did you do that?" Lou asked again, stepping toward him. The men flanking him raised their guns. Several pointed at her head. But the room wasn't well lit. If Lou was fast enough...

Dmitri, in a show of composure, pulled the handkerchief from his suit pocket. He wiped Piper's blood from his skin.

Piper's blood.

You will die tonight, she thought. She might go with him to the gates of hell, but she would deliver him herself.

"I wanted to know everything there is to know about you," he said, his voice matter of fact. "Happy birthday, by the way. I owe you a gift."

Lou refused to be distracted.

"Is it really your birthday?" Piper asked behind her. "Why didn't you tell me?"

"Hush," Mel said. "For heaven's sake. And hold up your hand like I told you to."

King and Konstantine shuffled on the edge of her vision, looking ready to jump into the fray.

Lou took another step toward him. It was obvious to her he had to force himself to remain in place.

"The only child of Jack and Courtney Thorne. Both murdered by *his* family." He jabbed a thumb in Konstantine's direction.

Konstantine did nothing. His body remained tense, ready for anything. He cast a look Lou's way.

"You were then raised by your aunt who shares your peculiar trick."

He seemed to gather himself now. "I would have killed her, if she were not already dead. That would have been a more even trade than this." He gestured dismissively at the others in the room.

"Because I killed your son," she said.

Hate flashed in his eyes. "And 416 other men that I can account for. But how many in actuality? Do you even know yourself?" He sneered. "I didn't think so. Your father is avenged. You're taking lives that are not yours to take!"

His words hit home. A direct arrow *plunked* through her chest. All the cold hunger building inside her ceased.

Petrov found strength in it. "I'm right, aren't I? You don't know what you're doing."

She said nothing.

"My son was a *good* boy. He only went on the convoy because I commanded it."

"Your mistake," she said.

He threw himself at her. She deflected him easily by folding her arm, and sending his energy past her.

"*Why?*" he screamed. He beat a fist against his chest. "You know the pain I feel. Here." He slammed his fist against his chest again. His face was beet red, veins bulging, spittle flying from his mouth with each accusation. "You *know* what I feel and yet you do it to others!"

Konstantine shifted nervously in the corner of her eye. He was waiting for her to do something.

"Are *you* God?" Petrov screamed.

He gestured at her.

"Are you his angel? Are you so righteous?"

No, Lou thought. *No, I don't deserve to be the one.*

She had no argument. She hated this man before her, hated everything he stood for. But she could not deny that he spoke truth. And more so, she *agreed* with him.

"Give me my gun," Petrov demanded. He turned to the men behind them.

"Now!" he screamed.

A pistol was put in his hand. He pointed the Smith and Wesson at Lou.

"You had this coming," he said.

"I know," Lou said.

And he pulled the trigger.

THIS WAS IT. THIS WAS THE MOMENT KONSTANTINE WOULD DISCOVER if all his efforts had paid off. *The best laid plans...* He only wished the moment of truth did not come with a gun pointed at his beloved's head. But that was faith, wasn't it? One had to have faith that the universe was with you, not against you. And Konstantine thought a life without faith was no life at all.

The gun clicked. No thunderous report. No bullet was discharged.

A second empty click. A third.

"Take a step back, gentlemen," Konstantine said.

The men behind Petrov retreated into the darkness, becoming only shadows.

"That's enough," Konstantine said to Petrov.

Petrov looked at the gun in his hand as if he'd never seen it before.

But silent disbelief quickly gave way to laughter. He laughed, but there was no humor in it. There was only mad, wild rage.

"How much?" he asked, turning to Konstantine. "How much did you give them?"

"Enough," Konstantine replied. To King he said, "Take them outside."

Unlike Petrov's men, they didn't obey him. It seemed Lou's people were as stubborn as she was. He understood. They didn't want to leave her behind. But they also didn't want to see what was coming next. Of course, he had no time to reason with them.

"No!" Petrov wailed. He threw the gun on the ground and stomped his foot like a child. "No! Why should *you* be the only one who receives revenge? Are *you* the only one who's loved someone? Are you the only one?"

Lou stepped toward him, now fully separating herself from the shadows. She stood in the spotlight above, in full view of Petrov.

"You'll have your retribution," she said.

It hurt Konstantine to watch her. It was like watching her disrobe for another man. But she removed her guns. She offered them to Konstantine.

He didn't want to take them.

"What are you doing?" Piper asked. "What is she doing?"

Lou didn't answer. She stepped up to Petrov, her eyes locked with his.

"He still has the knife," Konstantine said.

"I know."

"You don't have anything." He was dangerously close to pleading.

"Konstantine," she whispered. His name sounded like a warning on her lips. "Cut the lights."

He considered refusing her. After all, he could stop this here and now. He could keep her in the light forever. But he'd done that dance with her once before, and not only had he lost, but he'd promised not to interfere again. It didn't matter that he wanted to say something, anything to deter her. Hell, he wanted to put a bullet in Petrov himself and be done with this.

He was holding a loaded gun.

He could do it.

But he knew this woman, or at least he knew enough to understand that denying her will would only worsen this.

"As you wish," he said and raised his hand. The lights cut and darkness flooded the room. The women—and King too—cried out in surprise.

"Lights," he said again and they blinked on again.

But Lou and Petrov were gone.

31

"Whoa, whoa, whoa," Piper approached the man she'd never seen before, the one Lou had called Konstantine. He was taller than her by a good six or seven inches. His leather jacket hung loosely on broad shoulders. When he turned to look at her, she realized he had gorgeous green eyes, even by her standards. "What just happened?"

"Lou will take care of him," he said. He waved to the dark above as if he had friends up there. "That is all. Please go."

"Will she—" a man began. This voice came from the huddled group of assholes that Piper thought belonged to Petrov, but in fact, seemed to be taking orders from this other guy.

"You're safe." Konstantine cut him with a hard glare. "As long as you don't betray us."

They were satisfied with this answer and slid open the large door. A burst of freezing winter air rushed in.

"What do you mean she'll take care of him?" Piper said. She gestured at the pile of guns and—was that a freaking *grenade*? "Take care of him with *what*?"

Piper's insistence was lost in the shuffle of boots. Then it was only the five of them, including Dani, and whoever might still be watching from the dark above.

Konstantine peered upward. "Come down here, Luca. Stefano."

Boards creaked and a metal ladder rattled. Then two men appeared.

"We need to help her," Piper said, wishing this guy would look at her, and act worried that Lou was out there, by *herself* with a psycho who wanted to *kill* her.

Then Konstantine did look at her. "This is her fight. If she wanted our help, she would have—"

"*How* do you even know Lou?" Piper cried. "Did Dmitri say your family killed her family? Did I hear that right?"

"We need to get Dani to a hospital," Mel said, drawing all of their attention to the girl on the floor. "He took her finger."

"It's here," one of the men said. He stepped forward and offered Mel a bundle of cloth.

At this, Piper let the conversation go. As much as she wanted to know all about this Konstantine guy and where he fit into Lou's life, Dani didn't have the time.

Her face was swollen in a way that hurt to look at. Both eyes blackened shut and her lips so large that it was as if bees stung them. Her throat was also purple and no doubt her clothes hid more damage.

I forgive you, Piper thought, resisting the urge to brush the hair out of Dani face. Even a slight touch would no doubt cause her unbearable pain. Piper forgave her for being a snoop because she knew—absolutely knew—this could've been *her* lying there. Those guys could've easily gotten hold of Piper and beat her for information on Lou.

I'll forgive you if you don't die.

"Let me help," King said, trying to get to Dani's other side and lift the girl off the unforgiving concrete floor.

"I'll get the door," Piper said when it seemed that Mel and King didn't need any help. To Konstantine, "Do you have a car or something?"

He exchanged a look with his two henchmen.

"È fuori."

What was that? Italian? she wondered. It sounded Italian. She'd seen *Under the Tuscan Sun* about twenty times with her mother and she was pretty sure that's what she was hearing. So Konstantine was Italian. She resisted the urge to grumble and roll her eyes.

"Through here," Konstantine said, stepping through the door she held open.

The night air was freezing. January, even in New Orleans, wasn't the time to be going around without a coat.

The taillights of a BMW SUV flashed. Piper turned to see one of the men—again, no idea who was Stefan and who was Luca—hand the keys to Konstantine.

"I'll drive you to the hospital," he said.

"Let me," King said, opening his hands for the keys. "I know where it is."

Konstantine relinquished the keys.

"Piper and Mel can sit in the back with her. You can have shotgun."

Konstantine regarded them: King, Mel, Piper and the whimpering Dani between them. Piper wasn't sure how to read that expression. Okay, so he was somewhat attractive, she had to admit. If one was into muscle and smoldering eyes and dark brooding glares.

"No," he said, finally. "You go on."

"Thank you," Mel said, adjusting Dani in her grip. "You saved our lives."

"No," he said with a faint smile. "Lou is the one to thank for that."

Then he turned and walked away from the warehouse with his two men in tow. Already they fell into hushed Italian that Piper didn't understand.

Damn, she thought.

Dani groaned.

"Come on," Mel said, opening the passenger door. "She could be hemorrhaging to death."

"I doubt it," Piper said, sliding into the backseat. It was nice and reeked of leather. *I can't compete with this. Who the hell produces BMW SUVs on demand?*

She reached across the seat and placed Dani into the middle so Mel could slide in after her. King was already in the front seat, the whole vehicle rocking with his massive form as he settled behind the wheel. He moved the seat back and flipped up the visor.

"Nice," he said. "You think we'll get to keep it? Oh shit, Piper look in the back."

"Why?"

"Please look in the back."

Piper leaned over the headrest separating her seat from the cargo area. There was nothing but darkness back there, and a pristinely vacuumed floor. She told King so.

"It doesn't mean there aren't drugs in this car," Mel said.

"Drugs?" Piper said, buckling herself in. She tried to position Dani's head on her lap but nothing looked comfortable.

"Let's hope the car is clean," King said, wagging his eyebrows in the rearview mirror. He started the car and pulled away from the curb.

He's relieved that we didn't die, she thought. And Piper had to admit it, she was pretty damn relieved, too. She opened and closed her fist, staring at the two fingers she'd almost lost, as if to assure herself they were still there.

"Told you we needed an alarm," Mel said. She checked Dani's pulse for the fourth time.

"And the dog," King agreed. He met Piper's eyes in the rearview mirror. "You okay?"

"Got all my fingers!" Piper cried triumphantly. Mostly because the worried tenderness in his voice, his acknowledgment that what just happened to her might in fact haunt her dreams for years to come, made her heart ache. "But remind me never to get drunk and kidnapped by the Russian mob again. It was *not* fun the first time."

"You were drunk?" Mel said, snapping her head in Piper's direction as she continued to hold Dani against the seat.

"No," Piper said reflexively. "Who said anything about being drunk?"

Mel's eyes shot daggers, but she said nothing as they sped through the streets.

32

Lou heard the click of the blade extending. But then the world shifted and Petrov was thrown through the dark. The Alaskan wilderness formed around them. An amphibian chorus fell silent. Something splashed into the moonlit lake, causing ripples to radiate from its shadowed shore.

Petrov didn't lose his balance as most of the men did when suddenly landing on this bank. He lunged, thrusting the blade toward her. She dodged him, parrying the blow with her forearm striking across his wrist. The knife was knocked out of his hand.

The blade hit a large flat stone and skidded into the lake. He threw himself at her, growling.

The weight of him slammed into her stomach, knocking her back. For a moment, she was weightless, falling through the dark.

It became the night her father saved her. He lifted her up and threw her into the pool, before taking the gunfire himself.

She was in the air. She was flying.

But it wasn't the cold slap of a swimming pool that struck her.

Her back hit the muddy bank. All the air left her. Her lungs convulsed, burning.

Before she could recover, a hard fist slammed into her sternum. The impact rippled through her abdomen.

"*Why* my son?" Petrov screamed. "Why *mine!*"

He pulled his fist back again, and the knuckles flew through the dark. She moved her head at the last moment and he clipped her ear. It rang in protest. Pain radiated on the side of her head, mimicking the throb of her spasming stomach.

She bucked her hips and pitched the man to one side. He hadn't been prepared and toppled on his hands and knees into the mud.

Lou got to her feet.

World spinning, chest burning, it took her a moment to gather herself. Her limbs were weak with adrenaline. Her arms were transformed into something between wet bags of sand and live wires.

"I didn't kill him because he was your son," Lou said. "I didn't even know he was your son."

Her throat burned with the effort.

Why are you even explaining it to him? Another voice chided. *Because you aren't explaining it to him. You're explaining it to yourself.*

This new voice didn't sound like her dead father or her dead aunt. It sounded like a sinister version of her own voice.

"So I am to blame for this?" Petrov pulled himself to standing. The right side of his body was mud-slicked. He had a smear across that cheek, looking like war paint. "Because I sent him? Because *I* told him to go?"

She had no answer.

"Every man who obeys their master, who goes to the docks, who picks up the shipments, who does as they're told, you *kill* them? Is that justice?"

No, she thought. *No, it isn't.* But she hadn't known how to stop when Angelo died, so now here they were.

"He was seventeen! He was a good boy!"

Lou knew it was possible. Children couldn't be judged by the actions of their parents. She believed this herself.

"How many innocent people have you killed?" Petrov demanded. He looked ready to launch himself at her again. "Why should you be judge? *Executioner?* Did God give you this gift? Are you doing his work?"

Her stomach dropped.

It wasn't the hate and disgust in his voice.

It was the desperate pleading.

It was that he *wanted* her to say yes. He wanted her to give him a reason for his loss. He would accept anything strong enough for him to hold onto, any flotsam to support him in the sea of his despair.

"Why did you do it?" he asked, tears streaming down his face.

It was his tears that undid her. She knew he was a bad man. She knew he deserved to die far more than the son she'd slain. But it was his anguish looking so much like her own.

She couldn't bear it.

"I'm sorry," she said. And for the first time, in all of her years of killing, she was.

Screaming, he charged again and this time slammed full force into her body. She clung to him, holding on as they fell back into water.

Lou sucked in a breath before the water overtook them. She sank with Petrov in her arms.

The moonlit depths bled red. The water turned from icy to lukewarm.

She broke the surface on La Loon once more.

Petrov didn't notice. He was only interested in drowning her. Not in the twin-mooned sky. Not in the black forest with its twisted trees and heart-shaped leaves the size of an elephant's ear. Not in the white mountains in the distance.

Fine, she thought. *Let me die here.* Let this be justice in the truest sense. She would be one more body heaped on the shore of La Loon.

Only she found she couldn't give up. She couldn't simply die.

No matter what she had done, no matter what she did or didn't deserve, she wanted to live.

She kicked Petrov hard, forcing distance between them. Only then did he realize where he was.

She said nothing. She only dragged herself to shore. She stood there dripping and tired.

"This is where I brought your son's body," she said calmly, standing in sopping boots on an alien shore. "I put a bullet between his eyes, killing him quickly. He was afraid. He begged for his life, but there was no pain. Then I brought him here."

Petrov stood in the shallow water.

"Are you an angel of death?" he asked and she saw the anger leeching out him. There was no room for it as his bewilderment grew.

"I don't know what I am," she said. "But I *am* sorry about your son."

"And me?" he asked.

She still saw the blood on Piper's finger. She recalled the fear in her eyes as Petrov threatened to cut each digit off with his blade.

"I'm not taking you back," she said.

A monstrous shriek erupted in the eternal twilight.

Petrov forgot her entirely. Lou didn't take it personally. The first time Jabbers had thrown back her head and shrieked, Lou had bolted for safety.

The heart-shaped leaves rustled as something large bounded through the forest.

Petrov drew close to Lou as if she might protect him. But then the leaves parted and the six-legged beast revealed herself.

Jabbers raised herself to her full height and roared. Her reptilian bark split open the night.

Petrov dove into the water.

Lou could've told him that wouldn't save him. She could've told him that swimming toward that distant shore offered no more safety than this one. But she let him have his hope.

Jabbers rubbed her snout against Lou's stomach, then up the side of her head. It dragged a milk-white tongue over her face.

And this creature—was it evil? She ate every man that Lou dumped on this shore. Sometimes she killed them herself. Was she evil? Or did she simply need to eat?

You needed to eat, her mind told her. Every man she'd killed was feeding something inside her. The problem wasn't that she'd killed them. There was no need to wonder if she'd been right or wrong.

The problem was *that* hunger had left her, and she hadn't yet learned what to do about it. Perhaps her prey had changed and she didn't yet understand how.

"He's yours if you want him," Lou said, turning her mouth away. After all, while Lou might owe Petrov his life, the world hadn't pardoned him of all his sins.

But Jabbers only sat back on her haunches and watched him paddle away.

Until six dorsal fins rose through the water, surrounding Petrov.

He was jerked under by unseen mouths, his screams swallowed whole by the rippling waters.

33

"You can see her now," the nurse said.

Piper, who'd been ruthlessly wringing an issue of Cosmopolitan between her hands, popped up from the hospital chair. She was horrified to see she'd mostly rubbed the face off the pretty country singer gracing the front cover. She laid the magazine face down as if to hide her shame.

If the nurse noticed this tense exchange, she revealed nothing.

"We are keeping visits short," the nurse said, slipping her hands into the pockets of her smock. "But it will do her some good to see a friendly face."

Piper repressed a snort. *You're assuming she wants to see my face at all.*

The corridor was bustling with staff, patients in wheelchairs and doctors issuing orders. The nurse stopped suddenly outside a darkened door and rapped on the frame twice.

"Ms. Daniella, your guest is here."

Dani sat in the hospital bed, a tray across her lap with some nondescript meat in a sea of mashed potatoes and peas. Chicken maybe. Turkey? Pork? The dessert was gone, only the remnants of red gelatin stuck to the side of the plastic cup.

Piper stepped up beside the bed and gave a sheepish smile. She hoped that smile said *I come in peace.*

Of course, why in the world should she feel like she had anything to apologize for? *She* wasn't the one who lied. *She* wasn't the one who used anybody for their own ambitions.

She also wasn't the one who'd gotten her finger cut off.

"You going to be all right?" the nurse asked, reaching behind her to adjust her pillows.

"I'm fine," Dani said, poking at the meat.

The nurse frowned. "You want a soda or something? A milkshake? You've got to eat, honey."

Piper wasn't sure what a milkshake would do for the purple bruises shining from Dani's face and neck. The skin was yellow in places, giving her a corpse-like appearance. And her right eye was bloody—red from lid to lid except for the iris.

Christ. They beat her so hard her veins ruptured, she thought.

"I like chocolate milkshakes," Dani said, giving the nurse a weak smile.

The nurse patted her arm. "And fifteen minutes for a little chat so you don't overuse your voice, all right? Then I'll bring your milkshake."

Dani nodded. The nurse seemed pleased by this and slipped from the room without another word.

Dani pointed to the empty chair with her fork, clearly instructing Piper to take it. Piper felt like standing but under that glower she had no choice.

The door clicked shut.

"I'm surprised you're here," Dani said. Her voice broke, cracking on each word. She seemed to read Piper's mind. "They choked me and ruptured my vocal chords."

Piper flinched. "I'm sorry."

Dani tried to pull herself upright. Piper rushed forward to help her, getting her under the arms.

When she was adjusted on the pillows, Dani searched Piper's face. Finally she said, "Why are you here?"

"To check on you," Piper said. "I thought you were going to die."

"Why would you care if I did?" Dani asked. "It's what I deserve, isn't it?"

Piper's mouth fell open, her mind shocked into disbelief. "No."

"Aren't you mad at me? I lied to you."

"I was. No one wants to find out they were used for a story."

Dani didn't even deny it. She only watched Piper speak.

"But then you got your freaking finger cut off," Piper said.

Dani showed her right hand. The finger was reattached with thick ugly stitches and held in place with a fingerboard splint. "They put it back on. You can be mad again."

"No," Piper said, her heart dropping. "But that's what you did, right? You were trying to get information on Lou. You figured if you hung out with me long enough you'd meet her."

"At first," Dani croaked.

Piper's heart did a little leap. "Are you even gay?"

Dani laughed. It was a hoarse, raspy sound. "Yes."

"Did you actually move here from Baton Rouge?"

"No. I grew up on the other side of the lake. My parents have a house in Mandeville. I'm not subletting an apartment. I've got one more year at Tulane."

"Did you really dance?"

"Ballet until ninth grade and then I rebelled and took jazz."

We're going to have to redo every conversation we've ever had, Piper thought. "And you're majoring in journalism?"

"English actually, with a minor in journalism, but don't tell my mother. I got the job at The Herald for the resume."

"And what would be better for a resume than a big story," Piper finished.

Dani flinched and Piper regretted the snide anger in her voice.

"I'm not like Clyde, my boss," she said, putting her fork down. It looked like she was giving up on the mystery meat. "Did she kill him? Dmitri said she did."

Piper didn't know how to answer.

"They told me things about her while they were..." Dani didn't seem to know how to finish. "Does she really kill people?"

"Is this on the record?" Piper asked.

Dani quirked a smile. "Off the record. It'll stay between us."

"Yeah," Piper said. "But only bad people. Like guys in the mafia and sleazy politicians who screw people over."

"Did she kill Dmitri?" Dani asked.

Piper nodded. "I didn't see it, but I think she did."

"Then I owe her one." Dani searched Piper's face. "Tell me what happened. I was awake a little in the warehouse."

"It turned out to be a mechanic's garage, actually."

Dani wasn't deterred by this reveal. "I heard your voice and some of what was said, but it didn't make much sense."

Piper recounted the story for her, from the moment Mel slammed King's apartment door shut until delivering Dani to the hospital.

When she finished, Dani said, "She took the mob boss to...somewhere...and fought him with her bare hands."

Piper shrugged. It sounded more than a little vague to her own ears.

"That's what she does, isn't it? She hunts these trash humans and kills them."

Piper wasn't sure what to say. She wasn't even sure why she thought she could come here, and not expect these questions.

"Just bad people," Piper said, her defensiveness rising again. It amazed her how protective she felt of Lou. It was ridiculous. Lou could out-knife or out-gun her any day of the week. She didn't need protecting. But Piper wanted to do it all the same.

"Clyde was a tool," she admitted. "But I don't think he was evil."

Piper didn't have an answer for that. She shifted in the chair. It creaked.

"She going to kill me?" Dani asked. "Because I know who she is."

"Do you plan to go public?" It occurred to Piper for the first time that Lou might actually do it. She couldn't have her face in the papers. She couldn't have journalists beating down her door.

She wasn't sure what to think about that. Did Dani deserve to die because she couldn't keep a secret? Did she deserve to get beaten half to death for chasing a story—no. But people were responsible for the choices they made, right?

Piper had been stupid enough to think her mother could change because she'd wanted her to. And it cost her a deposit and lot of heartache. Dani investigated a woman she had no business investigating and now she was in the hospital.

It wasn't right. But it was what it was.

"*Is* she going to kill me?" Dani asked again.

"I don't know. I hope not. She isn't a bad person."

Dani gave a weak smile. "I didn't think she was. She believes in something. And she wants to protect herself."

Piper felt strange. This feeling in her chest, radiating out into her heavy arms. She realized she liked Dani, *really* liked her despite everything. Despite the lies. Despite how horrible she looked beaten half to death in this hospital bed and that one gruesome red eye. There was something in her that reminded Piper of Lou. Maybe it was her steely resolve or determination to see her cause to its end.

"Do you think we can convince her I'm not the bad guy?" Dani asked.

"Do you plan on leaking her identity to the public?"

She didn't answer right away. "I don't know."

Piper put her head in her hands and sighed. "You better figure that out before she shows up."

"You think she'll come back for me?" Dani asked. Her eyes widened with fear.

Piper thought of Lou Thorne. The Lou Thorne who took on dozens of men at a time. The Lou Thorne who simply strapped up and made magic happen.

"Yeah." Piper sighed, unable to imagine a world where Lou Thorne left business unfinished. "You'll see her again."

34

Lou stood naked and dripping in the bathroom. She raked a hand across the fogged mirror to reveal her blushing face. She met her own dark gaze as she slid the comb through her hair over and over again.

The water on her skin began to cool, raising goosebumps along her legs, stomach, and then arms.

She couldn't understand what had happened with Petrov. Why couldn't she kill him? In the face of his violence, she'd had every reason to.

The moments replayed in her mind. She still saw his face, beet-red as he screamed and the spittle flying from his mouth. Veins bulged in his neck above his shirt collar.

Why should your vengeance mean more than mine?

It was that question that haunted her.

She supposed if she had only been met with his anger, his violence, she wouldn't have hesitated. After all, anger was fear, and fear was about the self. It would vindicate rather than overrule her conviction if, in the face of his loss, he'd taken it only as a personal insult. In that case, Lou would've known it wasn't about losing his son.

But it hadn't been anger in his eyes. Lou had seen *real* pain. *Real* desperation.

And in that way, Petrov had delivered the killing blow.

She'd never lost to an opponent before. Petrov's life may have ended in La Loon, but he'd won the battle between them.

Lou padded into the living room. On her kitchen island, she saw the gun. A gun she wasn't sure she could raise again. Then she saw her aunt's letter, open-faced, with a glimmer of sunrise collected in its pages.

Lou lifted the letter from the counter, felt its weight in her hand and read it again.

It was in the second paragraph that Lou put the letter down, and dressed in silence. She plucked the letter from the counter, folded it and slipped it into her back pocket.

Pulling wet hair back into her ponytail, she stepped into the linen closet. She stood in the dark and felt them calling. King. Piper. Konstantine. No doubt they were anxious to know if she'd survived. If she was alive and well.

But they would have to wait.

She exhaled. She gave her mind over to the dark as one must do for safe passage through it.

She expected to hear cars, people. But instead what she heard was howling wind. She could taste the frost on her lips even before the darkness found its mark and pulled Lou down into it.

One step and Lou's boots found solid stone.

Before her sat an enormous statue. Buddha with his palm out as if to ward her away. This inner chamber was small. No pews. Nothing churchlike about it except for that enormous sleepy-eyed statue and the reverent hush cloaking all.

Lou heard small movements and realized she wasn't alone. A figure stirred at the base of the statue. It rose to its full height, apparently coming out of a low bow. Somewhere a bell tolled.

The figure approached. It was a woman, Lou realized, despite the shapeless robes of red and saffron. The face was too full, too round even with the shaved head. She was barefoot and padded silently across the stone floor toward Lou.

Lou wondered if she was in the wrong place. She wondered if she should turn and run before the woman reached her.

But then she was there, so short that she didn't even reach Lou's shoulders. Five feet tall at most.

"I'm looking for Ani," Lou said, removing the letter from her back pocket. The woman took it, opened it and read the first line before Lou could object.

Then she looked up at a Lou, surprise sparking in her eyes. "You're looking for me."

Lou stood in this inner sanctum, unsure what to do next. She'd come. She'd found Ani...and now what?

"Come this way," the woman said, waving Lou toward a door in the far corner.

Lou fell into step beside her, following the *swish swish swish* of her robes on the stone floor. They passed through the arched doorway into a narrow hall.

The place reeked of incense, reminding her of Mel's shop. There are many holy places in the world, she thought. Some less formal than others.

The Buddhist nun might be short, but she had quite the stride. It took effort to match her stride.

At last, they arrived at a door. Ani pushed it open and beckoned Lou inside.

It was a small space. Only enough room for a narrow bed and a table. Ani sat on the floor, cross-legged, waving for Lou to close the door. She obeyed.

"I can tell I am not what you were expecting," Ani said, her smile bright.

Lou sat on the floor, mimicking the woman's pose. It didn't feel right to remain standing, looming over this woman so slight she could be someone's child.

"You're white. Your accent is Irish," Lou said. And immediately she felt stupid.

But Ani only laughed. "Aye. You're right on both accounts. Like you, my life has brought me down a strange path, far from the life I'd expected for myself, when I was young and a dreamer."

Something in her pleasant tone relaxed Lou.

Maybe it wasn't the woman. Maybe it was the simple room and its intimate warmth. Aunt Lucy would often go on about energies and the feel of a place—none of which Lou ever believed.

But now, here, she suspected she understood. There was something in the woman's energy that disarmed Lou. She thought it was her open face.

"You're not what I imagined either, Louie Thorne," the nun said.

"You spoke about me with my aunt."

"Oh yes. You were the subject of many of our conversations. But now that I can see you for myself, I like it."

Lou's face warmed. "She died."

Ani only nodded. "I am sorry for your loss."

"And yours," she said. "You were friends."

The woman smiled at this. "We were. And I would like to be your friend, too."

"Even—" Lou began. But she wasn't sure how to finish.

"Even though you've killed people?" she asked. Her smile was amused.

"Yes."

"It's true that life is sacred to Buddhists. All life should be cherished and I certainly do my best, though some—certain politicians for example—make it difficult to cultivate those feelings of warmth and openness. But another tenet of Buddhism is acceptance. I don't want to change you, Louie. I cannot judge whether your actions are good or evil. My job is only to alleviate the suffering of the world until all beings are free. Are you easing suffering?" Ani shrugged. "I am not the one to say. But I see that you seem troubled. *You* are suffering."

"I don't suffer," Lou blurted.

The nun arched her eyebrows. "How enlightened you are. Perhaps you should be here and I there."

They laughed. The sound erupted from Lou's throat before she had a chance to understand what was happening to her.

"We all suffer," Ani said. "It comes with the package."

She gestured toward her body. "Is it your aunt's death that hurts you?"

"Yes," Lou said.

"But that isn't all."

Lou felt the desire to run. Suddenly the room didn't seem cozy, it seemed claustrophobic. Dangerous. As if monsters might begin to crawl from under that squat wooden cot, or this harmless bald nun might herself transform into something ravenous.

Ani must've sensed this fear because she smiled, sliding her intense gaze away.

"Your aunt was a little older than you when I met her. Almost thirty."

The promise of a story was enough to freeze the blind panic growing in Lou's mind.

"Oh yes. Scared the living daylights out of me," Ani said. "A woman who pops out of the shadows? Buddha help me. I almost peed myself."

Lou found herself smiling again.

"She was my friend for twenty years. I will miss her."

Lou's heart kicked in her chest.

"Perhaps not as much as you. She told me how afraid you were in the beginning, of your own power."

That seemed a lifetime ago. Lou, the horrified preteen who thought every slip in the bath or nightfall spelled her imminent death. It had been Lucy who had taught her to control that gift.

"She taught me to love the freedom of it," Lou said.

"Amazing," Ani said, arching eyebrows. "Especially considering how much she detested it herself."

Lou met that gaze.

"She was afraid you'd never love your power because she hated hers."

"Always? Until she died?" Lou asked, unable to stop herself.

"No," she said. "In teaching you its beauty, I think she fell in love with it herself. But before you came, she only resented it for what it cost her. Her family. Her friends. She knew she couldn't tell anyone and felt isolated."

Hearing her own history recited to her unsettled her. *How much did you tell her, Lucy?*

Everything.

Lou thought of her father's pleading tape. His desperation—*I'm sorry I didn't believe you. But Lou...* He'd been one of the people to reject Lucy's gift, even if he'd been willing to form a truce on Lou's behalf.

"You gave your father and Lucy a chance to reconcile before he died. And you taught Lucy to love her gift as well. Those are two positive outcomes I know you are responsible for—assuming positive outcomes exist." Ani flashed a mischievous smile. "So what is it that troubles your mind?"

Lou looked at the letter on the floor. *You can trust her.*

"I...I couldn't kill him."

Lou began talking. She wasn't conscious of where to begin so she simply started. Words formed and delivered themselves as if Lou was only a mouthpiece for another force, another will outside her own. She wasn't sure how long she'd been talking. Ten minutes? An hour? Time fell away. But somewhere in the middle she realized that she *didn't* talk. To anyone.

Not to King or Piper. Not to Konstantine.

She'd kept all her thoughts and feelings wholly to herself, yet *from* herself. And now that the floodgate was open, she couldn't stop.

"Then Petrov was standing there and I knew I couldn't kill him. I didn't understand why I couldn't. But even before I saw him, I didn't want to bring the guns. I didn't want to bring anything. It's like I knew I didn't want to give myself the choice."

"You have a powerful intuition. It has been your guide thus far," Ani agreed.

"Yes," Lou said, thinking of her compass.

"That's a wonderful gift, Louie," she said. "You're blessed to have it."

She drew her knees up to her chest.

Ani glanced at the wall as if reading something there. "It's interesting. You couldn't kill him, but you also couldn't let him kill you."

"No," she admitted. "I almost did."

"But?" Ani prompted.

"I wanted to live."

Ani nodded. "In the face of Petrov's loss, you thought you deserved to die. That perhaps you were no different than the others whom you've sentenced to death."

"Yes."

"But then you *wanted* to live. And you realized that all the others you've killed must have also wanted to live."

"Yes," she said and heard the truth in it.

"Why do you feel guilty for wanting to live, Lou?"

Lou glanced around the small room. Her eyes fixed on the small table with a book resting on top of it. Then they traced the ridges in the cold stone floor.

What am I living for? What reason do I have?

For a while, Ani said nothing. She only regarded Lou in that stony silence of hers. Then she spoke.

"Maybe your desire to live is also your intuition," Ani offered. "You may feel like you've lost your way, but maybe there's a part of you that knows you're not finished here."

Lou stood and brushed nonexistent dust from her pants. "I don't know why Lucy asked me to come."

"Your aunt asked you to see me because she wanted you to know there is a path for you. Buddhists call it the middle way. The path between lightness and darkness. The world needs both to be whole and so do you. It isn't about judgment. It's about balance."

Lou hesitated at the door. "I wouldn't know where to begin."

"We begin with intention," the nun said. "In the past, your intention was to avenge your father and to ease your suffering. But I suspect your troubles more recently, culminating in this showdown with Dmitri Petrov, is because that intention is not holding water for you anymore. Your father's name has been restored. The men who killed him are all dead."

"But I killed after Angelo. After Brasso and Ryanson."

"For a while you were able to distract yourself by taking up your father's work. But that was his work, Lou. Not yours. You haven't even begun to walk your own path."

Lou thought of Nico. She suspected that he, too, had been a distraction. His desire to have Konstantine's gang—Konstantine's *life*—hadn't concerned her at all. But somehow she convinced herself it'd been worth her time.

And now...?

"You're still running, love," Ani said gently.

Lou stood in the doorway ready to bolt. She smiled, understanding the irony. "You want me to stop killing."

Ani smiled. "I meant it when I said I accept you as you are, Lou. I can't possibly know your purpose in this world. If you are a tool of karma, or if you are working through karma of your own, I don't know. I only know that you are here now and I'm to listen."

"And what would you say?" Lou asked. "What do you think I need?"

Ani laughed. "If only it were that easy. The thing about Buddhism is you must accept that you've no idea what's going on. And to believe otherwise is an attempt to hold fast to the rock while the river beats you half to death. We are all afraid of not knowing. All of us. Me. You. Everyone you've ever met. Few of us have it in us to push off from the shore and let the river take us."

Lou found herself wondering how often Lucy conversed with this woman. They had a similar mannerism, a similar tone. Or did Lou only see what she wanted to see? Was she looking for a replacement?

"Where do I start?" Lou asked.

"You need a new intention. Before, your intention was to avenge your father. You've done that. Then you tried to continue his work, hoping that by doing as he'd done, you would continue to feel connected to him. And it's why I advise against coming to see me again."

Lou's heart fell.

"I'm not a replacement for your aunt," Ani said. "I'm only here to tell you that your intention must be your own. Your path must be your own."

A new intention, Lou thought.

"You don't need to know what it is today," Ani said with a light pat on Lou's arm. It was so like Lucy in its manner and sweetness that Lou's chest ached. "But keep your eyes open."

A new intention—a new reason to take on the Petrovs of the world.

"Be patient." The nun smiled. "It'll come to you."

35

Dani couldn't sleep. If it wasn't the pain wracking her body, it was the dreams.

In these dreams, sometimes Lou would only watch her from the darkness. Other times, she would reach out and seize Dani, yanking her into a suffocating black so complete that Dani woke up choking.

When Lou finally did step into her hospital room, she was awake.

"Am I dreaming?" she asked. Her throat still throbbed when she spoke, but it had improved vastly in the days she'd spent drinking milkshakes and smoothies.

"No," Lou said, stepping into the light.

Dani's heart took off like a shot. It ricocheted violently in her chest. It was a war drum, its pounding obliterating all thought.

"Have you come to kill me?" she asked. She wanted to sit up, and tried, but only managed to lift herself an inch off the bed before collapsing back against the pillows. Lou didn't offer to help her, for which she was grateful. She didn't want the woman to come any closer.

"That depends," Lou answered.

"On?"

"On you," she said.

"You don't want me to tell your story," Dani said. It was better to state the obvious. Now was not the time for coy games. She wasn't sure if she was capable of games after seven hours at the mercy of Petrov and his men.

"No," Lou agreed. "I don't."

"And you're prepared to kill me to stop me from telling it?" Dani asked. The question was saturated with curiosity. Part of her wondered if Lou could actually do it.

Lou couldn't be much older than herself. Two years maybe? Three at most? And yet she seemed like an entirely different creature. She was cut from the fabric of another world.

Part of it was the ice-cold resolve.

The other part was the unreadable eyes often hidden behind mirrored sunglasses.

No, more than either of those factors was her presence. The way Lou Thorne occupied a room was different than the other girls her age. It held none of the nervous excitement, the uncertainty, the indecision that she herself wrestled with.

What the hell was it about this woman?

She certainly understood Piper's attraction which in its own right should be a red flag against their budding—whatever. It wasn't a good idea getting into a relationship with a woman who had a death wish.

As these thoughts race through Dani's head, Lou remained silent and still, as if she had all the time in the world to wait.

"You aren't afraid for your own life?" Lou asked. She leaned a hip into the bed.

Dani's legs tingled as if preparing for a strike. "Yes, but truth is important. People deserve the truth."

Lou smiled. "What about my life do they *deserve* to know?"

Dani's bravery faltered. It was a good question. She could've made the argument that Lou's father deserved hero status. That the wrong people had been punished and must be set free. But none of those arguments applied here. Her father's good name *had* been restored. The men had been punished. Ryanson and Brasso both disappeared, and while the media might think they escaped with their lives, Dani had every reason to believe that wasn't how it happened at all.

What else could she say? Lou didn't owe the world anything. She'd already paid for more in losses than most would in the course of a lifetime.

But she had killed Clyde. Then again, Clyde had tried to feed her to a Russian mob boss. Didn't he get what he deserved?

"I can tell you're struggling with this," Lou said.

More tingles ran the length of Dani's body. Fear, she realized. Her body was electric with *fear*.

"I know what you do," Dani managed. The clenched muscles were near spasming.

Lou smiled. "Do you?"

"And I don't want to die," Dani admitted. "It wouldn't be fair of me to expose you like that when all you're trying to do is even the scales."

Lou said nothing.

"But maybe we can reach an agreement. Or an arrangement."

"You and me?" Lou seemed genuinely surprised.

Dani decided that if there was ever a time to be bold, now was it. "I know about Ryanson and Brasso. I know what they did to your father. Those are the people who deserve to be exposed. They have to be held accountable to the people they hurt. If they aren't checked in some way, the abuse will only get worse. It'll be normalized and we can't let that happen."

Dani wished she knew what Lou was thinking. Was this plea working? That placid face threatened to undo her sanity.

"Those are the stories I want to tell," she said, and it was true. She wanted to hold those in power accountable for their actions. Those who exploited the weak, who took more than their share, who profited from the oppressed—they must be held accountable. "Give me those stories, and I won't tell anyone about you. I'll never ask what you do or how you do it."

"You think men like Ryanson and Brasso deserve to die for what they do?"

"Killing them gave you justice," Dani said. She pulled herself up, forgetting her pain for one heated moment. "But it did nothing for the others they've hurt. The other victims will never know what happened to them. They'll think they got away. And I'm not talking about Ryanson and Brasso, but all these other men—they're not yours to kill."

Lou started, visibly jumped as if shocked.

This is it, Dani thought. *I've gone too far. She's going to dig a shallow grave and throw me in it.*

"I—I'm not criticizing your system," she added quickly. "But the peace you got from knowing your dad was innocent—"

"I always knew he was innocent."

Dani wet her lips and tried again. "Then the peace you got from knowing he was avenged. There are a lot of hurting people in the world who deserve that too. They deserve the truth. And by dragging their villains off before that truth is uncovered, before they can be held accountable—don't you understand? The victims will live the rest of their lives not knowing."

Lou pushed her glasses up onto her head. Dani immediately wished she'd put them back on. The direct and unwavering glare was far worse than looking at her own impassioned face begging for her life.

"Please," Dani said. "Accountability is essential. It's the only thing that changes the world. We *need* it, to heal and to move forward. And if you can just give me a chance to hold these people accountable, I promise I will never expose you."

"You promise?" Lou repeated as if charmed.

"I *swear,*" Dani insisted. She gripped the cold bars on either side of her bed. "And if it doesn't work and someone gets away with murder anyway, you can still kill them. Then we'll go to the family and explain or something."

"All right," Lou said and stepped into the shadows. Before her face was fully cloaked, she fixed those black water eyes on Dani again.

"If you break your promise," Lou said with a smile. "I'll show you where I put Clyde."

"Deal." Dani forced a smile, though everything inside her trembled.

36

Konstantine settled against the high back of his chair. The fireplace beside him roared, casting delicious warmth across his chilled legs. He hated winters. He considered the paperwork spread across his desk, wondering if he should make the treaty with the Canadian dealers. Their port was in a lovely position near New York City and Toronto. It would be a lucrative negotiation to say the least, if only he could make the numbers work.

It had been like this since his flight arrived four days ago. The procession from New Orleans had been long and silent. He didn't want to wait in the city, hoping she would return and deliver him home like a package. More importantly, he didn't want her to feel like she owed him anything.

He was perfectly capable of making his own way across the world, even if it was horribly slow.

Once he returned, he drowned himself in work. It was easier to focus on problems with solutions than let his worry consume him. Easier than asking the same questions over and over again and receiving no response: *Why hadn't she come back? What happened with Petrov?*

But he wondered how truly effective he was in his work. He reviewed this treaty for the fourth time, rereading the same paragraph again without seeing it. He would have to give this up soon and call for dinner.

The temperature of the room shifted. A pressure suddenly formed between his ears, and with a gentle *POP,* disappeared. He looked up from his papers and saw her emerging from the corner of his basement study.

The two men standing on the other side of his desk, silently awaiting his commands, followed his gaze. An audible gasp escaped Marcello, who stepped back. Instinctively, his hand went to his gun.

Lou wasn't remotely perturbed by this. She stood three feet from Konstantine's desk. Her lithe body remained mostly in shadows as she regarded him.

His heart leapt at the sight of her. She wasn't injured, but alive and well.

He'd known she was alive and well. He'd caught two snapshots of her from the internet. She was spotted in a 7-11 outside Dallas, buying a new pair of mirrored sunglasses and a hotdog. Another of her in Vancouver, only a partial profile caught by a security camera on the back of a jewelry store. But it had been enough to trigger the facial recognition software he had running on all channels at all times.

But knowing she was alive and well and seeing her here were two different experiences.

He could breathe again.

"*Vai,*" Konstantine said, waving his men toward the door.

Marcello had the door open and looked more than ready to flee with his life. Of course, he was not as loyal to Konstantine as Stefano. Konstantine knew this.

Stefano stayed put, his gaze locked with Lou's. However, he didn't go for his gun.

Lou seemed to accept this challenge. She crossed the firelit study to Konstantine's chair. And then in an act that could not have surprised Konstantine more than if the Virgin herself arrived to declare Konstantine's sainthood, Lou bent and wrapped her arms around his shoulders.

Her embrace encircled him, holding him back against the chair. Her cold cheek pressed against his warm one.

No, she *wasn't* trying to choke him unconscious. She only held him.

Stefano's eyes widened in surprise.

"*Vai,*" Konstantine said again, flicking his eyes toward the hallway.

Stefano nodded and left, closing the door behind him.

Lou released Konstantine immediately.

"Brazen," he said, turning his chair to face her.

She settled on the edge of his desk, her boots pointing toward the fire. This side of her face was alight in dancing flame. The other, he knew, was dark.

"He wanted to know if I was here to kill you or fuck you."

Konstantine swallowed against the hard knot in his throat.

"I hope I answered the question."

"For me you haven't," he said, his voice strained.

She gave him a wicked grin. "Neither."

He didn't bother to hide his disappointment. But he liked that grin on her face. Something had changed since he'd last seen her. It was reflected in that mischievous smile, in the gentle slope of her shoulders, in the casual way she regarded the fire.

She wasn't afraid to relax around him.

His gaze slid from her face down the length of her body. Yes, that was it. The tension was gone. Whatever battle had been waging inside her before was over. For now.

"Your face was cold," he said, replaying the press of her cheek against his. "Where did you come from?"

"Nova Scotia," she said.

"Dare I ask what interests you in Nova Scotia?"

She only smiled. That's when he saw the smear of blood drying on her chin. The blood-creased knuckles on her hand.

He raised his eyebrows. "Did you have a good hunt?"

"Yes," she said.

"And it puts you in a good mood," he said, smiling. She was infectious.

Her eyes were liquid amber in the firelight. A wolf's eyes.

"You're happy to be hunting again."

She looked like she might object, might reject the accusation that she had taken a break from hunting at all. But no one on this planet watched this woman's movements more than he did. He knew. Just like he knew it wasn't because there weren't enough men who deserved killing in the world. It wasn't because that ex-cop kept her busy. Lou

Thorne answered only to herself—and that was what scared him. Wars that waged within were the most dangerous. Inner violence was where one could truly lose.

"Petrov?" he asked.

"La Loon," she said. "I suppose whatever didn't sink to the bottom of the lake will be eaten by the birds."

"There are birds in La Loon?" he asked. He didn't like the name for her sacred dumping ground. Another world he could only imagine with morbid curiosity.

She shrugged. "Something *like* birds."

"What do they look like?"

"Terrifying vultures with shark mouths."

He shook his head to clear the image.

"I think they stay in the forest. I've never seen them by the water, but you never know."

Then his stomach dropped. "I owe you an apology."

"For?" she asked, without looking away from the fire.

"I believe the journalist learned your name because I was lazy."

Her eyebrows arched higher.

He licked his lips and continued. "There is a small window in my early hours when I do not pull your data from the internet. I suspect Petrov figured out that this window was his chance to track your movements. But I've corrected it. I've been able to set some autoresponders in place to pull, flag, or block any items that could pertain to you regardless of the hour. And I'm trying to figure out if I can reverse-engineer a virus, that should someone search for you or your information, their technology will be infected and any data they might have stored will be corrupted beyond repair. "

"It was only a blow job, Konstantine," she said.

He burst out laughing.

She regarded the fire again. "I want to thank you for what you've done. Not just for me, but for my...friends."

His heart kicked up a notch.

"I understand you do this for your own reasons."

"I do," he said.

"And you won't stop if I tell you to, because you think it's important."

"True," he agreed.

She crossed her arms over her chest, that gaze lost in the cracking fire.

"Thank you." She favored him with a smile. Not mischievous. Not a challenge.

It warmed him far better than the magnificent fire burning in the hearth. "Anytime."

37

Lou stood in her apartment, her bare feet cold against the wood floor. She drank from a Styrofoam cup of coffee courtesy of the café Le Bobillot. The sun rose over the horizon. The water began violet-red, growing to a burning orange reflected on the shimmering Mississippi River, before softening to a clear yellow light.

For the first time since her aunt died, she felt...calm. At peace.

I can't make any promises, she thought, seeing her aunt's gentle, unassuming face in her mind. *But it's beginning to take shape now.*

The Buddhist nun had said *it will come to you.*

And it had in the hospital room. The words had come from Dani's mouth, and they'd been what she'd needed to hear.

The picture that eluded her since the night her father died began reforming at its edges. For the first time in her adult life, Lou saw a path through the snow-covered trees. It was no longer about feeding the starvation in her bones. It was about enjoying the night.

A tug resonated through Lou's abdomen. She waited for the tug to strengthen as it whirled inside her. Then it snapped into place. The line vibrated with connection. She knew the destination at once. King. Perhaps the old man was up early, mulling over paperwork.

Perhaps he was tired of waiting to hear from her. She had set precedent, sure, by disappearing for months at a time. Maybe he was afraid she intended to stay away now.

Slipping on her boots and grabbing her leather jacket off the arm of the sofa, Lou stepped into the cedar-scented closet and into King's dark bedroom.

"Surprise!"

She pulled her gun and pointed it at the three smiling faces.

"Whoa," Piper said, setting down the cake she was holding down on the coffee table. "It's not that kind of party."

Lou regarded the balloons and the sign above the red sofa. Her eyes traced the colorful letters spelling out *Happy Birthday, Louie!* on white craft paper, taped at the edges to the brick wall behind it.

Melandra crossed her arms over a soft blue sweater. Her bangles clinked against one another. King stood adjacent, ready to pull a party popper and unleash confetti on the room. He was wise to stop lest the *POP* be mistaken for gunfire and provoke her shot.

Lou lowered her gun. "Sorry."

King pulled the popper and both Mel and Piper jumped. Thin strips of paper rained anticlimactically to the floor.

"Christ." Piper placed a hand over her chest. "Bad timing, man."

Lou took in the banner, the balloons, and the confetti on the floor. "What's going on here?"

"It's your birthday!" Piper said again, throwing in exuberant jazz hands now that the cake was safe on the coffee table. "Happy birthday!"

"It's not my birthday."

"Right. Technically your birthday was last week, but we were busy *not* dying, so we're having the party now."

"How did you know it was my birthday?"

Piper pointed at King. "And Petrov said something, didn't he?"

"You're throwing me a party. At six in the morning?"

Piper frowned. "We know you like to go out all night, so this is like dinner time for you, right?"

"No," Lou said. "This is not dinner time."

Lou looked from face to face. King still nursed his coffee, the hair standing up on one side of his head. Mel had an easy, open expression. Piper was holding fast to her bright smile.

Lou tried to understand what she was seeing. Finally, she said, "You didn't have to get up early for me."

"I was up anyway." Mel tugged at the gold bangles on her wrist, and in truth, she did look like the most lively of the three. "I wake at five every morning."

She was likely the only one. Piper had pitiful purple bags under her eyes and her ponytail was crooked. King crossed to the kitchen counter to refill his coffee mug.

"Would you like coffee?" he asked her.

"Oh, and there's Cherry Coke! You know, that's what you ordered from the bar!" Piper sprinted out of the apartment, leaving the door open behind her.

Mel jingled her keys. "My apartment is locked, which she will realize in thirty seconds."

That left King and Lou.

"How are you?" King asked, returning to the sofa with his coffee.

She shrugged. "Do you agree to many sunrise birthday parties?"

King flashed a lopsided grin. "No. But Piper's reasoning made a lot of sense at the time. Now, not so much."

Lou swatted away a balloon and crossed to the sofa. She took a seat beside him.

"I wanted to talk to you anyway," he said. He leaned forward and took a knife to the cake. He paused before cutting the first slice. "Do you mind?"

"Go ahead."

"I know you went after Sikes," he said. His voice was calm and near emotionless. But that's what gave it away. "You did that before I was sure he was guilty."

"I wanted to talk to you about that," she said, watching him dump a slice of cake onto a paper plate and offer it to her with a fork. She accepted it. "I spoke to Dani."

King froze in the middle of cutting a second slice. "She all right?"

"She'll live."

King arched an eyebrow. "Will she?"

"We talked about accountability."

His eyebrows arched higher. "For who?"

"For people like the Martinellis. Ryanson. Brasso."

"I'm fairly certain they've been held accountable."

"Dani..." Lou searched for the words, lifting a fork off the coffee table. "She made me realize that it isn't about me. I wanted to kill the Martinellis because it gave me closure."

She glanced at him from the corner of her eye, wondering if he was following her.

"I'm still with you," he said, sliding his fork through the cake.

"When I take these men, kill them, dump them in La Loon, I steal that closure from others."

King looked at her as if he'd never seen her before.

"I could go to the victims, and tell them what happened, and I suppose I will still have to do that from time to time when this doesn't work—"

"—when what doesn't work?"

"Your way. Dani's way," she said, poking the cake with the fork. "First we will find evidence and try to prosecute. Dani is willing to add pressure with high-profile stories, helping to uncover the truth. You'll help with the evidence, and the interviewing."

His eyebrows shot up.

"And I'll focus on what I do best. I'll hunt."

"But you said—"

She didn't let him get far. "Do you know how many cold cases there are? People who were tried but escaped justice? Plus there are serial killers, and those who were too rich to worry about the law. The system isn't perfect."

King smiled. "You have a plan."

"I want you to start me with a stack of cold cases." Then she saw his face. "What?"

"I'm surprised you arrived here on your own."

Not on my own, she thought.

"I'll see what I can find and get back to you," he said. "Shouldn't take more than a few days."

Lou stabbed her cake with her fork. It was too early for something so sweet but she wasn't about to say so.

The apartment door burst open and Piper appeared with a twelve-pack of soda under her arm. "Coke is here."

Piper handed Lou a soda.

"Thanks," Lou said.

"No, thanks to *you*," Piper said. "For not killing Dani."

"I did it for her."

"Right. She's clearly the main beneficiary here." Piper scratched her nose. "I just meant it was very decent of you."

Lou pointed at the cake. "You didn't have to do this."

"Yeah I did. And even with the sunrise party, you've still been more of a friend to me than I've been to you this week."

Lou searched for purchase. "You got Cherry Coke."

Piper waved a hand. "Doesn't compare to having all your fingers attached, man."

Lou smiled and opened the soda.

"I meant what I said. I'm going to be the best friend you've ever had. I don't care if I have to bury bodies—"

"I have the bodies covered."

"Oh good! I sort of have a bad back. Roller derby, you know? *Anyhoo*, I mean it. Whatever you need. I'm here."

Lou saw the blush spring to Piper's cheeks and she smiled.

"Now *that's* settled. Eat this cake!" Piper begged. She hacked off another slice and dumped it onto Lou's plate as if there wasn't already half a slice there. "I spent two hours trying to figure out how to pipe these rosettes!"

"You could've bought the cake," Lou replied.

Piper snorted, waving her attached fingers at Lou again. "The least I can do is pipe you some rosettes. Oh, and there's this."

Piper reached into her pocket and pulled out a card. Lou sat the cake plate down and accepted it. She pressed a thumbnail under the envelope flap, peeling it back to reveal the cardstock within.

"Read it aloud," Piper said.

"Happy birthday to the girl who always has your back."

Below the words was an image of a woman shooting a man in the back.

Lou's heart careened off course. It wasn't the sign, the balloons, the soda or the cake. It wasn't Piper's sweet earnestness or the way King leaned against the kitchen counter talking to Mel.

It was the card that undid her, which she closed slowly and slipped back into its envelope.

"You don't like it?" Piper said, frowning. "Sometimes my jokes are no good."

"I like it," Lou said, unaware that she was smiling. "But I'm not worth the trouble."

Piper grinned. "That's where you're wrong, Lou-blue. And I'm going to prove it."

ACKNOWLEDGMENTS

Many thanks to the fans who continue to support my work. You tell your friends and family about my stories. You ask your libraries to add my books to their collections. You write kind words and encouragement. You do so much and I am very grateful for all the love you continue to show me.

Thanks to Kimberly Benedicto, wife and beta reader extraordinaire. Your charming quips and "affectionate" input are priceless. As well as the food. Keep the food coming.

Thank you to Monica La Porta for her help with the Italian (any remaining errors are my own!). To Angela Roquet for her endless encouragement and graphics aplenty. To Kathrine Pendleton—whose humor reminds me how ridiculous I am when I start panicking.

Thank you to Christian Bentulan for the gorgeous cover. I can't wait to see what you come up with next.

Thanks to my assistants Alexandra Amor and Amber Morant who helped me tremendously as I made the transition from writing teacher to full-time writer. You two made it painless. I'm so grateful for your hard work. Particularly Alexandra, who formatted this book for your enjoyment.

And last but not least, thanks to my street team. You guys are amazing beyond words. You get the word out, you buy my books, you spot those typos—I love you guys. What would I do without you? I can only hope that I keep writing stories that excite you for years to come.

It's only the beginning. Let's do this.

Did you enjoy this book? You can make a BIG difference.

I don't have the same power as big New York publishers who can buy full spread ads in magazines and you won't see my covers on the side of a bus anytime soon, but what I *do* have are wonderful readers like you.

And honest reviews from readers garner more attention for my books and help my career more than anything else I could possibly do— and I can't get a review without you!

So if you would be so kind, I'd be very grateful if you would post a review for this book. It only takes a minute or so of your time and yet you can't imagine how much it helps me.

It can be as short as you like, and whether positive or negative, I cherish *every. single. one.* So do the readers looking for their next favorite read.

If you would be so kind, please find your preferred retailer here and leave a review for this book today.

Eternally grateful,

Kory

ALSO BY KORY M. SHRUM

Dying for a Living series (complete)

Dying for a Living

Dying by the Hour

Dying for Her: A Companion Novel

Dying Light

Worth Dying For

Dying Breath

Dying Day

Shadows in the Water: Lou Thorne Thrillers (ongoing)

Shadows in the Water

Under the Bones

Danse Macabre

Design Your Destiny Castle Cove series (ongoing)

Welcome to Castle Cove

Night Tide

Short Fiction

Badass and the Beast: 10 "Tails" about Kickass Heroines and the Beasts That Love Them

Chaos Cocktail: 13 Fantasy Bar Brawls

Learn more about Kory's work at: www.korymshrum.com

ABOUT THE AUTHOR

Kory M. Shrum is an award-winning and *USA Today* bestselling author of fantasy and thrillers—and something else that's a bit of each. She's an active member of Science Fiction and Fantasy Writers of America, Horror Writers of America, and the Four Horsemen of the Bookocalypse, where she's known as Conquest.

When not reading, writing, or battling her pug for the covers, she's planning her next adventure. She lives in Michigan with her equally bookish wife, Kim, and their rescue pug, Charley.

She'd love to hear from you!
www.korymshrum.com

Made in the USA
San Bernardino,
CA